CIRCLE OF
STONE

CIRCLE OF
STONE

VERNE JACKSON

*To Edda :
old friends are the best !
Best Regards,
Verne Jackson*

TWP
THIRD WORLD PRESS

Progressive Black Publishing Since 1967
Chicago

Third World Press
Publishers since 1967
Chicago

Queries should be sent to:
Third World Press
P.O. Box 19730
Chicago, IL 60619

First Edition
Printed in the United States of America

Cover design and interior layout by Denise Borel Billups

Library of Congress Control Number: 2009941115
ISBN: 978-0-88378-303-0
18 17 16 15 14 13 12   6 5 4 3 2 1

*All characters appearing in this work are fictitious. Any resemblance to real persons,
living or dead, is purely coincidental.*

ACKNOWLEDGEMENT

To Cynthia Bell, who typed the manuscript a dozen times—without her patience, understanding, and friendship over the years, there would be no book.

To my sister, Donnella Bishop Ward and my brother, Samuel Jackson, Sr. Without your support and encouragement I could not have swam the many rivers I had to cross.

And finally, to Randall "Randy" Dellorto, who loaned me my favorite research book. Thank you.

Thank you to my editor, Ms. Solomohn Ennis, who discovered my work. Special thanks also to Mrs. Rose Perkins of Third World Press, and Gwendolyn Mitchell, the senior editor at Third World Press.

A very special thanks to my last editor, Catherine Compton, who is an angel in disguise.

And to all of you who encouraged me and believed in me.

We Wear The Mask

We wear the mask that grins and lies,
It hides our cheeks and shades our eyes,—
This debt we pay to human guile;
With torn and bleeding hearts we smile,
And mouth with myriad subtleties.

Why should the world be over-wise,
In counting all our tears and sighs?
Nay, let them only see us, while
We wear the mask.

We smile, but, O great Christ, our cries
To thee from tortured souls arise.
We sing, but oh the clay is vile
Beneath our feet, and long the mile;
But let the world dream otherwise,
We wear the mask!

–Paul Laurence Dunbar

WARNING!

Negroes,
Sweet and docile,
Meek, humble and kind:
Beware the day
They change their mind!
Wind
In the cotton fields,
Gentle Breeze:
Beware the hour
It uproots trees!

–Langston Hughes

PART ONE

We wear the mask that grins and lies,
It hides our cheeks and shades our eyes,—

ONE

※

In this year of slack bellies and sparsely set tables, lucky to have a little meat, bread, and cold sweetin' water to drink, Lela Bailey's tables creaked with feast food and plenty. Duck, geese, and game of every description, were available and preserved fruits, syrupy with extra sugar, and bright vegetables of all kinds stood on shelves in her kitchen in rows of glass jars like well-dressed ladies off to The Ball.

So many neighbors had no store bought foods at all these days. No coffee, no tea. *Lawd, humans weren't meant to live without tea!* No cheese, no flour, or meal. No sugar or spices. No rice. No dried beans. No jobs. No money. No promise of better times. Although the year 1930 did promise changes: rougher times ahead and even more of less, the newspapers and radio announced.

But in Lela Bailey's house there was abundance: Fine clothes, fancy hats, good food, and *money*. Yes, money! Plenty of it! Hideful amounts! Amounts so large that the Colored must not be told of it—and white folks must not even guess! Colored with real money in these times? No, lord! Not these times, not *any* times.

But no amount of money could buy Lela any peace now.

There could have been happiness—or its twin sister, contentment—in Lela's house with all she and her beloved son, Dave, had. But no! She had ruined it all two weeks and three days ago.

Curiosity killed the cat they said, and now she knew what poor kitty suffered. Sleep had fled, leaving a clock that produced time in drum beats, splitting the night into tiny, noisy pieces.

I have important things in that closet, Mother. Don't ever open it, hear?

Lela had thought it was money. Sure. He keeps money in there. No one trusted the banks anymore. Anybody who had anything kept it stashed away now. It made sense.

And yet, something had prompted her to disobey her son's wishes. And now she had hardly slept since because money was not what she had found in there at all.

Her eyes had bulged and her breath had stopped completely before it started again in short gasps, and she quickly locked the closet again. And in that little room she locked peace of mind, sleep, hope, and everything that brought joy, for she had invited a large black crow to come and stand on her head and flap its dirty wings.

Now what to do? Two weeks and more had passed and Lela still had no idea what she should do, would do, or indeed, what she *could* do.

Lela rose this morning from another miserable night of fitful tossing. Sitting on the side of her bed she whispered her all-purpose prayer: "LawdhavemercyJesus!"

Three weeks without sleep that was a soft, dark, deep blissful hole into which you willingly slid, certain as sunrise that you would wake refreshed, left Lela with a jumpiness for even familiar sounds if they happened to be a mite louder than expected.

And it was getting worse.

Should she send for Dr. Echardt, the white doctor that she used to work for? He would come for her if it was serious, of that she was certain, but what she had was just a bad case of nerves, and who could cure that? Maybe John Candle, the herbalist and voodoo man, her best friend, Mattie Clarence, swore by. The herbalist was for cases when the regular doctor had given up hope, or when you needed to make some white person who had wronged you awful sick to get even.

Dat ain't what dis heah is about, thought Lela—at least not yet.

By the standards of the thirties, Lela Bailey was an old woman at fifty-eight. She had given birth to three children, fewer than most women her age. Her firstborn son died in infancy and for years Lela and her husband, Rex Bailey, thought that they would have no more children. But when Helena Bailey arrived six years later, Rex was so happy that he forgot to be disappointed that she was not a boy. After another six years, the third and final child was born to Lela and Rex. They named him Dave after Lela's father, and Rex after his own father.

Dave was a "chocolate drop" even at birth. The rims of his ears, the sure signal of the final color of a black child, were even then much darker than his face. Rex could not conceal his disappointment.

"All of my people is light skinned," he had said. Lela herself had a medium brown complexion. "You sure you didn't let that old coal black iceman in heah a time or so while I was gone?"

Lela always smiled at the joke, never letting on that it bothered her the tiniest bit that Dave bore so little physical resemblance to his father.

And in the end, although they tried to hide it, Dave became the favorite child of both parents. While Helena was pretty, she was hardheaded and whiney. Dave, on the other hand, was lively, friendly and apt.

"Gone be somethin' special," the midwife had said, "'cause he done been bone wit' a veil over his face!"

"He's a tough little bugger," Rex had remarked. "Ain't no tellin' what he'll be when he grows up."

Thinking of her husband, Rex, was also troubling. It had been seven months since she had heard from him, by letter, and four years since he had been home. They had been married nearly forty years now, and for many of those years he had been gone. In and out. A drifter. A hobo since Dave was five. He was sixty-two now and still he was on the road. She had long since forgiven him, long since lived down the shame of having a hobo husband—and of worrying that Rex had died on the road somewhere, never to be heard from again.

The fact was that he was responsible in his way, for he sent money regularly, very adequate sums from his latest job in Montana where he was working in forestry, or from New York City where he was a cook in a famous white cafe or from South Carolina where he was making furniture in a big factory.

Actually, Lela and her two children were better cared for than most of the families in West Steward that had fathers at home. She had money enough and Rex's letters were always interesting. Sometimes he sent a picture of himself and a friend he had met on one job or another.

Sometimes these friends were—unbelievably—white. Lela missed Rex terribly the first three or four years, but then she adjusted to his absences and built her life around her children, her church, and her community, where she was respected as a wise counselor and practical nurse to the Colored community. A nurse who had worked for and been trained by the beloved little white doctor, Henri Echardt.

Lela bowed her head and prayed again, not to God but to Rex Bailey, father of the son who had certain things hidden in the little room behind the closet.

"Rex. Rex Bailey. Wherever you is nah, would you please, please, please come home as soon and as fast as you can? Thank you. Amen."

Then she rose to start another day.

5

September was beginning to fade into October, and it was nearly a full year now since the Stock Market crash that had affected the Colored residents of West Steward, Arkansas hardly at all. Times had always been tough for the majority of Negroes in the South so the Crash had barely been noticed. Except for the extremely small number of blacks who had investments or regularly bought and read newspaper accounts of the dreadful event, the Crash and the beginning of the Great Depression was mainly White Folks Business.

Black folks had always eaten out of the ground, from the land, and from the rivers, and had not at any time been as store dependent as most whites. Peanuts, beans, sweet potatoes, all kinds of vegetables and fruits, as well as catfish, buffalo fish, crawdaddys—these things were as plentiful as ever, and then too, everybody had a little garden somewhere. What you didn't have you bartered for. Bartering was often fun, for it gave the work-worn women of West Steward a legitimate reason to socialize and gossip without the fear of being labeled a lazy housekeeper that preferred roaming the streets to taking care of her own.

Often, too, bartering was profitable. For instance, a good seamstress could salvage the best parts of a grown man's overcoat and make two, perhaps three, little winter coats for small boys. One coat could then be traded for a pair of shoes, or even sold for a dollar each, cash.

A core of the blacks of West Steward stuck together through their churches, quilting groups or other social gatherings and shared valuable information regarding their needs. Just last week Cutha Peabody's husband, LaSalle, had found a virgin grove of pecan trees, enough for practically the whole of Colored Town to supply their holiday needs.

Autumn had begun to set in, but the weather was still pleasant. Nice enough for Dave to sit by his tree stump in the back yard, his wooly head resting on the stump, his chocolate-colored face turned toward the sky that was no longer blazing with summer. He usually had two heavy wool blankets. He would sit on one and drape the other around his shoulders. Occasionally he would change positions and pull his long, young legs under his chin.

Lela would glance at him from time to time through the window of her kitchen as she went about her chores. Lately she'd been wondering what he was thinking and planning and why he didn't seem the least bit troubled when she knew he had all the trouble in the world stashed in that very house.

He was such a nice young man. The best son a mother could want. Lela and a precious few others knew Dave was well on his way—in spite of the Depression—to becoming the most well-to-do man in town, white or black, young or old.

Why, oh why, hadn't she seen fit to stay out of that closet? But then something might be cooking—something mighty big—and Lela would know nothing about it.

Maybe the Lawd works in mysterious ways.

Back in 1926 when business was booming, everybody in West Steward who wanted a job had one, and the level of satisfaction, not counting racial issues, was generally high. Dave Bailey was the boss of the Colored men at the Detroit Sawmill and had been since he was sixteen years old. His men spoke of his fairness, aptness, and most of all his willingness to go out on a limb for them. The older heads spoke of these things also, and added that Dave was uncommonly quiet and dignified for one so young.

Grant Fromm, Dave's foreman, thought Dave Bailey the smartest Colored man he had ever known. Not only did the boy work hard, he actually got the other niggers to work harder than most of them had worked before, as a matter of pride he had said. When the logs came into the mill, it was said of Dave's men that they could strip two hundred trees of bark and peel them down to veneer in the hot moist peeling room before a white man could eat his lunch—or that they could cut a hundred trees into two-by-fours or six-by-eights or whatever was ordered for the furniture factories in North and South Carolina, Alabama, Georgia and other parts of the South—stack them and have them loaded on the train for shipping before a white man could finish pissing in the weeds. During the time he had been boss Dave had performed a miracle—he had the men feeling good about the work they did. Hard work, ten hours a day, and eight hours on Saturday for ten cents an hour.

Until Dave was promoted to foreman of the Colored men, absenteeism was very high, especially on weekends. After Dave took over absenteeism went down a good deal and production, naturally, went up because Dave appealed to the men with what his mother had told him: any job worth doing is worth doing right. Out of the motley, discontent group of men Dave had forged a team and Fromm knew it. He also knew that niggers had a thousand ways to mess you up as a foreman if they didn't like you—and they didn't like him one bit, Fromm was sure. But Fromm was glad to have recommended Dave as boss of the Colored. Let him be blamed when things went wrong. That suited him just fine—at least he had a buffer between himself and the owner, Dayton Holyoke.

Dave had half of his sixteen men, ages seventeen to sixty, preparing the cottonwood "knock downs" that were too soft to be used for anything but crates in which eggs, fruit, and vegetables were shipped and stored. The other eight men were busy at their regular jobs of cutting the oak, gum, poplar, ash, hickory and other types of logs into planks for various uses: cypress planks were sent off to customers that built bridges, because cypress was imperious to water, wear, and rot. The best logs, oak, fruit woods, hickory, and walnut, were processed for fine furniture.

"Dave's boys," as they were called, also made simple solid storage boxes as well as pine planks in various thicknesses and lengths.

The work that Dave and his men performed was hot, fast, and often hard, but they were used to nothing else, and under Dave's supervision, were rarely discontent. There had been some trouble at the mill involvong one of Dave's best friends, Peter Frauzinou, and Dave had seen fit to leave Detroit Mill, taking his other best friend, Omar Williams, with him. He had started his own business almost immediately. In only two years, it had grown more than even his mother, with all her prayers, had expected.

Every Wednesday Dave got his crew together to start the "hot tamale train," as he called it, for the weekend. Dave had built a "factory"—a little cabin in the back of the house where he stored his food supplies and prepared tamales for sale on Friday and Saturday nights up on the car line in his five selected spots.

Dave could sell as many tamales as he and his crew could make. At first, there were just the three of them, Dave, Omar Williams and Peter Frauzinou. Recently, because of volume, Dave had taken on two more men; Will Henry Mead and LaSalle Peabody. Another friend, Tom "Fool" Leak, acted as a handy man and kept the cabin clean and did other odd jobs for Dave.

Clad in aprons and sweat bandannas they worked the "production line" as Dave tended his huge black pots of tamale fillings to make the tamales. Tom "Fool" Leak would spread four hundred moist shucks flat on the table, then Peter would plop and spread, plop and spread, plop and spread the seasoned cornmeal that Dave had made in his huge pots. Next would come LaSalle "wit' da meat," a heaping tablespoon full of ground beef and pork that had been cooked together with garlic, chili powder, cayenne pepper, onions and other secret spices. Plop, plop. Last, Omar

8

came along and rolled each tamale lengthwise so quickly you could hardly see his hands. He would tie them in the middle with a corn shuck strip and bend them upward making two tamales that would swell to twice their size after Dave set them in pots of boiling water to steam. It was hot, fast work—just the kind the men were used to when they worked at the mill.

As they worked, the young men hand-cranked Dave's Victrola and sang along with Bessie Smith, "Tain't Nobody's Bizzness If I Do!" Then they turned the record over and shouted out the "Down Hearted Blues." They told filthy jokes, drank Arkansas Gold, a potent delicious brew that Peter had taught them to make from the skins of peaches. They laughed and sang and felt like kings—they felt almost free.

The men made hundreds of hot tamales and sold them all on Friday and Saturday evenings. The tamales each man had never lasted until midnight. They were six for a dime—eighteen cents a dozen. The customers would already be waiting at 6 p.m. when the five men rolled out their "hot carts" to the car line where the three taverns, one whorehouse, and pool hall were located. Someone having a whist party would want ten dozen. Another twelve dozen would go to Mabel Conway, the whorehouse madam, if she was treating her best customers that night.

It wasn't even like work these Fridays and Saturdays. From their stations the salesmen witnessed all of the fun, fights, and good music the town had to offer.

Perhaps this evening, after the tamales had been stored in the ice house bins, they would go to the double feature at the Colored picture show over in Old Steward, five miles away. Peter, the picture show nut, could be counted upon to go—for, like Dave, he had no wife or children. Omar might go to "get away from da ball and chain and my three little nappy-headed chirrens for a spell." LaSalle always finished his work and went straight home as his wife expected. Will Henry would be welcomed, but nobody wanted Tom "Fool" Leak along, for he couldn't stay still long enough to enjoy a picture. He would be up roaming around the small theater if you didn't watch him.

Tom also had a habit of talking loudly to the actors on the screen and commenting on the action, itself: "Hey! See dat? He really let that bastard have it, didn't 'e? Ha!" And then his run-on laugh would explode. "Yahaheehee! Yahaheehee, oh, ya ha hee hee hee!"

Invariably someone would say: "I paid good money to see dis heah picture show! Nah set your crazy ass down!" Thus chastened, Tom would sit quietly for a full three to five minutes, then he would be up again like a Jack-in-the-box.

On Friday, after all the tamales were sold, Dave, Omar, Pete and Will Henry usually met up at Princess Thelma's between eleven thirty and twelve o'clock to listen to some Blues and eat the chitterlings, slaw, spaghetti and cornbread that Princess served on corrugated cardboard trays. Princess Thelma also served some of the best cat and buffalo fish sandwiches in the state, Omar believed.

Recently, Omar's wife, Ray Jean, had started to sell her crispy fried dried peach and apple pies at Princess Thelma's. Everybody was crazy for these fried pies, but nobody wanted to make them because they were too much trouble, so Ray Jean had the field all to herself. She made one hundred pies to be divided between Friday and Saturday nights each weekend, which added a tidy ten dollars a week to the savings she and Omar kept in the Rex Jelly Can in the ground under the house.

"I do believe," LaSalle had said to Omar in his slow deliberate way, "dat everybody who sticks around wit' Dave will come 'way with a right smart mount o'money after while. He seem to just print it, don't he?"

It was true. Everything Dave did seemed to prosper since he had left Detroit Mill, while the mills themselves fell to the Depression. There had been eleven sawmills in and around West Steward and Steward, Arkansas, assuring plenty of work for all, but in the deepening depression year of 1930, only two of these mills remained open and were only offering "short time" work of ten or fifteen hours per week during the peak shipping season. By the end of 1930, both Detroit and Vander Mills were closed for weeks at a time as longtime employees scrambled for the eight or ten hours of work per week that the mills offered as work wound down to nothing.

Dave, however, paid his men well—ten dollars a week for less than thirty hours of work. And the men were very pleased. At the mill they had received fifteen cents per hour-nine dollars a week for a sixty-hour, six-day week of very hard labor. The tamales work was a comparative breeze.

After Dave had paid his crew and deducted his expenses, including three dollars for the rental of the icehouse bin, he had nearly a hundred dollars left—a princely sum. Nearly four hundred dollars a month as opposed to the sixty dollars per month he had earned at the mill two years ago.

Of his profit, Dave spent less than seven dollars a month for "outside" food for home. He and his mother had their own gardens, fifty or sixty chickens, four peach trees, an apple tree, a fig tree, and at the beginning of the forest, way out in the back of the house, there were hickory nut and black walnut trees.

From their own fruit trees and gardens, Lela Bailey canned two to three hundred jars of fruit, fruit preserves, jelly and vegetables each fall for her table and for barter, so it was only necessary to purchase dry staples such as macaroni, beans, flour, rice, coffee; dairy products like cheese, milk, butter, and store bought meat. Steak was fifteen cents a pound, neckbones were one cent, a whole picnic ham was fifty cents, and liver was five cents a pound. Since neither Lela nor Dave were big eaters, their largest food expense was the sugar Lela used for canning and for coffee, fifteen cents a pound, and tea.

Recently Dave had expanded his investments by opening up a small school supply and candy store that the girl he planned to marry, Adrianna James, ran by herself. Profit after expenses, including Adrianna's salary, was between forty and fifty dollars a month. And this was just the beginning. Dave planned to open school supply and candy stores all around West Steward and Steward, Arkansas, wherever he found a Colored school without such a store.

Twenty-six-year-old Dave could boast an income of over four hundred dollars a month, when a very decent house could be built for less than three hundred dollars.

"Dave, you oughta start going back to church seeing as how the Lawd done blessed you," Lela had advised. "LawdhavemercyJesus! I wish yo' daddy would come home and see you nah!"

Two

Usually Lela Bailey was "up with the chickens" like mostly everyone else in West Steward, Arkansas. Four thousand and some odd souls, almost equally divided between blacks and whites, crawled off to bed by 8 o'clock and hopped up by 5 a.m. If West Steward residents varied from this routine "den dere wuz a damn good reason fer it," anyone would tell you.

But lately Lela had taken to dozing until seven to "rest her old bones mo'," as she put it. In the last year, Lela had started to feel a very pronounced stiffness in her joints upon arising. She felt stiff and wobbly now, as she walked down the middle of the wide hall to the kitchen of the house that Dave had laid out and practically built single handedly seven years ago when he was just nineteen years old.

Muddear's house, as Dave called it, was far more spacious and attractive than the average home in Colored Town. It was not a shotgun—a poor house consisting of three, maybe four rooms, one directly behind the other. No, this was a six-room "double shot," with three large rooms on either side of a wide hall. On the west side, Dave's bedroom was in the front of the house, his mother's room was at the back of the house, where it was quieter and closer to her domain—the kitchen. In between was a sitting room, a multi-purpose room really, that often served as a guest room or second parlor. Often Lela would find Dave in this cozy room with its own fireplace, reading newspapers and magazines, or even an occasional book. Lela also kept her sewing machine here.

In this room also, which was larger than either of their bedrooms, was a full size bed with a small table next to it and a cool window above. A davenport served as a divider between the sitting and sleeping area.

Because there were no Colored hotels in West Steward this large room often served out-of-town guests—free of charge and with daily meals thrown in to boot! If one were relatively well off, a small donation for the church was acceptable and should be left in a saucer on the night stand by the bed.

12

On the east side of the hall was the front room, or parlor, behind that the dining room, and directly following, the kitchen, which Dave had built on the east side of the house so it would never have to suffer the heat of the afternoon sun.

Lela's kitchen was a marvel for its day. It had a large wood burning stove with eight "eyes," two ovens, and a large warmer on top—the only one in Colored Town like it. The large, sturdy wooden table that sat in the middle of the floor could easily seat eight comfortably, and often did. A bright floral oil cloth that covered the table and the floor-to-ceiling shelves that held Lela's canning added a riot of color. And— most prized of all—a porcelain sink featuring cold running water right in the house.

On the back wall of the kitchen was a bank of three windows that allowed a view of the entire backyard. Under these low built windows Lela had placed another small table. This was where she sat each morning drinking her sassafras tea with its dollop of canned milk. And this was where each day was planned "in all humbleness of spirit through prayer and meditation, each day starting out wit' da Lawd o'glory."

"White folks would shit if dey sawed dis beautiful big assed kitchen Dave done set his mama up in, not be mention da rest of da house!" Aggie Pratt frequently exclaimed as she enjoyed tea and tea cakes with "Mother Bailey or Mother B" as she called Lela.

While Lela would chide Aggie for using bad language, she couldn't help feeling pleased about the statement itself. It was a remarkably spacious and comfortable house for a Colored woman to own in 1930.

This morning Lela had called her little friend over to help with canning, but she intended to try and find out—by the use of sly and cleverly worded sentences— whether Aggie knew anything about the contents of the room.

Aggie Pratt was a pretty, small, light-skinned woman of twenty-eight. She had waist length brown curly hair specked with copper that was usually braided in one long plait that hung down her back. She smiled, and laughed a good deal in a surprising husky voice for a woman barely five feet tall. She was only just taller than her two sons, nine-year-old Arky and eleven-year-old Villa, and she could often be seen running hot, dusty foot races with them up and down the streets of West Steward, much to the amusement or dismay of other mothers who "had sense enough to act more dignified."

Aggie cared not a "pickled peach" for what others thought of her. She was a tough little washerwoman with a dead husband—killed in some mysterious way when he went to Kansas City to bury his uncle—and two boys to raise. Folks who didn't like her could kiss her yellow behind, and she said so, loudly and often. The way Aggie figured it, she made her own living, and thanks to Dave and Mother B, it was a good one. And she had her own friends, the Boise sisters, Dave, Pete, Omar, Tom Leak, Mother B. It was enough. She cared little for most people outside of her tried and true circle of friends—and nothing at all for the heifers who thought that, because she had no husband and was considered a nice piece of yellow, she was after their little sad assed piece of nigger! Humph! There were more of those old clownish good for nothings after her than she was after them—that was for sure!

Lela knew Aggie was as loyal as one could be and closed mouth enough that Dave might have told her something to do with what he had in that little room, especially considering the "special work" that Aggie sometimes did for Dave. Who would have suspected that this freckle faced urchin, with her long plait was the best spy that Colored Town ever had?

Aggie was perfect for the job and she loved it—it made her feel important, useful. Very light on her feet she was, when she stepped up on the back porches of the houses in White Town to deliver her finished wash of shirts and waists which were her specialty. Like air she moved about, peeking, gathering, listening for what she could hear, for what she could bring back to Colored Town—information that could protect them all.

When Aggie was caught snooping where she didn't belong, she'd play dumb: "Oh! 'scuse me! Ise a-looking fer Susie or Mary (or anybody). Dis ain't the house of Missus Whitelady? Please 'scuse me! I 'pose to be working with 'er today as extra help. Dey be having a party for old Mistah Whiteman dis evenin'. I beg y'all most humble partners! I didn't steal nothin'! You kin check, miz (or mistah) and see. I'll wait."

They usually did check, and, finding nothing amiss, the pretty little bright-skinned servant was sent on—often with a smile. Everybody knew Coloreds were dumb and were likely to be found in places they weren't supposed to be.

If all else failed, Aggie had a ready answer that always worked: she was looking for another servant. It was as simple as that. She was so young, so pretty, so bright skinned that no one in White Town ever worried that she might be up to no good.

Aggie had only a fourth grade education but she was no fool when it came to sniffing out things. She was the best person Lela could try to talk to about what Dave had stacked up that room. But what if she truly didn't know anything about

14

it? Lela was sure she would be able to tell and decide what to do from there.

Did Omar or Pete know? Would Dave discuss his deepest business with his friends but not his mother? Lela could not be sure. Dave didn't like to worry his mama. They could all know, but Lela was at a loss to discover who did and who didn't, and she felt about to "burst wide open" from the stress of concealed knowledge and wonder.

Lawdhavemercy! Lela thought. She had never seen so many weapons! *Jesus! Jesus! What was dey fer?*

If Lela had hoped for a quiet talk over tea and cakes, she knew this morning's visit with Aggie would be anything but quiet the moment she saw the small woman running toward the house like the Devil himself was after her. While it was not unlike Aggie to be in an excited rush, somehow Lela already knew that this morning would not go as planned.

"Miz Bailey!" Aggie called as she came through the door. "I gots some news for you!"

Once Aggie had settled and caught her breath. She couldn't wait to get her news out.

A few months ago Dave had realized that there must be a snitch in Colored Town—someone who was passing information to the sheriff and his cronies. A watch was placed on the home and office of Sheriff Henry Birkens and Colonel Louis D. Stassen, known as Louie D, who was reputed to be in charge of the Ku Klux Klan. In a very short time, the frequent comings and goings of one Marko Horton was duly noted.

Aggie and Lela lowered their voices until they were almost whispering. This was not conversation that should be overheard by outsiders.

"Dat's who on the Sheriff's payroll—Marko Horton?"

"Dat be da one," Aggie exclaimed softly, angrily. She shook her head as if she could not believe it. "Why he do dis to us? We always treated him nice in dis community!"

Lela sighed heavily. "Lawd only know why we do what we does! You know Marko. He be a little bit different from the average main."

"He be a sissy!" Aggie spit out. "He crazy! Sometimes he puts lipstick and rouge on his face! And powder! Humph!"

"Not being quite like other mens," Lela continued, "could be we 'cepts him mo' den he 'cepts hisself. He probably carrying on a big fight inside hisself, you know? Maybe he feels like an outsider. Like since he can't be no regular ordinary person like other mens, he done bottled up all dat hate he has fer hisself and nah he just spilling it all on us. I dunno. I do know dis, he a strange bird ain't he?"

"A shitty bird is what I calls 'em!" Aggie said tossing her copper braid. "Blair Brown act like mo' a sissy den Marko, wit' his high squeaky voice, and da way he switches around, but he ain't like Marko! Everybody likes Blair. He be making some good cakes."

"What I called you over heah fer was the canning" Lela said, interrupting Aggie's musing. "I need you to help me can. Is you gone be 'vailable Aggie?"

"Sho' I bees 'vailable. You pays me mo' den da washing—not dat I'm just doing hit fer pay. You and Dave done been nice to me when I need it most. 'Sides, canning is fun. Mo' fun den washing. I'll give mah customers to a friend nex week."

Lela decided to leave well enough alone today. This business about a snitch was enough excitement for this morning.

That same Thursday morning Ralph Duster, a hot tempered twenty-year-old self-employed appliance and auto repair man was slapped in the face "like I was a little chile!" by one Leon Baycott, who was known to be very harsh in his treatment of Negroes. The forty-five-year-old Baycott had two claims to fame: one was that he had the biggest thang in Arkansas-even bigger than most niggers, or so he bragged. In the company of white men, Leon would not hesitate to offer visual proof, and therefore got the nickname of "The Horseman." The other claim was more virulent. With his self proclaimed "endowment," Leon considered himself somewhat of a stud. Around town he let it be known that he had slept with "a lotta men's wives." At present the lucky woman (someone would later remember that was exactly how he had put it) was Mrs. Luxury Tweedle, the wife of a traveling harness salesman by the name of Brentwood Tweedle.

Lux Tweedle, short for Luxury, which she thought she was, was a thirty-eight-year-old redhead who looked like she lied at least ten years off of her age. She wasn't particularly pretty but she had a good figure, slim legs, and was a real hot number according to Leon. "Soon as Tweedle leaves town I goes for some Twaddle" snickered the owner of Baycott's Feed and Grain serving West Steward since 1905.

Leon Baycott had slapped Ralph so hard for "sassing" him that morning that Ralph's nose had bled. The young man had rushed into the house from his little shop in the back yard bloodied and furious. It was all his parents could do to calm him down—for they didn't wish to see him lynched. Thomas and Eunice Duster had lived a long time in the South—long enough to know that a black man might get slapped at any time, and if he wanted to live, had to learn to get over it.

Later on that day Ralph was heard to remark, "I ought to kill that old gray bastard!"

"Ought" became "will" and was swiftly carried to the ears of Sheriff Henry Birkens after Leon and his lady love were found brutally hacked to death two days later on Saturday, October 4.

Leon Baycott and Luxury Tweedle were found "My God! Chopped up like chow-chow!" exclaimed the sickened milkman who found them at eight o'clock Saturday morning after he had sat the sweet milk in the ice box as usual then went calling for Mrs. Tweedle in order to collect on her bill. He had found the bedroom door wide open and at first could not believe his eyes. "There was blood all over everything. The walls, floor, the ceiling! I ran out of there 'bout to puke, honest to God!"

"Find the husband," said Sheriff Birkens. A neighbor said Luxury Tweedle had a daughter by a previous marriage over in Friars Point, Mississippi. Maybe she would know where her stepfather was.

The bodies had to be "morgued" Sheriff Birkens said. The fingerprint and lab boys were on their way from Monroe County, and deputy DeBell Hinkle was on his way South across the river to Friars Point. The milkman was not a suspect, but he was told not to leave town until further notice.

The Duster boy would be questioned, the sheriff decided without telling anyone but his deputy, who was then sworn to secrecy—for the sheriff did not want a mob on his hands.

Ralph Duster would have to be talked to, because by the time one hour had passed after the murders were discovered "certain information," the sheriff told Hinkle mysteriously, "has done come to ma ears."

THREE

L ess than an hour after the news of the double murders had reached Colored
Town, Dave dispatched Aggie Pratt to White Town with a load of his own shirts
in her big straw basket which she balanced on her head. Shortly before ten, Aggie
was back. Out of breath she related her findings to those gathered. Peter
Frauzinou, Omar Williams, LaSalle Peabody, Will Henry Mead, and Dave and Lela
Bailey, all sat around the table in Lela's big kitchen listening to the report and
talking in hushed tones. Tom "Fool" Leak stood guard outside to warn of any
approaches to the house. Tom was sometimes wild and scrambled but he was
pulled together enough to stand watch today, they agreed.

"Alright!" Aggie said, signaling for everybody's attention. "Y'all ready to hear
da report? Den heah it is: Sheriff Birkens, say dis ain't no darkie crime. They
wouldn't dare do what was done to dose two in dis county. Say what reason would
dey have anyways? Say man caught in bed wit' another man's wife pure and simple.
Say Leon was just axing for trouble—nah he done got it," Aggie continued in her
husky delivery, hardly catching her breath. "Sheriff Birkens, he say Negroes use
razors and sometimes pistols—not hatchets. He say he knows 'em —what dey do
and what dey don't do."

"Did they find the murder weapon?" asked Dave.

"Naw. But de doctor dat was called in—he say some o'it been done with a
hatchet. Yeeee Eee!" screeched Aggie.

"My Lawd in heaven!" exclaimed Lela. "One what done it was mighty mad or
mighty crazy!"

"Or both!" said Omar.

"Dats what the sheriff say," Aggie continued, "Say who ever done it was mighty
mad 'cause dey done smashed da brains right outta Leon Baycott's head!"

Recounting the story caused Aggie to shiver and Lela handed her a cup of hot
tea which she drank for several seconds before continuing.

"Say look like somebody, maybe Mistah Tweedle done came up on 'em, and wham! Bam! Done 'em in good fashion."

So, the sheriff didn't believe a Negro had committed the murders. They could all breathe a sigh of relief—for now.

"Good work!" said Dave. "How did you get all that information so quickly?"

"You know Oscar Manor? I calls him drunk Oscar. He's been trying to git to be mah boyfriend since I came back from Kansas City. Well, he was put in dis little old cell for two days, Friday and Sattiday, fer disturbing da peace—which he always does—dis time he was trying ta git in Mabel Conway's whorehouse—excuse me Mother B—which of cose you know jus' "services" white mens, even tho' Mabel be black as midnight without no moon herself!

"Well," continued Aggie, enjoying being the center of attention, "In dat little bitty jail you can hear everything. I bail Oscar. It only be two dollars, but Oscar, he ain't got it. Once I got 'em out, I sweets talks 'em you know—like I might go to Princess Thelma's wit' him one time and all dat, and he jus' tells me everythin' he knows. He be very upset 'bout dem bringing Ralph Duster's name into it. He 'fraid for Ralph, you know?"

Ever cautious, Dave asked whether she had asked Oscar to be quiet about her questions.

"O'cose!" Aggie was momentarily offended that Dave felt he had to "ax me such a question, you know I be highly careful!"

Dave gave Aggie a conspiratorial wink that said, "am I forgiven for asking?"

Of course he was.

It was no secret that Aggie had the "sho nuff hots" for Dave Bailey. To her snickering friends she had confided that "Nah deres a main! He can pull my bloomers down anytime! Why he laks that heifer Adrianna James mo' den me is beyond me! I knows I'm better looking!" When Aggie got to this point in her story, which was often, she would prance around the room switching her hips and flouncing her hair in a comically exaggerated manner that never failed to send her friends, including Omar's wife, Ray Jean, into spasms of laughter. And as long as they would laugh Aggie would clown, continuing her prancing and mimicking of Adrianna's whiny voice until the "girls" would keel over on the floor nearly dying of laughter.

"Lucky we got us such a smart gal!" Lela said, smiling the pleasure the entire group felt with Aggie for her spying skills.

After combining the various bits of information each of them had been able to gather along with Aggie's report, the group decided that Ralph Duster was definitely in danger, and they ought to take quick precautions—especially since Aggie had also revealed that Ralph had not gone home last night and wasn't seen again until around seven o'clock that morning.

Plans were hurriedly made and two groups were dispatched. Lela Bailey, Aggie Pratt and LaSalle Peabody in one group, and Dave, Peter Frauzinou and Omar Williams in another. The three young men piled into Dave's pickup truck and went looking for Marko Horton. It was not yet noon.

Lela and her group went to the home of Ralph Duster's parents, Thomas and Eunice, and confronted them with what they had heard: that someone had overheard Ralph wish Leon Baycott dead—indeed had threatened to kill him—and now he was dead.

The parents realized instantly that their son was in danger and Eunice began to cry soundlessly, holding her apron to her mouth in an effort to stifle her tears. Thomas swore quietly and the angry and helpless look that Lela had seen for more than fifty years came into Thomas' eyes.

The set shoulders, slack mouth, misty eyes—the low moans of injury and pain. *Well not this time!* Lela thought. *With any luck, not this time, white folks!*

"They're ain't no use in cryin', Eunice," Lela said kindly but firmly. "Now, heah what we gone do." Lela and LaSalle and Aggie took turns outlining the plan.

Although frightened nearly out of their wits, Ralph's parents agreed that the plan might work. Lela and her son Dave were leaders in the community and she had come to help them. They had to trust her. It was their only chance.

It was now nearly noon. Where was Ralph now? Sitting in the front room as peaceful as you please. Ralph showed no evidence of having heard them come in. Lela and her group were in the kitchen.

"Ralph had just got in not long ago," Eunice said with disapproval. None of her children had ever stayed out overnight before—but "Mistah Funky butt don got to smelling his drawers!" as Eunice pungently put it, for the moment forgetting the larger problem they had.

Suddenly Eunice stopped mid sentence and realized that they were all looking at her. Had the same thing occurred to them all—that Ralph might indeed be the killer?

LaSalle Peabody was a man of a little less than average height and made up right "bunchy," Aggie had remarked. Not fat, but with a round, clean head, a small paunch, and the high round buttocks that brought him a lot of teasing. He was of medium coloring, what Negroes called "brown skinned."

He always had a serious expression that belied his actual age, which was thirty. Most people thought he was closer to forty. Lela liked him a lot. In her book, it didn't do for a man, or a woman for that matter, to be too silly.

LaSalle was a stable, serious, hard worker. Lela looked at the young man with admiration that extended to her own son, for he had picked an excellent man in LaSalle. Both Lela and Aggie had agreed that LaSalle, being the man in the group, would ask the questions.

"Nah, ahm gone ax you some questions Mistah and Miz Duster—Naw, don't git Ralph, just let 'em sat where he at fer a spell."

"He say he tired," volunteered Eunice Duster, "Very, very tired. I say if you tired, git in bed—he say naw, 'I wanta stay up for a while. Don't wanna git no bad dreams.'"

LaSalle grunted loudly. "Is dat right?" he asked no one in particular.

"He setting in da chair sound asleep nah," Eunice added, "but still he don't want to sleep in no bed."

LaSalle had on his most serious face. "Please don't take no 'fense wit' my questions, but if we gone help, we gotta know certain things. Nah. Where your boy be last night? Did he say?"

"Naw, he didn't say nothin'," answered Thomas Duster. "He jus' come in round seven." He caught his wife's eye for possible correction.

"Closer to seven forty," she stated.

"What he do den?" asked LaSalle.

"I was waitin' fer 'em."

"What he do then?" LaSalle repeated, trying to keep his voice calm.

"I say, 'Where you been 'til dis time of moaning, boy? I say you hoingry? You want somethin' t'eat?' Again I ax 'em where he been."

"But he didn't say where. Right, Miz Duster? Yo' boy, he got a gal?"

"It's like I done tole ya befoe. I don't 'low no over-nightin'. Yas. He got him a sweetheart, but her mama and papa be very strict on her."

"Where are yo' other chirrens nah?" asked LaSalle.

"Da girls, dey helps the washerwoman, Hattie Mackie, to deliver on Sattiday moanings—she gives dem fifteen cents apiece. It helps. Joe Bee—he down at the church. He be cleaning it up fer Sunday. We figure dats a nice job for 'em."

They were talking quietly, almost whispering. Aggie could see Ralph from the kitchen as he sat in a chair, his head lolling in sleep. There was something strange about him sleeping through all this, Aggie thought, something unreal.

"So Ralph left last night. What time? Could he have been wit' some friends?"

"We dunno what time he left," Thomas Duster said with a pained expression on his face. "He was out in the shed workin' on somethin'. We got in da bed around 'bout eight. I didn't know he weren't heah 'til Mama woke me up. As fer friends, I 'spose he coulda been wit' friends—but I never knowed him or his friends to stay up past eleven o'clock—even on da weekends. Where would dey go? What would dey do? Dey ain't got no money. Sometimes dey play up a little cards—but like I says, dey all be home fo' midnight even den."

LaSalle made a mental note to talk to some of Ralph's friends then abandoned it because he didn't want to drag any other young people into this situation.

Finally LaSalle asked Thomas Duster to fetch his son from the front room.

Ralph, thin and slightly over six feet, shuffled in, still looking tired. He stared at the group curiously, blinking them into focus.

Lela told him why they were in his mother's kitchen—she told Ralph about the murders, which he professed not to know anything about. Where were you? Couldn't sleep so jus' went walking. Did anyone see you? Naw. Can anyone supply you with an alibi—in case one is needed? Naw. So you walked all night? Yes. I might o'slept under a tree for a while.

They all stared at him. "Slept under a tree?"

"It were cold outside last night," Aggie exclaimed incredulously. "I mahself slept wit' a quilt inside da house!"

"Son, you best tell us where you really was," pleaded the boy's father. "Dese peepers is heah because somebody heard you threat to kill Leon Baycott, nah he dead! Git some thinkin' into yo' head boy!" Thomas Duster said angrily. "You might have ta run out of heah in a hurry!"

"I ain't going nowhere. Can't lynch nobody for taking a walk."

"But it were cold last night!" Aggie persisted.

"I had a blanket," Ralph said sullenly.

"You done took a blanket? To walk wit'?" Eunice asked, her voice full of exasperation and fear.

Ralph did not answer. He had taken a seat at the table. He glanced at all of them again: the woebegone LaSalle, the pretty face of Aggie Pratt, old Lela Bailey, his daddy and mama looking tight and pinched and scared. His eyes came to rest on LaSalle Peabody and his bib overalls. And he said something that chilled them all to the bone. "Leon Baycott, he really sho' nuff dead? Good. I'm glad. I knowed somebody was gone kill 'em one of dese days. He weren't no good. He deserve to be knocked in the head. Whoever did it got my thanks."

Thomas Duster was on his feet. "Boy, you talkin' like a fool! Don't you let nobody heah you talkin' like dat!"

Ralph regarded his father calmly, coolly. "Is I'm talking like a fool? I don't feel like no fool—not no more."

"Lawd, Lawd, Lawd" exclaimed Eunice, bursting into tears.

LaSalle's mouth felt dry. "What do you mean by, 'not no more?'" he asked.

Ralph stared at the floor. A little smile crept over his handsome face. "Mean he can't bother me no more, and cheat me out o' what rightfully belong to me, dats all."

But nobody in the room believed that was all. Ralph knew what the South was like—he might be suspected of killing two white people—yet he sat there fearless as a rock, talking about how glad he was. They were all stunned.

Eunice had gotten control of herself to some extent and sniffled quietly at a corner of the table holding her husband's hand.

"Son," said LaSalle evenly. "I'm gone ax you jus' once mo'—where was you betwixt last night and dis moaning?"

Ralph answered LaSalle without looking up. "I was out walkin'. I stopped, sit down—den I musta fell asleep. I woke up, den I come home. I don't remember nothin' else."

"Was you doing any of yo' walking up in—White Town? Do you recollect?" asked LaSalle slowly.

"I don't reckoleck," Ralph answered dully, with a tinge of hostility.

Aggie stared at Ralph, her mouth wide open.

"Well, Jesus!" exclaimed Lela with some consternation, "I guess we done better git some kind of plan together as an excuse for Ralph without any mo' stalling."

"Nah, jus' a minute!" Thomas Duster burst out, jumping up from his seat again. "You mean to tell me dat if the sheriff ax you where you was during da time of dem peepers gittin' kilt you gone say," and here Thomas Duster adopted a high falsetto, "why I doesn't remember, boss! Jus' be walking all around. Jus' be sleeping under a tree, den I come home. Don't remember nothin' mo'!" Thomas banged the table, almost exploding with rage.

"Dat is the truf of what happen," Ralph replied mildly, ignoring his father's outburst.

"We'd better git y'alls plan a goin', Mother B, 'cause da way dis boy talkin' they'll have his behind hanging like an apple on a tree befoe night!" exclaimed the frustrated father.

Would Ralph even agree to a plan? Certainly, for he had always liked dramatic plays—had always thought if he were a white boy, he would try to get into movie pictures. He knew he was good-looking enough to be a screen star. Girls had told him so.

FOUR

~~*~~

Finding the snitch, Marko Horton, fell to "da three." Lela called them, her son Dave, Omar, and Peter, best friends since childhood.

The men left the truck downhill a short distance away and proceeded to move quickly and quietly through the fragrant high grass that had been baked a soft faded yellow by the summer sun. They moved single file until they reached Marko's small, overgrown, trash filled yard.

Quietly, Peter walked to the back of the house and stole a peek through the back window. Omar and Dave were right behind him and saw that Marko was alone, preparing a late morning breakfast as peaceful as you please, boiling a little pot of rice, frying flat brown pan sausages and eggs in the same skillet, baking his biscuits. The snitch's good coffee filled the air with an unbearably lovely scent that reminded the men that due to developments, they had not yet eaten. Omar's stomach let out a ferocious growl.

"Keep that big gut quiet!" Peter hissed.

"Ise trying boss," Omar whispered.

Dave went up to the door and knocked gently. It was just a two-room shack, hardly bigger than the playhouse Dave and Omar had built when they were boys.

Marko took a few steps and opened the door a tiny crack, smiling slyly as if he were expecting someone and this little peep of an opening was their private joke.

Bang! The three men busted into the crack like gangbusters, and it took them all of forty seconds to search the house for visitors, so poor and meager were the snitch's accommodations.

"Well, well, well!" lisped Peter. "I see us got us a little bitty table set fer two. Nah, who is we 'pecting on dis fine day? Blair Brown, maybe?"

Peter, who had been educated in good Catholic schools spoke good "proper" English, but loved to talk "flat" from time to time for effect.

Peter placed his hand on one hip and threw it outrageously out of place. With the other hand he blew Marko a kiss.

Marko's eyes popped with fear and his forehead beaded with perspiration. He knew these three were up to no good, and as he turned and tried to escape he was tripped by Omar and fell comically into Dave's outstretched arms.

"Sit down!" Dave ordered, roughly pushing Marko into a chair.

"Hey! What y'all want? What y'all doin heah?" protested the terrified man. "Y'all got no right to come bustin' in on me like dis! No right atall!"

"To put this nice straight razor on your worthless neck, Mistah Snitch?" asked Omar in a chillingly soft voice as he stepped behind Marko's chair. Omar pinned Marko's shoulders to the chair, crossing his right arm in front of Marko, he placed the hand with the razor against Marko's jugular vein on the left side.

"Move even a little bitty bit and yo' nappy head goes rolling across dis dirty flo'," Omar promised in his ice cold voice.

The pinned Marko let out a low primeval moan that filled the room with savage intensity: "Moomma! Moomma!"

"Shut up!" Peter yelled.

Dave moved around and sat in front of the snitch on the edge of the small table. "We have it on good authority that you are our little tattle-tale, Marko Horton. The one that tells Sheriff Birkens and all the other peckerwoods everything that goes on in Colored Town, aren't you?"

The pinned man tried to protest with another moan but they all saw the flicker of frightened guilty acknowledgment cross his face. Now he knew why they were here and the fear he felt now did not compare with what he had felt at first. He was frozen. He dared not breathe. So sharp was Omar's razor that when he moved his head a bit, he felt a slight nick that sent a little trickle of his life's blood spilling onto his collar.

"Everything!" Dave continued almost pleasantly. "Things we didn't mind the sheriff knowing and things we were trying to keep in the community, just between us, you know?"

No. Marko did not know. He could never experience how lovingly Dave's tongue wrapped around the word *us*. Although it was not so with other homosexuals—Marko knew that by nature he was an outsider and he felt fated, and until now, comfortable in his role. He felt no guilt for what he had done. Was he trying to please a father he never knew? An abusive mother he could never please? Well his tattling pleased, paid well, and made him feel important. Useful. Powerful.

Now bound by Omar's strong black arms and ignorant of what his future held at the hands of these intense men, Marko's mind went nearly blank with fear. What thoughts he could focus on turned to Sheriff Henry Birkens. Marko knew that the sheriff was in this mess somewhere. What a man the sheriff! He truly loved gossip, scandal and evil reports. Marko figured himself a poor man, direly in need of sources of income—it never occurred to him to get a job. He figured himself too smart to become a latter day slave in some factory, mill, or cotton field. As long as white men would pay for lies he would tell 'em! Neither conscience, nor loyalty, nor love was in his vocabulary—but money was.

When he, Marko, had raced up to White Town "wit' a really interestin' story," he found the sheriff, his deputy, and three or four of the sheriff's old jailhouse cronies sitting around a small iron stove drinking a potent brew of black coffee and canned cream heavily laced with bootleg whiskey.

"Heah come my telegraph coon!" the sheriff had said, meaning no offense. He liked Marko. "Dat boy sho' helps keep mah life from a getting' dull betwixt cases!" he often said with affection, and he paid him for big scoops relating to keeping Colored Town law abiding, and Marko, anxious to keep in favor with the Law, gave Sheriff Birkens tidbits of gossip and scandal for free. Such a boy was invaluable.

On the particular day that Marko was remembering at that moment, he had told the sheriff and his friends about Dabney Shell and her daddy. Well, the sheriff and his buddies wanted to hear more—and they paid a good piece of change for all he could tell. Before he left the five drunken men circling the little potbellied stove he had two dollars, more than a week's wages for many, in his pocket. And they still wanted to hear more. So Marko embellished, fabricated, and lied. He threw in a dog with Dabney and her daddy—Hell, Marko would have thrown in a goddamned horse and wagon the way the money kept rolling in as he told his story to the dirty-minded men up in White Town.

"Go down dere to Nisson's drug stow and tell Brady Nisson what you jus' don tole us. He'll gie you a piece o' change," the sheriff chortled. And on one of the few phones in West Steward, the sheriff called Brady and tole him to "git some of the boys together. Marko got a story to tell ya dats a dosier!"

Marko related his prurient story over and over, never once relating any of the heroics of the tale—never mentioning how a group of the Colored community men, learning what was going on between the unwilling Dabney Shell and her father, LeBow, after her mother's death, collected sixteen dollars between themselves and gave it to LeBow Shell, warning him to never set foot in West Steward again or have any further contact with his four children. Marko also never bothered to tell the sheriff and his pals how Lela Bailey, Mother Clarence, and a few others in the community sacrificed their own beliefs, their own Biblical sense of morality, for the fourteen-year-old who had been severely abused by her own father.

Hardly anyone in the black community openly believed in abortion. If a girl got herself "in a family way" and the boy refused to marry her, well-to-do families sent her away to relatives out of state, and the girl always came back without the baby which had been left with a childless aunt or a grandmother, etc. who adopted the child without benefit of law. To the ninety percent who were dirt poor, the child was simply absorbed into the family and no more was said about it.

Dabney Shell's case was clearly different. It was an outrage. "Da daddy will also be da granddaddy? It was a shame befo' da Almighty!" declared the good sisters of West Steward. Something had to be done.

And something was done. John Candle, the ancient herbalist, who had been to Africa sixty years ago knew all about herbs and roots and "potions." He would extend his legendary help to the girl Dabney Shell—but very reluctantly because "Good Gawd for sinners!" she was entering into her sixth month of pregnancy, and was "much too far gone," said the old man. But knowing the evil of the circumstances he agreed to help.

The greater reluctance was felt by the women who went up the hill near midnight to support Dabney's grandmother, Esta York. Lela Bailey, her best friend, Mother Clarence, and a few other close "old sisters."

The women hardened their hearts because they were convinced that this "devil's work" had to be done. When the abortion was finished, the "old sisters" stood in a circle and prayed while crying themselves dry.

And how did Marko know the entire story of what happened to Dabney Shell? Simple. Marko followed action to make his money. He hung around bus stations, car lines, cafés, taverns—juke joints—around barber shops and beauty parlors. Even around funeral homes. He was also a regular at Princess Thelma's and other places of action and entertainment.

There was usually a story in who left and who came into town, so when Marko saw the stout LeBow Shell half running to the bus depot very early one morning he followed him from a distance, then hid himself in the shadows and watched for what he might see.

So, in his travels Marko had heard bits and pieces of Dabney Shell's story. He assembled the pieces into a whole and relayed the entire, sordid incest story to his "paying" customers up in White Town.

But now, the three men in his room at this moment were going to stop him from this profitable business. Marko felt the blood drying on his neck. His own life's blood!

"Everything!" Dave continued. "Everything that goes on in Colored Town. Every birth, death—if someone farts down here you have the news in White Town before anyone in this community can smell it don't you, you piece of shit!"

Dave walked back and forth in front of the little table. "I'd say we had us a snitch wouldn't ya say? Speak up, damn you!"

"N-o-o-o-o-! N-o-o-o-o!" The sound from the snitch was a hoarse croak, a pitiful moan.

The sausages were burning, sending a pungent over-heated odor into the tiny house. Peter calmly removed the old skillet from the stove and dumped Marko's greasy breakfast out of the window with a malicious smile.

Dave stared off into space, a finger thoughtfully pressed against his lips. Finally he said to Marko: "I think you had something to do with Billy Binders death in 1928, you handkerchief head nigger! You gave somebody his name didn't you—as the one who played the prank on that ugly white girl. Because of a little childhood fun a boy is dead," Dave's voice broke with emotion remembering the sixteen year old fun loving boy.

Billy had been shot and then dragged through the streets of West Steward behind a pick-up truck until his body had literally fallen apart for allegedly chasing a white girl with a garden snake one evening, scaring her half to death. Now Marko knew, as did everyone else in Colored Town, that Billy was a prankster and had surely informed some cruel white man of this fact. Three days later, Billy Binder was dead—because the charge of intent to rape had been added to the story.

Later, a seventeen-year-old white boy confessed to the prank, stating that he had darkened his face with soot, put on a black wooly cap, and chased Martha Lou Henley because he didn't like her. By the time the confession was made Billy Binder had been dead two months. Billy's mother, Cressy had not yet accepted the fact of his death, and often made a pitiful scene walking around West Steward asking various people if they had seen her dead son. Usually her husband would be fetched to come for her, and he and her only other child, an eleven-year-old girl, would take Cressy home.

Meanwhile, Martha Lou, who was grossly fat with huge, short legs still came down to Colored Town to the Boise sisters' cafe for lunch whenever she pleased. The prankster, Wayman McMahon, was never charged with anything.

Dave castigated himself for not having placed a spy in White Town until after Billy's death. Why hadn't the old heads thought of it before?

"Where were you last night?" Dave demanded of Marko.

Marko's tongue lay frozen in his mouth. He let out another low moan.

"Don't tell me you were home in bed—or somewhere minding your own business. I know better. You are a thief as well as a snitch," Dave continued taking short steps back and forth in front of the man. "You swoop down upon drunks that have fallen out in doorways like a vulture, taking their money, cigarettes, even their clothes. You are out all times of the day like a slippery eel—sneaking, peeping, and poking around to see what you can pick up—see what you can overhear. What information you can sell to get us killed."

Dave's eyes bore into the snitch. He had never felt so much hatred for anyone in his life, not even a lynch mob, for this was one of their own.

"Now," Dave said, trying hard to control his emotions, we believe another young man may be in danger and you will try to find a way to profit from it."

"N-o-o-o-o!"

"Shut up you lying sack of shit!" Omar growled, pressing even closer with his razor and drawing blood for a second time.

"Did you see anything last night? Did you hear anything? If you did you'd better tell us about it now or forever keep your trap shut," Dave warned.

"What you tell dat sheriff, Marko?" Omar asked. "Somebody say dey seed ya talkin' to da sheriff dis moaning. What you tell da high sheriff den?"

Marko struggled to speak. "Da knife!" he croaked. "Take da knife off me! I'll—"

"Then you'll talk?" Peter asked.

"Yas," he muttered.

Dave motioned Omar to move away with the razor. Omar relaxed his arm but moved only inches away keeping his razor open and ready.

Relieved to have the razor away from his throat Marko looked around beseechingly.

Correctly assessing the problem, Dave stepped over Marko's feet, opened the small ice-box and handed Marko the fruit jar filled with barely cool water.

Marko grabbed it gulping the water like an affirmation of life. He was alive. Alive! His throat wasn't cut so bad! He was drinking water wasn't he? His joy was short-lived. When he handed the jar back to Dave his hands shook badly as he realized that nothing had changed.

"Ah don't know nothin,'" Marko said in a barely audible voice.

"Speak up, damn it!" Peter demanded.

"I sez I didn't see nothin'. Didn't hear nothin,'" Marko repeated. "True da sheriff did ax me—he say, 'tell me what done happen Marko?' —but me, I sez, all dis 'bout dem killins is news ta me, Sheriff."

"But you did tell him you would find out all you could, didn't you?" Dave asked angrily. "You promised to get him the names of some suspects—some Colored suspects didn't you?"

The snitch hung his head—if not in shame, in acknowledgement of the truth.

"I tell you what let's do!" Peter said merrily, placing himself in front of Marko's chair.

"Let's kill him."

"How?" said Omar.

"You asking me how with that razor right in your hand? Cut his throat!" Peter exclaimed with boyish glee. "Lay 'em out in the yard—naw, hang 'em upside down see? I hear when you slit the throat, the heart pumps out all the blood fast and easy."

"I see," said Omar catching Dave's eye and winking.

"Then," continued Peter laughing, "we take this bloodless snitch and hang 'em back yonder on that peach tree Sheriff Birkens has in his backyard up there in White Town. The sheriff gets up, goes out back to get some wood for the stove—and there he is. His snitch—his nigger—swinging to and fro just as nice as you please from his own peach tree! Won't that be something! I'll bet it would confuse the living shit out of 'em!" Peter said gaily.

Now it was Peter's turn to wink at both Dave and Omar.

"I like dat," exclaimed Omar. "A nigger lynched by other niggers! Bet dat ain't done a lot. I likes it. It's different."

"Oh, Gawd!" moaned Marko, as he tried once more to bolt for the door, but was stopped by Dave. Omar grabbed the terrified man and pushed him back in his chair so hard that the chair nearly toppled over.

"Oh, Oh, Oh! Don't kill me, don't kill me, don't kill me!" Marko screeched. "Lawd Gawd A'mighty knows I ain't seent nothin', I ain't heard nothin'! Lawd Jesus knows I ain't tole da sheriff no nothin'! Please, please, please!" Marko begged.

Marko had no way of knowing that the young friends were only toying with him—they had no intention of killing him. So he continued to plead and moan.

Suddenly, unbidden, Dave saw young Billy Binder's body in his mind's eye—he muscle all torn off the leg bones. His buttocks a mass of frayed flesh. Did Billy plead for his life as Marko was now doing?

Dave heaved a deep guilt ridden sigh. If only they had thought about a snitch sooner!

"Don't look back. Jus' look forward—and keeping a-going on down da road," Dave's mother had always told him. Good advice from Lela Bailey to anyone who wanted to cry over a lost opportunity. Dave sighed again. It was as good advice and he would take it. There was nothing else to do.

"We have a plan for you, Marko." Dave said leaving his perch on the rickety table. Omar had moved further away now and stood wiping his razor clean. He handled it gingerly as if it had touched the worse filth in the world.

Dave told Marko what he wanted him to say to the sheriff. He used exact simple words so there would be no possibility of misunderstanding. They needed Marko for a while still.

As Dave walked around Marko in the tiny room, his nostrils were assailed by a kaleidoscope of scents from the body of the frightened man—the lingering garlic, the rancid, tallow-like odor of his unclean body, and finally a faint but unmistakable fecal scent hung in the air.

Dave wanted to kill Marko himself, for he could feel his strong hands around his throat pressing out his life's air. Omar had drawn blood with his razor. Their hatred was palpable, immediate. They had to stop these homicidal fantasies from swirling around in their imaginations. They had to hold back. One reason was their need for Marko in their plan—the other was on a higher plane.

When Rev. Matthew Moses Clayton had opened the doors of the church for acceptance of new members three months ago, Dave, Omar, and Peter—who had been Catholic all his life—surprised themselves by joining the congregation. Clayton was different than any of the old "house" preachers they had known before.

Thou shalt not kill—they all knew that—so this worthless dog must be spared.

When Dave had finished instructing Marko, he asked him if he understood. Marko nodded that he did.

"Then repeat what I just told you," Dave requested harshly. Marko found it hard to speak. His mouth was totally dry. He looked around for more water, but none was forthcoming, so he repeated Dave's instructions in a raspy whisper while keeping his eyes on the floor.

"Good. You understand," Dave said. "No slip-ups boy—and don't even think of double crossing us or the whole world won't be big enough for you to hide in, and ten thousand sheriffs won't be able to offer you any protection. Do I make myself clear?"

Again a nod. Marko looked up in time to see Peter smiling at him as he spun the barrel of his .38. He walked over, put the gun to Marko's temple, "Lets shoot 'em now," Peter said laughing. He pulled the trigger.

"Aaah!" shouted Marko. His hair stood on end as he ducked the "air bullet." Grabbing his temples he started another round of pleading, "I ain't done nothin'! Please, please, please!"

Omar exclaimed, "Well, nah look at dis! He done gone and pissed on hisself."

It was true. A wide river of topaz water appeared under Marko's chair.

Omar's shoulders shook with laughter. "Dis fool is losing all his juices! His nose is snotty, he wet wit' sweat. Nah, he done pissed and done messed on hisself! I smell shit!"

"Captain Courageous," Dave said sarcastically. "Next week we want you out of town. Not sooner, not later. Out forever. Get me? Don't tell anyone you're going. Just disappear. And Marko don't ever contact anyone back here in any shape, form, or fashion for any reason. If you do, we'll find you wherever you are."

Peter held up the gun and pointed it at Marko again. "This time I got four bullets in here instead of one. Wanna take a chance?" he taunted.

Then they turned to go. "We'll be watching yo' ugly butt every step of the way Mistah Marko," Omar threatened. "Jus' gie us one mo' reason to kill you and you gone buster!"

Peter, the last to walk out of the door hesitated a moment, walked back to the chair and smashed Marko full in the face drawing an impressive amount of blood from his nose and lips. The snitch fell from the chair onto the floor and lay like a dead possum, not daring to move a fraction or scream in pain.

"That little love tap was just in case you had something to do with them beating the shit out of me at the mill in April 1928. Thank you," Peter said, bowing and doffing an imaginary hat. "Goodbye, you sad-assed sissy."

They walked back to the truck-back through the dry sea of sweet grass. "How can you be sure Marko won't go straight to the sheriff?" Peter asked Dave.

"He won't. I've never surer of anything in my life," Dave answered dryly. "We'll put Aggie on his tail day and night until we get Ralph out of here. I'll tell Mama and Aggie what we told Marko about Ralph being sick so we can have the same story. Until then, everything has to appear normal. If that boy makes one false move, I swear to God I'll kill him myself," Dave promised fiercely. "Did you hit him Pete?"

"Sure did!"

"Let's get our business taken care of, then maybe Mama will have time to fix us something to eat."

"Thank ya Jesus!" exclaimed Omar.

"Yassuh, dats what I done heered. Been sick wit' da piles, da pleurisy, da pnewmonias, somethin like dat—since round 'bout Thursday o'last week. Naw suh! No chance him gittin' up far from outta dat bed. I done checked up upon dat real good, sheriff, cause I knowed you'd be axing seeing as how his name done comed up in dis case. Been in his bed or mighty close to it pret-near a week. Shitting and a-puking he is, suh, ifn you'll excuse da language. Naw suh. I ain't heered nothin' 'bout no getting' even. Yassuh. I don heered 'bout Ralph being mighty mad at Mistah Baycott—his slapping 'em side da head and all, but since you axed," said Marko nervously licking his dry lips again and again, "I thinks dis-a-way about it: Step out yo' place, you natchelly stands da chance of hurt. We all knows dat Sheriff Birkens, suh," Marko stated humbly. "Ralph Duster, he be knowing dat too. Yas, he does. He ain't no complete fool. How far would a Colored main git doin somethin' like dat to..."

Marko Horton didn't have to finish the sentence. It was finished for all times and in all places South. Murdering a white man, and especially a white woman was unthinkable. A death sentence sure and certain. If you did happen to get that crazy, you'd be running for your life night and day.

But Ralph Duster was home in bed. This fact told Sheriff Birkens all he needed to know—almost. The sheriff decided to think on this whole situation a bit more and to visit Ralph and see what his condition was himself, because niggers could be tricky.

FIVE

✶

Everyone was talking about the "Love Nest Murders," as West Steward's *Arkansas Listener* had pronounced them in large headlines in their special Sunday edition. "No Clues!" the *Listener* stated. "Where Is The Husband?" *The Old Steward Herald* wanted to know.

"This is a hell of a thing!" Sheriff Birkens thought as he sat in his rocking chair on the porch of his neat little widower's house in White Town on Monday afternoon. So far all of them working together—the special agents from Monroe County, himself and his deputy, DeBell Hinkle—had turned up nothing.

After following the few leads they had received and some very extensive searching in the woods, creeks, along railroad tracks, and all around Luxury Tweedle's house they had nothing. No bloody clothes, not even a fragment that did not belong to the victims; no hair or skin samples belonging to the murderer under the nails of the victims; and no weapon or weapons had been located.

Nothing. Blank. A goose egg. The case was really no further along than it had been a few days ago. "Flustrating. Very flustrating," The sheriff mumbled to himself. There was one thing however that Sheriff Birkens felt very certain of-that this was too smooth, too slick—not a Negro crime. The sheriff prided himself on knowing the mind of the Negro. Not a one had fooled him yet. No, sireebob! Everyone knew niggers had only so much brain power and no more. No, he'd go with the theory of robbery being the motive—and yet there was Leon's watch—a gold watch mind you, that was still on his wrist. Then there was the thirty dollars. *Thirty dollars* in an unopened drawer in a night stand by the bed. And Luxury's fur piece, some real looking pearls and two diamond rings—all on the dresser.

Well, perhaps the would—be robber was scared off or something before he got to take anything. Shit.

The robbery theory was thin. Very thin. The whole thing was a great big "flustration!"

Now, when Colored was involved, Sheriff Birkens knew, the whole Negro community somehow got wind of it in no time flat and they all got skittish and started to give the Law sneaky looks and all. And at night, they could be counted on to sit in houses with doors bolted, peering fearfully from behind curtains. Well, there were none of these fear signals this time Birkens had noticed. In fact, some of the elderly Colored women expressed the same anxiety as the ladies in White Town. What if it wasn't her husband who done it in a berserk rage? Maybe there was a maniac among the many unemployed men that drifted daily through this town in search of jobs, food, or anything they could lay their hands on. True, most of these drifters were honest, decent men—but these were desperate times and theft of personal property was up a good deal.

For the first time in recent memory, West Steward residents kept their doors locked day and night.

Having nothing else, the two local papers advanced the robbery theory that the sheriff and the Monroe men had abandoned rather quickly. Since the fact that nothing had been stolen was kept from them, the newspapers presented the idea that Leon Baycott was a relatively well off feed store owner, and some drifter had got wind of this and began following him around. One night he was followed to Luxury Tweedle's house and had been killed in a robbery gone awry. That idea had frightened the residents of West Steward nearly out of their wits.

Brentwood Tweedle, the husband, and prime suspect at this point, the only one that perhaps had a real motive, had not yet been located.

Sheriff Birkens let out a stream of tobacco spit that splashed halfway across the road in front of his house without getting a drop of saliva on his shirt. In his youth, Birkens had won the greater Phillips County Spitting Contest more than once. The sheriff was pleased with his performance this afternoon. He spat again, further this time. Perfect. A good way to let some of the "flustration" out.

It was getting on to one thirty. Presently, he would have to take the few miles drive back to his office after having had his dinner at noon. He had pushed and poked at the good "somethin' t'eat" his housekeeper had prepared: smothered pork chops, candied sweet potatoes, fried cabbage, fried corn, hot water corn bread, and fresh sliced tomatoes sprinkled with black pepper, salt and vinegar.

"What you think?" exclaimed the outraged Nettie Lyons. "I got time to cook up a good meal what nobody eats?"

"Nah, Net don't go gittin' yo' feathers ruffled. You know dis heah old Love Nest thing done got me a-goin. Previous to nah, ain't I always been yo' number one hog?" the sheriff teased mildly. "Put dat some t'et in the icebox and I'll eat it fer supper. Dere nah! See how I done save you from cooking again?"

Nettie grunted and waddled off, pleased.

Based on information from a friend of Mrs. Tweedle's, and a few old letters found in the house, an address for a daughter had been found and the Monroe men had gone across the river to Friar's Point, Mississippi to locate her and bring her back to West Steward. Leon Baycott's ex-wife along with his four grown children would get him buried Wednesday, then they would start to carve up his estate, which was rather impressive for these times. One down and one to go, thought the sheriff.

Now he had to question that Duster boy. That would be wise—just to cover all bases. He had considered all the signs—nobody running in Colored Town—for the bus and train station had been watched. Nobody sitting in the dark at night. All the Colored present and accounted for. Marko Horton had informed him of that on the very first day of the killings.

Better just check him out anyhow, especially since he had heard from a source other than Marko—Merle Broomfield, the insurance man, to be exact—that Ralph had indeed had a run in with Leon over repairs he had made to his car last week. Merle had told the sheriff that Ralph had fixed whatever was wrong with the car and cleaned it thoroughly inside and out to boot, expecting maybe a two bit tip, over and above the six bits he had charged him. Well, Leon not only didn't tip Ralph a quarter or so for the extra work he had done, he refused to even pay him all he owed for the repairs, claiming to be dissatisfied.

"I figger Leon was dead wrong," Merle told the sheriff. "The boy had done done a real nice job, but you know Leon is death on niggers! Well, 'cording to another source o'mines," Merle continued, "Ralph was hot! So hot in fact that he refused to accept any money from Leon. Then he pointed his finger in his face and said 'you gone git what's comin' to ya one day old man!' "

Merle Broomfield had been known to exaggerate his tales and the sheriff didn't believe Ralph would have spoken to a white man so disrespectfully, especially since everyone knew Leon would as soon shoot a black man as a rabid dog. No. He didn't believe Ralph Duster had committed the murders, but all leads had to be checked out and he wanted to do it himself on the Q.T. There had already been enough of lynchings and violence in these environs, he thought. The way he figured it, this Depression wasn't going to last, and a lot of people—business people—didn't want to raise their children in a climate where there was a whole lot of shit going on all the time. The mayor, to whom he owed his job, was always talking about the importance of bringing new business—new life, is how he put it—to this town "ATD"—After The Depression. They had to keep a stopper on things until prosperity returned. That's why he wanted to check Ralph Duster out himself, nice and quiet and peaceable like.

Marko Horton was a good snitch. Reliable. The sheriff saw no reason not to pay him his dollar weekly retainer this week although he had given him no information on these killings to date. Well. He and the Monroe experts had not turned up anything yet either. And Marko had promised to try and find out something—and at this he was better than a pack of Monroe men, the sheriff thought. The boy was a regular blood hound. Perhaps he would come back this evening with a mouth full of news.

When Henry Birkens pulled up in front of the Duster's squat, sparrow hued house at two-thirty on that afternoon, Eunice Duster was on the sagging front porch shelling sweet peas as normal as you pleased. The sheriff was alone. Birkens got out of his state issued car—the only vehicle he had—and lumbered up the two steps, hoping—yes—there was the old overstuffed chair he had seen two weeks ago when he had come to collect the rent. The sheriff suffered from corns and bunions and now his "foots," he told Eunice, "was a-killing him."

"Well, take a seat den, Sherriff Birkens, dat old chair beat up, but it be real comfortable."

"Well, hi you doing, Eunice?"

It was October 6 now and it was starting to get cooler.

"I lak dis weather. Mo' lak Spring den Fall," the woman answered amiably, still shelling her peas. "Nah, what bring ya to dese parts sheriff? You wanna see me? I done paid da rent."

Sheriff Birkens owned five small non-descript houses in Colored Town including this one. They gave him a good added income of one dollar a week each.

An attempt at humor, the sheriff noted. More friendly than scared. Nothing out of the way here. A few people stared curiously at the police car as might be expected and kept on about their business—except skinny Missy Prentice. Her extremely slew-footed legs were headed straight for him, the sheriff saw with dismay.

"Well, howdy sheriff!" Missy exclaimed cheerily from under her parasol. "Hi you feeling? Howdy do, Eunice! Real nice weather we's having ain't it? But funny. First it be hot den it be right chilly, den it be hot again. Well now," Missy continued in her rushed delivery. "You done got da one who did it yet?" Moving up on the porch, Missy didn't wait for an answer. "So many old hobos goin' and comin' through dis town! It's terrible! Suppose it coulda been one of dem? Nah, I thinks—That woman could talk the fur off a bear, the sheriff thought. He gave Eunice Duster a pleading look. Missy, not catching the eye-hint, kept right on talking.

"Missy stop by later won't ya? Somebody done stole some o'my Rhode Island Reds and I wants to talk to da sheriff 'bout it," Eunice lied.

"Some o'yo chickens? Well nah, ain't that somethin'? Same thing done happened to Omar's wife yestiddy. Got a few of her Bodderocks; might be one of dem old hobos. Wit' this Panic on and no work, peepers gits hoingry. Den dey jus' takes anything that ain't nailed down. Why last Friday—"

Eunice stared balefully at the town busybody until she finally stopped jabbering and wandered off. The sheriff let out an audible sigh of relief.

"Nah, Sheriff tell me what you is heah fer," Eunice asked, returning to her fat sweet peas.

"I'm heah to talk to Ralph. Is he heah?" The sheriff removed his ten gallon straw hat and placed it on his knee. He took out a large blue and white bandanna and mopped his nearly bald head thoroughly. He was wearing his usual starched khaki shirt, khaki pants. He prided himself on always looking neat and professional. His tin star was pinned dead center on the pocket of his shirt. Clean and tidy was his motto. The sheriff wished his deputy would take a hint from him. Even though he had a wife at home, DeBell Hinkle always looked as if he had slept in his clothes, the sheriff thought.

"Better be heah," Eunice answered blandly. "As sick as he is. What you be wanting wit' 'em, Sheriff?"

"Oh, he sick is he?" Well, that confirmed what Marko had told him. "What seems to be the matter?" He wanted to show interest but not too much.

"He be having the runs, since—yes, 'bout Thursday evening it starts up. Ain't been outta bed much since. Throwing up he is—chills, fever. All dat."

"You mean Ralph done been sick five days? Big healthy boy lak dat? What done caused his sickness do ya think?" The sheriff showed unmistakable interest now.

"I know 'xactly what done caused it. His hard head!" exclaimed his mother.

"Oh? How's dat?" the sheriff sat forward now listening to every word.

"Bad saushit!"

"Bad sausage?"

"Yassuh! I tole him! I sez, 'Ralph, don't be eatin' dat saushit. It's been sittin' out all day long. The flies be done blowed it by nah. 'Sides, I don't believe it be cooked clean through. Yo' sistah done cooked it, and you know she ain't nobody's cook. But naw. He eats it anyway. Nah look what done happened."

"I guess that'll learn 'em!" Sheriff Birkens said, greatly relieved. "Listen, you think he might be up to talking to me a little bit anyhow?" the sheriff asked considerately. "I got me some trouble."

"Trouble?" All of the panic bells were ringing inside Eunice's head. Maybe Dave and Lela's plan was crazy. Maybe they should have just took off running into the night. Trying to keep her voice steady Eunice asked: "What kind o'trouble?" Now she had gone and done it! Sweet peas were spilling all over the porch.

"Ain't you done heered," the sheriff asked peevishly, "I got me two people kilt up in White Town."

"I done heered, sho', but what dat got to do wit' Ralph?" Eunice's heart was pounding. Run, run, run! It said, as she tried to retrieve her peas.

"Well, he be a mechanic ain't he?" The sheriff was determined to keep calm. His goal was to lay eyes on the boy. Then he could tell something one way or the other, he thought. No need to cause unnecessary alarm.

"I needs old Lucy more den ever wit' da places I has to go regarding dis case— up to Monroe County and all dis criss-crossing," he flopped his long arms "here and there to Steward and back trying to follow da leads. Nah, yo' son he 'bout the best mechanic in dese parts, young or old, white or Colored. Hi can I do what I has to do without no car?" the sheriff asked reasonably. "And she definitely gettin' ready to gie me a fit wit' her sput, sputty, sput! Jus' lemme talk to 'em to see when he thinks he may be up and about again."

"Well, why sho', Sheriff," said Eunice. *Thank you Mistah Jesus!* she said silently. *Praise da Lawd! He jus' be heah 'bout dat old car of his'n. Thank you Father Gawd!*

Eunice led the sheriff down the hall, dizzy with relief. "Baby," she called to

Ralph softly, "Da sheriff is heah ta see ya, 'bout his autty mobill."

The room was fairly dark, for the shade had been pulled to keep out bright light. The boy lay on an ancient wooden bed under a tattered patchwork quilt. His legs were pulled up to his chest and he moaned softly from time to time. There was a chifforobe with a cracked mirror on one side of the small room. Near the bed was a single chair with a large bowl of uneaten soup sitting on it. White lace curtains, one with a large hole in it hung clean in poverty and dignity at the window which was closed. A shabby robe of indistinct color lay at the foot of the bed.

Ralph had been instructed to get in the bed when he heard the sheriff coming, as he surely would.

The sheriff figured himself to be an observant man, especially where blacks were concerned. He noted that when Ralph peeked out over the covers, that his nappy hair was thoroughly matted down on the side he obviously favored sleeping on. That told him that this boy had been in bed for some time.

This was a sick room all right. A nauseating mixture of odors met the sheriff's nostrils when he entered the room. The slightly pissy, mildly shitty smell of the slop-jar combined with the harsh lye soap used to scrub the wooden floors in the airless room was nearly overwhelming.

The boy told the sheriff that he felt a lot better, and yes, he would probably be up and around tomorrow—surely by Wednesday, and he would fix his car because there wasn't a car made that he couldn't fix.

Cheered by the normalcy of this youthful bragging, the sheriff was totally satisfied that Ralph Duster had absolutely nothing to do with the crime. He had the shits pure and simple.

The sheriff got into his car feeling better. Kicking up dust, Birkens turned down Mulberry Street and headed for his office which happened to be sensibly situated halfway between Colored Town and White Town. While he felt a little lighter, the killings were still uppermost in his mind. The sheriff rattled along thinking this car did need some work, and thinking about the rooms where the victims had been found. Apparently Luxury and Brentwood had maintained separate bedrooms for a long time because the only fingerprints found in her room after a number of dustings were hers and Leon Baycott's. Luxury's room seemed to be their own private love nest. The affair, the sheriff and the Monroe men found out, had been going on for almost three years.

They had searched high and low for clues, questioned a number of friends and some relatives of Leon Baycott, and they were still looking for Brentwood Tweedle. So far, a donut hole—nothing.

The sheriff thought for a minute then stopped the car, turned around and headed back to Number Four, Apple Street, back to the Duster house in a huge cloud of dust as fast as the old Ford would push.

Couldn't be too careful, Birkens reasoned. Oughta git dat boy's prints jus' in case. He parked the service car, took out his little fingerprint kit, and walked back up to the Duster's porch, knocked and entered before he was asked to do so. The sheriff noticed that although he had left just minutes before, Eunice had already stopped shelling peas—and the ones she had spilled still lay all over the porch.

There was the rushing slap of feet in old "slides" coming fast toward the front door, before the sheriff could make it past the front room, sleeping room, then back to Ralph's room again.

Eunice rushed from the kitchen wearing her ever present apron with a blend of annoyance and fear on her plain face. "It's you again, Sheriff? You done forgot somethin'?" Her voice was a high whine just short of complaint. The mother stood in the middle of the door, in the middle room of the house blocking the sheriff effectively from the back where her son's room was located.

The sheriff stopped, his tall gangly figure slouching above the woman.

"Well, Eunice, seeing as hi we got us a double killing on our hands, and seeing as hi yo' boy—now, don't let's git excited—don't let's git excited!" he admonished. "It's jus' what dey calls da purliminaries. Yo' boy," he continued, "wuz not real fond, shall we say, of the deceased, Mistah Leon Baycott, I believes dey had deyselves a little squabble a day o'two ago?"

Eunice placed her trembling hands under her apron. *Lawd, Lawd! Would dere ever come a time when Colored people wuz not scared to death of white folks?* the woman wondered.

With a mouth full of sand, Eunice tried to answer the sheriff. "Mistah Baycott done slapped my boy in da face—fer nothin'—a week or so ago, Sheriff. Natural Ralph was upset but dats all he were," Eunice swallowed, then licked her lips and continued. "Anyone would be, somebody haul off and slap 'em. But you know, Sheriff, two peepers wuz kilt were dey not? Nah, Ralph ain't had nothin' to do wit' neither o'dem killings—of dat I be positive."

"What is you gittin' at, woman?"

"Jus' dis. Da one who kilt dose peepers had somethin' against both o'dem. My Ralph don't even know no Miz Deluxe Tweedle."

"Luxury Tweedle, not Deluxe dey call her," the sheriff corrected gruffly.

Eunice realized she was skating on thin ice. Colored people did not question the Law's judgment.

To Eunice's surprise the sheriff replied: "You got a point dere—mebbe, but you tell me hi dis person or persons gone kill just one and leave the odder to tell on him? You see, I got ya dere, Eunice."

"Yassuh. You right, I reckon," Eunice answered, relieved that the sheriff had not taken offense.

"If Ralph ain't done done nothin' den you got no cause to worry. I ain't lettin' nothin' git outta hand in dis town," he said not unkindly. "Nah, where Ralph? He still heah ain't he?"

"Yeah, he still heah," Eunice answered a little too sharply, as she struggled to keep her emotions in check. She had to remember to be humble. This man was the Law. "Where else he gone be? He sicker den a dog!"

"Did you call in Doc Echardt?"

"Doctors cost money and we got none o'dat." Of course money wasn't the reason. Dr. Echardt always saw anyone at any time, money or not. Colored or white. The man was a blessing to the entire community. By saying they had not called him in because of inability to pay, Eunice wondered if she had not accidentally aroused suspicion, but thankfully the sheriff didn't seem to notice her little slip.

"I'll jus' git some fingerprints," he said moving toward the boy's room. Ralph startled the sheriff no less than his mother by sitting up on the side of the bed in the dim room and extending both his hands in what the sheriff later thought of as in a haughty way. No. Not haughty, the sheriff thought on reflection. Amused. Like he thought the prints were funny. Not something to be taken quite seriously. Well, if you were not guilty, then a young man that was after all, still a teenager, might think it was funny. And yet the sheriff sensed something in the boy. Something that made the hairs on his arms stand up, he would later relate to his cronies at the jailhouse office.

Ralph's mother hastily let up the shade to provide more light. The sheriff pulled up a chair in front of him and carefully pressed each finger into the wide, flat tin box that held the wax which captured the prints. About now, the sheriff thought, most niggers would have shit in their pants from the implications of the prints—but this one's hands were as steady as a rock.

When he was finished, the sheriff told Eunice to bring a rag to wipe the residue from her son's fingers. Ralph curled back up on the bed, a funny little smile on his lips.

"Is mah boy what dey calls a suspect, Sheriff?" Eunice asked quietly. She felt like someone was holding a towel over her face to stop her breathing.

"Naw, naw. I tole ya! Hit's jus' da purliminaries."

Sheriff Birkens looked at Eunice's worried, earnest brown face and pinched off a little bit of the small amount of pity he felt for Negroes and invested her with it. Eunice and Thomas were alright, they were hard working—if any niggers could ever be thought of as hard working. Most of the old ones had accepted the ways of the South. It was the young ones—sometimes the sheriff noticed a look in their eyes that he didn't like at all. Someone from the North was probably talking that freedom shit to them—stuff that could get you in a whole lot of trouble down here.

"Where Thomas?" The sheriff asked suddenly in a tone that said he had a right to know whatever he asked.

"Out a-looking for work."

"Sho' ain't much o'dat around."

Eunice wanted to ask when they would know if any of Ralph's prints matched the crime scene, but that would be admitting that she thought there was a chance a print of his might be there wouldn't it? Now the boy's mother was assailed by new worries. What if the sheriff could not find a white person who committed the crime and accused Ralph? He could just lie and say they had found Ralph's fingerprints. What if the sheriff's little box of wax was actually a way to plant fingerprints? How could she know the difference? *Lawd, Lawd,* the woman thought. White folks were so low down you didn't know what to expect from them.

The sheriff was leaving again. "He ain't done nothin', den you got no worries," he repeated. He waved a slack handed goodbye, and feeling pretty confident about Ralph, Sheriff Birkens walked down the steps and got into the state owned car. Kill white folks in Phillips County and then lay around in bed as cool as you pleased? No sirrebob!

Eunice stood on the pea strewn porch and watched the sheriff drive off. Then she turned her eyes heavenward. "Lawd Jesus, you said you'd never gie us mo' den we can bear. I sho' hopes you won't go back on dat promise! Thank you."

44

SIX

Luxury Tweedle's daughter was located across the river in Friars Point, Mississippi and brought back to West Steward, Arkansas the Tuesday after the murders and the day before Leon Baycott was buried.

Mathene Eddy had not been easy to locate even given the fact that "everybody knew everybody" in small rural towns, for the simple fact that she had moved three or four times in the last two years. The woman now found herself in a large but mean old rambling house in a section of Friars Point relegated to poor white trash. "Mama woulda died to know how I was living nah. That's why I didn't write to her much," she told the Monroe men.

The Monroe men brought Mathene back to Arkansas, and when the lurid details of the heinous crime were related to her she promptly fainted dead away.

Mathene Eddy was thirty-five years old and the mother of six children. She blamed her "falling out" on the terribleness of the crime and "the low blood" the doctor said she had. "I got the chronic anemica," she told Sheriff Birkens. She also told him she didn't know anyone who might want to kill her mother. True, Brentwood was Mama's third or fourth husband and her mama's other husbands had been gone a long time ago, and far as she knew the other men had remarried "or somethin' and went on about they business."

No. She had not an idea in the world where any of the ex-husbands were. No, she didn't like Brentwood no better than her mother's other husbands, one of which was the father of her oldest child. Nevertheless she didn't think Brentwood capable of such an "arful crime." He was "fraidy" just like she was.

"Fraidy?" DeBell asked.

"Yes, 'fraidy cat.'"

Deputy Hinkle and the men from Monroe County filled the little office with ill concealed snickers. So. Brentwood was afraid of his own shadow was he? "Funny. Big old fat man like dat," the sheriff said aloud.

"Yes. He 'fraid of rats too," lisped the tall, stout, baby-voiced daughter.

DeBell and the Monroe men could not contain themselves any longer and let out yelps of laughter at Mathene Eddy's last revelation.

Sheriff Birkens cast DeBell a stern look of disapproval that caused him to twirl his large cap around and around on his index finger which evoked even sterner looks from the sheriff who liked "dignity and fitness" in the office, especially in the presence of "outsiders" like the Monroe men.

The men from Monroe County took a seat on the bench in the corner, and DeBell followed their lead by taking a seat at his desk and pawed in the drawers for nothing in particular.

They had questioned Mathene—the Monroe men and the sheriff, until it became quite clear that she knew nothing about the crime at all.

Another goose egg.

Oh, no! Luxury Tweedle was fifty-two, not thirty-eight? How did anyone ever get that idea?

"I was bornt when Mama was seventeen. She never could have no more children—that's why she was so good in bed wit' mens, she once told me when she had had too much licker," Mathene giggled displaying a mouthful of rotten teeth.

The four lawmen kept a mortified silence.

On Wednesday, the fingerprint reports from the County Seat came back, DeBell Hinkle informed the sheriff. There were no prints belonging to Ralph Duster found in the murder room.

Sheriff Birkens smiled a large yellow toothed and self-satisfied smile. At that particular moment he was happier to be right than to have caught the murderer.

"Jus' like I done said, DeBell," the sheriff declared in the pompous way the deputy knew so well. "Dis definitely ain't no coon case." The sheriff knocked on the side of his head with his fist. "Never let it be said dat I ain't got nothin' in the kettle."

The Love Nest Murders had gotten large play in the press in surrounding counties as well as West Steward, Arkansas in Phillips County. On Thursday, October 9, a picture of the husband, Brentwood Tweedle, had been printed on the third page of the Marianna Monitor, and a registered nurse from Marianna Memorial Hospital over in Lee County saw it.

"Why, that's our Mr. 239!" she exclaimed. After talking with her supervisor, the nurse immediately called Sheriff Birkens' office. Much to the chagrin of DeBell Hinkle, Ida Poders would speak only to the "high Sheriff" on this "very important matter."

When Sheriff Birkens returned from "chasing suspects" he liked to say, a sorry fabrication, everyone knew, he called Ida Poders.

"I know where the husband is," she told the sheriff. Apparently Brentwood was on his way home from an unsuccessful selling trip. It seemed fewer and fewer people wanted horse harnesses these days. To comfort his injured ego, Tweedle had stopped off somewhere, gotten miserably drunk, took to the wheel of his car and soon landed at the trunk of a large tree.

"He's here at Marianna Memorial over here in Lee County with a fractured skull and a broken leg. We got 'em last Thursday morning around three. Room 239. Isn't in no condition to read the papers, so he don't know nothin' 'bout his wife and all. He been right here in 239 since last Thursday. So he certainly hasn't killed nobody," Miss Poders said emphatically. "He'll be here for quite a while. He's got a lot of healing to do."

That was that. Well, if Brentwood didn't kill his old lady, who did? "Another blank wall!" the sheriff exclaimed, rubbing his head to stave off the headache he felt coming on.

The only thing that was finally found in the "murder room" by the Monroe men that didn't belong to either Leon or Luxury was a single footprint outlined in dried blood. So many people had been in that room that the footprint had been missed for three days. Missed because the sheriff had thought it belonged to one of the Monroe men or to other lawmen, newspaper men or photographers or someone from the coroner's office. But no. After a thorough check of all the many people who had access to the room for one reason or another, the unusually narrow long footprint stood alone. Size 14 Double A it was, found right over by the window where Baycott's body was found. Yes, indeed. The lawmen were elated. Finally they had a clue! Maybe *the* clue!

They put their heads together immediately, making plans for matching the bloody print to the guilty shoe.

Deputy Hinkle could be a little mouthy and excitable, and the Monroe men were not his men after all, so the sheriff had kept what he had heard about Ralph Duster's confrontation with the late Leon Baycott to himself. He would just have a look at

Ralph Duster's feet—for the life of him the sheriff couldn't remember anything about the boy's shoe size from his last visit. He would go alone to the Duster home again and just check things out nice and easy like. The Monroe men didn't have all the sense as Deputy Hinkle seemed to think—that was for damn sure.

Finding the footprint gave all of their spirits a much needed boost, but still it was getting late and the sheriff was feeling all of his fifty-eight years. He wanted nothing more than to go home, soak his "bad foots" in a foot tub of hot water and Epsom salts, rub them with his green salve, then stretch out and nap awhile before supper. He decided to pay Marko Horton a visit tomorrow, Friday, because nobody had seen him since last Sunday. Then there was Luxury Tweedle's funeral and cremation on Saturday. A bad business, this burning people up, the sheriff thought, but at least that part of it was over and both of them would be in the ground—or at least Leon would be.

The sheriff wondered what Marko would have for him. After all this time he was sure to have something. Everything could "hold cold" until tomorrow.

One of the "rocks in his shoe" today had been Mathene Eddy—the sheriff and his men had taken to calling her Big Mat. Mathene was staying at a local boarding house. It seemed to the sheriff that the big woman had been to his office at least twenty times between yesterday and today trying to show a concern the sheriff and the Monroe men believed she really did not feel-at least not to the extent that she pestered them.

"Y'all got no more on da case? No?"

That was around ten o'clock. At eleven fifteen, Big Mat was back. "Y'all think Colored or white done done it?"

Mathene was back again at twelve thirty. They told her about the footprints. DeBell told her of the call from the nurse in Marianna, Arkansas. Mathene refused to go to the hospital to see her stepfather. "I don't care no mo' 'bout him den a dog," Big Mat volunteered to DeBell in her soft whispery voice.

Finally she talked of what the men had decided was her real interest: The insurance policy which had been found. It seemed Mathene was the sole owner of the very substantial sum of $2,500. The young woman had decided to bury her mother using as little out of the policy as was decent. Didn't she have six children to raise and a husband, well a boyfriend anyway, who hadn't hit a lick at a snake in five years?

Big Mat had decided on cremation. It was the cheapest, pure and simple. But was she doing the "rat thing sheriff? Because some peepers in dese parts considered cremation right up dere wit' idol worshipping and all."

"hit's yo' decision, mam," replied the sheriff, his mouth puckering with distaste. Henry Birkens thought of Leon's funeral the previous day. A proper burial in the ground with casket and flowers and all. Truth be known, the sheriff never did cotton to no burning people up. It was damn heathen. What they did in China or India or somewhere—not proper or fitting for Arkansas.

The sheriff spat a large amount of brown tobacco spit noisily into the spittoon to show his disgust both with the whale of a woman before him and the whole "siteewashion." He barely missed her legs—on purpose.

Mathene hurried off, her thoughts in some disarray.

"She'll be back in a hour sure as shit," said the deputy.

When they were alone, DeBell Hinkle, ever anxious to show the Big Sheriff that he also had "somethin in the kettle," proposed a question.

"Twenty-five hundred tomatoes is a lot of vegetables," the deputy began with comic seriousness. Sheriff, do you think da big gal coulda thought o'having someone, oh, mebbe lak dat boyfriend of hern, come over from Friars Point and bop her mama over the head for dat insurance money do you? I mean dats mostly all she been in heah about, gittin' dat death certificate from da hospital and den gittin' dat policy paid."

DeBell's voice faded out in the silence of the room. Before the sheriff answered, the little deputy had time to examine the nondescript color of the small office's walls, the cheap dark linoleum floor, the fly specked ceiling fan with its tail of sticky fly paper that held three or four unfortunate insects.

The crowded office held three secondhand wooden desks, one recently purchased for the Monroe men. There were six chairs and one bench in the office. None matched. In the middle of the room stood a large potbellied wood and coal burning iron stove. Down the hall was an open door that led to four small holding cells. All were presently empty.

DeBell felt a trickle of sweat slide down his cheek. He heard Jeff D. Nickle's old truck clatter by. He could identify it by its distinctive sounding horn. He cleared his throat. The sheriff was glaring at him through his rimless glasses. The way the light slanted over the lens made Sheriff Birkens look especially furious, like he was behind a sheet of glass in a zoo DeBell had once visited in which a gorilla stood waiting to throw dookey in your face if the glass happened to be lifted.

Only a few seconds had passed, but if felt like an hour to the deputy. He had said something wrong. Really wrong.

"Gal have her very own ma kilt!" The sheriff burst out. "Her own dear mama?" It was too incredible for Henry Birkens. Then here it came: "You been reading too many dose Northern detective magazines boy! Dey pollutes up da mind. Heah we's got us a real problem heah, two peepers kilt—white peepers wit' narry a suspect after three or four days! The mayor on my butt! The newspapers on our asses! When you could gie me some real sho' nuff help—which I needs mo' den sinners needs da Bible—you come up wit' some detective shit lak dat from out some—some—" The sheriff reached in his frustration for the nastiest word he could think of. "Some Northern comic book!"

The sheriff looked down at DeBell Hinkle's five-foot, seven-inch, one-hundred-and-fifty-seven-pound body as if he had suddenly stepped on a large poisonous snake that he had failed to notice until he was bit.

"Shoally, shoally peepers ain't done got dat low-down. I mean to have yo' own mother kilt for less den three thousand dollars? Boy! You should be using dat 'magination on dis case! Nobody don't do things lak dat down heah! And you can bet yo' boots no nigger done done it either. Too smart of a crime."

There it was. All the days of frustration vented on him, DeBell Hinkle, when the Lord knew he was doing the best he knew how.

"Yassuh," said the deputy, hiding his hurt feelings and not at all convinced that he was wrong.

"Seem lak to me a smarter tack would be to look back at her husmon," said the sheriff. "She was fount buck naked as a jay bird wit' another main. Shoally Brentwood knew dat some other hoss was kicking in his stall. Maybe he knew who dat hoss wuz. His business is kinda petering out. Mebbe he thought his name was on dat policy and since he already sick o'her mess, he hired somebody to sneak back and do away wit' 'er. When dat somebody come upon 'er wit' somebody else, why he had to git shed o'dem both. Jealousy and revenge is powerful, powerful motives."

"We've been over that idea," said one of the Monroe men. "Makes sense. Was the best we had until the footprints."

"Still the best we got. The footprints could belong to the hired killer," said the second Monroe man. "And that would account for nothing being taken. The killer had already been paid, don't you see."

"Bull shit!" said the little deputy.

"What?" asked the sheriff, looking at the snake again. Hinkle had worked up a little anger of his own because of the harsh manner in which the sheriff had just spoken to him.

"I think that thinking is way off base. Don't no hired killer take the time to be so brutal. He takes a gun," said the deputy using his finger as a model, "and bang! bang! look at 'em. Make sho' dey dead, den he's gone. Da one who hacked dem two up was real mad—or totally insane! Good grief! Don't you remember? A hand was hacked off and Leon's brains were busted right out his head. Don't 'pear lak no hired killer to me. Too much savagery. Whoever did hit had a score to settle."

The Monroe men looked thoughtful.

Sheriff Birkens hated to admit that his deputy made sense. The maniac theory was potentially the most dangerous theory. He was glad more and more people were telling him they were keeping their doors securely locked until they solved the case.

DeBell Hinkle fumbled around in his desk drawer, finally extracting a magazine. He flipped through it a few seconds, then slapped the monthly detective magazine on the sheriff's desk. "Page 42," he instructed. "Dis is the news behind what happened up dere in Conway County four years ago in the town of Center Valley to be exact. You kin check hit out. Mebbe you will recall da incident. Man kilt his wife and mother for policies of eight hunnert smackers." To be sure the high sheriff didn't miss the point, Deputy Hinkle enlarged upon it. "Kilt two peepers for four hunnert dollars apiece, including his mama. I reckon it ain't no piece a fiction lak you think—I mean dat someone could kill dey very own mama for some money. I rest my case," the small man concluded, satisfied to the bone.

"You do dat," said the sheriff sourly. "I'm going home and rest my tired old ass for a spell!"

Marko sat at the table in his tiny, very sparsely furnished two-room shack. He had already packed his clothes in a small box and counted the cash in his money belt again. Four dollars and thirty-seven cents. It wasn't enough, which was why he had broken into a little Colored neighbor store last night and stolen three cartons of cigarettes. He could sell each cigarette for one penny to anyone along the road.

When the cartons were found missing, Marko would be blamed immediately. They always faulted him, and his neighbors were nearly always right. What difference did it make this time. He had to go. Now. So Marko, with two crocker sacks containing everything he owned, headed for the pike where he would walk to another place. He had no idea where.

Sheriff Birkens saw no reason to rush to see Brentwood Tweedle as soon as the nurse had called him—after all, he had an iron-clad alibi—the time of the murders had been set after Brentwood had his accident. *Gawd, I'll be one happy main when all dis mess is over and done wit' and dis little town is back to normal, the sheriff thought. All dis running to and fro can wipe a person clean out!*

Maybe he was a little scratchy with DeBell yesterday. Hinkle was a good man. But at thirty-six he still had a lotta boy in 'em and tended to get too excited and all that, but he was responsible, on time, mostly a good deputy—and young enough to run around and do all the little unimportant sheriffing jobs that the sheriff couldn't be bothered to do. *Dese killings jus' makin' me edgy,* resolved Sheriff Birkens. *Well, I'll make it up to 'em after while,* the sheriff promised himself.

Because he didn't want to unduly upset Ralph Duster's mother—and thus possibly the entire Colored community—the sheriff decided to ask Marko Horton to steal a pair of Ralph's shoes. The sheriff didn't want to "upset nobody and cause no running." The way he figured it, if no one felt particularly threatened as a suspect, everybody would stay put, then the killer—who Birkens felt was still close around—could be sneaked up on and caught before he knew it. At least that was his theory. Neither the deputy nor the Monroe men agreed with him. The three of them thought the killer was long gone.

Sheriff Birkens had left Lorraine Tweedle's service at Tops Funeral Home as soon as it was decent, and took the fifteen minute drive to Marko's place which was practically in the woods. He enjoyed the drive and noted with pleasure that some black field hands were hard at work picking cotton and would be picking until as late as the middle of December, which was near the end of the season. The cotton picking scenes infused him with pleasant memories of the "Old South," the South of his boyhood when things were not quite so hectic as they seemed to be getting now-a-days. Good darkies picking cotton. Not darkies all but sassing you to your face, giving you dirty looks when they thought you were not looking, and some even going into business like Lela Bailey's son—whom the sheriff suspected of making as much money as the richest white man in town. Sheriff Birkens heaved a sigh for a lost South that was changing too fast for his liking. The Negroes had their own newspapers now among other things—newspapers that spoke ill of the white men every chance they got. And that wasn't all. The sheriff had heard of an organization called the NAACP—"Nah dey really a bunch of trouble makers!" thought Sheriff Birkens. Trying to take the white man's laws and use them against him—and there were white folks in that club to boot. What was America coming to? he wondered.

Well at least there were a few blacks who were not ungrateful for what whites had done for them. Marko Horton was as good as gold. The boy knew his place and stayed in it like he had some sense, Sheriff Birkens thought.

Birkens parked closer to Marko's house than Dave and his friends had some days earlier. He proceeded cautiously through the waist high grass with his old hat pulled down so low on his face that it met the top of his spectacles. He knocked once—and the front door immediately swung open on its hinges revealing a single small table holding a kerosene lamp with a sooty globe. The sheriff called to Marko but received no answer. Without walking in, he called again. Still no answer. Cautiously entering the tiny room, he noticed an old run down bed with a striped feather tick on it, and the small battered desk and chair that he had given Marko years ago when they had bought better furniture for the jail office. There was an old pillow minus a pillow case, and several wooden crates in a corner. This was the parlor and bedroom he reckoned, and the crates seemingly had served as makeshift kitchen chairs.

The sheriff had not actually been inside of Marko's house before—he had driven up close to the place and Marko had come out to the car to talk to him, he remembered.

Although it was early in the afternoon, the two-room shack was dark, dank, filled with old, stale odors. The sheriff walked into the combination kitchen, dining, storage room behind the "parlor" and suddenly realized that Marko was gone. There were no covers on the bed, no clothes lying around, no food on the shelves in the kitchen, no dishes, nothing.

Let's see, the sheriff said to himself. *I done seent Marko 'bout five days ago.*

Henry Birkens lifted the top of the icebox and stared at the little piece of ice that remained. Maybe the boy left no later than yesterday.

It was the dishes that made him certain that Marko did not intend to return. When you're dirt poor, you take everything that you can carry.

Henry Birkens broke into an angry sweat. He felt deeply surprised and betrayed. Why had he left? The sheriff had never known Marko to make a serious move without informing him. What was going on here?

The sheriff got down on his hands and knees and shined his flashlight under the bed. He was looking for—there was one. A shoe left behind by Marko. The black shoe was beat up and wide, at least 2E, with biscuit toes. And it was no more than a size eleven. Why had he left without telling him? And where had he gone?

Sheriff Birkens walked back and forth in the rooms in a state of shock. There were a few cardboard boxes piled up in a corner. He looked in them knowing what he was going to find—nothing.

"Well, by Gawd!" The sheriff yelled. "Ahm a-going straight over to Ralph Duster's and look at his shoes mahself nah!"

SEVEN

On the Friday evening after Sheriff Birkens' afternoon visit, Thomas Duster and his wife had sat on the front porch. Eunice sat in the little swing that most porches had, and Thomas made himself comfortable in the old soft chair. It was a little too cool to be setting outside Eunice had complained, but they both wanted to be away from the "chirrens listening years."

In an attempt to understand Ralph's violent temper, Eunice said to her husband: "Lawd, hit's a wonder every main and boy in dis town ain't jus' lak Ralph. I means it! Dey done seent and heered too much evil. Too much-a lynching and beatins and castrations. Too much-a bending and bowing and scraping jus' tryin to stay alive. Some peepers kin take dat mess all dey lives—den some jus' can't. Da can'ts is most always on da chain gang, at da county farm, or dead, or gone up North."

Thomas puffed on his old pipe, sending angry little clouds of smoke into the air. He was not really listening to his wife. He was thinking that in another month he would be forty years old. Forty years! And nothing to show for it but the lines in his face and the muscles in his arms. Well, he thought, this Depression was sitting everybody back a mile. And now this business about Ralph and the sheriff's suspicions. It left him nearly numb.

"Sheriff done bent heah two times. Two times! Thomas, we gotta go! Can't you see dey tryin' to lay dis mess on somebody. And dat somebody may be Ralph!" his wife pleaded. "Thomas is you listin'? We's gotta git outta heah!"

"Ahm thinkin' on it Eunice. Jus' quiet down. I'm thinkin' soon dey gone find out dat da husmon done done it ahm reckoning."

"Thomas Duster you is a fool!" Eunice burst out again. "We shoulda done sent Ralph up North long fore nah. You done seed hi Ralph carried on when dat Binder boy was kilt. Lawd have mercy Jesus! I thought we wuz gone have to lock 'em up somewheres, he wuz so filled up wit' hurt and anger he was wantin' to kill up somebody! And when dey beat up dat bright-skinned boy Pete Frauzi, or somethin lak dat is his name, you 'member hi Ralph lak to have went wild again even doe he hardly even knows him."

"Yas," Ralph's father answered remembering. "He sez, 'nobody gone do dat to me. No suh. Never!' "

"Den, you do understan' what ahm sayin', Thomas?" Then she started her frantic pleadings all over again. "We's gotta get outta heah! You jus' turning forty. We can start out someplace else!"

"Wit' what? Nah who talkin' lak a fool? Ahm sittin' heah with two peanut shells and three red cents in my pocket, and you tellin' me we gotta move!" In frustration Thomas kicked furiously at a homemade toy one of the children had left on the porch, sending it flying clear out into the yard.

"Oh, I don't know what we should do!" Eunice wailed. "Mebbe you and me and da chirrens should just start out walkin'! I don't even know where Ralph at nah! Every time he leave da house ahm scared ta death! Dey could pick 'em up anytime. Thomas, ahm scared ta death!" Eunice repeated, gasping for breath as if she were drowning.

Later that evening Ralph came in after picking up a little mechanic work here and there. Silently he handed his father six bits.

"Did you keep anythin' fer yo'self?"

"I kept two bits," Ralph answered. "Anythin' to eat?"

His father took his plate out of the warmer section of the stove and shoved the pinto beans, salt pork and cornbread in front of him.

"You want some cold sweetin' water?"

Ralph looked hard at his father. "Why you being so nice ta me?" Ralph asked suspiciously, but with a smile.

"You lak dem beans? You know I make 'em better den yo' mama," Thomas said, sliding a little saucer of chopped onions and a bottle of peppers soaked in vinegar towards his son.

"Daddy you know yo' beans is good. 'Specially when you ain't had nothin' else to eat all day."

They both laughed. Ralph's father sat across the table from him waiting patiently until he finished his meal.

"Well," said Ralph, "you ain't sitting there looking at me because ahm so cute. What you got to say Daddy?"

The boy's father sat, his body all scrunched over, his face lined with fear and with caring. He had a question to ask. A question that must be asked but he was afraid of the answer. More afraid then he had ever been in his life.

Thomas looked at his handsome son. They had a fairly good relationship—not close, but open enough he reckoned. Ralph had always questioned everything he told him—not an easy boy to handle. Thomas remembered himself at his son's age. Whereas his frustrations over racial injustices had made him not docile, but quiet, watchful and careful. He would rather avoid walking on the cement altogether than taking a chance of being walked off of the sidewalk by a white man. Ralph was just the opposite. He would walk straight down the middle of the path daring whites to force him in the dirt. Seeing the wild and fierce look on his face, not many did.

When Ralph was sixteen, he had beaten a bullying neighborhood dog to death for grabbing at his trousers and tearing them. Ralph was always in a fight. Once he had a fight with an older boy in the house next door over a bowl of homemade peach ice cream of all things. Only a neighbor's intervention had stopped Ralph from shooting the boy with a shotgun. And he became especially aggressive after someone in the community had suffered at the hands of the white man.

Actually Eunice had more control over Ralph than Thomas did. He respected his mama because he knew she worried about him.

Now Thomas must ask his question, and he put it plain and simple, the only way he knew. "You didn't have nothin' to do wit' dem two peepers what got kilt last Sataday, did you boy?"

"Naw!" Ralph shot back, avoiding his father's eyes. "Why you go axing me a question lak dat fer? I didn't even know dat Miz Deluxery Tweedle. I knowed somebody was gone get dat old monkey one day though, him messin' with men's wifes and all, but it weren't me. Dats what you been thinkin' all week?" Ralph grinned broadly. "Somebody done jacked 'em up fer good, fo' I got a chance to. Ahm jus' jokin', Pa. For real. It weren't me." He touched his father's hand. "It weren't me," he repeated.

Ralph's fathers shoulders unscrunched and tears welled up in his eyes. He walked around the table, patted Ralph on the back, bit hard on his pipe and left the room.

Mother Bailey was known to give good advice, so not being able to sleep after retiring at eight thirty on the evening after the sheriff's most recent visit, Eunice got up at ten p.m., put on her clothes, including a clean apron and went to see Lela Bailey.

Mrs. Bailey served Eunice tea and tea cakes in her beautiful kitchen and didn't seem at all surprised to see her-although Eunice was very surprised to find her up this late at night.

"First of all Miz Bailey, I beg yo' most humble partners fer coming heah dis late at night."

"Don't you worry none 'bout da time."

"Thank you, mam. Well, I'll get right at da proint. Peepers 'round heah thinks the world of you and yo' son. Dey respects yo' advice 'cause it's good. Well, Lawd! I sho' do need some of yo' good advice nah."

Lela asked her if they had needed to use the plan they had made for Ralph.

"Sho did, Lawd. Sho did! Didn't I tell you what happened wit' dat plan?" Eunice asked excitedly.

Ralph's mother then related how the sheriff had come over on Monday—"He said it was about his police car, but I don't know." Eunice related all that had happened—how Ralph played his part about being sick for several days real well, and about how they had even left a large bowl of soup on the chair "lak Ralph was so sick he ain't been able to eat nothin'. We sho' did thank y'all fer dat plan. It worked out real nice, but still dat sheriff done been back two times mo'."

"Two times?" Lela exclaimed in surprise.

"Three times in all if I count da time he turned around and came back."

"*Lawdhavemercyesus!* Dis ain't no good! Eunice why didn't you tell us! Don't you remember? We told you to keep us told if the sheriff came, or any other white folks, axing about Ralph! Don't you remember?"

Eunice stammered and rung her apron.

"Nee mind!" Lela said. "What's done is done. Nah tell me Eunice persactly what dat sheriff be saying. Can you remember persactly?"

"Well," answered the flustered Eunice. "He be sayin' everythin' and nothin'. I mean he be real sly about it. Axin', you know, wit' doubt axin'... for example, sheriff say: 'dese be Ralph's tools?' to mah son Joe Bee. He say, 'yas.' Sheriff say, 'lookee heah hi he done gone and carved his initials on each and every one of 'em, real nice and neat lak. R.A.D. Ralph A. Duster. Joe Bee say he be doin' dat to cut down on someone stealin' 'em so quick. Sheriff say, 'Is dat right? Say any dem tools been stole lately? Lak mebbe a hatchet or somethin' lak dat?' Joe Bee say, 'naw.' Had, and he woulda knowed it 'cause he be in charge o'keeping up wit' each and every piece."

Lela moved up closer to the large table and lowered her voice. Her large expressive eyes were stretched to their limits. "He axed him about a hatchet? Naw!"

"Yas, he did. Dats what I mean bout him bein' sly. I knows dose peepers was kilt wit' somethin' lak a hatchet, leastwise dats what da talk in da papers sez. Sheriff ain't got no cause to suspicion my boy."

"No. Cose not," said Lela thoughtfully. She filled Eunice's cup with hot tea again. "What else he be axin?"

"Well," Eunice said trying to think. "Oh yas. He come back the third time today, Friday—this afternoon, and he comes justa looking at Joe Bee's feets all of a sudden. He looks at 'em and he looks at 'em. Finally he sez, 'Who got da biggest foots, you or yo' brother?' Nah, he real playful lak, but serious, you know what I means? Joe Bee say why, my brother 'cause he da oldest. 'What size he be wearing?' the sheriff axed. 'Oh! dats big,' sez the sheriff, 'and narrow. Bet he gotta git shoes somewha' special.' Joe Bee tells 'em 'cause he ain't got no reason not to tell 'em—he say, 'you know where all dem stores be all bunched up in Old Steward? Dresses and trousers, and others fer radios and iceboxes? Well, dere be jus' one sto' dat carries a size fourteen Double A. If mah brother had some money, dats wha' he would go.'

'What sto'?' he axed. 'Dat be Archie's Shoe Sto',' sez Joe Bee. 'I know where dat is!' says da sheriff."

"Eunice," Lela said, pushing her cup and the plate of cakes away. "Let's talk business. Don't let what ahm goin' ta say upset you. Whatever we do, we gotta keep a quiet spirit within us. You unnastan?"

"Yas," said Eunice quaking in every limb.

"I think y'all need to git outta town fast. It's clear to me nah dat dey gone look and look and search and search until dey can pin dis stuff on somebody—and you know who dat somebody usually is—us!"

"Dats 'persacly what I done tole Thomas!" Eunice exclaimed, hitting the large table with her fist for emphasis. " hit's been near seben days since dem peepers wuz kilt, and I think things are getting just a little bit too wurm fer comfort in dis town."

The chickens were making a clatter as if a hungry dog was circling the hen house and the night wind whistled through the trees signaling cooler weather.

It was time to stop dealing in delayed action that could soon find Ralph running for his life or grabbed and lynched as he went about his business trying to find work, Lela thought. You never could tell what the Law or the white folks up in White Town were thinking. Lela felt the deepest pity for the slumped woman before her, guilty or not guilty. What if it were her son? It could be anyone in Colored Town's son.

Eunice raised her tea with unsteady hands and tried to bring it to her lips and failed. "Who? Who?" Asked a hoot owl somewhere in a distant tree.

Lela could not bring herself to look into the face of the tortured woman sitting across from her. She toyed with her tea and listened to the ticking of the old kitchen clock.

"Dey already got deyselfs one young man who done had more'n one known fuss with Leon Baycott dat ends up with Leon slapping him in da mouf. Den Mistah Leon, he comes up dead. And Ralph Duster—nah, Eunice we gotta face the facts— is known to have a pretty hot temper..."

The women had been talking for nearly an hour. Lela felt that the time for talking was past. "Where is Ralph nah?" she asked Eunice, trying to keep any hint of anxiety out of her voice. Her spirit must be quiet enough for them both.

Afraid to answer, Eunice gave Lela a fearful stare.

"You know you can trust me, Miz Thomas," Lela added softly. Lela's heart went out to the mother as she watched her twist the apron she wore everywhere except to church. Hard working people, the Dusters, caught up in a trap of poverty intensified by "dis Depression" everyone called it. Poor, but not starving. Nobody was allowed to go hungry in this community if either Lela or Dave heard about it.

The mother and the son. "Two of the bestest peepers in the worl'." That was the general agreement of the residents of Colored Town. If you had a problem— medical, spiritual or even financial—talk to Lela Bailey, they said.

It was also widely known that Dave Bailey frowned on anyone in the Colored community borrowing money from a white man. He figured it could only lead to trouble. His friend, Johnny Straw, had been shot and killed by a white salesman over a fifty cent debt that could easily have been paid had the man asked for help. You had only to ask-and if you were not a known thief or liar, Dave would usually say, "come round tomorrow and I'll see what I can do." He almost never gave out loans on the same day, for he didn't want folks to know how readily he could get his hands on large sums of cash. Eunice had heard that Dave had loaned folks as much as fifty dollars—that was about what her Thomas had earned in the last six months!

If asked, Eunice Duster would have confessed that a loan was in the back of her mind when she came to see Mother Bailey. Well, she would pay it back if it was only at the rate of two bits a week for the rest of her life! The Dusters, Eunice thought, were nobody's charity cases.

It was quiet outside now, so still that you could almost hear people thinking, Lela was fond of saying.

"You gotta trust us, Eunice," Lela said.

"I ain't studin' 'bout no trust! You know that, Mother B!" exclaimed Eunice. "Why you and Dave—" Eunice got so choked with emotion that she had to take a few sips of tea before continuing. "Ifn you two can't be trusted, can't nobody in dis worl' be trusted."

Lela thanked Eunice for her sentiments in a distracted manner as she looked toward the front of the house.

"Please pardon me fer a minute, Eunice."

"Shoally."

Lela walked to the front of the house as quickly as she could. A door opened and Eunice heard muffled conversation. The door closed and the woman returned to the kitchen and took her seat again.

"Wuz dat Dave, Miz Lela? Ain't he down on the car line selling his hot tamales tonight? If I ain't being too busy-body."

"Yas. Dat wuz Dave," Lela answered. "It's near midnight, he been finished wit' da tamales. Dey go fast, you know..." Lela's voice trailed off. Clearly her mind was somewhere else.

"Dem hot tamales! I wish I had me one nah! Dey sho' is fine."

"Why, thank you!" Lela smiled with genuine pleasure and pride, for she had never really gotten over Dave's great success. It was still a wonderful dream, even though Dave had confided: "Muddear, those tamales are just the beginning."

"Da Lawd done seent fit to bless my boy over and above all dat I could think."

"And blessin' him, he done become a blessin' to all dat he meets," countered Ralph's mother.

"Amen! Bless da Lawd! Thank you Jesus!" Lela's right arm shot up in the air as she was suddenly caught up in a paroxysm of praise so often witnessed in black Baptist and "sanctified" churches during their services. Lela was "feeling the Holy Spirit."

"Guidance Lawd!" Lela fervently requested, her arm still waving slowly above her head.

"Lawd, guidance," Eunice repeated prayerfully, herself caught up in some of the fervor of Lela's outburst. Both women were crying now and both felt stronger—Lela in the knowledge of God's care, and Eunice in the humble trust of friendship.

After a few moments, both women dried their tears—refreshed in "the Lawd o'glory," Lela said, and wound down to the business at hand.

"Nah," Lela said wiping her face, "you didn't tell me where Ralph is nah. I heered he be at his grandmama's over in Poplar Grove."

Eunice smiled slyly at Lela. "Grandma Duster been dead two years. Ralph be nearby home. What we gone do, Mother B? What in the worl we gone do?" Eunice asked pathetically. Suddenly she was cold, chilled to the bone, her faith tottering again. The woman pulled her sweater closer to her. She felt like running—running clear out of West Steward, Phillips County, clear out of Arkansas.

"Quieten yo'self down," Lela instructed. "You ain't alone. Friends is all 'round you. Dave!" Lela bellowed. Her call was so loud and unexpected that Eunice jumped from her chair.

"Oh! Ahm so sorry!" Lela apologized. "Ah didn't mean to scare ya."

Eunice laughed nervously. "Sound lak you was calling da Devil!"

Presently Dave entered the kitchen dressed in dark cotton trousers and a light wool tweed jacket. He was wearing a cap pulled down low on his forehead which he did not remove. Dave sat down, tight—lipped at the table with the two women. He nodded sober greetings to Mrs. Duster and took a few sips of the tea his mother offered. Eunice looked at Dave expectantly. In his soft deep voice he asked Eunice Duster a few questions.

"Mrs. Duster, where is Ralph now?" She told him about the grandmother lie.

"Now," Dave continued quietly, if you had to leave West Steward right now—right now, where would you go?"

"To my sister's in Nebraska," Eunice answered without hesitation. "She living right outside o' Omaha. Her husmon got a pretty fair job still. He be working at a small packing house."

"And how many people know you have a sister in Omaha?" Dave asked gently.

"Not in Omaha, near to Omaha," Eunice corrected the dark handsome young man before her. He was so young! Funny, Eunice thought, that she really hadn't noticed that before. Why he was just in his mid twenties! Many thought Dave older because he was so "self possessing" and quiet. "Lak a wise ageable main, Harcaster Mabry had remarked one day to a friend of his after having paid on his debt of five dollars to Dave with one of his big sweet watermelons, delivered every Saturday this summer. "I've always thinked him as being 'round thirty-five," Harcaster had said. "Until you see him kicking up dust wit' dem frens o'hisn. Den you see dey little mo' den boys, although dey be some pretty smart boys, I tell you dat!"

"Not too many be knowing I got me a sister in Nebraska, she only jus' moved out dere a few months ago from Georgia. Her husmon thought dey ought try dey luck out West, and he wuz right—got him a job within two weeks."

"How many is not too many, Mrs. Duster?" Dave asked quietly. "Can you remember exactly whom you've told that you had a sister out West? It's very important."

"We got frens, but most in-gently we keeps to ourvaselves." Suddenly, the woman looked up and smiled at Dave. "Exactly, we ain't mentioned it to nobody but my fren Amy Delores Pages what lives rat next doe."

"Nobody else? Are you sure Mrs. Duster?"

"Ahm mo' den sho'. I remembers the reason bein' dat my sister wrote me dat dere might be some work out dere. If we could manage to scrape up da bus fare and all. We didn't tell nobody 'cause we thought it might lessen my husmons chances." Eunice blushed and fidgeted, shame-faced at her selfishness.

"I understand," Dave said.

"Nah, we's been working on gittin' da money we need ourvaselves. We wasn't planning on axing for no kind of a handout—until dose peepers don got kilt and da sheriff be snooping aroun'." Eunice's voice trailed off despairingly.

It was time to put the big plan into action. It was past midnight—Saturday again, a whole week had passed.

"Listen to me closely, Mrs. Duster," Dave said his voice low and intense. "We made some tentative plans yesterday concerning you and your family. I don't like those visits from the sheriff that my mama told me about, and the fingerprinting business. The Law has been known to lay things on people. The thought came to my mind was that was Birkens getting or planting evidence? The big white folks are squawking for results."

"Dem wuz my thoughts persactly!" Eunice exclaimed, thinking again how apt this young man was.

"Then you know that we have got to get you and your family out of West Steward fast. Tonight! We are not going to have another Binder family episode."

"All yo' family home nah?" asked Lela.

Eunice, choked up with gratitude for their concern and caring, and surprised by their cleverness and organization, whispered out, "at home sleep 'cept for Ralph. Tonight I jus' got scared and we put him in the woods nearby jus' in case. Doe I don't know what good it do, being in da woods, I mean. If dey 'cide to put dem old sniffer hounds on 'em. But we done gie 'em a whole bag fulla red pepper to sprinkle on da ground after hisself if he gotta run. I hear dem dogs can't be following yo' trail once dat cayenne pepper gets in dey nose, but I don't know if dats true."

Eunice looked around at Lela and Dave for approval. Her actions said, see, I'm thinking too.

"Very good!" said Lela.

Eunice flushed with pleasure. "We thought we'd better start taking some cares after old Birkens started to come by everytime you looked around."

"It's a shame 'fo Gawd da way peepers has ta rip and run from dese low down no 'count white folks!" Lela exclaimed bitterly.

Dave raised his hands gently to quiet his mother. "But you know where he is? You can get to him fast?"

"Yassuh, Mistah Dave." Eunice's facial expression was equal parts fear, confusion, and dogged trust.

"Mr. Dave? Who you calling mister?" Dave smiled. "Just plain Dave will be fine, Mrs. Duster."

Suddenly Dave asked, "Muddear, you ready to ring the bell?"

"I be ready."

"Alright then. Go give it a ring," Dave instructed.

There was a poem called "We Wear The Mask" by Paul Lawrence Dunbar that Dave especially liked. In fact, he was so fond of this poem that he had suggested that they call their group the Dunbar Mask Circle, and finally for short, just the Circle. The Circle had formulated a plan some five months ago to deal with situations like the Dusters now found themselves in. If whites went on the prowl threatening to beat or lynch some innocent black person, the Circle—Dave, Omar and Peter, and later Will Henry and LaSalle and now the two women, Lela Bailey and Aggie Pratt—would meet, find out all they could, trade information and form a plan that would hopefully avert a community tragedy such as the ones they had experienced in the past. Getting Thomas Duster and his family out of West Steward would be the first testing of this plan.

Lela pulled on her beloved old green sweater, and stepping as quickly as she could, she went into the back yard with a pounding heart and looked around her. It was a dead still moonless night, just the kind they needed.

It wasn't a bell really, rather a lightweight squarish grey sheet of metal, the size of a box of bonbons. When this metal was struck with the rod that Dave had furnished, it made a curious high pitched sound that could easily be heard in this quietness by Aggie and her boys Arky and Villa who were waiting in their small house a half a mile away.

Two, two, one. That was the signal. Ping-ping, ping-ping, ping! Lela sounded the metal twice, then went back in the house and took her seat, noting that the chickens hardly stirred.

"Aggie and the boys will be here in no time. You know Aggie can run 'most as fast as her boys!" Lela said.

"We are going to get you and your family out of here," Dave said resolutely.

"There really is no time to waste though. No time to discuss things with your family as anyone would like to. Do you agree? Good! When you get home you've got to move very fast. Just take a few clothes, that's all. We are shooting for fifteen minutes tops to get in and out of your house."

"Bless da Lawd!" exclaimed Eunice. "Dis is the answer to mah prayers. Lawd have mercy! I believes we can be ready in five minutes!"

Dave smiled. Then as quickly the smile faded into seriousness. "Just one question, Mrs. Duster." Dave glanced at his mother as if to get her consent to ask.

Eunice Duster braced herself for she thought she knew what that question would be.

As delicately as he could, Dave asked, "Where was Ralph last Friday night? Did he ever say?"

"No, he did not. Where he wuz when dese killins happened, between one and five in da moanin, I heered dey done set da time, I really does not know." Eunice looked down at the floor seeming to study the planks in it. After what seemed a long while, the time being elongated by the extreme quietness that comes only to rural and out of the way places at those certain times when early in the morning and late at night means the same thing. "Honest to Gawd, ah don't know wha he was," Eunice said, her voice was almost inaudible.

"Well, where do you think he was," Lela asked as kindly as she could. A tear slid down the mother's smooth, nut-colored cheek. She looked half her thirty-nine years now, a woman of more than average height, she shrunk in her chair.

"Cain't sleep 'til all my chirrens is in da house, so I got up and checked all night long. But he never come in, not 'til after seben thirty Sattiday moanin'. I ax him wha he bent. His daddy ax 'em what he bent. All he sez is dat ahm tied, real tied. I jus' wanna sleep, and he did—in a chair."

Dave wanted to ask if Ralph's clothing was torn or stained in any noticeable way, or if he appeared scratched or injured. Too obvious he thought. Instead he asked: "Did Ralph seem different in any way that you noticed, Mrs. Duster?"

"No. He looked clean and nice but a little bit rumpled up. He had on da same cloes he been wearing when I last seent 'em."

"And Ralph didn't make no practice of staying out overnight, Eunice?" Lela asked.

"No, mam. Lak I said befoe, I doesn't lie dat kinda stuff long as a chile is in mah house."

Lela found that she couldn't bring herself to ask Eunice if she thought Ralph had anything to do with the killings.

In less than twenty minutes from the time of the signal, Aggie walked into the kitchen, her eyes bright, anxious, ready. She was a little out of breath. "I left Arky and Villa outside," she said excitedly.

"Too cold for that. I'll get them," Dave said. Dave went out into the chicken yard and led the excited boys to the guest room where he lit a little fire in the fireplace to drive the chill from the air. The young man reached in his pocket and gave Arky and Villa a dime each, which brought large grins to their faces.

"Back in a moment, so keep your running shoes on, OK?" Dave gave them a wink and closed the door. Dave laughed aloud at the boys as he walked back to join the women. Arky and Villa were about to burst with excitement. Never had they been allowed to stay up this late. It was nearly midnight. They didn't know what was going on, but they were clearly glad to be a part of it.

EIGHT

———❧———

Dave and Lela Bailey, Aggie Pratt and Eunice Duster gathered at the large kitchen table, the four of them gathered at just one end of it. Lela poured tea for everyone again from her ever present pot.

Lela had turned off the overhead electric light and sat two bright coal oil lamps in the middle of the rectangular table. This was not electric light talk, they needed the quiet comfort of the yellow flickering natural light, she thought. The lamps seemed to provide a soothing focus to conversation. People seemed to talk softer and more calmly by lamp light.

Addressing Eunice, Dave said, "Muddear, Aggie and I thought this is what you should do Mrs. Duster: Leave a note for your best friend—and you've told us that's Amy Delores Pages—tell her in a sincere, friendly tone that you're sorry you couldn't say goodbye, but that your husband has a relative in, where?" Dave looked at Aggie.

"How's about Louisiana. New Orleans, 'cause dey figure Negroes always goes North. Dat oughta throw 'em off," she supplied.

Dave and Lela agreed that New Orleans sounded fine.

"Leave everything but a few clothes," said Dave. "Just take a small Crocker sack or suitcase of small things that have sentimental value, you know, like photographs, things like that. Nothing conspicuous, nothing to draw attention, you know what I mean? A small bag," Dave emphasized again.

"Leave all mah things?" Eunice wailed.

"Nah, Eunice, what you got mo' valuable den yo' boy?" Lela asked, not unkindly.

"Well, nothin' I reckon."

"You reckon?" asked an incredulous Aggie.

"Nothin' mo' valuable!" Eunice exclaimed with firm conviction. "I dunno what I wuz thinkin', all dis so fast. Family is the most 'portant thing to me in life o'cose."

"You're being asked to change your whole life, move away at a moment's notice from all you hold near and dear. It's a big step," Dave offered sympathetically.

"Hit's a big step, dats true, but we's ready ta make it, Mistah Dave," Eunice said firmly, now sure of her own mind. "Actually we *been* ready to leave Arkansas!"

"Good."

"Oh, jus' take some clean step-ins and a coupla brassieres," Aggie advised in her crude and practical manner. "A piece of face soap and a rag to wash out from under ya arms and between yo' legs!"

Lela looked at Aggie with shame and affection. "Aggie! Don't talk lak dat in front of mens. You make peepers shame!"

"I beg y'all partners," said the unrepentant Aggie.

Dave stifled a gaffaw as he reached inside of his jacket pocket and pulled out a wad of bills.

Eunice's eyes bucked.

"This is three hundred dollars."

"Lawd have mercy Jesus!" exclaimed Eunice falling back in her chair. "I didn't know dat dere was dat much money in all of Colored Town!"

Aggie smiled pleased, proud. This was big stuff, and she was part of it, right in the middle of it. Hot dawg!

"Let's not git side tracked," Lela stated wisely. "Come on! Let's git the note finished 'fo we start puttin' out any money."

"Of course you're right, Muddear. Aggie, get a sheet of paper will you? It's in the guest room on the bedside table."

Lela dictated as Eunice, who had only gone to the third grade, wrote laboriously.

Looking up from her writing, Eunice said, "Amy Delores is lak a sistah ta me. Me and her done got over a lotta rough spots together, her fambly and mines. I got me some pretty sheets made outta bleached flour sacks wit' hand work on 'em dat she jus' loves—nah dey hern. Also, old Miss Kelson dat I works—worked fer done gimme some nice throw outs obber da years."

Dave pursed two fingers to his lips in thought, as Mrs. Duster described various items that she regrettably had to leave behind.

Lela shushed Eunice when Dave was ready to resume speaking.

"Tell Ralph to take all of his small tools. It would look funny, a self-employed man leaving all his tools. And tell him to take his shoes. Don't leave any shoes in the house at all!"

"I tells 'em," Eunice said. "He ain't got but da two pair no how. And one of dose is old busted out work shoes."

Aggie's head shot up at the mention of shoes. She looked askance from Lela to Dave and back again. Lela cautioned Aggie with her eyes to keep quiet.

Dave counted out money in three piles. "I'm going go' give you one hundred and twenty-five dollars, Mrs. Duster. I'm going to have to do it that way because the plan is to split you up—and then have you all to meet up again in Nebraska—except for Ralph."

"Three hundred dollars!" Aggie said emphasizing the words. "That's mo' money than I'll ever see in one place again!"

"Omar will drive you and the girls to Memphis in a truck. It will take about five hours, going down back roads, not using the Pike or the highways. If you took the Missouri Pacific bus line, you could get to Memphis in three hours, but we can't take that chance. Y'all have to be split up to avoid suspicion."

Eunice hung on to Dave's every word, her eyes shining with admiration and gratitude.

"Now, Mr. Duster will go with Joe Bee. Will Henry has borrowed a truck and he will take them a little outside of Memphis, to Oleander, Tennessee, to take a different train at a different time. The whole family won't be on the same train at the same time you understand. I'll explain all this to Mr. Duster when we get back here tonigh—or this morning."

"Gotta take every caution." Lela said.

"From Memphis you can get a train to almost anywhere. You can get your ticket to Nebraska. It'll be a round about way—but the thing is you'll get there safely. Omar will give you directions once he gets you to Memphis. From Memphis to Nebraska gonna cost about twenty five dollars for all three of you. You'll have around one hundred dollars left."

"Dey gone have two hunnert dollars as a fambly, you count Mistah Duster's money, Dave," Aggie said, glad to be of help.

"I stand corrected," Dave said, doffing his cap to Aggie, causing her to blush a deep red through her white-tan skin. "Will Henry will follow essentially the same plan for Joe Bee and Mr. Duster."

"And Ralph?" Eunice Duster asked with motherly anxiety. "Who he goin' wit'?"

Lela and Aggie exchanged smiles. "He goes North," said Lela.

"In a disguise—jus' lak in da picture show!" exclaimed Aggie. "We dress 'em up lak an old grandpappy."

Lela produced a rude wig made of seagrass and doctored grey from its original white with smut.

"We gives 'em a cane, put a big old hat on his head and tell 'em to walk all bent over. He'll be fine. Nobody pays no 'tention to old folks, 'specially no old Colored ones," Aggie added gaily.

"I ain't even down gone think o'nothin goin' wrong," Lela pronounced, "'cause I know da Lawd gone take care his own."

"Yas, he will!" Eunice agreed.

Aggie broke in here to show Eunice that she was in on the planning. The young mother cleared her throat—rather importantly, Lela thought.

"Ralph goes to Old Steward wit' Dave and Pete in Dave's truck. From dere, he catches da Missouri Pacific bus to Clarkedale, Arkansas. Dere'll not be a whole lotta folks on dat bus so early in da moaning—ain't nobody got no whole lotta money fer no traveling dese days. From Clarkedale he go to Memphis, Tennessee, from dere to Chicago where he can take da train into Detroit, Michigan. Too many Colored end up in Chicago, so he better off in Detroit. Better in every way. My dead husmon's aunt be livin' in Detroit. I'm gond gie Ralph a note fer her. When he gie it to Alberta, dat be her name, she'll be helping 'em find some work and a place to stay an all. He'll have 'bout forty dollars when he gits dere. Dat should be 'nough to hold 'em 'til he gits situated."

"Lets move out!" Dave said pulling his long frame from the chair. "It's getting late."

Dave walked down the hall and loosed the boys to go in two directions to bring back Peter Frauzinou, and Will Henry Mead and Omar Williams who were waiting together. LaSalle Peabody, at his own request, was not included in this plan at this time, and Tom "Fool" Leak was too unstable for anything but the lightest work, such as standing guard at a door on occasion.

Overall, West Steward was a small town even if you added the little suburb of Epps to the west and Ketta to the east. North, in West Steward proper, was White Town, where eighty to ninety percent of the whites lived. If you went through White Town five miles north you would find yourself in Steward or Old Steward, as some called it, Arkansas. If one went north too far in Old Steward they would end up in the Mississippi River.

Aggie's boys, Arky and Villa, felt that they could run all over "dis little ole town" in a half hour or less. The boys were in friendly competition with each other and

70

prided themselves on how fast they could locate anybody at any time. When Dave "loosed" them that night, they went hurling and giggling into the night to bring the three men back to Lela's kitchen.

Dave would drive Eunice back home in his truck, which he would park a short distance away from the Duster house. Then, they would walk very quietly in the dark keeping to the side of the road and following Eunice's lead, for it was a pitch black moonless night and all the houses in Colored Town had long since been darkened in sleep, and in some cases, in fear—for the murders were far from solved and white folks might come for somebody at any time.

When the family was ready and the note had been slid under Amy Dolores Page's door, Dave and Aggie would put all six of them in the back of the truck, where they would lay on the floor and be covered with tarpaulin. They would then make the bumpy ride back up the hill to Lela's where the Circle would gather, anxiously waiting to put their plan into action for the first time.

Thomas Duster knew where his wife had gone, but not knowing exactly what to expect from her meeting with Mother Bailey, he had kept all the children-Joe Bee, Dorothy Pearl and Marystine—up and dressed. Although the children had fallen asleep, they could be easily roused. Ralph had been summoned from the woods and was now in the cellar that most people didn't know the Dusters had.

When Aggie and Dave arrived, Eunice found her husband and children sitting in the darkened front room waiting. Seeing this little family waiting—for God knew what-so touched Aggie that she begin to cry and had to be shushed and comforted by the strong arms of Dave Bailey.

Dave's respected presence lent credibility and a sense of urgency to the entire matter, thoroughly stifling any protest Ralph might have had. When he was brought up from the cellar, he was properly subdued and a little frightened, but he would never have admitted it. Ralph had decided long ago that he was prepared to die for kicking some cracker's ass if it came to that one day. However, expressions of bravery and actual courage were two different things. Ralph found that he was sweating profusely and when he stepped up from the cellar his knees were so shaky that they barely supported him.

In twelve minutes, the Dusters were lying closely together on the floor of Dave's truck headed for Lela Bailey's house—their last stop before, hopefully, escaping to freedom.

Dave ran through the traveling plans with Thomas Duster again, carefully avoiding eye contact with the man because the naked gratitude and admiration he saw there made him uncomfortable.

Thomas was nearly overcome with emotion. "I don't know hi to thank you peepers," he began hoarsely. "I jus' don't know hi."

"You can thank us," Dave said, "by arriving safely at your destinations."

"I got jus' one question," said Ralph, who to the amusement of hardly anyone, had already put on his sea-grass wig. "Don't this look lak we's runnin'? Won't da sheriff look at us leaving lak we's got somethin' to leave fer?"

"Shit on the sheriff!" Aggie burst out. "Nah what you 'pose to do den? Sat back and let dem swing ya from a tree, or drag you behind a truck 'til you dead? Is you crazy, boy? 'Sides yo' ma done left a note wit' her fren next doe 'plaining why y'all left, which her fren gond gie to da sheriff. Ain't you heered dat part of it?"

"I think that answers your question Ralph," Dave answered, thinking how immature Ralph was.

Suddenly the group heard one car then another pull slowly up the low hill. Dave's hand went automatically to the pistol in his belt a motion he tried to hide from his mother.

"Shhhhhhh!" Lela admonished, turning down the wicks on the lamps to darken the room even more. "I think dat be Omar and Will Henry. Dey should be driving wit' da lights out."

Dave got up to peek out of the window, for the trucks had pulled around to the back yard.

"It is Omar and Will," he told them, and everybody breathed a sigh of relief.

"You never can tell," Lela said, with a hint of scorn in her voice.

Looking at Ralph, Aggie said, "You better git shed of dat wig soon as you gits outta Arkansas. It be so ugly peepers might notice you jus' fer dat reason!"

The Duster children giggled agreement with Aggie. "Dat sea-grass hair is too straight," laughed Ralph's youngest sister Marystine. "Dats hi dey gone know it ain't yo' real hair. Yo' real hair is so nappy hit ain't funny," she said, making everyone smile.

Aggie joined Dave at the window. " hit's sho' dem. Heah dey come!" Aggie whispered as Dave opened the back door.

Lela turned the lamps back up. Dave took his seat at the table again. "Last thing," Dave said to Eunice and Thomas. "When you all have arrived safely at your final destinations." He handed them two envelopes, one for the parents and one for Ralph. "If everything is alright and you feel you have arrived without being followed or anything, send these to the post box number on the front of the envelopes." He handed them two stamped envelopes addressed to his mother with no messages or names inside, just a blank sheet of paper. It's just so we know you all arrived safely. Please send the envelopes as soon as you get where you're going. And sign your new initials on the blank sheet inside, not your new name. Just the initials, all right? And your post box number. We'll immediately destroy any letters we receive from you. But, we'll keep the P.O. numbers. I suggest you do the same. After a while we'll send you more of a letter when we feel it's safe. Nobody knows your new names except me and Mama.

But Thomas Duster was focused on an additional concern. "Hi we ever gone pay you back yo' money Dave?"

"Think about that after you're safe and after this Depression is over. The important thing now is the safety of your son, right?" Dave asked gently.

"We put on dis earth to hep each other," Lela stated emphatically. "You jus' hep somebody else who be in trouble when-so-never you can. Dat money will be paid back like dat."

Omar, Peter, and Will Henry walked in the back door with Aggie's boys. They removed their caps and spoke to everyone. The young men shook hands with Thomas Duster and Peter smiled assurance to the anxious Eunice. She thought he was the best looking man she had ever seen. Dave was right good looking hisself she thought, but Peter looked like an angel.

Omar surprised Thomas and Eunice Duster by handing them both a shoe box. When they opened it, they found fried pies and chicken that Omar's wife had made. The gruff Will Henry gave Ralph a flour sack containing a half dozen hard boiled eggs, salt, pepper, a chunk of cheddar cheese and a box of crackers. The sack also contained two apples, an orange and a large bag of McCully's coconut candies. He handed the bag to Ralph silently. Much to the amusement of Omar and Peter, Will Henry became flustered and his yellowish-red face flamed when Ralph tried to thank him.

"Alright!" Dave said to Peter. "Don't be shy. Let's see what you got in your bag, mister."

Peter, smiling, set a large basket on the table. In it were six medium sized cloth feed bags that had been washed and filled with nuts in their shells, raw peanuts, pecans, brazil nuts, even a few of the extremely hard shelled, but delicious, hickory nuts, and black walnuts. Pete also included twenty-four sticks of the skinny foot long peppermint sticks from Mr. Green's that everyone in West Steward loved because they were crunchy and sweet and not too minty. Finally, Lela uncovered her gifts that had been on the table all the time, but covered with a lace cloth.

"Oh, my!" exclaimed Aggie. "Dose is beautiful!"

Under the lace cloth lay six expensive white leather bound Bibles—one for each member of the Duster family.

"I believes," said Lela, "Dat everabody should have dey own Bible. Deres a place in front to record da major events o'yo' lives. Nah all da Bible is mighty good readin', but pay real close 'tention to da New Testament and what Jesus say most 'specially. Ifn you keep wit' Him, He'll keep wit' you. May God bless, and most 'specially, proteck y'all. Amen."

Eunice Duster burst into tears at this unexpected display of caring and generosity. The girls, Dorothy Pearl and Marystine joined their mother in sniffling, and Thomas Duster and Joe Bee blew their noses and stomped their feet to control their emotions. Only Ralph was unresponsive, taking it all in with an amused little smile on his face as if this bounty and show of support was somehow his natural due. He only wondered how they happened to get the presents and food together so fast. Asking Peter this, Peter had replied simply, "A wise man is always prepared. Besides we knew we were getting you out in a day or so, though you had no way of knowing it."

"And the hot tamales?" asked Thomas Duster.

"Finished. All sold out by ten p.m." Peter said. "We actually had a two good hours to get ready. Mother B, she bought the Bibles last week."

"Y'all is da bestes frens," Eunice began. "What in dis woil would we do without you? I jus' thanks da Lawd fer all y'all."

"Let's go-o-oo! Else we'll still be standin' heah chitting and chatting 'til the sun shows his face!"

"Quiet down Will Henry!" Lela exclaimed in an unexpectedly sharp tone to the red headed fellow. "We's got time fer one mo' thing. I wants y'all to jine hains. That's right. Move on around da table goils. Ralph! You, too. Come on! We's gone have a moment of prayer befoe we take another step further."

"Muddear, please make it a short prayer. We got a long way to go," Dave pleaded softly.

Lela met her sons eyes levelly and said sternly, "Yah! Da's right, make it quick! Everabody got a lot of time fer da Devil—very little fer Jesus." Taking her large old well worn bible in hand, Mother Bailey turned to the New Testament and announced one of her favorite passages: "Romans, twelf chapter, da ninth through da twenty-first verses. Y'all got dat? Den less us read together."

It was a moving selection that dealt with love and hope, and letting God avenge you rather than seeking revenge yourself. There were words about being kind to your enemies thus conquering evil with good. The reading took less than five minutes during which time Will Henry had managed to clear his throat six times.

Lela, with bowed head asked those present to join her in the well known benediction: "May da Lawd watch between me and thee, while we absent one from another. Amen."

Lela opened her watery eyes just in time to see Omar touch the inside of his jacket ever so carefully. In that second she saw the unmistakable glint of the gun at his waist. Lela's eyes flew open with alarm as she suddenly realized that all of them—Dave, Will Henry, Omar and probably Pete, were armed. What did they intend to do if they were somehow discovered moving the Dusters out of town? *Lawd have mercy Jesus!*

Seeing the weapon, Lela said to the Lord, "I jus' got to trust in you nah, Father to git us safely through. Please, Suh, don't let us down!"

Suddenly they were all gone. Omar with "the women folk." Will Henry with Thomas Duster and his son Joe Bee—and Dave and Pete with the most dangerous cargo—Ralph Adam Duster. The others could start on their journey immediately, but Dave and Pete had to wait awhile for the bus. They decided to wait in Old Steward.

"Aggie," Lela announced firmly. "You welcome ta stay as long as you wants ta, and you can jine me or not jine me; but I'm goin' in mah room nah and I'm gone stay in dere talkin' wit' da Lawd 'til I sees my boy and da others walk safe and sound back into dis house!"

To Lela's surprise, Aggie replied that she would put the boys to bed and then she would join the old woman in protracted prayer.

Aggie thought she'd better have a good long drink of water before joining Mother Bailey. When she entered the kitchen she noticed immediately that one of the lovely white Bibles had been left behind. Aggie knew it would be Ralph's bible, because in her heart she knew Ralph had no use in this world for a Bible.

NINE

———✦———

On Saturday morning, October 11, Ralph Duster was placed on the floor of Dave's truck then covered with large light bags of dried corn shucks.

Dave and Pete drove along the one paved road from West Steward to Old Steward, along the car line that featured a "Safety Sam" sign about every mile or so warning motorists to drive carefully. It was a path both Dave and Peter knew well. It was the road to town—Old Steward—where all of the "big stores" were located. The appliance shops, hardware stores, dress and shoe shops as well as most of the feed stores, all but one of the chain grocery stores, and both the white and the black picture shows. Everything was in town—and everybody shopped there—all of the towns and hamlets surrounding West Steward and Old Steward as well as all of the little surrounding towns across the river in Mississippi.

They drove briskly along in the misty cool morning towards the Missouri Pacific bus depot in town. The men had passed only two cars, both headed north as they were. The bus from West Steward to Old Steward would not resume its regular route until six thirty a.m., by which time Dave and Peter hoped to be in bed trying to get a few hours sleep.

Now, in the fall, the willow trees along the road stood in barren grace, fluttering gently in the morning breeze, perhaps anticipating the scant snow that would dress them in shimmering white lace later in the year.

It was almost too peaceful to break the soothing silence as they drove along, and Peter, never talkative to begin with, shattered the misty stillness with regret. Not turning to look at Dave he said very quietly, "I don't care for Ralph's attitude. He seems to think we are involved in some kind of game."

"You're right, Dave stated equally as softly. He was messing with the wig—putting it on crooked and backwards, playing with the cane."

Dave pulled abruptly over to the side of the road behind a clump of trees. It was only two a.m. and they had more than two hours to wait for the bus. Hand-signaling Peter to follow him, Dave went to the side of the truck and tapped. "Ralph! Listen can you hear me well?"

A muffled "Yas, but dese shucks is ticklin' me to death!"

A look of exasperation passed between the two friends. Quickly, Dave explained his concerns about Ralph's attitude. He admonished the boy to exercise extreme caution because the lives of his family, as well as his own, were in peril.

"We are all in danger here. Everyone is sticking their necks out for you and your family and we don't mind doing that, but this is no damn game, boy," Dave said purposely letting anger seep into his voice. "Just try to get where you're going in one piece, and don't do anything that will cause suspicion. Do you understand me? Dump that wig and cane as soon as you get out of Arkansas. You hear me?"

"Yas." And then, "Suh."

They thought the boy had finally been chastened, but just in case, Peter added: "We don't want any shit outta you, Ralph. A lot of people have put their asses on the road for you and your family. The best thing you can do for us is to get to Detroit— and don't come back to West Steward ever. For nothing. You read me?"

"Yas. I understands," Ralph mumbled from the bag of shucks.

"You better, you silly bastard!" Peter said under his breath as they got back in the truck.

Dave casted a surprised eye at Peter who was usually a lot more mild mannered than he had been in the last week. He smiled silently, his ready roll dangling from the corner of his mouth. Peter, a non-smoker, placed two sticks of gum in his mouth and chewed them viciously.

Dave and Peter drove straight to Old Steward and took turns napping in the truck as they waited for the bus. When the twice a week bus left at five thirty for Memphis, a stooped old feller of advanced years carrying a Crocker sack and a beat up old cardboard grip would be sitting way in the back in the Colored section. If asked, Ralph was to say he was going to visit a sick daughter up in Crittenden County, up near Clarkedale, Arkansas. Actually, he had been instructed to leave the bus in Clarkedale, discard the disguise, buy another ticket, and wait for the next bus to Memphis. From Memphis, he could catch a train to Chicago and change trains in Chicago for Detroit.

Dave had given Ralph another twenty dollars—just in case—told him to talk to no one if possible and to try to hide his young face which of course did not go with the wig, stooped posture and cane.

They let him out a block south of the Missouri Pacific Depot, where Pete and Dave helped him brush off the corn shuck silks and adjust his wig. He looked just right, they thought. Tacky, slightly dirty, and old. The right combination for not being noticed, they hoped.

Dave and Pete shook hands with Ralph. "Remember to keep your mouth shut," Pete warned again.

"You've got about a half hour to wait. Go in the Colored men's toilet until the bus is ready to leave. Keep your eyes open—and don't forget to send the envelope as soon as you reach your destination," Dave directed.

Ralph thanked the two men adequately—not profusely as one might expect—and hobbled off leaning heavily on his cane.

"He's overdoing it. Walking that slowly he'll never make the five thirty even though it's only five o'clock now!" Peter offered only half in jest.

Dave and Peter sat in the truck looking around them. There was virtually no one in sight except Ralph Duster. Old Steward sat contently on the South Bank of the Mississippi, snoozing away the last sweet hours before the sun rose to scatter the mist, and to bring trouble or pleasure to the residents of this small twin town.

Before turning the truck around and heading back home, Dave whispered, "I think we oughta wait to see him on the bus."

"You're right," Pete whispered back, "because the boy obviously doesn't have right good sense."

"So far, so good," Dave grunted. "You got your Peace Of Mind?"

"My Equalizer? Right here," Peter said, patting his coat pocket. "Snug as a flea on a dog's back. And she's loaded for bear."

"Or white folks," Dave replied dryly. "Although Lord knows I hope it doesn't come to that. We're not quite ready for big time action—yet."

"I know. I'll surely feel a heap better once we get this boy out of town. I'm not so much worried about the others."

Dave and Peter sat tensely in the truck watching as Ralph finally hobbled into the depot area.

Alert and armed they watched Ralph and listened for signs of trouble that they hoped would not come.

"I bet they had this depot watched for a few days."

"Yeah. But I don't see anyone around now."

Suddenly, Peter whispered, "Look, What is that boy doing?"

Dave squinted in the semi-darkness trying to see nearly a block away. Instead of heading for the depot and the Colored men's toilet as he had been told to do, Ralph slowly ascended the bus steps, and standing on its top step he turned around to face Dave and Peter, then he clasped both hands above his head and shook them in an unmistakable victory sign as a prize fighter might do-a young and vigorous prize fighter.

"What the hell...!"

"I told you that boy is crazy!"

"Where is the bus driver?"

"Went to the men's room probably—I hope."

"My gosh! What's wrong with him?"

"The nigger is crazy! Dave, let's get out of here," Peter said anxiously. "I mean if Ralph's gonna act like a fool!"

"I think you're right, Pete. If the boy is gonna act silly..., we've done the best we could. He's on his own now, and we won't know if he made it or not until we get the note with his new name, old initials and new address. Honest to goodness! What has gotten into him?" Dave exclaimed in a tone of disbelief. "We told him to be careful and here he is even before he gets out of Steward—clowning."

Both Peter and Dave thought it wise to leave now, but they could not. They sat watching and wondering and wishing the bus would leave soon.

Ralph finally entered the bus and Dave and Peter much relieved, headed back to West Steward, driving with the lights off until they reached the car line.

Simmering down a bit, Dave said logically, "Maybe the boy was just relieved to make it as far as the car line. After all, there was no one around to see him grinning and all."

"But it's the principle of the thing!" Peter burst out. "You never know who is around! You have to be careful."

"I agree, but you know what? Ralph was not as cool and calm as he would have us believe, boy got a little scared at the end! I noticed that. Maybe he was just acting silly to relieve his tension."

"Well, I hope you are right," Peter said unconvinced. "But all in all it makes you feel good though doesn't it? Possibly saving a man's life, I mean, and confusing the shit outta Old Man Birkens." The two young men laughed heartily, thinking of the sheriff and his reaction when he found the Dusters gone.

"Makes you feel great-us working our plan and all—for the very first time. I think they'll make it—all of them. They'll arrive safely at their destinations. With God's help as Mama would say."

"Now, we had the real keg of dynamite didn't we?" Peter said. "That Ralph is too much!"

"He's on that bus now and it should be pulling off pretty soon. I wonder what he's doing now," Dave asked not expecting an answer.

"Probably turning cartwheels in the damn aisles!" Peter volunteered.

They both burst out laughing. "Shut up, Pete!" Dave said, still laughing. "You gonna cause me to run into a ditch!"

They drove along silently through the easy dawn that was slowly lifting its veil.

Finally Peter asked, "So, do you think he did it? Hacked up Leon and his lady friend?"

Dave was quiet a good while as he shifted his little skinny ready roll to the other side of his mouth. Finally, he said in a voice that was barely audible, "Well. What do you think Pete?"

The two men drove straight back to West Steward without uttering another word, the deep silence of the coming morning clanging between them like an alarm bell.

TEN

Luxury Tweedle's funeral on Saturday, October 11, was surprisingly well attended considering that she was not a friendly woman, someone had remarked.

"Nothin but a buncha curiousity seekers!" pronounced the sheriff, "jus' come to rubber neck and gape at dat little jar dey done stuffed her in. It was a disgrace befoe Gawd!"

Mathene left a notarized letter with the sheriff for Brentwood Tweedle. In it she stated that he could have the house and everything in it, except the jewelry and the thirty dollars which she had already taken. Immediately following her mother's funeral, Mathene fled to Friars Point, Mississippi, cash in hand.

Leon Baycott's funeral had proceeded Mrs. Tweedle's by days and was well attended by relatives, friends and customers who cried out for the blood of the one that killed "this valued member of our community."

The sheriff finally had a real lead to follow. He knew where Archie's Shoe Store was and he had related this information to the Monroe men right away. This was their first real lead, and that's what they were here for, the Monroe men—to follow leads. This lead, said the county boys, suggested that they check not only this particular store, but all stores carrying extra large sizes within a twenty or so mile radius. They hopped on it with great eagerness. The mayor was called. Maybe they would be able to solve this case after all! They had something real to do at last.

DeBell Hinkle was a little too chatty for the sheriff's taste, so he had not been told that the other part of the report fitted Ralph Duster to a tee. Only he and the Monroe men knew that the killer was: a man, fairly strong, weighing, according to the cast print, between 165 and 185 pounds, and standing between 5-foot-11-inches to 6-foot-1-inch tall.

"Dat new technology is a bitch!" exclaimed the sheriff to the Monroe County boys. "Hi dey know all dat jus' from a footprint? And hi many mens in the state of Arkansas wear a shoe dat big and dat narrow?"

The sheriff swore the Monroe County law officers to secrecy about the report. He was doing the best he could to keep a lynch mob off of Ralph Duster for his own personal reasons and for the reason that this Depression couldn't last forever. The sheriff was pleased to know that most of the local businessmen in the Old Steward-West Steward Businessmen's Association agreed with him and expected him to do everything he could to keep the peace so they could have plenty of business. They would back him and give him their full support. He would report to them soon that they were "makin a good 'mount o'progress on da case." Now, all he had to do was keep the information he had from the sizable number of hot heads he had in town—especially the cousins, Parker Wilson and Willie "Red" Oakes, who had a constant grudge against the Colored community.

When Omar and Will Henry arrived in Memphis, they were to stay until the Dusters were safely aboard the train for Omaha. The Dusters had been told not to sit together and not to talk to each other until their safe arrival.

Once their mission was completed, Omar and Will would find a Colored boarding house, give phony names and rent separate rooms where they would sleep for five or six hours then head back to Arkansas. But first, they would find a telephone and call one of the five locations in West Steward that owned a telephone. It had been arranged that they would call Jones Meat Market located in the two story building near the car line and ask to speak to Fred Jones, a portly amicable man of sixty-one who had taken messages for Dave before. Omar was to say either one or two sets of words depending on the situation: Fine. Never. Which would tell Dave that everything was fine and that they were never stopped for any reason, or the other set of words: Problem. Call. Which would let Dave know that there had been some kind of problem and that he would call back to let Dave know the nature of the problem at noon sharp. Dave would stop by Jones at eleven a.m. hoping to hear the first set of words. If they heard: "Fine. Never." he and Peter would take to their beds again and sleep for a few unstressful hours.

When Dave stopped by Jones Meat Market, Fred said to him, "Omar called. Where he at? He said to tell you fine, ever. Does dat make sense to you? Or fine, never, he might o'said. He repeated it twice lak I can't hear good which ah kin—but you know you can't hear too well on dat telephone wit' all da noise up in dis sto.'"

Dave smiled broadly at Fred, thanked him, and went home to sleep more peacefully than he had in weeks.

Hearing the news Lela clapped her hands and shouted: "Thank you, Lawd Jesus! Da Lawd still answers prayers. Yas he do!"

Aggie, who had slept not at all, felt especially energetic after she heard the good news, so she left Lela's house, went home and packed her basket, placed it on her head, and begin delivering her beautifully ironed waists and shirts nicely wrapped in tissue paper which was her signature. As she went about, she was careful to let hearsay, rumor, gossip—anything that she could take back to benefit the Circle—stick to her like fly paper.

Henry Birkens was not an early riser as were most of his neighbors. He delighted in keeping "bankers hours"—the privilege of the man who enjoyed a better than average station in life, he thought. "Onliest ones that need to be up real early in the moaning was fools, niggers, and mules—and if you thought about it- fools, niggers, and mules were about one and the same," the sheriff often remarked.

So the sheriff arose at seven on Monday morning, October 13, and bathed, shaved and scanned the local papers, plus one or two newspapers from surrounding counties to keep himself informed, and pleased to see very little about the murder case, he ate the breakfast that Nettie Lyons had prepared for him.

"Dat woman is as black as hell wit' da lights out!" he remarked to some of his snickering buddies. "But dere ain't a nigger woman in the state dat kin out cook 'er!"

This morning was exceptional only because he had decided to pick up Ralph Duster for questioning on the advice of the Monroe men and his own thinking. For this reason he had risen one hour earlier.

The Monroe men had said they would "interrogate vigorously" to try to make Ralph confess. The sheriff was still sure that Ralph had not killed the "Love Birds," but then he did have some evidence—or possible evidence—on Ralph and no one else. Ralph had had at least one, perhaps two heated spats with the deceased-with all the different versions of the story travelling around he couldn't tell how many run ins there had been between the two. And then there were the shoes. Unmistakably the shoes were Double A's. However, the Monroe men had checked all of the stores in and around West Steward and Old Steward, Arkansas and had not been able to come up with any conclusive evidence to connect Ralph or any other black man, or white man for that matter, to large extra narrow shoes. None of the store keepers could remember selling any of the very few pairs of Double A's they carried to a young Colored man at any time, and they would have remembered, they said, because shoes in that size and width were expensive.

Sheriff Birkens was never to find out that Ralph Duster's shoes were always made by an old Negro man in Old Steward, Arkansas who had apprenticed himself to a shoemaker more than fifty years ago, and now made shoes for only three or four customers—if and when he felt like it.

Although both Eunice and Thomas seemed to have normal width feet—the sheriff had surreptitiously checked their feet on his last visit—Joe Bee already wore 13 Double A's at age fifteen, so narrow feet ran somewhere in the family. Then there was another disturbing fact that Henry Birkens did not want to face—one of the law officers from Monroe County had brought to his reluctant attention: that some niggers would kill a white man that got in his way no matter what the consequences were. There were a sufficient number of just such men on chain gangs all over the South to prove it—those who had somehow escaped lynching that is. They even had a woman who had killed her mistress serving time on the county farm, said the special men from Monroe County.

It was inconceivable to them that he did not know this. Yes, he had known this, but believing it was another matter. Henry Birkens would admit that he was a small town sheriff. He thought "his" Negroes a docile, passive lot. He had never seen any other kind. Oh, they raised a little hell on Saturday night and some ended up in jail for fighting and stealing among themselves, but that was all. That is why he did not resent the mayor having the Monroe lawmen sent in—for he knew that this double murder was more than a small town sheriff might be expected to handle with the tools at hand.

Sheriff Birkens couldn't honestly think of a soul in Colored Town that he thought was capable of killing a white man. Not even Ralph who had a bad temper—bad tempers always stopped short of white folks. That had always been his experience.

Not Ralph Duster. You didn't kill a white man and then just go lay down and take a nap. No. It made no sense. However, he would have to go along with the Monroe men. They were scheduled to pick Ralph up for questioning between eight thirty and nine o'clock. So be it.

Sheriff Birkens thought Nettie was a little grumpy this morning because he had asked her to change her schedule by an hour. He thought she had banged his plate of grits and pork chops and eggs down a bit hard on the table and he had given her a look of mild displeasure, which Nettie had returned with a displeased look of her own. Oh, well, let it go.

Then it dawned on him. Colored people in his town had an unbelievable grapevine. They seemed to know just about everything that was happening or about to happen. Somehow Nettie knew he was going to pick up Ralph Duster this morning. Worse, she was a distant cousin of Mae Bell Lewis. In fact, he had met Mae Bell when she had come to borrow some change from her cousin, Nettie.

Cadine Birkens had died sixteen years ago "of the ruptured appendix," leaving Henry a childless widower. Lately he had been keeping company with Irene Hopkins, a fifty-five year old widow up in Epps as a cover. But it seemed like every day more and more people knew about him and Mae Bell Lewis.

Sheriff Birkens did not want to pick up Ralph, but better he take some action himself, thus maintaining some control before hot heads entered into the picture.

Some whites were beginning to mumble in the direction of "a niggah" or "some niggahs" who might have done it. When crimes could not be solved quickly, easily, negative thoughts always turned to the defenseless blacks. Then too, the mayor who appointed him was on his ass to clean up "those killings." Stuff like that was bad for business, he said. Sure. As if anything was good for business right now, Henry Birkens thought.

But nobody liked living in a town with unsolved murders. No sirrebob! So the mayor was on his ass. This was Sheriff Birkens' first reason for picking up Ralph.

His second reason wouldn't stand the light of day—not in White Town. His reason was this: he had promised—promised—Mae Bell that there would be no more lynchings in West Steward. The sheriff had promised when the Lawrence family had been burned alive in their home, promised again after Billy Binder had been lynched and his body dragged to pieces from the back of a truck in 1928.

Oh, Mae Bell had gone quite berserk over that one—because everyone felt that Billy was quite innocent of the "crime" that he was accused of—raping a white woman.

Why Mae Bell had poured a slop jar of piss over him while he slept! And Mae Bell had threatened to drown little Birkey in the Mississippi River or cut him to bits or something. It did not matter to her that he knew nothing of the matter until he returned, too late to save the young boy.

"Outta da county mah ass!" Mae Bell had screamed. "Nah weren't dat lucky! You da sheriff. You 'pose to know what's goin' on!"

Her eyes were black pools of venom as she railed and ran around the room throwing things at him. In the end she had blamed him—the peckerwood Law— for all the woes of the black people for the last ten decades. There was no reasoning with her. She took Birkey, then two years old, and fled to Mississippi.

He was fifty-six, she was twenty-three, and the feelings he had for Mae Bell Lewis were beyond love, beyond reason. And then there was his son, Birkey, who unaccountably was nearly as white as he was. He had never had a son before. His late wife was barren, so he had forgotten about ever having children long ago.

Mae Bell was dark, but not nearly as black as her cousin Nettie. Birkey had his light brown hair, not straight like his own, but a mass of molasses brown ringlets. And his eyes were light grey instead of pale blue as his were. He would send him North—would educate him. He had already taken out a large insurance policy from a Northern insurance company and left it to Birkey and his mother. For he loved his little son even more than his mother—if that were possible.

And yet—and yet little Birkey and his mother were totally compartmentalized in some area of his mind. Sheriff Birkens accepted Mae Bell and Birkey, but not Colored people generally. He loved his Negro son—but yet he was not a liberal and thought little of blacks as a people. It was a puzzle, a dilemma that many white men in similar situations in the South did not even try to analyze.

After Billy Binders death, Mae Bell left the sheriff, taking her child. It was said that Mae Bell was living with a Colored man over in Mississippi. This rumor nearly drove the sheriff wild. Somehow it angered him more that she was with a black man rather than a white one. He didn't stop to analyze these feelings either.

It had gotten back to Henry Birkens, more than once, that some people were beginning to feel that he was "soft on niggers" because of Mae Bell, but all that mattered to him now was having her and his son back, so he called in his housekeeper, Nettie, and gave her a sum of money.

"Heahs five dollars fer yo'self," he had said as he handed her more than a week's salary, "and fifteen dollars for Mae Bell. Go on ovah dere and bring 'er back, Nettie," the sheriff pleaded.

Nettie was gone for three days. When she returned she looked well rested and rather smug, Henry Birkens thought.

"She won't come," reported the dumpy little servant. "She says what you gone do? Have yo' own son kilt one of dese days to please da white folks?"

The sheriff was deeply hurt by this accusation. "She know I got a good policy for her and Birkey! Why she go and say a thang lak dat? Holy Gawd Amighty!"

Henry sent Nettie back a second time with three dollars for herself and twenty dollars for Mae Bell.

"She living wit' another main?" the devastated old man asked, deathly afraid of the answer. His woman had been gone almost two weeks. He had lost weight and found it hard to concentrate on his duties.

"Chile, when dat main don't eat what I sets befoe 'em —all dem good pancakes and oven baked steak and gravy, and fried green tomatoes and lak dat—he sho' sick!" Nettie reported to her cousin.

"Nother main? Not as I knows of."

Henry Birkens' old shoulders sagged with relief.

Nettie went back to Mississippi and after a "nice rest" of two days, she returned again—without Mae Bell and of course without the money the sheriff had sent.

The sheriff could not go to Mississippi himself looking for Mae Bell, and he knew that when she came back and word got around, he might lose his job as sheriff—a very serious matter in these times. More than that he would lose the respect of all those who could hire him. If he had no job would Mae Bell be interested in him? She had made it very clear that she did not love him. He was simply better than taking in washing, which she thought beneath her. Birkey was an accident—but once the woman got used to having a child around, she lavished all of her affection on him as if he was hers alone and the sheriff had no claim to him.

She was a proud one, Mae Bell. And stubborn. And mean. And beautiful. And desirable. "Ax her hi much she want to come home," said the beaten man.

Mae Bell had anticipated this question. "She say she'll come back fer—" Nettie hesitated to tell him, "five hunnert dollars."

"Five hunnert dollars!" the sheriff burst out. "I ain't got dat kinna money! Is she done went crazy?"

"She say all white folks got money. She say she whip mah ass ifn I brings ya or tells ya wha she at. She say five hunnert dollars-not including what you already done sent," Nettie said hanging her head. Even she was ashamed of her cousin's greed.

"Have she done lost her mind?" Henry Birkens shouted again.

The sheriff had four hundred and fifty dollars—his life savings—before he used some of it up trying to get his woman to come back across the river. Now he had four hundred dollars in the world, and Mae Bell wanted five. He had the rent from the houses in Colored Town, twenty dollars a month—when he could collect it. The only other thing that he had was his real emergency stash—a gold watch with an extremely long and heavy chain that his wife had inherited from her father, and a gold picture locket. The watch was heavy and very ornate with unusual raised carvings on its front.

Beaten, the sheriff said to Nettie, "Tell Mae Bell I'll think on it. Send her a letter or somethin', no more goin' across da river fer you right nah—and keep yo' mouf shut about all dis."

"Yassuh!" Nettie knew as well as she knew her name that Henry Birkens would find the money somewhere for her cousin and his son.

The sheriff thought about his situation for two days. Finally he took the watch and locket to a businessman in town who had coveted it ever since Henry had shown it to him some years ago. He gave him one hundred dollars for the watch and locket. No questions asked—for the Depression had made questions about selling personal items unlikely.

Henry sent Nettie across on the ferry again.

"Tell Mae to come home. I have the money but I won't send it to her—she'll have to come get it."

Mae Bell came back with Nettie all smiles and sweetness—and later love making—after Henry Birkens had handed her five one hundred dollar bills.

Mae Bell and Birkey were back! And Henry Birkens' life was back on an even road again. At least he had that going for him, he thought.

It was strange how this slut of a girl, Mae Bell Lewis, who was despised by the whites who knew about her and barely tolerated by the black community because of her open relationship with the sheriff, so loved her people that she was able to extract a promise from the sheriff, who represented the Law itself, that a bus load of Baptist ministers would not have been able to get—no more violence against blacks. No more lynchings, no more beatings in this town. Of course, the sheriff could not guarantee his promises. The Klan, the Night Riders—even Parker Wilson and Willie Oakes—people like that could never be fully controlled. But Henry Birkens had promised Mae Bell that he would do all that he could do and he meant to keep that promise, for he was certainly not without power.

"Dats all a main can be expected to do, Mae," the sheriff explained in his hang-dog fashion. "Who do you think is makin' everabody take it slow on dis murder thang? Dats why nobody been picked up yet."

Henry thought it was enough. He figured himself an honorable man. One who went to church and "put in da plate" once in a while—although most Sundays he excused himself on "sheriffing business." A lot of dese old fellers had Colored babies around town, and dey made no provisions to care fer dems—now or ever. Most didn't even down recognize 'em as dey own chirrens, Birkens thought. Well— at least he wasn't that kind of trash! Yet Henry Birkens seriously wanted to "get shed" of the reputation he was quickly getting of being soft on niggers. That kind of thinking about a sheriff was death socially as well as politically. To be tough on blacks—not give them an inch, to jack them up at every turn—and still keep his angry black woman happy—"Dat," he knew, "wuz da dilemma."

Henry Birkens, DeBell Hinkle, and the two Monroe men arrived at the Duster house at just before nine o'clock on October 13, a full ten days after the murders, in two cars trailing an impressive amount of dust behind them. The sheriff had briefed the two special men from Monroe County on what to expect: Eunice, the mother would cry and plead, and Thomas, the daddy would talk as courageously as he dared to impress his son. Finally, the daddy would insist upon coming down to the jail with his son which he must not be allowed to do.

Just let him handle it—he knew how to keep 'em at bay. He, Sheriff Henry Talcott Birkens would be like iron—professional, tough, unbending. The Monroe men would be impressed this day, he thought. And he would tell Eunice just what he told her a few days ago. "Dese is jus' da purlimenaries."

While driving to the Duster house, one of the Monroe men—one was riding with the sheriff, one with the deputy—had mentioned that Brentwood Tweedle's shoes—there had been two pairs in the house—had checked out. Size 13 Extra Wide. They were presumed to be the husband's because the dead man wore only an eleven-and-a-half medium, and they certainly didn't fit the plaster cast print. Anyway the sheriff could check Tweedle's feet when he went up to Marianna,

Arkansas to the hospital, probably tomorrow, because he was behind his schedule.

The older of the Monroe men said to the sheriff: "If this Duster boy is guilty, we'll get it out of him. Trust us. We have specialized training. We are here to assist you in solving these baffling deaths—and you can rest assured we'll do just that!"

The sheriff smiled, somewhat reassured. They all knew it would look good to the Business Board of the town, not to mention the mayor, to have questioned at least one suspect roughly, thoroughly, no holds barred, using all of their technical criminal expertise. That's why they were here.

DeBell Hinkle was much excited by the talk of the Monroe men. At last he was a part of some real professional law work! Yes, just like in the detective magazines he read so avidly. Fact was, when the sheriff was out of the office and he was alone with the men, he never tired of listening to the exploits and adventures they had experienced as law enforcement agents. They talked ceaselessly of the big cases they had been involved in and especially of the crimes they had had a part in solving. It seemed it was easier to speak of past successes than their lack of success in these Love Bird killings.

When they pulled up in front of the Duster house, DeBell fairly leaped from the car and bounded up the steps ahead of the others, and found—nothing.

DeBell had collected the rents for the sheriff, off and on, for the last five years that Eunice Duster and her family had lived at Number Four, Apple Street. Therefore, he knew that Eunice Duster was as neat and tidy as they came, so walking through this small house and seeing the beds unmade, a coffee pot half full on the stove, the back door standing wide open and the screen door open—now everybody hooked the screen door to keep flies out, even when the main door was left open when it was hot. The fact that the screen door was left open told the deputy all he needed to know. They were gone.

"Dey ain't heah!" he called back to the others. "Dey gone!" he exclaimed. "Sheriff! The Dusters—dey gone!" he repeated for the third time with consternation.

The lanky old lawman hurried to his deputy's side. "Mebbe dey all done went out on a job." Sheriff Birkens suggested, his stomach suddenly knotting.

"I don't believe so," said one of the Monroe men examining the chifforobes and trunks. "I think the deputy is right. Just look at this place. True, most everything seems to be here and still..."

Presently, seeing the two cars and the four lawmen Amy Delores Pages came out of the house next door and walked across the porch.

"Good moaning." Four pairs of eyes swiveled her way. "Y'all be a-looking fer da Dusters mebbe? Dey gone."

"We knows dat!" shouted DeBell in exasperation. Ignoring the deputy, Amy Delores walked timidly down the steps and into the yard, her hand extended. She handed the sheriff a piece of paper.

"Here be a note Eunice done left me. She say I should show it ta ya."

Henry Birkens grabbed the note so quickly he nearly tore it in half. He jammed his reading glasses on his face and with the other lawmen closing in, straining to see, he read Eunice's note aloud: "Sorry to leave in such a rush but my sister in Louisiana, she say dere be work fer my man if we come real fast. Say work mebbe for Ralph too. We got nuthin' to stay fer 'cept frens lak you, Amy Delores. Take what you wants to from the house an sell the rest for money or use fer tradin' if you wants to, includin' the old car of Ralph's, which you may can sell for parts. The rent is paid up fer the month. Wish us luck. I will write as soon as we get settle down proper. Show dis letter to the high sheriff so peepers will know you got a right to what's in the house and they do not. God bless you and yourn. Mrs. E. Duster and fambly."

Funny. Amy Delores thought she could swear Eunice had said her sister lived in Nebraska somewhere. Had she dreamed that she saw people leaving Number Four, Apple Street? Some men with caps pulled down over their eyes when she had gotten up after midnight to use the slop jar?

"Did you see 'em leave?" asked the sheriff through tight lips and behind suspicious eyes.

"Naw suh," she answered, automatically sticking to the code: Never tell white folks nothin'!

"Did ya hear 'em leave?"

"Naw suh, Mistah Hinkle, suh."

The double *suh*. The bowing and scraping they demanded.

"When did dey leave?" asked a Monroe man yet again.

"Donno suh. Ain't saw 'em since Friday afternoon."

"All of 'em? Ralph too?" asked the second Monroe man.

"Yassuh. All o'dem, suh."

"Wha yo' fambly at?" The sheriff asked angrily as if it mattered.

"Out looking fer work, suh, my husmon is. He do dat every day. My chirren, dey all be in da house."

Now there it was, the shadowy figures peering from behind curtains, the sneaky looks, the doors probably locked.

When the sheriff had driven up, the street was filled with people going about their business—now Apple Street was utterly abandoned except for Amy Delores Pages and the lawmen. That grapevine knowledge that one of their own is hip deep in shit. The talking drums of Africa, Birkens called it. Mother Africa still at work.

Marko Horton. Gone. The Duster family. Gone. Something was going on here and Henry Birkens vowed that he would get to the bottom of it. That letter was innocent enough. Too innocent they all agreed. And too convenient. They would have the bus station checked—they would start asking some questions damn it!

"Did they take their black asses off in Ralph's car?"

"Naw suh! Ralph got dat old piece o'car dat hardly runs." Mrs. Pages volunteered. "Nobody could git far in dat thing. Yon it sit over dere." The woman pointed.

The old Ford sat rusty, black, and bent on the side of the house.

"Den somebody musta took 'em outta heah fast!"

The two men from Monroe County suddenly had single hard lines for lips. The sheriff's mouth hung slack, fearful and full of fury—and the deputy Hinkle was beside himself with excitement and frustration.

"Might I ax please, suh, what y'all be looking fer the Dusters fer?" Amy Delores asked shyly. As if she didn't know. Of course Eunice had told her of the sheriff's visits. Silently she asked the Lord for forgiveness because she was glad they were gone. The people in Colored Town didn't need any more trouble.

"You may not!" the little deputy spat out, not looking back as the four of them got in the cars again and sped off towards White Town riding on a cloud of dust and suspicion.

No, the ticket agent had not sold any tickets to a family of six. Only a few people had left on the bus in the past two days. None fitted the description of any of the Duster men as given.

"Gawd damn it!" Henry Birkens knew in his soul that they didn't all leave together.

DeBell Hinkle knew in his soul that they were probably taken out by friends—probably wearing a disguise—for he had read about stuff like that. Not much caught him by surprise since he had subscribed to *Master Detective,* he thought. They had left surely before dawn. It was now nine thirty. Should they try to notify the highway patrol? Which highway patrol? Which way did they go? The Dusters had at least a two-hour jump on them no matter which way they went, the Monroe men believed.

"They could be all the way to West Hell by nah! I sure in hell could use Marko nah!" exclaimed the sheriff in utter frustration and tried to come up with a plan of action.

He and DeBell would drive around looking for anything out of order— something going on, or not going on as usual. The sheriff decided he and his deputy would do this because they knew the town better than the men from Monroe County. They would visit the scene of the crime again for the umphteenth time. They would go back to Marko's, back to the Duster's—the sheriff had already told Amy Delores not to touch a thing in the house, and he had closed all of the windows and locked the doors. They would go back and read the coroner's reports again up at West Steward Community Hospital right outside of West Steward, even though by now they knew them by heart: Cause of death of victim one: a blow to the front of the head with a heavy blunt instrument. Victim one (female) was killed while apparently asleep in bed. Cause of death of victim number two (male): multiple wounds (35) plus a final blow to the head from the back with a heavy blunt object. Right hand severed at wrist.

Dr. Vincent Roadhill leaned back in his old creaky leather chair puffing on his treasured corn cob pipe that he had purchased "up out in the hills here in Arkansas."

"Way I figure it fellers, the woman was killed first to sort of get her out of the way. I'm certain she never saw the killer. Leon was obviously the real target. Who ever let him have it was mighty, mighty mad at 'em like I told ya—and pretty strong too. That knife was plunged in an out. In and out. Thirty-five times, so deep in some places that any two or three wounds woulda killed 'em in a short while. Yes sir! Mighty mad. Nah, like I said before. No fingerprints means the killer was wearing gloves of some kind, right? No hair or skin under the fingernails of Leon Baycott means, to me, the killer got the jump on Leon before he had time to gather his forces. He apparently got to the window where you found him, trying to climb out. Then bam! he hits 'em on the back of the head with the same instrument he used to kill the woman. Looks like to me one of the killer's weapons was a hatchet or blunt backed ax. But you never found weapons? No? Well there must have been plenty of blood. Just plenty of blood. The killer musta been slipping and sliding in it—cause he hit the jugular as well as the aorta. Vicious. Vicious!" Dr. Roadhill pronounced. "Worst I ever seen. Musta been a mad man. Nah, don't go gagging on me boys! You the ones that wanted to go over it all again. Y'all wanna see the pictures again too?"

The first thing the Monroe men had done when they arrived was to check Leon's books for evidence of a dissatisfied customer, or one that was heavily in debt to the feed store or to Leon personally. They had talked with his first wife, his children and any other women he was reputed to have kept company with—looking for jealous husbands or boyfriends. And the Monroe men along with the sheriff had asked anybody who had any information to come forward. Nobody did. After the Baycott son's had posted the very substantial reward of two hundred dollars two days after Baycott's funeral, the sheriff got one small lead from an informant: a woman by the name of Alvareeda Mallin was reported to have been the last serious affair of Leon's before Luxury Tweedle. According to the informant, Leon had grown tired of Alvareeda and was trying to get rid of her. So guess what he did? He offered the husband enough money—he believed it was twenty-five dollars—to take himself and his tall, blond, raw-boned wife out of his sight—back to West Virginia, and they hadn't been heard from since. "That was a good three years ago," the informant, a Mr. Hugo Gruely, said. He also stated that he had no other information, and looked at the sheriff expectantly.

Asked by the Monroe men who he thought might have committed the crime and what he reasoned the motive might be, the informant answered thoughtfully. "Well, seeing has hi—according to da papers—Mistah Leon done had forty-three dollars in his pockets and a gold pocket watch laying on da table, and also thirty dollars that weren't taken, plus da lady in question had herself a wrist watch, too, so I heard—den it weren't no robbery motive. Dat o'cose, would rule out a roving man wit' no job, ya see. And niggers also who, o'cose would steal the pennies off a dead man's eyes. I thinks hit wuz a crime of anger. Someone was mad wit' either one or both."

The informant's ideas mirrored the lawmen's thinking almost exactly. Rule out robbery. Rule out niggers. What was the motive? Anger? Yes, it must be. And where were the weapons? The bloody clothes? The sheriff had the deputy give the informant three dollars for his useless information and the man trudged off, his feet heavy with disappointment of not having received more.

Ralph Duster was really their only trump, and now he was gone. Henry Birkens, who had been hired by the mayor, felt he surely needed something at this point to show the mayor that they were doing their damndest to find the killer.

With an acid filled stomach, the sheriff ordered notices to be posted in every law office in every county directly surrounding Phillips County. Lee to the North, Desha County South, and Arkansas and Monroe County to the West. To the East of Phillips County was the wide and muddy Mississippi River.

Notices were sent all over the state of Louisiana as well. They had no pictures of Ralph Duster, so the flyers stated that one Ralph Duster was wanted for questioning in the murder of Leon Baycott and Lorraine Tweedle between October 3 or 4, 1930 in West Steward, Arkansas. Male Negro, age 19 or 20, slightly over six feet tall, medium brown complexion, weighing between 160 and 170 pounds. Any information could be forwarded to Sheriff Henry T. Birkens at the listed phone number or address in West Steward, Arkansas.

Now there was nothing else to do but wait to possibly hear from one of these notices and to visit the husband, Brentwood Tweedle with his perfect alibi up at Marianna Memorial hospital in room 239.

ELEVEN
※

After a totally exhausting week of trying to keep his ears to the ground in West Steward, the sheriff came up empty handed. On Friday, three weeks after the murders, the only difference that Birkens could see in the town was that the car line was much quieter than usual with a good fifty percent fewer of the regulars—but then that was to be expected. By now everyone in Colored Town knew that the Law had been looking for Ralph Duster in connection with the killings, and people were making themselves scarce as always when there was trouble brewing.

However, there was a small crowd for tamales near Claude Border's little shack of a tavern when Henry Birkens pulled up in his police car. The boy Pete Frauzinou had his stand there. When the sheriff bought tamales for Mae Bell as he was about to do tonight, he liked to purchase them from Peter rather than at any of the other stands. It amused him to buy from a nigger that was almost as white as he was. This boy was ambitious, he thought, because he knew Peter had aspirations of being a top chef one day.

The sheriff parked right in front of the tamale cart, got out and walked uncomfortably up to the little hot cart, his feet tired and on fire. "Evening Pete."

"Sheriff," the salesman greeted levelly. The other customers moved back quickly so the sheriff could be next in line. Most walked away altogether.

"Havin' a big evenin'?" the sheriff asked in a friendly tone.

Peter's pale grey eyes lit on the sheriff's face for a fraction of a second. He saw the muscles tighten in the pretty man's jaw on the side where the severe beating he had taken two years ago was evidenced by a long scar from his sideburns to the end of his cheek.

"Slower than usual," Peter replied, keeping his tone even.

"Oh? Why is dat?" Henry Birkens asked, wondering what kind of answer he would receive.

He got no answer. Just a sudden full toothed roguish grin as Peter asked smoothly, "And how many tamales for you lady friend tonight sheriff?"

"A dozen!" the sheriff snapped, caught off balance by the impudence of the question.

Peter deftly removed the hot little bundles from his pot, wrapped them quickly in newspaper and handed them to the lawman.

The sheriff slapped payment in the tamale man's hand more forcefully than he had to and walked away smarting. The grey-eyed bastard knew these tamales were for Mae Bell. These Gawd damn niggers knew everything! Peter probably also knew that he could not eat spicy foods anymore. Having some trouble with his stomach now, anything with peppers and onions seemed to "upset the apple cart," the sheriff often remarked. Fried foods upset him also, but not as much, and Henry Birkens had decided that he'd rather die than give up Nettie's fried chicken.

The scent of the tamales on the car seat next to the sheriff were almost overwhelmingly seductive. But forbidden. Like Mae Bell.

Later as he lay in Mae Bell's arms, he was too miserable to take any pleasure from her or little Birkey who had never failed to cheer his "da da" before. There was the memory of Pete Frauzinou snickering as he walked away with Mae Bell's tamales—and the constant painful fact that they were getting nowhere in solving the Love Nest Murders. One day soon the mayor would call him in sure as shit. It made a body feel low down and blue.

Mae Bell was uncharacteristically sweet tonight. She had removed all of her clothes and slid her warm, young body in the bed next to Henry's, smelling like a garden full of flowers.

"Thanks for the hot tamales. Dey wuz better den ever!" Mae Bell said in her high, honey pitched voice.

Henry grunted, wondering what the girl was up to, for she rarely thanked him for anything. There would be no loving tonight, for he was tired, and certainly felt older than his fifty-six years. He knew a lack of intimacy tonight—or any night— bothered Mae Bell not at all. She barely tolerated him anyway. Mae Bell was first and foremost interested in his money—they both knew that.

Now the young woman curled up next to the sheriff, rubbing her hand through the sparse haired sandy greyness of his chest. Mae Bell knew today was payday. When Henry Birkens went to sleep, she planned to steal five dollars from him— over and above the money he gave her every week. The five hundred dollar "bribe" for coming home was already squirreled away in a fruit jar in a secret place.

As she had confided to Aggie Pratt two years ago, she had very special plans for the money she had managed to hold on to over the years.

Mae Bell continued to run her smooth hands down the sheriff's chest in a soothing manner. "Henry, I heered dose Duster peepers done moved out and gone. Is hit true?"

"Yas, it's true, the sheriff answered irritably. "If you jus' heard of hit nah, you musta been deaf fer awhile."

"Why dey leave, Henry? Where you think dey be off to?"

Henry Birkens, sick with frustration and a creeping fear that he had been bamboozled, spat out, "I don't know and I don't give a gawd damn!" He turned his back to his woman and shut his eyes so tightly that tears ran down his cheeks.

Mae Bell turned her back to the old sheriff also and tried to smother joyous laughter behind her hands. They had gotten away! *In a little while all dis time of waitin' and savin' and, yas, prayin', I will get away too! Hot damn! Heah I come, Chicago!*

Mae Bell had other reasons to be joyful this night as she lay besides the old sheriff, who was already snoring loudly, "calling hogs" he had labeled it. Mae Bell lay on her back, her legs spread apart, a light quilt pulled up comfortably under her chin. This was her thinking position. She liked to lay in this manner and stare up at the ceiling, thinking about her Big Plan. *Oh! Won't dey be surprised,* she thought, wiggling her toes. Mae Bell knew herself to be a smarter little "black bird" than people thought.

She could just see them all now. All the high-class Colored people, like Miss Keller, the bright-skinned school principal, and Mrs. Wellsir Barr, the theater owner's wife and that prissy Lorine Aclavin with her lace dresses, who likes to listen to all that funny classic music by white folks. Them and all the rest of the high class folks in town. Wouldn't they just sit up and take some notice when she came back to West Steward, *if* she came back. But of course Mae Bell knew she would, if only to show off.

Yas!

One day, she would come back to West Steward, knowing how to dress pretty and how to eat proper and talk proper. And Mae Bell would have herself some money! Enough to choke a horse, she dreamed. A pocket book just stuffed with it! And Mae Bell Lewis herself would be famous and have her pictures in all the Colored papers from New York to Mississippi. "Yas, yas, yas! It was gonna happen. I knows hit in mah soul!" Mae Bell whispered with certainty to her confidant, the ceiling, where she saw her dreams spread out like a picture show.

The next reason for her joy tonight was that people in Colored Town who used to go out of their way to avoid her, folks who called her a slut behind her back, people who called her that little whore with the half-white baby by that old cracker sheriff were now speaking to her—well, some of them, anyway. And nobody in the community walked her off the sidewalk anymore. It was a miracle. And Mae Bell knew that miracle started with Aggie Pratt, and with her friend Billy Binder, who had been lynched two years ago.

Jus' lak Billy, Mae Bell thought. *So sweet and gentle and kind-hearted.* For it was Billy, she had later learned that had told Aggie about her. "She nice," he had said of her. "She ain't lak what peepers say she is. And she lonely. Do you think you could go and be her fren, Aggie?"

After seeing Billy's body dragged through the street that Sunday afternoon in May of 1928, Mae Bell had felt an urgent, no, desperate need to talk to someone. A female. Someone her own age. But she had no friends in Colored Town due to her relationship with the sheriff.

Mae Bell had turned around and around in her small parlor that day. She felt like a horse in a burning locked barn. Unbearably hot, Mae Bell had fallen on her knees and moaned. She felt her heart would break under her load of grief and misery. Never had she witnessed anything so cruel, so heartless! And there they had been sitting in the car—four fat white men, puffed up, swollen in their evil. They had driven slowly through Colored Town smoking large cigars and smiling as they dragged the body through by a rope attached to Billy's legs on the back of a car.

Oh, Oh, Oh! I have to git outta heah or I'm gone lose my mind! The baby, then one year old, was at Nettie's house. So the devastated woman started to walk. She had no idea where she was going. Her walk turned into a trot, her trot into a run. Somebody reported seeing Mae Bell Lewis flying through the town "lak she was wild."

Mae Bell ended up near the foot of a hill. Later when she thought about it, she realized she must have been headed for Lela Bailey's house. Anyone could always talk to Mother Bailey she had heard.

Usually Sunday was a work day, a day to fold her waists in tissue for delivery Monday, but there sat Aggie Pratt in her house out in a field just before you got to the hill that led to Mother Bailey's house. Aggie sat idly at a table in her little kitchen with a cup of something in front of her. Mae Bell looked in the window. Aggie looked so down-hearted, Mae Bell thought, she didn't even see her peering into her house.

Hesitantly the young woman tapped gently on the window.

Now Aggie was instantly alert. Bidding the boys—who were suffering from a mixture of frustration and confusion because she wouldn't let them out of the house on a perfectly glorious day—to hide under the bed, Aggie went around to the door and flung it fully open, her .38 special pistol cocked in her hand. That's how they met Mae Bell would later tell—at the point of a gun.

"It's jus' me, Mae Bell! Don't shoot that thing, please, mam!"

"Oh!" Aggie had exclaimed. "You Mae Bell Lewis, ain't you?"

"Miz Aggie, I begs yo' most humble partners fer barging in on ya dis-a-way, but I gotta talk to somebody 'bout what dey done did to Billy Binder and yo' house was the furst I done runt into when I got so tarred I couldn't run no mo'."

"No 'pology is necessary. Sat down, rest yo'self. You want some tea? hit's good."

"I sho' do thank you. It's nice of you to talk to me."

"It ain't no trouble at all. Jus' rest easy, Mae Bell. You real welcome heah."

Mae Bell was somewhat surprised at this warm reception—and grateful. Maybe there was some Christians in this town after all. Maybe everybody didn't hate the sight of her.

"It's 'bout to kill me what dey done done to Billy," Mae Bell burst out. "Lawd, Lawd, Lawd. He was such a nice young main—I knowed him—slightly," Mae Bell added, so there would be no mistaking their relationship. "He were kind to me. He spoke to me. Sometimes he see me with a heavy load of groceries he hep me. Sometimes he see me setting on the porch wit' my baby—I has my own house, I doesn't stay wit'—him," she said, not needing to explain who "he" was. "I has my own house!" Mae Bell repeated; her mouth twisted with the disdain of thinking what living with the sheriff full time would be like.

"When Billy see me with little Birkey, he sometimes come up and play wit' him a while. He were dat nice." Mae Bell searched Aggie's face for hints of scorn, because she had mentioned her baby, and the sheriff. There was none.

Seeing nothing but openness, and perhaps understanding, the young woman waxed bolder. Leaning across the plain little table she said, "Kin I tell you a little bit about mahself? I ain't lak peepers thinks I is. I ain't no white man's hoe."

"Have you done et?" Aggie asked simply, still showing no censure.

"I ain't been hoingry today."

"I know what you means," Aggie said, taking a seat across the table. "Me neither. Please do tell me about yo'self. I ain't gone do nothin' today. Peepers got waists and shirts dey gone have to wait 'til maybe Tuesday or Wednesday—and nobody better not say shit to me 'bout why dey didn't git no delivery Monday either. Dey gone lynch somebody and drag him through town lak a Gawd damn dog, den dey wants dey shirts and stuff delivered jus' the same? Well, to hell wit' hit!"

Mae Bell made a face at Aggie's language.

"Well, 'cuse my French, but that's jus' hi I feels today." Suddenly Aggie put her head down on the table and broke into tears, sobbing as if her heart would break. Mae Bell got up and put her arms around her shoulders. "It's gone be alright," she said over and over.

The boys burst into the room, eyes bucked. "Wha da matter, Muddear?" they asked simultaneously.

"You boys gwon out to play," Aggie sniffed. "But play real close to da house wha I kin see ya."

Having recovered somewhat, Aggie bade Mae Bell to talk about herself. "I needs to hear somethin' 'bout somethin' to take my mind offa Billy."

But after finally having an audience—someone who might possibly understand, Mae Bell found herself mute. Finally she burst out: "Dey had no call to do dat ta him! No call at all!" Then the tears came hot and plentiful and unstoppable.

"Gwon. Let it out. Hit's gotta come out." Now it was Aggie's turn to comfort. She sat Mother Bailey's remedy for all things in front of Mae Bell: a cup of steaming hot sassafras tea.

Mae Bell let it all out in a rush: "Friday night late, and all day Sattidy, dere had been talk all over town dat somethin' bad musta done happen to Billy cause he still ain't showed up. Billy's mama was in sich a bad state of mind! I felt so sorry fer her. I decided to do what I could, doe nobody ax me to. Everybody jus' look at me real mean lak I was da Law instood o'Henry, and dey know da Law ain't never been no hep wit' no missing Colored boy."

"Hell, dey don't care ifn all us disappear!" Aggie said.

"I know you right 'bout dat! Well, any hi, I went up to Henry's house. His neighbors think I works in da house. Nah, Henry done gie me a key long time ago. So, I goes on in the house and start bumping 'round pretending to be cleaning 'cause there is a real nosey old neighbor woman who live down da road. Sometime she come ova, pretending lak she got some kind ah complaint for Henry to listen to, den she look all around."

"You went up dere thinkin' mebbe da sheriff could tell you somethin'?"

"Dat's right. Henry pride hisself on knowing everything what goes on you know. I got dere about around six o'clock Sattidy evenin' but he weren't home. And he weren't at the jail. Nettie had already tole me dat."

Aggie was sitting forward now, listening with her whole body, her mouth slightly open.

"Well, by now, I knowed somethin' bad had happened to Billy. Ah jus' felt hit. I waited and waited for Henry. At eleven o'clock he finally came strolling in. Said he been away overnight on business up in Lee County. By nah everything was just jumping inside o'me. I knowed somethin' had done happened, some dirt had been done."

"And you think da sheriff knowed about hit?"

"Sho'! O' cose knowed 'bout hit, but couldn't stop it so he leave town Friday to gie hisself an excuse."

"Lawd, Lawd, Lawd!"

"He smile. I smile. He say hi glad he is to see me—surprised too. But I see he look funny 'bout da eyes. Lak he tryin' to hide somethin' in his head where o'cose nobody can see."

"Den?" Aggie was on the very edge of her chair.

"He say, 'Glad to see ya. Stay da night.' I say no, but I say I'll stay for a while. He say, 'I'm so-o-o-o tired, Mae Bell. I just want to lay down fer a while.' I say, 'go 'head. I be jus' sittin' heah a while.' I say, 'by da way, you know Billy Binder is missing? You done heered wha he may be?' His eyes buck lak dey do when he gittin' ready to lie. He say, 'no, I doesn't know wha he at. Why you axing me?' I say, 'because you know everythin'.' He say, 'ahm going to bed. Where Birkey at?' I say, 'he with someone,' which is true. He lay on down. By quarter to twelve, he sleep. Calling hogs. I waited until twelve thirty—'til he good and sleep. Dat's when I let him have it! Splash! A whole slop jar fulla piss, right in his face. I mean it wuz all ovah da flo', all ovah da tick on da bed! Da feather pillows wuz soaked!"

"Naw you didn't!"

"Wanna bet? Oh, I wuz mad, I wuz hurt, I wuz crazy all wrapped up in one! He had done promised me he weren't gone let nothin' happen no mo'. I tole him, 'Kill me! Kill me! Dat's what you do to niggers ain't it? Go tell yo' frens—go on!' I says, 'tell 'em to come git me and lynch me lak I know dey done done to Billy!"

At this point Mae Bell was on her feet re-enacting what had happened, eyes flashing, her hands grabbing the air. " 'Go tell yo' buddies dat a nigger woman done soaked your peckerwood hind part in pure I.D. piss. Den let 'em come and git me!' I says, 'Go on! Do it!' I musta looked outta my mind, I know dats hi I felt. All at once he was shaking me and shaking me. Den he slapped my face—not hard—jus' tryin' to bring me back to mahself. He screamed, 'I don't know nothin' 'bout no lynching! Wha Birkey? Wha Birkey? Wha my boy?'

"'I done kilt 'em!' I said. 'I done kilt him lak I tole you I would! What's the difference nah or later? He be a Negro, you know! Maybe you'll send some o'yo' frens to lynch him for somethin' he didn't do when he be sixteen, sebenteen years old.' He say, 'Naw, naw, naw! Tell me you didn't kill my boy! I say, 'I done took me a knife and cut 'em to pieces!' "

"And he believed you?"

"Sho', I be doin' some good acting jus' lak in the picture show. I be hollerin' and yellin'. It's a wonder da neighbors didn't come on ovah to see what's goin' on."

"When he find out you didn't kill Birkey?"

"Oh, he slick sometimes, Henry is. He went straight on over to Nettie's place and all, and there he found little Birkey safe and sleep. He cried."

"Well, my goodness! I guess he woulda."

Mae Bell had been jumping and shouting through her tears, and now she collapsed in a chair at the table.

"Lawd, we done turned out pitiful today, ain't we?" exclaimed Aggie through more tears of her own.

"This heah is a pitiful day, Miz Aggie," Mae Bell said still crying a little.

"Jus' call me Aggie, not no Miz Aggie."

"Yas mam," Mae Bell answered, wiping her face and eyes.

"Yas *mam*? Hi old do you think I is anyhow?" Aggie said with peevish humor. She was getting back to herself. She was trying hard to get back to normal. She knew she couldn't let this thing knock her out completely. This was not the first lynching in West Steward and it probably wouldn't be the last. She had to hold

Mae Bell up, Aggie thought. And there were her boys. She had to hold herself up for their sakes, too.

"You younger den me, I reckon," Mae Bell said.

"Well, thank you very much!" Aggie said, trying to smile.

They peered at each other through fresh wiped tears as they tried to be strong for each other, tried to think—and talk about something other than Billy Binder, trying to keep their hearts and minds intact.

"Nah. Tell me somethin' 'bout yo'self, Mae Bell, lak you said you wanted to."

"Alright."

Mae Bell composed herself, had a few sips of the reddish tea and began: "When I was four years old my mama gie me away."

"Nah!"

"Dere was some trouble between her and another woman. Dere was some trouble 'bout who mah real daddy was. Lak maybe dis woman's husband was mah daddy. After dat my mama left me wit' frens o'hern. I turned out to be a nasty, bad little girl dat nobody wanted. So I was passed from hain to hain so to speak. My mama was too young to have a baby anyway. She was but eleven when I was born."

"Eleven?" asked Aggie incredulously.

"Yassuh. Eleven. When she was fifteen she took off and I ain't seent 'er since. Wouldn't recognize 'er if I seed 'er on the streets. So I ain't had me nobody to teach me nothin'. No cookin'. No sewin'. No cleanin'. No ironin'. No nothin'. When I was eleven, one of the ladies dat I ended up wit' for a while—she was a kind Christian lady—taught me hi to make a lemon meringue pie. Da best you ever tasted. Dats all I know hi to fix. My cousin Nettie Lyons, you know her, she done tried and tried to teach me hi to cook but I weren't no good at it. More over I didn't lak to cook, or clean, or iron. When I was twelve I run away from the lady who taught me hi to make da pie because her husband was trying to crawl into da bed wit' me. So here I is. Twenty-three years old and worthless."

"Not worthless."

"Worthless! Least as far as makin' a livin' is concerned. Hi have I been living all my life? Boyfriends. One after another. Dey gie me enough to get by. I usta keep peepers kids—a real whole lot of 'em while other women went to chop cotton. Dey gie me fifteen cents a day for each one. I scaped by. I ain't never been nobody's hired hoe though. I wants dat understood."

Always one to hear an interesting story, Aggie sat with rapt attention.

"One time when I was between men frens and feeling pretty blue and low down, I went to Church. It was F.W.T. Edison's Church," Mae Bell said, rolling her eyes toward the ceiling. "I went back a coupla mo' times setting way in the back, but some hi he seent me, knew who I wuz, and you know what dat old nigger did? One Sunday night I come home and fount dis envelope under mah doe with some money in it. It was from old F.W.T. Seems lak he wanted me to be his woman."

"You joneing me!" Aggie cried.

"Nah suh! So he meet me and we talked. I says to him, 'What you gone do wit' yo' wife, Reverend?' He say, 'Don't nobody have to know 'bout dis.' "

"Why dat old bugger!"

"Girl, can you believe it! Wit' dat stinky breath o'hisn and all the sen-sens he tries to cover it wit'. He lucky his wife stays wit' 'em!"

"Well anyway," Mae Bell continued, "you wanta know what was in dat envelope? Guess hi much? Guess!"

"I don't know. Musta laked you pretty well, so I'm gone say...hum, hum, hum," Aggie squinted, trying to put a price on offered affection. "Ahm gone say twenty dollars. Is ahm close? I say twenty dollars."

Mae Bell laughed so hard that her knee went up and bounced against the table, upsetting the dishes, and while trying to catch a tea cup and saucer before they hit the floor she bumped her head hard against the wall as the cup and saucer clattered to the floor in a hundred pieces.

"Oh! Miz Aggie please! Ahm so sorry!"

"Girl, forget dat cup and saucer and tell me what wuz in dat envelope from this well-to-do minister," Aggie begged. The young woman was on her knees trying to retrieve the pieces.

Mae Bell looked up at her new found friend, and her expression was so humorous that Aggie started to laugh before she knew the answer.

"Two dollars."

"Two dollars?"

"That's right."

"Girl, you lying!"

"No I ain't. I told dat old stinky nigger to kiss my behind!"

"Oh, me!" Aggie howled, laughing and collapsing into the chair where she had so recently been crying.

"Stop laughing now. I'm not finished," Mae Bell pleaded.

"OK, OK!" Aggie said trying to stop giggling.

"So how did you—get together wit'...wit'..."

"Hard to say ain't it? You mean wit' Sheriff Birkens?"

Aggie nodded.

"I was in bad shape. I hadn't been able to get my life on da track after a love affair went real bad. I had some thinkin' to do. I was broke in mo' ways den one. I even thought of trying to learn to cook. I was trying to stop leanin' on mens. I actually went and picked some cotton. I musta picked about five pounds all day and I was so hot and tired and funky at the end of the day. Yet dere was peepers out dere—wimmens—who could pick a hundred pounds a day or mo'! Do you know hi little cotton weighs? I quit after the first day. It got to the place where I had nothin' comin' in. The mens I knowed didn't have no money no mo' neither. I couldn't wash or iron well enough to even git a job in some white woman's house, which I wasn't gone do, even if I knowed hi. Well, I had nowhere to turn, except my play cousin Nettie who worked fer da sheriff. She let me help clean up his house a few times—jus' bein' nice, 'cause I didn't do a very good job. Finally Nettie, who ain't my real cousin I don't think, jus' tole me frank like, 'Mae Bell, I'd rather *gie* you a dollar a week den to have you comin' up heah messing up and gittin' in da way!" Mae Bell's shoulders shook with laughter, remembering.

Coming up off her knees, Mae Bell asked, "What you want me to do wit' all dese little pieces I done picked up?"

"Throw 'em out."

They went into a fit of laughing again, as Mae Bell got up and took a seat.

"So," continued Mae Bell, "Old Birkens done seent me a few times and decided that he lakded me. To dis day I done know why. I ain't never been wit' no white man befoe. I know some peepers don't believe dat, but its da gospel truf. Well, anyway I come home, things so bad, mah close, everythin' done been set out in da streets 'cose I ain't paid a lick o'rent in five months. I set on my old grip and just cried. I had no place to go but back to Nettie. She mentioned mah troubles to da sheriff, not suspecting what hit would lead to. One day after I had been wit' her about three days, Nettie comes in wit' a big smile on her face. 'Go home,' she sez to me. 'Home?' I sez. 'What home?' Well, to make a long story short, when I went back where I usta live, da doe was open wit' a sign on it. It say welcome home, Mae Bell. Da furniture was back in da place. I had been storing thangs in Nettie's back room, and on da table was dis heah envelope addressed to me. 'Private', it said."

"Another envelope?"

"Dats right, and guess what was in it?"

"Oh, don't make me guess again!" Aggie said smiling.

"Thirty dollars."

"Thirty dollars? Dats a heap o'change!"

"Right. Well, I been wit' da sheriff every since, even doe I doesn't even lak white folks. Ain't dat funny? He pay my rent in my own house. When he call me, I come see him. It ain't no problem much. All he do is grunt loud. He know well as I do he finished in dat section. Dat's why we both so surprised about Birkey. When I was younger, the doctor tole me I wasn't never gone be no mother. Too many bad infections done messed up da works. So I didn't bother to use anythin'. Well heah come little Birkey—jus' 'bout knocked us off our feets. O'cose the sheriff had his doubts—until he seent dat pretty lil' ol' white thang. 'Dats mah boy,' he told the midwife, 'and ahm gone do right by 'em, by Gawd!' "

"And he has. Little Birkey is spoiled pitiful! Well, I felt different about Henry after Birkey. I ain't never gone love 'em, but after all, I got a boy by 'em. *Mah* boy! And I believe I done been able to do some good in ourva community fer ourva peepers. The sheriff listens to me. He better. He loves Birkey. I tell 'em I'll kill mahself and Birkey if he let anything serious happen to somebody in Colored Town. If he heard 'bout somethin' gone happen he best try to stop it—dat is if he wants me and his son. I tole him I mean dat."

"And he believes you?"

"Sho."

"But would you...?"

"Chile, no! I ain't killing mah son or me fer nobody! You heah me? If I was gonna kill us, I woulda done it today fer sho.'"

"So what you gone do nah? You gone stay on wit' da sheriff or...what?"

Mae Bell smiled a broad and beautiful sly smile, showing remarkably large even white teeth. At that moment Aggie thought Mae Bell pretty, in her own way, for a woman so dark complexioned that is.

"I can't stay wit' Henry da rest o'my life. He done settled a policy on me and Birkey—for when he dies. When Henry dies I might be ninety. His mammy jus' died last year. She was ninety-one. Henry was jus' a way for me to git somewhere, a stepping stone, dey calls it. I feel lak Birkey is my own baby alone. He gone carry on awhile 'bout us leaving but I don't even care. I'm gone leave heah when I gits enough money. I'm gone marry me a Colored man someday.

"What will you do until you find a husmon?"

Mae Bell stared at Aggie as if she was simple minded.

"I got me a plan," she said. "Can I trust you? No. I mean can I really trust you? We ain't been frens for no moren an hour. I don't want you to tell nobody nothin' 'bout what I done tole you, please!"

Aggie was obviously crestfallen—for she had already envisioned herself relating this juicy story to her friends, but she wasn't a fool and she was loyal to the marrow. So she promised not to relate Mae Bell's story to anyone—and she meant it.

Mae Bell studied Aggie's face a moment, then decided to trust her with the rest of the story although trust didn't come easily to her.

"I been wit' da sheriff for going on four years. Each week he gimme three dollars—moren I could make in any cotton patch—dats twelve a month. Nah, each and every month I steals an extry ten dollars from him. Den I begs him fer mo' money for Birkey. Count dat up. A sure thirty dollars a month for four years. Plus he pay mah rent, buy mah food. I save all I gits."

Aggie let out a whistle. "Dats a whole lots. I don't count too well, but I know dat musta be a lotta money."

"It was suppose to be around about a fourteen hunnert dollars. But over da years dis and dat come up so I had to pinch off it sometimes. Ahm gonna gie Mistah and Miz Binder a hunnert dollars fer Billy."

"Dat's mighty nice o'you."

"He were mighty nice," Mae Bell stated quietly. They were silent for a moment, each lost in their own thoughts of what life held for the future after this tragedy. The boys were outside playing relatively quietly. Birds screamed from distant trees, and Aggie knew, without looking, that her boys were chunking dirt and small stones at them.

Getting comfortable again in her chair, Mae Bell thanked Aggie for slipping another cup and saucer in front of her, pouring tea and laying two hard, but tasty, week old tea cakes beside the saucer.

"Nah!" she began again, slapping the table with her palms. "When I gits built back up to eighteen hunnert, maybe befoe dat, ahm gone on away from heah! If ahm careful I kin live nice, me and Birkey, for quite a spell on dat—until I kin get on mah feets doing mah real work," she allowed mysteriously, looking at Aggie with amused expectation of confusion on Aggie's part.

Mae Bell was not disappointed. Aggie's expression was one of total bewilderment. "What work is dat, girl? You done had me playing more guessing games today!" By now Aggie began to realize that this pretty dark girl was far more complex than anybody had ever imagined. Aggie stared at Mae Bell with dawning admiration. Right now she would not have been surprised if she pulled a fully cooked pig from under her dress.

Getting up, the young woman held Aggie's attention with a fixed smile of sweet coyness, as she proceeded to pull an old cloth table cover from a chair in the corner. Mae Bell shook it out and draped it around her shoulders like an elegant expensive shawl, and she—sang. Two spirituals: *Before I'll be a slave! I'll be buried in my grave—and go home to my Lord and be free! And Wade in the Water Children.* Next she did a rollicking blues number—*Good Morning Little School Girl.* Finally, she did what she called a white folk's song that she had learned from the radio called *I've Got a Crush on You.*

And her voice was glorious. Firm and sweet and husky, almost reaching the tenor ranges in the blues number, and then high and crystal faceted in the radio song. In the spirituals she out-did herself, for they were at once tear-filled and heart-rendering, as well as filled with joy and hope. Aggie was shocked and spellbound.

"Girl, where you learn to sing lak dat at?" Aggie asked, awed.

"When I use to get blue, I'd go out in the woods and sing to the top of my lungs. Dats hi I fount out I could sing. I was going to sing in the church a little. Dat's why I went, but old Edison...Well, I told ya about dat."

"His church don't know what dey done missed."

"Do you think I can make a living singing, Miz Aggie? Tell me da truf."

"Oh yas!" Aggie said enthusiastically. "Where you plan to sing? Is you going to Harlem, maybe?"

"I can't tell ya dat, yet."

"Well, I know you'll make it wit' dat voice. I ain't never heard nothin' lak hit! Hit's most nice."

"Does you really think so?" Mae Bell asked again, milking the compliment.

"I'm so glad you came today. I done really enjoyed yo' company."

"I'm da gladdest. Thank you, Aggie fer lettin' me talk to ya. You don't know what it means not to be looked down on."

"Oh, I think I does," Aggie said making a wry face. "Dere's a whole lotta ladies 'round heah dat ain't too crazy 'bout me neither!"

"Really? I can't hardly believe dats true," Mae Bell said, genuinely surprised.

"You ain't heered? Well, thank you, but I'm 'fraid hit's da fer sure truf!"

An almost palpable breeze of affection and admiration swirled around the two young women. They both swayed in it, let it envelope them without embarrassment or regret—both equally emotionally present at the birth of a new friendship.

"Kin I come see you again sometime—I mean when ain't nobody 'round?"

Aggie bristled with indignation at Mae Bell's humility. Aggie, the defender of any pitiful underdog, answered in her surprisingly heavy voice, "Honey, you come visit me anytime. Whenever you please! My friends don't have to be no secret from nobody. Dis heah is mah life and ahm gone live it lak I see fit! You don't have to hide to come see me. I don't even care what nobody in dis little ol' town thinks. You kin rest yo' mind on dat! Nother subject. Mae Bell, do anyone know you kin sang good as you do?"

The woman was pleased with secrets kept. "Naw," she smiled while trying to keep from smiling. "Jus' Nettie. Nah you. Not nobody else. Not Henry. Especially not Henry!" she laughed.

Mae Bell doused a hard tea cake in her steaming tea.

"Is dey dat hard?" Aggie asked.

Now Mae Bell raised the softened side of the cake up and began to nibble on it. While looking straight at Aggie, Mae Bell took careful small bites as if she was afraid of breaking her strong, white teeth. Aggie started to titter and they both ended up falling out laughing again.

"Oh, my!" said Mae Bell, "I never thought I'd laugh again and nah heah we is bursting ourva sides."

"Shhhhh!" Aggie cautioned, listening.

"What's dat?"

Aggie listened a while and after a few seconds, her body slumped in relief. "Hit's jus' dem nappy headed boys! Dey make mo' racket den a whole truck load o'heathens!"

"Dey cute," Mae Bell complimented.

"Aha. You wouldn't think so you had to be 'round 'em twenty-four hours a day."

Mae Bell doused more cakes as Aggie spoke of the boys with disparaging affection. Finally they got around to a subject both had been avoiding: possible funeral arrangements for Billy Binder. Billy's desolate mother could not yet accept his death and was acting peculiar, they said. They spoke of "BeBe's" sweetness and childlike naiveté, and his fondness for playing harmless pranks.

The black community later had reason to believe that the actual lynching had taken place sometime between Friday night and Saturday morning, but the evil men had, for reasons of their own, delayed dragging Billy's body through the Colored section until the Sabbath.

"How could they do this on the Sabbath? On Sunday morning? The Lawd Gawd Almighty would not forget to punish all that were involved in this mess!" was the consensus of the Colored community. And The Almighty would have to—for they could not—and the wind of their sorrow carried the stench of their powerlessness all through the Colored community.

Since there was no body left to speak of—Billy Binder had been dragged behind the truck until his body had fallen to pieces—a memorial service was being planned for the young man instead of the traditional open casket funeral. Almost everybody in the Colored community was planning to attend, so the service was to be held at Rev. Edison's Church, because it was the largest church building in Colored Town.

Finally Mae Bell Lewis rose to leave and she and Aggie sealed their new found friendship with hugs.

"Nah, 'member Aggie," Mae Bell said. "You done promised you ain't gone say nothin' to nobody 'bout mah singing."

"Chile, don't you worry yo'self one little minute 'bout dat!" Aggie answered. "When Aggie say she ain't gone say nothin', den dats da end of dat!"

"Thank you, Aggie. I shoally 'preciates what you done done fer me today. Deep in mah heart, I 'preciates it."

Aggie placed her hands on both hips and stared at Mae Bell with real surprise. "What? What is I done done fer you today? Don't you even down be thinkin' dat away. We maybe done heped each another. You think about it dat way, OK? And you come back ta see me anytime, you heah? And ahm gone come see you sometime another. I know wha you be livin."

Before Mae Bell left, she stood in the door and shared another item about Rev. Edison just to make Aggie laugh—because she was grateful for the open way Aggie had accepted her into her home.

"You know what some of the young 'heathens' and 'infidels' Rev. Edison calls 'em, say the F.W.T. in the reverend's initials stands fer? Farts Wit' Turds."

Aggie let out a yelp of shocked laughter that nearly knocked her off her feet.

"Naw! Girl, you joneing!" Aggie exclaimed falling into a chair.

Pleased with Aggie's reaction, Mae Bell continued, giggling. "And dat ain't all. You should see the young folks laughing when Rev. Edison goes struttin' through the neighborhood on one o'his 'pastoral visits'. He is a sight wit' dat stripedy, swallow tail frock coat he likes to wear. Here he come," Mae Bell said, mocking the reverend's pompous walk. "Honey, I lak to have *died* laughing when I seed him in dat frock coat and dis wide brimmed, black wool hat all sauged down on dat big head o'hisn!"

Now Aggie, in real pain, was holding her sides as she fell across the table laughing. "Girl, git outta mah house!" she said to Mae Bell through gasps of laughter. "You gone be the death of me! I done been to his church a few times. Dat main really puts on a show! You don't hardly learn *shit* about da Bible, but when he gits to twirling around in dat pulpit he will make you faint from laughin' and he ain't even trying to be funny!"

The women parted laughing as they had met crying, each having succeeded in dispelling a small amount of the hurt and anger and pain that the other felt. They had been through a war together. It was the stuff that deep friendships were built upon.

Many of the relatively better educated people in Colored Town despised F.W.T. Edison's brand of hysterical preaching, but most had to admit that Billy's service was conducted with a fair amount of dignity, and that the minister had done a fine job of lifting and offering for the Binder family in this year of plant closings and the severe winding down of the economy. The Binders left the church with a little over two hundred dollars—enough to show how much the community cared. Enough to show that the community was standing together as well as they could, even though they were mostly dirt poor and had become even worse off since the Depression began.

"Lawd, Lawd, Lawd!" Mae Bell uttered quietly. "What we go through wit'!" Fresh tears filled her eyes and ran uninhibited down her smooth cheeks meeting under her chin. "Nah you see why I had to throw dat slop jar fulla piss on Henry!" she exclaimed, smiling a wide smile full of pleasure and pride through her tears.

She had done something after all. In her own way she had *stood up*. And she would do more. In the end she would take her very self away from Henry. Would Henry fall out and have a stroke when he heard where she was and what she was doing when she went away up North to sing? She did not care. She had taken what she wanted from Henry—Birkey. Bell Lewis. Not Birkens, for she did not even want Henry's shameful name. She had made up her mind. When Birkey was grown, he would be told his daddy was a Colored man. A light-skinned Colored man that had died when he was three. There was really no reason for Birkey to know—but people being what they were, Mae Bell knew somebody somewhere would eventually tell him who his real father was. *Well, I'll cross dat bridge when I gits to it, she thought. Right nah ah'll jus' let it be.*

TWELVE

On the Friday after Thanksgiving in 1923, Ralph Duster, age 12, went for a solitary walk in the woods. It was time to start picking up pecans for Christmas, so the boy had a medium sized crocker sack with him—the size that twenty pounds of potatoes might fit into.

It was a nice day—cool enough for a light jacket but not chilly enough for gloves. Ralph whistled a nameless tune as he trudged along through the fallen leaves, happy as only children and wise men can be. Pleasant thoughts of Christmas skittered through his mind, mingled with the equally pleasant impressions of Thanksgiving one day past.

He had eaten so much goose and dressing! And sweet potato pie and jelly cake, and ambrosia. So much chocolate marble cake and banana pudding! So much cabbage slaw and greens and cha-cha! So much rich egg nog laced heavily with moonshine whiskey.

"Mama!" he had cried. "Ahm sho nuff drunk!"

Times were good. All the Colored men had work, food was plentiful from the gardens, and from the woods as well as the stores, so everyone was in a festive, easy mood.

"Shut up, boy! You want yo' daddy to hear you? Go lay down a while and sleep off dat egg nog. You so mannish! You had no business in dat egg nog in da furst place! Dats fer grown peepers! You drink dat orange soda water. You hear me? or make yo'self a cold glass o'sweeting water. Nah go lay down!"

Eunice was feeling pretty mellow herself, for she and Thomas had been drinking strong homemade brandy and wine all day and going from house to house partaking of "Thanksgiving."

Up and down the block, neighbors were indulging in their favorite pasttime—playing cards. Coon cane, black jack and finally the hours long bid whist. The whole of Colored Town was joyful and happy. The grown people were joneing each other, laughing, drinking and eating their fill.

114

Ralph loved holidays because they were gay and fun and all rules for children were relaxed—indeed the grown folks hardly noticed them at all, so the children took advantage and ate more than they should and stayed outside longer than they were allowed, teasing and yelling and generally getting into all sorts of mischief. It was a glorious time.

Ralph's father had even let him burn a whole box of the stick sparklers that he loved so much. He thought them the most beautiful things he had ever seen. He even liked the heavy metallic odor they left in the air after they had cast their colorful dazzle of flashes and sparkles in the air like a thousand lightning bugs, and sputtered out.

The boy walked along going deeper into the woods, as happy as he could remember, looking for a large pecan tree. Suddenly he spied one and ran the few feet to it. He fell to his knees beneath it almost in a gesture of prayer. He smiled at the good big tree and began to pick up the dull brown black striped nuts that seemed to be everywhere on the ground. Six here under a clump of rotting leaves, twenty or thirty here on a pile of dried grass. He would pick up the plump undamaged ones, for they would stay oily and sweet well past New Year's—if they lasted that long.

Although he was not hungry, Ralph fairly drooled as he thought of eating the tasty pecans with foot long peppermint sticks from Mr. Greens little store in Colored Town or with the hard beautiful candy ribbons his parents bought over in Old Steward for Christmas.

Abruptly Ralph became aware of a presence but glancing around him, saw no one, but a chill went over him just the same. He continued to pick up the choicest pecans for his crocker sack. After a few minutes, Ralph again was aware of someone or something. Having enjoyed his fill of ghost stories around various fireplaces and stoves in the neighborhood, his first instinct was to run as fast as his twelve-year-old legs would carry him, but he had taken some teasing of late from his father regarding his fear of the dark and was therefore trying to act more grown up. But as he stood up and turned his eyes upward into the branches of the pecan tree, his knees shook.

Looking up, Ralph noticed a very gentle swaying, but there was little wind. What is it? Then his eyes widened in horror and all of the carefully gathered nuts scattered across the ground rolling everywhere.

"A main! A main!" he screamed. "A main hanging in dis tree!"

Ralph turned to run, tripped and fell backwards. Now the figure in the tree faced him clearly and directly seeming to sway down upon him as he lay paralyzed with fear, confronting the lolling bulging tongue and the staring half opened eyes. The man's bib overalls and light colored shirt were stiff with dried blood. He got up and stared at the horrible thing, belted by waves of nausea. He felt extremely lightheaded, and suddenly he was at home. He did not remember how he got there.

Now they were running back with him; men with shotguns, pistols, somebody with a big knife to cut the man down. His mother was the only woman that would come.

As they cut the stranger down the grown men cursed and raged. Finally they said a prayer. They inquired of the sheriff-another sheriff, Farris A. Walters, not Birkens then. Sheriff Walters knew nothing of a lynching. He seemed amused by the little party.

"Y'all got a shovel? I suggest you bury 'em. Y'all don't know who he is? Well, I doesn't neither. If he ain't rotten much, he couldn't a been dere long."

"Dirty bastard!" Thomas exclaimed as they walked back through the woods with shovels. "Been a white main dey woulda been all over dese woods thick as thieves tryin' to find out who dis po' main wuz. Naw, Eunice, don't take Ralph home yet, let 'em see hi dey do a black main in dis life!"

The identity of the lynched man was never learned—nor the reason for the cruel deed. Nobody ever claimed the corpse. If some person or persons, for a lynching always involved more than one, admitted to the foul deed, nobody in Colored Town ever heard about it from that day to this.

By the time Ralph was nineteen years of age he had witnessed or heard of countless acts of violence against Southern blacks—men, women, and sometimes children. A good friend of his father's from boyhood had been castrated in Florida. His aunt's brother-in-law had been roasted over a spit like a pig. Another knew personally of a man who had been buried in the ground up to his neck, and then had starving dogs sicced on his head. A woman was held under water and drowned in a tub by the husband and son of a white woman she had reportedly slapped after the woman had slapped her first over some small misdeed.

Every black person Ralph knew had a dreadful story—or several—to tell. There was no end to them. The stories made him physically ill. They gave him the heaves.

They made his head swim. Try as he might, Ralph could not shelve the memory of the horrible stories from his mind completely. Sometimes a particularly bad story he had heard would surface to "discombobulate" him, his mother said, in ways he couldn't explain. After such an experience, Ralph remained sad and angry for days at a time. He also felt lightheaded at these times, and often would cry uncontrollably.

When Ralph was fifteen, he had seen Dave Bailey reading a book from the principal's, Mrs. Keller's, locked library room of "adult themed" books, books on sex education that she tried to interest young couples in reading—if they could read. There were also books on health and nutrition, black history, and newspaper clippings from all over the country on various subjects, foreign cook books, "and anything else that would interest a grown person," Mrs. Keller had said. "Colored people need to read more to open up their world!" She had devoted a room to reading for "mature" people.

The book Dave Bailey found so interesting was a black book with a gold circle on the front of it. The title was Nat something. It was a popular book because he had seen men taking it out before. Ralph was determined to get his hands on the book. Maybe it had some pictures of naked women in it.

Not being scholarly or even mature, Ralph finally got the book by bribing the library assistant, a thin scholarly bright-skinned young man who was the principal's pet because his father was a dentist, and he himself had finished grammar school and was now a high school student.

There were no pictures of naked women in the book Ralph found out, but he wasn't disappointed for long, for there was enough violence, mayhem, and murder between the book's pages to hold a boy's attention for days. The book was the life story of Nat Turner, who lived from 1800 to 1831. Nat, Ralph read, was a black mystic preacher and terrorist leader of the most violent and sustained slave insurrection that America had ever known. On one bloody day, the book recounted, Nat Turner and his gang of recruited slaves killed over sixty whites, mostly women and children starting at the home of Nat's master in Virginia.

Having finished the seventh grade, Ralph could read well, although he still tended to talk flat, "because you associate with people who talk flat," Mrs. Keller had told him. You could do much better if you tried, she had said to Ralph one day before he left school for good to tinker with his true love—cars.

Becoming interested, Ralph got permission from Mrs. Keller and read more books on black history. He read about Frederick Douglass. He read Booker T. Washington's autobiography, *Up From Slavery,* and he even read about Denmark Vesey, a free black man who had attempted to lead a slave revolt eight years before Nat Turner.

Ralph admired Nat Turner more than all of the other black heroes he had read about put together. Douglass and Washington were powerful men—intellectuals, Mrs. Keller had told him, but Nat Turner—he had put the fear of darkest Africa into much of the South for a whole two months. A black man had stood up! A black man had fought back! So what if Nat was caught and hung after only two months, ending his short life. At least he was lynched for something that he had done, not for something he was innocent of, like a lot of black people he had heard of. A black man had the entire South in an uproar, and before they got him, he had taken a lot of sorry-assed white bastards with him. Nat, in Ralph's opinion, had proved himself a man. He took action, Nat did. He didn't just sit around talking all day about what ought to be done. Nat got up off his mystic hind-part and whipped some ass. That was how to handle it!

Ralph Duster, minus his disguise, now sat in the Colored Section on the sparsely populated train headed first for Chicago, then Detroit. He was finally on his way to a new life far away from West Steward, Arkansas. Waiting for a connecting train in Memphis, Tennessee, he had experienced the momentary fear that all of a sudden a whole army of lawmen would burst on the scene looking for him, looking for his family; but nothing happened. So far the trip had been uneventful. Probably most people were more concerned about where their next meal was coming from then about a bunch of Colored folks trying to get out of Arkansas, Ralph figured. In the station, people milled about quietly, forlornly going about their business.

As Ralph passed fields and farms the wheels of the train beat out a rhythm that almost sounded like speech to him: "Clackety-clack, clackety-clack. Never go back, never go back," the wheels said.

Having traded some of his boiled eggs for chicken back at Lela Bailey's, Ralph now bit into the tender meat suddenly realizing that he was starved. He had piled his crocker sack up on the seat next to him as Dave had suggested, for he wanted to be left strictly alone.

His family was headed for a small town in Nebraska. Ralph wondered when he would see them again. Ralph rehearsed in his mind what he would do if they stopped the train looking for him. First he would try to hide in the luggage closet if there was time. If he failed to find a hiding place quickly enough, he had another choice: inside of his daddy's musty old tweed jacket that he had insisted upon wearing, was a .38 special and two straight razors, sharp enough to cut through a bail of cotton. Nobody knew he had these weapons. Ralph had decided back in Arkansas that if the Law came after him, he would not go alone. He would shoot some cracker right between the eyes or he would cut some peckerwood's head clean off. That settled in his mind, Ralph patted the weapons and felt a little more free and confident. Actually he felt that if they didn't catch him in Memphis, they would not catch him at all.

The North and heading in that direction held a kind of magic for him as it had for thousands before him. Negroes, his father told him, had been leaving, leaving, leaving the South since around 1915. Now only the Depression slowed the pace. "When dis Depression is over, Colored people jus' gone gush out da South like a river," said Thomas Duster. "Ain't nothin' in da South fer da black main but pickin' cotton and trouble."

Now, the magic of hope spread its golden wings before his eyes. He saw freedom, a good job as an auto mechanic, and grand, unlimited opportunity before him. The northern air itself is different, someone had told him. Ralph found himself breathing deeply of this expected air.

Ralph ate quickly, hungrily, but allowed himself to think of his family. Generally nobody paid much attention to Negroes, not to mention giving them much credit for being intelligent and courageous enough to be slick. It would be an easy thing for his forty-year old father to change his name as Dave had suggested, Ralph thought as he took the folded envelope from his pocket. There it was. Smitty Kane and Lurlean Kane. These were to be the new names of his parents, because his mother once had a teacher she liked by that name. His brothers and sister would have new names also. Later he would write to his mother and father in Nebraska and find out the new names for everybody from his new place in Detroit, and he would use the new name that he had picked for himself—Lee Monroe—the name of the two surrounding counties where he had been born nineteen years ago. This new name thing, it made him smile.

Ralph thought of the headaches and blackouts he had experienced occasionally, usually after something "real bad" like a lynching or beating had happened in the Colored community. He wondered if the floating feelings—the feeling of being somewhere and witnessing things happening, but not really being a part of those things—like he imagined a haunt felt-he wondered if those feelings would stop now that he was leaving Arkansas?

He was enjoying his ride North: thoughts of his escape mixed and melded with the peaceful, pastoral, and rural life scenes that sped past outside his window. He thought of Dave and Lela Bailey and the others. They were good. Warriors. What every Negro should be and was not. He counted them among the very few people he admired and respected.

Finally he thought of his girlfriend, Shirley Ann Booth. Well, she was more in love with him than he was with her, which was for sure. The way some men carried on over women was a pain in the ass. Women were easy. Easy found. Easily left. He would find another Shirley Ann before he had set his crocker sack down in Detroit, Ralph mused. No problem.

Freedom, freedom, freedom! That's what the train wheels were saying now. Ralph moved his right hand in a half circle to the left of his body touching the .38 special, the razors, and finally the money belt as he passed around. He gave everything a fond pat, and then got more comfortable in his seat. He would let the rails lull him into a peaceful kind of alertness—for he dared not sleep.

The young man smiled to himself at first tentatively, then broader and broader. Ralph looked around. No one was paying him the slightest bit of attention. In fact there were only four other people in the car, all immersed in their own thoughts.

He was going North! He was going to Detroit, Michigan! *Well, Sheriff Birkens and all of his peckerwood friends can kiss my black ass nah!* Ralph exulted. *Ahm clean gone!*

PART TWO

This debt we pay to human guile;
With torn and bleeding hearts we smile,
And mouth with myriad subtleties.

THIRTEEN

F inally it was too much for Lela Bailey. She had to tell someone but, who? Why, Matthew Moses Clayton! Of course! He was Dave's preacher.

Now, why hadn't I thought of him before? Girl, you are gittin' old and foolish! Lela chided herself, but then they had been so preoccupied with this Duster thing. *Yas! Rev. Clayton.*

She would get Vera Marie Taylor to drive her down the hill to where he lived first thing tomorrow. She would try to get Rev. Clayton to find out the reason for what she had seen in Dave's private room a month ago.

Had it only been a month? Lawd!

It seemed like a lifetime. Because of that old room, *I ain't hardly had a lick of sleep in a whole month!* Lela thought to herself.

Indeed the contents of the room had made Dave's mother lose weight. Made her think she was "gettin' as po' as a snake!"

She and Vera Taylor rambled down, she called it, to the boarding house where Rev. Clayton lived in Vera's husband's old rickety third-hand truck. Rev. Clayton was out on the back porch, the boarding house proprietor told them.

"He be bringing in some fie wood fer me. He right helpful."

Vera's face twisted with disgust. "Did you see all dat snuff dat woman had in her mouf!" Vera hissed to Lela. "I mean slobber was 'most running down her chin!"

After finding Rev. Clayton, Lela told Vera politely that she wanted to speak to the reverend alone. "Dis be a highly personal matter."

Vera could barely hide her disappointment, but she took out one of her cigarettes and went out to the car and waited. She knew Mother B would tell her all about it sooner or later.

Lela told the minister why she had come, then she pulled out a sheet of paper and handed it to him.

"Dis is what I done fount in my son's room 'round 'bout da furst week in

September," Lela said quietly. They were sitting in the small parlor where residents of Miss Hashell's boarding house were allowed to receive guests—for half an hour only. Fearing immorality, Betty Hashell, a self-proclaimed "highly respectable" woman, did not allow guests in the boarder's rooms for any purpose at all.

Rev. Clayton took the paper from Lela's unsteady hand, but not before telling her comfortingly: "Whatever it is, Mother B, you and me and the Lord can handle it."

On the sheet Lela gave to Rev. Clayton was a listing in Lela's large scrawly handwriting:

3 razors

27 rifles

30 shotguns

18 pistols all differen kinds

10 hachets

7 ax

30 nifes - big

10 nifes - little

15 hamers

7 ice picks

4 baseball bats

1 pitchfork

A hole shef of bullets and shells

Rev. Clayton, looking down the list exclaimed: "My Lord in heaven!"

"Yas," Lela agreed. "Mah Lawd a-mighty. What you reckon he aiming to do wit' all dem fie arms an' things, Reverend?"

Lela was somewhat calmer, after sharing her long held secret. Whatever happened now somebody else knew—and she was even going to get some advice now, she hoped.

Strangely, she suddenly felt sleepy, as if her body was telling her that she could now finally relax, go back to normal. She felt she could sleep tonight, thank God. Lela yawned out of place and felt ashamed. She explained to the minister that now she might get one good night of sleep—after five long weeks.

Now the reverend turned the question Lela had asked back to her: "What do you think he means to do with all of those firearms, Mrs. Bailey? Do you think he's going to sell them? Is he thinking of opening a hardware store maybe?"

"Naw suh. Ahm sho' dat ain't it. Why we got hardware stores a-plenty what sells guns all ova da place. Naw suh, dat ain't it. Dose guns wuz hid away on purpose." Lela felt nervous and uncertain again. Perhaps she should have just kept quiet about the room after all.

Sensing her distress and concern, Rev. Clayton said: "Everybody in these parts says Dave Bailey is one of the most level headed young men they know. If he is collecting guns or anything else, I think he can give a good reasonable account for his actions. Don't worry." He looked at the list again as he hid a feeling of icy cold fear that went all the way down to his toes.

"But do you have any idy whatever o'what all dem weapons be fer?" Lela stammered.

Matthew Moses took Lela's hand in his. "Now, let's not wonder about it, Mother Bailey," he said in his comforting tone. "Let's ask him."

"Oh, my goodness!" Lela exclaimed suddenly, wide eyed and fearful.

"What is it, Mrs. Bailey?" Rev. Clayton asked releasing Lela's hand.

"Nah, Dave gone know I done bent in dat room, and he done told me specific to stay outta dere! Oh, dear me!" Lela wailed. "Ifn I wanted to ax *him*, I wouldn't come to *you*!"

"Set up a date, a dinner date," Rev. Clayton said, smiling at Lela. "And I'll come over and see if we can't shed some light on this situation, OK?"

A date was set as Lela continued to turn things over in her mind.

"I'll tell 'em I thought I smelled smoke in dat room. Dat's what I'll tell 'em. I'll say I jus' went in to see what was burnin'. If somethin' was burnin' in dere, why o'cose I had to go in."

Rev. Clayton did not comment.

"I mean I know hit's a lie, and I hates to lie but..."

Rev. Clayton changed the subject. "By the way!" he said excitedly, "the way you and Dave handled getting the Dusters out of town was truly wonderful!"

"Who tole you?" Lela asked stiffly. "I sho' hopes hit ain't all over town." She stood up as if ready to defend something or somebody.

"Oh, no! It isn't. Sit down, Mother Bailey. Will Henry Mead and LaSalle Peabody filled me in. Dave knows they told me. I think it was a magnificent act," the reverend enthused. "I hear you gave each member of the family a Bible!"

"Ralph left hisn behind."

"So I heard."

"We didn't mean to leave you outta it," Lela began apologetically, "but you a minister and all, and..."

They were speaking very softly now, turning their heads this way and that watching for Betty or anyone else that might carry all or a part of this conversation to the wrong ears.

"... you somewhat of a newcomer ta West Steward ... only been over heah a year."

"Well, I'm glad you trusted me enough to come to me with this situation of yours today. I hope I'll be included in the next...plans. I'd like to be of help."

"Ahm sho' you will be included in the next... whatever," Lela said too quickly. " hit's jus' yo' being a minister and all..."

Lela found herself flustered as she rarely was, before this "tight little black main," as she called him.

"I doesn't mean no disrespect ta you personal, Reverend, but..."

Matthew Moses Clayton let out a loud howl of laughter at Lela's efforts to backtrack and soften her words.

"Don't worry yourself," the minister said for the second time. "We'll get to the bottom of everything. You pray for me and I'll pray for you."

"Why thank you, Reverend!" Lela said, pleased and surprised at the way he had expressed himself.

"By the way. This killing thing. You think it's drying up? Have they got any suspects?"

"Yo' guess is as good as mine, Rev. Clayton. I ain't heard nothin' much mo' about it. Lawd willing dey won't come up with another Colored suspect."

"Mrs. Bailey, I don't mean to alarm you, but what if they come up with another black suspect? What then?"

"Do you think dey will, Reverend? You know, I ax dat same question o'Dave. He say 'Mama, we'll jus' have to cross dat bridge when we come to hit.' "

They sat in silence for a while, watching the yellowed lace curtains flutter at the window. Then Lela said, "You know, Rev. Clayton, when I think about it, I know in mah heart of hearts dat all dem guns and nifes and things got somethin' to do wit' da answer to dat same question."

Rev. Clayton studied Lela as he had not done before. Here was a woman without book learning, but a powerhouse in her own way. He felt a rush of admiration for her and for all black women like her. Strong, resolute women, usually well liked and respected in their communities as Lela was. Long suffering, fearless women. Where would the South be without them?

"Betty Hashell sho' don't mean for ya to stay in this little bitty room long, do she? It's as cold as ice in heah, and dis bench is hard as a sack o'potatoes! Jus' look at hi da wind is zipping through dat winda."

"Betty is a rascal alright," Rev. Clayton admitted smiling. "And you might be right about what you said. But let's just wait until I talk to Dave."

"What you want me to fix fer you to eat, Reverend?" Lela asked.

"I eat anything and everything," Rev. Clayton said, smiling his self-effacing smile. "Just don't put yourself out too much, now. A little snack will do nicely. Or just a cup of coffee and a few cookies."

But Lela—a very fine but frustrated cook who hardly ever got a chance to show what magic she could perform in the kitchen because she had no family at home anymore " 'cept Dave and he eat most lak a bird"—was already planning a feast. She pulled her coat about her and got ready for Vera Taylor's cigarette smoke and the rickety ride back home.

After leaving the room that held the weapons, Dave carefully placed three small splinters at the top of the door so if the door was opened in his absence, he would know because the splinters would dislodge and fall to the floor. He had noticed several weeks ago that the little signal pieces were on the floor. At first he wasn't sure if the culprit was simply the wind driven by the changing autumn weather, but after the third time he was certain that his mother had been in the room.

That was problem number one.

Problem number two was that she had become frightened and taken her knowledge to an outsider, Rev. Clayton, instead of approaching him. Although he liked Rev. Clayton a great deal, Dave had not been ready to trust anyone outside of his close circle of friends with his plans.

Problem number three was that he was angry with his mother—an emotion he so rarely felt that he was having trouble reconciling it. When he sat still and thought about it, he had to blame himself. He knew he should have spoken with her when he first suspected her snooping, but he put it off. He never thought she would tell someone else.

As she cooked the sumptuous dinner for Rev. Clayton, Lela kept glancing at Dave through her kitchen window. He was sitting in his usual spot by the stump and she could see that he was thinking hard.

Lela breathed a sigh of relief that brought very little actual relief and went back to the pounding of her steak for tonight's supper. When she announced that the reverend was coming to dinner, the whole mess had come spilling out.

I'm making a plan you see, and those guns and things may just be a part of that plan. I don't want to talk about it to too many folks because I really don't know what direction I'm going in yet. That's why we have to keep this quiet. Very quiet!

Dave's words kept replaying in her mind.

"Dave, I want to ax you jus' one mo' question, den ahm gone leave hit alone," she had said.

"Alright," he had answered, already standing to take his anger outside.

"Does yo' friends, Peter and Omar and Aggie and all dem, know about your having all dem fie arms or anythin' 'bout dese plans o'yourn?"

Dave had hesitated a moment at the kitchen door. His mother's question had not surprised him-he had anticipated it.

"Up to a point, Mama, yes. They don't know everything. *I* don't know everything. I'm just trying to prepare myself—and the rest of us—just in case."

"In case o'what?" Lela had asked, squinting up at Dave.

Dave had sighed deeply before answering.

"In case of anything, Mama. In case of whatever comes up."

Lela had known already but she had wanted to hear it from Dave himself. She knew very well in case of what. *In case trouble from white folks came—dats what in case of,* she thought.

After Dave left, Lela sat down at the kitchen table for a moment with her arms stretched out in front of her.

"Lawd, I stretch mah hains to thee, no other help I know," she prayed. "Please, please take care o'mah son. He means all da worl ta me. Thank you, Lawd fer heering da prayers o'yo' chirren. Amen."

FOURTEEN

Rev. Matthew Moses Clayton was on his second helping of everything—the smothered steak and candied sweet potatoes, the macaroni and cheese and fried white squash with onions, the fried cabbage, fried corn, the pickled beets, the corn sticks. He was eating as if he hadn't had a meal in a week. It seemed that each forkful was punctuated by a "Uh uh uh! This sho' is good! Nah this is some good eatin'!"

Dave Bailey felt a mild revulsion for all of this gnawing and chewing and slurping. Not a big eater himself, he had delayed eating all day in order to be truly hungry so his mother could not accuse him of "picking at his plate." But now he was anxious to get to the discussion and the reverend was still too busy shoveling food into his mouth to talk.

"Will you pass the sweet potatoes and macaroni and cheese again please? My! I don't believe I've had such fine tomato dumplings in my life!"

It was no use. Rev. Clayton had arrived promptly at five and they had begun eating at five-fifteen. It was now six-thirty and they were still at the table, both Dave and his mother having finished eating long ago.

Rev. Clayton had told several amusing stories about his childhood in Mississippi. Most of them revolved about how much he could eat even then.

As Dave watched his mother enjoying watching the minister eat, he realized that he hadn't seen her laugh so much in a long, long time. He began to appreciate the Rev. Clayton's presence a little more. Now if only he could get him away from the table!

Suddenly Rev. Clayton noticed Dave looking at him, and stopped mid-fork, ashamed.

"You know, Dave, I live in a boarding house. I don't often get a meal like what Mother Bailey cooked here tonight. It was magnificent," he said, looking at Lela.

"That's all right, Reverend. Enjoy yourself. You surely have brought a lot of fun into dis house tonight. We is both enjoying yo' company," Lela said.

"Yeah, but I'm gone stop eatin' now. I don't wanna wear my welcome out." He smiled again at Lela and put down his fork and pushed his nearly empty plate away.

Dave followed the minister's lead in pushing his chair back from the table. Both he and the minister went through the polite motions of offering to help Lela clear the table and put the food away in one of her ice boxes and wash the dishes. Of course Lela would have none of it. The kitchen was her special place—and that was the way she liked it, she said as both Dave and the minister tried to hide their relief at not being pressed into service.

"Now, Dave," Rev. Clayton began glancing around, his table napkin still firmly tucked in the front of his shirt. "Where do you do your serious talkin'? 'Cause we got us some jaw jabbing to do. Of course you know your mama invited me over here for a reason, don't you? And I imagine you know pretty well what that reason is."

"Yes, I do," Dave answered warily.

"Well. Without further ado as they say, let's git at it."

The two men ended up in the middle room that was often used as a guest sleeping room for out of town travelers. It was a fairly large room with a stone fireplace and Dave lit a fire as Rev. Clayton settled in the rocking chair and lit his aromatic pipe.

When the men were comfortably settled in Dave's mother brought in two steaming cups of tea. She then placed a saucer of tea cakes slyly in front of the reverend and both she and Dave chuckled when he made no attempt to conceal his interest in the cakes even after his enormous dinner.

"You got the nicest house, I do believe, I've been in anywhere here in West Steward," Rev. Clayton said by way of putting the young man at ease.

"Thank you," Dave answered. "It's comfortable." Then Dave asked the minister an unexpected question. "How old are you, Rev. Clayton?"

"Nah you trying to git in my business!" The minister answered amicably as he sipped his tea, and pretended to ignore the cakes for the moment. "I'm thirty-two."

"Why you're just six years older than I am!" Dave exclaimed, surprised.

"I know, I bet you thought I was a hundred, didn't you? Seriously, people usually think I'm over forty. I guess I'm just one of those old looking little niggers."

Dave laughed again, thinking how much joviality this man had brought to his house tonight and how grateful he finally was for it. Although he found that he was still uncomfortable with calling the reverend by his given name of "jus' plain

Matthew," as the minister had suggested, he thought he saw a man here that he could like. Rev. Clayton was certainly different from the ministers he had grown up with. These were very formal men who expected and demanded respect—even if they were totally without education or formal training for the ministry, their only credentials being a "call" to preach by "da Lawd." Most of these men were known as self-styled "jack leg" preachers, who lacked vision, courage, or even plain goodness. They were self serving and subservient to the calls of the white man and as fearful of being lynched as any ordinary man. Yet many of these men rose to positions of relative prominence like F.W.T. Edison of Greater Peace Baptist Church.

Dave did not think the Lord would call such a motley crew to do much of anything, and in his mind they retained their jack leg status no matter how large their congregations grew.

Lela had assured her son that there were other types of ministers than most of those seen in West Steward—ministers who were deeply spiritual men full of race pride, good works, good guidance, courage and leadership ability. Well, until the appearance of Matthew Moses Clayton, Dave knew he had not seen such men. The ministers he had seen were at best leaders of "religious social clubs."

Dave could not imagine calling The Right Rev. F.W.T. Edison by his first name. "Old F" as he was often called behind his back, was a man given to loud and inaccurate use of the English language. A fat, posturing, pompous creature, who admitted he only had a fifth grade education, but when "gourd calls ya, gourd prepares ya!" the Right Reverend was fond of saying. Dave found him despicable.

If Rev. Clayton had not become Rev. Edison's assistant pastor and preached quiet little lectures on the power of love, courage, patience, and loyalty when Rev. Edison was away from his pulpit for some reason or another, Lela would have despaired of ever getting Dave "in da church."

Rev. Edison did not once suspect that he had any competition whatever in the calm, very black little man that sat to his right every Sunday and got the opportunity to preach only five or six times a year.

Dave poked the fire, then bent and placed another thick log on the flames. He stood up and paced a bit, his tall frame nearly bumping into the single shaded electric light bulb that hung from the ceiling before sitting down on the davenport again.

"I really don't know where to begin," he said.

The minister stopped his slow rock, pulled on his pipe a few seconds, and then looked directly at Dave. "How about starting with the arsenal," he said. Then he set back in the rocker and simply puffed on his pipe and waited.

Finally Dave spoke.

"It all comes down to this, Reverend..."

"Matthew."

"Alright, Matthew then. We are exhausted. Tired. Tired of sitting here waiting to be maimed, shot, lynched, or God knows what. Just sitting waiting to be destroyed. To see our relatives and friends dragged off, beaten, raped. Anything they want to do. Just sitting not lifting a finger of help or protection, afraid of being killed ourselves. We are all so damn scared of white folks, we could dirty our drawers everytime the White Man says boo!"

"Go on," Matthew said quietly.

"If something happens to someone down here, we lock our doors, turn out our lights, or blow out the lamps and watch fearfully from behind the raggedy curtains like a pack of scared rats." Dave gave a short mirthless laugh. He was on his feet pacing again now. "Omar Williams and Peter Frauzinou are like brothers to me. We grew up together. Mama calls us 'da three,' as in the three musketeers. I will die before I let someone come in here and take them somewhere and beat or kill them. I think they feel the same about me."

"Oh, I know they do," Matthew said earnestly.

"You heard they beat the shit out of Pete two years ago. He was bleeding like a damn dog when they found him. They had tried to disfigure him by kicking him in the face. They cracked his ribs, broke his arm. Damn near killed him. I was up at the mill at the time."

"My, dear Father!"

"Yeah. Right. They brought him here. Mama and Mother Clarence took care of him-stopped the bleeding and all. Then they called Dr. Echardt. He got him admitted to the hospital. Down in the basement where they reluctantly look after a few Colored patients."

Dave's voice was thick with anger and bitterness as he kept up his pacing, his hands shoved in his pockets. He seemed almost to be talking to himself.

"Some of our friends came to the mill to get me. When I saw him, saw all of that blood, I wanted to kill somebody! I remember Mama screaming 'it ain't as bad as it looks! It ain't as bad as it looks! Face wounds bleed a lot but his wounds ain't deep, he's going to be alright.'

"Ha!" Dave spit out. "His wounds ain't bad, Mama said," Dave spun around and looked at Matthew, who was now totally spellbound by Dave's recounting of what had happened to Peter.

"What Mama meant was at least he isn't *dead!*" Dave stopped and looked at the ceiling as if the information he was trying to recall was written up there somewhere. "Not dead. No, not dead, but his face required twelve stitches. His left arm was broken. It still pains him. His ribs were all kicked in. Both eyes were black for a long time. His lips were swollen up like baseballs. And for what?"

"Yes, tell me why. I never knew why. Naturally, I heard rumors, but you know a lot of lies get mixed up with loose talk."

Dave was silent for a minute then he laughed loudly. Taking a seat he continued to laugh moving his entire body in a spasm of merriment, using exaggerated body motions to squeeze the last drop of humor from a story. The young man placed his large hands between his knees in an effort to stop laughing.

The minister was completely dumbfounded by this turn in emotion—from deep bitterness and anger to explosive laughter. He stared at Dave, waiting. And his perplexed expression made Dave laugh even harder.

Finally gaining control, Dave asked, "Do you know a woman named Martha Lou Henley?"

"Seems I've heard the name."

"Sure you have. Well, Martha Lou Henley went to the Boise sisters' café at least three or four times a week for dinner. The food is excellent there. Pete used to work there before he started to work with me and the hot tamales. He still works there part-time."

Dave was up pacing again with Rev. Clayton watching his every move.

"Martha Lou is a fat, ugly little blond. She is barely five feet tall and weighs, I swear, over two hundred pounds. Way over two hundred pounds. Lord forgive me, but she is one of the ugliest white women I've ever seen. I'm telling you how she looks for a reason."

"Go 'head on," the minister said without censure.

"She has these very small, very round blue eyes, and her nose is so short and turned up that she looks just like a little pig. And her legs! Huge. As big around as some people's waist. And she has a nasty, uppity personality. Even white folks don't like her and very few of the Colored women will work for her. You get the picture?"

"I got it," the reverend said, sending his sweet pipe smoke around the room.

"Now you've seen Pete?"

"Sure, of course."

"Even with the facial scars that he now has, women can't keep their hands off of him. He's not exactly ugly."

"No, not at all," Matthew agreed. "He's very handsome. Extremely so."

"And just as nice as he is good looking," Dave said. "He's the furthest thing from conceited about his coloring or his hair or his eyes or anything. I mean, let's face it. On the outside he is far more white than black. He could pass but he never would. Now here's what I was laughing about. Martha accused Pete of making eyes at her. Of wanting her."

Now it was Matthew's turn to laugh.

"You jokin'? That boy is good looking enough to have anybody he wants."

"Exactly. Yet here comes this little dumpy bitch—excuse me, Reverend—saying she had to stop having dinner at the Boise sisters' because Pete was always after her. Said he took every chance he could get to rub up against her, you know—feel her, touch her breasts."

"Wait a minute, wait a minute!" Matthew exclaimed, remembering. "Is this the same little woman that comes down here to Kung's to buy those little Chinese steamed buns that Mrs. Kung makes every Thursday?"

"One and the same."

"Why, she must be insane. Oh, that's so pitiful, really," the minister said sadly. "She'd be lucky if any man wanted her, Lord forgive me, but she is not exactly one of nature's most beautiful creations."

"Now you got the complete picture, Matthew. Well she went even further, finally accusing Pete of coming up to White Town one night to get at her. Hell, he didn't even know where she lived! Well, anyway she said he was trying to climb through her bedroom window and that he had rape on his mind."

"Oh, no!"

"Oh, yes. Of course we found all this out later. I understand the sheriff didn't even believe her and he delayed taking any action, but she was able to talk several white men into believing her story, and a few hours later Pete was set upon by this bunch of poor white trash, taken outside of town and beaten on the pretext of protecting a white woman's honor. Her honor. Can you believe that?"

"Did Peter know the men who did it?"

"Sure. It was four men from the mill where I worked. Pete knew two of them slightly. I knew them real well. Two of these were those cousins Parker Wilson and Red Oakes. They are always involved when anything racial happens. I think they are in the Ku Klux Klan."

"She said Peter was trying to rape her? That poor crazy thing!" The minister mused. "No wonder you were laughing yourself to death."

Dave was smiling again. "They said she came bustin' outta the house screaming for help buck naked as a jaybird. She said Pete snatched her gown right off."

"My goodness! I'm glad I didn't have to witness that! Seriously though, I wonder what a good nerve specialist would have to say about her condition," Matthew said shaking his head in disbelief. "Dear, dear, dear! Life is sure a challenge some days. What did the sheriff finally do? Did he question Miss Henley about her story? Anything like that?"

"I'm surprised you asked a question like that, Reverend, when you know very well that black people have no protection under the law."

"Of course you're right. I just thought..."

Dave interrupted him. "You thought that just this one time justice would prevail because you know Pete is a good man and well liked and Martha Lou is a lying, crazy—" Dave stopped himself and sat down again, and the two men stared at each other, sizing up each other and the situation as it stood.

Dave half expected a reprimand because of all his swearing—one did not curse in front of a minister—but Rev. Clayton offered no reprimand, nor had he seemed surprised or offended by Dave's use of what was called "strong language." He simply took a large white handkerchief from his back pocket and wiped his thick glasses carefully. Placing the glasses back on his nose he continued to study Dave, his ebony head cocked attentively to one side.

"I left the mill because of that incident. I didn't have another job. I didn't know what I was going to do or what my future held. All I knew was that I couldn't stand to see those white men at the mill go free and laughing and smiling every day about it. Laughing at Pete—at me—Mama was the first one to bring that to my attention—that they really wanted to beat me but they didn't dare because of my standing with the mill owner. What their laughter said was 'well, smart ass nigger! You can get a raise for your boys, and the mill owner obviously likes you, listens to you, but we beat the hell out of one of your close friends, nah what you gone do about dat!'"

Dave was silent for several minutes, then he spoke again. "You know what those guns in that room say, Reverend? They say no more. No more! Enough is enough. Sheriff Birkens didn't believe that woman, and I honestly don't believe any of those men really did either, but Peter was beaten anyway just to 'keep the niggers in line!' "

"So you have a definite plan? I mean for the guns..."

"We are going to fight them, man to man. That's the plan. If they want war they'll get it. Ain't gonna be no more of this 'I kick, you holler' shit anymore."

"I see," said the minister calmly. "Now explain to me exactly who 'they' is."

Seeing nothing but intense interest on the face of the minister, Dave obliged.

"They, are the white folks in White Town—or anywhere else that come down here messing with us. The next time they come looking to hurt someone that has been accused of one thing or another, they are going to be in for a little surprise. You can bet your bottom dollar on it. We are going to have all of the lights on and most of the men in this town will be standing in their doors with a gun in their hands."

"Really? All of the men? How did you manage that," Rev. Clayton asked mildly.

"Well, perhaps not all, but a good many of them," Dave corrected. "We've been busy organizing, Matthew, and a good many people feel the way we do."

"But not all?"

"No, of course not. A lot of people are still scared to death. It's going to take a lot more persuading, but I think we have momentum on our side. Anyway, you know black folks outnumber white folks here, by several hundred, that's a fact."

"It is also a fact, Dave, that white folks have guns also, and something else we don't have: power—and the law on their side," Rev. Clayton continued in his reasonable manner.

Dave laughed out loud.

"Power, you say? Well, there is quite a lot of power in a nigger behind a gun, especially an unexpected gun. There's nothing like the element of surprise," Dave said dryly.

"So. You've thought this whole thing out very carefully, have you? Well, let me just ask you a few questions to clarify things in my own mind. If you have organized a group of armed men as you say, and they are ready to do battle to protect themselves and this community, won't a lot of people get hurt, possibly children and women on both sides?"

"Are you suggesting that we sacrifice one for the many?"

"I'm not suggesting anything, Dave. I'm just trying to understand how you came to this drastic decision."

Dave could not figure out the meaning of this new tone he heard in the minister's voice and he vacillated between continuing and not continuing.

Did Matthew understand or not? He decided to try to explain himself further.

"Do you think a plan to protect ourselves in the only way we know how is drastic? This is 1930. Five years ago, my friend John Straw was shot and killed by a white man over a tiny debt. John originally owed Victor Gaffin, The Blanket Man, fifty cents-plus interest. Every week interest. When the fifty cents became eight dollars over the months, John refused to pay anymore and Victor Gaffin shot him dead. Two years ago Sam Lawrence's family was totally wiped out by a gang of whites that set his house on fire because of a dispute Lawrence had had with another white man over bootleg whiskey. I'm sure you've heard about it. That same year Billy Binder was lynched, and Pete was brutally beaten."

The minister held his hand up to ask a question.

"No, let me finish," Dave said. "Tom Leak is the way he is now—half crazy, afraid of fire—because in 1920, when he was twenty-years old, his mother, father, two sisters and a brother were locked in a burning house early one morning, and his whole family except for him and one sister perished. He and his sister, Edelle, were at their grandmother's at the time. Do you know why they were set on fire? Because Tom's father was angry about being cheated. He had sharecropped all year expecting around three hundred dollars or more at payout time. He was given eighty dollars. For a whole year's work. The owner of the fields told Preston Leak that he had spent all of his money taking up things on credit at the company store.

"They are burning us up, shooting us, hanging us. It's too much, Matthew."

"Can you believe men can be so evil?" Matthew said in disgust. "Lord help us, Jesus."

"Now, Matthew, the things I just related to you are what I call drastic acts. We are just trying to defend ourselves because the law won't defend us. Is that wrong?"

The minister rocked and puffed. Finally he spoke. "So you're looking for revenge, are you? To show the white folks a thing or two for a change? Is that it?"

"Are you starting in on a sermon, Reverend? Because if you are..." Dave's voice trembled a bit from anger and disappointment and he didn't know what else. He thought at that moment that if Matthew started preaching a turn the other cheek message—a love thy enemy speech—that he would scream and totally lose control of himself.

"I did not come here to preach a sermon," Matthew said tautly. "I'm a minister, true, but I'm also a black man—and for that reason alone I'm with you, totally." Matthew smiled a humorless smile of encouragement at Dave.

Dave felt such a wild sense of relief that he was embarrassed to find that this little man's approval meant so much to him. He picked up the tea cakes and extended them to Matthew. It was a subtle way of saying thank you.

Matthew took three cakes and ate them, washing them down with cold tea.

Dave shook his head in mock disapproval. "Still room for another little snack, huh?"

"Always," Matthew replied. "Don't misunderstand me, Dave. I'm a little older than you, so I've heard and seen even more violence than you have. It's a shame that every Negro in this town or in any other Southern town, who is over the age of ten could match every terrible story that we could come up with in this room. And I agree with you that enough is enough, but I'm concerned about you, about us. And there's something else, too—I'm also concerned about the good, decent white folks around here—and there are a few. Like Agatha Brooks and Dr. Echardt, and the Italian family with the store. People like that. I just want to make sure your plans extend past your anger."

"I'm not at all sure that it does, Matthew, but we've got to do *something.*"

Matthew saw before him a young man of resolute raw courage. He wanted desperately to build on that courage and at the same time to protect Dave—to protect them all. Having heard a number of good things about Dave, he wanted to know this man better. Rev. Clayton liked the idea of becoming his confidential counselor. He felt eons older than Dave—perhaps more mature but certainly not smarter.

Dave walked over and stared briefly out of the single window at the back of the room above the bed. The town was quiet—and black. Not many Colored families in Steward had "wired" houses. Most still used coal oil lamps and without much electric light the darkness of the town was nearly total.

"What are you looking for?" Rev. Clayton asked.

"I'm not looking. I'm listening."

"For what?"

"We are four miles from the city proper, but you'd be surprised what you can hear from up here—breaking glass, arguments, gun shots. Sometimes I stand on the porch and just listen. There goes the bus down the car line headed for Old Steward. You hear it?"

"Naw."

"This is Monday. Everything is about closed up at this hour but listen—I hear Roger Mulright's truck going—" Dave pointed south. "Probably going home from work somewhere in White Town."

"You hear Roger Mulright's truck? From here?"

"Sure."

Dave put more logs on the fire, and they both watched as orange flames started to lick the logs and chase the chill that was now in every corner of the room. The fireplace made this room entirely comfortable and cozy, the reverend thought, and the fireplace lingered in his thinking for a minute as Dave started to pace again. After a moment he sat down abruptly, staring into the fire. A sigh with a good deal of pain in it escaped his lips.

"Take your time, take your time," the minister said gently. "We got all night long."

Matthew Moses Clayton was thin, wiry, just under average height and, unlike Dave, who was the rich color of good black coffee with a dab of cream in it, Matthew was black with tones of grey in his ashy, dry complexion. Thick metal rimmed glasses sat on a nose which was neither broad nor narrow. He wore his hair in the bangs most men featured now. These bangs, a curious three-to-five-inch wide line of hair on the front of the head on an otherwise very low cut head of hair, often stood straight up unless plastered down with a heavy waxy grease, then brushed very hard with a stiff brush until the hair rebelled into something called waves. The most unique thing about the reverend was his surprisingly deep voice. He usually spoke softly but his voice had such carrying power that some of the church ladies had remarked that he sounded like "one of dose radio announcers from New Yoke City."

Matthew had small, even, white teeth, and when he smiled, certain young women in the community thought he looked not handsome, but "right nice." When he did not smile in his disarming, self mocking way he looked much older than he was, sad, and full of sharp perceptions and secret regrets.

Dave, studying the man before him thought he saw a measure of strength not necessarily noticed by others. He liked the way the man caught your gaze and held it, and he had an air of dignity about him that Rev. Edison could never duplicate. His mother was a good judge of character. This man was no fool, and Dave believed he could be trusted. He sat forward on the davenport and began again.

"No, I have not planned much past my anger, as you so aptly put it, Matthew. All I know right now is that I'm not going to be target practice ever again. Nor will any of my relatives or friends. I just want to repeat that and get that completely straight."

Matthew was puffing on his pipe again. He looked perfectly relaxed and attentive, and Dave suddenly realized that the minister's calm attitude had the effect of calming him. He found that he was feeling a little lighter in spirit now and he lowered his voice a bit as he continued.

"Now, you may think that some of us will be hurt or killed. Isn't that just what's happening to us now? The White Man can do anything he wants to do to us. We have no real protection under the law. Justice and fair play doesn't extend to us. So you take your pick. You can be killed fast—and take some of these peckerwoods with you—or you can die slowly a day at a time, inch by inch, until when you officially die they won't even have to dig a hole for you. Because they wouldn't be burying a man—just a dried up hull—a scooped out shell. They could just as well lay you on top of the ground. You know what I mean, Reverend? A grave is for a whole man not an empty vessel."

Dave leaned back on the davenport, a little spent by his speech. He stared again into the flickering flames and Matthew could see that his eyes were filled with tears that stubbornly refused to flow down his cheeks. Matthew gave his pipe several animated taps on the arm of the rocker and rocked back and forth for several minutes.

"I see," he said. Obviously touched by Dave's words, he rubbed his head fiercely back to front, causing his grease-stiffened bangs to stand straight up, giving him an unintended clownish look. "Thank you, Dave, for telling me how you feel. I'm with you completely, as I told you, but I feel you should exercise great care and the tightest planning you can think of, because you know," he said, catching and holding

140

Dave's eye, "that situations full of feeling and emotion have a way of getting out of hand more than anything else."

"Yes, I know that," Dave answered quietly, a little apprehension flowing into his bones. "So what are you saying, Matthew?"

"I'm saying I'm you and you are me. All of us are definitely in this together. And a man has a right to defend himself, certainly. When one of us hurts we all hurt, that's for sure."

"But?" Dave asked with just a hint of anger in his voice. "I hope you're not getting ready to quote scripture."

"Now, what scripture did you have in mind, Dave?"

"Ho! Good comeback, Reverend!" Dave said, slapping his thigh and smiling.

Matthew waited, smiling patiently.

"How about 'he who takes up the sword will die by the sword?' How about that one?" Dave said half teasing.

The minister looked off into space, puffing on his sweet pipe. Suddenly he leaned forward in the rocker, ignoring Dave's comment on the scriptures.

"I remember a lynching back where I came from over in Fair Damsel, Mississippi. I was fourteen or fifteen years old. The man was a pretty well respected fellow and the people were terribly upset about it. Much more then they would have been had this man been just a regular person. He was a school teacher you see. After he was lynched on some trumped up charges, something quite unexpected happened. Without a discussion or a plan of any kind, the Negroes started to boycott the stores to show their outrage over what had occurred. Now, Fair Damsel was about ninety percent Colored—still is. But all the businesses were owned by whites, except for a few little bitty candy stores where they sold cookies, sour pickles, snowballs, stuff like that. Anyway as soon as the people stopped buying from the white stores, things got very bad for the store owners. They had no customers! Well a few store owners actually started coming through the town asking Negroes to shop with them. 'Y'all come ta mah sto'. Y'all come down and buy from me!' They were practically begging in the end."

"Did anybody buy?" Dave said smiling hopefully.

"Nope! Not a soul. Slowly the Negroes begin to realize that we *did* have some power. I remember Prunell Douglas personally coming to see my daddy and asking him to buy something from his store. 'Two reason ah can't, Mistah Douglas,' my daddy told him. 'One, I ain't got a quarter. Two, I got everythin' ah needs.' But as soon as Prunell was out of earshot my daddy jumped up off the porch and started dancing around in the dust like a crazy man!" Matthew laughed out loud remembering.

"Dancing? What for?" Dave asked, smiling.

"We were all sitting on the porch and Daddy hollered as he danced: 'I got me jus' plenty money but dat somebitch Prunell Douglas ain't gone git a dime of hit!' " Matthew was laughing heartily now, as was Dave. "When I go home we still laugh about that day."

"How long did the boycott last?"

"For a good five months. We had about four stores that sold various things. Three of them went completely out of business. Prunell's was one of them."

"And everybody shopped over here in Old Steward doing that time?"

"Sure did. So I'm asking you, Dave, before you think about using your guns, think about organizing a boycott of some kind. I think it could be very effective. Nobody can force you to spend your money where you don't want to. A boycott. That way nobody would get hurt. Will you think about it?"

"Yes, I will, Matthew," Dave answered flopping his legs about. "Did the black people ever get together and talk about why they decided to boycott? I mean all at once?" he asked.

"Yes, a few of us did. People were just tired of abuse, Dave, just like you are. It was almost spontaneous. And over a period of two days everybody just stopped buying. Then the Negroes begin to notice the effect their boycott was having and they got right hinkty! They started giving the little ol' Colored stores lots of business to show that they did have money. They played pitch pennies in the dirt while store owners watched, and they played with half dollars!"

Dave threw his head back and howled with laughter. "I love this!" he exclaimed.

"Some of the white store owners took to going down to the dock and watching the ferry bring Negroes back from Arkansas with sacks of grub, new shoes, hats. Oh, they were mad as could be, I remember. They would ask some man, 'thought you sayed you didn't have no money boy?' 'I ain't, boss!' he would answer. 'All dis stuff was gave to me!' "

Both men laughed for several seconds. They were enjoying each other, and both had a sense of having started in the direction of accomplishing something, one through the other.

FIFTEEN

"Sshhhh!" Dave said, suddenly stiffening. In a flash he was up and standing by the window, listening for a few seconds as he put on his jacket in one smooth move. Then quick and quiet as a cat, he bolted across the room and grabbed the shotgun that sat against the wall by the fireplace.

"Dave! What's going on?" Rev. Clayton whispered loudly. "What's wrong?"

"Someone is outside creeping around. Don't you hear them?"

"Naw!"

"There are two or three of them."

"Who are they?" asked the astonished minister who had heard nothing at all. "What do they want?"

"That's what I'm going to find out!" Dave whispered hoarsely.

"How do you know it isn't some of your friends, maybe Omar or Peter?"

"They would drive up with the lights on, not sneak around in the dark bumping into things."

"Muddear!" Dave called, not too loudly.

Lela was already down the hall with a shotgun in her hands. She pulled a box of shells from her pocket and gave them to Dave without comment.

"You heard, Mama?"

"Yas! I blowed out da lamp and turned off the radio. I was fixing to go ta bed."

"Here," Dave said, shoving a gun into the minister's hand. "You know how to handle a shotgun, don't you?"

"I reckon," the minister said uncertainly.

"Good!" Dave said giving Matthew a handful of shells.

From a drawer in the hall Dave took a pistol and shoved it inside of his belt. From the same drawer he also removed a large flashlight. All of this was accomplished inside of a minute. Not waiting for their eyes to adjust to the darkness, they could barely see as they moved along the hall to the front door.

143

"Stay at the back window, Mama. Do you have the bell?"

"Yas, and I'll give hit da emergency code if I hears you shootin' in da air fer help. Three sets of rings in a row if you want Aggie's boys to run fer da men folk, is dat right?"

"Right. I'll shoot twice if help is needed because you won't be able to see what's going on."

"Lord Jesus!" muttered Matthew, as the men came to the front door.

"Let's go out the front, then around to the back, because they're already out back in the yard. Maybe we can sort of surround them."

"Alright," Matthew said, praying and quaking at the same time.

Dave stopped just inside the front door and, asking Matthew to hold the flashlight, he loaded his shotgun, then held the light for the minister so he could do the same.

As they loaded their guns, Dave whispered hurriedly. "When Ralph Duster was twelve years old, he found a lynched man in the woods while he was picking up pecans for Christmas. Nobody ever identified the body. Well, they are not going to hang nobody on any trees of mine!"

Dave slid off the front porch and into the blackness of the night without making a sound. Rev. Clayton followed right behind him, trying to be as quiet and quick as he was.

Their eyes having adjusted a bit more to the darkness, they moved carefully towards the back of the house, Matthew marveling at how cold it had gotten. In the cozy room with Dave he had not noticed the sharp change in temperature.

Rev. Clayton pointed his shotgun down toward the ground and tried to keep up with Dave's long confident, stealthy strides, which was not possible. It was so dark that he couldn't see his hands in front of his face but Dave knew his land and had no need for light—yet.

There was movement now, away from the back of the house, a definite running, rustling sound. Suddenly someone seemed to stumble and fall.

"Git up, damnit, and come on!"

"Wait! I done hurt mah ankle!"

"Never mind dat! Let's git off dis property. Look lak private property. Dey may got dogs! We too close to da house!" "Stop!" Dave called loudly, as he turned his powerful flashlight on the prowlers. Three young white men stood in the circle of his light. Two standing and one sitting on the ground nursing his ankle. All were wearing caps pulled low on their heads.

The minister finally came up beside him.

"Take the flashlight, Reverend," Dave ordered, as they both moved in on the men, shining the light in their eyes until it pained them and they threw up their hands as shields.

The two men pulled the redheaded man with the twisted ankle to his feet and they stood before Dave and his double barrelled shotgun.

"This is my property," Dave said to them in the low steady tone that his few enemies had come to fear. "What is your business here?"

The older man, about thirty, with yellowish hair, badly cut, stepped forward a bit.

"Ifn you could just take some of that light out our faces, sir."

Dave took the flashlight from Rev. Clayton and pushed a button that reduced the light to medium, then he shined the light in his own face. He then shined the light on Rev. Clayton.

The redheaded man, who seemed the youngest of the three, shrunk back from the two men after seeing Dave's face. It seemed to him like a polished black mask—and those eyes! Huge eyes nearly square. He wanted nothing more than to limp out of here as fast as he could go.

Dave spoke again: "This is Rev. Matthew Clayton. My name is Dave Bailey. This is my property. State your business here," he said a second time, giving the flashlight back to Rev. Clayton and again aimed his gun at the three.

"Well, sir," said the blond man in a less than steady voice. "We ain't got no business. We are jus' some men looking for work. We wuz over yonder," he pointed in back of him, "sleeping in a lil' old 'bandon house, and we got so gosh awful hoingry and cold we just got up and started walkin.'"

The tallish dark haired man spoke next. "Da ground is clean picked for nuts. We wuz jus' lookin' for somethin' to eat, mister. We didn't mean no harm. We maybe jus' be goin'..."

Seeing the double barrel shotgun and the .38 stuck in Dave's belt, Raymond Parteen, the dark haired man, thought: *they could just as soon shoot us here and bury us and no one would ever know the difference. From way out here mebbe nobody would even down hear no shots...*

"We wuz jus' lookin' lak he say, fer somethin' to chew on, mister," said the light haired man. "Looking fer a smoke house or somethin'. We decided not to steal no chicken 'cause we ain't got no way to pluck it, or cook it. Hell, we don't even have one knife betwixt us."

Dave lowered the gun. Never before in his life had he been called "mister" by a white man. It was strange, stunning.

"Where might y'all be from?" asked Rev. Clayton.

"Me?" said the blondish man, "I'm Stanley Chester. I'm from Oklahoma. Red here, by the name of Petey Elkins, and Raymond Parteen—dey from Southeast Texas."

"Oooh!" wailed Petey. "I gotta git off dis leg."

Dave and Rev. Clayton studied the three men a minute longer. Rev. Clayton looked. Dave listened. He didn't hear the sound of anyone else nearby. He flashed his light quickly in all directions. The three men were alone.

Finally he said: "If you want to come up to the house I'll see if my mother can give you a sandwich."

"Y'all would give us a samich?" said Stanley Chester, removing his cap. "We would be mighty grateful! Yes indeed!"

"Follow us," said Dave turning his back to them, and thinking of his daddy, Rex Bailey, who could have been in a similar situation at some point in his travels.

Stanley Chester helped the equally enthusiastic Petey, who hobbled after the two black men, but Raymond Parteen did not move.

"I'm thinking I'll just stay out here and wait on y'all. I'm got no money to pay for no somethin' to eat." he said.

Both Stanley Chester and Dave stopped and turned to look at the man.

"Well, den you jus' suit yo'self," said Stanley. If dese peepers is good enough to offer us somethin' ta eat, I sho' ain't fool enough to past it by."

"It's jus' dat I can't pay," Raymond repeated in his hang-dog fashion.

"Nah, who done axed you for some money?" Stanley Chester said harshly. "I should think dese gents know we ain't got a nickle betwixt us."

Stanley looked at Dave and Rev. Clayton for confirmation.

"Nobody's asking you to pay for a sandwich," Dave began with a chuckle of surprise.

Petey Elkins moaned in pain again.

"I'm gone get Petey off dis leg. Nah you can stay out heah and freeze yo' ass off—'cuse me, Reverend—if you wants to. Please lead da way, gents. We's right behind you."

Lela met them at the kitchen door, her eyes circles of surprise and fear.

"It's OK, Muddear. Turn on the electric light."

Lela, ever alert to hurt or ill, exclaimed "Oh! You've been hurt!" to Petey, who was limping badly—more actually than he had to.

"Set 'em down right here," Lela said to Stanley Chester.

The two men could not take their eyes off the jars and jars of fruits and vegetables in the floor to ceiling open shelves. Their mouths literally hung open. Then they looked at the rest of the spacious, spotless kitchen in awe.

"Nah, is dis heah yo' house, mam?" asked Stanley Chester.

Dave, removing his jacket, tossed him a look that made Stanley wish he hadn't asked.

"This is my mother, Mrs. Bailey. This is her house. This is my land," Dave said simply as if talking to a child. "Why don't you find a seat and sit down."

Stanley Chester immediately caught the tone of annoyance in Dave's voice and knew he had said something wrong and he knew what it was: he hinted that this house was too fancy and clean, and that they were perhaps too well off for Colored. He was thinking that sure, and this smart looking Colored man had caught it all in a flash.

"I mean it's just so pretty and fine!" Stanley said, sitting down, hoping to back track a bit, and hoping he sounded admiring, not so jealous that the offer of a "samich" and maybe some hot coffee would be withdrawn. That possibility gave him a chill greater than what he had felt out in the woods.

They got Petey in a chair and Lela applied a bright green salve that she had gotten from John Candle to Petey's ankle as he sat at the kitchen table, his face scrunched up in pain. She wrapped the ankle loosely with a cloth from her great store of "nice clean rags," and had him prop his leg up on the seat of a chair.

"Hit ain't bad atall," she told the relieved Petey. "You just done twisted hit a mite. Hit'll be good enough to walk on after while."

"Is dat right, Missus? Well, I be dog! I'm sho' obliged to you, Mam," Petey Elkin said sincerely.

Stanley Chester was trying to peer down the dark hall. He was glad they couldn't hear him thinking: *Hi do Colored live dis good in dese bad times? Why, dat cook stove alone with its six eyes musta cost...*

Lela, watching Stanley's expression as he tried to look around without seeming to do so, could almost read his thoughts, and thinking it prudent never to let white folks know how much you had—even poor, harmless looking men such as these—she said, "I see you laks my canned stuff?"

"Yes, mam! It's right pretty looking," Stanley said, eager to please in order to eat.

"Well, hit's all we've got!" Lela said lightly.

"How's dat mam?" Stanley asked puzzled.

"Well," Lela said putting the coffee on the stove that was never allowed to grow cold because it was bad luck to let fire go out in your house. "All me and mah son got in dis woil is dem fruits and vegetables—and a few chickens."

Dave and Rev. Clayton passed a knowing look between themselves and smiled.

"See, when we need somethin', I use dem jars to trade wit' if I kin. Yassuh! Dem peaches and tomatoes and sich is most of da money I has."

"Ooooh, I see," said Stanley Chester. He was relieved to know that these people were not so well off after all, they were just a little bit better off than he was.

Dave opened the back door and shined his flashlight. Raymond Parteen gazed sadly up at him from the steps. Raymond found the scent of Lela's coffee nearly unbearable, and he could not remember ever having been so cold, miserable, and hungry in his life—even when he and other men were hopping freight cars all over the country looking for work.

Dave closed the door gently again without speaking to the man.

As he did so a rush of warm food-scented air gushed out from the kitchen leaving Raymond Parteen weak with desire.

"Hey, Ray! You gone stay out dere and freeze lak somebody dat ain't got right good sense? It's mighty nice in here and we're about ta eat!" Petey called in a comically seductive sing-song voice.

"Why doesn't he come in?" Lela asked Dave.

Her son shrugged his shoulders.

Lela made six ham sandwiches and spread them with the mild yellow mustard she had gotten from the Jones Brothers' store. She sat four of the sandwiches in front of the men along with two steaming cups of coffee. Although Lela did not wish the men to see the leftover feast that the ice boxes held, she thought it not too much to include two hunks of blackberry cobbler.

The two men pounced on the sandwiches and coffee unashamed and grateful, but when they saw the dessert they nearly cried for joy.

"My mama's prayers is following me sho' as you born!" Petey exclaimed reverently.

"I honestly never expected no meal lak dis, Mam. We don't know hi to thank ya," Stanley said as he accepted a refill of coffee. "We ain't had nothin' near no meal in four or five days. Jus' bits and pieces heah and dere as we got off one boxcar and on to another. One day all we ran up on was jus' a handful o'peanuts between us all day long. It was better during the summertime when there was gardens and fruit on da trees."

"They keep on acting this nice and humble and all, Mother Bailey will give them everything in those two ice boxes!" Rev. Clayton whispered to Dave with mock concern.

There was a soft knock on the kitchen door.

Stanley winked at Petey. "Is you folks got an old cat scratching to git in from da cold?" he asked smiling.

It was Raymond Parteen.

Dave opened the door and the man walked in grinning shyly and removing his cap.

"Is dat samich still 'vailable?" he asked with such pitifulness that everyone laughed, including Dave.

Fleetingly Dave thought—as men have time immemorial upon meeting an enemy in a momentarily friendly situation—that in another time, in another place, *I would have liked these men. We could have been friends...*

The thick ham sandwiches, coffee, and cobbler were set in front of Raymond Parteen, but instead of eating, he just sat looking at the food. Finally he took a sip of coffee. "I'm near too hoingry to eat," he explained to another round of smiles from his friends.

After they had eaten, the men told of riding the rails, roaming around from one town to another looking for work-mostly in vain, for there were thousands of men doing the exact same thing so competition for any kind of work was fierce.

They spoke of women folk and families left behind. Only Petey was unmarried. He was eighteen.

Much to Dave's surprise Raymond Parteen, who was about his own age, said: "I tole dese two dat I hoped dis was a house wit' Colored peepers in it when we wuz deciding whether to come up to the house or stay away."

"Oh? Why is that?" Dave asked, raising an eyebrow.

"'Cause Colored peepers has mo' feeling, mo' heart. I've always found that out to be true. If dey Colored, I told Stanley, didn't I, Stanley? Dey will share what so never dey got. Didn't I say dat, Petey?"

"You sho' did," Petey replied. Having finished eating he tried to stand, testing the ankle.

"Hey! Hit don't hurt me no mo'!" Petey looked at Lela in wonderment. "Well, thank you, lady! Look. I can put mah full weight on it!"

"Well, if you felt that way—why did it take you so long to come in?" asked Matthew.

"I was ashamed." Raymond said simply.

"Ashamed?" Dave asked, perplexed.

"Sure. Put yo'self in mah place. We come busting into the house of peepers we don't know—begging. We ain't got a penny betwixt us. We starving, we cold, we tired, and we ain't had a bath since I don't know when..." Raymond stopped at a lost for words looking around the table for understanding.

Now it was Dave's turn to feel ashamed. Of all the reasons he had thought of for Raymond not wanting to come into the house, he had never thought of plain shame. That being human, Raymond may have felt as he might have in the same situation. Racism, racial hatred and suspicion was robbing him of his humanity, Dave thought ruefully.

"Your situation is not your fault," Rev. Clayton said kindly. "This whole country is in an uproar, bad—and getting worse, so the papers say. You can't blame yourself because there is no work."

"I know, Reverend," Raymond said, but it sure do feel good to hear somebody say dat to you once in a while."

"So what y'all planning to do nah when you leave heah?" asked Lela.

Outside the wind was whistling, and it was much colder than usual for November. The men heard it too, and flinched at the thought of having to leave this bright, warm kitchen. And even though they prolonged their stay with several cups of coffee, and second desserts, the meal finally came to an end.

"Well," said Stanley in a resigned way, "we sho' do thank y'all fer yo' kindness. We best be moving out," Stanley said, shuffling his feet and moving his chair as if to go. "Mam, is there anything I kin do fer you? I kin clean up dose dishes in a flash. I used to wash 'em all da time fer my mama—and I never broke a one," he added.

"As to what we gone do after we leaves heah, I don't rightly know, Mam."

Lela refused his offer with a surprised and pleased smile.

Dave sat at the table with the three white men thinking. Finally he said, "Hold on a minute. I'll be back." And he made off down the hall.

The three men looked at each other not knowing what to expect.

"We may git cold tonight, but at least we ain't cold and hoingry," Petey offered by way of cheering up his companions who had fallen into a state of melancholy and dread of what their immediate futures held.

Dave went into his bedroom and into the closed "arsenal," as Rev. Clayton had called it, and getting down on his hands and knees, he reached under his desk and opened a small trap door in the floor that even his mother did not know was there and lifted the steel locker box from its hiding place. The box contained bundles of bills, nothing larger than a twenty.

Dave never carried more than five dollars on his person unless he was going shopping, so he had to open his box.

Pursing his lips, Dave thought about what his mother had told him so many times: *Never, never let white folks know your business. For there is nothing worse than a white man jealous of a black one. If they're jealous long, they will try to git back at you some hi.*

Dave took a large bundle of singles from the box and peeled off nine one dollar bills. He went back into the kitchen and sat at the table.

"Do any of you men know where Old Steward is?" he asked.

"I do," Petey piped up.

"Alright, Petey, you're the guide. There's a place over in Old Steward or Steward—this is West Steward you know—where you can get a room for the night, a hot bath and a heavy breakfast in the morning for a dollar and twenty-five cents. You don't have to leave until two in the afternoon, so they tell me. The place is called Elmer's Hotel."

"Sounds nice," said Raymond Parteen. "I wish I had the price of it. You go there a lot, Mister Bailey?"

"Well, no, it's for whites only," Dave said.

"Oh. Yas." said Raymond, flustered.

"The bus fare is a nickel from here to Steward," Dave continued. "That's a total of a dollar and thirty cents."

"All the money in the world to a poor man," Stanley Chester whistled.

Dave took the nine dollars out of his pocket. He pushed three dollars towards each man.

"I don't have much," he lied, "but a man ought to have a good hot bath once in a while. Oh, yes," Dave added, "for fifteen cents more you can have all the clothes you're wearing washed and delivered back to your door before breakfast."

The men stared at Dave in total disbelief. Three dollars! You could get a stamp and an envelope to write home for three cents. You could have a full dinner for twenty-five, thirty cents. You could buy five cigarettes for a nickel. You could. It was, given the times, a goodly amount of cash. No one touched the money.

Finally Stanley said, "Mister Bailey, we can't eat up yo' food *and* take yo' money."

"It's a loan," Dave said smiling.

"And this is how you are gonna pay it back," volunteered Rev. Clayton. "You are going to get back on your feet again although that is hard to imagine now, but you will. And when you do, pay this loan back by helping anyone who needs help— Colored or white—however you can. Is that fair enough?"

"My mama's prayers is sho' nuff following me!" Petey exclaimed again.

"We don't know hi to thank you enough," Raymond began.

"I just told you," Rev. Clayton said. "Just help someone else along the way, then you'll be thanking Mr. Bailey."

They all looked at Dave as if to ask if that were true.

"That's good enough for me, sure. That's the way I want it," Dave assured them.

"The bus line is west of here, down the road about four miles. You could probably ride down there in the back of Dave's truck," Rev. Clayton said, turning to look at Dave.

Dave nodded that he would take them.

He and Rev. Clayton delivered the three young men to the bus line, and were greatly amused to see how much better they all felt.

They sang all the way into town in back of the truck. They smiled broadly when they found warm wool blankets to drape around their shoulders during the ride in the truck, for none of them were dressed for colder weather.

At the bus stop, they piled out. Stanley Chester stepped forward.

He had tears in his eyes as he shook the hands of first Dave and then Rev. Clayton.

"We are much obliged," he began and then got choked up.

"We ain't gone forget what y'all done done for us, mister," Petey finished. "And please tell yo' mama thanks again fer my ankle."

"Thanks," said Raymond Parteen, solemnly. "We ain't gone ferget yo' kindness."

Dave told the men that they could keep the old blankets for warmth. Then he and Rev. Clayton left the men at the bus stop and started back up the hill.

"You wanna go home now, Reverend, you pretty near there, or you wanna go back to the house—it's getting pretty late."

Rev. Clayton frowned at Dave with mock hostility.

"You just take me right back up to the house, young fella! Didn't you see that your mother has prepared a sack for me to take home. It wouldn't be polite not to take it. I imagine it's a good little midnight snack!"

I don't believe you!" Dave cried, laughing loudly.

"And I just weigh 148 pounds." Rev. Clayton said, smiling. "Seriously though, Dave, that was very generous what you did for those men."

"I think you helped them most of all, Reverend, by lifting their spirits, but do you think that maybe we were too nice to them? I mean after all, I doubt whether one of us would have met with any hospitality at all had the situation been reversed."

Rev. Clayton started to smile, but when he looked at Dave's face and saw that he was serious, he said, "No kindness is ever lost, Dave."

"I didn't mean the money itself."

"I know you didn't. Kindness is never lost," Matthew repeated. "They didn't seem like real bad fellers—not Klanners do you think?"

"When you're a Negro in the South you can never be sure of any white man and his motives," Dave said sourly.

"Well, we'll go catch 'em then! Take that money back and give them a good butt whipping to boot! What about that?" Matthew suggested.

Dave and the minister stared at each other for a fraction of a second before they both collapsed in laughter, filling the truck and the night with merriment as they proceeded back up the hill.

Rev. Clayton looked at Dave admiringly. "Now, I'm a preacher," he began. "I'm suppose to be nice to folks. It's my job, you know," he said half seriously. "But you. Your attitude toward those men was, well, shall I say surprising. I mean considering the trouble you've experienced with white folks, your friend John Straw, Peter Frauzinou, and all."

"Reverend, every Negro over the age of two has had trouble with white folks," Dave said reasonably. "My mother never taught me to hold hatred in my heart for long. Neither did my dad. I believe in fighting the battles where they are, when they occur, Matthew. You can't just lock up war inside yourself for life."

"You're a smart young man. No, I mean it. A lot of old heads couldn't have said it better. Let me ask you a question, Dave. What if those three had been up to no good-that Stanley, and Raymond and Petey. What then?"

"Then I would have shot them straight through the head and buried them under my fruit trees out back," Dave said without smiling.

They came to the bottom of the mild incline that led to Dave's front yard and Dave turned in, moving slowly up the hill.

"Did you hear all of that mistering? I have never before in my life been called mister by a white person. Neither have I ever heard a black woman called 'lady' or 'mam', have you?" the reverend asked.

"Never," said Dave. "It was kinda funny to hear it, wasn't it?"

"Yes! It is truly amazing what effect a little piece of change can have sometimes."

"Yeah. You're right. I don't think I'll ever see anybody in my life that grateful for three dollars again. Say, Matthew after you git yo' sack," Dave said humorously, "I'm gonna take you home, OK? because I'm getting a little tired."

"Me too. This has been a long day."

"I imagine you want to lay your stomach on a separate pillow and rest it," Dave teased.

"Sound like a good idea!" Matthew smiled.

"We didn't finish our talk. We still have a few things to thrash out."

"I was just going to ask you to come back. I've enjoyed talking with you— seriously. It's helped me straighten out a few things in my head."

SIXTEEN

———✻———

A week after their first meeting, Dave and Rev. Clayton met again as planned for dinner and to discuss what they could do to protect themselves and the community against the violence that blacks all over the South had experienced for longer than either one of them could remember.

After Dave and Rev. Clayton were settled in the room, and Dave had gotten the fireplace going to his satisfaction, the men took the seats they had before—Dave on the davenport and Rev. Clayton in the rocker with his pipe.

"Actually," said Dave, "there isn't much to tell. This discussion of plans will probably be shorter than you expected."

"Go ahead," Matthew said, sticking a match in the bowl of his pipe.

"Well, there are about eighteen of us, that's all—including the men you know— Omar, Pete, Will Henry and LaSalle. The age range is from about twenty-two—we don't want anyone too young—to about fifty or so. We meet way back up in the woods—the Colored Woods," Dave explained. "We've been meeting Tuesday mornings at 11 a.m. Those who have jobs meet with us at Omar's or Will Henry's house Tuesday evenings at eight o'clock. I attend both meetings. The only real commitment we have right now is to protect each other."

Dave took a breath and continued.

"All of the men who have joined us feel the same way—they are sick of the abuse, the violence. Many have lost relatives, brothers, cousins, nephews. One man's father was killed, another's sister. Even the youngest men have seen enough."

"How do you propose to protect each other?" the minister asked quietly. As Dave had talked, Matthew rocked slowly in his chair, puffing on his pipe, seemingly lost deep in thought.

"I'll tell you by way of a story, something that happened when I was eight years old. My father happened to be here, off the road at the time, and I never forgot it."

"Go on," Rev. Clayton said. He had stopped rocking and now leaned forward attentively in his chair.

"Dad had an old bachelor friend by the name of Napoleon Powers. We called him Nappy for short. He was somewhat of an alcoholic, a jicky head—but very lovable. He always had candy in his pockets for me. I was crazy about him. He was a lot older than my father and he used to call my daddy Little Red because of his reddish complexion. Everybody thought him calling my daddy 'little' was funny because my daddy, Rex Bailey, was at least a foot taller than Nappy, but of course he was referring to my dad's age. Well anyway, whenever Nappy got drunk, he would start to run down the sheriff, at that time a big man named Joe Newly, in a good natured way. He would say such things as, 'I wonder how many niggers' asses Joe Newly done kicked dis week,' or 'Joe Newly drinks as much whiskey as I do,' or 'I hear Joe Newly cheats at cards.' Things like that. Harmless within themselves. He really disliked Sheriff Newly because he was always putting him in jail on drunk and disorderly conduct charges. Had Nappy been a white man nothing would have happened."

"So what did happen?" the minister asked anxiously.

"We found out later that some snitch had told Newly that there was a nigger down in Colored Town that talks about you like a dog everytime he gets drunk. Apparently we had snitches even then," Dave said angrily. "Well, the next Saturday about mid afternoon, the sheriff's car pulls up with three men in it. Daddy and Nappy and me were sitting on the porch. They were playing checkers and I was watching. To make a long story short, three big burly men, including the sheriff, hauled Nappy away, beat him senseless, then brought him back hours later to the very spot they had taken him from and threw him up on the porch like an old beaten dog."

"Oh, no!" Rev. Clayton exclaimed.

"Yes indeed," Dave said. "That's exactly what they did. Well, I was hysterical. I was screaming and hollering when they took Nappy...I was worse when they came back with him. I was yelling at my daddy, 'why didn't you help him? Why you let 'em take Nappy away? He's your friend. Why didn't you help him? Let's go after them now,' I begged my father. "My father took me in his arms and he cried. I shall never forget it. 'Son,' he said, 'there's nothing nobody can do to help Nappy. Now, the Law came got him. You understand?' But of course I didn't understand and I blamed my father for what had happened. I thought he should have gotten together with some of his friends and gone and rescued Nappy."

"But of course you understood later that his fear was not so much for himself" Rev. Clayton began.

"As for his family—me and Helena and Mama. Yes, I understood that later. Much later, I'm afraid. These peckerwoods have been known to come back and wipe out whole families of people who have crossed him—and that within the law."

"Yes. I know," Rev. Clayton said sadly.

"When they threw him out of the car six hours later, Daddy and Mama and a lot of his other friends and neighbors had been agonizing all that time about Nappy, people just swarmed around him to help him, thanking God they hadn't hung him. Turned out his wounds were not life threatening—black eyes, busted lips—they had knocked out all of his front teeth. No, they had not taken his life—just his spirit. They had succeeded in totally crushing his spirit. He had been a jolly man, always carrying on a lot of foolishness, Mama called it. Everyone loved to see him coming. But after they beat Nappy, he became very quiet, very solemn, and you couldn't get a joke out of him no matter how you tried. It really hurt my father to see Nappy changed that way."

"What happened to him?"

"Nappy? He died about five years ago without ever regaining his sense of fun and humor. We tried to contact my father but we didn't know where he was at the time."

Rev. Clayton leaned back and puffed on his pipe and resumed his slow rocking, waiting for the rest of the story.

"It's simple, Reverend," Dave stated. "We have decided to die if necessary."

Matthew stopped rocking and leaned forward in the chair again.

"Do you really think I'm going to stand here and let Sheriff Birkens and that little old crazy deputy of his—what's his name? DeBell?—drag off Peter or Omar or anyone else for that matter? No indeed!"

"So you're committed to protect each other. How?" asked the minister for the second time.

"I told you there were eighteen of us. Well, since we started last year, our numbers have grown to forty-one."

"Wow!" exclaimed Rev. Clayton. "That many?"

"That's only a small fraction of the Colored men that actually live in this town, Matthew."

Dave was on his feet walking around the room. He looked down at the minister.

"The plan is this: If they pick up one of us for anything, one of us from the original eighteen will go down to the jail and try to bail the member out, or talk him out, or something. Just one of us—one of the calmer ones, LaSalle Peabody, Peter-or me. We don't want to appear to have a definite leader. You're just targeting that person for trouble that way."

"But you are the leader," Rev. Clayton said with conviction.

"Naw, naw, Reverend, I wouldn't say that. LaSalle Peabody is a hell of a negotiator, and Peter Frauzinou is nowhere slack."

"I see," said Matthew, unconvinced. "Then what?"

"Well, if we can't talk him out of trouble, or pay someone off to get the person out, the next move is theirs, whether it the Law or a lynch mob."

"The next move is theirs? What do you mean?" Matthew asked, squinting up at Dave.

Dave stopped pacing, sat down facing the minister, and said calmly, "Nobody's going to be beaten and nobody's going to be lynched ever again in this town. If they do it it'll be over my dead body."

"Oh, my!" exclaimed Matthew.

Not waiting for the minister to gain his composure, Dave continued: "If one person can't reason with the sheriff, then we'll send another person along with the first one to try to talk things over. If they refuse to talk and want to start some shit— "Dave smiled apologetically to the reverend for the number of cuss words he had used again tonight, "then everything—every weapon in that room of mine—comes out and every single man in the group comes up to the jail ready to do whatever is necessary. You understand, Reverend?"

"My Lord!"

"Yeah," Dave said dryly. "We'll be needing Him."

SEVENTEEN

❧

The weekend being past, Dave and his crew would not have to give serious consideration to the tamale making for a few days. Sunday, Monday and Tuesday were free days for "Dave's boys." Ironically, his men were living better and had more leisure time during the Depression than they had had at any other time in their lives. No corn shucks were needed, so there was nothing at all for Dave's friends to do except enjoy themselves until it was time to rev up the tamale train again.

Will Henry Mead, formerly a frustrated abusive father and wife beater who could not even put a name to his pent up misery, now never ceased to marvel at his good fortune in working for Dave. Now he said, he felt "lak a main."

"Dave Bailey saved mah life when he let me come to work fer him," he would say.

Will's wife and children were delighted with the change in him. Today he was taking his oldest son out with him to fish a little he said, and try to pick a few nuts off the ground for the holidays if there were any left to pick. He kissed his wife good-bye before he left, and because he had not taken the slightest interest in any of his children for a long time and had certainly never kissed his wife good-bye when leaving the house for many years, Emmie Lorraine Mead burst into tears, causing Will Henry to laugh with shame, and beat a hasty retreat, his red face flaming.

Tom "Fool" Leak was helping his favorite washerwoman, Hattie Mackie, with her work. Sometimes he washed, making expert use of the strong lye soap he had made and the large tin washboard. Sometimes he cleaned her house while she washed, getting down on his knees to scrub the wooden floor until it was almost white. Today Tom ironed, which he liked best of all.

"I'm a sho'nuff good ironer," he often bragged. "No cat face wrinkles and buckles on nothin' I irons! If Dave hadn't gie me mah job being a handy man, I could make me a good ol' livin' justa ironin' and ironin', " he said, pleased with himself.

Tom Leak was so thoughtful and helpful and full of foolishness when not thinking about the fire which made him sick, that Hattie Mackie had remarked, "There ain't hardly a house here in Colored Town wha Tom Leak can't sleep at and eat at whenever he wants to, fer as long as he wants. Peepers thinks jus' dat much o'him. Even Miz Keller and her old maid sister loves Tom."

Omar Williams spent most of the day getting ready for winter by chopping wood and putting in a small bin of coal.

Peter Frauzinou was busy at the Boise Café helping to prepare the meals, or "chefing" he called it, in preparation for owning his own fine restaurant one day.

LaSalle Peabody had gone out into the countryside to make a deal on a shoat for Thanksgiving dinner, because he preferred baby roast pig to goose.

Lela Bailey visited her post office box up in White Town, and finding two letters, she slipped them in her sweater pocket.

There was trouble in these letters. She could feel it.

One was from her husband, Rex Bailey, after three long months. It was post marked Baltimore, Maryland. So. He was back in the East again. His last letter had been from Oregon.

The second letter was from Helena. It had been four months since she had heard from her. The two letters being in the post box on the same day—one from her husband, the other from her daughter—Lela considered it a bad sign and they weighed her sweater pocket down like rocks. She would read them at the "prayer table" under the kitchen window where Jesus sat with her, but as Lela walked as fast as she could—which wasn't very fast due to her rheumatism-she felt an almost overwhelming desire to stop and rip the letters open and read them right there in the street.

Instead, Lela moved along the streets of White Town and thought about the Dusters. There had finally been a letter from them last Friday. They were doing well and using the names of Smitty and Lurlean Kane. Thomas had found work in a small packing house right away, and they felt very blessed, Eunice said, because of Thomas' work and because of having such good friends back in West Steward. She and her husband had received a short note from Ralph, and for some reason he had decided to stop and stay in Chicago instead of Detroit. Eunice said Ralph had given himself a new name, but that he didn't want anyone to know what it was. Eunice and Thomas had enclosed eight dollars on their "bill."

Lela had given the money to Dave and promised herself she would write a long letter to the "Kanes" as soon as she could. Meanwhile, she had burned their letter at their request after Dave had read it, but she carefully saved the address: Mrs. Lurlean Kane, 1214 Menokott Lane, Drover, Nebraska. Lela had glued three large letter envelopes in the back inside of her Bible. These envelopes held her most "importantest" papers. She placed the address of Smitty and Lurlean in one of these envelopes, far away from prying eyes.

Now, with steaming tea in front of her and trembling hands, Lela opened her husband's letter first. A blank page, carefully folded, tumbled out. Inside was a twenty and a five dollar bill. He never forgot to send money home even though Lela had written to him long ago, when he was in Washington State for a while, that there was no longer any need to send money home. His last letters still contained small sums.

There were three words inside of her husbands letter: "I'm coming home."

Lela sat for a long time with her hands around the tea cup for warmth; for she had grown suddenly cold. Without a doubt. Trouble. Lela dropped her head and prayed: "What-so-never hit is dear, Lawd Jesus, help me to understand it. To git around hit. Thank you, Lawd. Amen."

After a long sip of jasmine tea Aggie had given her, Lela was ready to read the next letter which was considerably longer:

Dear Mother,   *November 3, 1930*

I am fine, how are you and Dave? Have you heard from Daddy lately? I hope everyone is well. I am coming home for the Christmas holidays. Is that alright with you? I want to bring my children with me although Merry doesn't want to come (smile) you know how she is.

Please write and tell me right away if there is room for us for a while. I thought we'd stay a month are so. Write soon mother. When we get your letter we'll come around December 15th.

Your loving daughter,
Helena

Helena who wrote infrequently and had not spent more than ten days at home since she was married fourteen years ago, wanted to come home for a month? Something wasn't right. Lela would write a letter this very day inviting her daughter home. Then she would spend the rest of the afternoon in prayer and meditation locked in her room next to the kitchen. She would ask the Lord "in all humbleness of spirit" to give her strength to bear the burdens she knew would come.

Dave was taking some time to ponder his relationship with Adrianna James. It was odd that all the reasons he was attracted to "Adri" in the first place, her tomboyishness, ribald humor, and frank and open sexuality, all but repelled him now. He could now see the wildness in her that his mother had commented on in the beginning.

"Why, she's as wild as a jack rabbit!" his mother had remarked half in jest. "I hear tell her mother sent her down here to make a new start. Say she too wild fer Ohio."

Adrianna was loud and unladylike and she drank a little and smoked in public. Also she loved the scene at Princess Thelmas; a place where respectable women were not seen. Dave himself was wary of Thelma's because, though the music was good at all times, and often great, and the atmosphere was open and friendly, it was still a place where drunken fights sometimes broke out; and once in a while someone got cut up because almost everyone brought bootleg liquor and things often got out of hand. Then there were the rooms upstairs—rented for an hour or two at a time to unmarried men and women.

Often the entertainment got very raunchy—the jokes and songs highly suggestive. It was, Lela had heard, no place for a good Christian. It was in her estimation a "devils den."

Then there was Thelma herself. When she got a "head fulla bad whiskey" she became wild, personally throwing anyone out who, in her judgement, did not purchase enough food to warrant their staying for the entertainment. "Alright you cheap ass niggers!" she would growl. "Rise and shine!" And off would come her wild hat of the night revealing an all but bald head. "You ain't gone sit heah all nite fer free! Buy somethin' or git yo' shaggy ass outta mah place of business!"

"Decent" women would have nothing to do with Thelma Kyle.

"Humph!" Adrianna had exclaimed to Dave. "If it's good enough for you, it should be good enough for your future wife!"

On Friday night after work, Dave went to meet Pete, Will Henry and Omar at

Thelma's to hear a terrific new blues band and their female singer Hi-hat Jean, who while singing like nothing they had heard before, did her "nasty" bumps and grinds that brought down the house. Hi-hat Jean and the Mississippi Mud Boys were the most popular group Princess Thelma had ever had.

Because Princess Thelma's was on a hill, just east of the city proper, one could hear the good music pretty well without actually going in, and some of the more adventurous girls would come with their boyfriends in warm weather, bringing blankets or quilts to sit on as they listened to the music from the bottom of the hill. If their friend had thirty-five cents, the young women would often ask their sweethearts to go up the hill and bring them back a treat: Thelma's famous catfish, white buffalo, or crispy fried chicken sprinkled with pepper sauce. For fifty cents, a corrugated tray of chitterlings, slaw, spaghetti, and corn muffins could be had; and icy cold Coca-Cola was five cents in the store, fifteen cents at Thelma's.

Good music and perhaps a snack at the bottom of the hill, yes, but "nice" girls never actually went in to Thelma's—especially after 10 p.m.

When Dave arrived at Princess Thelma's and entered the smokey, pleasantly dim, noisy room at nearly midnight, the first person he saw was Adrianna James. She was dressed in a tight fitting lemon yellow lace dress, with a small matching hat. She was sitting alone or trying to. Men with greasy hair and oily lust in their hearts swarmed around her like bees to a daffodil at her tiny table.

Dave stiffened as he stood in the door of the club watching her. Adrianna, pretending not to see him, was flirting outrageously. She kicked out her long dark legs with glee and laughed excessively long and loudly at a joke one of her admirers made.

Dave walked over and slid into a seat beside her, staring at her in disbelief. Adrianna's fans started to slide away, but one said to Dave before leaving, "Is you da one? Man you sho' got yo'self a fine looking woman! Chocolate candy! If she ever git tired o'you, tell her to come and see me! Pretty woman lak dis can have everythin' I got in dis woil!"

Adrianna laughed up at the departing bold fellow, and then looked at Dave, her eyes full of defiance and mischief.

Seeing Dave's obvious anger, Pete pulled Dave aside and quickly told him how he and his friends had tried to sit with Adrianna to protect her, but she wouldn't let them. She wanted to sit, by herself and think she said.

Dave thanked his friends and they moved away with difficulty in the packed room to a table nearby and sat watching the couple furtively.

"I didn't care for that performance, Adri," Dave said quietly.

"What performance you mean?" Adrianna giggled. "I just like to have me some fun," she said, standing up to kiss Dave on the mouth to sighs and applause from some of the little tables.

Nearly always the aggressor in their lovemaking, she asked, "Ya wanna go upstairs, honey baby? It's been a long time!"

Dave did not answer. Sitting down again she fondled Dave's knees under the table. "I know you ticklish about the knees," she laughed.

"The show is about to begin. Why don't we just sit down and watch it?" Dave suggested, ignoring Adrianna's advances.

Adrianna pouted and sat back in her chair watching the front of the room, which held a simply built stage with white sheet curtains on either side of it. Someone had turned off all the lights except the ones directly over the stage.

"Ladies and gentmens! We's got a real treat fer you tonight!" Princess Thelma bellowed from the stage.

Fifty-two years old, tall and stout, Princess Thelma moved with an exaggerated smooth swishing of her hips that some men found exciting and yelled lewd remarks at her. Tonight she was dressed in red from head to toe, wearing a hat that shot feathers twelve or more inches from her nearly bald head in every direction.

"And nah! Before we bring out Miss Hi-hat Jean and the Mud Boys! A little break to gie y'all time to order up some of da nice fish and chittlins we done prepared for you—'cause when dose Mud Boys comes out heah wit' Hi-hat Jean, y'all ain't gone have time fer nothing but holding on ta your seats!" Thelma said.

As waitresses came out to take orders, Adrianna said, "That piano could stand a little tuning, don't you think?"

"Sounds OK to me," Dave answered, watching Adrianna. What was she really hinting at?

Dark skinned, but lighter in shade than Dave, Adrianna was considered a great beauty, tall, sleek and shiny with dazzling white teeth. She smiled at Dave and arched her back up drawing attention to her perfectly formed melon breasts.

Dave sighed deeply, looking at his fiance with his intense wide-eyed stare.

Adrianna, mistaking his look, moved closer to him and whispered, "Let's leave now. We can do it in that old shed out in back of the house. We used it before."

"I don't have any protection with me, Adrianna!" Dave sighed.

Adrianna drew back and looked hard at Dave. "You know I really don't care!"

"Adri, we have to be careful!"

"Why? I'm twenty-two years old—all my friends got three babies by now. And you! You're almost an old man!" she teased. "Besides, we gonna git hitched anyway. Let's go!"

Dave pushed his seat back, got up, and reluctantly left the club with Adrianna on his arm.

Knowing how much Dave wanted to hear the Mud Boys, his friends looked at each other and shrugged.

Once they were outside and down the hill a bit, Adrianna turned to Dave, her eyes bright and teasing.

"Do you feel like doing something you never did before?" she asked, biting the lobe of Dave's ear.

Dave's eyes went wide with question.

"Oh! You are the brave man alright!" Adrianna burst out with irritation. "But you're so cautious about us! You're gitting chilly on me, ain't you! You don't wanna marry me no more, do you?"

"That's not true, Adrianna," Dave said.

"Yes it is. Look at your face! You look like the cat that swallowed the bird!" Adrianna cried.

"Adri, you dead wrong!" Dave answered, startled that his girlfriend had read him so accurately.

"Really? Am I?" she asked huffily.

"Yes, you are, Adrianna," Dave lied looking into her eyes, hoping that he looked and sounded sincere. His mother had told him that she could always tell when he was lying. Dave hoped that every woman did not have this ability.

"I said, do you wanna do somethin' exciting?" Adrianna asked again, tossing her head defiantly.

"What?" Dave asked trying to keep his voice steady so this wild beautiful girl would not pick up the apprehension he felt. He might marry her yet, he thought— but he didn't want to disappoint his mother with a shotgun wedding.

Adrianna's casual attitude towards sex—and everything else—had increasingly annoyed him in the last few months. She was not keeping the store clean, she often didn't open on time—and some days not at all.

"Well," Adrianna said, becoming coy again. "Your overcoat is wool ain't it? My coat is wool, too." She gingerly slipped out of her coat, laid it on the hard cold ground and lay on top of it shivering from the cold and from excitement at once. Her eyes stared up at Dave bright with challenge.

"Out here? Now?"

"Sure," she giggled. "Why not? There ain't nobody out here but us now."

"But somebody could come by any minute, Adrianna!" Dave exclaimed, his voice a little short of a wail. He had meant to sound as casual as his sweetheart, but he knew he had missed the mark.

"So? You can use your coat to cover our faces!" This statement of hers struck Adrianna as so funny that she lay on her coat writhing with laughter even as she removed her step-ins and tossed them some distance away in the dry branches, where they fluttered flippantly in the breeze.

EIGHTEEN

Aristotle Gillis trudged along across the wide, yellowed, frost bitten field of wild greens after hopping off the slow moving train. The train's box cars were spotted with men, white and Colored, riding the rails looking for work. Aristotle was hungry and cold and this place—West Steward, Arkansas, he had seen on a large sign a few blocks back—seemed as good a place as any to hop off because it advertised two or three sawmills on the side of barns. He was hoping they just might still have a bit of work.

The icy wind bit through his inadequate jacket, the only one he had. He did not own a pair of gloves. Aristotle had started to downgrade himself for not listening to his wife. Maybe he should have stayed at home.

Aristotle Gillis, like thousands of others, thought circulating was better than sitting still and starving. His wife thought differently: "Best stay heah wha you be safe," she had said. "Peepers don't lak white mens roaming 'round in through dey towns—hi you think dey feel 'bout niggers? I hear tell dey lynching strange Colored mens dat dey finds. And I ain't da onliest one done heered dat."

Aristotle had left them—his father, mother, his wife and their four children—in the care of each other, and explained to his wife for the one-hundredth time that he was just trying to find a way to take care of them all, as both his wife and mother had recently lost their jobs as maids, and his father was ailing now with dropsy. So being the man of the house he felt he had to go.

When the Gillis family was down to three dollars, Aristotle left taking one of the dollars—but not before his wife had rubbed his chest down with goose grease and covered it with red flannel the night before he left to ward off colds. She had also gone to the local voodoo woman and got a small grey sack filled with charms—some black cat hairs, a few bones from the spine of an eel, a toenail from a dead man's foot, things like that—to keep her husband safe. She had purchased the sack on credit and hung it around Aristotle's neck on a long thick white string that had been soaked in the grease from a fried catfish.

It was nearly noon when Aristotle hopped off the train in West Steward. He was hungrier than he could ever remember, but he dared not spend any of the dollar, because if worse came to worse, he would have to use some part of it to get back home to Carson City, Arkansas.

Aristotle touched the curious smelling little sack of charms around his neck, which he did not believe in, hoping it would bring him luck anyway. Smiling cynically, he walked towards what he could see was the least built up section of town, for he knew from personal experience that the raggedy part of town, the part with few two-story buildings, would be the Colored section. At night you looked for the section of town that had the fewest lights burning and that would be Colored Town, or the section where most of the Negroes lived.

He walked with his shoulders hunched against the chill looking down at the wide, hard expanse of ground before him. Aristotle wished he could find something, anything, a dollar or two—or maybe even five dollars laying on the ground—something to take back home. He wished he could get his hands on a big bag of nuts, a sack of sweet potatoes, a large sweet smelling ham from a smoke house. Something—even if he had to steal it.

Aristotle broke into a trot now, trying to out—distance the icy wind and the sharp insistence of his hunger pangs. He trotted, trying to get to somewhere fast— to warmth, to something to eat, even to talk to someone about the worry of his situation—for Aristotle could not remember having ever felt so alone in his life.

When you made it to the Colored section of town, some individual or church would always offer you a meal from the little they had. Right now Aristotle thought of how welcomed a plate of greens—even without salt meat—would be, or a saucer of black-eyed peas.

A small shabby house came into view. *Colored?*

If there was a man and his wife, a family, then they would likely share what they had with him, but a lone woman would probably be a little shy of helping a single man roaming around. He hoped and prayed that a Colored family lived in this little house, which sat all alone in the middle of a patch of dead wild greens.

Aristotle knew he was in West Steward, Arkansas, a sawmill town, but what he didn't know was that two white people had been murdered there a little more than a month ago.

From a distance the house looked like a smaller three room shot-gun. It seemed a poor little house, but even poor little houses had vittles, and because he had not eaten since one o'clock yesterday afternoon anything would be welcomed. His good wife had not packed him a lunch because there was nothing to pack. Collie Dean had fried him the last two eggs in the house, given him a hard dry square of cornbread, a cup of hot sweeting water and kissed him good-bye.

As he came closer to the house he saw a very small chicken coop. There would be eggs. At least they might give him eggs and biscuits. Maybe a piece of fried chicken. Aristotle hated to think of what he might do for a few pieces of fried chicken now! Never again would he take food lightly—as something common and plentiful. Food was a treasure, a blessing. From now on he promised he would pray over each meal as his mother had taught him to do more than thirty-four years ago.

When Aristotle reached the small house he was nearly out of wind. His breath huffed out in front of him in little icy white clouds. Leaning against a window, he peered in. His heart sunk. He saw a woman. It was a white house. Now he would have to keep going quite a distance across town yet before he reached the Colored community.

Aristotle peered in again, unable to believe his bad luck. A lone white woman that seemed a little under forty cast her cold blue eyes his way. Their eyes locked for a fraction of a second before she dropped the bundle she was carrying and let out a scream so loud that the few chickens in the hen house started to cackle and fly around.

Aristotle turned to run and found himself staring into the double barrels of a shotgun. Moments later, he was in the back of a pickup truck. The woman with the icy eyes was driving while her dumpy, bad-smelling husband kept the shotgun aimed at the captured man's middle as they delivered Aristotle to the jail in West Steward. The whole trip, the dumpy white man kept his greasy hat pulled down over his beady eyes, a pleased smile on his face. He never uttered a word.

Aggie Pratt heard about a black man being brought to the jail almost immediately. There was a new handy man working for Sheriff Birkens whom Aggie had quickly befriended and paid forty cents a week out of her own pocket for information on the activities that went on in the jail. On the pretext of having to return home for a few minutes to pick up forgotten medication, O'Neill Edwards had quickly found Aggie.

"He a medium dark main, kinda young, dat dem French-coxs from up in da patch done brung in dey truck. Dey say he be tryin' to break into dey house. Nah, what he want to do dat fer? Dey ain't got nuthin'. Dey ain't nuthin' but po' white trash. Dey be looking to git dat reward money the Baycotts is offering, dats all, 'cause dey sayin' he da one what done kilt dose two white folks last month, although I doesn't know hi dey came to dat result!"

Aggie asked the man's name. Perhaps she had heard of him.

"By da name of Aristo-dell Gilly. I talk wit' him a little bit when he in his cell. He just be looking for work, Miz Aggie, jus' lak everyone else. He ain't done nuthin' tuh nobody. He doesn't have no iddy why dey done grabbed 'em. When I told him dey think he done kilt someone, you shoulda seed his eyes buck! I believes dey 'termined to make some kind of example out o'him cause dey can't find somebody to pin dose killins on, dats what I believes—specially dat lil' old DeBell bastard. Dis Aristo-dell Gilly, he be awful scairt, Miz Aggie. Did what I tell you hep him any? Lawd, I sho' hope so."

Aggie assured O'Neill Edwards that his information had helped, without going into any details.

"Nah, you know you can't never say what I tell you," O'Neill said, looking around fearfully. "I would lose me mah job—or worser."

NINETEEN

Times were extremely hard for Cora Lee and Rendell Francox, as they were for almost everyone now. All three of their children had died over the years, leaving them bitter and poor. Two hundred dollars would be a small fortune. Two hundred dollars reward money would enable them to make a new start, if the man they had brought in could be connected with the murders—and Rendell and his wife hoped in their hearts that this Aristotle Gillis was guilty. They thought most niggers were usually guilty of something anyway.

Rendell Francox brought Aristotle Gillis into the jail, and keeping his gun on him, explained the circumstances of the man's capture to Sheriff Birkens and his deputy.

"Look at 'em!" Deputy Hinkle said gleefully. "He shaking lak a bowl of jelly and sweating lak a hog!"

"He looks plenty guilty ta me," one of the sheriff's drinking buddies exclaimed before the sheriff asked him to leave. "Y'all best git dem Monroe fellers back down heah."

Sheriff Birkens said "Alright, take 'em to da interrygating room."

Mebbe, jus' mebbe, the sheriff thought, his spirits lifting a little, da Lawd done seen fit to deliver da killer into mah po' old hains.

Like all good interrogation rooms, the room where they would question Aristotle Gillis was small and nondescript. It contained a medium-sized square table and three wooden chairs. A single bald light bulb hung from the ceiling and an unexpected regular sized ice box sat in a corner. The peeling paint on the walls was grayish beige in color.

The sheriff ordered two more chairs to be brought into the room, because DeBell Hinkle was calling to have the Monroe men sent back to Phillips County after they had already been in West Steward as extra investigators for more than a month.

171

O'Neill Edwards had cleaned the musty little room this morning, placing clean coffee cups on top of the ice box. It had never been used as an interrogation room before—the sheriff used it mainly to entertain his friends, and to eat the meals that Nettie Lyons sent over. In fact, O'Neill had been getting ready to pick up the sheriff's dinner from his house just before the prisoner arrived.

While the Francoxes waited in the main office to be told something or another, O'Neill thought he would ask the sheriff if he still wanted his dinner. He had to get out again—he had to tell somebody what was happening.

"Yah. Sho'. I think dat mebbe dat will be the onliest other meal I'll git today, cause we got us some work to do heah!" the sheriff exclaimed enthusiastically.

O'Neill could tell the sheriff was feeling more hopeful; his voice sounded lighter, more in control than before when he thought he did not have, and possibly would never have, a suspect.

Well, O'Neill thought, his spirits were not lifted—quite the opposite, for when he went back into the interrogation room to get the keys for the truck, he had caught the unfortunate man's eye for an instant. He thought him the most pitiful looking man he had ever seen. Clearly he was filled with fear—and he expected no help from O'Neill Edwards. In that flicker of eye contact, all was said. They both knew what was going to happen to him now. They would question him on his whereabouts on the night of the murders. They would beat him—badly. They would lynch him. His body would be handcuffed, weighted down and thrown in the muddy Mississippi River. He would be tied across a railroad track. He would be swung from a tree as a large crowd watched. Then the sheriff could tell the good people of West Steward, Arkansas that they could rest easy now because they had found the killer, he had confessed—and justice had been done. Oh, not in the way that the sheriff knew was right and proper—but then the crowd had gotten out of hand.

Already the beatings had started. As O'Neill Edwards walked out to get into the truck, he heard DeBell Hinkle ask the captured man in a high self-important voice filled with rage, "What you go peeping in white folks windows fer?!" Whack!

As Aristotle received the blow, he thought about his family. Why had he not listened to his wife? And who would look out after them in these hard times once he was gone?

O'Neill Edwards pushed the old truck as fast as it would go. He had to hurry. He had to get the sheriff's dinner back to him and find his friend Roger Mulright. Roger, the rocking chair maker—he knew everybody in town. Perhaps he would know what to do. There had been talk around town that somebody—Colored—had gotten the Dusters out of town before their son Ralph could be questioned. Maybe this mysterious person could help this poor man. *Lawd, Lawd, Lawd!* O'Neil thought.

O'Neill drove down past Soliz's Chili parlor at the "back door" of White Town. Then he turned and drove further into White Town, past the shedding trees and large neat houses that were so much bigger and better kept than the houses in Colored Town.

As O'Neill drove, he thought of the sheriff's offer. He was looking for another "boy" to replace his sissy snitch Marko Horton.

"Whatsa matter O'Neill? You ain't got no ambition to step up? I could pay you a dollar mo' a week den you gittin'. All I wanta know is enough to keep down any ruckus dats a-brewing in Colored Town fore anythin' get serious down dere. I calls hit bein' a good citizen. I don't see no hurm in hit."

Well, I sho' could use an extry dollar each week, but ahm no white folks snitch! O'Neill thought hotly as he drove along, *Birkens jus' gone have to find hisself another sissy boy!*

O'Neill Edwards pulled up to the sheriff's neat little clapboard house and hopped out, calling to Nettie Lyons as he took the steps two at a time.

"Nettie! Dey got a main captured up in da jail house and dey fixing to lynch 'em sho' as I'm telling ya!" O'Neill exclaimed after Nettie had opened the door to his insistent banging.

"Quieten yoself down nah and tell me 'zactly what done happen. Here, take a seat, and keep it low," Nettie suggested.

"Yas, alright Nettie," O'Neill said, and sweating profusely and running his words together in urgency, he related the story from beginning to end as he had seen it unfold.

"Good Lawd Almighty!" Nettie exclaimed after she had heard all O'Neill had to say. "Ahm goin' wit' you to Roger Mulrights!"

"You can't leave heah! Da sheriff gone see you in da truck wit' me!"

"Naw he ain't," Nettie replied, "'cause you gone first take me over to Mae Bell's, den you take da dinner basket up to da jailhouse."

"Well, alright," O'Neill said reluctantly. Scared and confused, he didn't quite know what should be done.

"And you go back and sat in dat jail unless dey throws you out! Me and Mae Bell will git a-holt to Roger. He'll know what ta do."

O'Neill was feeling somewhat better now after confiding in Nettie—women folk always knew what to do. From his mama on down, *dey knows hi to git da ball rollin'*, he thought.

When they came to Mae Bell's tiny rental house, Nettie gave the dinner basket to O'Neill, and got out of the truck without looking back.

"Go!" she said, "and try not to let nothin' happen to da main before we can git us a plan up."

"Nah, hi in da woil ahm gone do dat?" O'Neill cried.

"I don't know. But if dey look lak dey fixing to make some kinda move, you run outta dat jail and find somebody you heah?"

As soon as Nettie told Mae Bell what had happened she said three words: "Let's find Aggie."

"I thought one of the men folks, mebbe Roger Mulright—he right level headed."

"No. Aggie Pratt is da one to find. She right close to Dave and all. I talked to her dis moaning. Dis is Wednesday. Da day when Dave and Pete and a lotta others takes off, but Aggie kin find 'em wit' her running boys."

"Running boys?"

"Yas, dats what dey calls 'em, cause dey be running all over town finding folks."

Mae Bell put on her winter coat and the two women set out down the road, asking as they went.

Finally they spotted Aggie with her basket, on her way back from White Town, wearing a frayed blue coat many sizes too big.

"Hey, wha you two goin' in dis cold weather?" she called cheerily.

Seeing their serious expressions, Aggie said, "What done happened? Y'all look fit to be tied!"

"Sheriff got a main locked up in jail dat dey trying to pin dose killins on!" Nettie burst out. "Dose no count Francoxes brought 'em in. Dey looking to get dat ree-ward money dat Baycote family done offered."

"And Henry wants to solve dis case by puttin' it on someone to please da white folks, even doe he done tole me mo' den once dat he didn't think no Colored person done kilt dose peepers!" Mae Bell retorted heatedly. "I oughta go up at dat jail and kick his ol' broke down ass!"

"Anyhow, if dat main done kilt two white folks, why would he be comin' back any wha near dis town?" Nettie asked sensibly.

Aggie was calm. O'Neill had already told her about the jailed man, and she felt they still had time. The sheriff could not afford to show that he couldn't exercise any control. If things were going to finally break down it would probably be later in the evening. They had to bank on that—and work as fast as they could.

Both Nettie and Mae Bell seemed close to tears as they walked along towards the paved bus line, further into Colored Town.

"Hit ain't no need to cry y'all" Aggie said. "Everythin gone be alright. Let's git to Will Henry, he be livin' right near here. He jus' done come back from fishin' wit' his son. I passed dem comin' back when I was on my way to White Town. He say hit's too cold fer fishin' after all. He say he gone go home and eat dinner," Aggie said, subtly taking charge. "You know how Will laks ta eat!"

When the women arrived at Will Henry Mead's, the family was eating dinner. Will's wife, Emmie Lorraine, scurried around the table serving her husband and their five children.

They looked so mismatched, Aggie thought. Will was so big and red skinned with the flaming red hair that a good number of Southern Negroes had—and Emmie so tiny and black.

Aggie knew Emmie Lorraine only slightly. They often waved to each other and passed the time of day in that excessively familiar and friendly manner that Southerners have. It was necessary to speak, and to talk to everybody you met if you didn't want to be considered hinkty.

"Hey!" Will Henry called out to the women. "What three fine looking wimmens lak y'all doin' comin' to mah doe in the middle of da day? Come on in. Make yo'self comfortably!" Will bellowed. Apparently he had not heard that the sheriff was holding a black man in jail in relation to the Love Nest case.

The more sensitive Emmie Lorraine stared at the women with wide eyes. Nettie and Aggie were working women. They did not visit in the middle of the day. She knew something was wrong. Emmie Lorraine looked from one woman to the other, trying to make sense of their presence.

"Y'all want some nice cold lemon-aid? Y'all want something ta eat?" she asked still watching the three women closely, especially Mae Bell and Nettie, whom she had never met before, but she knew who they were. Nettie worked for the sheriff, and the other one…

Aggie, attempting to lighten the situation and not frighten the children, asked, "What ya got? Hit sho' smells good," as she walked closer to the table. The parlor and dining room was one medium sized room, the small kitchen directly behind it.

Will Henry knew Nettie Lyons vaguely. He knew Mae Bell "to speak to," but nothing more—except she was Sheriff Birkens' whore. Everybody knew that. He wondered what on earth she was doing here, but he showed no emotion except pleasant hospitality.

Aggie would tell him everything in time, he was sure.

Aggie said to Emmie, "Chile, everythin' looks so good, and Lawd knows I'm hoingry, but I'm 'fraid we gone have to 'cept yo' nice offer next time. We's got us some business." Moving closer to Emmie, Aggie placed her arm around her shoulder and whispered, "Girl, dey got a main locked up in da jail, dey trying to pen dem killings on 'em."

"Oh, no!"

"Yas, dey has. We heah on business. We need to borry Will fer a spell. Where kin we go ta talk?"

Emmie led Aggie to a back bedroom beside the kitchen. "Is dis OK? Da chirrens can't hear nothin' from heah."

"Dis is fine. Tell da others to come on in heah. You wanna be in wit' us?"

"No. no!" Emmie answered, her eyes going wide again. She had been scared all of her married life—of childbirth, of poverty, finally of Will Henry. It would take more time before fear was leached from her soul. For now she was content to live on Will's newfound courage. "I'll jus' stay and eat wit' da chirrens."

Will Henry sat on the bed in the small immaculate bedroom. Aggie and Mae Bell found a perch on a heavy old trunk that set against the wall and Nettie settled gratefully in a rocking chair that had a comfortable pillow in its seat.

Aggie related the story of the jailed man to Will Henry in as much detail as she knew. "Da sheriff don't believe he had nothin' to do with the killings, but somebody heard him say dat dey needed some action on dis case."

Will Henry listened much more calmly then he would have in the past—before he met Dave, before he became a member of the Circle. For he felt more in control now, safer and more courageous, because they had their developing plans, and none of them were alone anymore. Will Henry wanted to handle this himself, to show Dave—and the others in Dave's brief absence—that he could be cool and decisive, not the wild hot head he once was. Aggie, looking at Will Henry mistook his bland, placid expression for just the opposite of what it was. She thought he didn't, wouldn't know what to do in order to free the imprisoned man.

"Wha Dave at?" she asked a little crossly. Maybe she should not have stopped at the first Circle member's house she came to. Maybe she should have looked for Peter or Omar, even Roger Mulright.

Watching her face and hearing the slight skitter of irritation in her voice, Will Henry read Aggie exactly.

"Dave is out of town, up at da sto' in Epps, I think," Will said. "We can handle dis, Aggie. First let's do what Dave always do, but let's be quick, although I think we still have a good amount of time left befoe da sheriff makes a move. Those no good peckerwoods usually wait until da nite to do dere nasty work."

"What does Dave do?" Mae Bell asked Will Henry. "You said let's do what Dave always do."

Again Will Henry looked at Aggie before answering. He still did not know why the sheriff's woman was here. This was Circle business. And why was Nettie Lyons here? The sheriff's housekeeper and the sheriff's woman. What was their interest in this case?

"I see you looking at me funny, Mistah Mead," Mae Bell said. "I think I know what you be thinkin', but let me tell you somethin', Mistah Will Henry," Mae Bell said fervently, "and I'll be quick about it."

Mae Bell told Will Henry how she had poured urine over the sheriff when Billy Binder was lynched, how she had made the sheriff promise he wouldn't harm anyone in Colored Town or she would leave him, how she felt about her people, her son. She stopped by telling them all, "I got enough money saved up nah. I'm going to leave dat sorry assed old peckerwood any day nah anyhow! Ain't dat right Aggie? Ax Aggie. She done knowed 'bout mah tru feelins for nah on ta two years."

Aggie nodded vigorously. "She tellin da truf, Will. She done kept down a lotta stuff in Colored Town over da years. She wit' us!"

Now it was Will Henry's turn to show wide eyed surprise. He looked at Mae Bell as if for the first time. "Well, I'll be damn," he said smiling.

Mae Bell smiled back at him. "I jus' want y'all to do one thing fer me," she said looking from Aggie to Will Henry. "When dis is over and ahm gone, will y'all please let da peepers of dis town know dat I had a hand in doin' somethin' fer mah peepers?"

Aggie and Will Henry smiled and nodded. "You kin count on dat,"Aggie assured Mae Bell. Will Henry shook his head still unable to believe what he had just heard. Up to this moment Will Henry had thought he had Mae Bell's number—a Colored woman of the worse kind. Still looking at Mae Bell, Will Henry exclaimed "Well, I'll be got dog!"

"Dave always sez let's pool our iddys, Miz Mae Bell. Anyone got any iddys?"

"Dis is mah idear," Mae Bell said. "Why don't I jus' go up to dere jail and say ahm his cousin and dat I wants to pay da bail and git 'em out. Da sheriff don't dare to cross me," Mae Bell said haughtily. "He know what I do when he make me mad!"

"But you can't go up and shame him in public in front of everyone," said Will Henry.

"I think Mistah Mead is right, Mae Bell," Nettie agreed. "Hi dat gone look? Lotta peepers knows 'bout you and him—and Birkey. You might make matters worser."

"How? I doesn't believe y'all! We talkin' 'bout a main's life. Alright den, I'll say he my main and he was in da bed wit' me da whole nite dem peepers was killed if I has to," Mae Bell said.

Both Aggie and Will Henry laughed out loud.

"Girl, you a sight!" Aggie said. "But, I don't think nobody would believe yo' story."

"What we gone do?" Nettie asked tiredly. She didn't harbor any hope that anything could really be done.

"Y'all all know dere herb main, Mistah Candle? Back up in da woods?" Will Henry asked.

"Yas."

"We goin' ta see him. Aggie, git yo' coat on. Me and you is got a trip to make," Will Henry said. "You other ladies jus' make yo'self right comfortable 'til we gets back. We ain't gone be long. Aggie, we got to git da running boys ready. Dave might be at da sto' and he might not. We ain't got no time to go looking fer 'em."

Finding Dave first probably would have been the best thing to do, but Will Henry was anxious to show that he could handle this situation in an effective way himself, so when Aggie made this suggestion in the tidy little bedroom, Will Henry pretended not to hear her.

Aggie's boys, Arky and Villa, as everyone knew, could run and find anyone who needed to be found in a very short time. Everyone also knew there were only five telephones in all of Colored Town—all in places of business, but there was no phone in Dave's store yet.

"If the boys ain't located Dave by da time me and Aggie get back, den I'll look for him in da truck," Will Henry said, as he and Aggie walked out of his house heading for the "herb man's" place.

TWENTY

A ggie Pratt and Will Henry Mead arrived at John Candle's old sprawling house in the truck Will Henry had borrowed. They drove up into his yard, which oddly still held budding summer flowers in great profusion.

They were met at the door by Miss Rindton, John Candle's assistant and long time "companion," as she liked to be called.

Aggie figured Martha Rindton was at least eighty-five years old, but she "lookted good," Aggie thought. Her face "was jus' as good and smooth and all, and she wasn't all stoopedy over or nothin'!"

The little woman, even shorter than Aggie, peered up at them. "Good afternoon, howdy do," she said in a friendly tone. "Hi y'all lak mah flayers! Dey real pretty aint dey? Come on in."

Miss Rindton sat them down at a large round table in the parlor. Six chairs were the only other furniture. Although the sun was shining brightly, the house was dark, dank, even brooding.

"You must wait awhile," Martha informed them. "John Candle be takin' his herbal enema rat nah. He be finished shortly. Y'all sat down and make yo'self comfortable. I'll git y'all a cuppa tea," Miss Rindton said, not surprised by these visits, for many people came to see John Candle.

Will Henry started to light a cigarette.

"Uh-uh!" Miss Rindton exclaimed, wagging a finger. "Ain't no kind o'smokin in heah!"

Will Henry fidgeted, looking at the clock. "What you say he doin'?" he asked the assistant.

Seeing their questioning expressions, Martha Rindton was glad to elaborate. Eager to share knowledge she had spent years obtaining. "An enema is the best thing in da woil fer ya. Hit clean out all da poisons in yo' system, and enable ya ta live a long time—almost till you ready to die yo'self!" Martha said, laughing.

Aggie looked at Will Henry disdainfully. "Humph, humph! I sho' hopes he washes his hains good fo' he comes out heah." Aggie whispered to Will Henry.

After a few moments, Miss Rindton returned with tea.

Will Henry looked at it warily.

"Go head and drink hit," Aggie whispered, "hit ain't nothin' but mint tea—nothin' to be a-scared of!"

Aggie drank her tea and smiled at Martha, who had sat down facing them. She did not inquire as to why they were here.

Aggie was fascinated by the room she found herself in.

"Dem shelves and drawers and all," she asked of Miss Rindton, "is dat where Mistah John keeps his stuff?"

"Yes, mam!" Martha said, pleased at the young woman's show of interest. "And in dem jars too. The master got about a million different potions in heah—and he knowing dem all!" Martha said proudly.

"Lotta white folks creep up heah for medicine, but dey don't want nobody to know a Colored main done done dem some good. Nah ain't dat a shame! Well, white folks is lak dat. Dey don't wanna gie the black main credit fer nothin'! Some o'dese white folks—and you'd be surprised hi high up some o'dem is—dey come up heah...some o'dem ain't even down worth helping 'cause dey be so low down to Colored peepers. I say to master, let 'em die! But he say naw. I'll just charge 'em ten times what I charge da black folks! Hee, hee, hee, hee!" Martha chortled, bending in her chair from her neck to her knees with laughter.

"Dis enema he taking," Aggie said to Miss Rindton, "what kind of stuff he be using, do you know?"

"Why sho' I do!" Martha said merrily, and she rattled off the names of several herbs: "Wild alum root, shepard's purse, chickweed, white oak and bayberry bark, and two, three chopped dried leaves from Africa dat he grow in the back out yonder."

"Goodness!" said Aggie impressed.

"Yas, yas," Miss Rindton said, pleased to show how well she knew her business.

They had been in Candle's waiting room ten minutes, and Will Henry had started to pace nervously around the room. It was nearly two o'clock. There was still time, he thought, but he wished the old man would hurry and finish his douche. The whole house had an odor that Will Henry could not place in any memory slot—a scent strange, yet familiar. As he walked around with the uneasy scent of this house assailing his nostrils, Will became more and more tense. Perhaps it was just this whole mess, he reasoned. At any rate he was happy to hear someone coming swiftly down the hall—for he wanted to leave this mysterious house as soon as possible.

Suddenly the slight form of John Candle appeared. The fit looking herbalist greeted everyone pleasantly, then he sat down at the round table with Aggie and Will Henry.

They explained why they were here to see him.

After hearing their story, John Candle's hands flew to either side of his head, and he held his ears and shook his head as if what he had heard was too distasteful to stand.

"Mah, mah, mah!" he exclaimed. "Dey jus' will not leave da black main alone will dey? What y'all want me ta do?"

"Kin you gie us somethin' that mebbe kin be slipped in a drink what will knock dem lawmens out so as we kin git da main out? Somethin' dat can't be traced?" Will Henry asked.

"Sho'. I kin do dat," John Candle said with calm assurance.

"We got a main working up in da jail. He kin git dis main out once we git the lawmens outta da way, I believe," Will Henry added.

"Den what?" the herbalist asked.

"Well," Will Henry said, unsteadily making it clear to all that his plan was still forming in his head, "we gets him outta town, see? Den we go git his fambly and git dem out too—gie him some money to git somewhere jus' lak we did…"

"Sshhhh!" Aggie warned.

"Oh, yeah!" Will Henry said, catching Aggie's warning before names were revealed, but both Aggie and Will Henry got the distinct feeling that it was useless to try to hide anything from the hooded eyes of the old herbalist.

"So y'all knows wha dis main and his fambly lives?" asked the herbalist.

Will Henry turned lamely to Aggie, hoping she had the answer.

She did.

"A Colored main dat works in da jail," Aggie said, not wishing to disclose a name unnecessarily. "He done writ down everything. He listens real good. Main by da name of Aristodell Gilly," Aggie said mispronouncing the jailed man's name, "He and his family live over in Carson, Arkansas. We got da street and house number from da records."

"You mean O'Neill Edwards?" the little man said smiling, amused that these two young people thought he didn't know what was going on in West Steward and Steward just because he rarely left his house.

There was no need to leave. All the news came to him—and since he was one hundred and one years old, there was nothing else left out in the world to see, he figured. He had been a slave. At age thirty-nine, he had made his way to Africa and remained there for twelve years. He had lived with many women and fathered many children. Most of the women he had outlived—most of his children were scattered to the four winds. Before taking Martha as his last companion, John Candle had fathered his last child by a thirty year old woman. He had been over eighty at the time.

Sitting at the table, his face resting in his hands, John Candle was lost in reverie, as he was often these days, even though his mind remained as sharp as ever.

"Mistah Candle?" Will Henry said thinking the old man had fallen off.

"I got jus' what you need," the old herbalist said as if there had been no lull in the conversation. "Nah keep quiet and listen. Don't interrupt me!"

Martha Rindton was already bringing a jar without being told what was needed. "Mozumbo Kelè?" she asked.

"Dat's da one, sugar!" the herbalist exclaimed. "Yo' memory is still right fine!"

The old woman smiled at the compliment.

The herbalist opened the jar releasing a very pleasant sweet scent into the room. The scent was of tobacco and—cherries? With a little hint of roses?

Will Henry pulled back, trying to rid his nose of these alien scents.

John Candle removed a few of the fat shiny balls from the jar. They were black in color, and resembled large beads such as a woman might wear around her neck.

"Dese" he said, holding four of the beads in his palm, "is mahzumboo kele-lay," he said, drawing the word out dramatically. "Dese black ones is nice. Dey make you sleep and nothin' can wake you up until dey wear off. Dey use dem over in the mother country—dat's Africa in case you never heered of it," the herbalist said with mild sarcasm. "Dey use dese to put peepers to sleep when dey operate on dem or somethin'. Dey last most exactly five hours. You wake up feeling rested and good, no matter if you even down slept on a hard flo'."

Will Henry was about to ask a question, but the herbalist stopped him.

"Keep quiet, I say!" he exclaimed sharply. "You ax questions when I finish. If you got a question den."

183

Will Henry reddened and kept quiet.

"Da black ones is pretty and mostly harmless, but dese," he said, taking red beads in his other palm, "dese red ones will kill yo' ass in five minutes flat!"

John Candle broke into high, shrill laughter at his last statement.

"Dead," he continued, chuckling, "as a wurm stepped on by a two hundred pound main!" The herbalist threw his head back and lifted his sandaled feet up from the floor laughing with all of his might.

Aggie giggled and Will Henry smiled indulgently.

"Well, nah!" John Candle exclaimed, trying to stop laughing. "Which one of dese you want? Da black or da red mozumbo?

"Never mind!" he said before anyone could answer. "Y'all don't aim to kill no one right? Den take dese heah black ones and dis is hi you gone use 'em: make a small tiny pin hole in da pill lak dis."

John Candle showed them how to puncture the beads. "Da liquid won't run out none 'til you squeeze 'em. Put dem in some cellophane paper 'til you ready fer 'em. Nah, you don't put dem in no drink. No. No," he said emphatically. "You put dese in da coffee cups. A few drops a piece in each cup. When the air hits da mozumbo kelé, hit dry clear right away. Nobody know hit's in da cup. Dey drink coffee from dat cup, dey git sleepy, regular lak, in about fifteen minutes wherever dey at, dey go to sleep, boom! Jus' lak dat. Dis also work in a water glass if necessary. Let's hope dem lawmens be drinkin' some coffee while dey whippin' dat po' main's head. Nah! You got any questions?

"We jus' got to git dis some hi to O'Neill," Aggie muttered under her breath.

"What if someone catch our main in da jail wit' dese beads?" Will Henry asked.

"Drop 'em on da flo' and step on 'em. Dey don't look lak nothin' dangerous. Is dat all da questions? Well den good luck. When O'Neill Edwards washes da cups out, all traces of da pills disappear. Even down if he don't wash da cups and pot, dat stuff jus' disappears after while, and dere ain't no way in da woil to trace hit," John Candle said, smiling.

Aggie noticed that the old man had most of his teeth!

"'Course dere ain't no charge," the herbalist said. "Just remember dere is lots of good stuff over 'cross da pond in da motherland."

A confused look passed between Aggie and Will Henry. This was the second time the little man had mentioned some motherland. This wasn't the Africa they had heard about, was it? Surely not. Everyone knew there was nothing there but jet black savages with filed down teeth. If you went there you were likely to end up in a dinner pot. Both Aggie and Will Henry knew that was true because they had seen it at the picture show more than once.

They promised to let the herbalist know what happened.

"No need to do dat. I will know," he said, smiling mysteriously like a naughty child.

TWENTY-ONE

---※---

When Aggie and Will Henry returned to Will's house with the black beads, Aggie immediately sent her boys to look for Dave. She assumed that Omar was at home and that Peter was at the Boise Café. Will Henry could pick them up on the way back from the jail.

Will Henry drove Nettie back to the jail on the pretense of having forgotten the dessert, which she had. Knowing that Deputy DeBell Hinkle was crazy about sweets, Nettie knew he would want her come back with the baked banana pudding.

When Nettie got out of Will Henry's truck and went into the jail house to get O'Neill Edwards, who would bring back the banana pudding, Nettie would have ample time to pass on instructions on how the black beads were to be used to the jail house handyman.

The group had discussed approaching the sheriff and offering bail or something back at Will Henry's house, because that was the plan they had originally talked about with Dave, but everyone present had agreed that offering bail would not work in this case: this was a murder case, and the Law was more than willing to pin the crime on the man they were holding—and since a crowd had already formed in front of the jail, they felt the sheriff could not negotiate if he wanted to.

So the group dropped the bail plan altogether. They would go with the black beads, if Dave agreed. They hoped they could get to use them in the way the herbalist had described. Right now the black beads were their only hope of rescuing Aristotle Gillis from a lynch mob.

When Nettie, Will Henry and Aggie were a good distance away, they could see that a mob had gathered in front of the jail, a bunch of unemployed, frustrated, hateful men. It was such men as these that made violence possible and likely.

As Will Henry came even closer in the old truck, the stench of hatred was so heavy in the air that Nettie remarked that she could almost smell a lynching.

Nettie got out of the truck and walked through the mob of about eighty men

186

that had gathered. As Will Henry tried to turn the truck around and head for home, the crowd eyed them suspiciously and with glee.

"Well, look lak dey done cot da coon dat don kilt dose white peepers! I say let's us string 'em up!" one man said loudly from the crowd. He meant for Will Henry and Aggie to hear.

"Yeah! Yeah!" the men roared.

One man had a rope. "It would pleasure me ifn you used mah rope to hang him wid," he exclaimed. "Bring dat nigger on out heah! What Birkens talking 'bout a trial! We got da justice tree right out side o'town!"

Nettie walked up the steps of the jail, relieved to see O'Neill appear at the door at her insistent knocking.

He was sweating profusely.

"Lawd!" he said quickly, nearly hysterical. "Y'all gotta git dis main outta heah! Come nite, dey gone lynch 'em fer sho'! Dey done already beat 'em half to death! You see dat crowd out dere!"

"Cool on down. Everythin' gone be alright," Nettie said quietly, trying to calm her friend.

"OK! OK!" O'Neill shouted, about to jump out of his skin.

"Nah, where da sheriff!" Nettie called out almost gaily. She went swiftly towards the interrogation room before O'Neill could stop her. She wanted to see Aristotle Gillis for herself.

"Hey!" O'Neill called loudly to Nettie, "You not allowed back dere!" he yelled without trying to stop her.

Nettie knocked on the interrogation room door and burst in without waiting to be asked. After all, she had delivered the sheriff's food to this room many times before.

"Good Gawd A'mighty!" she called out after seeing the captured man. Nettie dropped her pocketbook and ran back down the hall screaming. She would never forget his face, even though she had only seen it for a few seconds. The man's face was a massive bloody blob of flesh.

One eye was closed and swollen tight. His lips were huge, bloody, rubbery things. There was blood all in his hair running down his shirt. He raised his head and looked at her with his one good eye. He looked utterly abandoned and hopeless. He looked like a dead thing still moving.

Nettie stumbled down the hall with the sheriff running after her.

"Nettie, Nettie! What you heah fer? You got no business coming back to da interrogatin' room!" the sheriff exploded. "O'Neill! I done tole you not to let nobody back heah!"

"She was too fast fer me, Sheriff Birkens, suh! She rant pass me!" O'Neill explained, trembling.

Nettie had collapsed in a chair retching. "Oh Lawd! Oh Lawd!" she said over and over again.

"Nah, Nettie!" Sheriff Birkens said in a soothing tone. "Ain't nothin' wrong wit' dat prisoner. Ain't nothin gone happen to him. We jus' questioning him a bit—den we'll probably let him go."

"I got eyes and I can see!" Nettie snapped, surprised at her own anger and courage. "Y'all done beat dat main half to death and you doesn't even down know if he be da one!"

"Nah, Nettie! dats enough," the sheriff exclaimed with a firmness that he did not feel. He felt numb, sick. He knew the deputy and the Monroe men had been allowed to go too far—much too far—and then there was all that mob outside ready to take the law in their own hands.

"Dat main, fer yo' information, has done confessed," he said somewhat lamely.

O'Neill looked dumbfounded at this revelation. He gave Nettie a wretched look of complete misery.

"Dats right!" Nettie shouted out bitterly. "You whip me lak a dog all day long and I'll confess I kilt Jesus!" Raising from her chair, Nettie said, "I came heah lak I do a heap o'times to bring yo' somethin' to eat! I forgot your sweets. Do you want dat banana pudding or no?" she asked loud and angry.

"Well DeBell will sholly be wanting hit," the sheriff said weakly.

"Well come on, O'Neill!" Nettie said before the sheriff had time to protest O'Neill's leaving.

"O'Neill will bring hit back to ya," Nettie said, moving briskly towards the door. O'Neill hesitated, looking at the sheriff, thinking about the crowd outside.

"I say come on O'Neill!" Nettie shouted, giving the helpless servant a fierce look. The man jumped at the tone in Nettie's voice and the ferocious look on her face.

"Yas, yas! I be comin' rat nah!" he said following Nettie reluctantly out of the door.

The sheriff followed Nettie and O'Neill to the door, and seeing the crowd that was growing by the hour, he shouted with real anger, "Y'all gwon on away from heah nah! Dis ain't no gawd-damned circus! I say git on away from heah! We ain't 'stablished dat the main we got is da main what done hit."

There was a great roar from the crowd. "Hang dat nigger!"

"He da one!"

"I say let's pour some coal oil on 'em and set 'em a fire!"

"He gone git a fair trial," the sheriff yelled over the crowd.

"Who sez?!" the man with the rope cried.

Nettie turned an angry face to the sheriff and said before she got in the truck, "I thought you said he done confessed already!"

The crowd continued to roar for blood as Nettie climbed with difficulty into the cab of the old jail-house truck with O'Neill. When Nettie was in her seat she turned to O'Neill.

"What in da woil is da matter wit' you O'Neill?!" she cried, her face swollen with rage. "Ahm trying to git you outta da jail so ah kin talk to you 'cause you a big part of our plan to save dat main, and here you is astanding dere lak a gawd damn fool lookin' in dat peckerwood sheriff's mouth! I declare! Sometimes you act lak you ain't got right good sense! Move over!" Nettie said bumping the sheriff's man hard with her elbow.

Ironically, the plans to free Aristotle Gillis were made at Sheriff Birken's kitchen table. The sheriff's house was separated a little distance from the houses on either side of him, and banked with bushes and hedges on both sides.

Aggie and Mae Bell had taken the bus, then walked the rest of the way to the sheriff's house, where they waited for the others, grateful for the bushes that covered them as they waited for Nettie.

When they were seated around the table with the shades pulled down, Nettie showed O'Neill the beads and told him how they were to be used. Then not wishing to stretch friendship so far out of shape that it would not snap back into its old familiar curves, Nettie apologized to O'Neill for losing her temper at the jail. O'Neill accepted her apology graciously stating that they were all nervous and upset and that Nettie's behavior was "understandable."

"Did you see da main?" Aggie asked. She wanted to hear and she didn't-for she knew how brutal jail house beatings could be.

"Yas. I seed 'em. His face be so bloody look lak somebody done throwed a bowl o'red jelly on hit. Dats hi dey done beat 'em."

Unexpectedly, Nettie started to cry.

Never since she had known Nettie Lyons had Mae Bell seen her cry—in fact, had she been asked she would have said no, Nettie does not cry-she is too tough, too independent. Other women cry—not Nettie. She had seen her eyes fill with tears, but they never rolled down her hardy cheeks.

Harboring these thoughts of her cousin, Mae Bell found her tears shocking— and deeply touching. They brought out every ounce of her pent-up rage for "peckerwoods" in general and Henry Birkens in particular.

"Henry Birkens, you gone pay for all da pain you done caused, you hear me!" Mae Bell shouted, her heart twisted with hatred so deep it startled even her.

Nettie reached out and touched Mae Bell's arm, using her as a brake to stop her own tears. "Don't do nothin' crazy on mah account Mae. Hit's gone be alright. We gone be alright." Abruptly her tears ended and Nettie looked around at the concerned faces at the table, somewhat ashamed by her display of emotion.

TWENTY-TWO

The boys, Arky and Villa, knew where to look for Dave, they thought. If he was at his stores, he would be coming back down the pike through West Steward. If Dave did not come through this way "after awhile," Aggie had told them, then the boys must go and ask Lela, Dave's mother, where he was.

They didn't want to ask Lela right off because, Aggie and Will Henry agreed, it would worry her unnecessarily. Will Henry wanted to tackle their problem himself in the absence of their leader, but final decisions were always left to Dave.

The west entrance to West Steward was called "the gate" because you could get on the pike there and follow it down to several little towns on either side.

Arky sat on one side of the gate in the road, Villa waited on the other, bundled up against the chill in their large wool coats. After about twenty minutes, they agreed that they had waited "awhile," and were about to start running toward Lela's up the hill on the other side of town.

"I hear 'em!" Arky said.

"Sho' sound lak his truck," the other boy agreed.

Presently Dave's truck appeared in the road and the boys started to run towards it as fast as they could, their coats flapping in the wind like blankets on sticks.

When Dave saw their unmistakable figures running towards him, his heart froze. The "running boys" they called them, usually meant trouble. Mama? Omar? Peter? Dave put his foot on the gas and sped towards the runners.

When the truck was close enough, the boys jumped on either side of the running boards before Dave had come to a complete stop.

Always glad to be a part of grown folks' business, the boys were terribly excited about this lynching thing, and the twenty minute wait had only served to excite them more. Both of them started talking at once: "Mama say come to Will Henry's right away. And she say don't leave dere and comin' looking fer dem if dey ain't back dere yet. Yeah! she say you stay put."

"What's going on boys?" Dave asked, trying not to show alarm.

"Dey cot a main. Dey say he dont kilt dose white peepers. Dey fixin' ta lynch 'em."

"Get in and hold on!" Dave said to the boys.

He drove as fast as the truck would go, and the boys were so agitated that they started to giggle uncontrollably while holding on to the side of the truck door.

Dave had a hundred questions he wanted to ask the boys, but he thought better of it and settled for just one: "Do you know who this man is that they've caught? Is he a friend of ours, you know, Omar or Peter or LaSalle?"

"Naw. Mama say he a stranger."

The relief Dave felt made his arms and legs quiver. "Thank God," he said under his breath. A stranger's problems were easier to handle. A stranger's problems would not necessarily leave the soul in shreds.

Dave and the boys arrived at Will Henry's house at the corner of Pine and Elm, and nearly ran in to each other getting up the steps and into the door.

"Dey ain't back yet," Emmie Lorraine told Dave flatly.

"Shit!" Dave burst out without apologizing.

"Well then, Emmie, tell me what you know," Dave said, trying to conceal the extreme irritation he felt.

Will Henry's wife, having chosen not to be a part of the bedroom discussion, didn't know much. She gave Dave a sketchy account of the facts.

Dave started to pace back and forth in front of the parlor window.

He didn't have long to wait. Presently three trucks stopped in front of the house and Will Henry got out. In fact so many people got out of the trucks—Omar and Peter, LaSalle Peabody, O'Neill Edwards, and Aggie, Nettie and Mae Bell Lewis— that people began to stare out of the windows, and Dave wondered if it was wise to have a "summit" meeting here because the wrong person might have something to tell the sheriff. The advantage of his own house was that it was relatively isolated and sat on a small hill where you could see anyone making an approach during daylight—and it was a large place.

After greetings were made and everyone had a seat, Will Henry said, "We ain't never had dis many folks in our house befoe! Y'all must come back under different times and we'll have a party!"

"Let's get down to brass tacks," Dave said abruptly. "Somebody fill me in."

O'Neill told how the man had been captured by the Francoxes, who were interested in collecting the reward money, then Will Henry told Dave about their visit to the herbalist. Nettie Lewis related how they had beaten Aristotle Gillis.

"Oh, dey done beat him so bad!" she told Dave. "Nah, the sheriff say he done up and said he done did it. Dey jus' done beat him so bad he'd confess any thin to them!" Nettie said and started to cry again, much to her own shame. "Sorry, sorry," she said apologetically, as she wiped her face with a rag she had taken from her old brown pocketbook.

"Dats all right Nettie!" Emmie Lorraine exclaimed, near tears herself after hearing the story. "You cry much as you wants to!"

The Meads' five children, plus Aggie's boys had been shepherded into a bedroom with enough toys and books to keep them busy, although Aggie's boys were obviously disappointed at being treated like the rest of the children.

Will Henry wanted to distance himself a little from the black beads, in case he had made the wrong decision.

"All I know," Will Henry said, clearing his throat, "is dat we had to figure some way to get Gillis out dat jail. I couldn't think o'no way but jus' to knock everybody out, den take Gillis out da back way. Nobody else could think of anythin' better." Will said, his voice trailing off with a defensive edge.

"Whatever we decide we better git together fast," said Omar.

"That's right," Peter agreed. "There is no telling what is going on at the jail right at this moment."

"If anythin' happens to dat main, I'll stab Henry Birkens right through the ass!" Mae Bell promised loudly.

"I think we oughta git dese wimmen folks outta dis. Maybe dey kin go up to Dave's house?" LaSalle said slowly.

"I gotta git dis banana pudding up to da jail!" O'Neill exclaimed. "Dey gone be missing me."

Dave had been listening, taking it all in before making a decision.

"Alright," he said, here we go. Will, I think you and the ladies did just fine. The man is in jail and we have to get him out—now. The question is if those berries work, how do we get him past the crowd that you say has formed in front of the jail?"

"Dere's a back do' to da jail dat leads out in the alley," O'Neill said.

"They'll be all around that jail," Peter said, "back door included."

"I once done saw a picture up at Wellsir Barr's picture show," LaSalle began, "it was called...oh, I don't remember the name!" He shook his cleanshaven head trying to remember. "Anyhow," he said, "it showed where dese mens was trying to get outta some prison somewha in London, England so dey come jus' a making all dis noise so dat da ones dat was keeping dem would look some wha else sos dey could get away."

"*Flight of the Sparrows,* 1927!" Dave said.

"Yes! Dats hit!" LaSalle said.

"They used a diversionary tactic" Dave said. "Something to keep a person's mind on one thing while something else is being accomplished. Gentlemen, I think we have a solution. We will use some sort of diversionary tactic. I have one in mind, but first let's get the ladies up to my mama's. Aggie, please fill mama in on what's happening and tell her not to worry, OK? Me and Peter will get our cave weapons just in case. I think we can leave the extra weapons in my closet up at the house for the time being."

"Oh, no!" squealed Emmie Lorraine at the thought of weapons.

"Never kin tell!" said Will Henry, not unhappily. "Don't worry, baby," he said to his wife. "We men, we kin take care of ouva selfs. We ain't alone. We got us some back up dis time!"

"LaSalle, drive the ladies up to my house, and Will and Omar, trail O'Neill back to the jail. O'Neill, everything depends on you. Do you think you can get them to drink some coffee with that banana pudding?" Dave asked.

"I reckon," O'Neill said quietly. He wanted to help, but he was having second thoughts. What would happen to him after they got Aristotle Gillis out safe and sound? Surely the sheriff will suspect he had something to do with them falling to sleep since he was the only one serving them in the jail. He really didn't want to go back to the jail at all. Neither did the other men, but it was something they had to do. Everyone was aware that a confrontation might start right there as they were trying to deliver a banana pudding and get the beads into the jail. But it was a chance they had to take.

"If you men are not back in fifteen minutes..." Dave said.

"We'll be back," Omar said.

"Wha is Tom Leak?" Aggie asked suddenly.

"Good question," Dave said. "Find him Aggie, and take him up to the house with you."

Dave discussed starting a fire in the Old Storage House that was about a quarter of a mile east of the jail as a diversionary tactic. Everyone agreed that this was as good a plan as anyone could think of.

"When the crowd leaves the jail to check out the fire, we'll have time to get Gillis out. Who can resist a good fire?" Dave asked.

"Wha we gone hide 'em?" LaSalle asked.

"With the herbalist until we can get him out of town."

"Alright!" Will Henry shouted enthusiastically. He was rearing to go.

"Aggie, I want you to tell mama to give Tom some of her sleeping tea. I want him to sleep through this whole thing, OK?"

Both Aggie and Mae Bell fought going to Lela's to be with the "women folk," but in the end they gave in, as Dave hoped they would.

Dave hated the looseness of their plans, the spur of the moment aspect of what they were doing, but thinking about it more deeply he realized that given the situations they were likely to encounter, their plans were always going to be rather spontaneous and quickly thought out.

Dave heaved a long sigh filled with anxiety and dismay.

He and Peter left to pick up the other weapons from the cave where they had been hidden, realizing how wise they had been to store a second cache of weapons five minutes outside of town where they could easily get to them.

Dave was concerned too about all the people that had left Will Henry's house at one time. People were watching out of windows and wondering, but it couldn't be helped. They would have to depend on the code of silence.

Dave could only pray that everything would go smoothly. He regretted not telling Aggie, "Tell mama to pray for us."

Tonight Omar and another man from the Circle would go over to Carson, Arkansas, and remove Aristotle's family from harm before anyone knew what was happening.

As they drove the truck swiftly down the pike to the cave, Dave said, "After we stack the weapons in the truck, Peter, we've got to check the storage house out to see how easy it's going to be to get in and out fast. Then all of us have to use these next hours before dark to pick up all the Circle members we can find to give us a hand—and hope to God the mob doesn't storm the jail before then.

"I told O'Neill you would be in the crowd to relay his signal back to us. Oh, you're gonna be a helpful little rascal tonight with that white skin of yours. We're gonna pass you off as a white man in the crowd."

"I do what I can with what I've got," Peter said, not smiling.

"That's what I've heard from your women friends," Dave said, punching Peter in the side and laughing.

"Now, you're getting as dirty as Omar," Peter said.

"I could never be that dirty if I didn't bathe for a year!" Dave retorted.

"I told O'Neill to look for you right up front in the crowd wearing that big old ugly black hat you used to wear pulled down to hide most of your face. You still have that hat, don't you Pete?"

"Of course. That's a very nice hat."

They were coming to the cave after a short drive.

"I've got two flashlights in the back," Dave said.

"We could get shot tonight. Have you thought about that?"

"I don't intend to get shot," Peter remarked, "not without taking someone with me. Can you believe all this?" Peter said with some amazement.

"Yes, of course I believe it. What's not to be believed is our response this time."

"I hate to admit it, but I'm a little—well, you know."

Even though the two men were the best of friends, neither wanted to give voice to the thing that lay between them like a stone—fear.

"Are your little pink tootsies getting cold?" Dave said half jokingly to his friend. "Well, mine are too," Dave said as he unwrapped guns and rifles in the high, dark, dry cave. "Not so much for myself, but for the innocent people a jail break might effect. They'll probably be grabbing random Colored men off the street, beating them just for revenge after this.

"It's them I worry about, Pete. The black people who are not connected to us. Who don't know anything about this—the people who live on the outskirts of town without any protection from us."

"Yeah. I know what you mean," Peter said. "I've thought about them too. Do you have enough light?" Peter asked, turning the flashlight up to full intensity.

"Yeah, I can see just fine. Well. Shall we call it off, Pete?" Dave asked, looking sideways at his friend. They were loaded up and driving back to town with their weapons. It had taken twice as long as they had figured to unwrap the weapons from their cloth sheets and load them, adding to their anxiety.

"Call it off?" You must be joneing! Hell no!"

"Good" said Dave. "Because this shit has got to come to a head sometime."

"You're right about that."

"Listen, Peter, I told O'Neill to holler out the window to the crowd that the sheriff said to disperse when the drugs have taken effect on the lawmen. That'll be our signal. You'll then make your way out of the crowd and come back and tell us. After that we'll torch the Old Storage House."

"We should divide the men up into as many trucks as possible for a fast getaway."

"Right. During the confusion, you'll have to make your way back to the jail and get O'Neill and Gillis out the back door. That'll be the tricky part. Will Henry will be waiting with a truck behind the jail about a block away. Go straight to John Candle's house. Of course he knows we're coming. I sent Aggie with LaSalle to tell him. Stay there until we come for you, OK?"

"Hell, I hate to miss the excitement, but I'll do that."

"Peter, you know I'm depending on you to get Will Henry out of town and keep an eye on him."

"I know."

"You know Will Henry can be dynamite. All we need is him deciding to shoot into a crowd of white folks."

"Yeah, you're right. Getting him clean outside of town was a smart move."

"Wanna know another smart thing I did?" Dave said, laughing at himself. "I picked you to drive. You look white—no offense. O'Neill and Gillis can lay down in the padded bed of the truck covered with straw until you all get across town. People will have heard about what's going on at the jail and get curious about an injured Colored man in the cab of a truck, but they won't stop a white man. It's best to be safe," Dave concluded.

With their plan in place, Dave and Pete and some of the others went to check the Old Storage House. The storage house was easily seen from a distance because it was the only three story building in the area. The building was old and dry, and would burn fast.

"In and out," Will Henry said. "Boom! Burn it down and get on outta heah!"

Dave had told O'Neill about the signals when they were at Will Henry's house, and that they were going to get him out of town to Buffalo, New York—with money in his pockets to rejoin his wife and children, it was the first time Dave had seen O'Neill Edwards smile. O'Neill had reached for Dave's hand and shook it.

"Thank you, Mistah Dave!" he exclaimed. "I'll do mah part real good in dat jail. I'll have dose bastards knocked out soon as I kin git da coffee on!"

197

Twenty-Three

———✦———

With the beads in his shirt pocket and the banana pudding in a basket, O'Neill Edwards drove up to the jail, got out of the truck and walked towards the gathered mob on cotton legs. Puffing and sweating, O'Neill nearly panicked as the crowd's eyes swiveled to look at him as one.

"I woiks fer da sheriff! I woiks fer da sheriff!" he hollered out. " hit's me, O'Neill Edwards!" he called, coming closer to the crowd. "I got some'o da sheriffs dinner he done ordered up in heah!" he said, frantically pointing to the basket and holding it aloft for the crowd to see.

"Let 'em through!" one of the Francoxes said loudly to the crowd. "He da sheriff's boy."

O'Neill banged on the jail door for what seemed several minutes before anyone from inside could hear him above the crowd noise. Finally DeBell Hinkle cracked the door, his gun drawn, and O'Neill fell in with the brown basket.

"Oh, I see you got mah puddin!" DeBell said almost gaily, as if nothing unusual was happening.

Well, two can play dis game you lil son-na-fa-bitch! O'Neill thought of DeBell's unconcerned attitude.

"Yas!" O'Neill said, without noticeable rancor. "And you'll be wanting some nice hot coffee wit' dat puddin. I'll just git da cups and wash 'em up front in da zink. Dey git so dusty ya know!"

"Oh, I've been dying fer some coffee!" DeBell Hinkle said gratefully.

"Yas," said O'Neill dryly, he was warming to his part. He would get everybody to drink and drink and drink.

He took the coffee cups into the little toilet where there was a sink. He put water in the large pot and poured coffee into the percolator from a paper sack, a little extra to make it strong and rich. Then O'Neill sat the coffee pot on the little potbellied stove in the office, put a few more pieces of wood in the stove both to make the coffee and to force the chill from the November air.

Soon the aroma of the fresh brewing coffee filled the air with its irresistible odor.

"Jus' smell dat!" the deputy remarked. "Why is hit dat coffee always seems to smell even better den it taste? And dat coffee gone taste plenty good, O'Neill."

"Thank you, suh," O'Neill said blandly. O'Neill took his four earthenware cups and dried them thoroughly. DeBell Hinkle had walked back down the hall to the interrogation room and closed the door.

They were all in there. Good.

Removing the black shiny beads from his pocket he made a tiny hole in four beads with a safety pin from his shirt, and squirted the thin opaque liquid from them into the bottom of the cups. In a few seconds—it seemed like much longer to the nervous O'Neill, who had dropped two beads on the floor twice before he succeeded in puncturing them—O'Neill could no longer see the liquid in the cups. He sighed, pleased that they were working as the herbalist said they would. He walked over to the stove, opened the door with the latch, and threw the collapsed shells from the beads into the fire.

Next, O'Neill took the cups back to the interrogation room and placed them on top of the icebox.

"The coffee will be ready in a few minutes, gents," he said amiably.

He glanced at Aristotle Gillis who now was slumped over with his face in his hands, grunting softly.

It could be me, O'Neill thought with a wild rush of anger for the white men.

Having already finished one saucer of pudding DeBell said, "I'll have me another saucer of pudding wit' mah coffee."

One Monroe man stood in a corner, the other against a wall. They both looked tired, slovenly. Both had blood on their shirts. So did DeBell Hinkle. Only the sheriff would be able to tell Mae Bell after this was over. "Honest ta gawd! I never hit 'em one time. No, not once!"

The sheriff looked worn out too. Only the deputy Hinkle seemed ready to go on and on.

"That crowd is getting unruly looks like," one of the Monroe men said.

The sheriff grunted, irritated and frustrated.

Aristotle prayed. "Father I lift mah hains to thee..."

"Shut up!" DeBell said.

"Oh, let 'em pray," the sheriff said in a weary tone, walking down the hall to the front office. "O'Neill, keep dat front door locked tight, you heah?"

"Yassuh!"

"Is dat coffee ready yet?" the sheriff asked, holding a cup in his hand and rubbing his stomach.

"Not yet, suh. Won't be long."

"Well," the sheriff said, "I don't think I want none. I wuz gonna have some, but..."

O'Neill froze in place. "What wuz dat suh?"

"I sez I don't want no coffee. I had enough fer today. Hit done gimme da sour belly. Don't worry hit won't be wasted. Dey waiting fer hit back dere. Hit sho' smell good, doe."

The sheriff did not want any coffee! Oh no! Then nobody could be given coffee, O'Neill knew, for the sheriff couldn't sit in the room and watch everybody fall out but him. *Den he'll know I done bothered wit' da coffee. Dey'll lynch me too! Dey'll think I had somethin' to do wit' dose killings! Oh my, my my!*

While O'Neill was thinking these panicked thoughts his face was a blank. It was if time had stopped. Finally, he was to say later, his mind started "to workin' again, lak somebody was tellin' me what to do. Mebbe hit wuz da Lawd..."

O'Neill looked at the sheriff's face. He had not seemed to notice his alarmed state at all.

"But you has yo' cup, suh!" O'Neill exclaimed too loudly. "You musta want some coffee."

"Thought I did. I want somethin', but not no coffee."

Think, think, think!

O'Neill took the cup from the exhausted old sheriff's hand. He had been at the jail all day. O'Neill knew how much he liked to take a nap in the afternoons.

"I think I got somethin' fer ya, Sheriff," O'Neill said with false brightness. "I'll bring hit to ya in a minute."

The sheriff let O'Neill take the cup from his hand without thinking twice about it.

Presently the man brought the steaming pot of coffee in.

"Don't she smell fine," he said, then checked himself against over doing it. These men were waiting for coffee. He didn't have to sell it to them. *Careful, careful.*

O'Neill decided to go ahead and serve the other lawmen, and he poured three cups of steaming coffee for the men and watched the lawmen greedily putting in sugar and cream, except for DeBell Hinkle, who drank his black.

The sheriff was still massaging his abdomen, trying to spread the acid around.

O'Neill left the room and returned shortly with a steaming hot brew for the sheriff. He had used his tin cup to quickly heat water on the stove, then dump the hot water into another cup—with the liquid from the Mozumbo Kelè berry bead. Next he placed canned cream and sugar in the cup that he had taken from the interrogation room. But he needed something else to make it taste slightly strange and different.

"Oh, Lawd! What if the sheriff refused to drink it? Please, please, please father!" O'Neill prayed. "What, what, what can I put in dis cup?"

He looked quickly through the deputy's desk drawer. He was always smacking on something. He must hurry for they had to fall asleep at the same time!

There it was! A little cellophane of salt and one of pepper that Nettie had twisted into little packages for one of the dinners. Salt. Pepper.

And—a little cellophane of mustard. *Thank you, Lawd!*

O'Neill quickly mixed a little of the salt and pepper and all of the mustard and placed it in the sheriff's cup and stirred it well. He wanted to taste the contents of the cup, but decided he'd better not. He walked back to the interrogation room and handed the cup to the sheriff.

"Dis," O'Neill said to the sheriff in a grand manner, "is somethin' mah old grandmammy use to gie me when I had your same condition—da sour belly. Hit works lak magic if you drink it down fast. You can't let it get cold or hit don't work as well."

"What's in dis," the sheriff asked, taking the cup and sniffing the mixture. "Medicine?" he turned up his nose.

"Oh, no! hit's jus' a few herbs. I carries dem around wit' me sometimes jus' in case. I always takes dem on a picnic wit' me and when I eat at frens houses. Sometimes dey uses more spices den I'm used to and dey gits to me. More coffee gents?"

The sheriff frowned into the cup and sniffed it again.

"You gotta drink hit sheriff—not just peek at hit!" O'Neill said, trying to sound humorous.

The sheriff brought the cup reluctantly to his lips, hesitated, frowned some, then turned the cup up and drank half of the portion.

201

"Don't taste all dat bad," he said. "I sho' hope hit do me some good." He turned the cup up again and drained it.

Thank you, Jesus! O'Neill exhaled. What if the salt and pepper and mustard made the sheriff's drink less strong? *Well, mebbe he'll jus sleep less den the five hours*—three hours would be enough, O'Neill thought. *But its gotta knock him out. It's gotta!*

O'Neill made a show of drinking a cup of coffee himself out of his tin cup—then he gave Aristotle a cup—using one of the sheriff's cups that had not been doctored.

Aristotle took the cup from O'Neill's hand and thanked him hoarsely for the steaming coffee, but it was too hot for his swollen lips, so O'Neill took the cup gently from the mans hands and placed it on the table.

"I'm going back ta watch da doe," O'Neill told the lawmen.

O'Neill had to admit he was becoming very scared for himself. There was a real mob outside now. He wished this was over with. A lot of "what ifs" assaulted his mind. *What if dey break down dis doe and haul me and Aristotle out to a tree?* Well, they were out there somewhere, weren't they?

With guns? Dave and his men? O'Neill was afraid to go to the window—suppose someone threw a brick at his head?—But he had to look for Peter in his big hat that he had gone back home to get—the one that Dave said made him look like a rogue. He hoped he could find him in the crowd.

O'Neill made his way to the window and squinted out cautiously in the gathering dark, looking for a face with a large black hat in the crowd.

There he was! There was no mistaking that awful looking hat that Peter had pulled down low on his face so that no one in the white crowd would recognize him as one of the "hot tamale boys."

Seeing O'Neill at the window, Peter touched the old hat a few times in an exaggerated manner as an unmistakable signal to O'Neill, then he started screaming and joustling like the rest of the crowd.

O'Neill felt better now. They really were out there! What a mess! O'Neill thought, noting that the day had started out so mild—and now all this! There was a picture at Wellsir Barr's picture show that he had wanted to see tomorrow. It was called *Coconuts* with Groucho Marx, now O'Neill thought sadly that he would probably never see it at all. It was a small thing, seeing the picture, but it stuck in O'Neill's mind as an example of how quickly a good day could turn unexpectedly bad.

O'Neill decided to go back to the interrogation room on the pretext of telling the sheriff that the door was securely locked, and that nobody had tried to storm the jail—so far. What he really wanted to find out was whether the beads had started to have any effect.

Looking into the room he asked politely "Is everythin' alright heah gents? Y'all want some mo' coffee?" Only ten minutes or so had passed, but the Monroe men were sitting down now.

O'Neill thought they looked much more tired than before. He hoped it wasn't just his imagination. Only DeBell Hinkle showed no signs of slowing down.

"You know you done kilt dose peepers on Honeysuckle Lane, didn't ya!" O'Neill heard the deputy yell as he had for the one hundredth time today.

"No suh, no suh, no suh! I ain't kilt nobody never in my life. Ah ain't dont nothin', suh. Please suh! Ah jus' come over lookin' for me a job of work of some kind," the man said through swollen lips. Then he started to cry. Great gasping sounds escaped from his chest and rocked his whole body.

"You lying burr head!" the frustrated deputy yelled, delivering another body blow to the prisoner, as O'Neill flinched and swore in the hall.

The blow set the captured man to sobbing again as O'Neill crept back to the front office.

In the little interrogation room, Sheriff Birkens sighed deeply again.

" hit's been a long day," the sheriff said, yawning widely, and stretching his long arms above his head.

He had seen the Monroe men use all of their expertise—they had cajoled and threatened—promised and lied, been kind and understanding and finally brutal and vicious, and still the innocent man would not confess to the murders he did not commit.

"We done been heah all day long, DeBell. Put dis main in a cell."

"But, Sheriff," Deputy Hinkle started to protest.

"I said put his ass in a cell Gawd damn hit! We'll question him some mo' come tomorrow. DeBell, you gone have to learn to do lak I say!" the Sheriff burst out. "And don't hit dat main no mo'! You been defying me and defying me all the life long day and I'm gettin a little sick o'hit. You heah me?"

The deputy sulked, walked over and stood against the wall, glaring at the prisoner because he dared not glare at the sheriff.

"O'cose we all gotta stay heah tonight. Dat includes O'Neill. Y'all might as well go somewhere nah and get a nap," the sheriff yawned again.

"Gawd! I ain't never been dis sleepy in mah life! Must be dis weather and weakness from not eating—plus not having my afternoon nap," the sheriff mused to himself. "And dem Monroe boys is out fer dead! Dey must be terrible exhausted from goin' at hit so hard fer so long. Is you sleepy DeBell?"

"Not a bit!" the little deputy snapped. "Hit ain't even six o' clock. Ain't nobody going to sleep dis early," DeBell said, as scornfully as he dared. "Besides, hi can anyone think of a nap wit' dat mob outside," he asked incredulously—but under his breath.

O'Neill looked at the clock. The old herbalist had said fifteen minutes or so, they told him. How long was "or so?" O'Neill wondered.

Fifteen minutes had already passed.

O'Neill figured the sheriff would be the first one to fall asleep. He was the oldest and the most tired. But it was DeBell that worried him. He had read all those detective magazines and all. If he was the last to fall asleep and the sheriff just dropped everything and fell out in the middle of the floor all of a sudden, surely DeBell, with all of his detective learning would suspect something, O'Neill thought.

O'Neill felt panic rising in him again like foam on a windswept sea. Would this day ever end? he wondered.

Now he had to coax the sheriff to a cell. He had to get him to a bed! But it was not the sheriff but the Monroe men who had begun the slow slide to oblivion first. They were now sitting at the table struggling to stay awake. One man's arms were stretched out in front of him, his jaws going slack from the pull of sleep upon his face. The other mans arms had fallen to his sides, and he laid his head on the back of the chair as if to rest and collect his thoughts for a moment.

"If y'all wanta sleep, y'all would be mo' comfortable in one o'dem cells," the sheriff said to the Monroe men.

But the men were already in the first throes of sleep and could not respond to this suggestion. The deputy looked at them with thinly disguised disgust.

"No staying power," he said out loud. "Sleeping lak two babies and hit ain't even good and dark. Well hit sho' won't do for everybody to go to sleep in heah what wit' dat crowd out dere. I ain't got no kinna plans fer sleeping tonight." The deputy finished with a grandiose air.

DeBell had put Aristotle Gillis in a cell and locked the door. He walked back to the front of the jail with the keys in his hand.

The sheriff, who had been checking something in the interrogation room came back up front.

"Boy! mah legs feel lak lead," he remarked.

"Hi your stomach feel sheriff? Did mah old mammy's stuff do you any good? You ain't had yo' nap today Mistah Birkens, suh," O'Neill said, his voice filled with concern. "I'll go in dere and fluff up da pillow fer you, suh."

"Why thank you, O'Neill," the sheriff said, touched by this solicitude. "Yas, I think dat cup you gimme did help break up somma dat gas I was feelin', I done farted twice. Say listen DeBell, we gotta move dis boy over to da big jail over in old Steward early tomorrow moaning-ahm talkin' four o'clock da latest. Fore dat crowd wakes up and gathers again. hit's mo' safe and secure over dere. Don't and dey gone bust in heah fer sho', what wit' dem Francoxes whipping dat crowd up to red hot."

The sheriff looked towards the back and smiled. "Nah, ahm old. You'd expect me to need me a nap—but dem young Monroe boys done fell out 'fore I did. Ain't dat somethin?" the sheriff asked.

"No staying power," DeBell said again, curling his lips in scorn.

"O'Neill, you wake me up after one hour on da dot, you heah?" The sheriff staggered to his feet and fairly dragged himself back down the hall where the four small cells were located.

O'Neill followed him, watched his every step with mounting anxiety. He had to make it to the cot without falling out! When he got into the cell, O'Neill said, "Come on sheriff, sat on down on dis cot. My! You is sleepy! Heah. Jus' let me fold back dis blanket fer ya."

But Sheriff Birkens suddenly collapsed like a punctured balloon, and fell on the bed without removing his shoes or eye glasses.

Working swiftly, O'Neill removed the sheriff's shoes, and then lifted his glasses from his face. Deciding not to touch his gun, he gently pushed the old man over on his side and covered him with the heavy gray wool jail blankets.

There now. He looked more natural—even though he was sleeping with his gun and holster on.

Now they were—thank Gawd—all asleep—except DeBell Hinkle.

O'Neill returned to the office after having wiped his sweating face with his bandana.

"Lawd, Lawd, Lawd!" he repeated over and over under his breath. "Hep me git through dis day!"

"So. Everybody sleeping under dese conditions huh, O'Neill?" the deputy said. "A mob out front and all da lawmens in heah sleeping. Don't dat strike you funny, O'Neill?"

"Suh?" O'Neill said, pouring sweat again. *Gawd, he suspected somethin'!*

"Is you hot, O'Neill? Some peepers jus' can't stand no strain. No sirree! I ain't gone be sleeping tonight. If that mob tries to get in heah..." He looked at O'Neill and patted his gun.

"Wanna play some checkers?"

So they played a nervous game of checkers until the deputy asked O'Neill to get him another cup of coffee and another saucer of banana pudding. Nearly forty-five minutes had passed since the men had drunk the coffee. The herbalist had said in fifteen minutes or so the beads from Africa would do their work. Had he accidently missed putting a bead in DeBell's cup? No. No. He was sure he had been very careful. The others were out for dead—the sheriff was snoring loudly. He just had to be patient.

O'Neill fingered the two beads he had left. Should he try to slip both of them into the deputy's coffee?

"I don't intend to sleep a wink tonight," DeBell repeated again, smiling at O'Neill as if he expected some praise for this decision. "Somebody gotta stay alert."

O'Neill was scared silent. He moved his men around the board, hoping that the deputy didn't notice how badly his hand was shaking.

"Is dat crowd gettin bigger or smaller?" the deputy wondered out loud, walking towards the window to pull the shade back and peek.

As he headed towards the window, DeBell swayed a bit for a few seconds, then fell heavily to the floor, coffee in hand. The earthenware cup broke into pieces and coffee spilled in a black line over the wooden floor like blood.

O'Neill stood immobile for several seconds daring not to breathe.

When he was sure the deputy was fast asleep, he took his keys. The handyman's thoughts were muddled and slow. *Think, think boy!* he demanded of himself. *Soon dis will be all over.*

He thought he must put the deputy on a cot with the door to the cell open, then if the crowd busted in before they could run their plan, it would look as if the lawmen were merely sleeping.

O'Neill removed the deputy's gun from its holster and then dragged him by his feet—belly down—to an empty cell. He then walked down the hall and looked in on the Monroe men. They were deeply asleep, their chests moving up and down in the slow rhythmic pattern of normal sleep.

Tears welled up in O'Neill's eyes. "Thank ya, thank ya, Lawd Gawd Almighty!" he whispered fervently. When this was over, O'Neill made a promise to "da Almighty Gawd in Glory" that he would start going to church as his dear dead mother wanted him to, because he could "truly see dat da Lawd had been wit' him dis day!"

O'Neill made his way to the window. He opened it just a crack and instantly the noise from the crowd gushed in on a wave of frigid air, surprising in its savagery. Peter was out there somewhere in the crowd wearing his large black hat.

Peter, seeing O'Neill at the window, stepped forward just a bit and adjusted his hat. When O'Neill saw that gesture, he hollered as loudly as he could the prearranged signal: "Da sheriff say y'all is to dispurse and go home!"

Having heard the loud but quaking voice of O'Neill, Peter pointedly adjusted his large hat again, and O'Neill waved his hand to show that he had seen his signal.

The nearly white man then headed for the Old Storage House to tell the others that the black beads from the Motherland had done their job admirably.

TWENTY-FOUR

Ten men. That's what was needed, ten more courageous men willing to risk their lives to save a man they had never laid eyes on, willing to risk their safety and their futures here to show whites they were not powerless, and that they had had enough.

They were all wearing dark clothes as Dave had suggested, and talking in whispers.

The Circle was more than forty strong now, men he knew who were dedicated to the cause and not given to talking too much, men who could be trusted completely.

The knot in Dave's stomach would not dissolve. He knew their plans were so bold and audacious as to be ridiculous. It was a plan that depended on one man and a few black beads from Africa. Would it work? Could it work? Even though they had received a positive signal from O'Neill that the lawmen were definitely knocked out, Dave still felt queasy, and dared not think of what would happen if their slender strategy went awry. He was not at all afraid for himself, but for the men.

He did not wish to lead them into a blood bath.

Dave was a believer, but he did not pray often. Now he found that when he wished to pray, he could not.

The knot tightened.

Dave squinted at the four men before him. He could barely make out their faces because they were not using light, but he could see Omar's teeth flash in a smile.

"Don't worry boss," Omar said, "we gone make out fine. I feels hit in mah toes!"

The other men, LaSalle, Will Henry and Peter, laughed and grunted a little in agreement, showing no fear whatever.

Dave was a little cheered by their attitude and he said, "Well then, let's hit it! Tell the ten to each pick up another one if at all possible. We'll be needing all hands on deck once we get back to Colored Town. Tell everybody to wear dark clothes and bring their pistols. If we need more weapons, of course we have the ones we brought from the cave. Tell them to leave all personal identification at home. We don't want anyone to drop anything that will later identify them. Also, tell them to bring a large hankerchief to cover their faces. We've got plenty of rifles and shotguns—tell them that too—and nobody in their families is to know where they are going. OK?"

A chorus of agreement.

"I'm sure dey done heard a plenty about dis main being in jail by nah," LaSalle said.

"So when we come for dem, hit won't be no total surprise," Omar added.

"That's right," Dave agreed. "They are probably wondering where we are right now. I'll bet they are looking for us."

"We ready to move out, gents?" Dave asked.

Peter had been silent until now. He looked much younger than his twenty-four years, clothed as he was in his over-sized dark coat and big black slouch hat. His white face seemed to glow in this darkness as he spoke to the group. "What if the crowd doesn't leave the jail and come to the fire? What if only some of the lynch mob comes to watch the fire and the others stay back? How are we going to get Gillis and O'Neill out then?"

Dave, who had also turned this question over in his mind, thus adding to the tightening of his gut knot, said, "That's a good question, Peter. A valid question. That's what I meant about the possibility of getting shot. All we can do is plan as tightly as we can and hope for the best. We're going to make a great deal of noise, banging on tin tubs, shooting in the air, and hollering our lungs out. We are going to try to create so much chaos that it will be irrestible. That's all we can do," Dave finished rather solemnly, but thought, *Dear God! What have we got ourselves into?* "Be with us Father," he sighed, in as much of a prayer as he could muster.

But Will Henry laughed. "Nah did you ever know anyone what could resist a good fie?" he asked still laughing.

"I think he right," LaSalle said.

"Just thought it ought to be mentioned," Peter said.

"You're right for asking Peter. Everything we can think of should be brought up," Dave said kindly.

They went over the plans again. Each truck or car was to carry four or more armed men plus extra shotguns, rifles and ammunition. Once the fire was set, the men would scatter and head for Colored Town. They were only coming out to the site of the Old Storage House to receive all the information regarding the plans they would need for this night and to be a part of the noise making. Once everyone knew exactly the same thing, and they had made all the racket possible, they would immediately drive to Colored Town as fast as they could.

Dave shook each man's hand firmly. "Be very, very careful," he cautioned. "And good luck to all of us. We'd better get going. It's dark enough now."

LaSalle and Omar headed for Colored Town to pick up the additional men. Peter struck a match and checked his watch. It was six-thirty. He would go back down to the jail to wait his chance to get O'Neill and Aristotle Gillis out. Will Henry was to park his borrowed truck around in back of the jail about a block away as soon as LaSalle and Omar returned. They figured it would take perhaps an hour to locate the men Dave had asked for. That would put them to seven-thirty—if anything went as planned.

In forty-five minutes Omar, LaSalle and five other trucks and cars began to roll up to the Old Storage House yard, and in these cars were an astounding twenty more men!

"All we said was dat Dave Bailey needs help," LaSalle said, smiling broadly. It was the first time anybody could remember seeing LaSalle smile lately.

One of the older men had brought a lantern. "She don't give off dat mucha light," he said. "Jus' enough sos we kin make each other out."

Dave walked over and looked at the men and was almost overcome with emotion as he looked into their good, decent faces. Suddenly his gloom lifted, for now he knew he was doing the right thing in getting these men involved to save one of their own. Aristotle Gillis was one of these men. Aristotle Gillis was *all* of these men. Hard-working, life worn, life torn, mostly gentle men, thrust, Dave thought, into the lion's mouth of poverty and segregation—and yet here they were in a show of support on the most dangerous mission of their lives.

Dave looked at the men in the dim light of the lantern. No sir! They were not going to be lynched—sacrificed to the whim of some white folks—not now, not ever!

At that moment, Dave had a sharp insight: Was his whole life a cry against his father's inability to help his dear friend Nappy long ago when he was a small boy? Was that his reason for being so determined to protect his friends?

Dave struggled with this unsummoned idea until Omar pushed him gently forward, saying, "Dis yo' Circle, Dave. Why don't you go shake hains wit' everybody?"

Dave noticed in the dim light that there were tears in Omar's eyes.

Lincoln Foster, a stocky, black-skinned man of forty-two, told Dave apologetically, "We woulda had everybody heah 'cept fer da fack dat time was running out fer findin' peepers."

Dave smiled at the man. "You all did fine, Lincoln. We got enough men here to kick some ass ain't we?"

The men were to stay beside the cars and trucks, ready to roll out fast after they made their commotion. But in spite of the seriousness of the situation, there was nearly a party atmosphere at the storage house. Only Mister Daniels, the oldest man among them, so named because his parents had decided sixty years ago that their son would never be called Mister in the South by a white man unless they *named* him Mister, was sad and reflective: "Ah've been waiting all mah lafe to strike back at da white main. Even if I die tonight, Ah will have done had me a chance and kin die happy!" he said intensely.

"We are going to do it right." Dave placed his arm around Mister Daniel's shoulder. "Nobody's going to get killed," he said, hoping with all his heart that this was true.

The men gathered around the single lantern and Dave went over the plans again, carefully and slowly. They thoroughly discussed what they were to do when they returned to Colored Town. Everybody seemed to understand, to agree, but even so Dave thought uneasily that their plans could go haywire at any point. Pray and hope for the best, Lela Bailey always said. Well, he would do that tonight. Unexpectedly, Naisbitt Patterson, whom nobody ever thought of as the least bit religious, said, "Well mens, how 'bout let's us jine hains? I'd lak to offer up a prayer."

There was a murmur of agreement in the group about the fitness of this suggestion, especially from the suprised and pleased Reverned Clayton, and all the men moved together and joined hands in a circle as Naisbitt Patterson prayed:

"Oh Lawd. We hope dat we don't have to kill nobody tonight—and by dat self same token, we shoally hope dat nobody will kill us. So I ax you, Lawd, whatsonever happen tonight, I hope you will be 'ponsible fer our souls whichever way dey go, up or down. Amen."

"Thank you Naisbitt," Dave said sincerely as Omar stifled a snicker. He looked at the man on his right, which was Dolittle Auburn, and whispered, "Whichever way dey go? Up or down?"

Auburn's lips trembled as he tried to stifle a guffaw also. "Keep quiet you black fool!" he whispered harshly to Omar. "You ain't nothin' but da devil!" he laughed.

The men walked back to their cars and trucks and removed the tin tubs and flat boards they would use to make a racket, as well as the shotguns they would shoot off to add to the clamor, and as LaSalle and Dave hurled their flaming gasoline soaked branches, the men began to yell and bang and make a terrible din as soon as the flames crackled and sizzled their way to the top of the building for the whole town to see.

Nothing in his forty-eight years of life had ever made O'Neill so happy. Not his marriage to his childhood sweetheart, not the birth of his son or daughter; nothing compared to the feeling he had when he walked into Aristotle's cell and said, "Git on up Mistah Aristotie Gilly! We gonna git you outta heah. Ain't nobody gone lynch you today, tomorrow, not no time!"

The man had simply lain where he was, too confused by this news to move. He tried to move his swollen lips. "What you say?" he whispered fearfully.

O'Neill held the keys up and jangled them for Aristotle to see.

"You believe me nah? Yo' cell doe unlocked ain't it?" He said giddy with happiness.

With a pounding head and sore muscles in every part of his body, the jailed man struggled to sit up on the side of his cot. Upright, he continued to stare at O'Neill in one—eyed disbelief.

"Wha day at? Da Sheriff and all?"

"Come see fer yo'self!" O'Neil said feeling lighter than air even though the mob was still humming around the jail, more than one hundred strong now.

Aristotle limped slowly behind O'Neill. Scared and weak, he held on to the wall for support.

"See! Dere be da sheriff—snoring!" O'Neill said grandly. "And dere be da deputy sleeping sweet as a baby!" he said, walking to the next cell. "Da other two is back dere in da 'terogation room flopped out fer dead on dem tables." O'Neill laughed. "Ain't dat somethin'?"

Aristotle crept down the narrow hall and peered with frightened eyes into the room where he had suffered so much just hours ago. He saw the sleeping men for himself. Still terrified, he asked, "How?"

"Poison! Ah put in dey coffee cups mahself. Hit won't kill 'em—jus' make 'em sleep five hours exactly." O'Neill said with authority. "And ain't no way you kin wake dem up 'til dat five hours is up—even if you set dis building on fie!"

212

"Is dat da truf?" Aristotle wheezed, still in a state of shock, stunned by the possibility of staying alive.

"Dats right!" O'Neill said proudly, feeling more powerful than he had ever felt in his life. Was this the way a white man felt every day? he wondered. Well, it was a mighty fine feeling!

O'Neill explained the plan of escape to Aristotle, and when he heard how much men he did not even know were willing to do for him, he became overwhelmed with emotion and started to cry again.

"Dis is a special, special town," he said over and over through his tears.

"Stop dat crying nah," O'Neill said, not unkindly. "We got to git to da back doe."

O'Neill led Aristotle to the back door with its peeling buff colored paint, and O'Neill peeped out carefully.

"You stay up against da wall," he warned Aristotle. "Ahm gone see hi many dese peckerwoods is round to da back."

"Well nah, I be dog!" O'Neill exclaimed as he looked out the back window. He beckoned to the prisoner. "Come over heah and look. See. Dere ain't a devil's soul back dere! Well glory be!"

O'Neill made his way back to the front of the jail with Aristotle limping behind him. He wanted to be at the front so he could see when they set the fire.

"Kin you run on dem legs?" he asked the prisoner.

"I expects not, but I'll be one hobbling fool!" Aristotle lisped through his puffy lips, trying to smile.

"Heah dat noise?" O'Neill exclaimed excitedly. "Nah dey goin' ta set da fie! When you see da fie, we got to head fer da back quick! Two mens will be out dere somewha in a car or truck to git us outta heah. Dey got fie—arms aplenty too."

"I can't believe hit. I jus' can't believe hit!" Aristotle croaked to O'Neill.

Momentarily the noise from the direction of the Old Storage House grew louder and more intense: screams, yowls, banging, pistol shots, and pitiful calls for help were heard as O'Neill tried hard not to holler with excitement himself.

"Won't be long nah befoe—" O'Neill started to say, but his sentence was interrupted by a series of short explosions, then flames shot skyward like a spear illuminating the night for miles around.

"Hit's dem!" O'Neill shouted. "Dems ouva boys! Git to da back doe!"

"Won't all dat noise dem wake up?"

"Naw! I done tole ya. Dey out fer dead. Come on, let's move! When dey gets heah, watch and be careful, dere is two steps to go down out back so hold on to mah arm—you can't be falling down."

When the crowd heard the noise, saw the sudden flames, and heard the screams for help, they ran to the next bit of excitement as fast as they could. Indeed, some of them almost ran over each other in their haste to be among the first at the scene.

Only Cora Lee Francox and her husband Billy hung back a bit watching the jail, then they took off with the rest of them, unable to contain their curiosity.

Nobody stayed at the jail long enough to wonder why the sheriff and his deputy did not run out immediately to see what was going on.

Peter easily made his way to the back of the jail in the running confusion. O'Neill was at the back door with the bloody, sore prisoner.

"Come on! The truck is just a little way away!" Peter said as they got on either side of Aristotle, holding him up by the arms to help him limp along faster.

Will Henry waited in front of the truck so he could crank it when the men were settled in. Peter and O'Neill helped Aristotle into the truck bed, which they had been thoughtful enough to pad; then O'Neill got in and carefully lay beside him, and Peter and Will Henry quickly covered both of them with blankets and straw.

"Ride up front with me," Peter said to Will Henry. "If we are stopped, you're my handy man and we are out to pick up something, OK? I'll drive," he said, walking to the front of the truck.

"Yassuh, boss!" Will Henry said, smiling broadly. "Look! Dey done started a right nice fie. I can feel dat heat from heah!"

"Me too," Peter replied. "God, we really did it! Now the hard part. Getting these two out of town."

"Oh, we gone git outta town!" Will Henry exclaimed. "Ain't nothin' gone stop me from gittin outta heah fast. Hit jus' wouldn't do to be caught heah back o'dis jail at da present moment nah would hit?" Will said half jokingly to Peter.

"You got dat right," came O'Neill's muffled voice from under his straw and blankets.

Peter started the truck and Will Henry cranked fast and furious trying to get the motor to catch, then Peter gave the old truck some gas. The truck did not move. Stepping back in front of the truck, Will Henry stooped over and cranked the truck up again. It hacked and wheezed and fumed a little, seeming to catch, but still did not move.

Peter and Will Henry looked at each other in the glow of the fire just blocks away. Peter's eyes narrowed when he was alarmed. They were mere slits now, but he appeared calm; his movements were quick, but smooth and methodical.

"What you wonder is wrong wit' dis truck, Peter?" Will Henry whispered, sharp and insistent.

"I don't know! You borrowed it. Did you check it over carefully?" Peter said with uncustomary irritation.

"Yas!"

"Carefully?" Peter asked again.

Looking warily at Peter, Will Henry opened the cab door of the truck, and taking a large flash light they had, he lifted the hood and looked under it. Peter got out to join him in looking as the light from the fire died down some. That meant their men were gone. The voices they heard now belonged to the jail house mob that now would be slowly returning to the jail. Their men were gone. They were on their own!

"I don't see anything wrong, Will, do you?"

"No, no!" Will answered. He was sweating now, realizing that they were isolated here. They should have made a better plan! A different plan! Maybe two trucks, one to back up the other.

"Damn!" Peter exclaimed as he got back into the cab of the truck.

"Nobody counted on the truck stalling!"

"What's da matter? What's wrong?" O'Neill shouted, peeping out from under the straw, why ain't we moving?"

"Stalled!" Will Henry told him, his voice edged with panic.

"Oh, Lawd!" Aristotle and O'Neill said in unison.

Will Henry cranked the truck hard again until he thought he heard the motor turn over, and Peter turned the key in the ignition again. The truck jumped, sputtered, and bumped forward a few inches and stopped.

"Lawd!" Will Henry exclaimed.

Nobody in the Inner Circle knew that the truck had stalled. Soon enough the mob would realize that the fire was a ruse and return, now two hundred strong. Already he thought he could hear the footsteps of some of the mob making their way back to the jail, their voices wild and wondering. It would be just a matter of time before they were found in back of the jail.

A look of cold alarm passed between Will Henry and Peter.

"Will, give O'Neill a gun," Peter said, with some resignation.

"Alright."

This afternoon Peter had put a rosary in his pocket that had belonged to his grandmother Blanche Giteau. The rosary was beautiful and delicately made of white seed pearls. Touching it now comforted him—seemed to help clear his mind.

When Will Henry gave the gun to O'Neill, O'Neill showed it to Aristotle. The gun was a dull, black, rather harmless looking thing.

Aristotle looked at it and said, "We ain't gone make it after all, is we?"

Then he laid his head back down on the floor of the truck, his breath coming in short fearful gasps.

"O'Neill! Come out and help Will push," Peter shouted suddenly, and O'Neill scrambled out from under the straw, putting the gun in his jacket pocket.

Will Henry cranked again with all of his might. He was soaked with sweat as he, hearing the motor turn over, ran to the back of the truck to push with O'Neill.

Peter, back in the truck, put his foot on the gas, worked the steering wheel and prayed.

"Careful you don't flood da engine!" Will Henry warned loudly, as he and O'Neill pushed the truck with all of their strength.

Abruptly the old truck lurched forward, jerked a few times, sputtered a bit, lunged forward again, and kept going as Will Henry ran and swung into the front cab with Peter.

"Keep 'er goin'!" O'Neill hollered as he ran along behind the truck, trying to hop into the back as the truck took off faster and faster.

O'Neill barely made it as Peter sped off, daring not to stop, but yelling to O'Neill, "Get in! Get in!"

Jubilantly the men reached the bus line that led north to south through Colored Town. From there they could go across town, get on the pike for a few miles, then cut through the woods to the house of John Candle the herbalist who was expecting them.

"Made it, made it!" O'Neill sung out.

"Not yet," Peter said, looking behind him. A Ford had been following them ever since they had hit the bus line.

"We're being followed," Peter said to Will Henry.

"I know," Will Henry answered, glaring straight ahead.

"There can't be more than four of them in that car," Peter said, tensing.

"Can we take them?" he said, turning to look quickly at Will Henry.

"Gawd damn right!" Will Henry said a little too recklessly for Peter's taste. He thought again of how right Dave was to send Will Henry into the woods tonight.

"What'll we do, Peter?" O'Neill asked, his voice filled with anger and anxiety.

"I'll slow down and let them pass us if they will," Peter said. "They just might not be following us as we think," Peter said, looking at the rifle that sat across the window and touching the gun at his waist.

Peter slowed down. The Model T Ford pulled ahead of them and crossed in front of them, cutting them off.

"Stay in the truck!" Peter cautioned. "Let them come to us," he said, placing his gun between them.

A tall dark Negro man threw his long legs out of the car and quickly walked back to the truck. He was smoking a cigarette and smiling.

It was Dave Bailey.

"What took you so long?" He asked in a jocular manner that hid the real sense of concern he had felt when he realized his friends were overdue. "Towerland's truck has a history of stalling. I thought about that the minute we set the fire. We were waiting here at your crossing point. When you all were later than we figured you should be...well, we were only going to wait about thirty seconds more, then we were going to head back to the jail. We're going to stay with you now until you get all the way to John Candle's."

Peter and Will Henry smiled with pleasure and relief. Their plan seemed to be working after all.

"We did stall!" Peter explained. "It was pretty scary there for a while."

"We better git," Dave said, looking up and down the dark empty bus line. They were more than a mile away from the jail and the mob now, and the next bus was not due for another twenty minutes.

"Wait a minute," Dave said. "You know I've never even laid eyes on the prisoner? I'd like to meet him—in a hurry of course," Dave said, making his way to the back of the truck with his flashlight.

Will Henry got out and helped Dave remove some of the straw that covered Aristotle Gillis. Then he peeled back the blanket and Dave aimed the light towards, but not directly on Aristotle, so that the light would not hurt his eyes.

The other men were piling out of the car. They wanted to see the freed man too.

"Hurry!" Dave beckoned to them.

"This is our leader," Will Henry said proudly as Dave reached for and held Aristotle's hand. He nearly burst with anger when he saw Aristotle's face. It was swollen, bloody, with two black eyes, one closed. His lips were nearly too puffed up to speak.

Aristotle, laying in the truck, raised up and rested his sore body on his sore arm. He held Dave's hand.

"I'm much obliged ta ya, Mistah..."

"Dave Bailey."

"Mistah Dave Bailey, I sho' do thank y'all fer saving me," he whispered. "And I won't be forgetin' dis heah no way soon," Aristotle said passionately.

"My pleasure," Dave said in a tight whisper. He was outraged—again. But this time his anger was not as white hot. It was cooled a little by their activity to rescue this man and get him back to his family. This time he would not have to walk through the woods for hours thinking murderous thoughts and feeling helpless. This time there was some joy in the pain he felt for Aristotle Gillis—the joy of victory, the defeat of powerlessness.

"You are going to a place where nobody can find you!" he told Aristotle. "There is a man out yonder in the woods who helps us. He is a healer. You'll be well in no time. Don't be frightened. You're well protected and safe now. There are a lot of us working together."

Quickly Dave introduced the men that were with him: Amos Shackelford, Mister Daniels, Lincoln Foster.

"Good luck!" he said to Aristotle.

Aristotle tried to see the men that accompanied Dave but could not, until Dave thought to shine the light briefly in their faces. They were all smiling and wishing him well. Aristotle looked at them all and tried to smile, tried to talk a little.

Dave tapped him lightly on the shoulder. "Don't try to talk anymore. We understand," he said. The men walked briskly back towards their car, as Aristotle Gillis of Carson, Arkansas, and soon to be Buffalo, New York, laid his badly bruised face on the floor of the truck and prayed and cried through tears of happiness.

Across town Lela Bailey, Aggie Pratt, Mae Bell and Nettie saw the flames as they leaped and flashed against the midnight blue sky, signaling courage and power, and a new day.

"Dey done done hit!" Aggie yelled. She grabbed Mae Bell and they danced gleefully around the room like two mad birds.

"Thank you Jesus!" Nettie exclaimed. "Hallelujah! Nah ahm really sweatin'!"

Only Lela was utterly silent as she stood at the window watching the flames. She was a pillar of strength and comfort when it came to other people's children—indeed one of the first people most anybody thought of calling in a time of crisis was Lela. But with Dave, Lela was different. She simply could not bear the thought of him being hurt—or worse. Thoughts of his safety were constantly on her mind when he was away from home. Lela felt better now with the existence of the Circle and their vow to protect each other, but not much.

And now this handful of men were going up against the Law in their effort to save one of their own! Lela knew that they had pledged themselves to protecting each other, but still it was almost too much for her mother's heart.

And that huge fire! And not knowing what was happening! Lela felt numb, frozen into silence. She was worried that if she spoke at this moment, she might start hollering and lose control of herself, and she did not wish to lose her "peace" not in front of these women—especially not before Aggie, who depended on her so much for strength.

Help me Lawd Jesus in dis mah hour of need! Lela said over and over in her mind, not even daring to move her lips.

At Lela's request, the women had read a good deal of the Psalms while they waited, especially the twenty-third Psalm, which they had read twice.

Mae Bell did not read with them, but sat apart at the little table under the window with her own coal oil lamp and a hot cup of tea in front of her. While the others read from the Bible, she sang soft and low, one spiritual after another-songs she had learned in churches here and there on her sojurn to adulthood.

"You got a right nice voice Miz Mae Bell," Lela had remarked after the readings, and Aggie had caught Mae Bell's eye and winked.

Aggie could tell that Lela was nervous about Dave tonight, although she was pretty good at hiding this fact. Aggie herself was frightened about this, their first case where they actually put themselves up against the Law and the Klan. What if in that good group of trusted men there was a snake, another snitch—maybe better paid than Marko Horton, and therefore willing to risk more, give up more, tell where the meetings were held, and who the leaders were? In her heart Aggie knew Lela was thinking these same thoughts.

Lela pulled herself away from the window and sat down at the kitchen table again, and when she lifted her tea cup, her hands shook so badly that she had to put the cup back on the table, complaining that the tea was too hot, to cover her shakiness. Aggie looked hard at Lela through the lamp light. It was now very dark outside, but they were using only one lamp—for no good reason except that one lamp could more quickly be blown out than several, if that became necessary.

"Nah, let me tell you somethin', Mother Bailey, since you done been so nice to set me straight mo' den once," Aggie began her tone so loud, harsh and firm that it caused all of the women to sit up and listen. "Dave is smart and he tough. He ain't bout ta git hisself and dose Circle mens into anything dey can't git outta, believe you me! If he got who I think he be having wit' him, sich as "Teak" Moody and Dolittle Auburn and Amos Sackelford and Lincoln Foster and lak dat, dey ain't no ways slow either. So you just rest yo' mind and git up all dat faith I know you has and take a grip on hit. Dem mens gone be alright. Dave a grown main nah. You gotta learn to trust his own thinking 'bout things."

Lela looked at Aggie through tears of gratitude. Her mouth moved several times before she could find words to thank her. "I know you right, Aggie," Lela said softly. "I just gotta trust in da Lawd to take care o' my boy. Take care all dem. You know how hit is, Aggie. Sometimes you jus' git besides yo'self and start worryin' when you should be prayin'."

Mae Bell smiled a broad pleased smile at Aggie, and Nettie grunted appreciatively, for they too had noticed Lela's distress and were glad for Aggie's helpful words.

Mae Bell passed tea cakes around the table. "Dese ain't hard," she said, teasing Aggie about the time at her house two years ago that she had tried to eat the rock hard cakes that Aggie had made.

Helpful words. Joking. Now some of the worry and fright they all had felt was evaporating away.

"Nah, ahm gone check on mah boys in da guest room, Mother Bailey, 'cause hit's about dey bed time, den we gone finish reading da next selection dat you done picked out. I speck we'll stay heah wit' you tonight, if dats OK."

"And we'll jus' rest easy 'til dem mens gits back wit' da news," Nettie said, looking around. "I ain't never done bent up heah befoe, Miz Bailey. You sho' is got a pretty place."

Lela was fond of saying she had Bibles all over the house, and she did, so each woman had her own.

"Let us," Lela suggested in the solemn, slow voice she used for scripture readings, "turn to the eleventh chapter of John, verses twenty-five and twenty-six, and give up some praise."

As Lela read from the Bible, Mae Bell sang softly, "Jesus is mah harbor, Jesus is mah light. He will bring me safely o'er da waves!" It was a song from years ago when someone had briefly forced her to attend Sunday school to try to help her forget the burning hurt she had felt inside because her mother had abandoned her.

"Nah let us read John eleven, twenty-five and twenty-six," Lela said.

The women read together: "Jesus said unto her, I am the resurrection and the life: He that believeth in me, though he were dead, yet shall he live: And whosoever liveth and believeth in me shall never die. Amen."

Lela thought the selection a good preparation in case any lives—God forbid—were lost this evening.

"Nah," Lela said to the three women, "Ah will turn to another one of mah favorites, da one hundred and twenty-first Psalm. Heah hit is," she said, reading alone: "Ah will lift up mine eyes into the hills from whence cometh mah help."

Lela read on until she came to the seventh verse, which she read with great fervor: "Da Lawd shall preserve thee from all evil: he shall preserve thy soul."

She continued on until she finished the last verse. Then, feeling a good deal better, she turned to Mae Bell, who many thought too wicked to join the church and associate with "nice peepers" and said, "you know you really has a pretty voice, girl. You oughta gie thought ta jineing da choir. You could easy be a solo. Rev. Edison would be sho' nuff glad to have ya ahm sho'," Lela said sincerely.

"Why thank ya, mam! I really preciates you axing me to jine yo' church. Dat sho' do mean a lots to me. A whole lots," Mae Bell said fervently. Then, trying to keep a straight face, she asked, "Did you say you think Rev. Edison would be glad to have me? Well I'll certainly think on dat Miz Bailey," she said, glancing at Aggie, a giggle bubbling up between them.

TWENTY-FIVE

I t was after eight o'clock and colder than normal for this time of year. Most of the residents of West Steward, black and white, were getting comfortable for the evening, eating supper, not planning to venture out again until morning. Many of the elderly residents were already in bed. But as the fire burned down the Old Storage House, many people doned robes and slippers and went to peek out of their windows to investigate the ruckus. Many of the mob at the jail reported the next day that, although they had responded to the noise and fire at the Old Storage House in a flash, they had seen no one and nothing, except the well fed flames shooting toward the sky that finally consumed the Old Storage House completely.

Moments after arriving at the fire, the Francoxes, who were much more interested in claiming their reward money than watching the flaming spectacle, began to consider the possibility that they had been duped into leaving the jail.

"Git back to da jail!" They yelled to the crowd. "Niggers is tryin' to bust dat main out! Dey tryin' to fool us! Get back to da jail house!"

Many of the mob headed back to the jail, but more than half stayed to watch the fire light up the town.

The small group, led by Rendell Francox, found the prisoner, Aristotle Gillis, gone, the back door to the jail wide open, the lawmen knocked out.

"Gawd damn hit!" Rendell exclaimed. "Dese niggers is takin' us fer a ride! Come on, boys!" he said to the cousins Wilson and Oakes. "Let's us go over to Old Steward and git Sheriff Lynn. Da mayor is outta town!"

On the way to Old Steward, the men hotly discussed recent events in the town: Two white people had been killed just last month, and the deputy sheriff had leaked that the Duster boy, their only suspect so far, had disappeared—with his whole family. Now another suspect had been caught and brought in, and a bunch of niggers—yes, niggers! Who else would set a fire to distract folks? Who else but niggers would have busted a Colored man out of jail?

The cousins knew from DeBell Hinkle that the snitch Marko Horton had also left town suddenly and unexpected, leaving White Town without its best source of information.

"Dese burr heads is jus' dancing a jig on our private parts—and hit's gone stop!" Rendell Francox exclaimed angrily.

Someone had gone the short distance to alert the sherriff of Old Stewart. When Sheriff Jethro Lynn and his deputy Ansell Morrissey, a loyal young man half his seventy years, arrived at the jail, they found the four lawmen still sleeping peacefully, the sheriff and deputy in a cell, the aids from Monroe flopped out in the small back room.

"Lawd will you look at dis heah!" the old sheriff whistled, walking back and forth through the jail.

The Francoxes had squeezed into the jail along with the cousins Willie "Red" Oakes, Parker Wilson and Louis D. Stassen, head of the Klan in Southeast Arkansas, who had finally been located and had made his way to the jail. Deputy Morrissey pulled his pistol on some other members of the mob who were trying to shove their way in to see what was going on.

Sensing unnatural sleep among the lawmen, Sheriff Lynn ordered his deputy to immediately call West Steward Community Hospital for ambulances. As early as he could tomorrow morning, he would go to the county seat and ask for two or three more men—whatever the evertightening budget allowed—for West Steward. Sheriff Lynn was certain everything could be brought under control again. There had been "problems" before and they had been dealt with. They would pick up the handyman, O'Neill Edwards, then there was the cook. Yes. She must be found right away also.

Who knew where they were? Nobody. Well, as soon as the sheriff and his men were on their feet again, all of the loose ends concerning the cook and the handyman could be tied together. Sheriff Lynn didn't know where either Nettie or O'Neill Edwards lived. Birkens had better find them himself when he woke up.

While he waited for the ambulances, the sheriff examined the four men himself, especially Sheriff Birkens. He asked the cousins, who were young and strong, to aid Deputy Morrissey in getting the two Monroe men into a cell and on a cot where they could be looked at more easily. When Sheriff Lynn had the men where he wanted them, he began his examination.

First Sheriff Birkens and his deputy, who looked as normal as could be under the bright single light that swung from the ceiling: No obvious proud flesh in the face, legs and arms, no noticeable stiffness of the limbs, no great looseness of the joints. Their faces were not blotchy and discolored—yet no amount of cold towels to the face, or shaking of their bodies, or calling their names aloud woke any of the four men.

Deputy Morrissey had some ammonia in the little first aid kit that he had brought in from his police car. Getting the sheriff's permission, he passed it under the nose of each victim. Nothing. "Not even a flicker of an eyelid," he was to tell his wife later.

"Poison," the sheriff announced to the room. "Real smart poison."

Who? They exclaimed in unison. What? The old sheriff did not answer, but he knew. African voodoo shit probably. He had run up on this "harmless" poison before, many years ago. The circumstances were different but the poison was the same. Exactly. And there was only one man in these parts that had that kind of stuff—John Candle. But he could prove nothing. And he knew quite well that it did not pay to mess with John Candle! If you did you might very well end up cold and stiff the next day. Everyone knew that. John Candle was off limits—even to the powerful. That man was friends with the devil, it was said.

But he was a healer of some reknown as well. And everyone, black or white, knew the ancient man could often cure what the "big white doctors" could not.

"Louie D" Stassen, Parker Wilson and "Red" Oakes had no trouble loading up three truck loads of men to go to Colored Town. This was the usual procedure: When Negroes acted up from time to time, they had to be put back into their place. A ride through the town hollering threats, breaking out windows, shooting into the air and giving any unfortunate man they meet a good ass beating was usually enough to scare the tar out of Colored Town residents and restore law and order. The next morning would find the Negroes quiet and docile again. A lynching was rarely necessary—although if one was, there were always plenty of volunteers.

Sheriff Lynn knew that he could not stop the three trucks that were already rolling out. A decent enough man, he hoped nobody got lynched. He would never admit it, but he put his money on the Negroes this night. They knew how to lock their doors, put out their lights and hide—unless their houses were set on fire.

Whoever had done this was bold, and even smart. He had to give it to them. They had killed two white people and had not been caught. In his mind, he believed it was unlikely that they would be. And they had burned down a great big storage house and rescued the Gillis fellow.

And four white lawmen lay drugged and useless. There was no doubt in Sheriff Jethro Lynn's mind that it was nigras who were doing these things—and the same ones that burned down the storage house killed the white folks down on Honeysuckle Lane, he was sure of it. The only thing he had not figured out was why.

Obviously, they had burned down the Old Storage House to rescue a man, but why had Leon Baycott and Luxury Tweedle been killed by these same people? He and his friends in Old Steward and up in White Town had talked of little else in the last month and a half, and they had all just about come to the same conclusion: Somebody had a grudge against Leon—one of the Negroes—Luxury was just in the way.

The old sheriff thought he finally heard the sirens from the ambulances coming. He told Ansell to have them come as close to the door of the jail as possible and to be as quick as possible. If the remaining crowd saw the four lawmen stretched out for dead in the ambulances, they would likely go wild, the sheriff thought.

Well, what could he do? Age and experience had introduced a certain amount of fatalism into the old sheriff's personality, he thought. Hell, what was gonna happen was gonna happen. The night was already one of the worst of his life. He would tell the mayor when he got back into town that he had done the very best that he could—after all, he wasn't sheriff over here.

Sheriff Lynn thought going to Colored Town in trucks was very unwise, but no one would listen to him. Privately, he welcomed the ride to the hospital to get away from some of this mess! Clearly something was happening to the niggers lately. He was not the only one who had noticed it. Even when they came to Old Steward, to his town to shop it was noticed. In the five and dime, in the Piggly Wiggly, in the various dress shops and shoe shops, in the furniture store where droves of young blacks used to go, back when people had some money to buy their phonograph records. A new boldness in many, a lack of meekness, a lack of fear—something was different.

Maybe hit wuz all jus' comin' together in dese latest events dat had happened, the old sheriff thought.

Cautiously, he looked out of the window. There they went-three full trucks headed for Colored Town. Somehow, the sheriff thought, the situation in Colored Town was not going to be like truck loads of men had always found it in the past—

dark, extremely quiet, everybody behind locked doors and scared to death. Although he didn't know what, the old sheriff smelled a rat. Something was going to be different this time; he felt it in his gut where he felt everything—not in his heart. Hell, he had not been the sheriff for twenty-five years and learned nothing!

He was old, sickly, tired. The sheriff thought it best that he was going in the opposite direction of the trucks. He was taking care of the sheriff, getting him back on his feet so he could take care of his own town himself. Nobody could fault him for that. He was sure the mayor would approve his actions here tonight.

The events that had happened recently—taken together—were grounds for a lynching most of the white men agreed. A lynching had a way of quieting things down. So they talked back and forth as the trucks headed for Colored Town. Some of the men were armed, although most were not.

Everyone knew of Louie D's Klan connection and looked to him as their leader.

"I bet if we shoot every nigger in sight tonight, and then burn a few crosses on these hills things will quiet down a plenty!" he exclaimed.

"Can you believe it?" One of the other men asked in disbelief. "Niggers done poisoned a whole bunch o'lawmens and busted a killer outta jail—and done got away clean so far, and we ain't got no iddy who dey is."

"Do you suppose it were outside niggers or no?" someone asked. "I think dey musta be, 'cause our niggers wouldn't dare to do no sich a thang as dat!"

The trucks roared towards Colored Town in a straight determined line, covering the ten minutes of distance in half the time. The night was clear and cool enough to blow wispy, frosty breaths back into the faces of the men, as the bright moon which had finally came out, ducked back and forth between the clouds like a peek-a-boo spectator.

As the men neared the black area, they watched angrily for a single man that they might "whip the piss out of," Louie D. said, to teach him or them, and thus the entire community, a lesson. The cousins were talking lynching, and the trucks full of men could have been easily persuaded had a victim shown himself. But there were no Colored people on the street. Not one.

TWENTY-SIX

D̲ave and his group had accurately anticipated the moves of the white men and had prepared themselves for the trucks they knew would be coming down the main street, Chinaberry, any minute now.

After the fire had been set, the Colored men sped in all directions. They had less than ten minutes to roll down the main streets in Colored Town shouting, "A fire! Trouble in White Town! Put out your lights and lock your doors!"

After the town had been alerted, all of Dave's men met in the middle of Chinaberry Street for further instructions. They laughed, pleased at how quickly and smoothly they had carried out their task, and surprised by their own lack of fear. It was as if all of them had been waiting all of their lives for this moment—like Mister Daniels.

Chinaberry was not the real main street, but it was the first wide neighborhood street of little houses one came upon when entering the Colored area from White Town. This was the street that the white men would drive down, shooting and hollering and threatening to do injury to anyone they could find.

Dave had divided the men roughly into five small groups stationed at the beginning, middle and end of both sides of Chinaberry Street so they could converge when needed. For dramatic effect, he told his men he would put six of the younger men in low, "climbable" trees with their weapons. When he signaled to these men, they would jump down from the trees to give the white men the notion that the trees were full of Colored men ready to pounce on them.

Minutes later, the three trucks of perfect white targets rolled directly into the line of fire as Dave's men stood waiting, wearing the suggested dark clothes, their faces covered with hankerchiefs so they would not be recognized.

The black men had been instructed not to shoot first. If the white men started shooting, then the black men would shoot first into the air and into the ground.

227

Dave hoped this surprise "barrage" would be enough to rout the white men—for an unseen and unexpected enemy was hard to fight against.

If they could not scare the volunteers from White Town off with their surprise "attack," it had been thoroughly discussed at a number of the meetings that they had held in the woods, if it came to shooting to kill to protect their own lives, they were prepared to do so. The twenty or so extra men that had joined them this evening had been briefed and were as prepared as the regular Circle men could make them in the short time they had spent together.

Dave hardly knew what to think of the "new" men they had picked up. He was surprised and glad to have them, he reckoned. But trusting this, their first real case against the Law into the hands of men who had not been in on any of the meetings, did not know of their dedication and committment to avoiding violence at all costs, did not know who the team leaders were—Dave found all this more than a bit unnerving. He certainly hoped he could trust all of these men who had bravely joined in on the operation tonight. Right now the only thing he could rely on was their blackness, their sense of the rightness of their cause and their action. He prayed that it was enough to carry them through.

Rev. Matthew Moses Clayton, who had insisted on being a part of "this battle," as he called it, tried to control his shaking knees and hands. He was not afraid, just deeply saddened by this turn of events.

Actually a mixture of three emotions assailed him, and sadness was their leader. Sadness, anxiety, and a wild joy that they had stopped a lynching. These three feelings entertwined like snakes and nipped at his heart before finally melting into one curious sensation: That of a strange, dreamlike uneasiness. Like knowing you are dreaming, but being unable to wake.

Rev. Clayton wondered how the other men felt. When the moon flitted out from the clouds he could see their faces briefly, and tried to weigh their sentiments as best he could. From what he could see and feel, they looked ready and able.

Watching the men, the minister felt deeply proud. He allowed his Christian spirit to push out thoughts of impending disaster and fill all of the empty quivering spaces with faith. He truly hoped he would not have to preach over anybody tomorrow, and standing in his position with his gun, he prayed without ceasing.

"Heah dey come!" Dave's men called. "Git ready!"

The trucks made their way down and across the bus line that separated the town into East and West, and turned onto Chinaberry Street as the men had expected.

The black men tensed in their places, their weapons ready to shoot to "heaven or hell," as Naisbitt Patterson had put it. The young men balanced themselves more securely in their trees, their blackness hiding them in the darkness of the night.

Dave prayed that everyone would keep their emotions under control. Three or four dead white men could cause a riot of the worse kind.

"Control, control," Dave chanted under his breath, knowing full well that this entire situation has been generated by a lack of control on the part of the white men.

"Heah dey come," a man whispered loudly as the white men proceeded in the night. "Alright nah!"

The trucks had slowed considerably after the drivers had turned into the residential area, and was conducting what looked like a friendly, pleasant drive through town, but seeing the darkened windows and very probably locked doors enraged and enboldened the truck loads of men and they began to shout, "Come on out you scared assed monkey niggers! Come on out so's we kin string ya up!"

"Who done set dat fie at da Old Storage House? We know y'all hiding da Gillis boy! Y'all better bring 'em on out chere! Don't and y'all gone suffer fer hit! Bring 'em out! Don't and we gone set all dese shanty shacks on fie!"

"Some o'you nappy headed coons done burnt down dat storage house knowing full well hit was a white main's property! You niggers is gittin' scandalous but we gone fix yo' black asses!"

The trucks rolled along in the semi-darkness until they were about halfway up the street, surrounded by an unnatural silence except for their own periodic rantings.

The black men stood waiting, waiting. A slight wind drifted through the trees, ripping away a few more of the more willing autumn leaves with each windy breath.

Various voices from the trucks continued to ring out: "We know y'all know who done kilt dose two peepers last month! Y'all better tell da sheriff or we gone jus' start to fillin' dese trees wit' lynched jigaboos! Is all o'y'all ready to swing? Where dose Dusters peepers at? Where so ever dey is we gone find dem! We wanta talk ter dat Ralph boy!"

All of these remarks were aimed at the houses on either side of the tree-lined Chinaberry Street. Not one of the men in the trucks had given any indication that they saw any of the dozens of dark men that stood at their posts behind and in the trees, between little houses, hunched down behind fences.

So, Dave thought. Word has gotten around that somebody got Ralph out of town. Dave's mouth slid into a smile again. He noticed with pleasant surprise that his hands were very steady now, and that all anxiety had left him.

The houses all over Colored Town were utterly silent. It was as if they were empty. Empty of peace, empty of justice, they stood as a rebuke to the white men, as well as fuel and targets for their fury.

Suddenly somebody from the truck threw a brick, shattering a window, and the sound played upon itself in the extreme quiet, becoming more full and self important than a mere brick thrown through a single window would normally be. The stillness continued.

Next a man from the trucks pulled his gun and aimed directly into the window of one of the houses. Glass shattered and a scream immediately rang out, followed by a child's loud crying.

"Pay dirt!" A toothless man grinned and hollered from the last truck in the line.

Instantly more than a dozen shots rung out from several areas of the street, and the tires from the middle truck were quickly shot out, and sat flat on the ground holding six astonished white farmers, shop keepers and mill workers in its back, two more men in the cab.

The mouths of the men in the trucks literally dropped open at the boldness of what they could now see was scores of Negro men like black shadows in the dim light slowly circling them, cutting off running escape—if they had not been too stunned to take off.

Never had the twenty-five or so white men witnessed—or heard of—a group of Negroes attacking white men. And yet here they stood watching black men with drawn weapons and hankerchiefs over their faces coming upon them!

The black men, weapons ready, got within several feet of the trucks, but not close enough for their dark faces to be recognized—and stopped. Somebody in the trucks thought they had seen a definite signal from one of the black men to stop the others.

Now another sure signal, and three men from the side where the shot had been fired in the window quickly ran over to the house to check on its occupants. Everyone could still hear a child screaming.

In a few minutes, while the world stopped its rotation, the three men were back to report that nobody had been shot. A young mother, ignoring her husband's advice, had suffered minor cuts on her face and hands because she had been peering out of the window that the man on the truck had shot out. Her child had screamed in fright, but was unharmed.

Silas Benson, one of the young men that had gone to check on the occupants of the house, moved up to the truck where the shot seemed to have come from. He was pointing a gun. His face was a sweaty black mask of hatred under his hankerchief. He could not tell who had fired the shot but it did not matter.

"Lucky for whatever one of you crackers fired dat shot dat you didn't hit no one," he said loudly, boldly. "If you had kilt someone in dat house den I would be obliged to shelve dis shotgun up dat main's ass and pull da trigger!"

Having said this, the young man stepped back into the crowd and smiled, more pleased with himself than he could ever remember—even when he had caught his first fish over in Alabama at his grandmother's house, and it had weighed more than twelve pounds.

Perhaps later when he was alone, and some of the white men had put a name to his voice and came after him to hurt or kill him, perhaps then he would become afraid and regret his reckless speech. But not now!

Now all he felt was jubilation! A wild thumping of his heart that he could barely contain. They were standing together—finally—after months of talking and planning and talking some more. They had these white men cornered! They had the upper hand! Silas Benson felt lightheaded, like he was about to join the moon in the clouds and float away.

No matter how long he lived, Silas knew he would not forget this night and his part in it.

"Why you sonafabitch!" the toothless man shouted, stepping forward in the truck, courage riding on his anger. "I'll teach ya a lesson!" he screeched, bringing his shotgun up and pointing in Silas' direction. "Come on up wha I kin see ya, if you dare! Don't en I'll shoot into da crowd!"

The man thought he had made a pretty good show of bravery against the black man, as he looked for Silas, and back at the other white men for support. But the white men in the trucks were still so confounded by this turn of events that they had barely moved.

Silas stepped out of the crowd again and pointed his gun directly at the toothless man that he could now easily identify because the moon had decided to show itself again.

"Go ahead," he said cooly. "Shoot me."

The two men stood pointing their guns at each other—one confident and determined, the other gasping with rage and amazement.

A voice cried out from the lead truck, "You got us nah, but we'll see ya again real soon. One at a time! Den thangs gone be different!"

"And you can kiss mah ass den, and nah!" someone shouted out of the black crowd, to approving titters by Dave's men.

Finally Silas and the toothless man, both glowering at each other, lowered their guns. Silas was careful to lower his several seconds after the man in the truck did so—he could afford to. The black men had him covered.

Dave Bailey, still wearing his mask, stepped out of the crowd.

"Who is the leader here?" he asked.

"We ain't got no leader! We don't need no leader! Who is yo' leader?"

"Why did you come down here?" Dave asked reasonably of the bib overall-clad man who was doing the talking.

"Ta git dat main you niggers done busted outta jail, dats why!" the bib-clad man answered gathering courage from his own anger and frustration, and bringing the truck loads of men back to a semblance of life. "You lettin' a main who done kilt two peepers get away!"

"You goin' outside da Law. What you bastards think ya doin'?" someone from a truck shouted. "Burnin' down property! Killin' white folks! Shoally y'all don't think we jus' gone let dis rest?"

"Nah, if y'all would jus' see fit to step on back a bit and let us gone on back home, we could possibly see dat it don't go too bad fer all o'y'all," another voice from the truck suggested in a concilatory manner.

Walking up to the first truck, Dave smiled and touched the arm of the bib-clad man who had first spoken. The man jerked away roughly and stared at Dave with wide-eyed surprise and anger.

"Don't go puttin yo' hains on me!" he hissed.

"Look," Dave said to the man in a pleasant and friendly voice. He pointed up into the trees.

Reluctantly the man's eyes followed Dave's pointing fingers and let out a strangled sound as he squinted into one tree and then another as the moon barely illuminated figures of black men with their pistols and shotguns pointed at them.

"Gawd damn!" the man exclaimed. "Look at dis y'all!" he said to the men in his truck. "Dese trees is filled wit', wit'..." He found himself hesitating to say niggers, to say coons, to say shines, burr heads. "...mens!" Suddenly he was finding it hard to breathe. His face reddened and he broke out into a sweat as he began to realize for the first time that he and the rest of the white men in the trucks might be in real danger. That he, Louis D. Stassen, head of the Klan in Southeast Arkansas, was surrounded by niggers with guns who did not seem at all afraid—in fact, this tall one, who seemed jet black in this darkness, was easy and confident and seemed to be smiling broadly and frequently behind his mask.

Dave gestured to one of the men in his group, and the man stepped backwards, outside of the twenty or so men that surrounded the three trucks, and standing like a soldier, straight and erect, this man raised his shotgun to the sky and shot into the air three times. Pow! Pow! Pow!

Then he lowered his gun and smiled and walked up to Louis D. Stassen.

"You who dey call Louie D, ain't ya! Da Klan main?"

The regional Klan leader looked flustered and put out by this second familiarity from a Colored man. How did he know who he was? His position in the Klan was supposed to be somewhat of a secret.

"Well, nah," the man said to Louie D. "Mah name is Death and Destruction. Dese mens," Omar continued, smiling, "is all friends of one another. We looks out fer one another, know what I means, boss?"

A few minutes after Omar had shot into the air and had given his small speech to Louis D. Stassen, there came a bursting, rushing noise from either end of Chinaberry Street—the quiet but quick sound of footsteps moving in the direction of the trucks.

Suddenly the men in the trucks saw what was causing the shuffling sounds and their hair stood up on the back of their arms and necks.

"What the Sam Hill!?"

"Gawd damn! What's goin' on?"

"Shit, dey gone kill all of us!"

"Oh, Lawd! Jus' look at da niggers!"

From the west and east ends of Chinaberry Street, Omar's three shots brought the rest of the men. They walked with slow and steady resolution towards the trucks.

Later, the white men who would talk about it at all would speak in hushed voices of the "five or six hunnert niggers coming on them wit' hankerchiefs over dey faces and dey hats pulled down over dey eyes so's we couldn't make dem out. And all o'dem had a shotgun apiece, a pistol in dey belts and a razor in dey hat band! We wuz outnumbered twenty or thirty to one!"

Actually it was less than forty black men, but it was to be remembered as the strangest of nights—later some would wonder if it happened at all, if indeed the whole confrontation had not been a dream, or a nightmare; the kind of raving mind pictures you got when you went to sleep with a stomach full of watermelon and fish, which every sensible person knew should never be eaten together.

Black men confronting white men? Threatening them, scaring them? In 1930, a year when scores of black men were lynched for much less. Surely a dream!

Dave had to hope this show of force and togetherness would be enough to cause the white men to think twice before coming to Colored Town again with bad intent. Or would it backfire? Dave would not let himself think of that possibility.

Now LaSalle Peabody stepped forward out of the circle of black men. Although he looked boyish, and lacked real height, LaSalle conveyed a certain dignity that caused the men, black and white, to quiet down and take notice.

LaSalle removed his cap respectfully and began to speak in his careful studied manner:

"All day long we been hearin' talk dat dere gone be some trouble in White Town tonight, so me and my friends heah," LaSalle pointed at the black men surrounding the truck and those a short distance away, "we done got together to protek ourvaselves. We didn't know what kinda trouble, we didn't even down know trouble fer who or fer what or when dis trouble gone start. So we jus' decided to git ready fer whatever come, and ta look out after what's ourva own—ourva chirrens and ourva wifes and ourva houses same as you would," he said reasonably, walking slowly back and forth between the trucks.

"Cause," LaSalle continued, "If truf be heard, when deres trouble up in White Town, hit most-in-gently ends up spreading down heah fer some strange reason, whether hit be concernin' Colored peepers or no."

"Somebody done knocked dem lawmens out, done burnt down da Old Storage House, and while dat wuz a-goin' on, dey done sprung a guilty main from outta da jail house and let 'em go free! Nah you gone stand dere flat footed and tell us y'all don't no nothin' and ain't had no hain in hit?" one of the men snapped loudly from a truck.

"Why, boss," LaSalle said innocently, "we mens jus' heah to protek what belongst to us lak I done tole ya. We heard trouble is headed dis-away, so heah we is. See, boss," LaSalle continued. "We jus' can't 'law nobody to come 'tacking us no mo'. We got so little dese days as hit is, we natural feel we got to look out fer hit."

Other voices from the truck were sharp and indignent:

"I doesn't believe a word you sayin'! We knows hi to protek ourvaselves too! What ever y'all aim ta do, you sho' is hell ain't gone git away wit' hit! Somebody gone pay fer busting out mah ties! Nah, git on out da way and let us through!"

LaSalle, unperturbed, donned his cap again and stepped back into the crowd, back into the dark.

The assembled black men made no effort to move back and let the trucks pass. They stood silent and shadowy in the moonlight, causing many of the white men to wish they had not volunteered for this mission.

Now Dave stepped out of the group again. His manner was easy, nonchalant. "We don't want any trouble," he said in a firm voice, as if he were addressing a group of errant school boys. "We know nothing of what happened in White Town tonight. Like the gentleman said, we heard there was going to be some trouble. We don't want any problems, but neither are we running. Not anymore, gentlemen. We are law abiding citizens," Dave said, looking at the men in the trucks. "Unlike yourselves who have come down here with evil intent."

The men in the trucks murmured and whispered at this bold accusing speech.

"You know everything 'bout what happened tonight, you lying assed nigger!" someone from the truck burst out.

"You cannot prove that anyone here knew anything about either a fire or a jail break," Dave said. "Fact is we know nothing. What happened in White Town is your business, not ours."

"Why you sass talking bastard!" yelled one of the men in the bed of the middle truck, who had let his emotions get the best of him in spite of the threat the black men represented. "I'll blow ya nappy head offa ya shoulders!" he shrieked, bringing his shotgun up and pointing it at Dave.

But as soon as he pulled his gun on Dave, every man close to the trucks drew their weapons on him, ready to blast the man to pieces.

One could hear nothing but the dry scrape and sharp click of pistols and shotguns being cocked to fire.

Abruptly, the six men who had been standing on low branches in the trees jumped to the ground guns in hand.

"Mah Gawd! Dey got jus' hunnerts of niggers in dese trees!" one of the men in the truck gasped.

Now more than one of the white men's breath came in short pants and more than a few had broken out in a sweat as the scent of real danger thickened the air like a heavy vapor.

"Go ahead," Dave said quietly, his voice falling like velvet in the sudden still. "Shoot me. What are you waiting for?" He stood gunless with outstretched arms in a mocking posture of resignation, of surrender.

Walking ever closer to the truck, his arms still outstretched in surrender, Dave suddenly lunged forward and tore the gun from the man's hand. Then, backing away from the truck, he raised the gun and slowly aimed it.

"Or shall I shoot you?" Dave asked gently, the hankerchief over his face again sliding up his cheeks, hiding a smile.

"Yaaaaah!" one of the older men yelled out, as he fainted and fell backwards out of the truck to the ground.

A ripple of snide titters floated through the black crowd, and Silas Benson burst out laughing and could hardly bring himself under control again.

Slowly, slowly Dave lowered his gun and the man he had been threatening collapsed to a sitting position on the floor of the truck, shaking unashamedly with relief.

The next thing that happened was unplanned and unexpected and caused a stir of respectful moving back and careful watching among the black crowd.

A very black man of barely average height moved out from the crowd. He wore thick glasses and moved his right hand nervously back and forth across his head as if trying to rid himself of a pesky insect. He removed his mask, folded it carefully and placed it in his shirt pocket, then he moved up to the side of the lead truck.

He looked into the face of Louis D. Stassen for a long while, as if by looking he could see his mindset and thus fathom his soul.

Louie D looked back at the man, not recognizing him, barely able to see the features in his black face in this light.

The man looked up at the trees now, and all of the white men's eyes followed his, wandering at the scores of black men they still thought they saw there.

"Good evening, gentlemen," the small man began. "My name is Rev. Matthew Moses Clayton," he said, looking steadily at Louis D. Stassen again. "I'm the assistant pastor of one of the churches down here."

Now walking back and forth between the trucks, he said, "I want to tell you men in the trucks something that I think you oughta listen to closely," he said, looking at the white men, making sure that he had their attention. The black men had moved all the way up now, forming a rather tight circle in order to see and hear what was going on.

"I'm a man of peace. Peace and prayer. That's what I believe in. I don't like trouble, but sometimes it just comes to you. No matter how you set your mind against it. Now we got us some trouble tonight! Place burned down. Man gone. Now y'all here in your trucks. Things like that. But you see it's a serious, serious matter," the minister said. He walked back and forth, now rubbing his head with both hands, causing his grease laden hair to stick up in spikes, as the men both black and white strained to hear him. "When men will die to protect themselves—and I think that's the thinking these good Colored men have finally come to, you see," he continued, sounding more and more like the preacher he was. "When you are ready to actually *die* for what you think is right, that's when all natural fear leaves you and you get ready to go if need be."

Rev. Clayton looked at the white men. "You understand what I mean, gents?" the minister asked amiably.

The white men looked at each other in disbelief for the fourth or fifth time tonight. "Now, how many of you men in these trucks believe what happened up in White Town tonight is worth lying down your very lives for? Will you raise your hands?"

None of the white men in the three trucks moved. They could have been statues carved in chalk.

Rev. Clayton bowed a little to the men as if to say, *There. You see?*

"Make no mistake," he continued. "We will protect ourselves. No doubt about it."

"Him dat takes up da sword will die by da sword!" a man hollered out from a truck.

Rev. Clayton looked toward the voice. "Good! I'm glad to see you know scripture," he said pleasantly. "But that goes for you too, you know."

Another ripple of laughter went through the crowd of black men.

"If you come back down here," the minister continued, "you'll always find us just like this," he said, turning slowly, pointing to the circle of men. "And that," he said, finally pointing to the trees that the white men thought were infested with black men.

Now a very audible angry buzzing among the men in the trucks was heard.

"Is y'all threatening us, Reverend whatever yo' name is? Is y'all puttin' us on notice?" a red faced, outraged man asked.

Rev. Clayton ignored the man's outburst, which served to infuriate the white man even more. It caused him to fill with so much fury and frustration that his nose burned inside. He was sure before this was over he was going to have a stroke.

"We shall never be alone. When you see one man, there will be ten, twenty, nearby. We are committed and dedicated to protecting each other from this day forward. We want no misunderstandings or trouble. We aren't going to make any trouble if given a choice. We just want to be treated fairly and left in peace." The minister paused, looking up at the white men. "Gentlemen, the rest is up to you. Thank you for your patience," Rev. Clayton finished, stepping back into the arms and admiration of the Negro men. There was a smathering of applause from them, and Dave smiled at the minister and touched his shoulder in affectionate approval.

This unexpected speech of Rev. Clayton's brought the standoff to an end. The black men lowered their shotguns and pistols, and Omar closed his weapon of choice, his very sharp razor, and placed it in his shirt pocket. The others who had knives or razors put them away.

Omar stepped out and bellowed, "Y'all pick up dat brave main what done fainted and fell out da truck on his ass, and turn around and move dese gawd damn trucks outta heah!"

"What 'bout da truck y'all done shot out?" someone from the trucks whined.

"I'll have the tires replaced and have the truck setting in front of the jail by noon tomorrow," Dave answered. "You can bank on it."

The white men and the black men stared at each other for perhaps a full minute, then the men in the shot out truck clambered aboard the two good trucks, and the vehicles were turned around and slowly moved off, rapidly picking up speed as they went. And it was over. Less than an hour had passed, but it seemed like much longer.

The black men let out whoops of joy and victory. They hollered and slapped each other on the back and many of the older men cried with relief and amazement.

"We turned 'em back, didn't we?" they yelled to each other.

"We ain't powerless atall!"

"I wuz ready ta die!"

"Well, I'm glad we didn't have too!"

Always the realist, LaSalle said gloomily, "Dey'll be back wit' hunnerts."

"Let 'em come! We'll be waiting fer dem-in da trees!" Omar said, howling with laughter.

Dave and a few of the other men quickly sped back to his house, and after having a brief and reassuring conversation with his mother and the women, he and the men removed all of the weapons in the closet and took them back down to Chinaberry Street. This frightened Lela so badly that she started a series of prayers all over again.

The black men waited all night in various houses for the white men to return with a mob, with ropes, with guns, with fire. The men took turns sleeping and waiting. They waited with guns and pistols, machetes, hammers, hunting knives and pitch forks. Waiting, waiting.

At dawn no one had returned.

At noon, that evening, that night, the following day, not one white man had set foot in Colored Town. Not even to pick up rents, sell dress material to the women, or to collect insurance payments.

But the black men stashed their weapons and kept them ready.

When the story of all that happened spread, most of the Colored community was proud, but many were more afraid than ever. Dave's old enemies from the mill, Benjamin Carter, Rosebud Vickers and Charlie Abner, were incensed. Especially Benjamin Carter.

"Ah tole ya!" Benjamin shouted. "Young crazy niggers gone git us all kilt! What about peepers dat ain't in dey secret group? Who gone protek dem? Nah, da Klan and all dem gone be aftah every nigger dey see! Dat Dave done made us all unsafe! I know he had somethin' to do wit' hit! I could whip dem niggers' asses good!"

TWENTY-SEVEN

The four lawmen were whisked away from the jail, brought in and laid out on the waiting examining tables in the emergency room at Old Steward Community Hospital.

Dr. Theodore Chantel, Chief of Emergency Service that night, started to work on the men immediately. He and his resident rushed around taking blood pressures and checking the patients' eyes. They found all four of the men to have normal pressures and all of their eyes contracted to light in a normal manner.

"Did these patients suffer any kind of head injuries? Is there a history of diabetes in their backgrounds?" Dr. Chantel asked Sheriff Lynn.

"Hi da hell would I know! Nah, hi you think I know da medical history on dese mens?" Jethro Lynn asked incredulously. "Anyhow, no matter what dey history is, Doctor, do you think dey affliction would grab 'em all on the self same day? Nah, dat don't make no sense," the sheriff continued in a flabbergasted tone of voice.

"Yes, yes," Dr. Chantel hurriedly agreed. "Of course you are right." The doctor and his assistants examined the patients again. Finally Dr. Chantel asked the sheriff what he thought had happened to the men.

"Poisoned." The sheriff answered simply. "Dat's fer sho."

"Poison? Really? What kind of poison, Sheriff Lynn?"

"Hi da hell do I know? You da doctor," the old sheriff snapped.

"If you don't know what kind of poison we are working with here," Dr. Chantel said reasonably, "then how do you know it is poison?"

"I jus' know," the sheriff answered stubbornly. It was no use to tell them about John Candle's strange potions. They would never believe him. No use to go ask John Candle for the "wake up" potion—he would smile and deny everything.

"Oh, I see," said the doctor aridly, rolling his eyes toward the ceiling.

The neurologist, Dr. Phillip Batten, was sent for. He came down to the emergency room and repeated all of the physical testing that had been done, then with a lighted instrument, he peered at length into each man's eyes, checking the fundus, the very back of the eyes, for some indication of swelling of the brain. He found none.

"Strange, strange case," Dr. Batten murmured to himself, ticking off in his mind what was *not* wrong with these men.

"Umph!" the sheriff snorted. "Voodoo African shit pure and simple," he mumbled to himself.

Just then Sheriff Birkens yawned, kicked his legs out, looked puzzled as he felt for his pants which had been removed, and opening his eyes wide, he struggled to sit up on the side of the examining table.

Recognizing Sheriff Lynn immediately and seeing the white brightness of the room and the medical uniforms, he feared the worse.

"Jethro?" he said hoarsely. "What's happening? Where is ahm at?"

In fifteen minutes the other men were awake, even DeBell Hinkle, who was the last to fall asleep. They were all relaxed and very rested, but floored to find themselves in a hospital emergency room.

The astounded doctors examined the men again. They were made to touch their toes, fling their arms out to their sides while standing, hold their arms above their heads, and walk a straight line.

"I've never seen anything like this!" Dr. Batten exclaimed over and over. "How do you all feel?"

"Fine. Fine!"

In the end there was nothing to do but release the lawmen and send them home, or wherever they wanted to go.

"Voodoo!" said Sheriff Lynn.

"What?" asked Dr. Chantel.

"Jungle shit!" the sheriff exclaimed, removing and lighting one of the larger recycled cigar stumps he kept in a small flat tin in his jacket pocket.

"Now there'll be no smoking in here sheriff!" one of the nurses snapped. "There is oxygen and ether in here! Don't you know that? Put that stinky thing out this minute!"

"Bossy little thang, ain't she?" Sheriff Lynn said to his deputy, smiling.

"Yes, sir. She is that," Deputy Morrissey agreed. "Now, what did you say about the jungle, sir?"

"Oh, nothing," the sheriff answered.

As the old sheriff and his deputy drove the lawmen back to West Steward in two cars, one loaned by the hospital, he thought about all that had happened in the last six weeks. He was convinced that a bunch of Negroes were going around doing mischief.

It was growing late and he was tired, as both age and weight bore down on him. Sheriff Lynn was glad to have Deputy Ansell Morrissey driving.

Good man Ansell. When the time came he would slip Ansell into his spot as sheriff. There was talk of having just one sheriff for the two towns anyhow as a money saving effort.

But this nigger thing had to be thought out carefully. When the mayor returned, he planned to have a long talk with him about just what was going on in West Steward of late.

When the two sheriffs returned to the jail after midnight, Nettie Lyons was waiting for them. She had gone in and sat down, ignoring the taunts and remarks made by the few stragglers that were still left milling around the jail.

"Huh, huh, huh," she said to herself. "Dis po' white trash is finding what happened heah tonight mo' better den a picture show—and cheaper too!"

Trash! Dey ain't no earthly good! she thought as she held herself tightly in the chair, showing by the slant of her head and the way her arms were folded and pressed together what disdain she held for the poor peckerwoods outside.

The women at Lela's house tried to dissuade Nettie from going back down the hill to the jail, but finally agreed with her that she should make herself available because she would be one of the first people the sheriff would be looking for. Aggie promised to get word to Dave. She was sure that he and his men would protect Nettie.

Sheriff Birkens walked in the door looking pink skinned and refreshed, although his mouth was pinched with worry and "botheration," Nettie called it.

"Evenin', Sheriff Birkens," Nettie said, rising from her chair.

All but Sheriff Birkens seemed surprised to see her, and one of the Monroe men shouted, "This woman outta be locked up! She slipped something in the food!"

"Will you jus' shut up?" Sheriff Birkens said quietly but firmly to the man. "Can't you see Nettie done come heah on her own? She ain't hiding from no one."

The Monroe men bristled in the background, wondering what they might do to gain a foothold again, because tonight had been a sad night for all respectable lawmen.

DeBell Hinkle was uncharacteristically quiet for the moment. "I jus' feel lak somebody done knocked da stuffins outta me," he had told Sheriff Birkens with unaccustomed candor, as they had ridden back to West Steward in the back of Sheriff Lynn's police car.

"I knowed da sheriff would be waiting ta speak to me 'bout da dinner since dey say y'all all done been poisoned," Nettie said simply.

"And who is dey!" Deputy Hinkle asked, coming alive.

"Dey is everybody!" Nettie answered. "Everybody in town done heered whats goin' on down at da jail. Everybody knowed dey done carted y'all off to da hospital dead to da woil. I ain't de onliest one!" Nettie said indignantly.

"Nettie, what you know 'bout all dis heah? I mean da poisoning and so forth," the sheriff asked.

"Not a thang, suh."

"Well somebody knows somethin', dats fer sho'," Henry Birkens said quietly.

"Sheriff, kin ah sho' you somethin'?" Nettie asked, rising out of her chair without waiting for an answer.

All of the lawmen regarded her suspiciously, except for the old sheriff, who sat in the large old rocker seeming to doze. Where was the handyman? That was the question in all of their minds, but they had to let Sheriff Birkens lead.

Nettie walked over to the basket she had prepared and sent to the jail much earlier in the day.

"Look. Ain't nobody tiched a lick o'dis somethin' ta eat. See?"

Nettie looked around encouraging all the lawmen to come over and look in her basket, and all of them did except the old sheriff.

" hit's even down laying in da exact same way I done placed hit. Nobody ain't tiched a thang! See? I sent over one whole chicken, which is ten pieces da way I cuts hit. I sent eight biscuits, and heah dey is. I had some sliced tomatoes wit' beets and onions in some sweet vinegar, a baked corn pie, some boiled eggs fer later. hit's all heah."

"Except da banana puddin'," DeBell smiled.

"Dats right," said Sheriff Birkens. "And ain't nobody et none o'dat 'cept you."

The day had been too upsetting and nobody had eaten anything except breakfast and a small snack, lunchmeat, crackers, pickles and soda DeBell had purchased from a store. The entire supper basket was there just as Nettie had already known it would be.

"She right," Sheriff Birkens said. He was smiling for the first time today, relieved because he hated to think his house maid and cook of six years thought so little of him that she would poison him.

"It's very clear what happened here," the younger Monroe man said impatiently. "The poison had to be in the coffee—and we all had coffee. And your handyman, O'Neill Edwards, made that. Where is he, by the way?"

Sheriff Birkens looked at Nettie.

"He home, I reckon," she lied. "But he wouldn't poison no coffee. Ahm sho' he don't know nothin' 'bout no poison."

"DeBell, when we finish talkin' heah in a minute, I wants you and da agents ta go pick up O'Neill and bring him back heah right away."

"Right!" the agents answered with snappy enthusiasm. Maybe in time the frayed edges of ineptness could be carefully woven together again into something like a workable cloth, the men hoped.

"Nah, I wanna say dis—I didn't have no coffee, but O'Neill made da drink ah did have. Somethin' funny tasting come to think of hit," the sheriff remembered.

"Therefore he slipped something into all of the drinks. That's how he did it!" the younger Monroe man said, pleased with his deduction.

"Let me jus' git dat pot!" DeBell Hinkle exclaimed. What's left in hit can be sent to da lab."

Sheriff Lynn burst out laughing, his full belly shaking with glee. "You must be joneing!" he exclaimed. I bet you a nickle to a dollar dat dat pot is been washed out—da cups too. Dat nigger is 'bout in West Hell by nah. Do you really think he not only would leave some evidence but would be settin' around his house some whar waiting to be hung?"

The old sheriff fell forward in his chair laughing so hard at their lack of common sense that his hat fell to the floor. He guffawed some more trying to retrieve it.

DeBell Hinkle fetched the pots and cups anyway. They were washed and dried as Jethro Lynn had predicted. This fact threw the old sheriff into another fit of laughing.

"Well, Sheriff, you wuz da one what tole me to pick up O'Neill Edwards in da first place. You thought he would still be 'round heah too," DeBell said as roughly as he dared in an effort to spread the blame.

"Den go on ahead and see if he still might be heah by some small chance," the sheriff told the lawmen. "Leastwise we gotta try."

But there was a cloud of anxiety looming over Sheriff Birkens head growing heavier and darker by the minute. It was clouding up to rain.

The search for O'Neill Edwards would be Ralph Duster all over again. He just knew it.

TWENTY-EIGHT

---※---

O'Neill Edwards' wife, Vergie, a fine seamstress and cook, had left for New York City with their two girls four months ago in search of work in some rich family's home. If she found such work as a cook or a seamstress, for she refused to be a house maid, then she would seek work for O'Neill as a chauffeur or gardener or handyman—that's why she was looking for rich folks, some family that had not lost all of their money in this Panic and could still afford more than one servant. This dream of the Edwards family had come true and O'Neill was a week away from leaving West Steward, Arkansas when this Aristotle Gillis thing came up.

O'Neill rented a small room from Mrs. Rosielean Liggins and her husband on one of the many tree-named streets, Pine, in Colored Town, and worked at the jail for pennies while he waited for news from his wife.

The deputy and the Monroe men arrived at Rosielean Liggins' house shortly before midnight and banged on the door hard enough to wake the entire neighborhood, had they been sleeping.

When Rosielean opened the door, the lawmen shined their flashlights right into her face.

"Wha O'Neill Edwards at?" DeBell Hinkle bellowed.

"Dunno. Ain't seed 'em since yestiddy," Rosielean lied from her crack in the door. A Circle member had already been to her house and explained why O'Neill was leaving and warned her the lawmen would be coming.

"Open this door, woman!" the Monroe men shouted, pushing in and shining their flashlights all around the darken rooms.

They searched. They passed through the small shotgun house three times "makin a mess!" Rosielean wailed.

They found nothing. Not even an old sock or a necktie.

"Did he say why he was leaving in such a rush?"

"Oh, yassuh! He goin' to be wit' his wife and chirrens."

"Dats right," said the previously mute husband of Rosielean. "He done went up Nort."

"North? Where North? Chicago? Detroit? Harlem?" one of the Monroe men asked hotly.

"Jus' Nort is all ah knows," Rosielean said with finality, as if all Norths were the same to her. "Whole lotsa peepers done left and went up Nort. Dey gits nice letters from Nort. Say da money was big for Colored. Say nobody don't come bustin' in yo' house all time o'night axing questions and thangs."

"You watch yo' mouf, woman!" Deputy Hinkle lashed out.

"Yassuh," Rosielean said, unafraid. There was no need to be afraid anymore, O'Neill had said.

The three lawmen left, cursing to themselves. Another dead end.

O'Neill Edwards was gone like the Dusters were gone, like Marko Horton was gone, like Aristotle Gillis was gone—and they still had two unsolved murders on their hands with cold leads and no suspects.

"Gawd damn it to hell!" muttered DeBell Hinkle.

There was an article, and a dramatic picture about the burning of the Old Storage House in both West Steward and Old Steward newspapers, but there was absolutely nothing in any of the papers regarding the confrontation between the black and white men in Colored Town that same evening. Sheriff Lynn had seen to that. The mayor, who was in Little Rock on business, would have wanted it that way.

No matter. By noon the next day, even the children in both Colored and White Town had heard about the "Tree Incident."

Then an unexpected thing happened, without the white men even conferring on it. It just happened naturally, so to speak. The whites who had been in the trucks that night in Colored Town all denied their presence there to a man.

"Who me let niggers jump down out of a tree and threaten me? You must be carrying on foolishness! Where you hear dat at?" was what every single one of them claimed.

But the black men knew differently, acted differently, were different after that night. Moses had finally come down from the mountain, and a new day's dawning was seen in the folds of his garments.

White men now regarded black men, if not with respect, with a new sharpened interest, realizing for the first time that there was a different man behind that black skin than they had imagined.

Now the whites watched blacks as never before. Subtle movements became wide, meaningful gestures that must be analyzed and weighed and talked about and endlessly speculated upon over both cold drinks and meager meals.

The black men that went around in groups, or were thought to be in groups, were as polite and civil as ever— yet there was something different about them that the whites could not quite place, and ironically the whites started to avoid the usual situations where confrontations might arise; they did not insist on butting the line in Piggly Wiggly's or walking a black person off of the sidewalk as they used to. Small victories, but victories just the same.

But the week after the jail break and the Tree Incident was a tense time. The whites professed not to trust their servants of many years anymore. Many said they were afraid of being poisoned. But there were no servants except Negroes for those who could still afford help, and so an uneasy truce existed. Older heads among the whites thought that things would get back to normal soon. They always did.

But Dave and his group knew better. They may not have been entirely clear on which direction they were headed in, but they knew they were not going back!

It was noticed that most Negro men and women were walking taller and holding their heads up a bit higher since it was whispered all over town—even in Old Steward—that *somebody* had gotten the Dusters out of town, and *somebody* had run the notorious snitch, Marko Horton, out of town, and *somebody* had set the Old Storage House—white folks' property mind you—on fire and burned it to the ground. And *somebody* had been in those trees that night, and now white folks were sitting up and taking notice because *somebody* had promised that there just wasn't going to be any more lynchings and beatings in this town anymore without somebody doing *something* about it!

But a small group of determined white men had chosen not to forget what had happened a few nights ago, and they had no intention of letting it rest.

This tight little group of men dedicated themselves to revenge against threats and deeds both real and imagined. And they acted as cool as the black men now did, "not bothering nobody" and "not causing no trouble"; they avoided black men they felt sure were involved "that night"—they had taken to calling it—and bided their time waiting and planning for an opportunity to avenge themselves.

TWENTY-NINE

—✶—

ettie Lyons arrived at the sheriff's house earlier than usual. She would make Sheriff Birkens a good heavy breakfast—something that would help erase what he had suffered last night, the hospital and all.

Nettie had been Henry Birkens' housekeeper for six years, and in spite of everything, she felt some affection for "her white folks." The man was, being the father of her cousin's child, almost in the family so to speak, Nettie reasoned. She could not bring herself to hate him, even after Aristotle Gillis. What Henry Birkens was was a weak man, not a bad one.

Nettie could not figure out, she had said many times, how they had elected someone like Henry Birkens to be sheriff. He missed as many things as he caught, she thought.

There was a saying in Colored Town: A sorry man. That's what Henry Birkens was—a poor excuse for a man. But then in Nettie's experience, most men, white or Colored fell into that category—especially Colton Lyons, the husband she was separated from, wherever he was.

Nettie had in mind a Sunday breakfast although it was only Tuesday. Fried chicken with lots of tomato gravy, hot buttered biscuits, creamed potatoes, creamed sweet peas, and a big pot of the hot tea that the sheriff had been preferring lately to coffee.

Nettie was to be disappointed.

"Naw, naw Nettie. Not dis moaning. What you thinkin' on is way too heavy. I'll jus' have me a cuppa tea wit' lotsa cream in hit, and three or foe pieces of light bread buttered jus' a lil' bit. Dat's all ah wants."

"Umph! Nah dat don't make no sense atall if you ax me!" Nettie exclaimed, and for some unaccountable reason tears came to her eyes and rolled down her plump black cheeks. *Why is ahm tearing up lak a fool?* she asked herself. She had only to think a minute before she realized why.

When she had gotten home last night Nettie had walked through the dark house to the kitchen and lit a coal oil lamp. As soon as she lit the lamp, she saw the letter lying in the middle of her kitchen table.

Nettie wiped her face with her apron before the sheriff took notice of her tears. Then she brought the sheriff the tea and toast, spread with more butter than he had asked for, and with a big glob of blackberry jam to boot. The sheriff asked her to sit down.

"No, not dere. Come on over heah and set at da table wid me, Nettie, and tell me wha Mae Bell is, and wha is mah son? She ain't been up heah and she ain't at home."

"Ah don't know, suh."

"Don't know ah won't tell?" the sheriff asked, his heart sinking like a stone in a sea of mud. Still in his pajamas, the old sheriff pulled his fraying robe around him, tightening the cloth belt around his thin middle.

Nettie was quiet. She slapped her hands together nervously as if her quiet slapping helped her to make a decision.

"Nettie I done axed ya a question. Wha is Mae Bell and mah boy? Is she done took and runt off again?"

Nettie stopped her quiet slapping.

"Yassuh she has."

"Mississippi?" the sheriff asked, taking a small bite of toast, a small sip of tea, pretending to be unconcerned, as if he had but to ask and Mae Bell would return to him this afternoon. But his heart was thumping, his stomach contracting, acid spewing into it from every direction.

He had no more money to give her. No jewelry to sell, nothing.

He could not buy her back this time. The sheriff sat his tea cup down slowly, hoping Nettie did not see his hand shaking, hoping his face had not gone completely white.

"Naw suh. Not Mississippi dis time. Ahm 'fraid she done gone heap further den dat."

"Wha den Nettie? And when did she leave?"

"She left I don't rightly know when. Between last night and dis moaning, I reckon. I seen her last yestiddy. When I left da jail last night, I went home and found a letter on mah kitchen table."

"You still got holt of dat letter?"

"Naw suh. I done tore hit up."

The sheriff did not ask Nettie why she had destroyed the letter.

He sighed deeply and sat firmly back in his chair waiting for his housekeeper to finish. There was more to this story and he wanted to hear it all.

Coming forward in her chair, Nettie said, "Ahm mighty 'fraid she gone fer good dis time sheriff, suh. You see, suh, Mae Bell sangs."

"Sangs?" the sheriff repeated, as if the word belonged to a foreign language. "Sangs? What? Songs?"

"Yassuh. Songs. Lak you hears on da radio or in da church house. She got a real pretty voice too, suh. You didn't know dat."

"I never heered her sang nothin'!" the sheriff exclaimed, totally confounded.

"I know. But she sangs jus' da same. She looking to make herself a life wit' her singing. She reckon on sanging in a club or somethin' lak dat. Somewha lak Princess Thelma's. Only she didn't want to start doin' no singin' 'round in dese parts. She want to sing up Nort."

"Up North?" the sheriff repeated with stunned stupidity. This new information about Mae Bell simply would not soak in.

"See, she been saving up fer years and years to go to da Nort fer singin', and dats wha she went. Nort. Where, I doesn't rightly know. She didn't say. She said she were gonna write me—sometime," Nettie said truthfully.

"And she done stole my boy 'way from me and left without saying boo?" the sheriff asked increduously.

"I reckon so, suh. She say long time ago she gonna eventually go to New York— maybe to dat Harlem?" Nettie said, uncertain of the place. "Or she say maybe to Chicago or even New Orlins. Someplace big wha day pay you good fer singin' songs." Nettie's voice was high and rushed. "Leastwise dats what she tole me. Say soon as she gits da money she gone."

"You say she been doin' her planning fer years?" the sheriff asked, his voice quiet and muffled with disbelief and despair.

"Oh, yassuh."

"And you knowed 'bout hit?"

"Yas, I did Mistah Birkens, suh," Nettie said, her voice unsteady and edged in contriteness.

"And you didn't say a word to me about hit? Not nary a word!" He was angry. He was deeply wounded. He was mixed up. All of these feelings Sheriff Birkens hurled at Nettie Lyons, making her responsible because there was no one else to blame. "You knowed all da while!" he spat at Nettie, emphasizing the words, making them sound like a lynchable offense. "Dat dis woman wuz takin' mah money each and every week dat da good Lawd sent, all da while stashin' hit away, and plannin' to steal mah child from me? You knowed dat? You know about dis terrible plan fer years and you ain't said not no nothin' ta me, Nettie?"

"Well, suh, it weren't none o'mah business." Nettie answered quietly. She felt sweat trickle down her face and meet under her chins.

"Ah, Nettie!" Henry Birkens exclaimed, "I wouldn't do a dog da way you two wimmens is done me! Not a dirty low down dog! Nettie, I ain't never done nothin' in mah life to harm neither one of y'all, has I Nettie? Has I Nettie?" the sheriff wailed.

With a red and tear-stained face, the sheriff suddenly got up from his chair, went into his bedroom and closed the door.

"Good Gawd amighty!" Nettie heard the sheriff cry out as if his heart would break.

Nettie sat frozen, tears streaming down her face. "Lawd, Lawd, Lawd," she cried under her breath. *He gone go off in dere ta shoot hisself wit' one of dem old guns o'hisn like white folks sometimes do,* she thought, and actually steeled herself by pressing her feet hard against the side of the table while waiting to hear a shot.

Jesus! She had not meant to hurt him so—but what could she do but tell him the facts, Nettie thought.

Nettie was greatly relieved to hear the sheriff just using the slop jar to heave as if he would never stop.

Presently Sheriff Birkens returned to the kitchen looking pale and helpless, wiping his mouth with a large handkerchief. He seemed to have gotten a grip on himself to some extent and avoiding Nettie's eyes, he sat back down at the table.

"Fix me another cuppa hot tea willya? Den you kin go on home. I wanna be by mahself a while."

"Thank you, suh."

He was most in general a good man, a kind man Nettie reflected.

"You think you kin hold down some mo' tea, suh? And mebbe a little piece o'dry toast?" Nettie asked with great tenderness.

Having just lost two earlier cups the sheriff replied, "Who knows?"

While Nettie heated more tea the sheriff said forlornly, "You know ah gotta go befoe da mayor Thursday moaning at ten o'clock."

"Naw suh! I didn't know dat," Nettie said sympathetically because that's what the sheriff needed more than anything now—understanding.

"Yep, yep, he wanna see me," the sheriff said dryly. "Ah talked wit' him on da telephone in his hotel room over in Little Rock early dis moaning."

"Does you know what he wanna talk ta ya about sheriff? 'Bout dat jail break?" Nettie asked, placing the steaming tea in front of the sheriff.

"Dat amongst other thin's, Nettie. As you know we done had some curious goin's on of late. Peepers gittin' kilt, peepers breakin' outta jail, peepers goin' and comin'. Thangs lak dat. Fies. Distrebances. Lak dat," the sheriff said without emotion.

"Well, da best o'luck ta ya, Sheriff," Nettie said, meaning it, for she knew that "her white folks" was in deep trouble. "'Course you want me ta be back tomorry, Wednesday, is dat right, suh?"

"Yeah. Sho," Henry Birkens said without interest. "Say look, Nettie, I would drive you home but da way it is ahm plumb wore out."

"Oh, dat's alright Mistah Birkens. Ah needs da walk I 'spect. Ahm gittin' fatter den an old hog."

Nettie was half way down the block, her sturdy cuban heels clicking against the sidewalk, when she heard the sheriff calling after her.

"Nettie! If you heah anythin', anythin' atall about—you know—will you let me know?"

Nettie turned and ducked her head in the sheriff's direction in what she hoped was neither a "yes" nor a "no" gesture. She pulled her old coat around her, and kept on walking down the sidewalk toward Colored Town.

THIRTY

—✶—

Mayor Robert McShane, was an elegant man, a true Southern gentleman, women said—"Shirt and Tie" McShane, one of his few enemies had coined him. The only undignified thing about him was the name: he let people call him Bob. It gave him a certain common touch that he felt was necessary for political purposes.

Bob McShane smoked an occasional good cigar, took an occasional drink of hard liquor when it was available. That was all. He was not one of the boys. Very few knew his background was hillbilly. He had successfully lived down his poor white trash background years ago. When he was thirteen, he had run away from his ne'r-do-well father and his slovenly toothless mother with her passel of fourteen children. He had never looked back and had few regrets.

Mayor McShane was five-feet-eight-inches tall, but his carriage was so erect, his body so slim, that he appeared taller. He had slicked back nearly black hair, and piercing blue eyes that seemed to look right through you.

The mayor was so well dressed at all times that he even wore a shirt and tie to picnics. Other men, unless they were extremely secure, tended to feel uncomfortable in his presence and could be noticed straightening their ties, hitching up their pants, pulling up their socks.

McShane knew this and cultivated it.

He also made a point of knowing the dirt on his acquaintances.

Know the shit, and don't be taken by surprise. Surprise was the enemy of the unprepared, he liked to say.

Robert McShane had few friends, none close, and he liked it that way.

McShane had been mayor of West Steward and Old Steward for nine years. He was forty-six years old.

Sheriff Henry Birkens had been a disappointment to him. When he saw to it that he was voted in four years ago, he had thought he was the right man for the job—not too bright, but steady and reliable. Certainly not a man ambitious enough to come after his job. Henry was not controversial, took orders well, and seemed to know how to deal with

254

his Colored people, but lately he had been messing with a young Negro woman and there was a child. That certainly was no problem. A whole lot of white men had "messed" with Colored women at one time or another in their lives, and they usually kept it discreet. But Henry Birkens was not discreet, and his truck with the Colored gal had become the talk of the town because she supposedly told him what to do—a bad position for a white man to be in, especially a sheriff. What a fool this man had become!

McShane castigated himself for his lack of judgement, which in most cases was very sharp indeed.

The door to the mayor's office opened, Miss Thesault stepped back, and Henry Birkens walked into the mayor's office, exactly on time.

"Good moaning, Mistah Mayor. Hi you feelin' dis moaning?" the sheriff said, removing his hat.

"Henry," the mayor said standing and stiffly extending his hand. "Please sit down." His voice was bland, cool, non-committal.

Henry Birkens had decided his best bet was to say as little as possible and to answer only those questions he was asked. He would be truthful, frank, open. Yes, he was aware that there had been some trouble, he rehearsed as he drove over to Steward, to what was commonly called the Business Building. The mayor's office was on the second of three floors. There was no elevator—one had to walk up, face Miss Evelyn Thesault "wit' her great big titties," then one was let in if she saw fit.

Say as little as possible. Agree to everything. Take the necessary blame. Then perhaps, perhaps...

"Henry," the mayor said, shuffling papers on his fancy desk as he swiveled a little in his fancy chair. He did not look directly at the sheriff but looked to his left and right as if he was looking for something. "Henry," he repeated, "we have a problem of some magnitude here."

A fancy talker, the sheriff thought. What was it? Two or three years at some college in where? Arkansas? Tennessee?

"Yas, we has, Mistah Mayor," the sheriff said, straightening his tie, fooling with the cuffs of his shirt, trying to get his tall frame comfortable in the too small chair that sat in front of the mayor's desk.

"Yas, we has, Mistah Mayor," the uncomfortable sheriff repeated.

The mayor produced a sheet of paper from his top drawer and studied it with some distaste, as Henry Birkens sat forward in his chair trying to guess what the paper held. As the mayor continued to scrutinize the paper, the sheriff found himself fascinated by Bob McShane's tie, which was a robin's egg blue with a little navy pattern. *Silk?* he wondered.

The mayor finally laid the paper down and looked directly at the sheriff in front of him.

"Now. Let's take our problems in chronological order, shall we?"

"Oh, yassuh. Certainly." Now the acid in his stomach was flowing like a river.

"First, two white people were killed, murdered. When a possible suspect was fingered—one Ralph A. Duster—he and his entire family vanished. Then you lost your snitch, Marko Horton. Gone. Disappeared. Now why would a snitch being paid good money leave town, Henry?"

Robert McShane did not wait for an answer. "Another suspect appears on the scene. Maybe a weak suspect, but a man who should have been held over and questioned thoroughly just the same."

"We did question dat main!" the sheriff protested.

The mayor held his hand up flat signaling for silence, and continued as if Sheriff Birkens had not spoken. "Then unbelievably you are poisoned—all of you, sheriff, deputy, and special agents from Monroe County."

"Poisoned!" the mayor said spitting out the words as if the poison that had been used was coating his own tongue. "In your own jail, and the suspect that you had is whizzed away, right out from under you by a person or, more likely, persons unknown—who, of course, have not been located."

The mayor stopped talking, sat back in his chair and watched Henry Birkens with his mirror eyes, his thin lips pressed together in a tight line of disgust. Then he leaned forward again in his chair and continued, not reading from any of the papers that he had on his desk. "You are all knocked out for hours. You are taken to the hospital and the final story is that the kind of poison which you were given couldn't be identified. And the man who obviously administered the poison, one O'Neill Edwards, a man whom you hired, has also—guess what?—disappeared! I believe your house girl, Nettie, was seen to be in the clear, is that correct?"

"Yassuh. Dat's right, suh."

Burning, aching misery assailed the sheriff's entire body. He could not remember such a misery in his life. He was trying not to sweat, trying to look dignified and in control, but both he and the mayor knew that he was losing the battle.

The mayor was looking around the sides of his desk again, rocking gently in his fancy carved chair. "To distract the large crowd that had gathered in front of your jail, Henry," he continued in the absence of words from the sheriff, "a fire was started at the Old Storage House, burning private property to the ground. And that's not all. You do know about the three truck loads of fellers that went down to Colored Town to straighten things out and the trouble they encountered there don't you?"

"Yas, I does, suh."

"Trouble, Henry. Negroes jumping out of trees like monkeys. Threatening white men, blowing out the tires on their trucks. And you and your men stretched out in some hospital emergency room instead of keeping order!" The mayor pounded on the desk in his first—and rare—show of emotion, and this rare flare-up struck terror in Henry Birkens as nothing else had. He begin to have doubts about surviving in his position as sheriff of West Steward, Arkansas.

"Now one of these incidents is bad enough, but taken together they are quite a shocking mess, don't you agree, Henry?" the mayor asked, regaining calm.

"Yas, hit is pretty bad, suh, but..."

"Do you know what is being whispered all over town, Henry?" The mayor asked rocking, looking undereyed, moving his head this way and that.

"What is dat, suh?" the sheriff said fearfully, holding his breath.

"That your gal Mae Bell Lewis is connected up with the problems we've been having here—or was. I understand that she has now left town also." The mayor gave a short mirthless laugh. "Looks like everybody is leaving town. Went somewhere up North," he said, waving his hand in dismissal—a flea out of his collar. "Gone to pursue a singing career I hear."

How on earth did the mayor know about Mae Bell's singing when he had just learned about it himself? the sheriff wondered. It occurred to the sheriff that the mayor had been having him watched, having Mae Bell watched. By who? *Mah Gawd!* The thought was terrifying.

The sheriff shifted in the hard chair, now looking at the dapper man before him with icy fear. Did he know how much money he had given her over the years? About the insurance policy? Did somebody report when Mae Bell had emptied the piss pot on him? *Lawd Gawd Almighty!* Did this slick as shit mayor know how many times he had begged Mae Bell to come back to him and how much he had paid to get her back?

Trying hard to keep his wits about him the sheriff said, "I don't think Mae Bell had nothin'—not a thang to do wit' da incidents what been happenin' at all. Why you think she do, Yo' Honor? Mae Bell is jus' a simple ordinary gal."

"Really?" the mayor said frostily. "I was hoping you could tell me why people are laying the blame for some of this disorder at her door step."

Actually the mayor had been digging when he told the sheriff the town was whispering about Mae Bell. Robert McShane had heard nothing about Mae Bell being connected with the "recent events." The mayor merely wanted to see what kind of a response he would get from this inept man. Virtually everyone in town knew that the sheriff was crazy about a Colored woman who was pulling him around by the drawers. So, undoubtedly some people were connecting Mae Bell at least to the jail break. Apparently, this peckerwood sitting before him couldn't even spell discretion.

"You let your Coloreds get too strong, Birkens. They don't seem to know their place anymore. Do you realize that we could have had a riot the other night? Where else in the South have you heard of a mob of Negroes meeting armed white men with guns of their own? All of this is bad, Henry."

"Yassuh. I know, suh, but..."

"Bad for business. Very bad for the reputation of these twin towns, Henry," the mayor continued, respecting no interruptions. "This Depression, or Panic, or whatever you want to call it, will not last forever. Read your history, Birkens. When this is over and things start going again, we're going to be left behind if people don't see these towns as a good place to settle and raise a family. We can't expect prosperity to stop here if there are unsolved killings here and niggers running wild in the night, can we, Henry?"

"No suh! You right. I know you right, and we intends to git a hain on matters!"

The mayor rocked back in his chair and, giving another little laugh, slicked back his already slick hair with both his hands, releasing some of the scent of his good hair oil. Then he stood up, causing Henry Lee Birkens to disentangle himself from his chair and stand too, thinking the meeting was over—and it was.

The sheriff extended his hand. The mayor did not take it.

"Sheriff Birkens, I want you to turn in your badge and gun to me, now."

"Suh?" the sheriff asked, holding his large hat in his hands.

"The Business Board and I have discussed the recent events at length, and we have made a decision. The gun and the badge, please."

"Suh?" Henry Birkens heard himself repeat.

"I'm truly sorry, Henry, really I am, but our decision stands. I'm relieving you of your duties as sheriff as of today."

The mayor stood waiting as slowly it dawned on the sheriff that he was out. After four years he was out—no longer the "high" sheriff of West Steward, Arkansas, Phillips County.

"What about—mah deputy," sheriff Birkens asked thickly. He was burning at both ends—his head flamed, his feet scorched.

"DeBell? Oh, he'll be reassigned to work in the office of Jethro Lynn until the election in April."

"Who—who den will be takin' mah place?" the sheriff asked thickly through parched lips.

"The acting sheriff in West Steward will be Ansell Morrissey—Jethro has agreed to that. I haven't talked to DeBell yet but I shall," the mayor answered without missing a beat.

Henry Birkens slid his gun, then his badge, across the desk, and turned and walked out of the mayor's office.

Robert McShane said something about a last check already made out waiting for him at the cashier's on the first floor. He would pick it up another day. Right now he wanted to get out of this building, out into the fresh air.

The sheriff found it difficult driving home from Old Steward to West Steward, a trip he had made hundreds of times. Everything looked strange and unfamiliar, even though he had driven through this part of town, the business section, less than an hour ago. The words ran together on the many large "Going Out of Business" signs, and the boarded up stores had a scary, threatening, ominous look about them, as if their boards were blank eyes staring at him. The little bit of snow that was falling seemed to be a blizzard, and even the trees along the busline as he headed for West Steward appeared different, too stark and black against the overcast sky.

When the sheriff finally reached home he wanted to collapse in bed and not start thinking again until next week. He was glad he had had the presence of mind to tell Nettie not to come in today. He wanted to be strictly alone.

Henry Birkens wanted to lie down forever, but he told himself no.

Lay down nah and you'll never git up no more. So, feeling washed out, wilted, burned up, the sheriff sat on the side of the bed listening to the mayor's voice inside his skull again: "The Business Board and I have made a decision..."

The big important men of the twin towns—if the hard times had left anybody big and important anymore.

The sheriff took off his shoes, and finding the green salve that Nettie had gotten from John Candle, he massaged his feet thoroughly, focusing all of his attention on their care. There! That was much better.

Now that he could walk comfortably on his feet again, Henry Birkens got up from the side of the bed, walked over to his "chess o'drawers," opened the top drawer and removed a large round sweet snuff tin that had belonged to his mother from behind his B.V.D.s. His mother used to keep the tins to store small items like pennies and buttons, but she also hid folding money in her tins and it came out all circular and bent.

Since his last episode of ransoming Mae Bell had left him broke, the sheriff had started to stash a little something away each month against an emergency. Nobody, including Mae Bell, knew the small keepsake tin was there, and nobody had any reason to open the drawer where he kept his underwear because when they came back from the washer woman, he put them away himself. Sheriff Birkens fumbled for the round tin. There should be fifty dollars in the tin now, tight and circular like his mama's paper money.

He would start over. He would sell the house if he could. There were still a few people in this town with a small piece of change. Someone who could invest for the future. It was a nice, clean house. Then there were the five sparrow-colored row houses he owned up in Colored Town from which he was still able to get a little rent—when the residents had it.

With the final payroll check that was due him and the fifty dollars, the sheriff reckoned he could get by until after the houses were sold.

Feeling around, he found the tin with his fifty dollars in it that represented all he had at present. But something was wrong. Somehow he had used too much "lift," expecting the small box with its curled paper money to be a little heavier. Henry Birkens slowly pulled off the top of the old shiny dented tin and peered into it. It was empty.

Nettie would not do such a thing. He had never known her to steal so much as a red cent in all of the years she had worked for him.

It had to be Mae Bell. She had taken all the cash he had in the world, not because she needed it—*Lawd knows she done squeezed me dry over the years,* he thought—but she had done it as a last act of spite just to break his heart, he figured.

"Nah she done got me! She done really got me!" the sheriff muttered, and feeling old, despised, and utterly forsaken, he crumpled up on his bed, and pulling his knees up toward his chest, he cried.

PART THREE

Why should the world be over-wise,
In counting all our tears and sighs?

THIRTY-ONE

❧

In the end, there was really nothing more to do. Helena had finally to admit that there was nothing to hold on to anymore and that she had slid to the very bottom of a slippery incline.

Now she knew that she should have never married Norman St. Quatran in the first place. He of the pretty name and the handsome face. If she had had any good sense, she would have passed him by—or, having taken up with him, dumped him fast at the very first sign of misgiving. But, instead, she had stayed fourteen years in a marriage that was essentially over in the first four years.

Well, it was time, Helena thought, to focus on her new direction. For once she was sure that what she was doing was going to come out right. She was going back home—back to Arkansas.

Yet it gnawed at her to realize that her action was not born of pure logic. It was a decision forced on her by circumstances too obvious to ignore. She would divorce Norman because he no longer supported her financially or emotionally. He rarely even came home.

Now, his daughter, Meredith Ashley St. Quatran, nicknamed Merry, was not at all merry. It is believed in some circles that the disposition of the mother during pregnancy affects the unborn child. Whether this thinking was an old wives' tale or not, it was certainly true of her daughter. When her mother, Helena Bailey St. Quatran was five months into her pregnancy, she had discovered some distressing facts about Merry's father, and from that month on, things had never really been the same between her parents. So Merry was born "blue," an irritable cry baby. As she grew older, she was a somber child, prone to dark moods and given to a sharp tongue and divided loyalties. Merry had been "back South" twice—once when she was too young to remember anything, and again one summer when she was nine years old, and remembered everything. They—she and Helena and brother Basil Jann, who was then three—had stayed for nearly two weeks, and she had hated every minute of it. And now they were going back! Not even on the train, on the bus! All the way from Chicago!

Yes, it had to be the bus, her mother had explained. It was the cheapest way, and they had no money. No money? Then it had to be her mother's fault, because when she was five or so, her father had brought home buckets of money. He used to pile it all up on the bed and show it to her, letting her stuff her pockets with change. Why, the last time she had seen him he had slipped her a five dollar bill, which she still had hidden, of course, from her mother.

Helena had gotten no thanks for spending nearly her last dollar to give Merry a memorable send off party so she could say goodbye to her friends—perhaps forever.

In all, there was a party for fifteen girls and boys, all of whom were the sons and daughters of the well-to-do, the only kind of people her father would let his children associate with. Upper classed people, Norman Newbridge St. Quatran said, people like themselves. Most were light skinned, most were handpicked by Norman. These people, professional Negroes, were destined for all kinds of success. They were not a bunch of slum dwelling coons who were satisfied with nothing and had plenty of it, Norman said.

Before he had a car, Norman Newbridge St. Quatran went out of his way to avoid lower classed people on the city bus. People who would spit on the bus floor as if they were still in the cotton fields, or eat a hot buttered sweet potato just purchased under the "El" as they sat their shabby stinking selves in their seats, talking and laughing too loudly, and embarrassing Norman and all the other right thinking Colored people riding home from respectable labor.

Meredith's party had been a great success, as it should have been. Helena had a huge amount of experience giving parties for her husband.

Norman had been anxious to show off both the size and the beauty of their flat, with its waxed caramel floors, velvet burgundy sofas, and brand new ebony grand piano, all togged down with a silk fringed scarf. Neither Norman nor Helena could play the piano. Norman had bought it, at no small expense, solely for a friend, a professional entertainer with a local name that usually attended their parties.

Not even the one black bank president, or the doctors, or other successful businessmen and their wives gave parties as lavish as the St. Quatrans' parties. Witty and stylish, Helena and Norman were on everyone's party list. But behind closed doors the gossip about the St. Quatran couple could be much less than flattering. Most agreed that Helena was charming, beautiful, and a terrific hostess. But Norman was quite bossy to his wife, and pinched asses behind her back.

Merry stalled as long as she could, claiming horrible headaches, stomach pains and diarrhea, but in the end, her mother fried the hated, greasy shoe box of chicken they would take for their meals on the way to Arkansas, as well as a few pieces of fruit, candy bars and little store bought cellophane wrapped cakes.

The rent for the month had not been paid, and Helena had nightmares that old Mrs. Silverstein would get wind of their leaving and figure she was not planning to pay or return—which was true—and there would be a scene, the lie Helena had prepared in advance sticking like peanut butter to the roof of her mouth. "We are just going to visit my mother, Mrs. Silverstein. Just for a week. When we come back, I'll have the rent for you."

Helena liked Mrs. Silverstein. She was fair. She saw to it that repairs were made. It was not wrong to expect your rent. Helena simply did not have it. The woman would have to try to chase down Norman.

"Sure Dollink," the old woman would smile, but think bitterly, *Slicked by the Schvartzers. Again.*

Helena did not know where her husband was, so she left him a note. Enough was enough. She had not seen Norman in eight days. The note explained that she was taking the children to West Steward so they could have a decent Christmas. She did not say when she would return.

Then, Helena took the suitcases out to the cab along with the shopping bag that held the shoe box of fried chicken, and they headed downtown to the bus station. Even as broke as she was, Helena could not bear climbing on the city bus with two suitcases, two children, and a shopping bag of greasy food. She was deeply grateful to her mother, Lela Bailey.

"Come on down. I would sho' love to see you. I got a letter from your daddy too. He say he coming home soon too. What a blessing. The Lawd done answered my prayers right good," she had written.

Merry kept her eyes glued to the scenery as the bus made its seemingly endless journey from North to South, stopping a hundred times in between. God! How she hated the South! And if she admitted to the truth she did not much like her grandmother either. Neither did she like her house or her grandmother's friends who were always demanding hugs and kisses and slobbering snuff. And the way her grandmother talked! Even at nine, Merry had known Lela did not talk "right."

"She talks flat, darling," her father had explained to Merry without defending his mother-in-law. Then, there was the heavy southern food you were forced to eat—food that later made you feel you had swallowed a log, her father had complained, and once Merry had been exposed to it she found herself agreeing. Well, at least her grandmother was not all fat and shiny and black like the grandmothers or mothers of the nappy headed girls she had been forced to play with. Not one of these girls were bright skinned. Not one had the smooth, long curly or straight hair of her Chicago friends. They were mostly an ugly, backwards bunch. Now that these girls were twelve or thirteen, Merry hated to imagine how ugly they had become!

And there were the creatures! Rabbits, and squirrels and possums that people actually ate, and old mangy, rabid looking dogs that hung about looking as sad and stupid as their owners. And the snakes! They were the worst of Merry's remembrance of things terrible. Encountering one as she made her way down the strange orangey clay hills that became bright red in strong sunlight, sent her yelling and screaming—which Mother Bailey called "hollering."

"Girl, what you doin' all dat hollering 'bout? Hit ain't nothin' but a snake. Jus' keep outta hit's way," her grandmother had said.

Merry gritted her teeth as she thought about the plumbing—or lack of it—in her grandmother's house. At night they actually had to do "their business" in something her grandmother called a slop jar. Her mother tried to pretty up the thing by calling it a chamber pot. In the morning the slop pot had to have its nasty contents dumped out back somewhere where you might easily meet a snake. It was all unbelievably filthy Merry remembered with a quiver, even when you took a scoop from the sack of outhouse lime and sprinkled your "business" with it. If the outhouse had not run out of lime.

At nine, one is curious about many things. One day after emptying her pot of its "business," Merry decided to get a good look into the filthy hole where she was to dump the contents "carefully," her grandmother had warned, "don't be splashin' nothin'." As Merry peered into the semi-darkness of the hole, she seemed to see a constant, swirling white movement in there. Maggots! Gallons and gallons of maggots!

Meredith Ashley St. Quatran dropped the white enameled chamber pot, spilling the contents over her feet, soaking her socks and shoes with overnight urine. She ran back to the house screaming and hollering, Lela said later.

After Helena was able to calm her daughter down a bit, Merry, still crying, sweating, and retching, told her what she had seen.

"Why honey," Lela had said, unperturbed, "dat's what a outhouse is lak. You puts yo' waste matter in dere. Natchel da flies gon' git at hit if peepers don't use dat lime."

Through tears, Merry vowed never to go to the outhouse again. Never, never, never!

"I hate this place!" she had wailed. "Why can't we just go home?"

They had stayed five more days. And Merry had nearly suffocated amid the nightly pots of rags burned on the front porch to keep mosquitoes at bay.

Finally Merry had returned to her spacious clean Chicago home with its wonderful indoor plumbing—but she had heat rash, scores of mosquito bites, a wasp sting, and scratched knees she had gotten running away from the maggots in the outhouse.

It had been a trip to hell, and now they were going back! Only Basil, who was going on six now, and a true simpleton if there ever was one, Merry thought, looked upon the bus trip to Arkansas as a great adventure. Even when his older sister warned him that he would have to pee in a pot, Basil smiled and stated that he rather liked the idea of peeing in a pot. It sounded like great fun and he couldn't wait to do it.

THIRTY-TWO

Setting tea up in the kitchen for the "ladies," Esta York, Mother Clarence, Lula Mae Simpson, and Vera Marie Taylor, Lela apologized for not serving them in the dining room, explaining that her daughter Helena was expected anytime. They would be visiting for the holiday and the dining room had to be kept "straightened up."

The friends had met to discuss the future of the daily meals they served to the poor in the basement of Greater Peace Baptist Church.

"We gone have to cut down on what all we be servin'," said Lula Mae.

"Dat or cut down on da days—or both—right after da new yeah," Mother Clarence added.

Esta York agreed. "Deres too many hoingry nah. We can't feed everbody in dis town what's needy, plus all da Colored hobo men what be travelin' through."

Lela looked glumly at Vera Marie Taylor. "What you thinkin' 'bout dis, goil?"

"Da ladies is right, Lela. We ain't gittin' near as much as we usta git from da community no mo'. Dey jus' don't have it to give. Most peepers is working real short hours—or not none at all."

"Lela, I know seeing peepers hoingry really hurts yo' heart, and I know da Lawd done blessed you real nice. But you can't feed all dese folks by yo'self, you know. You wearin' yo'self out. Peepers jus' gone have ta tighten dey belts a little bit mo'. Hit's really all in God's hains. Ain't dat what you done tole us?" Mother Clarence said wisely.

"Dats right," Lula Mae said. "We doin' our level best wit' what we got. We stretchin' and stretchin', and doin' da bestest we kin. We ain't required to do no mo' den dat. We ain't da cause o' dis Depression, ya know."

Finally, after much discussion it was settled among them these five days before Christmas: The meals would be cut to three days a week instead of six, and the hobos would receive only a substantial soup, good bread, and coffee. Full meals would be reserved for the needy of West Steward. Even Old Steward was left out.

"Nah! Nah dat dats behind us, Esta hi your granddaughter gittin' on?" Lula Mae asked, daring to bring up the subject.

"Oh, she alright," Esta York answered not wishing to dwell on the matter, but the women had sat forward, alert, ready for news, needing to put even a little salve on the still sore spot of guilt that they all felt about their part in that night that had to be—the deed that had to be done.

"Hi is she really? I mean in her heart?" Mother Clarence ventured again, treading thin ice over dark waters.

"Shoot!" Esta York said in her direct way. "You ain't gone forget somthin' like dat ifn dats what you means."

"No, Lawd!" Lela allowed. "But she seem to be comin' on jus' fine."

Just fine after the incident of incest between Dabney Shell and her own father, whom a group of Colored Town men had run out of town.

"Actual better den I expected after bein' forced to get rid o' dat baby. No nightmares or nothin'. LawdhavemercyJesus! Was dat just three months ago? Seem lak a lifetime, don't hit? Yas, she alright," Esta continued, noticing that most of the women had tears in their eyes from remembering the terrible event.

Esta smiled to break up the gloom that had dropped like a blotter on the room, soaking up the joy of friendship, and pleasant thoughts of holidays ahead. "Come on y'all. We did what we had to do and nah hit's over and done. Listen, I even let 'er do a little bit o'courtin, to git bad feelins 'bout mens out her system fore hit git too big in her mind, ya know?"

"Nah, dats a right smart thing to do, Esta," Lela said, smiling a little through her tears.

"But fer sich a thang to even down happen!" Vera Marie Taylor persisted, unwilling or unable to let go of her horror of it.

"I feels dis-a-way: if Dabney's own grandmother kin have as good an outlook on hit as she do, why we jus' got to follow in behind her," Mother Clarence said to the group.

"Nah, ain't dat right!" Lela agreed as the women turned their faces toward the front room. They all heard a truck or car approaching.

"Ah wonder who dat could be?" Lela asked. "Ain't da sound of Dave's truck, doe."

Since the "recent incidents," the Bailey house was guarded around the clock, so none of the women were alarmed by the sound of an approaching vehicle, which had now pulled up and stopped.

Lela made for the front door with Mother Clarence right behind her. There was a muffled knock and Lela pulled the door and opened it wide-eyed and expectant.

"Look what I done fount down at da bus depot!" Roger Mulright hollered out. "Nice Christmas present huh?"

The young woman was very beautiful in a delicate way. Slender, almost fragile, she was a whitish tan, with wavy black hair rolled tight in a conservative bun. A surly, tired looking pre-teen girl of a slightly deeper color stood beside her mother, daring anyone to speak to her, kindly or otherwise. The other child, a tallish boy, curly headed and definitely brown, pushed his way in, all smiles and expectation.

"Helena! Oh, my Gawd!" Lela exclaimed, grabbing her daughter to her bosom. Embracing her was like taking a lovely bunch of fragrant flowers that melted compliantly in your arms, so thin was the woman she held.

"Oh, my!" Lela wailed. "Why you let yo'self git so po! Why, yous no bigger den a sparrow! Is you sick? Dat's what hit is!" Lela said, pushing her daughter quickly out from her body in order to get a better look at the eyes, the skin, the hair, the things that told you about good or poor health.

Noting Helena's dark circled eyes Lela began a soft round of wails: "Lawd, Lawd, Lawd!"

"Now, Mother," Helena protested. "I'm really fine." Helena smiled too brightly at her mother's friends that she wished were not here.

"Is you sick, goil?" Lela repeated, unconvinced, as the old friends, the old hens, closed in to become another pair of eyes for Lela.

"Mother, please! I'm tired as the dickens. Can I come all the way in the house— please?" Helena asked walking in the door, trying to smile and make light of Lela and her questions. "So I lost a few pounds. You haven't seen me in years—and I was always a little too plump," Helena said smiling again at these friends of her mother's. Sharp old buggers. They were eyeing her every limb, every strand of hair, every rise and fall of her voice. A woman coming home without her husband, looking bony and worried, didn't fool anyone, least of all these sister-friends of her mother's.

"Come on in heah! You late! I thought you wuz comin' way sooner den dis heah. Hand me one of dose grips. Your room is all ready fer ya," Lela said in a nervous jumble of words. The women had never seen her so totally unraveled, and they marveled, ready to help, to support, if help and support was needed.

When Helena finally got to the middle of the parlor, Lela said, "You know my frens?" and she introduced them all, even though Helena had known all of them since childhood.

Merry had barely moved inside the door.

"An dese is mah grandchirren!" Lela said proudly to her friends, who made the usually expected comments about how beautiful they were, how much the two of them had grown, how smart they looked.

Meredith thought she would throw-up if one of the women approached to hug, to kiss, to squeeze and slobber.

"And hi is Merry?" Lela said as gaily as she could manage, trying to ignore the scent of trouble in the air so thick, you could almost fan the aroma from it around the room.

"Sick!" said the sullen girl. "May I be excused please? I have to lie down. Where is my room?"

"I seed her down at da bus depot, and I sayed to mahself, dat sho' look jus' lak Lela's pretty daughter. I recognize her even though she done fell off quite a bit since I last done seent her." Roger Mulright said, smiling.

"Well, mucha obliged to ya fer fetching her, Roger. Dave were gonna pick her up, but we didn't rightly know what day she were comin.'"

Knowing that she needed to be alone with her daughter, Lela's friends departed after many hugs and kisses, which Merry mercifully escaped by going into the guest room and throwing herself on the bed.

After Helena was settled into her room, she whispered out of earshot of the children, "Where is Dave? When he comes in, we'll talk, OK?"

Her mother protested. "Tomorry—when you done had you some rest."

"No! Tonight. Mother, when is Daddy coming home?"

"Shouda done bent heah," Lela said, feeling that dropping emptiness in her stomach she felt nowdays when she spoke of Rex. She wouldn't share her feelings with Helena though, she decided. She had enough of a load right now—of that she was sure.

Dave arrived twenty minutes after his sister, after having met up with Roger Mulright in town and been told that his sister was home.

Dave had been out taking the "feel" of the town, checking his store in Epps. It was December twentieth. The Circle had already had their meeting back up in the

271

Colored Woods yesterday, and it was agreed that if there was going to be retaliations of any kind, no doubt it would be after Christmas; even after the New Year. The Circle was prepared, and had been warned not to let their guard down for a minute.

Walking in the back door, Dave saw Basil first.

"Hey, man! When did you get here?" Dave smiled.

"Are you my Uncle Dave?" Basil asked hopefully.

"I sure am. Don't you remember me?"

"No. Do you have a dime?" Basil asked staring up at the tall man.

"I reckon I do," Dave said, amused by the directness of this pretty child. "Where is your mother?"

"Down the hall with grandmother." Basil pointed.

Dave told his nephew that if he would be very quiet, he would give him two dimes. "I want to surprise your mother," he told him.

Creeping down the long hall, Dave saw Helena, her back to him, sitting on the rarely used sofa in the rarely used parlor. His mother saw him coming, but he put his fingers to his lips, as he continued to creep upon his sister. Suddenly his hands were over her eyes, and Lela and Dave were laughing over Helena's head.

"Oh!" Helena cried, going along with the game and pretending to be surprised and frightened. "Now, let's see. Rough hands. Large hands." She grabbed his wrist and turning around she faced the one who had held her eyes. "Why, it's Dave!" Helena said laughing, and then standing up to look at her tall brother. "Have you grown since I last saw you? Oh, my! You've gotten so handsome! Really you have. Let me look at you!" Helena marveled.

"Thank you, mam. I must have been uglier than Satan's cat the last time you saw me," Dave teased.

"No! That's not what I meant at all. I mean you've filled out—become a real man. Really you have. Look at him Mother! He's so good looking!"

"Shoot! Ah always knowed dat!" Lela said beaming, feeling her heart lift a little as the love her children felt for each other swelled and filled the room, pushing out some of the ache of the double home coming she felt meant pain and trouble.

Dave stooped and gathered his sister in his arms. She was so thin! Like a homemade rag doll, Dave thought.

"So how's it goin'?" he asked, smiling down at the circles under his sister's eyes, the beginnings of long lines down the sides of the nose. The plump and oily yellow and rosy girl he remembered had faded into a woman of dry and wispy tan with strands of gray in her once shiny black hair.

He didn't really want to know how it was going. The truth of it, he thought, would break his heart. His mother had warned him that the letters she had received from Helena and Rex would bring pain—now he saw it before him.

Helena sat looking at her brother, undiluted and sincere praise for his good looks shining in her eyes. At thirty-two, she was six years Dave's senior. Now it was unbelievable to realize how much she had hated Dave when she was of courting age. When she was fifteen, Dave was nine—and the worst peeper, tattletale, and unofficial chaperone one could imagine.

Once Helena had threatened to blind his eyes with cayenne pepper, and to cut his tongue out so he couldn't follow her around and tell their mother everything she even thought about doing.

At nineteen, Helena had married and moved to Chicago, so she had never gotten to know her brother as a young man and could not believe in his true redemption until now.

"So I look OK?" Dave asked again teasingly, giving Helena his dazzling smile.

"Absolutely!" Helena said, smiling back.

"Yeah, maybe. But you'll notice that I'm still black as tar, and my hair is still as nappy as a sheep's behind. Do you remember when you used to make me wear all of those caps, both summer and winter, Helena, to hide my nappy hair?" Dave said, smiling without malice.

"Oh, Dave! Can you ever forgive me for that silly, childish nonsense? I was such a vain foolish girl!" Helena said, near tears.

"Hey, hey, hey!" Dave exclaimed. "I was only joneing! Don't take it so hard. I'm just playing with you, girl!" Dave said rushing to her side and hugging her again.

"Besides," Dave said slyly, "I never cared two figs what you thought!"

"You rascal!" Helena shouted, jumping up from the couch to punch her brother playfully about the middle.

Lela watched her children, her heart as content as it would get without knowing the whereabouts of her husband. How long had it been since both of her children and her husband had been under the same roof at the same time? "Lawd, Lawd!" Lela mused. "To have dem all at home. Nah dat sho' would be a satisfying feelin'!"

Helena had gratefully crammed herself and her two large grips into the guest room. Basil was very excited when told that he would be sleeping in Uncle Dave's room—and peeing in a chamber pot, he hoped.

Helena was satisfied. She was home. She had done the best she could by coming. Her children would be assured of a Merry Christmas—Grandmother and Uncle would see to that! And there—mercifully—would be three meals a day. And shelter. There would not be the possible humiliation of being set out in the frigid Chicago streets.

Usually, coming home to family dead broke and in need would have required a bit of pride swallowing. After working as little more than a house maid, pride had shrunk now—as had most of her self-esteem.

But she was home now, hoping for mercy. Understanding would have been too much to expect.

THIRTY-THREE

—✳—

Merry got up long enough to give Dave a disheartened greeting and promptly announced that she was going back to bed at three in the afternoon, because she was tired and sick. Basil was already curled up napping in his uncle's bed, the long bus ride having sapped all his intentions to play and explore.

"Let 'em sleep, dat bus ride wuz mo' den ten ourvas long! Why didn't y'all come on da train?" Lela asked.

Helena reached in her purse and laid three silver dimes on the parlor table, her lips parted into a painful smile. "Those dimes tell the whole story. That's all the money I have in the world."

Lela gasped and pulled away from the coins as if they were spiders.

"Why—" Lela began, and Dave had a question also, but Helena put a finger to her lips, shushing them both.

"There is something I want to tell you finally—Daddy too, but he isn't here yet. I want to tell you the truth. I've been covering, lying, hiding the truth for fourteen years, fourteen long years! Now after all those years, the lies and deceptions have risen to the surface like grease in a pot of stew."

"Mah, mah, mah!" Lela moaned. Just like she had thought—trouble.

"Mother, maybe you should get your tea. Dave, coffee?"

"Nothing for me, thanks," Dave said, his eyes riveted to his sister's face.

Lela suggested they move from the parlor to the big table in the kitchen, near the hot drinks which would doubtlessly be needed.

When they were settled again, Helena said, "Well! Shall I begin at the beginning?" She was almost gay now, giddy with the possibility of finally giving birth to this heavy load that had strained both mind and body, making every day one to be endured, never enjoyed.

"Mother, you looked up the road and you saw it, I believe as you often do. You said, 'Baby, be careful, please be careful!' I really didn't know what you meant. I was

275

just too immature, too starry eyed at the time. I thought if I married Norman I would be able to live like the women I had read about in the books and magazines."

Helena was thinking of Mrs. Keller, the principal of her high school, who had introduced the students to stories of people who lived in New York, Chicago, even London and Paris and Italy, women who were married to men who were businessmen, physicians, lawyers. Women whose lives bore no resemblance to the lives of poor Negro women in the South. All those books and magazines! All those picture shows! They nearly ruined her life. Poor Mrs. Keller! She was just trying to open up her poor students' view of the world a bit. She never meant to harm them. Quite the contrary. But when she told Helena that a few Negro women actually did live as well as the women she read about in books and magazines, she became determined to become one of them. Her hands would never pick cotton!

Lela poured Helena a cup of tea without taking her eyes from her face and without spilling a drop.

"When Norman came along, I even loved that name of his. A handsome, yellow man with good hair and a pretty name: Norman Newbridge St. Quatran. What more could I want?"

Norman was six years older and from Chicago. To the residents of West Steward he was a man of the world. He had come to town because his aunt had died and left him a small fortune—thirty-five hundred dollars. Born in Wisconsin, he had never been to the South and was curious, so he stayed two weeks.

"When he got the insurance check he cashed it out in small bills and showed it to me.

"Of all the pretty girls in town, he asked Daddy if he could call on me, remember, Mother? Later, I found out that even our courtship was tainted."

"What do you mean, Helena?" Dave asked, frowning.

"I was Norman's second choice. He told me that himself after we were married three or four months. He laughed about it. He said it was time for him to get married and he had heard Southern girls were special, so he wanted a Southern lady, but he wanted the daughter of a professional man, not a laborer. He presented himself to Marisa Post, you know, the dentist's daughter, but Dr. Post didn't like him and told him not to come calling again. He asked Marisa to sneak and meet him in Mr. Green's candy store. They had a heated little fracas that ended with him saying, 'Alright, I'll show you something! I'll marry the next girl that comes in that door!' "

"And you walked in?"

"You know me, Dave. I was always death on Mr. Green's sour pickles and peppermint sticks. Yes. I walked in. To save face, so to speak, he started to ask me out. I was already over age, waiting for my prince. Most of my friends were already married or engaged. Norman looked right and was well-to-do, and had a big bank job back where I wanted to escape to—a big city. I was more than willing to overlook any faults he might have had."

"Lawd, Lawd," Lela exhaled.

"Oh, it wasn't bad at all in the beginning," Helena assured her mother. "We lived very well. We took small trips, went to plays, nightclubs, all kinds of fashionable happenings. All of Norman's friends seemed to have their own businesses, small ones, but important for Colored—barbershops, restaurants, funeral homes. Well established people in the Negro community. The kind of people Norman catered to—people on their way up, successful folks. Later we even counted the president of an insurance company, a doctor, a dentist, and a banker among our close friends—or so we thought."

There was nothing to be heard in the kitchen now but the ticking of the clock.

Helena coughed a little, took a sip of tea and continued. Her mother and brother had barely stirred.

"We gave the best parties. We had the best food, the best drinks. We were fun, stylish—both me and Norman stayed togged down. We had a large lovely flat. It hardly occurred to us to notice that Norman and I were spending most of the money. We were the ones who were always giving parties—other people not so much. We really lived it up for two whole years. I tried to be a good wife to Norman, be what he wanted. Lookswise, I fitted in. Everything seemed OK."

"Until you come up expecting," Lela said.

"Norman never wanted children. He would have been satisfied to go on forever like we were, roaming around in a flat much too large and expensive for us. Four bedrooms and two baths. That's where we live now. Or did.

"When I was five months pregnant," Helena continued, "I decided to treat Norman to a bright, sunny lunch in the park. Norman had told me to come down to the bank anytime, I guess he thought I never would—or—well, I'm getting ahead of my story. I packed a bottle of iced soda, a small cake, baked chicken, potato salad, things Norman liked, and I called a cab. But when I went in the bank and asked for Mr. St. Quatran, the vice president, the receptionist could barely contain herself. She turned her head and tried to keep from laughing. Finally she said, 'So you're Normie's little wife?' Normie's little wife indeed! Not Mr. St. Quatran, mind you. Normie! Well, she said, 'He ain't in just now, but that's his booth over there. I don't know if I would wait, honey. He be taking some long lunches.' "

Helena paused, looking at her mother and her brother, as the clock ticked and the tea cooled.

"Shall I make a long, long story short?" she asked. "Norman was not and had never been a vice president of that bank. He told me he was in the teller's booth that day because one of "his" tellers had called in sick. But I saw the sign, Mother. It said Norman St. Quatran: Teller."

"Did you have lunch with him that day, Helena?" Dave asked, feeling all the old dislike he had felt for Norman from the beginning surfacing, being vindicated.

"Are you kidding?" Helena scoffed. "I went home and cried until I was sick. After that I didn't see Norman for two or three days."

"What do you mean, Helena?"

"I mean, dear brother, Norman simply didn't come home. That wasn't unusual though," Helena said, her voice muffled by tea and cakes that suddenly seemed the best she had ever eaten. "I was about used to it. You see, Norman is a gambler."

"Oh, no!" Lela exclaimed, as Dave expelled a harsh breath.

"That's what you probably saw in him that I didn't see, Mother. Hard edges, a soul stained by all the low down places he had been in his young life. A mind twisted by greed, and seeking and not finding. By wanting and not having. What did your preacher once say? 'Wading deep in the rivers of inequities.' That's what he was doing. Wading deep."

"That was pretty eloquently put, Helena," Dave said.

Helena laughed harshly, ignoring Dave's compliment.

"There was just the two of them. Norman and his big sister, Collie. And they spoiled him rotten, Mama, Daddy and big sister. They spoiled the little yellow child absolutely rotten. He had been gambling seriously since he was in his teens, and nobody stopped him or called his hand. Even now when he goes home the three of them act like he's the King of Jordan or something—he can do no wrong. His mother was absolutely no help to me—except she often watched the children when my regular sitter was sick and I had to go to work."

"Work?" Lela lifted her eyebrows, her palms, her feet from the floor in dismay.

Helena made a sound between a snort and a giggle.

"Oh Mother!" she cried in mock despair. "I've been working for ten years."

"For white folks?" Dave asked with distaste.

"For a woman named Paulette Greenbrier."

"Was you a housekeeper, Helena?" Lela asked sadly.

"Yes, Mother—a sort of lady's maid."

"Child, dat weren't atall necessary. None atall! You shoulda writ!"

"Now, Mother," Helena began waving a slender hand that shook slightly. "I have some pride. You wrote me that my brother was in business for himself and doing great. Now what would I look like, the older sister, coming back begging? Dave's doing a fine job of taking care of you. In fourteen years I never sent you a penny."

"But I didn't need—"

Helena continued over her mother's objections. "Marrying Norman was the biggest mistake of my life. I made my bed hard, now I have to lie in it. I just needed to come home for the holidays that's all!" Helena finished, her voice becoming higher, quivering. She was near tears.

"But, Helena!" Lela protested again.

Helena held up her hand for quiet, trying to steady and calm herself. Finally she said, "Let me finish. Please. It's important that I get this all out."

"Well... all right," Lela said reluctantly.

Helena told her mother and brother that she wasn't a housekeeper, but a combination secretary and lady's maid to a young and pretty but uneducated woman with social pretensions.

"Paulette Greenbrier used to work in a cold cream factory. She caught the owner's eye and old Mr. Greenbrier divorced his wife of twenty years and married Paulette. She was twenty. He was forty-seven."

Lela gasped. Helena smiled. Dave shook his head.

"Paulette was very ignorant but not dumb. She recognized her need to learn, to fit into society, so she placed an ad in the paper and I answered it, never expecting I'd be hired. I was picked because Paulette told me, quite frankly, she didn't want nobody better than herself! Even though I knew how to do what she hired me for: 'Write some of dem lil' thank you notes, en show me which is which wit' da forks in all, en help me pick da right dresses, en give the right kinda parties en all,' " Helena said, mimicking Paulette's nasal white trash voice with a giggle.

"I lied. I told Paulette I had gone to a lady's maid school to learn the proper things a lady's maid did. And you know, she never questioned what I told her."

Dave laughed out loud, but Lela kept quiet, for she didn't think it Christian to tell such a big lie to get a job, but she didn't want to hurt Helena's feelings by criticizing her actions. She felt that her daughter had been through quite enough already.

"Well kin ya beat dat!" Lela exclaimed. "My daughter working fer some heifer who done stole another woman's main!"

It was one of the most angry statements that either Dave or Helena had ever heard Lela utter and they looked at each other with surprise and humor.

"Ten years! Ten years, Helena! And you never said a word to yo' own mama!" Lela wailed in a grieved voice.

"Mother, it's over and done," Helena said firmly. "I had to bring some cash into the house, don't you see? I never knew if or when Norman would give me anything, and the bills had to be paid. Well, anyway, I've gotten way ahead of my story. Two months after Merry was born, Norman lost his job at the bank. He had gone from being absent frequently, I was later to learn, to not showing up at all, because he was in pursuit of games—some in rather rough parts of the city. And he gambled on everything. Horses, sports, dog races, you name it. About two weeks after Norman was fired from the bank he won a great deal of money. Thirty-three hundred dollars, he told me. He gave me seven hundred dollars, and I took care of the house off of that money for a year. I had to count every penny because he never gave me another dime that year and Merry was still an infant. I knew I had to find a job. Norman was now running the streets and trying to sell insurance in his spare time. That didn't last, so he submitted a written column for the society page to the *Chicago Black Guardian*. It was witty, it was knowledgeable—they hired him on the spot. He loved the job, and he actually kept it for nearly a year, but the gambling caused him to start missing his deadlines. And that was the end of that!"

"You sent me one of his columns. I showed hit to Miz Keller. She thought the woil of hit!" Lela said.

"After that job went under, Norman opened a café," Helena continued.

"A café?" Dave asked, amazed. He had not liked Norman St. Quatran fourteen years ago. His sister's new husband had made more than one joking remark about his color, asking him, "Davey, how come you the only fly in the buttermilk?" A reference to the fact that he was the only truly dark member of the Bailey family. Dave had thought him too "color struck," too much the braggart, always pulling out a twenty dollar bill when a single dollar would do. Dave thought Norman, as he remembered him, an unlikely candidate to work in a lowly cafe.

"Norman had won at gambling—again," Helena said. "This time on the numbers wheel they called it. He won forty-six hundred dollars, paid the rent for three months, had a big party, and gave me three hundred dollars. With what he had left, he opened a small café. It was an excellent idea—even then people were leaving the South. Most men were coming without their families. They would find a job, then send back home for their wife and children. Meanwhile they missed home cooked Southern food terribly, so Norman had the idea to open a small cheap cafe called Beans and Greens. He found a great cook and two good women to manage the place, and he opened on Saturday, April 9, 1921. From the beginning the place stayed packed. By then I had been working for Paulette Greenbrier for a good while," Helena explained. "Norman asked me to quit because it didn't look good for his wife to be working since he was such a success. Anyway, I got pregnant again right after Norman opened Beans and Greens. I wanted at least three children, and since we had regular high income again I thought we could afford another child."

"But?" Dave asked.

"Paulette was awfully nice about taking me back when Basil was six months."

"You left yo' house to work leaving a six-month-old baby?" Lela exclaimed, her voice filled with both pity and anger.

"Mother, I didn't want to risk losing my job," Helena said peevishly. "Especially since Norman was showing signs of messing up again. And I had really grown to love it because I talked Paulette out of the loveliest, most expensive gowns by telling her they were too garish, not suitable, not dignified enough for a woman in her position. In this way I had dresses that very few Colored women in Chicago could afford. And Paulette only wore her clothes for one season—then gave them to me. I'm telling you, at one time I had more clothes than I knew what to do with! Gorgeous outfits! Then there was the food, the best of everything—and I got to take the leftovers. As Paulette's personal lady's maid and assistant, I got first choice even over the rest of the house staff, white or black. Why, I often had teas and parties off of food from Paulette's parties!"

Lela looked stiff and disapproving at what Helena was revealing. She did not think it honest to lie to get a pretty dress. She wished again that Helena had written to her about her situation.

"Norman was spending the profits from the cafe as soon as they came in. Due to mismanagement on Norman's part, Beans and Greens closed two years after it opened. Good thing I got my job back. Meanwhile, our friends thought we were doing just grand. We still gave small parties, went out on the town, dressed to kill, but our marriage had fallen apart. So I worked for ten years to hold my family together. What money Norman brought into the house came from gambling, because he never worked another day after the café closed."

"Mah, mah, mah!" Lela exclaimed.

Helena looked at the dour expression on her brother's face and actually laughed. "Oh, that's nothing at all!" Helena said lightly, tapping Dave's hand playfully across the table. "One night I got a call to come to the emergency room of Chicago Memorial Hospital. It was for Norman. Because he had less money now, Norman was associating with people he despised, and I hear he never passed up a chance to let them know it. He was chasing games in rougher and tougher neighborhoods, and it came out later that he had insulted some man down on Thirty-ninth and State Street by calling him an ignorant black bastard. That was Norman. Bright skinned and always calling someone black this and black that. There had been some drinking and cheating, and emotions were very high among the men who were playing this card game; anyway, I understand the man took insults from Norman all night. Finally enough was enough. This man jumped up and slashed him across the chest with a razor. Norman said the man meant to kill him and was really aiming for his throat, but when he saw the razor coming, in a flash he reared up pulling his chair back and standing at the same time, causing the razor to catch him across the chest from his shoulder to his navel. They stitched him up and I brought him home. I hired a woman to look after him and Basil."

"Well I'll be!" Dave exclaimed. "You mean Norman was stabbed?"

"Cut," Helena corrected, "just like a regular tramp on the street."

"LawdhavemercyJesus!" Lela yelled. "Helena, you shoulda done been home!" she said, tears welling up in her eyes.

Helena's laugh was small, dry and brittle. "Yeah, yeah," she said, toying with her cup of tea.

"Where is Norman now?" Dave asked, not all that calmly.

"I don't know, Dave."

"You don't know?"

"Nope. I left him a note telling him to call me at the Jones' brothers store if he came home. If I don't hear from him in a week..." Helena's voice trailed off.

"Well is he OK, you reckon?" Lela asked.

"I don't know that either, Mother. But I do know this! After nearly fourteen years I'm nearly past caring. We had a few good years of marriage before Merry was born. It's been downhill ever since. Before we left, I hadn't laid eyes on Norman in more than a week. He stays in the street. When he does come home, he bathes and sleeps, hardly talking to me at all. He's very jumpy now, on edge. I think he owes money."

"Mah mah mah," Lela exclaimed again.

"So that's my story," Helena finished, smiling a tight little smile again.

"This can all be straightened out," Dave began.

"It's my problem, Dave," Helena said quickly, and then thinking she had sounded a little too short, she added, "But thank you. I'm going to have to take care of this myself. I'm going to get on my feet, go back to Chicago, finish my schooling and become a teacher. That's my plan."

Helena said rather defensively, "I brought the children home because I couldn't bear to see them suffer through the holidays with nothing. Mr. Greenbrier, his wife was the woman I worked for, was one of the ones totally destroyed by the crash last year. They lost everything. Naturally I lost my job—but not until October of this year. I had a little money saved, but it's gone now," Helena said. "That's why I didn't come home much over the years, Mother, or even write that often. I was afraid you would detect something of the truth of what was happening between the lines in my letters. I wrote you short, careful little letters."

"Yas mam you did!" Lela agreed. "You didn't never write but one little page."

"I was so ashamed of how things had turned out."

"Shame? In front of yo' mama?" Lela exclaimed. "Don't be silly!"

"I'm not going to stay here long... I can find some kind of work. I know it. I just had to get away from Chicago for a while. Norman was driving me crazy!" Helena said, trying to smile again as if her statement was hardly more than a joke.

"Helena," Lela said, rising, "we done listened to you, nah I want you to listen ta me and Dave. Nah!" Lela exclaimed, slapping her hands together. "I told you we had somethin' to tell ya, me and Dave. Cose hit's really Dave's story," Lela said, looking at her son.

Dave's brows went up in question.

"And what story is that, Mama?" he asked.

Lela looked at her daughter, her face all sly amusement and pride barely concealed. "Yo' brother is real well ta-do, chile." Lela said, smiling. "Ax him hi much he makin' in a month. And he got four, five mens workin' fer him. Pays 'em good too!"

Helena looked at her brother, and now he was smiling a little, but somehow talk of his success always embarrassed him, and his expression was halfway between pride and shame.

"Mama wrote me that you were doing real well in the tamale business, but I have no real idea..." Helena began haltingly, not knowing if she should really ask him how much he made, although she was curious—especially since her mother brought it up with such obvious pride and enthusiasm.

"Ax him! Ax him!" Lela insisted.

Dave was still smiling in his shy hesitant way, but now his expression contained mischief as well.

"Guess," he said playfully to Helena.

"OK, give me a minute." Helena thought of the big new stove in the kitchen, the only one in Colored Town, her mother had written, with six eyes. The two radios, when most of Colored Town had no radio at all, the comfortable, plush sofas in both the parlor and the middle room, her mother's *two* ice boxes—they must be doing very well indeed.

"Dave got hisself a new truck last year," Lela giggled. "Is you through guessing?"

"Well, seeing how fine everything in this house looks..."

"And I have a helper!" Lela shot out. "I have trouble bending now because of my rheumatism. I got a girl, Aggie, helps me with scrubbing and washing, and everything once a week—just lak white folks!"

Dave laughed at his mother's eagerness now, and at Helena's growing bewildered expression.

"You did say a month?"

"Yas, yas!" Lela sang out impatiently.

"Is that after all expenses?"

"Yas, yas!"

Helena hesitated a moment longer, calculating in her head.

Finally she said. "I'm going to say one hundred and fifty dollars." She looked from Dave to her mother and back. "Plus or minus fifty dollars," she added, hedging her bet, not knowing what to make of their silence.

"You better plus up mo' den dat!" Lela exclaimed with delight.

"More?" Helena asked not able to believe it could be more than two hundred dollars a month. Two hundred dollars a month would be a huge sum.

"Come on up some, goil! Don't be scared!"

"Dave, is Mama teasing me?" Helena asked.

"No," Dave answered, trying not to laugh.

"I sayed yo' brother is a rich main! Is two hundred dollars what you think is rich?" Lela taunted her daughter. "I thought everybody in Chicago made at least dat much!" Lela said, laughing, playing the tease.

"Oh, quit now!" Helena begged. "Just tell me how much. My last guess is two hundred and fifty dollars. There. Am I right?"

"Over foe." Lela said with solemn pride.

"Over four hundred dollars? A month?" Helena asked incredulously.

"Yas, and climbing. When Dave gits his other lil' school and candy sto's goin' out in the New Addition, ain't no telling hi much he'll be makin'."

Helena stared at Dave, sitting impassively in the rocking chair, a little smile still playing on his lips. She had never heard of a Colored man making so much money! Perhaps a doctor, perhaps a dentist—but her own brother? It was dazzling!

"Is it true, Dave?" she asked quietly.

"Yes. I've been able to do pretty well for a nappy headed boy," he answered jokingly.

"My God!" Helena exclaimed.

"Don't take da Lawd's name in vain, Helena," Lela said seriously, although her own constant use of the Lawd's name was not blasphemy in her way of thinking.

"Why, this is wonderful, Dave! I've never felt so proud."

"So you see. You shoulda done been home. You didn't have to stay up in no Chicago takin' stuff off no Norman," Lela said hotly. "As you can tell, Dave make enough to take care ten families real well!"

"I see!" Helena said, and she couldn't help thinking that even Norman Newbridge St. Quatran would be impressed, and might find it hard to run through that kind of money in a month.

THIRTY-FOUR

After they all enjoyed a light supper, with even the reluctant Merry being coached into eating a slice of cake and a glass of milk, Dave had promised to tell his sister how he gotten into the tamale business.

"First, I'll tell you what you asked about my little business, then I think you should know about the murders that took place here not long ago, because they are at the center of everything here now. You noticed the guards outside?"

"Someone was murdered? White or Colored?" Helena asked, aghast. "Mother never told me...I did wonder about all those men outside...Oh, my goodness!"

Dave waved a hand as if dismissing the subject of the killings—at least for the time being. "Let me tell you about the business first. That's a more pleasant story—and easier to come to grips with."

Suddenly Helena felt a chill and pulled a light, small "baby" quilt around her shoulders.

"Do you remember old Mr. Dubbins? Luke Dubbins the 'hot tamale man' we used to call him. Well, he got sick, and became almost totally blind. He was looking to give up the business. He showed me how to make the wonderful tamales he had been making for over forty years. So I bought the business from him."

Dave told Helena about why he left the mill and about the attempt on Peter Franizou's life. "I had to leave the mill, Helena. Can you understand that. If I hadn't left it would have just been a matter of time before I killed one of those men."

Helena looked doubtful.

"No. I believe I could have actually killed one of the men that had beaten Peter. Anyway I didn't want to look for another job in a sawmill. I was frustrated working for white folks. I just wanted to take some time off and think, and that's what I did. I had saved my money and me and Mama's needs were small. And Papa never missed sending money from wherever he was, although we really didn't need it," Dave said, smiling broadly.

"I had taken to going up on the bus line on the weekends, mostly to listen to music and take in the sights, and old Luke Dubbins was always there five days a week selling his hot tamales from six to midnight. But he had gotten quite old and sickly and a group of young boys who had not been raised properly took to taunting him. He was nearly blind now, and these boys used to give Luke a dollar and swear it was a five or ten. When he wouldn't give them change for the bill they lied that they had given him, the boys would start to raise all kinds of hell with poor old Luke."

"My, what a pity!" Helena said.

"Yes, it was," Dave continued. "Finally Luke wouldn't accept paper money, just exact change, which he could feel and identify by size, but those little buggers still found a way to bother the old man. Well, I wasn't doing anything, so I started to sit with him, make change for him and serve the customers. He's been knowing me since I was a kid."

"He'd say, yah! Lela's boy. I kin trust him," Lela added proudly, sipping her tea, listening to the wind, thinking about her husband—and thinking about the short time before Christmas and all the things yet left to be done. She knew the story of Mr. Dubbins and Dave and the tamales, so she did not have to give this telling her full attention. It was for Helena to hear after all, but she wanted to be with her children to feel their warmth, enjoy their rare company, so she had no intention of leaving the room no matter how long the telling and retelling of the story took.

"I got to like him a lot. He was a sharp old man, or had been. You know he's been selling hot tamales for forty-seven years? He made a job for himself when he was thirty-four and he'd been at it ever since. His wife died a while back. They had two children but they died. However, he did have a great number of nieces and nephews and grandnephews and their husbands and children he helped financially, some of whom lived in his house. Mr. Dubbins kept offering to pay me for helping him but I would never take it. I just wanted to help the old feller out and keep those bad young niggers off of him. Well anyway, he kept inviting me up to his house to see his "operation" he called it, and finally I went."

"Uh, uh, uh!" Lela exclaimed, remembering. "What a mess!"

"Yeah. It was. Where he made the tamales was the filthiest place I'd ever seen! Children were all over the place, and dogs were running around eating out of his stock pots. It turned my stomach to know that I'd eaten many a tamale from this place! It was terrible."

"Why was it so dirty?" Helena asked, making a face, for she had grown up eating Luke Dubbins' hot tamales herself.

"Mr. Dubbins explained that his place had not always been this way. All the nieces and nephews were supposed to be helping him. Helping him cook, keep the place clean, make up the tamales. He said that over the years they had gotten pretty slack, not even helping him make enough tamales to meet his demand. And they stole from him every chance they got. They were the worse bunch of Colored folks I ever met!" Dave said angrily.

"So when he asked me to manage the operation for him, to shape up his ungrateful clan, I accepted."

"Oh, he did a beautiful job!" Lela said proudly. "He made da wimmens keep dat place clean as ah bean! And da ones dat was suppose to be heping, great big old mens thirty and forty years old, Dave made dem woik, baby. He turnt everything around and upside down!"

"And they didn't like it one bit," Dave said, laughing. "One morning all of his relatives—there were about eight of them, counting their children—gave old Luke an ultimatum: Get rid of me or they would all move. They were blood. I was not. They resented me being brought in over them. 'Next thang you know dis Dave be done talked you out all yo' money you got hid,' one of the teenage grandnephews told Luke. Well, at that old Luke finally exploded! He called them a worthless bunch of trashy niggers, and he told them to git! He told them he had been praying that they would leave for years because he had never seen such a bunch of no account coons! Oh, he let them have it. They didn't think he could function without them you see, at his advanced age—he was eighty-one—and they had a fit every time he tried to bring in other help over the years."

Helena was excited. "So did they leave?" she asked.

"Not immediately. They were so surprised they didn't know what to do at first—especially since they had been bluffing. But a few days later when I went up to Mr. Dubbins—he had this big old ten room house—there was a "big man," all five feet three inches of him and the leader of the pack, sitting out in the yard with the entire group all dressed up in brand new clothes. 'We's leavin',' he announced. 'Good!' Mr. Dubbins said. 'Ya shoulda been gone!' So they left."

"All of them?" Helena asked.

"Every last one!" Dave said.

"But I got to thinking after they were gone. Something wasn't right. They had been with their uncle for four or five years, ever since he started to lose his sight almost completely, and all of a sudden they pull out just like that? And they had seemed rather in a hurry, too. Then it hit me. Everyone was wearing new clothes. Luke Dubbins paid the adults for their help, but they were looking a little too prosperous. And where were they going? What were all of them going to do when they got there? In 1927-28, things were already tightening up, some of the sawmills were already starting to slow down. Do you know what I figured?"

"What?" Helena asked excitedly.

"I figured that those niggers had found some hidden money around the place, dug it up, split it up, and were anxious to leave before they were found out. I told Mr. Dubbins what I suspected. Remember I told you he was almost blind. They must have followed him and watched him as he hid some of his money. After all, he couldn't see them watching him."

"What did he say?"

"He was well aware that they had been stealing from him. He told me to go look in the hen house and I did. There was evidence of digging in there, and a large empty glass jar. I thought they had gotten it all. I felt very badly for him. After all the man had been saving for years. But after they left, Luke offered to teach me the business and sell me the operation. I thought about it, and Mama prayed about it, and finally I decided to give it a try. Luke was tired and getting up in age and it gave me a chance to be my own boss. I had a lot of ideas from the beginning, and I started out with three carts, not one, from the very first weekend. And the rest, they say is history," Dave concluded.

"Now dat ain't all," Lela said, looking at Dave. "Mistah Dubbins was so grateful to Dave fer bringin' some order into his old life! He treated Dave most lak a son until da day he died. Dave got 'em a woman ta keep house and cook fer 'em and keep 'em comfortable dere rest o' his days—out his own pocket. Mistah Dubbins lived until just six months ago.

"Dave," Lela said looking at her son. "Ain't you gone tell yo' sister da rest?"

Dave smiled again, a smile Helena would come to recognize as a mixture of embarrassment, modesty—and pride.

"What I'm going to tell you, Helena, is for the ears of the three of us only, OK? Can you keep a secret? Because this is definitely not for your husband's ears."

"Do I look like I have a husband to you?" Helena asked archly. "I don't even know where that man is! And if I did I wouldn't tell him what I had for supper!"

"OK," Dave said convinced. "Several months before he died, old man Dubbins called me up to the house. 'Dave you been lak mah own boy dat I never had—just nieces and nephews. I shoally 'preciates all dat you done done. Because o'you I got me some peace at last!' he told me.

"I said, 'I was glad to help, Mr. Dubbins.' He was totally blind by then. He reached in his pajama pocket and handed me a folded piece of a brown bag. 'Look at dat note, boy. Can you read hit? Dat was drawed years ago when I could see. Nah, I can't see good enough to even down point nothin' out, so you'll have to listen. Dem two squares on dat paper stands fer da two turrets on dis house. Dose bushy thangs is trees. You see dat? And dose lines is pointing to dose trees on dis property.'

"Mr. Dubbins' carefully drawn out note was a treasure map, Helena. His brother and two sisters were dead, so he left the map to me. It pointed to where he had hid most of his money over the years before his sight failed. Mrs. Hall had been holding the note for him all these years without fully knowing what it represented. In the last few years before he lost his sight almost completely, the relatives who worked for him had been digging up his money as fast as he hid it. He knew that—but it wasn't a great deal—nothing like what he had hidden before they came, and there wasn't a lot he could do about it. He told me that over the last five years he had given most of the money he earned to Fazy Ruth Hall who was more than a friend. He said she was well taken care of, was very satisfied and was not to receive anything more. Besides, she's eighty-one years old and in poor health. Mr. Dubbins also said that in addition to the caches on the map, he had money hidden in so many other places he would never remember them all, and 'dem lil' dumb bastard nephews and nieces were too dumb to find it.' He said after he died that I should 'git ta lookin' and that I could have every penny I could find!"

"So have you looked, Dave?" Helena asked, her face becoming splotchy with excitement.

"So far I have only been able to locate twenty-eight thousand dollars." Dave said with a straight face.

"What!" Helena screamed nearly falling off her chair. "What will you do with all that money Dave?" Helena asked, her voice compressed with awe.

"Listen, girl. When this Depression is over, I'd like to open a decent hotel for Colored people with a place for entertainment where respectable people could come—not some juke joint up in the weeds like Princess Thelma's. I'd like to help black people open their own stores and get more independent of white folks, I'd like to see white folk coming to some restaurants we owned, some bakeries we owned, some laundries we owned, because they were the very best. We do all the work Helena, but when pay day comes," Dave's voice drifted off ruefully. "I got plans Helena," Dave continued, and I want you in with me. I'd like a family business to start with, even though we are a small family—but then some of my friends are almost like family, Peter, Omar..."

"Oh, Helena would be good wit' most anythin'," Lela added. "She would give a little high tone to everythin.'"

"Well, I don't know..." Helena began. "Although I certainly appreciate you thinking of me. My gosh!" she burst out, her hands flying to her face that was no longer colorless but spotted again. "This is all so sudden! So unexpected! I'm getting hot and cold flashes!"

"Shoot! Dave don't need no answer rat nah. You got plenty time to think on hit," Lela said cheerfully. "Don't you want to nap, Helena? That bus ride must have been a killer."

"No, no, no! I'm too wound up to ever sleep again! I want to talk! I want to listen! Tell me everything that has happened since I was last here. Go ahead, talk!"

So they talked-away into the morning, each energizing the other, Dave and Lela taking turns to make sure nothing was left out, that the right emphasis was added to the right stories. They went into detail about the lynching of Billy Binder, they told her that Sam Lawrence and his wife had been killed, about the circumstances surrounding Peter's beating; Lela told her about LeBow Shell being run out of town. Dave told her why the Circle had been started, about the murder of the couple up in White Town and how they had spirited the Duster family out of town because their son, Ralph, had become a suspect, how they had rescued Aristotle Gillis from a lynch mob, and finally about the tree incident.

When Dave had finished relating that story, Helena expressed pride in the purpose of the Circle, but a deep fear of retaliation.

"Oh, Mother!" she exclaimed. "We are in mortal danger! White folks will never let you get away with things like that," she said, and started to tremble with alarm.

"Hey!" Dave said gently, "Don't worry. We've got it under control Helena," Dave said walking over and taking her frigid hands in his large warm ones. "We have always been in mortal danger, huh? The difference now is that we've decided to do something to bring about some changes. Not just be picked off like birds for sport. You hit me, I hit back. Maybe pretty soon you start thinking. Maybe you start to realize if I shoot this nigger, he will shoot back. I could get killed also. Maybe I better stop messing with these niggers, better stop being so rash in my actions—especially when I'm not being provoked. Maybe I'd better start being a little careful. Especially when I see that they are prepared to *die*."

"Oh dear!" Helena wailed, her head spinning with yet another revelation.

"Helena, how could you respect me if I did anything less? We have just sat and took it too long as it is." Dave said tersely, letting go of his sister's hand.

"But they have all of the power! The Negro is nobody down here!"

"Yes, they have power—for now. But they don't have all of the guns, all of the courage, all of the sense!" Dave said fiercely. "And in every county we even outnumber them."

"Mother!" Helena cried alarmed, seeking help.

"Child, I have been through dis already. Nothin' I kin say. Dis Circle got dey minds made up!"

Helena stared at Dave, wondering what she had come home to. She felt an involuntary shaking of her limbs begin, and wondered if this was a nervous breakdown.

Lela noticed her condition immediately. "I'm gone put some brandy in dat hot tea and pull dat quilt up 'round yo' shoulders. You 'zhausted from dat ride, from staying up all day and night. You need to sleep, but if you too up to sleep, den drink all dat tea and brandy, and stay still. You gone be alright."

Lela was right. After the hot drink Helena started to feel herself slowly pull back from the very edge of panic. Her body relaxed and she announced at 1:30 a.m. that she would like to try to sleep, and she left and went into her bedroom and kicking off her shoes, she rolled over into the bed beside her daughter and fell asleep immediately without undressing.

The following morning, Helena slept until a little past ten o'clock. Lela had kept the house quiet and when Helena finally came into the kitchen, Lela said, "dinner?" teasingly.

Dave sat, eating a rare breakfast of fried potatoes and onions, biscuits and coffee.

"Now you look like the old Helena! Got a few roses in those cheeks," he said when he saw how much better his sister looked after sleeping. Basil had eaten and was down the road with Aggie's children and a guard. Merry was still in bed, awake but pouting, refusing to get up.

Lela had spread a small feast: Jars of peach and tomato preserves had been opened, and there were plump hot biscuits, crisp sweet thick sliced bacon, fried potatoes with onions, fried eggs, and eggs scrambled with brains, and both sassafras tea and coffee. Additionally, Lela had made cinnamon and raisin biscuits with powdered sugar frosting especially for Merry.

"Mother, this is heavenly!" Helena beamed surveying the heavily laden table, her eyes becoming hungry before her stomach. She sat down and piled her plate high, much to Lela's satisfaction.

"Eat like that every day and you're gonna find those hips you lost," Dave said.

"I don't care!" Helena answered. "It's so good to have some real Southern cooking! I'm gonna clean this table up!"

"Well, look lak I ain't gone be cookin fer no one but you and me. Basil didn't eat nothin' but sweets and meat. Not one tater did he eat!" Lela complained.

"I'll be right back," Dave said abruptly, walking down the hall.

"Now where's he going?" Helena asked, biting into a biscuit loaded with peach preserves that pushed the fragrant scent of cloves, cinnamon, allspice pleasantly up her nose.

Dave was back in five minutes. He handed his sister a pillow case.

"I want you to take this," he said, not smiling. "I was going to send it to you anyway. You are just getting your Christmas present a few days early."

"A pillow case?" Helena asked, looking adorable, Dave thought, with biscuit crumbs in her hair, around her lips.

Helena pulled away from the case.

"Uh uh. I ain't taking it! You probably got a rat or something in there," Helena said, looking to her mother again for aid and assurance, remembering Dave's childhood tricks.

Lela shook her head at Helena. "Child, I ain't got no iddy what he got in dat case, but he wouldn't gie his sister no rat nah," Lela said, siding with Dave. "Go 'head on an take hit. Hit might be somethin' that you gone lak," her mother said smiling.

Helena took the case that was tied loosely at the top with a piece of grosgrain ribbon, all the while watching to see if Dave's eye lit up with the sign of a joke.

"What is it?" Helena asked, her eyes large with fear.

"Why is it that when people take an unopened gift from you, they shake it to death, smell it, turn it over, everything but open it, all the while asking the person who gave it to them what it is?" Dave asked, smiling at his mother.

Helena cleared a small spot on the kitchen table and carefully dumped the contents of the bag slowly on the table.

"I know it's not something that will break," she said to Dave. "But I can't imagine—"

Suddenly Helena screamed, and kept screaming as the bills tumbled out on the table. Small bills, fives, tens, some twenties.

"Sssshhh! you gone wake up Merry!" Lela cautioned, but Merry, still lying in bed watching a spider in a corner, gave no evidence of interest in anything outside of her private and dreary thoughts of Southern life.

When all of the bills were jumbled on the table, Helena asked with an awe stricken voice, "Is this for me? How much is it?"

Dave pretended to sigh with impatience and did not answer.

Lela laughed and slapped her thighs like a playful schoolgirl at the expression on her daughter's face. "Why don't you count hit up, honey?" her mother laughed, enjoying herself more than she had for months.

This heap of money made her nervous, and Helena fumbled to bring order to the heap, the fives here, the tens there, the twenties. Finally, to her amazement, she had counted five hundred dollars.

"I don't know how to begin to thank you Dave," Helena whispered through her tears. "This is the best Christmas present I could ever dream of. This is—well— unreal. These two days have been unreal. Dave, you realize you have just given me my salary, I mean about what I earned in a year!"

"Well, I'll be dog," Dave said, unimpressed but smiling at his sister's joy.

"Go hug his neck Helena!" their mother urged, tears sliding down her face.

Dave submitted to the sweet wet kisses to his face, chin, neck, with a scowl as he did when a boy, as if he could hardly stand such a show of gratitude and affection, but both women could see that he really did not mind Helena's joyful kisses as much as he pretended; in fact, he was happy to see that Helena did not refuse the money out of pride, as he thought she might.

"I'll accept this only because I know you have a little teeny weensy bit more left," Helena teased, and all three of them laughed heartily at her joke and at her delight.

"Nah, I 'magine you'll be wantin' to fetch a play pretty or two fer da chirrens over in Old Steward tomorry?"

"Oh, It'll be so wonderful not to have to pinch every last penny!" Helena said, starting to count the bills again. "I can buy everything I need for around thirty dollars. Merry a few dresses and a pair of shoes and some under things. Pants for Basil and a few little shirts, shoes and a cap. You know what else? Ribbon candy and Brazil nuts, and a game for each of the children," Helena exclaimed, her eyes sparkling. "Why, Dave, this is a fortune! Thank you so much!"

Dave thought how right he had been to give his sister money instead of anything else he could have thought of. He had seen it time and time again: A little money in an empty pocket could make a big difference in how one felt about the world. It made him proud to be in a position to help—especially family.

Tears welled in Lela's eyes again thinking of her daughter's needless years of suffering. Well, that was over now. Helena was home. They could have been truly happy in this moment, except for the recent events and not knowing the whereabouts of Rex Bailey, husband and father.

THIRTY-FIVE

~~✦~~

Both Dave and Helena had noticed how their mother haunted the windows in the last two days, looking down the road in front of the house, staring out back where the woods began, jumping at every visitor's steps upon the porch. Listening. Praying. Waiting. Waiting for Rex, her husband, who had written weeks ago that he was coming home.

The children began to worry about Lela's daily vigils at the windows—until she sat them down over a cup of tea.

"Listen, chirren," Lela began, "I know I been lookin' and listenin' a lots of late, and I know you done noticed hit, but I'm alright. Really I is. I was just hopin' against hope dat Rex would be home 'fore Christmas but he won't be. New Year's either." Lela said with finality.

Helena and Dave looked at each other.

"What makes you so sure, Mother?" Helena asked. "Did you get another letter?"

"Naw. No letter. But when I was at mah prayer table yonder under dat window dis moaning, I seent hit jus' as clear. Jus' lak dere Lawd was talkin' ta me. He say in a clear voice inside mah head—He say Lela, Rex is fine in dat he ain't hurt or nothin', but he won't be home 'til after New Year's. I heard dat voice clear as anythin', so I'm gonna stop lookin' and peepin' and listenin' every little while."

And Lela did. She stayed away from the porches and the windows and continued to cook and prepare for Christmas, as it was now already December twenty-third.

"My," Helena remarked to Dave some time later. "I wish I had half of mother's faith."

Lela had learned to "let go and let God" over the years, and so she really had relinquished Rex's care over to "Gawd's capable hains," and she was actually experiencing more happiness than she had known in years. Her daughter and grandchildren were home. She had someone to prepare her glorious meals for, and that made her quite content. Lela's only disappointment was that Rev. Clayton would be unable to come for Christmas dinner because he was going to Mississippi to be with his family. That was nice, Lela thought, but she had so looked forward to Helena seeing the minister eat!

Christmas was a magnificent affair. Lela had decided there would be no scarcity in this house for Christmas! Even Merry enjoyed herself. In the Southern black tradition, enough pastry was prepared to last until New Year's—and to share with even casual visitors that happened in.

With Helena's help, Lela had baked her usual twelve cakes. However, there was no counting of the pies she baked. Mince meat and cherry, chess and lemon meringue, pecan and dried fruit, and stacks of sweet potato pies.

"We ain't rich in money, but we sho' rich in somethin' ta et!" people liked to say—even now, during this Depression, there was enough to eat in Colored Town for everyone during the holidays. The church ladies saw to that.

Every room had been decorated for Christmas with bowls piled high with apples, oranges, nuts and candy, especially the beautiful ribbon candy that everybody prized. In addition, there were bowls of grapes, raisins, and dried figs. There were heaping bowls of mixed nuts: black walnuts in their rough hewn hulls, dull-skinned, long, sweet pecans, the extremely hard shelled hickory nuts—even the lowly peanut was represented.

Helena was having a hard time keeping Basil away from the sweets, especially the ribbon candy, until dinnertime while she made the center piece, a large bowl of fruit and nuts with foot long peppermint sticks shooting out all around it. Lela thought her daughter's creation so beautiful that she cried.

The guest started arriving for Lela's grand dinner before the appointed time of two o'clock. Shouting loudly back and forth, "Christmas gift! Christmas gift!" as they came out of their coats and were led proudly to see Helena's Christmas table decoration.

There were to be around sixteen for dinner. Mother Mattie Clarence and her husband, Turner, who were alone now, their children scattered about the North. Esta York and her four grandchildren, including Dabney Shell. Aggie Pratt and her boys, Arky, named loosely after Arkansas, and Villa, after a magazine article about Italy, and Dave's fiancée Adrianna James, Helena and her children.

"Mama, where you gonna seat all those folks?" Dave had asked with some concern, for the room was not huge.

With Rex Bailey coming home, Dave knew he had to help Helena find a suitable rental house of her own as soon as he knew whether she was going to stay. Perhaps something in The Clearing with an indoor toilet, Dave thought, because even now they were pretty crowded.

Helena was very excited about meeting Adrianna. Not knowing how the moody Adrianna would choose to behave today, Dave felt nothing but anxiety when Helena said, "I bet your young lady is very beautiful."

"She is," Dave said, his delivery so abrupt that it sounded like an angry retort, even though he followed the response with a smile.

Helena decided to say no more about Adrianna for the time being. She concentrated on helping her mother with the dinner: A fat roasted goose with rich sausage dressing, a large Virginia ham, a number of baked hens so each guest would have "tomorrow's dinner without cooking," pots of snap beans, and greens cooked with salt pork, sliced beets and onions with sugar and vinegar, mounds of rolls that everyone in town bought from Lucille Aclavin's house bakery because no one could make them better, huge bowls of potato salad, macaroni and cheese, dishes of fruit preserves, relishes, ambrosia, candied sweet potatoes with oranges and honey— the food was endless, and magnificent. The Depression had not touched this house.

The guests brought gifts for Lela, too. Handmade towels, pillow cases, and tablecloths, a set of glasses from White Town, a long robe lined in satin, a white waist trimmed in lace, two pounds of sweet butter in a clay pot, cinnamon sticks, whole nutmegs, a gallon of strong applejack from Turner Clarence, and more.

While Dave went to fetch Adrianna, Helena set the table beautifully with her mother's "good plates."

"My, ain't you pretty!" Aggie said to Helena. "I had no idea Dave had sich a pretty sister," the young woman said without guile or envy.

Suddenly Aggie became nervous and shy. Perhaps she had been too loud mouthed with this lovely woman—too familiar right off. Maybe she was hincty like some people from the North were, looking down on poor uneducated Colored people such as herself. Maybe she was not as nice as Lela or Dave. *Dat shoally was possible,* Aggie thought as she stood looking at this "classy" woman, waiting for her to say something. Anything!

"I knew you were Aggie Pratt the minute you walked in the door the other day" Helena said warmly to Aggie. "Mother mentioned you so fondly in her letters. She said you were her little helper. Your two youngsters are so handsome! I know they are going to become great friends with my children, Meredith and Basil."

Then Helena called her children over and formally introduced them to Arky and Villa Pratt, and the four of them went off in the middle room with the other children to play games until dinner time.

"Girl, we better git busy!" Aggie said, greatly relieved that Helena was not the least bit full of herself.

"You've done enough already. You are a guest too, remember," Helena said graciously.

"Guest my foot!" Aggie said attacking a chunk of ice with an ice pick and placing large pieces in each dinner guest's glass. "Lets git dis food on the table while hit's hot. Everything smells and looks so good and everybody is hoingry to death! Da chirrens can be set up in da kitchen."

"Dave isn't back with his fiancée yet," Helena protested with some concern.

Aggie made a face. "Dat one? Adrianna James? She'll do her level best tuh make 'em late. She dat kind, sorry to tell ya. We best to start tryin' to feed da ones dats heah!"

Aggie was right, but Lela insisted upon waiting for Dave to return with Adrianna. However at a quarter to three Lela said, "Lets us eat," with a slight edge to her voice.

"My ice is most melted in all da glasses by nah!" Aggie said peevishly.

The guests fell upon the food with great gusto, praising the dishes, and everybody laughed and joked and piled their plates high, enjoying themselves greatly. But Lela herself ate sparingly and watched the clock.

"Scuse me fer sayin' dis, Miz Helena," Aggie said heatedly as she cut peach cobbler into generous squares, placed them on saucers and surrounded each piece with hot buttery juice.

"Just plain Helena will do fine, Aggie."

"Well Helena then," Aggie hissed under her breath. "But I could kick Adrianna's dark behind rat nah! She know hi upset Mother B. git when Dave a little late dese days due to what's been happenin' down heah. Dey tole ya?"

"Yes, but perhaps it's not her fault Aggie. Perhaps there was trouble with the truck, or—"

"Not hardly!" Aggie shot back, licking her finger. "Adrianna a ornery, hinckty heifer! You jus' wait and see. Hit's gone be all her fault da reason dey late. She can't get her stockin' seams straight, or she can't find her bloomers! Somethin' silly assed!" Aggie fumed.

"Aggie!" Helena exclaimed, a little taken aback by Aggie's frankness.

"Oh! Please excuse me. Dat wasn't no fair. You gotta judge Adrianna fer yo'self. Please look over me! Please," Aggie begged.

"Of course," Helena said pleasantly. "We are both getting a little tired."

"But personal, I hates 'er fer a no good cow!" Aggie said, squinting her eyes up mischievously.

"Aggie, behave!" Lela said, hearing the young woman's remarks.

This time Aggie did not apologize, but threw her head back and laughed for all she was worth.

"Dabney, you jus' getting prettier by da day!" Mother Clarence said to Esta York's granddaughter, to give her confidence, and because it was true.

They listened to music and talked only of "nice pleasant things today," as Lela had insisted. After everyone was comfortable and served at least twice, Aggie and Helena slid into seats next to each other like two comrades that had just fought a successful battle and fed themselves.

"Where could they be?" Helena asked, her voice now showing some concern, because she noticed her mother becoming more agitated by the moment and trying not to show it.

"Oh, dey'll be along by New Year's," Aggie said, smiling around a mouth full of mashed potato salad.

At twenty minutes to four, one hour and forty minutes late, Dave and Adrianna walked in the door.

Lela looked at Dave sharply, the way he looked would tell her everything—never mind Adrianna.

Dave helped his girlfriend remove her coat then walked over and planted a kiss on his mother's cheek. "Sorry," he said. "Everything is fine, Adrianna just kept changing her clothes!"

"Why?!" Lela asked Dave.

He shrugged and removed his jacket, and took the two seats together his mother had saved for them.

"Hello everybody!" Adrianna said loudly. "Is we late? I thought the dinner started at three-thirty."

"You lying heifer!" Aggie hissed quietly so that only Helena heard her.

Lela looked at Adrianna with something akin to pity. Such a pretty girl—and such a liar.

"Well, anyway, we here now!" Adrianna said, giggling and looking all around trying to charm the guests.

Aggie stared at Adrianna with abject hatred. She had heard more stories about her than Dave ever knew, and none of them were nice. She wanted to tell Lela or even Helena about Adrianna but she would not. She prided herself for keeping her mouth shut. Aggie felt that one day the girl would break Dave's heart, Dave whom she loved like a brother—and more.

Helena looked across the table at the girl with interest noting that she was indeed a great beauty. She was dressed modestly in a conservative grey suit with a high-necked lace-trimmed white waist. Her hair was brushed back, shiny and sleek. If she was trying to look like a school teacher, she had succeeded.

Adrianna's and Helena's eyes met and Helena smiled in a friendly manner, but Adrianna did not return it, and stared blankly at Dave's sister for a moment and then looked at Dave, as if for an explanation for her presence. Helena could not quite hear her above the noise level, but she could see her lip movements and half hear Adrianna ask Dave, "Who is that?"

Dave looked at Helena and smiled. "My sister," he answered proudly.

"Oh?" Adrianna said with little interest. Then she stared at Helena again, unsmiling.

Aggie was watching Adrianna's unfriendly exchanges and said, "I wish Mother B hadn't invited that hinckty heifer!"

"Aggie!" Helena said, feeling a little hurt by Adrianna's lack of warmth. Helena so wanted the girl Dave was going to marry to like her. Perhaps the woman was shy...and perhaps they would meet on better terms after everyone had eaten and left the table, Helena thought, covering strange behavior with gracious excuses.

Again Aggie said, as if reading Helena's mind, "Honey, that wench don't hardly lak nobody dat wears a dress! If she don't git to lakin' you don't let it bother you. Hit ain't none o'yo' fault."

But Adrianna was out to charm the mother and tried again. "Miss Lela has sent me so many sweet things this year until I have gained some weight. I can hardly fit into any of my clothes anymore. I had to search and search for something to wear.

That's why we are a little late. I beg you pardons, Miss Lela. It wasn't Dave's fault."

This statement warmed the air a little as Lela decided, of course, to forgive and forget.

After dinner everybody retired, at Lela's insistence, to the parlor to let their dinner "die down." Surprisingly, Meredith did not balk against helping to wash the dishes. She and the young people made a game of it and were soon finished.

The last guest left the house at eight-thirty, after marveling at the sumptuous dinner and their personal good fortune at being so warm and well fed in times such as these; for in addition to the Depression, most of Arkansas had experienced a terrible drought this year, and being able to say you had a twenty-five pound sack of flour, some meal, a sack of rice, beans, sugar and coffee, was a great blessing these days. The dinner the guests had just experienced left them with a happy, prosperous feeling that would last all week.

Before she left, Adrianna had finally come up to Helena, and eyeing her sharply, she said, "So you Dave's sister, huh? Well, you certainly don't look anything like I expected you to look." Then she smiled broadly. But the smile held neither warmth nor friendliness and left one to wonder why she had bothered to smile at all.

Helena would not have wondered had she known that Adrianna had been told that she was especially beautiful when she smiled. Well, she wanted Dave's pretty yellow sister to see that smile—the one that would "break a hunnert hearts," a silly man had told her a while ago.

"I guess I'll see you again," Adrianna said airily to Helena, and turning she slipped on her coat and Dave took her home.

"Dey sho' stayed long enough, so I suppose dey enjoyed deyselves," Aggie said.

Helena was still looking rather stunned after her encounter with Adrianna. Seeing this, Aggie said, "So hi did you lak yo' sister-in-law ta be?"

"Well, she was a little...different," Helena said, not wanting to be unkind.

While Aggie threw her head back and laughed loudly at this understatement, Helena was struck with pangs of envy and guilt. Obviously Aggie had been the daughter that she had not been all these years. Even Dave treated Aggie with the deference and sweetness reserved for a favorite relative.

Aggie had taken her place while she was in Chicago being miserable with Norman. There were feelings of guilt, but Helena also liked Aggie a great deal already.

THIRTY-SIX

D ave turned his truck around and drove home. It was getting quite late by the time he left his girlfriend's house. The three men that had followed him blinked their lights at him and Dave waved.

Adrianna's behavior with his sister had been unacceptable, Dave was thinking on his way home. His fiancé's attitude was becoming increasingly annoying to the extent that Dave decided to make some time in his schedule to sit alone and give their relationship some serious thought.

The three men followed him home, called good night to Dave again when he reached the house, and took their post out of sight in the trees across the road from the house.

So far so good, Dave thought. The days they all thought they had to fear were the days directly following the New Year—and he was pretty sure they were right.

Dave would not be making hot tamales this holiday weekend or the next—a paid vacation for the men. But Dave liked working, was used to working, and this two week vacation he was giving left him with more time on his hands than he would have liked. But Helena's company was a Godsend, and took up a good deal of the evening slack. And so on Saturday, December 27, Dave and his sister found themselves cozily ensconced in the kitchen, enjoying each other's company as usual, long after Lela and the children had retired.

After bedtime, Helena and Dave spoke quietly, thus adding to the mood of peacefulness, and the exclusiveness of each other's company.

"Norman called today," Helena told her brother, keeping her voice very low.

"He did? What did he have to say?" Dave asked, using the same quiet calmness of his sister's tone.

"Asked me why I left. Asked me if I had any money I could send him. He said he's broke."

"Helena, I could—" Dave began.

"No, no, no!" Helena said harshly. "You have been more than generous already. I told him to sell something from the house. I told him I was broke too. He told me when he got back on his feet he was going to send for us. Sure. Bet he thinks I'll go running back too. Like a fool."

"Wanta go digging?" Dave asked, changing the subject, but not too abruptly, in order to lighten his sister's mood.

"Digging?"

"For the money Mr. Dubbin left me. I told you there's thousands still left on that property. I just have to locate it."

"I'd love to go digging!" Helena exclaimed, her eyes sparkling with the thought of a real live treasure hunt.

"I was on the property today. The guards followed me, but I had them stay on the road and I went up to the house alone. I have it boarded up good and I have the house watched pretty carefully. The group knows something is going on up there at Dubbins' old place but they don't know what. I never told anyone. Not even Peter and Omar. I have a key to the one door I didn't board up. Anyway, I want to show you something."

Dave went to his room and returned dangling a greasy looking little cloth bag. "I let myself in the house today and I was just peering around in the dark with a flashlight because all the windows are boarded. There was a picture on the wall of a house and wagon painted very amateurishly, maybe old Luke painted himself before he lost his sight. I had a feeling about the painting, so I took it down. I found this bag nailed to the back of the picture frame."

Dave handed the small cloth tobacco sack to his sister, who pulled away from the dirty, nearly rotted little sack.

"It's nearly falling apart!" she cried. "Do you think there are bugs in it?"

"Maybe," Dave said laughing. "But from the weight of it, it contains more than bugs unless they're mighty fat. I haven't opened it. Wanna be first?" he teased.

Helena took the sack, laid it on the table, pulled the rotted cloth apart with her fingers, and stared wide-eyed at the clump of yellowed bills rolled lengthwise. She tapped the bills gently with her finger and when no bugs exited the roll, she and Dave laid out fifty twenty dollar bills, which they had to weight on each end to keep from re-curling.

"I cannot believe this!" Helena exclaimed. "That place is a proverbial gold mine! How soon can we go digging as you call it?" Helena asked, running her hand gently across the bills, her face splotching red with excitement.

Dave drank his weak coffee and laughed at his beautiful, enthusiastic sister. "We'll go as soon as possible, Helena—maybe right after the holidays. It will be fun, but I doubt if we'll ever find it all."

Since Helena had been home, Lela had taken to retiring earlier, and at eight o'clock had retired for the evening. Merry and Basil, being city children, were allowed to stay up until nine o'clock, quietly listening to the radio and playing games or reading. The rest of the evening after nine was free for Dave and Helena's "talks and tea," Helena fondly called them—and they talked far into the night every night that was not a working night for Dave.

One night Helena hit Dave with a question that was loaded with emotion: "Dave, why did Daddy leave home and take to the road all these years? I know I'm the oldest and should have asked Mother, but to tell you the truth, I was afraid to. I used to hear Mother crying in her room sometimes late at night. I thought over the years she might have told you."

Dave was quiet for a long while, sipping the hot but weak coffee he preferred at night. Finally he said, "I asked Mama about that one time when I was about seventeen. I'll tell you what she told me."

Helena set her tea cup down, determined to strain out even silence in order to hear what Dave would tell her, to solve this mystery for herself once and for all.

"Mama said it took her a good while to figure it out herself. It's a rather short and simple story actually. She blames—if Mama ever blames anybody for anything—the old men Daddy listened to."

"The old men?" Helena said, puzzled, moving her small stomach even closer to the kitchen table.

"Sure. Men like old Rebler Cornfield, Beasley Buckman, Saint Glow Hall, men like that were seventy or older when Daddy was a young man. He used to listen to all of their stories about places they had been, things they had seen. Like the Great Smokey Mountains, Niagara Falls, New York City, Chicago, California, Montana. He also used to go down and talk to hobos every Saturday when he got off from the mill, Mama said. He was the first person at a traveling side show of any kind, talking to the people—if they would talk to Colored. He was just so curious, that's all. He finally wanted to see the things that he heard about, Mama said. Her first clue was that Daddy started to scrape and save every single penny. I remember he was even reluctant to give me a penny for candy."

"Mama told me that a year before he left he worked two jobs—at the sawmill and then at the chicken plant. He wanted to leave Mama well fixed and have some money to take with him as well. When he had what he felt he needed, he sat Mama down and had a long talk with her. He told her that he loved her and that there wasn't anyone else, but he didn't want to be like so many men in this town—they were born here and they died here. Most without ever setting foot outside of Phillips County. He said he wanted to see a bit of the world while he was young, before he got too stiff to hop trains."

"I remember Mama crying and crying after Daddy left," Helena said. I was twelve, you were six, she got us up, told us Daddy was going on a trip for a while. He talked to us for a while. He gave us a dollar apiece. That was impressive! Then, he kissed us and hugged us—hard—and he hugged Mother a long time and—he left. Just like that."

"But he was back in three weeks with stories of New York, Michigan, Canada. Mama was so happy. She cried and prayed."

It was true. Lela told her friends, "Honey, he got dat hotfoot outta his system! He back. He done seen a little somethin' and he back. Naw. Hit's alright. Main got a right to go see somethin' 'foe he die!"

Lela had been proud of her husband Rex's sojourn after she thought about it. He had a right to travel a bit, didn't he? But after just two weeks Rex told her he was going again. This time he stayed two months. The short letters came from the West—Colorado, Wyoming, Idaho, finally California.

"But he was home when I graduated from the eighth grade," Dave said with some satisfaction.

"And he had Mama worried to death, but he did show up to give me away when I married. Remember how the people cheered when they saw me walk down the aisle with 'Hobo Rex,'" Helena laughed.

"And he always worked somewhere and sent money. As much as we needed really. Mama is used to his wandering ways now, I guess."

Helena looked at her brother sternly. "Dave, a woman never gets used to her man being away from her—out of her home by choice. I often wonder what Mother really thinks about Daddy. Does she ever talk about it—her feelings, I mean?"

"No. She speaks fondly of Dad—when she speaks about him at all. But I noticed after she says these nice things, she gets quiet, you know? Like she's thinking, and she doesn't like what she's thinking about—as if she's a little blue and down-hearted."

"I reckon!" Helena huffed. "Twenty-one years is a long time to be gone. What's the longest Daddy has ever come back and stayed since he left, Dave?"

"About a month. Middle of December to the middle of January one year."

"Dave the man is getting old!" Helena exclaimed.

"Yeah. I know. I wonder if he plans to die on the road."

THIRTY-SEVEN

For days now, Dave had been trying to see Adrianna James, but her aunt, Dura Webster kept telling him that she was not at home in such a pitiful and shamefaced manner that Dave knew she was lying for the girl. Adrianna had also stopped opening the school store over in Epps without explanation. He couldn't figure out why she would not see him. She had played such games before when she was angry at him for some slight, real or imagined, but this time he was annoyed at her irresponsible abandonment of the store and he quickly resolved to ask Omar's wife, Ray Jean, to run the store for him.

Ray Jean was overjoyed, but she and Omar argued about it. His wife was already making pies on the weekend for Princess Thelma's place. If she ran the store six days a week, who would care for their four children?

"Cook his meals?" Ray Jean exploded. "We have a chance, when peepers is *starving*, to git three jobs between us and you heah talkin' 'bout who gone fix yo' dinner? Man, sometime you acts lak a chile! You *fix* da meals! Shit, you only workin' two, three days a week! Can't you gie me no hep?!" With that, Ray Jean slammed out of the door and began working for Dave that very day.

Omar never told Dave about the argument, but he continued to simmer about his wife's new position for weeks—not angry at Dave, but at his wife.

The appointed Circle members faithfully patrolled the twin towns each day looking for something out of place, and Aggie Pratt continued with her spying.

"Da town be very, very quiet." Aggie reported, and the "captains of ten" that the Circle had been divided into reported this information back to the over one hundred men and the scattering of women the Circle had now attracted.

Nobody trusted this quietness, and the Circle waited and watched, going about their business, figuring that "some stuff" would start up after the holidays—and they were right.

On the Wednesday morning after New Year's Day, Dave decided to go to White

Town and shop for the purpose of checking out the temper of the town for himself. Nearly all of the things that had to be purchased from stores for Christmas—Brazil nuts, apples, oranges, fresh coconuts—had been eaten either by the family or by the many guests that had visited during the holidays, so Dave had a small excuse for shopping.

Marrow's Country Store in West Steward was a gathering place for the local "bib and tobacco" set, and Dave knew that all of the local gossip filtered down to this place, so he decided to go there first.

When Dave walked in, there was a lull in the conversation of the mostly middle aged and elderly white men, but not much. They looked him over to see who he was, thought maybe for a second of what his business might be. A can of peas? Oranges? There was no obvious hostility that he could see. The three other Negroes in the store cast him friendly smiles.

Outside, the security truck had pulled up behind Dave's, and the men sat patiently as always and waited for him. Dave would bring them a little treat; maybe rat cheese and crackers and soda water. One of the men was very fond of hog head souse. He would include a pound of that too.

Dave knew Carson Marrow, the son of the owner of the store. A broad man of average height with prematurely graying hair. Friendly and curious, Carson prided himself on knowing everybody in West Steward, black or white, and he welcomed them to Marrow's—"The Friendly Store"—because everybody's business was badly needed.

Negroes found the Marrows fair enough, except they did not "keep a book of credit." Locals had been known to spend hours in the store, doing more lying than buying. The Marrows didn't mind. What the hell? They were good men, and when they did have a piece of change, why they generally spent it at The Friendly Store.

"Afternoon!" Carson boomed as Dave walked up to the counter. "Where you been hidin'? And what kin I do fer ya today? Nice weather we gettin' ain't it?" Carson expected no response to his questions. They were just questions from page one of his "Friendly" catalog.

"Got everythin' ya need?" he continued. "I reckon you don't, lessen you wouldn't be here. Ha ha ha!"

Dave smiled. The Friendly Store. Well, they were certainly trying to live up to their name he thought.

"Any Brazil nuts left?"

"Heels?" the storekeeper asked, careful not to offend by calling the rough crescent shaped nuts by their commonly known name of "nigger heels" or "nigger toes." He needed all the business he could get. "Yas! matter o'fact we got moren we usually has left over at this time. Hi many you gonna have?"

Looking Dave over, he figured more than a nickel's worth. Perhaps fifteen cents? The man standing before him was neat and clean—he didn't even wear a moustache like most of the niggers favored. He knew he ran a little hot tamale cart business part time up on the car line. Not much change here, Carson thought, adjusting his figure down to ten cents. Anyway, he would talk loud and push hard, because an extra nickel was an extra nickel. "This bag'll hold up to a quarter's worth," the shopkeeper said amiably, showing Dave a paper sack. "You want ten or fifteen cents worth?"

Dave smiled inwardly, still young enough to pull pranks with enjoyment, and howl with laughter at the later telling of the story among friends. With studied casualness, Dave said, "Give me four quarter bags," then, looking around as if he had all the time and money in the world, "a dozen apples and a dozen oranges too. And how about two pounds of strong cheese and a pound of hog head souse while you're at it?"

Carson Marrow had not had such a large order all day, and he rushed around nearly ashamed at his own eagerness to fill this order before the apples went mushy, to get shed of some of his mounds of nigger heels that the Negroes had usually purchased long before now. He was almost working up a sweat.

"Nah, will that be all?" Carson Marrow asked. Of course it would be. He had figured it up—this boy had already spent the rent!

"No. That's not all," Dave said, as the shopkeeper's eyes bugged in disbelief.

"No?" Carson said weakly, his fat palms resting on the counter.

"Four quarts of orange soda water and a large box of salt crackers should do it," Dave said calmly while Carson Marrow sacked and wrapped.

Sixty cents for two dozen apples and oranges, forty cents for four quarts of soda water, a dollar's worth of heels, two pounds of cheese, forty cents, one pound of souse, twenty cents, crackers, ten cents—it came to more than a day's pay, two dollars and seventy cents.

"Now, you know you up over two dollars?" Carson Marrow said to Dave, looking at him intently as if to say, *You got that kinda money, boy? 'Cause if you ain't—don't waste my time, even at The Friendly Store.*

Dave was in a playful mood, made so by the fact that he had confirmed everything to be fine, as his security people had told him earlier. If there was a plot or plan being hatched somewhere, these men would surely know about it. These "store locals" seemed no more concerned or tense than usual, and that was cause for a little fun in Dave's mind.

Dave took some bills from his pocket and slowly, carefully pulled a twenty from his roll, giving the pop-eyed shopkeeper plenty of time to check the fatness of his stack. Dave handed Carson Marrow the twenty.

Carson took it, turning it over reverently in his hand. "Where you git all this money?" he asked Dave, trying to smile.

"I beg your pardon?" Dave answered dryly, not replying to the question. But his mother had warned him, never make a white man jealous—never let them know what you really have. Well. A man had to have a little fun sometimes.

Carson's face was flushed. "Ain't you got nothin' smaller? If I break this twenty, it'll put me plumb outta change."

Dave obliged, placing two singles and three quarters on the counter.

The shopkeeper pushed the bags and a nickle towards Dave. "All I can say is the hot tamale business must be doing right fine."

There was a subtle hint of envy in his voice Dave thought.

"Oh, I creep by," Dave said, already a little remorseful over his foolish display of the worker's payroll. "I creep by," Dave repeated, taking his bags. "Nothing big at all."

"Is that right?" Carson Marrow said, almost hopefully.

Turning to leave, Dave literally bumped into Dayton Holyoke, his old boss and owner of the Detroit Mill.

"Well, hey Dave! Hi you doin?!" Holyoke called putting out his hand as if greeting an old friend. "Hi did Christmas treat ya?"

"Howdy, Mr. Holyoke, I can't complain." Dave answered, taken aback a little by the old man's extra friendliness—and something else. He looked awful.

"You looking well," Dave lied. "How is everything?"

"Shitty!" The old man bellowed so loudly that customers turned to stare.

Holyoke took Dave by the elbow.

"Step on over here and chat me up a bit!" he said, pulling Dave into a corner by a wooden barrel full of small greasy oil sausages.

"I hear you got a business going? Hot tamales, right? And I hear they gooood! Too bad I'll never know. Anything with grease, even good grease, and spices, sends me right to the slop jar!"

Dave knew he was hearing evidence of Holyoke's legendary earthiness, as he referred to his well appointed indoor toilet as a slop jar.

"Is that right? I'm sorry to hear it," Dave said, and he was. The old mill owner had lost a great deal of weight, and the black circles around his sunken eyes and his flour white face gave him a frightful look—rather like he imagined a haunt would look like from all the ghost stories he had heard as a child.

"Look at me!" Holyoke rasped loudly. "You lied when you said I looked well." The old man smiled, showing dentures that now seemed too large for his mouth. "Can't you see hi I done fell off? Done got po' as a snake! And gittin' weak as a baby chick. Doctors don't know what the hell is wrong with me."

"I'm sorry to hear that," Dave said, feeling foolish because he didn't know what else to say.

The mill owner rescued him by changing the subject.

"Business is bad at the mill. Real bad. We're just barely holding on. I'm using six men now, and that's part-time. I used to employ around two hundred, three shifts a day, as you know."

Dave was quiet, hoping a look of deep, sincere sympathy would suffice, for he liked old Holyoke a great deal and deeply regretted that there was so little work for everyone. Finally Dave asked if Grant Fromm, his old supervisor, was still at the mill. There were rumors and Dave hoped to get some facts.

Holyoke eyed Dave with suspicious amusement. He pulled him even further into the corner. "Come on! Little bitty town like this? You know you done heard what happened to Grant!" he said, smiling.

"Only rumors, sir, really." Dave answered, dismayed that his question about Grant had been so obvious to the old man.

Holyoke laughed, low and strained, and then looked grave, and poked his lips out so far that his whole face was drawn into a pucker of hundreds of dry lines.

The customers were casting furtive glances now, especially the Negroes, as they wondered what a big important man like Dayton Holyoke had to say so quietly over in a corner to young Dave Bailey. Some craned their necks, perhaps he was being offered work? Nobody could make out a thing.

"They had to take that bastard to the Garden of Eden."

"I didn't know that, sir. What happened?"

A state mental institution was located in Eden, Arkansas in Phillips County. Over the years it seemed almost inevitable that it would become known as the Garden of Eden.

"Sonofabitch got a holt to somethin' from one of them moonshiners up in the hills. Whatever it was drove him wild as a rabid dog. Which was a short trip for him, know what I mean? They took him straight from the hospital to Eden two months ago. He's been there ever since. You know his wife is a cousin of mine. They stayin' with me and my wife for a spell."

So Grant Fromm had ended up in the crazy house? Dave was not at all surprised and he said to old Holyoke, "Well, well."

"Yes." Holyoke returned, catching the full meaning of those two words.

In parting, Dayton Holyoke told Dave that when things picked up at the mill, "You'd be the first man I'd call back, if you'd come, 'cause you were the best damn boss I ever had, Colored or white. I ain't shittin' ya!"

What a great old guy! Dave thought. Just talking to him, Dayton Holyoke had casually and deliberately broken taboos: one, you did not mention the weaknesses of white men to Negro men, and two, you did not stand and talk in an "old friend" manner to a Colored person nose to nose as if you were equals—and you did not tell him loud enough for all to hear that he was the best boss you ever had, even if he had only been the supervisor of the Colored men.

Dave thought of telling Dayton Holyoke about John Candle. Surely he would be able to help him. John Candle especially liked cases where "da big white doctors had done gaved up." He planned to talk to his mother as soon as possible—after all she had been a doctor's helper for many years—then have one of Holyoke's servants, perhaps old Gepline, who had been with him for at least fifty years and had long since lost his first name, persuade his boss to see a Colored healer who might be able to do him some good.

THIRTY-EIGHT

———✺———

Dura Webster got up very early in the morning and dressed carefully. She was nervous, and her hands shook as she took the whisk broom to her stiff old wool tweed coat. They were poor, she and her mister, and would be poorer now that...well. That thought could wait.

In a way what happened was a blessing, for now she could rent the two back rooms again, and if they rented them carefully to two nice responsible people, they could be sure of getting the fifty cents a week from each room. Heaven knew they needed it.

Dura, aged forty-six, like most Colored women in West Steward, worked for a family up in White Town. Her lady, Mrs. Esse Pons, was good. She allowed Dura to take leftovers from her table—in fact, the coat she would wear today was a gift from Mrs. Pons. But now her "good white lady" wasn't sure she could pay anymore, and it was just a matter of time before she would have to do her own house work as so many other white women were forced to nowadays.

Lawd, Lawd! I justa gotta rent dose rooms or we gone be just swept away by hard times, Dura thought, feeling tense and stressed. But first it was her duty to talk to Lela Bailey. She owed the good woman that much, she thought, so she tried to steady her shaking hands.

When Dura finished brushing her coat, she chose between the two dresses she owned—a deep wine-colored one with a detachable white lace collar for winter and church, and a cotton one with large yellow flowers. Dura picked the wine-colored one. The other was too full of flowers and too summery for this occasion.

Besides, Lela was a well-to-do woman and the floral dress was beginning to look frayed. Dura did not want to look "po' and tacky" in front of Lela Bailey.

Lela's house was a good long walk, but Dura had no way to get there except to walk, so at six thirty in the morning on Friday, January 9, 1931, Dura set out for the Bailey house. Nearly every step of the way was spent rehearsing her speech.

You all is sich nice peepers...you and yo' son is so highly thought of by all...I think therefo' hit's only proper to let you know...

The woman arrived perspiring and tense at the foot of the small incline that led to Lela's front door. She stopped, wiped her face with a clean handkerchief she carried in her pocketbook, pushed sprigs of graying hair back up under her hand-crocheted hat, pulled up her thick cotton stockings and headed for the door.

The men in the security truck had seen Dura approach and now they sat up, alert, looking her way, wondering what brought her to Dave Bailey's house this early in the day.

Dura stood at the door perhaps two minutes, gathering courage. Finally she knocked, too lightly she thought, but it was enough to bring the slow steady sound of footsteps toward the entrance.

In the moments of waiting, Dura thought it would have been better to come later, but then she was due at Mrs. Pons at eight thirty...perhaps for the last time.

When the door was opened, Dura stood speechless before Lela in her fine satin robe, just like the one she pictured her wearing.

"Why good moaning Dura! Come on in. What brings you out so early?" Lela inquired.

"Oh, dear!" Dura cried. "I hope I ain't done woke up yo' house!"

"Chile, naw! I been up at least an hour. Mah daughter and her chirrens is heah visiting from Chicago. Dey won't be up fer quite a spell."

"From Chicago? Ain't dat nice!"

"Even Dave is still sleep. He usually up by nah, but he put in a big night wit' his frens."

"He heah?" Dura asked with some alarm. "I didn't think he gone be heah! Hit's after seben o'clock in da moaning," the woman cried, as if Dave had no right to be in his own house.

"Nah settle yo'self down, Dura. Take a seat and tell me what dis is all about." Seeing the woman's anxiety, Lela said calmly, "Dave ain't gone be up for least an hour—mebbe longer, so we got us some time. Nah what's dis all about Dura? Adrianna?" Lela asked quietly, guessing correctly.

"Yas, hit is—and Dave."

"Oh?" Lela said, feeling far more uneasy than she showed. It had been her experience that unexpected late night and early morning visitors usually meant trouble. Lela was sure that this visitor was no exception. "Well, why don't you tell me about hit? Is you had yo' breakfast yet?" Lela asked as Dura slid into a seat at the kitchen table, still wearing her coat.

"Naw I hasn't, but den I ain't hoingry. A little somethin' hot to drink maybe."

"Shoally."

Lela poured the woman a steaming cup of tea and watched in dismay as she struggled to control herself.

"Lawd, Jesus," Lela murmured. *Bad trouble.*

"Since I can't remember hi I was gone put hit, Miz Lela, I'll jus' go 'head and say hit lak hit is. Adrianna is expectin'," Dura said very quietly.

No! No! No! Lela's heart screamed. She felt angry, hurt, betrayed. She did not like this girl at all and felt in her soul that she was not the woman for Dave, that she would pull him down, possibly hurt him deeply, keep him in an uproar. Now Dave had to marry her. There were no two ways about it. He would marry her, no matter how he really felt. And although he had not discussed it with her, Lela knew that things were not like they used to be between her son and this woman's niece. Love had faded. Love had gone cold. Possibly love had died. And now her son, who was the most honorable man in the world, had to marry this woman's wild—yes, and slutty—niece. *Well. Lawd, help us Jesus,* Lela prayed, but felt like screaming, *This little whorish girl has tricked my son!* She could not yet appreciate the fact that he had some part in this and was not totally innocent in this matter. Men being what they were, it was the woman's responsibility to hold herself up, it was the woman who should be careful, Lela thought.

While these thoughts collided around in her head Lela was the soul of calm outside.

"Do Dave know?" she asked softly.

"No."

"No?"

"No, mam. He don't even suh-spect."

"How could he let dis happen?! But den dey wuz engaged. And dey wuz young. And, I mahself wuz young—once," Lela sighed, reason seeping back into her bones. Her facial expression of friendliness, of kind graciousness, did not change, but Lela took a few moments to pray silently.

During this time, Dura Webster only noticed a slight lowering of her hostess' head.

"Well, shall we wake up Dave and git him in heah, Dura? I think he oughta heah 'bout dis," Lela said, somewhat more peaceful in spirit. The prayer had helped. It always did.

"Oh, I don't see why we has to go disturbing yo' son," Dura said, smiling and sipping some of the slightly cooled tea.

Lela looked at the woman, bewildered. What could she be talking about? Of course Dave should be told, the sooner the better. And where was Adrianna now? Why hadn't she told Dave? Could it be that she was ashamed? Is that why he had not been able to find her home for over a week? Lela watched Dura for a clue, but found nothing on her face but a small smile that was neither pleasant nor unpleasant—it was blank and filled with mystery.

Dura Webster was comfortable now in her cheap dress, sitting in a kitchen such as she had never seen before for beauty. Dura was enjoying herself, watching Lela, who pretended to be alright, but, she, Dura, knew her insides were in an uproar. Oh, this was real satisfying!

Now Dura leaned forward towards Lela like an old confidant. Her eyes were shining and she smiled with delight as Lela fastened her wide-eyed confusion and frustration on her face, trying hard to fight the anger she felt seeping into her veins with the soothing remedy of prayer, for Jesus' sake.

"No need to talk to Dave. No sir-ree!" Dura repeated, almost gaily.

Lela waited and prayed some more.

But Dura sipped more tea, taking her time looking around, admiring Lela's kitchen.

Finally Lela said, "Dura, Dave gotta know sometime. Ain't dat why you done come?" she finished doggedly.

"No, he don't. Cause you see, Miz Lela, dat baby ain't non o'hisn. Dat's what I come to tell ya!"

The words exploded like fire crackers.

"Not Dave's!" Lela exclaimed, stunned, praying she had heard right. She stood up and then fell back into her chair again. "Not Dave's?" Lela repeated, hearing her own voice as if from a distance, thin, high like a scrape on tin.

"Dat's right," Dura said. Pleased at Lela's reaction, the little smile had never left Dura's lips.

"Den who? What?"

"Dat child which my niece is been carrying fer four months nah, ain't none o'Dave's. Adrianna done told me dat and I got no cause to doubt 'er. None. Cause you see, Miz Lela, Adrianna got an eight-year-old daughter back in Ohio."

"No!" Lela exclaimed.

"Yas. Dat's right," Dura said. Then she told Lela why she was here: "When Adrianna was thirteen years old she came up expectin.' Unlike her other two sisters who ain't near as pretty as she is, she was always fast, always womanish, her mother couldn't do a thang wit' 'er. So she talked to Adri, she say, 'girl, you fixin' to make a hard life fer yo'self!' But it didn't do no good. When she wuz fourteen she had dat baby. She wouldn't tell her mama and daddy who wuz da father for almost a year! Well, dey take dat baby in, accept dat baby, and Adrianna went back to school. Although she dumb in life, she smart in school, good pupil, do right well. She still running wild as a deer at near sixteen, nah. I go to Ohio to visit my sister, she say you take her down South for a while. We can't do nothing wit' 'er. I musta been a fool cause I took her, though she still ran pretty wild down here too. Den she met Dave Bailey and he da sweetest nicest main in da woil, she say. And at furst he don't touch 'er! Naw! He say we has to be married first he say, even though she were mo' den willin' to come outta her step-ins. I say you gone tell 'em 'bout yo' little girl Susannah? She say later, Auntie Dura. Well, she never tell 'em! Not to dis day."

"Mah Lawd, mah Lawd!" Lela moaned under her breath, but it was a moan wrapped in relief and thank you cloth for God's mysterious ways.

"She really try hard 'cause she want Dave's respect. She say later on after dey engaged and he did touch her up nah and den, she say he so innocent he could not even tell she ain't no virgin, didn't never notice she got stretch marks on her belly. Lawd, I done talked so much, I done got hoingry!"

Lela quickly and quietly fixed Dura a plate. Grits, thick sliced fried bacon, hot biscuits and pear preserves that were the waiting breakfast for her guests from Chicago. But Lela was so relieved to hear that Dave did not have to marry Adrianna James, she would have given Dura Webster everything in the kitchen!

"You want some eggs?" Lela whispered.

"Is hit too much trouble?" Dura whispered back.

Eating hungrily, Dura continued her story as Lela added fresh eggs to her skillet.

"My niece ain't no good," Dura confided frankly. "She done more worst den git pregnant. I jus' don't feel lak talkin' 'bout hit at da moment—well, I'll tell you one thing, doe. She done sneaked men in her room even after she 'gaged to Dave—and befo'. She can't do without no mens. She say Dave don't take it, others will."

Lela's face hung down in displeasure. The girl was an out-and-out whore, there was no two ways about that. *Good Gawd A'mighty*!

"I wanted you to know, cause y'all are sich nice peepers, so highly thought of, so highly respectable, I wanted y'all to know the truth from someone who knows, so dat when peepers start shootin' dey big lips all which-a-ways wit' gossip, you and Dave would know when, and what, and like dat. Da girl left yestiddy moaning," Dura said, dipping a grateful fork into her sunny side eggs.

"I ax, you say goodbye to Mistah Dave? Well, she didn't turn me no answer."

"Hi she leave?" Lela asked, thinking she could have left crawling for all she cared! Thank the Good Master she was gone!

"He came got her in his lil' ol' car, all the way from Ohio. I mean the daddy of the little girl, though she ain't little no mo'. He been heah befoe. He see Dave, look at Dave, but yo' boy didn't know who he were. Once Adrianna sent him to git two dozen hot tamales. She say go to the tall black one wit' da pretty eyes. Dat be Dave. Later on she and Clifford Davis, dat be his name, dey be up in her room laughing."

"Dey don't wanna git married? Her and dis Clifford?"

Dura Webster clanged her fork down in disgust.

"Marry? You joneing! He ain't *nothin'*, you heah me?" Dura said vehemently. "He don't care hi many mens Adrianna done stepped outta her drawers fer long as dere somethin' left for him!"

Dura looked under eyed at Lela. "Is ahm being too frank, Miz Bailey?"

"Oh no, mam! You go 'head and say what you wanna say. Don't mind me, 'cause I done heered hit all," Lela said, thinking that nothing could be too terrible to hear- as long as Dave did not have to marry Adrianna James!

"We don't lak hit, but he stay overnight. He little ol' bright skin feller. Don't look lak nothin' ta me, lessen you crazy fer yellow. He ain't near pretty as yo' boy."

"Thank you, Dura. Mo' tea?" Lela felt something akin to love for Dura at this moment—love for her truth telling. "Po' thang. She young. She got a lot to learn," Lela said.

"Po' thang mah foot! Dat gal insist on takin' two mah rooms, and all doe she makin' good—or wuz—at dat soap factory, she pay me when she get good and ready—and ready didn't come too often, let me tell ya!"

Finally, it was time for Dura to go to Mrs. Pons. Lela hugged the woman, giving her a teary thank you of great sincerity.

"When you come home dis evenin' dere will be a box sattin' in yo' kitchen. I'll have Dave take it over." Lela knew the Websters were struggling.

"Miz Bailey, nah I didn't come fer no handout," Dura Webster began, but her protest was weak because her pantry was bare except for a small cloth sack of rice and a tablespoon of coffee, so she watched Lela pack a box, trying not to seem too anxious or even too grateful. That would have been tacky, but her heart leaped with joy as Lela filled the box for her son to deliver. A large smoked ham, sweet potatoes, a good wedge of "rat" cheese, boxes of crackers, several jars of home canned vegetables, preserves, fruit, two mince pies that had been baked for Rev. Clayton, but Lela would bake him two more. The grateful mother also included meaty homemade souse and, Lela explained, a half gallon of apple-jack "fer da chills." Then she added even more: coffee, tea, canned cream, sugar, rice, a dozen eggs from her hen house, a home sewn apron from her store of Christmas gifts; and in the apron pocket she slipped twenty dollars.

Finally gratitude overcame any sense of dignity and Dura Webster fell on Lela with hugs of gladness and tears of appreciation.

Dura begged Lela not to wake up her son until she had left for "her lady's," because she was skittish about having had to lie to him about Adrianna not being home during the many times he came to see her niece and didn't want to face him yet, she said.

When Adrianna's aunt had left, Lela sat at her prayer table a long while in a near ecstasy of praise and thanks to God. Then she went to awaken her son.

Dave was quiet for several minutes after hearing the story. Finally he said, "Well, I'm surprised, especially about Adrianna and other men after we were engaged. My God! And she has an eight-year-old child? I don't really know what to say. I'm surprised, even shocked, but not broken up about it, Mama. So don't worry about me. You see, there hasn't been any real love between Adri and me for quite a while. We were at the crossroads—just sort of going through the motions you know. When we were together lately, we always fussed and fought. Any little thing started a big argument. That alone was a pretty clear sign that things were not right between us."

"Yas. So you ain't bothered 'bout hit real bad?" Lela said with great pity for her son, for she knew that you didn't just stop loving someone so quickly. It was going to take time.

Dave was raised on one elbow in his pajamas, considering the darkness.

But Lela was looking at the light. The girl and her son had been courting for two years. What had stopped them from getting married long ago? Perhaps it was her prayers in which she had constantly asked, *Lawd, is this really the one for my precious boy?*

His mother left him in the silence and privacy of his room, and he lay for a long time listening to the winter morning, the gentle clacking branches as wind brushed through the barren trees, the stirring sounds of barnyard animals that could be kept on the hills, but not in town. The racing of his own heart.

She had sent Clifford Davis to look him over? That was cold. Damn cold! Dave strained his memory to conjure up the small bright man: Kinda pigeon toed, slicked backed hair, small eyes, the color of a pecan shell. No. His memory would not belch up Clifford Davis. And Adrianna never even said goodbye. Never even hinted that she was leaving. Leaving before her disgrace was displayed to all.

"Dura say she was probably mo' then four months, 'cause she was already poking out some," Lela had told Dave.

Logically, Dave thought himself well out of it. Then why had a lone tear gathered in the corner of his eye and slid slowly down his face, followed by another and another? When the tears ceased, Dave got up, poured cold water from the pitcher on the dresser into his porcelain water basin, washed his face, and went into the kitchen to have breakfast with his mother, although he had less of an appetite than he had ever had in his life.

But the day still had more trying news. Later, Aggie Pratt came walking up the hill to the house clad in her old gray mothballer, she called it, and spoke to Dave's security detail. They were surprised by her news, and asked if she wanted one of them to go into the house with her.

No, she said, and walked up and knocked on the Bailey door. Dave opened it.

"Hey, Aggie," Dave said, playfully pulling her waist-length copper plait. "Come on in. Want me to cut off some of this hair for you? Here, let me take your coat."

"Well! I'm glad to see you in a fine way," Aggie said, thinking too much bad news at once was hard on even a person as strong as Dave. Aggie had thought Dave might be pining.

"Why shouldn't I be?" Dave asked knowing full well what Aggie was referring to.

Aggie looked up more than a foot into Dave's handsome face.

"Well. You know..." she said, somewhat shamed faced. Lela had told her about Dura Webster's visit, about Adrianna.

"Adrianna?"

"Yeah," Aggie said, removing her coat, then pulling her sweater around her face as if to shield a hurtful answer.

"Aggie, what's gone done went!" Dave replied with unexpected merriment, and they both laughed. It was the relieved and easy laughter of old friends whose problems needed no long explanations, did not need to be hidden behind face saving lies.

"What's up?" the young man asked, leading the way to the most important room in the house, Lela's kitchen. Dave had been expecting Aggie, the Circle spy—or somebody—or something. The New Year was well upon them.

"I got some bad news. I was jus' up in White Town. Dey done fount dat Mistah Holyoke stretched out dead."

"Lawd in Heben!" Lela said, looking at her son. Dave sat down heavily at the table.

"Dead? Dayton Holyoke?" Dave shook his head. "But I just talked to him in Morrow's grocery store a few days ago! What happened, Aggie?" he asked, his voice full of sadness.

Aggie loved to be the first to bring news, whether it was bad or good. It was a struggle for her to keep the enthusiasm out of her voice, the excitement she always felt when she was the first with the tale to be told. And Lela had warned Aggie time and again about the sin of being self important, of being full of herself on occasion. So Aggie put on her most solemn face.

"Old Mistah Geplin what done worked fer da Holyoke family fer moren fifty years, fount him dis moaning when he went to gie him his moanin' coco. Mistah Geplin is eighty-one. Dey just keep him round 'cause he been round so long, says Carrie Lee Murchison. She da housekeeper. Old Geplin ain't good fer much but helpin' fetch da moanin' food, den he plumb wore out fer da day."

Dave wished Aggie would get to the point of the circumstances of Dayton's death, and he bent forward slightly.

Aggie caught this delicate hint of impatience, which jogged her out of her tendency to stretch and extend her stories.

"He just died real peaceful, I guess, in his sleep. He jus' old, and he ain't been too well, so he jus' up and died," she finished.

"That is bad news," Dave said. "I respected him. He was a good man."

THIRTY-NINE
---※---

On the night of January 10, 1931, the second Saturday night of the New Year, Circle members who had volunteered for duty positioned themselves on a hill overlooking the house of Louis D. Stassen, head of the Ku Klux Klan in Southeast Arkansas. The men were looking for anything out of the ordinary that would tip them off to future Klan plans. They found it. Huge planks lying on the ground, enough for three crosses to be burned on a hillside as soon as they were nailed together and covered with pitch.

Louie D's "nigger" dogs had picked up the scent of the men on the hill and were going crazy, but the men inside of the leader's house had grown drunk and were too careless to wonder at the commotion the dogs were making. The dogs were thrown meat scraps, half-eaten sandwiches, boiled eggs, then the loud gathering, with fiddles, singing of country songs, dancing and laughing, went on.

Silas Benson liked being with the "old mens." Men like his father who were between thirty-six and forty. Men who were considered "ageable" now due to hard life experiences. These volunteers had not been young for a long time. In the "old days," most of the volunteers tonight had begun working full time at the age of eleven or twelve. At sixteen or seventeen, many were fathers. Now thirty-eight, Curty, Silas' father had two grandchildren.

Curty Benson had not wanted his son along tonight. Being a member of the Circle was dangerous enough, and he did not want to risk another foolish show of bravery such as his son had displayed on the night of the "tree incident." So Curty made Silas sit between himself and the driver of the truck, "Old Man" Wiggins, who was forty.

"We'd better move out," Edmond Wiggins whispered. "Dem dogs done caught dem a good scent. We don't want dem drunk peckerwoods to finally come out to see what dem dogs be raisin a ruckus at."

As the small convoy of three trucks made their way quietly down the hill without lights, they saw the planks again.

"Yep! Dey fixin' to start some shit! We got bad times getting' worser, but peckerwoods still got time fer shit." Old Man Wiggins spat a mouthful of tobacco juice out of his side of the truck.

The men in the other two trucks were silent, but their stomachs lurched up for the old fight as their spirits and hearts dragged the ground with the misery of both bad and uncertain times and bad and uncertain white folks.

But Silas smiled at the crosses, at the yowling dogs. A smile born of courage and youth. Turning his voice to his father in the dark cab of the truck, he said, "One day Louie D's nigger dogs gone come up against da wrong nigger!"

The men sat talking far into the night, and down the hall the children listened, not understanding the planning but enjoying the energy of the voices, the obvious friendships among them gauged by their frequent laughter. The two grandchildren liked the regular—and irregular—rise and fall of the speeches, and they listened excitedly until they fell asleep, sure that something big, something fun, was being discussed.

Louis Devon Stassen, at sixty-one, was the oldest man among the group, and personifying the myth of wisdom embodying age, the younger men found themselves beginning and ending their complaints to him, looking for approval, for verification, for understanding, finally for judgment on the plan itself.

Louie D, as he liked to be known, was proud of being the head of the Klan. He was of average height and muscular, with a high pink forehead set off by a full head of black hair mixing with silver. A good fisherman and hunter, a good family man, a devout Baptist deacon, Louie D was well liked among the gathered men. Having finished the eighth grade, he was considered "pretty well educated."

Earlier in the evening, Lafete Gorman had given his "report," which was kind of a summation of all that had happened in the town since the fall of 1930: The double murders, the fire at the Old Storage House when the man they planned to lynch was somehow slipped away from them, the other suspect in the murders, the Duster boy, being slipped out of town, and finally, reluctantly, the tree incident was passed over briefly because that incident above all, where white men were so bested, was better forgotten.

Gorman and the others in this room felt that niggers were responsible for each and every thing that had happened, and the unspoken knowledge was that they—the Klan and other interested white folks—had responded to each incident that happened, but their actions, so far, had been ineffective. Now it was time, said Lafete to "stop all dis shit, cause hit's totally outta hand."

It was bad enough that all this shit had taken place in such a short time span, the gathered men agreed, bad enough that they, the power structure of this town, had not been able to "control their niggers," Louie D's boss, the Grand Kleagle, had told him in a threatening way. But what was now absolutely unbearable—and had brought these twenty-three men here tonight—was the attitude, the new attitude of the town's niggers, including the nigger women, Gorman said.

Examples were given: "Nah, everybody know we been walkin' niggers off da pavement for as long as there been cement and niggers. Who gone move over fer a nigger? Up to nah dat was always understood," said the blond headed man giving the example. "Niggers always understood dat," he continued. "But nah a nigger, especially a young one, was liable tuh look you straight in yo' Gawd damn face, and look lak he wuz gone walk straight through you ifn you didn't git outta his way!"

The men nodded and grumbled their assent. Some had also had the experience the blond man had spoken of, much to their amazement. Then, too, the men had taken to travelling in groups: "You never see one man no mo'. Look like if one come to my store for six cigarettes, there'll be four of them! And they're all armed to the backbone, flashing their pistols where you can see them!" said Pryce Keys. "How did they get so brave so fast?" the group asked themselves. Why it's almost like a whole new set of niggers!

Louie D chewed his cigar end to a wet mush listening to the compilation of misery, taking it all in, waiting for the time that he would speak.

Finally he said, "They still selling rope down at the hardware? 'Cause if they is, we can handle this."

The men laughed loud and long, some sending up rebel hoops of renewed confidence as Louie D stepped out in the middle of them in his bib overalls.

"I know what you gents is sayin'," he assured them. "Enough is enough and too much stinks like hoss shit," he said.

Louie D talked with the men for about twenty minutes. He told them their situation was not out of hand, far from it, he said. The holidays were over and it was time to get down to business and, more significantly, back in business.

A great cheer went up from the men who were farmers, small shop keepers, clerks, managers of small stores, husbands, fathers, and sweethearts.

"The Law gonna have to stay out of our business," Louie D warned, "But I guarantee you that inside a month's time our nigger problem is gone be plumb rested."

When the men left their leader's house it was past two o'clock in the morning and they had a firm plan: They would burn their crosses which always scared the dookey out of the Negroes—especially the ones that lived on the outskirts of town. Also, the Klansmen had identified the leader of the group that was probably responsible for, or knew a great deal about, all of the trouble lately—even the murder of Leon Baycott and Luxury Tweedle—the one who surely had a hand in getting those Duster people out of town. They had the leader alright, indeed he had identified himself on the night of the tree incident: It was the preacher called Matthew Moses Clayton, the one who had stepped out of the crowd and clearly showed his face.

"Cut off da head and the body will die each and every time," Louis D. Stassen had told the men confidently. So the Rev. Matthew Moses Clayton was targeted to be lynched when he returned from Mississippi, where he was known to be visiting.

"Ifn we have to, we'll catch 'em when he goin' to the outhouse to shit. Niggers still shit alone, don't they?" said the blond man.

"'Til da preacher come back," another man said, raising a glass of Homemade, "we'll scare da outskirts some!"

Two nights after the meeting at Louie D's house, the men began to execute their plan of beatings and terror. Three young black men that lived on the outskirts in an unincorporated area known as The Bottoms had seen a huge burning cross and started running for home after a futile day of looking for work. They were running along in the dark and terrified when they were set upon by a mob and beaten nearly to death.

All three were given a verbal warning: "Stay in your place, niggers! And no mo' sass. Next time we'll string your black asses up!"

The Klan, remembering the unsolved murders, the tree incident, the unsolved escapes, were hesitant to lynch anyone just yet, for the Negroes flashing guns these days had shaken their confidence. The guns, the strange new attitudes of the blacks, carved down their egos a mite, and made them a little more conservative in their night riding—though they would have been the last to admit any fear of "nigras."

"Let's just see how dese ass beatings do," said Louie D with much more bravado than he actually felt. "We'll make our adjustments from there."

FORTY

———✦———

The three young men were left nearly dead in a gully by the side of the road. They were found by a mother with a lantern, horse and wagon who was looking for her son, who should have been home long before.

Somehow the mother, Saturday Westover, pushed and pulled the three slippery and bloody young men, who had little strength of their own left, into her wagon and roared yelling and screaming toward West Steward, where there were people who had money, where there was a good doctor, Saturday had heard, who treated the Colored, where there were Negroes who were unafraid.

The mother hoped she was not too late, for she had seen too much blood, had to struggle too hard to bend and lift limbs that bowed and bent the wrong way.

"Lawd! Somebody! Hep dese mens!" Saturday cried when she was scarcely within the limits of the town that looked like heaven to her. Dr. Henri Echardt was sent for, and Lela Bailey and Mother Clarence came immediately when they heard. Even the herbalist, the "old African" John Candle consented to being driven into town. When Dr. Echardt surveyed the bloody chaos he gritted his teeth in anger.

"Vhy! Vhy!" he cried. "Such brutality! Such a vaste! Such cruelty! Vat for? Huh? Vat for?" he asked the angry crowd that had gathered.

Mrs. Keller, the principal of both the grammar school and the high school, had volunteered her spacious home with its indoor hot and cold water faucets and bathtub, and several men, unmindful of soiling themselves with the blood of the injured men had tenderly carried the three men into Mrs. Keller's parlor and laid them on the wooden floor.

Blankets and quilts were brought and rough pallets were made on the floor, and the men were gingerly lifted on to those.

Lela and Mother Clarence, whom Lela had trained, went to work, expertly cutting away clothes dripping with blood to expose wounds, and holding flashlights so that the doctor could have bright close light to see what must be clamped off

CIRCLE OF STONE

promptly, what could be sewn later, and whether all of these men could avoid a trip to the white hospital where they would be most unwelcome.

Seeing all of the blood soaking her son's pants, Saturday Westover hollered out without shame, "Dey done cut off mah boy's dick! Oh, mah! Dey done cut off mah boy's dick! Nah, I'll never git no grandchildren from 'em! Oh, Lawd!"

Lela's lips moved in constant silent prayer, and as she worked the prayers became more fervent almost audible as she aimed her strong light between the legs of the young man.

Lawd God almighty! Don't let hit be!

Lela shined the light and forced her eyes to look as the doctor, who had the man laid high on the dining room table, probed and used his wads of white bandages, returned in seconds to the tin pan soaked with the blood of hatred and malice.

Finally he was able to get all of the blood stopped and Lela, her knees about to collapse, her stomach churning in spite of faith, shined her light full and searching, gasping a final prayer: "Please Lawd! Don't lemme look and see nothin' wha somethin' is suppose to be!"

Lela looked sharply at Dr. Echardt to make sure she was correct. As she looked, he smiled.

"Tell da mother she vill get a grandchild," he said simply and went back to work on Saturday's son.

When Saturday Westover was given the doctor's message, she slumped over and slipped to the floor in a dead faint while a great cheer went up from the group that had gathered, because there had been whispers that all three of the men had been castrated. Some of the men sobbed openly.

John Candle was not recognized when he arrived in Roger Mulright's truck because he was wearing a shirt and pants, but instead of a coat, he was wrapped in a blanket like an Indian.

When the herbalist saw all of the bloody discarded clothing, he hissed, "Dogs!"

"I quite agree," said Dr. Echardt.

Dr. Echardt knew of John Candle's restorative powers, his use of natural medicines and was in agreement with him nursing two of the young men back to health, but one had to go to the hospital, for he had lost much blood. Dr. Echardt would see that he was admitted—to the place where Colored patients were accepted, the hospital's basement.

328

Lela had been too busy to wonder what Dave's reaction—what the Circle's reaction—would be. But now that the three young men that Saturday had brought in were out of danger, Lela's worries turned in a different direction and she began a different prayer.

Since the "tree incident," the Circle's membership had grown substantially, and Dave had started setting up three meetings a month, with the new members, far back up in the "Colored Woods" behind his property. The meetings dealt with organization, dedication, commitment to future plans of action. Surprisingly, about twenty-five of the men who offered themselves for membership were from areas outside of Steward and West Steward, and Dave was in the process of creating a whole different unit for the eleven women who insisted upon joining. Dave saw their work as valuable, but different from what the men would do.

"Gentlemen, the vow we have taken is the most serious thing in the world," Dave said to his group—some nearly old enough to be his grandfather. "And nothing will get us expelled from this group faster than acting rashly—or acting alone without the consent of the group, or at least your team captain; and as you know, every ten men has a captain he can go to quickly for advice. Also, I want you to know that nothing will get you killed faster than talking to outsiders about what goes on in this Circle. I want us to be very clear about that."

When Dave said this, the men who were sitting around a large fire noted that Will Henry Mead, the big red-headed fellow that always sat or walked close to Dave Bailey, smiled broadly as if he were the designated executioner. He was not. Nobody had been designated. Dave was bluffing at the moment and the Inner Circle, the original group, knew it. What they also knew was that if such a measure became necessary it would be carried out, and there would be no problem getting a "designated executioner" or two.

"So whatever happens, remember it is not just us—our members against the Klan or anybody else. What we choose to do involves our families, wives, children— the entire community. If they can't get to one of us they will get to them. So be very, very careful. We must think before we speak. We must think before we act. Most of all, we must think before we strike."

A murmur of approval for what Dave had just uttered started to go through the crowd, but was cut short by the rumpling sound of trucks approaching and the cracking of tree limbs under their tires. There were two trucks, and they pulled up as close as they could get to the clearing in the woods. Immediately, one of the sentries from a nearby tree let out a high pinging sound from the curious piece of metal that Dave had given all of the sentries. Ping! Ping! *Our men approaching.* Two pings meant that they were not being followed, there was no need to douse the fire, no need to pull pistols, ready shot guns, rifles.

The six men walked hurriedly into the clearing. The gathered men could see that they were highly agitated, but striving for control. A large, tall man named Cannon Seacourse stepped forth as the spokesman. He was sweating. Something had happened. Many members had been in the group less than two months, only since the tree incident or the jail break.

Would these new people remain cool and calm under duress? Dave wondered. Or would they go off in all directions in spite of all the talking he had done, causing many people to possibly lose their lives as the Klan and other angry whites sought to punish blacks, any blacks they could get their hands on?

Dave did not think the men would chicken out after their vow. That was not a big worry. The concern was that the vow and the sense of solidarity and bravery it had conferred might make the men too rash, too eager for action, too willing to explode long held and pent up emotions of anger, frustration, hatred. But he, Dave, and other cooler heads like Peter and LaSalle were hoping for, praying for calm. Whatever had happened was going to be a test.

Dave stood up.

"What's going on, Cannon?" Dave asked, his voice tight with the effort of control.

"Everythin' in control, Dave," the large man said twice. "So you men's can just take you hains off dem pistols for nah. But we done had us some trouble."

The relatively calm attitude and posture of the big man helped to soothe the entire group. Cannon was following the rules. He was trying to remain calm, logical.

Cannon Seacourse outlined the trouble, from beginning to end, and the men's faces tightened in anger, and there was some swearing here and there, but the group stayed peaceful waiting for Dave, looking at him for instructions.

At that moment Dave felt such love for this group of men that he would have gladly died for them on the spot. Such was the tenderness that he felt that he prayed one of his relatively short rare prayers: "Lord, please don't let us lose anyone this night!"

"Clearly something will have to be done," Dave said, walking slowly out of the group and turning to face them all.

"I want you men to disperse now. Your captains will get back to you very soon with instructions—meanwhile, keep your ears open. I think something may happen real soon that will change things a bit in our favor," he said, actually smiling broadly at the men through the hurt he felt for what had happened.

Seeing Dave's smile lightened the situation a great deal, for most of the men knew Dave was not one for idle words. If he said they were going to respond that was it. You could bet on it, and the men started to leave for town quickly and quietly as they had been taught to do. Except for one man.

He pestered his captain to know exactly what they would do and when, and then he asked, "Dave is the real leader, ain't he? He the one who has da final say about everythin', right?"

Peter Frauzinou's head snapped up when he heard Elton Seal's questions. He thought them too incisive to be just idly curious questions.

The man had not struck some of the members just right. He seemed sincere enough but there was a fetid air about him, a scent of less dedication, less commitment—an air that he thought this Circle was a plaything, a show of some kind.

Wilder Peau had reported to his captain, Omar Williams, "I don't know 'bout my new man, that Elton Seals feller...hit's nothin' I can rightly put mah hains on, but I smell some shit somewha."

Omar and Peter stared at the man as he walked away. He had medium brown, nearly straight hair under his old railroad cap, a long shaggy mustache, was of medium height, and was nearly as bright skinned as Peter, but he always looked like he needed a shave.

"Poor white trash in a brown wrapper," Peter remarked to Omar.

"Goes by the name of Elton Seals. Lives in town. Usta work at the chicken processing plant number three. Nah lak many, he don't work no wha. Come here from Georgia looking for a better situation, engaged to a town woman. I don't know her name, yet. I don't think things got better," Omar finished.

"I say we put a tail on him, can't hurt," Peter said.

"Right. What you feeling 'bout him, Pete? You sometimes hits it right on da head."

"Bad. Real bad."

"OK den, he got a tail longer den a monkey," Omar promised.

There was nothing in all of the South like the physical safety and economic security members felt within the arms of the Circle. The only way anyone had left so far was to have died, moved out of the state, or had been asked to leave for security reasons. Many wanted to become members, but the group had decided to whittle their number down to an even one hundred by attrition. During times of danger and crises, these numbers were prepared to swell to four or five times as many volunteers.

People were so proud to be in the Circle, until those who were not often lied and said they were and tried to behave accordingly by sticking together "lak Colored peepers should," they said, "and acting dignified." When someone was cross and uncooperative on any issue, often a scathing remark such as, "Well! I can see you ain't no Circle member!" was hurled at them.

Only two people, one man and one woman, had been asked to leave the Circle so far. Sudie Mae Smith and Andy DutWiller, had both been ousted for the same offense: endangering the security of the Circle by bragging about its power.

Sudie Mae's ten-year-old son, Rodie Lee, had his foot broken for stealing a piece of chicken his mother had fried for her employer, Amos Fitler. Seeing the young hungry boy run out of the back door with the hot chicken thigh so enraged Amos that he chased Rodie and smashed his foot with a small log.

Dr. Echardt explained to Sudie Mae that the bones of the foot were delicate and that he would do his best, but Rodie would always be crippled from the blow.

Sudie Mae took the matter to her Circle captain, Aggie Pratt, begging for help.

"I knows da Circle heps in cases lak dis..."

Two days after the incident, all six of Amos Fitlers huge, healthy razorback hogs lay dead in his back yard. They represented all the wealth he had and he had been fattening them for market. Amos laid in his backyard and howled like a mad man.

And his howling was the finest music to Sudie Mae's ears. The vet was called. The sheriff was called. No reason could be found for the death of Amos' hogs.

"Keep yo' mouf shut," Sudie Mae was told. "You know the rules. No leaks. Nothing hurts a duck but his bill."

But the woman could not keep quiet. The taste of revenge ran through her body sweet as honey and came out on her tongue. A week after the hogs had been buried, Sudie Mae said slyly to Amos, "Seem lak yo' hogs done died o'da same thing kilt dat farmer's animals a while ago, remember? Ain't a soul done fount out what happen to dem neither. Onliest thing I know is dat farmer wuz real low down and mean to Colored peepers, too."

Amos stared at Sudie Mae, his mouth dropped *lak he lookin' fer a fly*, the woman thought, laughing inside as the man caught her meaning.

"'Nother thang, Mistah Amos Fitler. Dere ain't no charge fer mah work dis time 'cause I don't want no mo' yo' washin' and cookin', thank ya!" Saying this, Sudie Mae turned and walked down her former employer's back steps, her head high, an exaggerated sassy sway to her large behind.

Amos exploded. "Ifn you know sometin' 'bout somebody poisoning mah hogs, gal, you better tell me rat nah, you black heifer!"

"Who says!" Sudie Mae turned and hollered back at Amos, her face sweating, boldly displaying the hatred she would have swallowed just a year ago. Now the woman spewed her mouthful of venom at the poor hogless man. "You better watch dat old snuff dippin' mouf o'your'n, Mistah Fitler. Don't, den maybe dey gone find you laying out heah in da yard 'stood o'dose hogs! Colored peepers got dem a circle o'friens nah! We ain't all so hepless and hopeless no mo'. No suh!"

By evening Sudie Mae's "sass story" was all over town, and Dave had to extinguish it quickly. He took the matter to Sudie Mae's captain, Aggie Pratt. In the space of ten minutes and in the presence of two other witnesses, Su Mae, as her friends called her, was out. Banned from the Circle forever.

The three Circle ladies expressed sorrow, and they meant it, for they knew how hard Su Mae's life would now become. Another Circle woman would be assigned her duties of collecting the sometimes laughably small but mandatory items for trade and barter from the town's very poorest families. Items that made these families feel the dignity, Dave said, of being contributing members of the community, not just receivers: two mismatched socks, three eggs, a small handful of beans, six homemade tea cakes, a shirt that was more patches than shirt.

The other women would not come to tease her any more with, "Su Mae! What you collect today, girl?" And she would show them her pitiful collection, her large collection box never even half full, and her friends would laugh good naturedly while showing the fine things they had collected: pretty dresses, nice trousers, two or three live chickens donated by the school principal "for our poor," good shoes, hardly worn, from a fortunate Colored woman who had bad feet. They were a social group as well as a service group, but it was all over now.

Not only could Sudie Mae no longer trade and barter within the Circle, she would not enjoy its special protection and "payback," which she had just experienced with the hog incident, and she could not borrow money from its rich fund, receive discounts from the merchants it dealt with, or receive free overripe, but good for canning and eating, fruits and vegetables from its gardens.

The worst was that Sudie Mae was no longer guaranteed a livelihood of some sort within the Circle as employers of the last resort. After the meeting with her captain and the witnesses, Sudie Mae was just another Depression-era Negro woman with five fatherless children to feed. Her service to the white community had been ruined by her threat to Amos Fitler, her value as eyes and ears in White Town to the black community destroyed by her need for power and vengeance.

Andy DutWilder's case was virtually the same. He would not keep quiet in White Town about the deeds of the Circle. He was asked to leave even before Sudie Mae, and left with the same deep regret for the loss of Circle privileges.

Both were made to understand that further betrayal would mean that they would find themselves facing the wrath of the furious whites who were looking for someone to blame for the Circle's dirty tricks—and being between the mysterious, powerful Circle and the enraged whites was a frightening no man's land. Too many people had disappeared without a trace.

PART FOUR

Nay, only let them see us, while
We wear the mask

FORTY-ONE

———✦———

The original Circle was at Lela's kitchen table when there was a loud knock at the back door, and before anyone could get up and open it, one of the sentries whose job it was to ride around the town every hour along with several others, checking things out, burst in.

"What's da matter?" Aggie asked, bug-eyed as Helena, in a reflex action of fear and dismay, grabbed Aggie's hand.

"Dey done fount dat Miz Martha Lou Henley dead up in White Town!"

"The one who had Peter beaten up?" Helena asked.

"Yes, ma'am. Missy Prentice fount her. 'Bout thirty minutes ago. Say her face was all black and grey lak—lak someone done put smut on her. We hung around fer a few minutes but dats all we fount out."

"Aggie, git in da truck wit' one of dem boys and go on up to White Town and find out what happened. Don't tarry. Go on up dere and come on back, you heah?" Lela commanded.

"Yesm," Aggie replied obediently.

Once in the truck, Aggie asked not to be taken to White Town, but straight to the house of Lottie Mae Stevens, the seamstress. Lottie had been working all day at the house next door to Martha Lou's. Helen Denver's mother had given her a new model sewing machine that she had never learned to use. Now Lottie Mae worked out of a room in Miss Denver's house all day, turning collars, replacing buttons, letting out hems, and otherwise repairing clothing that Mrs. Denver and her friends would have sent to Colored Town in better times. Business was good, and for the use of her machine and for the space to work, Lottie Mae now paid Mrs. Denver, who she had formerly worked for, one dollar a week, and repaired her clothes for free.

It was after eight in the evening and Aggie was sure Lottie Mae would be home by now.

"Yes, I was dere when Missy Prentice came out dat house hollering and screaming. Chile, dat woman died three hours ago. Dey wuz trying to keep it quiet. Thought hit might been another killin'. Missy did some house work for Martha now. Missy bout da onliest one what can stand her. Dey in da same boat—know what I mean? Both lonely, manless, mean old heifers! As you know Missy run da streets night and day, I don't know when she work! She constant knee deep in other peepers business cause she got none o'her own."

"What happened!" Aggie asked, not caring if her impatience showed this time. Lottie Mae talked slow and tended to run on.

"Weren't no killin'." Lottie Mae said looking a little hurt because she had not been allowed to finish the long version of her story.

"No?"

"No."

"Hit were dat juice what kilt her. Least wise dats what da doctor dey done called say."

"Da juice?"

"Chile, Martha Lou was losing weight lak nobody's business, as you know. Gettin po' as a snake I tell ya! Missy Prentice told the doctor over and over, 'I done tole her to leave dat juice alone! Just look under dat bed!' And when dey did, dey fount crates and crates o'grapefruit juice in cans. Missy say all she was eating lately was eggs and grapefruit juice, maybe as much as a gallon a day, morning, noon and night. I magine da acik in dat juice just ventually kilt her dead."

"Da acid?"

"Yep. Dat acik got 'er. Ain't nobody kilt her, the doctor say. She done kilt her fool self. Ain't dat somethin? She read 'bout some crazy grapefruit diet in one of dose white lady magazines. Missy say, 'nah look what it done done for her! She tryin' to git skinny, to git a man. Nah she ugly and dead!' "

Aggie did not tarry but reported what she found out directly back to the Circle.

"Well, dats dat," Lela said. "Lease wise her death ain't gone cause us no problem—I hope."

Always sensitive to the feelings of others, Dave asked Peter, "Pete, how do you feel about all this? After all, Martha Lou Henley caused you a lot of hurt."

"Right now if I'm feeling anything, it's indifference. I don't care whether Martha Lou is dead or alive. She was a miserable, unhappy woman and now she's dead," Peter said, shrugging his shoulders.

Even Lela Bailey, who was the soul of caring and concern, did not waste sympathy on Martha Lou Henley. She sipped her tea and was silent.

The following night was relatively quiet. It was Saturday and the captains had reported to Dave that the town seemed to be accepting Martha Lou's death as natural, and they did not think her passing would cause a problem in the Colored community.

Dave also reported that the young man that had been hospitalized after the beating was expected to be released in a day or two and would recuperate further in the home of John Candle.

Everyone was being extremely careful, and the men and women in the Circle were being humble and subservient as they had been instructed in order to lull the whites back into a sense of security and a feeling of control, before the Circle carried out their plan of retaliation.

Some of the Circle members were carrying their play acting rather far, and with some comic effect and were thoroughly enjoying their perfomances.

Cannon Seacourse, who was a great hulking man of six-foot-eight with nearly jet black skin, had taken to standing outside the Piggly Wiggly grocery store offering to tote bags for grateful segregationists "fer anything you kin spare, Boss, 'cause I sho' is hoingry." The whites rarely hesitated to flip the poor, humble Negro a penny or nickel, leading Seacourse to say at the end of a day, "I could make a livin' off white folks by jus' being humble and pitiful—dey loves pitiful niggers!" And then the big man would collapse into laughter, his whole body shaking with glee.

Likewise, Silas Benson was courteous—for the first time—to the people his mother worked for as a cook. He even chopped some wood for them.

"How very nice!" his mother's mistress exclaimed. "I'm so glad Silas has grown out of his surliness. That kind of attitude could cause him a good deal of trouble down the path."

For chopping the wood, Mrs. Winn gave Silas fifteen cents and a blueberry muffin. Silas bowed his gratitude and smiled broadly, his eyes flashing with merriment.

"You know, you're not a bad looking boy when you smile, Silas," Mrs. Winn had said.

"Thank you, mam!" Silas had responded through gritted teeth.

By the following week, most of the residents of White Town and all of the members of the Klan were convinced that the cross burning and the beatings had certainly been the right things to do as the nigras' manners were much improved.

Louis D. Stassen was now also sure that a good lynching would be just the way to cap things off-to make sure that the fine behavior they were now experiencing from "their nigras" continued because, after all, the Colored had brought these beatings and the planned lynching on themselves with their unbelievable boldness of late. The Negroes had done things—a number of things—recently that could never, under any circumstances, be allowed to happen again.

FORTY-TWO

---❋---

The four sentries at Dave Bailey's hilltop house had found a young white man creeping around the side of the hill leading to the house and promptly delivered him to Dave at gunpoint.

Dave and Helena were in the kitchen, tea, coffee, and talk between them. Jumping up from the table, Helena stared with alarm at the young man with fire for hair.

But Dave recognized the young man, even in his big tattered overcoat, and winked at Helena, putting her more at ease.

"Mistah Bailey!" Petey Elkins exclaimed fearfully, finally realizing the danger he was in from the serious men with the guns. "Suh, I don't mean no harm," he said, glancing backward at the men and their weapons. "I'm heah on business, Suh. Personal like, I wants to speak wit' you alone."

Dave's mother had found her house slippers, donned her robe, and came towards the noise. Lela sucked in her breath sharply. "Why, it's Petey Elkins!"

"Yes'm! It's me, Petey!" The red headed young man said, turning to look at Lela.

"Oh, Miz Bailey! I'm so glad to see ya!" Petey said, as he respectfully removed his cap, relieved to see a friendly face.

"Take the guns down," Dave said quietly to the sentries. And then to Petey, "What's going on, Petey? Why are you here?" Dave's tone was not unfriendly, but then neither was it friendly and welcoming. Seeing Petey again was a shock. Where had he come from after all these months, and what ever could he want?

Dave tried to raise questions and answer them in his mind as everyone does, but he couldn't quite figure this one out, except that this man's presence must involve a loan—but surely he was bright enough not to come down to Colored Town at midnight to borrow money!

The sentries glowered at the white man.

"We found dis man creeping 'round out back," one man began, with the easy

341

anger black voices could affect when talking about white folks.

"It's OK. I know him," Dave said, but didn't ask the sentries to leave, not out of fear for safety, but out of respect for their judgment in trying to protect his family.

"When you come back to West Steward, Petey? And wha da other boys at?" Lela asked.

"I never did leave, mam," Petey answered. "I thought I would stay heah and try my luck. I got me two or three little hustles heah and dere. I fix up cars and trucks over in Old Steward on the weekends at Bixly's. Know wha dat is? Den I works up in White Town at the big grocery sto' sweeping up, taking out cardboard boxes and stuff. I do other work. Whatever I can find. Raymond Parteen and Stanley Chester, dey hopped a freight and kept on going West. I don't know wha dey at nah."

"You never left?" Lela asked incredulously.

"No, mam, I never did. And it's a good thing da way I figure. I wants to talk to Mistah Bailey, but you know, mam, I thinks you should hear dis too maybe," Petey said, becoming visibly uncomfortable.

Now he wasn't so sure the young man had come to borrow money. He was more than "borrow" nervous, and there was more fear in him, Dave thought, than shame.

"Kin we talk alone, suh?"

"Sure," Dave said. "We can go in the middle room." Petey was eighteen, but looked younger. He still had his "three hair" mustache and he was still unfailingly polite.

"Uh-uh!" one of the sentries said firmly. "Stand up heah before you go any wha!" He ordered Petey roughly.

Petey obeyed, looking askance at Dave. Dave smiled at him slightly but did not interfere.

The sentries patted him down expertly, even feeling around in the tops of Petey's socks.

"Nah turn yo' pockets inside out and put everything in dem on da table."

Petey obeyed and placed the contents of his trousers and overcoat pockets on the table. A pack of gum, a grape lollipop, a rubber band, safety pins, a small comb, a piece of string, thirty five cents and a small pocket knife.

The sentry patted the young white man down a second time. He found nothing more. He looked with suspicion at the little dull knife and back at Petey. Petey looked at Dave and then at Lela with child-like confusion.

When the sentries had finished their search, Lela led the way down the hall with Petey in the middle, Dave behind. They came to the cozy room with the fireplace and Dave motioned Petey to sit down. A sentry appeared at the window and looked in on the group, his pistol ready.

Now Petey was more comfortable. At last he was alone with friends.

"So hi you been, Miz Bailey? Still making dem good preserves?" Petey asked, smiling a twisted nervous smile.

"Oh, I speck so," Lela answered, tense with wonder and question.

Dave noticed that Petey's hands were shaking a bit. He wished he would get to the point, but he felt a little sorry for him too—he was probably a decent enough kid.

As if reading Dave's thoughts, Petey said, "Listen, Mistah Bailey, I ain't heah fer no foolishness. And I ain't heah to git no money. Maybe dats what you thinking. I've been doin' all right. Sometimes I can send two or three dollars home to my mamma. I'm heah because you and yo' mother wuz so good to us when we wuz down. I ain't gone never forget dat. Dat's why I'm heah. But can you help me to git back outta here safe without being seen? And can you not tell nobody I been up heah to talk to you? I mean kin you tell yo' friends outside not to say nothin' bout me being here? Cause they would kill me."

"Who?" Dave asked, sitting forward and upright in his seat, every bone, every muscle alert.

"The Klu Klux Klan and dey friends."

"Listen," Dave said, turning his whole body around to face the young man sitting beside him on the sofa. "I understand what you are saying. Yes. Now I understand. And I can guarantee your safety out of here, don't worry about a thing. I can send you back home tonight if that's what you want," Dave continued softly. "Now tell us what you've come to tell."

The young man was visibly relieved. He had taken a great chance coming up here, even without knowing that he would be running into a half dozen guards! What if Dave and his mother somehow didn't understand, didn't believe his story? The thought had made him perspire under his arms, but now he was feeling much better and he began his story:

"You and Miz Bailey, and dat preacher, was just so fine to us, I couldn't bear to see nothing happen to y'all and dat preacher. Where he at now?"

"Over in Mississippi on some business," Lela said, trying to hide her impatience to know what had brought Petey Elkins here at this late hour.

"Dat's right. I heard da Klan say dat. He over in Mississippi rat now."

"What?" Dave exclaimed, knowing such knowledge could only mean one thing.

"Has Rev. Clayton been picked out by the Klan in some way, Petey?" Dave asked with a steadiness in his voice that his body did not feel—for he was thinking: *My Lord! They could be over there right now tracking Matthew down!*

"Dat's right. Da Klan say he da leader of a group dat's causing a whole lottsa trouble. Dey say he led the group dat burned down dat storage place, and dat he got some people outta town—twice—dat da Law wanted to question. Dey say he probably even know somethin' he ain't tellin' 'bout dem two people what got kilt up back in October. Dey say dey know he the one, 'cause one night he jumped out of a tree and told dem his name and said he wasn't afraid of nobody!"

"My Lawd!" Lela exclaimed, listening to this warped tale that the Klan had manufactured to hang injustice on.

"Go on, Petey," Dave said calmly.

"Well dat's about all except dey say when he jumped out of da tree, da preacher say he ready to die and den some of them laughed and say dey ready to help him."

"LawdhavemercyJesus!" Lela exclaimed.

"Da places wha I works, I hears lotsa things," the young man said almost apologetically.

"Petey, you did the right thing in coming here this way, and I want you to know we appreciate it," Dave said, standing. Petey stood also and Dave placed his hand on his shoulder.

"When you get home, you can tell your mother that you saved a man's life. She'll be proud of you, no doubt."

Petey's legs were shaking slightly and he held on to the back of a chair to steady himself.

"Come on over heah, boy, and let me hug you!" Lela said. And she did hug him, enclosing the slender young man in her arms, her head coming up to his chin.

"Don't worry about a thing and don't be afraid. You're going home tonight. Back where you came from," Dave said reassuringly.

"But," Petey protested. "Mah stuff!"

"What do you want to go back and get? How many changes of clothes do you have? What is so precious to you that you can't leave it?"

Dave smiled inwardly at himself. He was getting to be the "transportation man," the man in charge of getting everyone out of town, it seemed, using the same speech: "What is so precious to you that you cannot leave it behind?"

"I ain't got but da one pair shoes, da ones ahm wearing. I got me two mo' shirts and one mo' pair o'trousers, but..."

"Yes?"

"Well, Mistah Bailey, it's just dat since I been heah, I saved up near ten dollars. It's back in mah room, hid. I can't leave dat money. Hit's all I got in da world."

"Leave it." Dave said firmly.

"Leave it?" Petey said pitifully, his face screwed up in pain thinking of the lost of such a large sum.

"Tonight someone will take you to Memphis and buy you a ticket home." Dave reached into a box on the stand by the bed and pulled out some bills. He handed the bills to Petey.

"Why dis heah is a hunnert dollars Mistah Bailey! Is dis fer me?" Petey asked stunned as he counted the money again. He had never seen so much money in his life.

"Sure it's for you, Petey. You've done a good thing."

"I didn't do hit fer no money, Mistah Bailey," Petey said sincerely, looking around at Lela.

"We knows you didn't, honey," Lela said.

"But this here is a hunnert dollars!" Petey said again, still stunned, raising his voice, looking at the bills as if such a sum should be aired, talked about, given respect.

"The sentries will take you to Memphis and buy you a ticket so your hundred is free and clear," Dave said, smiling a little at the young man and his windfall which he could not have saved in months of working in these times.

"You do want to go home, don't you, Petey?"

"Oh, yes sir, Mistah Bailey! My mama will be proud to see me!"

"I'll pack you a lunch to eat on the way!" Lela said, and went off to look for a shoe box.

So Petey Elkins had to be spirited out of West Steward, as had the Dusters and their son, as had Aristotle Gillis and O'Neill Edwards. There was no sleeping that night. An emergency call had to be made to Rev. Matthew Moses Clayton in Fair Damsel, Mississippi, to the one Colored store in town that had a telephone. The reverend would be told to hide himself until early tomorrow morning, at which time at least ten heavily armed Colored men would board the ferry, separately to pick him up and bring him safely home.

When the Rev. Clayton was informed of Petey Elkin's visit, he was quiet and thoughtful as usual, and yes, he would return immediately with the men who were being dispatched by ferry. He suggested a meeting place and said that he would take Dave's advice to wear a disguise of some sort.

"But there was something else in his voice," Dave confided to Peter and Omar. "What I don't know, he sounded—well, funny."

Peter and Omar both agreed that perhaps they would sound funny too if they had just been told of a plot to lynch them! But Dave, who could be as sensitive as his mother, was not convinced.

"Maybe he concerned fer da family he leavin' behind?" Omar speculated.

"No," Dave said. "The Klan was not after his family." In this case, both he and Peter believed they wanted only the minister—although the Klan had often been known to involve more than one family member.

"Well, if he got somethin' on his mind, he let us know when he git heah. He did say he were goin' home on business, though he didn't say what dat business were," Omar said.

The ten heavily armed men, who took pains not to appear to be together, paid their fares of ten cents each for the short ride across the river to Mississippi. The reverend would be waiting in some sort of disguise and would identify himself to Omar. Dave would have transportation ready when they came back to the Arkansas side.

The ferry shoved off at five o'clock and arrived on the muddy banks of the Mississippi thirty-five minutes later. Omar left the ferry, ignoring the other nine men who scattered themselves about John's Ferry Bank Café, and went directly to the side of the small café where Colored were served standing up. He ordered cocoa and two buttered biscuits with jelly, while looking around. There were only two other Colored men on the stand-up side. They paid him no mind.

The huge biscuits—cat heads they were called—were hot and heavily buttered, and the jelly was smooth, very sweet, and fruity. The small meal was very good, and

Omar felt a twinge of guilt because he hoped he could finish them before Rev. Clayton made his appearance.

He ate fast, planning to have a good look around the place when he finished. Just as he savored the last bites of the second biscuit, a small boy of about five came directly up to him and said, "Mistah Williams?"

"Yassuh! And who might you be, little mistah?"

"Huh?" the child asked looking up at the big ebony hued man.

"I said what is yo' name, son," Omar asked smiling at the child's momentary confusion.

"Frederickdouglasclayton," the boy answered, running his name altogether in a sing song manner, as if such a long name had to be sung to be remembered.

"Mah daddy, he say, he waiting for you outside. He say come wit' me."

"Whoa! Who you say yo' daddy is boy? You sho' he want me?" Omar asked not having caught the name.

"My daddy is Matthew," the young boy said with some impatience. "He say you come wit' me."

"Well I be dog!" Omar exclaimed. "Heah I come, boy! I'm rat behind you!"

The other men that had come over with Omar lounged at a casual loaded pistol distance away, fully aware that Mississippi had the worst reputation for lynching of any state in the union, and they were ready. Just in case.

There was a small man outside the café, hiding behind a tree, and the others had not spotted him.

"Hey, boy," Rev. Clayton said when Omar's large frame appeared, "I'm packed and ready."

"Rev. Clayton! Hi you doin'?" Omar asked with relief.

"Fine, fine!" The minister said, smiling.

"Dis boy he say..." Omar said, bucking his already large eyes with question.

"That he's my son? He is," the reverend said, smiling again. He looked rested, relaxed, not at all frightened and not in disguise.

"This," Rev. Clayton said, pushing forward a small pretty woman the color of an English walnut, "is my wife Quella. We call her Q."

Omar held out a dumbstruck hand to the pretty little woman who was still half hidden behind the large dark tree. "Howdy-do, mam, name is Omar Williams."

"Proud to meet you," Quella said shyly, coming out in the open and taking his huge black hand.

The boy, Frederick Douglas Clayton, was seven. He had his mother's coloring and good looks, his father's quiet manner. The four of them went back into the café to wait the thirty minutes or so for the next ferry and to alert the other men to be ready when the ferry came back.

The Circle had known the reverend for how long? A whole year? And not a peep out of him to anyone about a wife and a child! Omar could not wait to see Dave's face, to hear Lela Bailey exclaim, "LawdhavemercyJesus!"

FORTY-THREE

K.D. Whitmore, second only to the Exalted Cyclops, Louis D. Stassen himself, was known to be a "solid thinker." As such, and especially because, as owner of the largest furniture store in Phillips County, he was—or had been—a well respected rich man. So when he spoke, the gathered Klan tended to listen carefully. Besides, Louie D was out of town on business and had left K.D. in charge.

The assembled members loved to meet at K.D.'s place because the snacks were always first class and his house was the largest and the most attractive of all the houses in West Steward. Meeting at K.D.'s gave the Klan a heightened sense of importance—more fruit in the pie, so to speak.

K.D. had been giving a lot of thought to their plan for a lynching. While lynchings were necessary every now and then to let the niggers know once and for all who was really in charge, and where the source of all power truly lay, K.D. Whitmore's good solid thinking told him their plan to lynch the minister was frought with possible problems. He knew that preachers were almost as good as God himself to niggers. If you passed within a mile of one of their churches on a Sunday you could hear such hooping and hollering and stomping and clapping, you'd think they'd all gone plum crazy.

K.D.'s solid good sense told him clear as the big yellow moon that the incident that nobody even wanted to even taste in their mouths, much less talk about—the "tree incident"—was most disturbing because of the reckless bravado that the black men had exhibited. While it made sense to make an example of their leader, he didn't like the idea of all that church crazy coming loose, and he was certain that whatever sudden bravado this minister had whipped up in his followers, it would evaporate like morning dew if handled *correctly*.

He wanted to suggest a different way of handling the situation, but he knew he had to tread lightly and cast the idea delicately out on the water, and in the end, if the gathered men agreed—why, he just had to make the group feel that it was their good sense that made the final decision.

Now, a group of Klan grabbing a lone black man off the street in the dead of the night and stringing him up—that was something they were familiar with, comfortable with. And so K.D.'s plan was readily adopted, each man being careful not to show too much gratitude for K.D.'s suggestion, which suited them all just fine-a lynching would cap this all off and end all of this "New Nigger" shit for good, the men agreed.

Older women in the community treated Tom "Fool" Leak like a son. He would take on the tiring tasks of shelling bowls of nuts for holiday cakes with no thought of pay except to eat wherever he wanted, when he wanted, which was no problem at all. The old women loved stuffing anyone with their one sure wealth—food— well cooked and usually plentiful. Tom would sometimes peel mounds of fruit for canning for someone before getting the urge to wander off. Tender with children, Tom kept them busy for hours with nonsense games and wild stories while their mothers washed and boiled the White Town clothes in their huge black iron tubs of hot soapy water in the often communal backyard laundries.

Frequently, when the women were too tired from their work to scrub their own floors, cook their own meals, Tom would be found, and he would help cook, clean and iron, accepting nothing but gratitude, smiles and snacks to fill the bottomless pit that was his belly.

Hattie Mackie, widowed with three small children, had been telling everyone that Tom "Fool" Leak was getting better—more stable.

Dave had noticed it too. When Omar took with the shits Thursday he called it, surprisingly Tom had filled in for him, making the tamales almost as well as Omar.

"Hey Tom! You did real well today," Dave said, praising him. Tom had blushed and hung his head in a comical fashion.

"I been watching y'all make dem tamales a long time. Nah I can do hit too!"

"You sure can," Dave said, patting the man/child on the shoulder.

"Gotta find a real job now, you know," Tom said, looking directly at Dave. "Kin you gimme one?"

Dave found Tom's direct eye contact unsettling. He had known this child-like and often childish man for five years and he had never seen him make direct eye contact with anyone. Neither had he been stable enough to work anywhere an entire day without running off to White Town after a while to jump and dance and sing for any change thrown his way—much to the amusement of the White Town peckerwoods, Omar called them.

Tom had never been "quite right" since his family was burned alive in a fire in Mississippi by a group of white night riders ten years ago. He was thirty now.

Dave sensed that something very fundamental had changed with Tom, and he was curious to know what it was.

"Tom, can you come up to the house this evening? We'll talk—I mean about a better job for you," Dave said, wondering why a "better job" was now needed.

"Could we, Mistah Dave? Gosh, I sho' would lak dat. I needs mo' money for mah fambly nah, you see."

"Your family?"

"Yassuh."

Dave wondered, *What family?* As long as he had known Tom Leak he had always been completely alone—except for one sister over in Mississippi that no one had ever met.

"What time, suh, shall I be dere?"

"Oh, for goodness sake, Tom!" Dave said, laughing. "When did you start calling me sir? I'll ask Peter to bring you up around what? Five o'clock—after the tamales are stored."

"Dat would be fine wit' me—Dave."

My Goodness! He looks perfectly normal! Dave thought with a shock. Just like anyone else. What has happened? Is this the same wild man we use to hide from in the picture show as recently as a month ago?

Tom arrived promptly in the truck with Peter at five o'clock and whispered to Dave, "Kin we talk wit'out Miz Lela? What I has to say is main talk."

Dave smiled, surprised, and Peter's eyebrows shot toward the sky, remembering that Tom always seemed to have secrets that were only secrets to him.

"Can Pete stay?" Dave asked.

"Sho'. He a main, ain't he?"

They settled in the middle room with coffee and cake.

351

Well, Tom wasn't completely stable after all, Dave noticed. He still ate fast and furiously as if someone would snatch his food away at any second. His cake and coffee disappeared in less than two minutes.

When he looked up at Dave and Peter, crumbs strewn all down the front of his shirt, cake on his chin and lips, they were looking at the old Tom "Fool" Leak they were familiar with and both men began to smile.

Tom, with a determination that was as new to him as it was to his friends, noting the trail of crumbs, brushed at them fiercely as if they had appeared to embarrass him through no fault of his own, and said very distinctly, as normal as you please, "My old lady, Hattie Mackie, is expecting. She is right along—nearly seven months and she been sick all da way. I got to set her down. Git her off her feets, you know? All dat bumping up and down in dat wash tub all day ain't no good, you know? I heps her a whole lots, I irons the clothes, but she don't trust me to deliver. And I hep her wit' the other children, which ain't mine, but belong to Denester Mackie, her husband what is dead. Dis one be mines."

Here, Tom squinted up his eyes and smiled proudly.

"Well I'll be da da do!" Peter said with a surprised smile. "Congratulations, Tom!"

"That's nice news, Tom," Dave said, a little envious.

"Well, yo' mama wouldn't think so—so don't go tellin' her. We aim to git married up. I'm just looking for mo' steady work what pays a little bit mo'."

"You got it," Dave smiled.

"For real, Mistah Dave? For real?" Tom asked, delighted. "What is ahm gone be doin'? I'll do anythin', you know."

"I have something in mind," Dave lied. "Let me get it organized and I'll get back to you in a couple of days. How would twelve a week suit you?"

It was more than twice what the man earned weekly now, and Tom could hardly believe his luck.

"Did you say twelve? Well, you won't be sorry, Mistah Dave!" Tom said, standing, then sitting two or three times nervously.

"Who is Mistah Dave?" Dave asked, laughing.

"Well, Dave, den! You won't be sorry! I'll work real, real hard. And I won't take off marching around like I used to. I kin stay put! You'll see."

Tom was smiling, showing all of the teeth he had left, and having sat down again, he placed his hands on his knees and held on for dear life, trying hard not to show any more signs of trembling and quaking and being "loose in the noggin," as Hattie Mackie often said.

The guards had told Dave more than once that Tom enjoyed sneaking away from them, which he considered a game of wits. He was fond of roaming the town in the middle of the night, listening, he said, "to da stars doin' dey shining." Lately he had taken to roaming much less at night because he was not so loose in the head anymore, but he had not stopped sneaking away completely, for he enjoyed the befuddled, angry, and finally relieved look on the face of his guard for the night when he was located.

"Where you been at, Tom?" his angry guard would inquire.

"Oh, around," Tom would giggle, covering his mouth and swaying back and forth like a mischievious child.

"Tom, hit's dangerous for a Colored main to go poking around—especially up in White Town at night alone."

"Nobody bother me," Tom had said flatly. "Nobody mess wit' me. Dey all know Tom. Dey all lak Tom, even da white folks."

Now, he couldn't wait to go window shopping and think about all the things he would buy for his new wife and child.

Dave had barely had two days to consider this abrupt change in his friend before Hattie Mackie was in Lela Bailey's parlor, her eyes red from crying. Lela noticed that Hattie was more than seven months expecting, because her stomach had dropped.

"LawdhavemercyJesus! Nah, dis ain't right, Sylvester. You and Douglas know better den to jus' let dis go. Near two days? Mah mah mah!" Lela scolded the two grown men standing before her.

"We can find him. We always found 'em befoe," Douglas began doggedly.

"And he ain't never been hurt or nothin' yet," Sylvester Miles said. "He jus' playin' wit' us."

But Hattie Mackie was beside herself with agitation.

"Hit's been going on two days and y'all didn't see fit to tell Dave? And beggin' me not to tell 'em? I shouldn't have listened ta you two! What earthly good is guards ifn dey both fall out and go to sleep at da self same time?"

"Nah, Hattie." Sylvester whined. "We didn't fall asleep! He jus' slip off lak he do all da time."

"We jus' tryin' to find out what da best place to start lookin' for Tom again is," LaSalle Peabody said. "As you knows, we done been near every whar already soon as we heered he gone missing—Aggie done tole us. White Woods, Colored Woods, checked all da cricks and ponds. Been up and down the shores of the river, up and down the rayroad tracks." LaSalle shrugged his shoulders. "We jus' don't know what ta do no mo'. But we ain't gone give up, doe, I'll tell you dat!"

"You see, Dave," said the other guard, Douglas Card, "I'm sho' you done heard what a game Tom makes out of us guarding him. He never understood da seriousness. Nobody wanted to guard Tom and dats a fact. He considered hit a joke, a plaything to gie us da slip."

"I know," Dave said tonelessly. "Tom never really understood the seriousness of our situation, we were bound to lose him for more than just the usual hour that it sometimes took to find him."

"But dis heah is most forty-eight hours nah and he still missing!" wailed Hattie Mackie. "Y'all ain't never took dis long to find him befoe!"

It was true. Tom could always be found in an hour or so. Less if he had not hitched a ride to The Bottoms, for he rarely left West Steward, Lela reminded the group.

After Tom "Fool" Leak had been missing a full three days, Dave and the Circle had drawn the following conclusion: If Tom had been harmed by the Klan or anyone else in White Town, there would be no point in not revealing it. The Klan was going to let them know what had happened to Tom soon, Dave thought with a sinking feeling in his stomach and a coldness around his heart.

But Aggie Pratt was ahead of the men this time. She figured the Klan did not care if Tom was ever found "as long as he stayed missing," she said. So after making discreet inquiries and talking to key people she had long ago designated as "peepers who always knowed a little bit o'somethin'—peepers who could help you put pieces together enough so you could begin to see da sides and edges and corners of a problem," Aggie told Dave some time later. Using her methods, Aggie found Mr. and Mrs. Ford Pasterway and sat them before Dave in Lela's kitchen on day three.

The couple introduced themselves with quiet dignity to Dave. They were very poorly dressed, but "presentable," Lela would say. The husband and wife were both sitting at Lela's kitchen table with steaming all purpose saffafras tea in front of them.

"Jus' tell 'em what you done saw,"Aggie prompted, glancing at the entire Inner Circle that sat at the table or stood balanced against the kitchen walls.

"Well nah," Ford Pasterway began, "Me and the missus was 'bout to go to bed— we live at the very end of what's called the Colored Woods. Our house is little and small. In the dark you could pass right by hit wit'out noticing hit, which is what dose peckerwoods did."

"Go on," Dave said, sitting forward in his seat as his heart began to quicken. He folded his arms across his chest, as if that effort would help him get control of its pumping.

"Dey say, 'Maybe we should string 'em up in da middle of da woods, dats where dey have dey meetins and think we don't know hit. Dat way dey find him right quick.'"

"Nah listen tah dis!" Aggie interrupted, her eyes blazing in the lamp lights.

Orin Pasterway, a lumpy little woman, grunted with distaste. "Say dey didn't know 'bout no meetin's in da Colored Woods until somebody told 'em a few weeks ago. Seem lak he somebody dat be comin' to y'alls meetin's—or whatever. We strain ourvaselves, but couldn't hear da main's name although dey called hit."

Peter Frauzinou dropped his head as if praying as he stood against the wall. "We'll find Tom," he whispered. "And the snitch."

"If dose son-of-a-bitches done done somethin' ta Tom!" Will Henry burst out.

Dave raised his hand for silence.

"Please continue," Dave bade the couple quietly.

"Dere was a buncha dem, maybe eleven, twelve. We was glued to ourva back window in da dark, scared to breathe a breath. We could see some o' dem, but o' cose they couldn't see us."

"Hit's a small little bitty house," Mrs. Pasterway repeated.

"At first I couldn't see da main's face, but when dey held up dey lanterns, I seed hit wuz a Colored main dey had. He were all covered wit' blood, but he weren't dead doe, 'cause he holler. I was surprised when I hear 'em, 'cause wit' dem lanterns I could see he was whipped pretty bad, all covered wit' blood. Look lak he didn't have a holler left in 'em," Ford said.

"Gawddamn hit!" Omar roared.

"Den dis older peckerwood say again naw, not in the middle o' da woods. I got a better iddy. Let 'em *search* for his black ass."

"Then what happened?" Dave asked. His voice was thick—he was trying to think clearly but finding it difficult. Maybe these people were snitches themselves. This couple lived in the Colored Woods and even he had never stumbled upon their house. Perhaps somehow they had heard too much. Surely they had seen groups of black men coming and going.

The Circle knew a few Colored people lived around these woods. It was a chance they had to take. They had kept their voices low, even talked in fragmented sentences at times, sentences that outsiders would find hard to make sense of. They had also put some faith in the code of blackness—don't tell white folks nothin'!—but there was no real protection from that reality of existence since slavery—the snitch for money.

LaSalle rose from his chair and walked around to face the seated couple. He stared at them coldly, suspiciously, all the cool calmness he was known for was absent from his manner now.

"Hi we know you peepers ain't lyin'? Hi we know you peepers ain't snitches fer da white folks?" LaSalle said, his voice harsh and accusatory on purpose—for he could see the couple was certainly poor enough to open their pockets to snitch pay.

Ford rose from his seat and faced LaSalle, his expression a terrible mixture of hurt and anger, his voice full of indignation and long suffering.

"Ahm forty-eight years old, and ifn I lives to be forty-eight mo', I will never in all mah days tell da white folks *nothin'* what Negroes do. White folks never did me a bit o' good in mah entire time on dis earth—never. I swear on da grave o' my dear mother Hilda Betty Pasterway dat I ain't told nobody no nothin'!" Ford held LaSalle's eyes, his own afire.

"Dey done lynched my husmon's brother fifteen years ago down in Texas," Orin said quietly, adding a period to her husband's pain and rage.

"Alright," Lela said. "Alright." The old mother's words held all of the belief and conformation the group needed. It was as if Lela's two words had cast a beam through the darkness of uncertainty that the room held, and trust was once more illuminated.

"Go head on, Mistah Pasterway." Aggie urged. "What you think done happened to dat main?"

Ford told of seeing Tom Leak in White Town "once or twice" himself and of recognizing his peculiar run on way of speaking.

"He say, 'Leemelone! Leemelone! Leemelone!' Lak dat, three times if I remember correct," Ford finished.

"Oh, mah Gawd!" someone in the room exhaled. "Dat was Tom alright!"

"What I think happen is dis: Dey done got hold o' him when we heered dat rumbling dat night sho' as you bone. Dey headed straight out to da back o' da Colored Woods. When me and my wife couldn't hear dem no mo', we put on ourva coats and headed straight for mah cousin's house heah in Colored Town quiet as two thieves in a church house. Dats where yo' Aggie fount us. We ain't been back home since. We didn't rightly know what ta do. We right glad to see you, Miz Aggie. We wanta tell somebody."

"So he right out dere somewha by the Pasterway house!" Omar Williams exploded.

"Probably. My God. Why didn't we find him? We've been that way twice already," Peter said, looking at Dave. There were tears in his eyes.

"Possibly because they have hidden him in plain sight" Dave said logically. We have probably passed by him"—Dave refused to say "his body"—"more than once while searching."

Feeling chilled and wretched, Dave asked Ford if he would be willing to help them close in on the area they had missed.

"I'll do everythin' in mah power," Ford answered without hesitation, but his wife wanted to stay with the women—which Dave thought was fine.

"You'll have mo' niggers protecting you den ever in yo' life!" Omar said taking his pistol from his jacket pocket and giving it an unnecessary inspection.

"I got me a little piece o' trouble mahself," Ford said, lifting a small pistol from his pocket. "Let's go. I ain't scared no mo'."

"Dere wuz a group of Colored operating in dis town dat was takin' care of things. Dat wuz da talk—but nobody seemed to know who dese peepers was." Ford smiled to himself in the beautiful kitchen as he looked into the eyes of the fearless and armed young men and women before him. Now he knew. Now he knew at least who a bunch of them were. Later he would ask if they took men as old as himself into their group—because he intended to join them.

FORTY-FOUR

———✦———

Aggie could not be talked into staying with the women so she left Lela, Helena, Orin, and Hattie Mackie, who could not stop crying, and piled into the two trucks with the men of the Inner Circle.

Aggie, who could shoot as well as any man, had her pistol in a holster strapped to her waist as she swung into the back of the truck with Will Henry and LaSalle, covering herself with heavy wool blankets and thick quilts for the ride. It had been her idea to ride in the back of the truck "so I kin see everythin' whats tah see."

Dave thought it best if just this tight group of original Circle members should be the ones to look for Tom, given the new information they had. He figured involving even ten more Circle members at this time might create chaos and possibly cause unnecessary loss of life. No. Their search should be tight and orderly at this point.

"Shall we send someone to tell Rev. Clayton what Mistah Pasterway done tole us?" LaSalle wondered.

"Not yet," Dave said. "Let him stay hidden where he is for now."

It was a little past two in the afternoon when the two trucks arrived in the "Colored" woods on the opposite side of town from the "white" woods, which featured a large clearing with benches and shade trees, widely used for picnics, parties and strolls. The Colored Woods were dense and tangled, still full of wildlife—birds, snakes, small animals, and some said occasional bears and wildcats.

Following a relatively open trail, the trucks stopped in a small area that was slightly cleared, and Ford led the group to his tiny house that he thought they should use as a starting point and landmark.

The day was overcast and gloomy, so the Circle took their lanterns and flashlights, even though there was still adequate daylight for a few hours more.

"Let's use the rest of this daylight to make a general search," Dave suggested. Ford Pasterway led the group straight down from the side of his house, about a mile back into the woods. The men and Aggie walked the ground that was now stiff with January cold, lifting their heads, shifting their eyes, carefully placing their feet. Looking up into the branches of the skeletal trees, their hearts and minds flowing in two directions at once—hoping to find Tom, if he was in these woods—and hoping he was not in these woods, but alive somewhere—still laughing and dancing and being his old fool self.

The group searched for more than an hour, growing warm in their anxiety and heavy coats. Another half hour led the Circle members out of the woods and onto the Pike, so they turned around, and now instead of marching in a straight shoulder to shoulder line of six men and one woman, they broke into three parallel groups, putting thirty feet or so between them as they searched the middle and both sides of their space. The group covered the woods in this manner for another hour, then, more tired than they would admit, Ford suggested they build a log fire and "warm up awhile." The group reluctantly agreed.

After a scant half hour by their log fire, the search party carefully put the fire out and was up again, this time moving around and around the parameter of the now dark woods with lanterns and flashlights, moving in closer to the center all the time, covering ground already covered, looking up into trees already checked, but in a different way, at a different angle for something they perhaps missed. After more than five hours of searching, the group had found nothing. They returned frustrated and discouraged to the trucks, and wrapped themselves in quilts and blankets and tried to contain their emotions.

"I thought sho' we would be able to find somethin' by nah!" Ford repeated more than once, as if it was somehow his fault that he had not been able to lead these distraught friends to Tom.

"Oh, we aren't near through searching yet," Peter said adamantly. "Not nearly through."

"If he's out here we shall find him," Dave added, and whispered, "Please. Please. Not Tom, Lord," under his breath.

The group searched beyond hunger, beyond cold or exhaustion. They moved around the woods like driven shadows, their feet like machines that crushed and kicked small branches and fallen leaves unmercifully.

Finally, darkness not only fell but closed in on the woods, rendering the flashlights and lanterns puny and nearly ineffective.

"Mistah Dave," Ford said, almost afraid to speak to a face so set in pain, and anger, and hurt. "Mistah Dave, mebbe we should start up again tommory? Hit's so cold and so dark."

Dave heaved a deep resistant sigh and the search party left the woods without a clue, and headed for Lela's kitchen.

"LawdhavemercyJesus! Y'all is half froze!" Lela wailed, as she ushered in the members of the search party and began to spread food before them. None had eaten since breakfast—even Omar had not thought much of food this day.

Hattie Mackie, who had been unable to sleep, came quickly into the room when she heard the group return at nine o'clock, and burst into fresh tears when she heard they had not found Tom. Of course, everyone knew that whatever the outcome, there would be tears aplenty, and Lela had tried to prepare the women as much as possible by sharing her favorite scripture verses with them all day.

Lela had made a thick rich beef stew and corn muffins. It seemed to be just the thing, and suddenly realizing that they were starved, the search party ate quickly and heartily, taking second helpings.

Helena served hot tea, hot coffee, and to keep herself busy, Orin Pasterway had made two large creamy pans of butter rolls for dessert in Lela's kitchen.

"We'll search more tomorrow, Hattie," Dave said almost apologetically to Tom's "wife," who was being attended around the clock by Lela and Helena, and now Orin Pasterway.

The Pasterways went back to their cousin's house for the night, and Aggie and her children spent the night at Lela's in order to be ready to move out again after breakfast.

Lela could not persuade anyone to take food into the woods.

"We ain't goin' on no picnic!" said the mouthy Will Henry Mead, who immediately apologized for his sharp tone with "Mother Bailey."

The next day, the fourth day of Tom's disappearance, after an hour of searching, Ford Pasterway sat on the hard, cold ground rocking in confusion and frustration. "I coulda swore we would have done fount somethin' by nah," he said, his voice full of hurt and anger.

It was colder than the day before and early into their search. Dave suggested that they build a log fire, but everyone sensed that he had more than keeping warm on his mind. When everyone was seated around the fire, Dave said, "Let's summarize.

"Given the description of the Pasterways, the man they grabbed was definitely Tom," Dave said.

The Circle members sat on logs and stumps around their fire and murmured in agreement. Aggie humped her small shoulders several times to force a chill out of her small body.

"Now, we have looked everywhere. Down railroad tracks from here to Epps— even over in Ketta. We have searched all of the ponds and cricks, we have been all up and down the banks of the Mississippi river over here, and we must have looked in the branches of every tree in these woods, and we have kept our ears open to hear of a body being found. Where have we not looked, assuming they want us to find him?" Dave asked, but he had an idea swirling in his own mind which he would advance alone or mix with whatever was offered by this group of friends.

"Dey wants us ta find 'em? Well dey sho' ain't makin hit easy!" Omar snarled. "One thing I knows fer sho'. He out heah some place."

"He is obviously hidden in plain sight," Dave mumbled, a thought he had repeated before.

Aggie looked keenly at Dave, for she had known him long enough to know his mind was "working up a smoke," she called it.

"Dave, what do you think?" asked Peter.

"Well, let's try looking at the trees themselves, not just passing them rather quickly as we look up into their branches," Dave suggested. "Let's look at the tree trunks."

"Dere is a helluva lot of trees in dese woods." Will Henry grunted.

"We know they went way past your house on its west side, isn't that right, Mr. Pasterway?" Peter asked.

"Mah friends, dey jus' calls me Ford," the guide said to this nice and good looking white boy that was a Negro.

"Then let's start straight down from Ford's house again," Peter proposed.

"We already done done dat," LaSalle protested.

"Yeah, but dis time we looking more closely and we lookin at da *tree trunks*," Aggie said.

Will Henry plunged ahead of the group, walking with fierce and determined strides, his face set in iron as he examined first one tree, and then another with angry glares and pokes, as if daring any one of them to reveal the body of their beloved friend.

"Don't lose us, Will! We all gotta stay together!" Aggie called from several yards behind him.

The woods were always blanketed by a dimness that held back some of the warmth and sunlight, making it a pleasantly cool place in the summer, the green leaves acting as a natural parasol. In winter the naked tree branches still shielded the scant rays of sun, causing the forest to seem colder and more foreboding than it was.

As Dave moved amongst the trees, a heavy primitive chill that had nothing to do with the temperature of the forest gripped his shoulders, spread down his back, and finally up and around his heart. The chill left a sharp ache that had no physical cause—and having no physical beginning, the pain could not be ended with pills or poultices. It was just a worrisome ache filled with tears that stayed locked up in his soul, giving his body no peace.

"Oh, God! Oh, Lord Jesus!" was Dave's involuntary sigh as he surprised himself with the multitude of his prayers. He had to stay strong, to stay pulled together for all of them. Especially for Aggie, but also for Will Henry, who might explode if they found Tom. As Dave steeled himself and gave a loud order, even small animals scurried and scattered looking for their nest, their holes, before the feet of this resolute group.

"Turn around! We are coming out of the woods and onto the Pike again."

The small party obeyed and was about a quarter of a mile back into the woods again, now proceeding in a staggered and rather random manner, when Will Henry stooped and picked up something.

"Dave, look at dis!" he called. "Ain't dis one of Tom's shoes?"

The group rushed to join him around the shoe as one, eager to see, afraid to see, what the ground had yielded.

Will Henry held the left shoe gently, carefully, as if it were a treasure. It was a brown lace leather high top, the kind that thousands of poor working men wore—but none probably tied just the first three eyelets over to the right side and left the other holes open, the easier to slip in and out of without tying and untying again. And hardly anyone—even during these tough times—let their shoes get this scuffed and run over. Tom "Fool" Leak had worn these laughable "ankle breakers" everywhere.

Dave took the shoe in his hand, and they all just stared at it.

"Hit's Tom's shoe alright," Omar said quietly.

"Yes," Dave said, feeling his soul chill again. "It's Tom's shoe."

"Gawd damn it!" Will Henry yelled, clutching his fist.

Abruptly Aggie ran away from the group. Fast as a deer, she ran, first zig-zagging, then in a circle, then she stopped for a fraction of a second and was off again in a straight line running and running.

Thinking her hysterical even though she had not uttered a word, Peter took out after her, but she was faster than he and they both ran in a circle now wider and wider, Aggie's hair coming undone and flying in the wind behind her. The others tried to head her off.

"Catch her before she hurts herself!" Dave shouted, as all of them crashed through the woods after Aggie Pratt, a woman who was almost as swift as her two boys, Arky and Villa.

But Aggie suddenly stopped and pointed. "I knowed he was right around heah somewha!" she cried her chest heaving, her long old coat caught with hanging, dry twigs.

The men looked where Aggie pointed, where the sunlight filtered prettily through the trees making nice neat afternoon patterns on the ground. And suddenly they saw it. A dark grayish piece of tarpaulin weight fabric wrapped tightly around a large black tree. The man was encased from shoulders to heels, standing upright, his body held in place by the cold and the stiffness of death. His head lay towards his right shoulder, his tongue protruded from his lips and his eyes were slightly open. The lynch rope was still around his neck.

Without warning Aggie fell straight forward and Ford sprung out and caught her. He picked up her small body and sat on a nearby tree stump with the woman cradled in his arms like a child. Aggie revived quickly and stood up unsteadily on her feet.

"I ain't gone faint no mo'!" she said between clenched teeth, and forcing herself to draw closer, she looked into the face of Tom Leak, who had so recently helped her to iron the few waists she still had orders for, had played all day with her children to give her a rest, had made her some lye soap in her backyard tub.

The man had been severely beaten, his bib overalls were covered with dried dark stains they knew was blood. His face was badly swollen and disfigured, but there was no doubt. It was Tom.

LaSalle and Omar carefully cut the holding cloth and unwrapped the stiff tarpaulin like fabric from the body and laid Tom on his back on the ground. It helped that he did not look quite real—the cold open air had preserved him some and left him with the appearance of a badly banged up store mannequin.

Peter kneeled down and removed the note that was written on cardboard and placed on a string around Tom's neck.

"Read it, Peter," Dave said to the group that had now fallen into an eerie silence. Even Will Henry was mute.

Peter held up the ten by ten inch board and read:

Quit going around in bunches and stay in your place or the same will happen to you.

"That's all it states," Peter said quietly.

"OK. Let's get him back to the truck," Dave said through clenched teeth and hands. "Let's get Tom home."

Ford Pasterway didn't know much about the Circle and their plans, but this calm and quiet among the men—and the lady—seemed dangerous to him. If only they would holler or curse! Ford could understand that. But the group did neither— not even the big redheaded fellow who had been exploding all day. But their faces! Jesus in heben!

There was no fear—none, but he had never seen such pain-and hatred!

These peepers were jus' gone explode afterwhile, he thought. Well, he was going to get his ass back to his cousin's house, thankful for the envelope that the white-looking boy had slipped him for his helping—although there was no charge—Yes! He was going to get his ass back to cousin Kempies in Old Steward and hope it was far enough away, because *sho as you wuz born ta die some shit was comin' down da Pike!*

FORTY-FIVE

*

Hattie Mackie was kept heavily sedated with herbs from John Candle that Lela had sent for.

"Da leaves will keep her away from her feelin's and would not hurm dat baby chile," the herbalist had said. They were to be used until after Tom's funeral.

Nearly everybody in West Steward and many from Old Steward were present at Tom Leak's funeral, which Dave insisted that Matthew preach, much to the annoyance of F.W.T. Edison.

Rev. Matthew Moses Clayton preached a beautiful sermon about the lovely spirit that resided in Tom, and humbly admitted that he believed that Tom had died in his place.

Everyone struggled to remain calm, but Will Henry Mead had to be physically restrained when a few white parents showed up with their children to attend Tom's funeral because he had so amused their children, and when one asked to speak and kept referring to Tom Leak as Tom the clown, Peter and Omar saw to it that Will Henry was given a brief drive down the Pike.

Even the Catholic Mexican Soliz brothers, who had never sat foot inside of a Protestant church before, attended and wept loudly.

After the funeral, Dave's captains called their men together in groups of ten and informed them of all that had happened in the past few days.

Elton Seals, the man from Tennessee, was immediately picked up after the men who were set to tailing him found out certain information: Elton Seals had left a wife and six children in Bolton, Georgia looking for a "better situation." If that included another wife that happened to have some money, that was just fine with Elton, and he had already proposed to Benjamin Carter's daughter, who was ugly as a bull frog but had saved up three hundred dollars to give to some lucky man in exchange for marriage.

Several times Elton and Flo Lee Carter had been headed for the altar, but Elton had been successful in delaying the nuptuals while borrowing another twenty dollars from the lucky bride to be. In the two months he had been in town, Elton had borrowed one hundred and twenty dollars from Flo Lee and had successfully increased his funds with snitching. It had taken only a few days of watching by Silas Benson before Elton Seals went directly to lay his "wares" before Sheriff Ansell Morrisey, the new sheriff. Being on the sheriff's payroll could only mean one thing: Sooner or later, for perhaps as little as two dollars, five dollars, some Negro's neck could be in a noose. The entire Circle had probably been betrayed.

Two days after Tom Leak's funeral in early February of 1931, Elton Seals, the white trash in the brown wrapper, disappeared from the hopeful dreams of Flo Lee Carter, leaving her with less bait to catch another fish, and was never heard from in West Steward, Arkansas again.

On Monday, five days after Tom was laid to rest, McCoy Harper came roaring into town from the New Addition on the back of a borrowed horse-borrowed because his three horses, eight pigs, four hundred chickens, four cows, and two mules were all dead.

"Had to be poison!" The distraught small farmer told the sheriff.

"Nah, Lawd have mercy! Ahm ruint," McCoy mourned. "I got nothin' mo' left but a wife and seven hoingry children! Who would do sich a thang to me?" he sobbed unashamedly.

Now, the Circle knew that Harper was Klan but they did not know until much later that they had the very man that hung the cardboard note around Tom's neck.

"Do you think hit wuz da feed?" McCoy asked the sheriff pitifully as an investigation was started.

In the end nothing was found. Not a drop of poison of any kind was found in the stomachs of the animals tested by the State Laboratories of Vetinary Medicine.

"Lordy!" exclaimed old Sheriff Jethro Lynn over in Old Steward when he heard the results from the laboratory. He was remembering a night not long ago when a sheriff, a deputy and two lawmen from Monroe County were taken to the emergency room. No poisons were found then either.

"Lordy!" The stout old sheriff exclaimed again. It was dat old African nigger back up in the weeds again. He just knew it. But he had no proof. And there was never going to be any way of getting any either.

The black men were making themselves scarce up in White Town.

Louis D. Stassen pronounced himself satisfied. A lynching always put niggers back in their box. A lynching was a cleaning thing, Louie D gloated. In the end he had agreed to K.D.'s plan of choosing a less inflammatory target in order to frighten the uppity preacher's followers out from under him. He could still be dealt with later if necessary. This McCoy incident was probably just a personal grudge, pure and simple. McCoy Harper carried enemies, that Louis D. Stassen knew. It was a very unfortunate thing to happen, especially in these times, but then every dog had to stand on his own two hind legs. And that was that.

Willie "Red" Oakes got stinking drunk on bootleg every Saturday night, and his cousin Parker Wilson enjoyed the ritual of arriving at his house a little before noon Sunday morning to rouse him with a bucket of ice water.

Willie had an unidentified medical condition that his friends found more laughable than serious. If Willie was "out" from drinking, and was not "drowned" with water he wouldn't wake up on his own until very late in the evening, and then would remain foolish, he called it, well into the next day. His cousin was glad to perform the wake up service and had done so for six months, every since Willie's wife, Clarice, had left him, taking his seven-year-old son, the only other thing he loved in the world besides his dog, Bitcha.

Parker arrived Sunday morning to do his duty.

His pail, which he had filled with water and left out overnight, now had a thin coat of ice across its top.

Even after dozens of times, Parker never tired of watching Willie Oakes holler and sputter and finally come alive from his dousing and say, "Thanks a heap! I sho' 'nough 'preciates hit!"

It was Willie's heartfelt gratitude that never failed to send Parker into a such a fit of laughing that it made leaving a hot woman in a warm bed every Sunday morning worth the trip.

Parker had left his water pail on top of the outhouse, and as he fetched it on his way up to his cousin's house, he thought it odd that Bitcha, Willie's big, old sloppy mixed breed hound, had not come lapping towards him by now, anxious for the tied up rag of scraps he always brought for him.

Pail in hand and a huge smile on his face, the cousin walked up to the back porch and stopped in the middle of the yard. His eyes saw it but his brain refused to register the scene. The pail of water flew from the man's hand and he froze momentarily, while his mind tried to assemble what he was seeing into a rationale whole to be imprinted on both his eyes and brain at the same time, in order to form a complete picture. Finally, the picture completed itself and the whole was staggering, causing Parker to trot backwards in such a rush that he nearly fell.

Slowly forcing his eyes upon the scene again, moving closer, he crouched in a running mode, puffing chilled air in front of his face. Parker looked up on the porch. Suspended by the neck on a chain from the ceiling of the back porch, directly at the entrance to the steps was the stiff cold body of the dog, Bitcha. The dog's stomach had been slit neatly from neck to tail, and congealed blood and guts spilled out on to the porch and down the steps. The body of the animal weighed heavily on the chain, causing it to twist and squawk plaintively in the frigid wind.

Parker's body bent itself in half and bitter greenish bile spewed from his belly. He was wet with sweat now, and having no weapon, he straightened up and hurriedly grabbed a large fallen tree branch, climbed over the side of the porch to avoid the dead dog, and, quaking in every limb, he prepared to face the dead body of his cousin and possibly be killed himself—perhaps by the same person who had killed Leon and Luxury. Parker had meant to enter the house carefully, quietly, but once he entered, anxiety and fear took over and he began to holler and kick open doors, then jump back with his branch, ready to foil escape attempts.

But hearing nothing but silence, Parker was sure he would find his poor cousin stretched out dead and bloody. Then he heard the familiar loud snoring coming from the small back bedroom. Quickly and more fearfully than he was willing to admit later, Parker searched the small four-room house, his stick at the ready. The man immediately found his cousin sleeping peacefully fully clothed, except for his shoes, waiting to be dragged out of bed and doused.

Breathing a heavy gasp of relief, Parker searched the house again and found nothing missing; this was a wrongdoing against Willie himself. Parker was greatly upset by how things were stacking up in West Steward—first McCoy and now

Willie. *It shoally did look like some kinda plan,* Parker thought, but his mind flitted and did not long rest on this idea.

When Willie was doused awake, his grief was "heavier den a mountain," he said, because he had slept "drunk as a skunk" while his beloved dog was "kilt lak a nigger."

Parker could not persuade Willie that the "person or peepers dat kilt Bitcha could have easily killed him, too. Dey didn't wanna kill you, dey jus' wanted to hurt ya real, real bad."

"Well, dey sho' done done dat!" Willie lamented.

"Why? Who? When?" The men asked each other. And what could the sheriff do in a case like this? the men asked each other. Nothing.

"Let's take dis whole entire thang to Louie D and go on call the sheriff if you wants to, Willie. 'Bout all he kin do is come look at a dead dog same as me."

It would take Louis D. Stassen, head of the Ku Klux Klan in Southeast Arkansas, to figure it out.

Louie D and a group of his boys, they called themselves, came back to Willie's place to look at the gutted dog.

Well Lawd have mercy!" Louie D. spat out, walking back and forth, eyeing the swinging animal. Seven of the ten men that came back with Louie got sick.

"Please!" Willie pleaded. "Let me take Bitcha down and bury her nah!"

"Naw. Not yet," Louie said. "I want all the boys to see dis. And let's keep dis quiet. No sheriff. I got a strong feelin' dis is pure Klan business and nobody else. So keep hit closed mouth, you heah?"

After most of the boys had seen the dog, Willie tried to dig a hole in the hard cold earth for a grave and the Klan met at Louie D's house that same night.

"Gentlemen, hard as hit is to believe," Louie D began, "I think some of dese niggers in dis town is going for bad and is putting themselves up against the Klan, if you can believe dat." Puffing out his jaws, he paused for dramatic effect. "Foolish, I sez. Real foolish!"

A relieved ripple of laughter now floated through the room, trying to push out the uneasiness that power was being stolen, challenged. But Louie D had just assured them such things would not be tolerated. They were white. They were all here together. They were the power structure here. There was nothing to fear— surely. Still, it would be comforting to hear Louie D's plans.

"Niggers powerful afeered o'fie," Louie D said, swaggering confidently among his boys. "Feered o'fire as dey is o' haunts!" he said, puffing on a cigar and smiling the devilish smile that he was known and loved for.

"Nah, boys, heah what we gone do."

Louie D. outlined the plan for the men, and they smiled with pleasure. It was safe, it was spectacular—and it would scare the living shit out of the burrheads. Soon, Louie D said, the Colored of the town would be begging whoever among them was responsible for this foolishness to cut it out, but quick. After they carried out this plan, Louie was sure things would quiet down again. They were disappointed that the lynching had not stopped the Negroes as expected, but now everything could get back to "white man's normal," Louie said.

FORTY-SIX

The Klansmen rode into the Bottoms at three in the morning two days after the dog had been found. They rode like a plague into the least protected and most poverty stricken area in Arkansas. It was said that people in the Bottoms existed mainly on wild greens and gruel, and that they wore their clothes until they fell off their backs. Bottoms babies often died in infancy, mothers often in childbirth, and Bottoms men in despair. Many Bottoms men and women were once sharecroppers who now lived on defunct farms, finding themselves with no money and no place else to go. Some folks worked for people in "town," white or Colored, when work could be found, but driven by the endless whip of crushing poverty, some Bottoms folk were given to stealing, lying, and cheating to gain a small advantage. And the few had given the many a bad name. To be labelled a "Bottoms Nigger" was fighting words among working class Negroes in Colored Town.

It was against these hapless souls that the Klan rode, trapping them in a circle of flames with kerosene soaked stakes flung at the roofs of shanty houses, so dry and poor that the fire seemed to sprout spontaneously.

One hundred and sixty-eight souls shattered the morning quiet with their screams as they ran in every direction. Bottoms residents sucked hot air and smoke into their throats and lungs as they cried out for family—husbands, wives, children, mothers, fathers—as the smoke burned and blinded their eyes, the flames licked at their bodies.

The Klansmen stood on an incline nearby watching, laughing, complimenting themselves on a job well planned, well done. It was better than a picture show, they said, as they quickly faded into the night, leaving three crosses on the incline.

It was a miracle that only two people were killed—a small baby left in the confusion and an old man who had suffered a stroke and could not move fast enough to escape before his shack exploded around him, trapping him in flames.

More than fifty heavily armed Circle members arrived at the scene of the fire just minutes after the fire had burned and destroyed the ramshackle homes in the desperately poor community. And Circle women arrived to bring order, organization and help to the hapless Bottoms people in their time of need, and they were speechless with gratitude.

"Klan work," Peter Frauzinou said bitterly to Dave Bailey as they watched the last of the flames crackle and destroy, and noted the three crosses.

"Of course," Dave said mildly. "We'll take care of it," he said with an arid little smile.

Meanwhile, Dave called a meeting of all the Circle captains and told them to get ready for some serious work.

"Serious work," Dave had said, as somber as anyone had ever seen him. Something much closer to the hearts of the white men than dead animals was about to be dealt with this time.

Aggie Pratt summoned her eleven Circle "wimmens" together and outlined the job that Dave was depending on her to handle. Aggie stood before them as they crowded around her kitchen table and outlined the plan. When they heard all of the details, many of the women, ages nineteen to sixty-three, could not contain themselves and burst out laughing, their whole bodies shaking with celebration.

"Well hit's about time!" was the sentiment of a number of those gathered, as they smiled and laughed and enjoyed the idea thoroughly. But Aggie's mouth only hinted at a smile and she even cut that in half, reshaping her lips for "very serious type business."

"Dere is a heap o' danger in takin' dis type work. Y'all know dat, don't cha?" Aggie asked.

"Sho'. And dere is danger in takin' a squat in der woods too. A snake might bite yo' behind! We gotta do what we has ta do!" Lucy Harvard said to a ripple of agreeing laughter.

"Ahm de oldest heah, I thinks," said Reza Mae Long, standing up, "and I'd be most proud tah gie hit a try—fact about hit I'd lak to start terday!" she said to loud applause from the women.

Helena came along to be of assistance to Aggie she said, and she busied herself unwrapping the dishes the women had brought to serve after the meeting. Now she said, "You don't seem to have any opposition, Aggie."

"Looks lak dat," Aggie smiled, this time wide and friendly.

"Nah, y'all see why dis is kinda wimmens work, don't cha?" Aggie asked, striving for inner calmness, but she could hardly wait to get started! Her heart hopped like a rabbit inside her chest. "I see y'all bustin wit' spirit lak I is," Aggie begin, earnestly, struggling to act "dignified" like Mother Bailey had told her to be. "And possible some y'all already may have an answer."

"I do!" a young tan girl called Howdy Abbot hollered out.

"Den don't say no mo'," Aggie suggested. "Does yo' white folks sospect dat you knows?"

"No mam! Not a thang!" Howdy nearly shouted again.

"Nah see," Aggie said again making every effort to call on that quietness inside herself that Lela said she must strive for as a leader, "we real excited, but 'member, too much of dat excitement draw suspicion—even death. Hi many y'all don't know what ahm talkin' 'bout?"

Nobody raised a hand.

To emphasize her point, Aggie pulled out her pistol. It looked surprising large and menacing in her small hand. She pointed the gun out at the women, her face tight and hard.

"Dis gun fully loaded and I see y'll ain't flinching a bit. Good. You is good brave wimmens. But let me tell you somethin'. I know hah to use dis pistol. I kin shoot da titties off a rat. And if ahm one o' you wimmens even down breathe one word 'bout what we doin'—to anyone, husmon, mammy, pappy, anyone—I swear to Gawd I'll shoot you right betwixt da eyes, or any wha else you wanna be shot, you heah me? We dealin' wit' life and death heah. Y'all all knowed Tom Leak. We doin' what we doin' fer him, as well as fer ourvaselves. Nah I could picked different wimmens," Aggie continued. "Dere is near twenty-five wimmens wit' us nah, but I picked y'all."

There were no questions. Everyone understood what they were to do. Both Lela and Aggie expected the older women who had worked in White Town the longest to report back first, and they did. If the women could not easily handle a "clean out," the Circle men would take care of the identified hiding place.

FORTY-SEVEN

~~~~~~

Reza Mae Long had worked for the Comfreys, owners of the largest dry goods store in Old Steward, for twenty-one years. In 1924, the Comfreys had proudly opened a smaller store in White Town in West Steward, and it was quite successful also, so the Comfreys were pretty well-to-do, most folks agreed.

Reza Mae enjoyed the pay but not the atmosphere of the Comfrey home because she knew that Scottsdale Comfrey, the forty-year old son and heir of the two stores, was a known Klan sympathizer.

Lately Reza Mae had been called on more than once to stay overnight to look after Scottsdale Comfrey's mother who was in failing health.

"Dats hi's I happened to be in da house when dey was doin' dey countin'. I was overnighting once mo' wit' dat sick old gal," Reza Mae now related to Lela Bailey and Aggie Pratt in Lela's kitchen as they sat talking quietly with Reza Mae Long, sixty-three, their first "return."

Reza Mae was very excited and would not be denied the long version of her tale, although Aggie was anxious to have her questions answered.

"Dey got a private graveyard see, way out back behind da house. All da big Comfreys be buried dere. Ain't suppose no mo' private graveyards in da city limits, but dey rich so dey do what dey please. Well, anyhow, I kept noticin' dat when I'm up real late at night wit' old Miz Comfrey, sometimes Miz Carol Anne and Mistah Scottsdale be wanting some hot cocoa and lak dat you know, and sometimes dey be talkin' real low. Well, I didn't think too much 'bout hit—jus' wonder why dey didn't carry dey selves to bed. But two, three times lately 'bout three, four in da moanin', I catched dem using dat big kitchen table to count up money—lots of hit wit' a big iron pot on da table. Dey thinkin' I done fell off sleepin' up near old Miz Comfrey. You run up on a lotsa things when you walk real quiet lak I kin do," Reza Mae said, praising her own cleverness.

374

"Anyway, I pretend I don't see no nothin'! Ain't hit funny hi if you act lak you don't see nothin', peepers think you actually don't see nothin'? Well anyhi, I say y'all want a nice cuppa cocoa? If dey got money all over da table dey jump, surprised a little by me, and dey say no, den I goes on 'bout mah business, after I git some hot tea fer old Miz."

"Yas, yas!" Aggie said trying to push things along a little.

Reza Mae cleared her throat and continued at the same pace.

"Pret soon Mistah Scottsdale, he git up, go outside."

"So, where he put hit?" Aggie asked with thinly concealed impatience, trying to hide rudeness with enthusiasm, but eager to know, especially since Reza Mae was the very first one to come back with information.

"In de family graveyard!" Reza whispered loudly, her eyes shining with mischief.

"Naw!" Lela whispered back.

"Yas mam! Rat out dere wit' dem dead folks! I be watching from an upstairs window in da dark."

The woman adjusted her old shawl, took a sip of tea and a few bites of the fried peach pie Lela had sat before her, and continued her story. "See, all white folks think Colored peepers be scared to death o' haunts. Well, I ain't scared o' no haunts! Hit's the live peepers you gotta watch out fer—not no dead ones!"

"Amen," Lela said, smiling at Reza Mae's good sense.

"Mistah Scottsdale had done dug a lil' ol' pretend grave, lak for a baby see. Hit had a headstone and everything. Even had a birth and death date on hit jus' lak hit wuz fer real. 'Cept dem Comfreys ain't never had no lil' boy name Thomas A. Comfrey. Never! I looked at dat stone real good one day in da daylight when ain't nobody home ta see me. Well, anyway, pret soon one nite heah comes Mistah Scottsdale. He got a shovel and he come jus' a-digging. He git him a hole, den he put somethin' in hit, da round iron pot I was tellin' you about. After he put dat pot in da hole, he fasten on da clamp lid, den he shovel back on da dirt, and he stomp hit down real smooth and good, den he rakes some leafs over hit. All dis time he keep looking round hisself every few minutes lak a squirrel hiding some nuts."

"Now, Reza," Lela said quietly, "when da money is removed, is dere any way dat you kin think of dat you could be blamed fer hit? Do anyone know you know hit dere?"

"No mam," Reza said proudly.

"Is you sho'?" Aggie added, with deep concern.

Reza Mae offered proof with another story: "One day last summer Miz Carol Anne ax me to come to the graveyard wit' her to clean up da graves. Mistah Scottsdale say rat in front o' mah face, 'Carol Ann, let your girl do somethin' else. Reza ain't goin' to go to no graveyard. Don't you know niggers scared o' haunts?' Den he laugh. Well, I didn't make hit no better, and no worser. From den on, I 'tend lak I'm really is 'fraid o' graveyards! Nah dem Comfreys think dats da last place I'd be fount!"

The women continued to come in with the requested information: Life savings cleverly hidden above a nailed up door frame. Small jars of paper money very tightly sealed with wax and cellophane and then hidden by pushing them down inside of larger jars filled with dark jams and jellies. A box with a considerable sum was placed in a hole in a wall then plastered and papered over. In the graveyard. In the ceiling. In the floor. Places clever and common. Money hidden in fruit jars in holes dug under the plentiful shit in the hen house, money in tin cans buried under the house...

Many of the Klansmen and Klan sympathizers, and many other men and women known to be troublesome and dangerous to Negroes, had money hidden all over West Steward and Old Steward. In many cases, these hidden hoards represented every bit of cash these men and women and their families owned in an increasingly bleak and financially terrifying world. Their stash was their hope, their joy, and fondest, surest security. And soon they would lose it all.

"Jus' tell me dis," Aggie asked one of the women who had identified a particularly clever hiding place. "How on earth did you find out wha dey had dat money hid at?"

Three of the women had found out where hidden money was in almost identical ways: There had been a small fire and master or mistress had run first to rescue hidden treasure—to save a single painting, to knock a hole in a wall in a certain spot, to save a single large jar of jelly.

Servants in the South, like servants the world over, missed little and pretended to see nothing. Black Southern servants used their assumed stupidity to their advantage in many ways.

Dave also told them that they would leave Reza Mae's graveyard job until last, and when they robbed it they would make it very sloppy and obvious, thus alerting everybody to check on their stash of money if they hadn't already, hoping a general panic among their enemies would be the result. And in that panic would be the Circle's continuing victories.

Will Henry Mead made the trip up to John Candle's place along with Peter Frauzinou, and LaSalle Peabody.

"Hi much you want?" the ancient man had asked.

"How much do we need?" asked Peter. Will Henry had stayed in the truck, for he had been exposed to "no hound powder" before and it made him sneeze violently.

The herbalist handed Peter a bag containing about two pounds of fine powder. He told them to wear gloves when handling it and not to get it in the eyes.

"When sprinkled very lightly all around da house you gone be working in, no dog in dis woil can pick up yo' scent," he giggled. Then, looking very serious and small, the old man said, "Is I done been any hep to y'all dese past weeks?" he asked, squinting his already tiny eyes at the two men.

Peter gently hugged the old man.

"Without you, very little would have been accomplished, Mr. Candle."

John Candle's eyes disappeared in the pleased wrinkles of his smiling face.

Would every one of the Klansman be hit? Rev. Clayton wanted to know when he was finally told what was being done.

"Of course not, Reverend." Dave said. "There were too many evil people involved to target them all. What will happen is *all* of them will be put on notice that they are not invulnerable, and we are not powerless! What we are taking is something more precious than money. We are taking away their self confidence, their sense of safety and security, and with that goes a great deal of their feeling of power and invincibility. Once a man's sense of being in control, of having power, and relative financial security is gone, what's left?" Dave asked.

"Faith," Rev. Clayton said simply.

"Not for these people, Reverend, do you think? If they had Christian faith we wouldn't have had a lynching would we?" Dave retorted.

At this statement, the pastor looked pensive as he puffed his fragrant pipe and sighed deeply, wondering what he could do or say to stop this insanity—on both sides. He gave another sigh, deeper and sadder this time, thinking briefly of their scattered plans for an all out economic boycott. It seemed that no one but him thought such a boycott might work—especially after Tom Leak was lynched. A boycott would have been too "iffy," to "indirect," the Circle thought, and one Circle member, Will Henry Mead, had caused the minister to shudder when he said, "Enough of dis pussy footin'! Hit's blood and guts time nah!"

Louis D. Stassen rarely missed attending church at True Love Baptist Church. The whole house, Louie D, his wife Theodora and their two grandchildren who were staying with them, left the house early so the children could attend Sunday school. Theodora was a member of the choir, and during these hard times, Rev. Garland Reeves thought it a fine idea for the woman folk to bring a little something "eatable" to share after the service.

What with the length of Rev. Reeves' sermons and the socializing afterwards, several pleasant hours were spent each Sunday at True Love Baptist by the Stassen family.

Louie D's habits were known, and when it was sure the family had not forgotten anything and would not be returning until around one-thirty in the afternoon, two young black men approached the Stassen house, each carrying large heavy cloth sacks. In one of these sacks was three pounds of beef chunks for Louie D's "nigger dogs." The dogs were reputed to be especially trained to tear Negroes apart on sight.

"Well, well," Silas Benson said, walking up to the fence to face the largest dog, who was already spinning around and running and jumping in a fury, trying to scale the fence and get at the young black men, or the fresh meat they smelled, or both.

"I told ya me and you wuz gone meet up one day Mistah Red Devil—ain't dat what dey calls ya? Well. Nah is yo' time and nah is mah time. Come on over heah. I brung you somethin'," Silas said reaching in the bag and standing back from the fence. He and his companion threw the chunks of meat in the center of the yard, and the dogs that Louie D kept half starved on purpose to make them extra fierce pounced on the meat, ripping and snarling, the young men forgotten.

In five minutes the dogs would be sleeping peacefully and would sleep for three hours. They would be awake and alert when the Klansman returned home. John Candle had promised them that.

The Stassens employed a black servant after their Mexican girl, Rosita, had gone off to Texas to bury her sister and had never returned. The Stassens had counted the money at least once since Rosita had left. The black woman—their girl—knew nothing of their hiding place, the Stassens were sure, because for one thing, she was not allowed in the bedroom. Now the woman, Charley Mae Davis, had left to work elsewhere three months ago and had not been replaced.

After slipping into rubber gloves and sprinkling their No-Hound powder, the two men who entered the house quickly found the papered over spot in the bedroom with the picture of a vase of lillies hung above the bed. Silas and his partner moved the double bed to the side. The wallpaper peeled down relatively easily without tearing, as if it had been only glued around the edges and had been taken down before—which it had.

The walls behind the painting revealed a discolored spot about twelve inches across and about eight inches high. The plaster was weak and powdery, held in place by chicken wire, easily punched out, and as easily replaced.The men quickly punched out the hole, pulled out the chicken wire, and shined their flashlight into the opening. Silas saw a small flat metal box in the wall opening which was about six or eight inches deep. There was nothing else in the opening.

Silas removed the box, and looking at its small lock, placed the box in the cotton sack he carried over his shoulder, then the men stopped and listened intently. A truck horn would signal an approach being made to the house, or something wrong. They heard no signal, so they replastered the hole, using a small hand cranked fan to quick dry the plastered spot as much as possible. They re-glued the wall paper and re-hung the painting, cleaned up the area, again sprinkled around the door where they had entered with No-Hound, got back in the truck and sped off. The entire job had taken less than an hour.

They noted on their way back to the truck that the five Klan dogs had finished their meal and were still sleeping "as peaceful as if dey had died and went to heaben," their driver remarked, laughing.

When the Circle men returned with Louie D's money, they found that Aggie had discovered through her "informers" that another family had left to visit aged parents over in Old Steward, would be away from their home for hours, and were also Klan. The opportunity to do a second clean-out, although unplanned, was too good to pass up.

Jimmy Boggins often joked that he did not consider his day complete unless he had walked at least half a dozen big strong niggers off the cement.

Once LaSalle had slipped into the Boggins' house, it was easy to remove the frame above the door. When he was finished, he replaced the now empty envelope back under the ledge and nailed the frame neatly back to the wall, then he slipped out of the back door and down to the truck where Omar and Will were waiting.

"Did you git hit?" Will asked.

"Sho'." LaSalle said confidently. "Nah lessee hi many niggers Jimmy Boggins gone feel lak walkin' off da sidewalk when he find his four hundred and eighty dollars gone!"

Three days passed as the Circle waited anxiously, hoping the two completed clean-outs were not discovered yet, hoping hidden money was not checked on, was not disturbed until badly needed.

The Circle wanted to finish the other jobs before the jig was up and stashes were removed from other known hiding places—from the ceiling above the light fixture, from the large tin tobacco can that was stuffed tightly then cleverly placed in a hollowed out log, to the money sewn inside the pillows on a couch, to the envelope taped to the back of the dresser drawers, the money pushed up in metal pipes that were lying innocently in the attic.

The money.

Once all of the known stashes had been raided, then the little fake burial plot that Reza Mae Long had identified would be very obviously dug up, thus alerting the other Klansmen to check their hiding places—too late.

"And there will be weeping and wailing and gnashing of teeth aplenty!" Dave had laughed, loosely quoting the Bible.

Helena continued to express her deep concern that the housekeepers would be the very first ones suspected.

"No mam, lak I tole ya befoe, and Mistah Dave knows dis," Smitty, an elderly woman belonging to Aggie's group, explained. "White folks think we too scared to peep and poke where dey say not ta go—and o' cose dats percisly where we be most interested in. I done peeped and poked to mah old heart's content, but nobody knows hit. Dats hi we see what we see. Besides not a one o' us got a job in nobody's house up in White Town nah. Nah everybody done gone and forgot we ever did have a possible chance to see somethin', I bet ya."

Hearing this, Helena relaxed a bit. If these former housekeepers, out of work now because of the Depression, were not afraid, she decided to try and adopt their brave attitude—with mixed results. Helena knew she had simply forgotten how to fine tune herself to many aspects of Southern living, and was having adjustment problems on occasion. She still could hardly bear going into stores and waiting for all the whites to be served before her own request was taken—not to mention other indignities—she told Dave, which those who had never left the South bore as a matter of course.

Luck—Rev. Clayton liked to think prayers—were with the group.

After a month the "clean-out" work was nearly finished, and without one incident. Only one woman had never known the hiding place of the family she had once worked for, and her failure caused her to cry bitter tears of regret.

As an added bonus, the merchants in both West Steward and Old Steward were complaining loudly because "the Colored" were not shopping with them hardly at all since that man was lynched, but were taking their business to the Jones' store, or going without. And since blacks were seventy to one hundred percent of their business, the merchants suffered and offered credit and nearly begged.

"Buy from me, won't ya, Sam? You know I got a better product den dat peckerwood Larry. Buy from me and I'll throw in..."

Their begging caused Dave to remark to Rev. Clayton that he had his boycott after all.

"They are desperate, but they still serve a white person with a dime before a Negro with ten dollars," Peter Frauzinou said crossly. "Well, we'll see about that in a little while!"

"Yes, we will, Peter," Dave said to his friend smiling and winking good naturedly. It was another one of the rare times anyone had seen Dave Bailey smile since Tom Leak had been lynched.

FORTY-EIGHT

Although Mason never gave her a snippet of credit, Jane Biltree, Mason's wife, was the smart one in the family. Because she had persuaded Mason not to put his money in the bank in Old Steward, when the run on the bank started the Biltrees lost not a cent.

Two years before the Crash, Jane had fought to purchase a large, seven-room house for their expanding family, and Mason had been loath to part with the eight hundred dollars it took to buy the house and the five acres of land, but now it was he who was always eager to show off "their place" to his friends, and watch them go ga-ga over the large kitchen, the indoor toilet, the grove of fruit trees, and the black walnut pods falling off his trees. With thrift and good sense, Jane Ash Biltree, who was as plain as she was smart, had, by canning and sewing for her family and owning chickens and livestock, managed to preserve most of their capital. After the house was purchased, there was nineteen hundred dollars left. Except for feed for the livestock and chickens, Jane never spent more than one dollar a week of their money now.

"If we are careful," she said, "we'll come out of this Depression with enough money to start a little business."

Mason wanted to be thought of as one of the big business boys, like the mayor's crowd over in Old Steward. Hell, with nineteen hundred dollars in his possession, he could hardly be thought of as "po' white trash," he thought proudly.

It was a good match, people said. Jane married Mason because he was the best looking boy at Washington Heights High—and the dumbest.

And Jane Ash was the smartest girl—and the plainest, even though she had sky blue eyes and hair the color and texture of corn-silk.

Jane Ash wanted Mason and she never allowed herself to think of what a whole lifetime spent with a stupid man would be like.

Jane Ash wanted a steady boyfriend, which she had never had, wanted someone to moon over her like the boys did over pretty girls, so she went after the dumb as a stick Mason, whom she knew she could easily trick into getting her pregnant. A few well placed tears behind a swelling belly and the deed was done.

They were married a month after high school graduation—she was first in the class, Mason was second from the bottom.

The things Jane did not approve of about her husband were legion, but the most disturbing was his Klan connections. Jane Ash did not share her husband's mindless hatred for Negroes and she often told Mason that, "One day, hanging around with that Klan trash is going to land you in trouble."

Jane had been extremely displeased when her husband told her, "You know that feller what usta dance and carry on up in White Town? Well, I was there when they roped him a few days ago."

Their money, Mason and Jane's, was hidden in an envelope taped behind a dresser drawer. Jane had been after her husband to move it for quite a while. "Put it in a metal box in the ground," she said. "Earth does not burn."

"I will," he said. "Next week." Next week turned into a year.

"What if we have a fire?" Jane wailed.

"I'm the man of the house, I'll take care of it. Don't you bother dat money! It was left to me by *my* folks! Next week I'll go into town and get a metal box and bury the money in the ground."

Jane took the children, all five of them, including Fig, the three-month-old baby and the only boy, for an outing, she called it. Exercise was good. They would walk the two miles up the road to visit her mother and father, who did not care for their dumb son-in-law, but doted on their beautiful, smart grandchildren.

Mason was glad for the peaceful silence of the house without the constant buzz and hum of the women folk. He could use the absence of his family to do something else that had been on his mind for weeks. Mason wanted to put some money in his pockets. He had heard that even now, during these slack times, some of the big business men over in town had one hundred dollars in their billfolds each and every day! Of course they never spent it, but just imagine having that kind of money for show! Although his wife had warned him about bragging, the idea nipped at his heels, and would give him no peace. He had to put some "flash" money in his pockets, too. Hell, it was his money! Left to him by dead parents. He had a right if he wanted to.

Mason decided he would be very content with only fifty dollars "walking around" money. That was more than a respectable "walking" sum these days.

Jane Ash Biltree, Mason thought, would give him five hundred dollars worth of hell, if she knew he was even thinking about the money that was hidden behind the "chesterdrawers" —that is why he would not tell her about it. Mason would pull out the drawer and set it on the bed, then he would carefully slide five ten dollar bills out of one of those envelopes, go out and break three tens down to thirty single dollars and sandwich them, top and bottom between two tens, creating a fat looking roll.

Jane would not need to take anything out of the envelopes for another week. Next week she would remove her monthly money to buy things they could not grow: coffee, sugar, a little cheese, perhaps a jug of sorghum. Mason figured a week would give him time to come up with some reason to offer as to why he now had fifty dollars from their hiding place in his pockets if Jane bothered to count how much was left.

Mason went into the largest bedroom and pulled out the sizeable middle drawer. He was quick, careful and quiet, even though there was no one in the house to hear noise. Carrying the long deep drawer to the bed with shaking fingers, the man turned the drawer around to face him. The heavy brown money envelope was puffy but not greatly so, for the cash was mostly in twenties.

Mason carefully removed the tape. He was being careful, almost respectful. Lifting the flap of the envelope, the man gazed at newspaper, cut precisely the size of bills. The envelope flew to the floor, scattering some of the paper "bills" and, with trembling hands, Mason stooped and picked it up. His first thought was that his wife had removed the money and was playing a bad trick. The second thought pushed the first one out rudely: Jane Ash Biltree was the most serious women in Arkansas. A trick was unknown to her way of thinking—even a smile was nearly a stranger to her face.

Where then was the eighteen hundred and seventy-five dollars?

Just twenty-five cash dollars had been spent all of last year.

Had it been stolen by thieves so smart that they stopped and cut paper?

In a frenzy, Mason wrecked the house. He pulled out every drawer in every room, strewing diaries, pressed flowers, and private and precious young girl secrets all over the floors. But no money was found.

Not a dime.

Wet with perspiration, Mason finally jumped in his truck and headed for his in-laws' house. He arrived in less than five minutes.

Jane Biltree was relatively calm when Mason told her the story, showed her the envelope with the precisely cut paper bills.

"Was a note left with this cut paper, Mason?"

"No!"

"Do you have any idea who may have done this, Mason?"

"No. No, I shoally do not!"

"But you will agree that some pretty curious things have been happening to white people in this town lately, won't you, Mason? Things that have never happened to white people before?" Jane said, pulling on her coat, rushing the children around to leave.

"What you mean, sugar puddin'?" Jane's father asked, rocking in a chair he had made himself. "You think Colored done took that money?"

"You know what I mean, Daddy. People gitting killed. Jail breaks. White people being run out of Colored Town at gunpoint after Colored people jumped from trees and threatened them. Burning down property owned by white people. All of that, Daddy, and not one soul in jail, not even one suspect!"

"She right, Taylor," Jane's mother grunted. "Not narry a suspect," she said to her husband as if he didn't know.

"And that's not all, Mama. Now, Colored people are starving white people," Jane continued pushing the girls out of the door.

"Now hi is that, sugar puddin'?" her father asked again, not rocking now.

"Why, they refuse to buy a thing from the merchants. Not a slab of salt meat, not a bag of beans, nothing!"

"Why, honey, Colored ain't got no money jus' lak the rest of us nah."

"Mama, please! Surely you know better than that? Just ask anybody that happens to go through Colored Town on Sunday morning! You smell steak frying, and liver and onions, and biscuits baking, coffee, everything! The Negroes are buying from somewhere, I'll tell you that!"

"But what about our money!" Mason howled again. "What niggers is doing I don't care about! Where is our money?!"

Jane Ash Biltree smiled one of her rare smiles. "Don't you see? It's all connected." Jane said simply. "Come on, girls. We're going to ride back home."

"What you mean connected up?" Mason said when he had his family in the truck. "If you know where that money is, you oughta tell me!" Mason raged. "This ain't no kinda trick, Jane!" But Jane held the baby and said only, "We'll discuss this when we get home—mister."

When Jane, who prided herself on a clean and orderly house, saw the wrecked state that her husband had left things in, she held her temper just long enough to send the children into the oldest girl's, Delilah's, bedroom.

"Kindly lock the door, Delilah, and do not come out until I tell you," Jane said, handing the baby to her oldest, who was fourteen.

"Yes, Mama!" The children said in unison, glad to escape those now pencil line lips, those darting eyes, that certain angle of Mama's up-thrusted chin that told them she was real mad!

When the children were safely locked away, Jane was ready to deal with her husband.

"Now, mister!" Jane began. "Haven't I been a good wife? Haven't I come near death five times to birth your babies? Haven't I scrimped and saved every penny you ever brought into this house trying to secure our future somehow? And now you have ruined this family! You have taken our pearls and thrown them to swine!"

"What is you talkin' about, Jane?" Mason asked, his dark eyes blank with honest bewilderment. "You better have a seat, you gittin' all excited."

"I will not sit down, mister! Don't you know that money was stolen and we'll never see it again? Never! We are now destitute, mister! And you brought this on us!"

"Me? How you figure that?"

"This was a clever deal, mister! That money was taken and someone knew exactly where it was. No doubt due to some of your drunken bragging!"

"No, no, no!"

"And someone took the time to cut newspaper to the exact size of paper money. Now that took forethought. That took planning, Mason!" Jane shouted.

Lord, he could not stand it when Jane stood up to him this way, when she hollered and screamed and called him mister! Mason would bet that the children's ears were plastered to the bedroom door. What would they think, this house full of women, the mother getting the best of the father this-a-way?

"Klan," Jane said. "Don't you see the Klan is responsible for this? I begged you to stay away from them, but no, you had to be the big man. What were you doing messing with that money anyhow, Mason? Answer me!"

Jane was in his face, so close he could see the little hairs in her nostril, smell the onions she had for dinner. The plainness he thought he had gotten used to, resigned to. The buckteeth, short chin, too wide cheeks, small piggish blue eyes, the long and flaring nostrils, the thin as goodness on earth lips. Gosh Almighty, the woman was the ugliest of all his friend's wives, and even more homely in her red faced anger.

"Hi you figure the Klan had something to do with the money, Jane? You think the Klan stole our money?"

The weight of her husband's ignorance hung around her neck like an affliction, and Jane knew she would never be free of it—and no amount of good looks could make up for his stupidity.

She sat down and patiently told her husband her theory. She thought that the Negroes had organized into some kind of a group and were punishing those that were unjust to them. Jane then ticked off the recent events in the order that they had occurred: first the murders, which may or may not have been committed by Negroes, Jane said. Then she had heard that the Duster boy, who was a possible suspect, had left town with his entire family. Next the sheriff's snitch, whom everyone knew was a snitch, disappeared. Another suspect appeared, Jane continued, and he was sprung out of jail and a white man's property was burned to the ground as an obvious distraction. Then, there was the incredibly bold tree incident up in Colored Town, and finally things got much worse as livestock was killed, the dog of a known Klansman was slit from stem to stern, and now, after a lynching, instead of things getting better for white folks, they were getting worse!

"I bet you anything that more Klan money is going to disappear—or has already!" Jane concluded.

Mason stared at his wife after her tirade. As usual, he was unconvinced by her logic.

"Whataya mean things are gitting worse, Jane? You know, none of what you said makes any sense to me."

Suddenly Mason felt terribly uncomfortable. He wanted to leave the room for a piss, a cup of coffee, a smoke, anything, but he dared not—not when Jane's hair had come undone this way and her thin lips were curved in that hateful, know-it-all smile. When his wife got this way, which was fairly often, Mason knew from personal experience it was better to control your bladder than leave the room.

"Whataya mean? Whataya mean? Mason, you are an idiot! A four-star dunce.

A moron. An out-and-out fool! Whataya mean! Is that all you can think to say?"

"Jane! The children! You don't want them to hear their daddy and mama fussing and fighting like this, do you? Please don't call me a fool, Jane."

"A complete packaged up fool!" Jane hissed. "Can't you see that the Negroes are striking back? What's the matter with you all?"

"Well, if that's what they trying to do, all we gotta do is go to the sheriff, or Louie D," Mason Biltree said indignantly. "I know they got a hand on it already!"

Jane threw her head back and laughed bitterly.

"Yeah, you all go 'head and take it all to the sheriff—even the mayor!" Jane laughed. "And if you just can't find out who is killing dogs and poisoning livestock, murdering folks, and stealing money and replacing it with cut paper, then why, you all can just get busy and lynch each and every Negro in Phillips County. That should be easy," she sneered.

Mason looked thoughtful, as if considering this possibility momentarily.

"Come on out, children!" Jane yelled, and the children tumbled out of the room, where they had been pressed up against the door listening to every word.

Mason found himself walking the mile and a half down to his friend Scooter Fend's place. Jane made him leave the truck. She was going into town—without him, she said—although she had only a quarter in her pocket for shopping. But she was not going shopping, she was going for air. Going to keep from losing her mind.

Mason had stuffed his hands deep in his pockets for warmth, and his thighs moved quickly against the wind that had suddenly become biting and filled with little chips of ice. As he moved along, he felt his heart beating from the briskness of his walk, and the twenty extra pounds he had put on in the last months of "just sittin' around doin' nothin'." He was also gripped by hard cold fear. *Gawd!* What would they do without that nearly nineteen hundred bucks? The only other money they had was the six bits he had in his pants pocket and the quarter Jane said she had. *Gawd-a-mighty!*

Mason stopped along the road to relieve himself. Having already used the toilet before he left home, this was a nervous piss rather that a necessary one.

Jane said she was positive that Scooter Fend's money was gone too if the Negroes were avenging themselves like she thought they were. She said she was sure Scooter's money was gone, if nobody else's, because he was always bragging about his one accomplishment in life so far: his "secret" Klan membership. Well, he would just prove Miss Know Everything a liar. Niggers would not dare to break into Klan homes. Would not dare!

Then who had taken his money—and then rubbed it in his face, Jane said, by not just taking the money and leaving, but by laughing at him with cut paper? Surely not some old tramp, Jane said, just passing through.

Mason's mental powers did not take him far. Someone else would have to figure out the whys and whens of this one. He was sure Louie D or the sheriff could do so, and Mason was content to leave the solution in someone else's hands. He was sure his wife was wrong. This was stuff for men, not his wife, to figure out.

Reaching Scooter's small rented house, Mason pounded on the door and rushed in with such force after Scooter's thirteen-year-old son opened it that he nearly knocked the boy over.

"Where's Scooter?" Mason shouted. Instead of being calmed by his walk, it had the opposite effect. Now Mason felt near panic.

Scooter's wife Marjean, raw-boned and red-headed, met Mason with blood-shot eyes, her lips scrowled down. She had obviously been crying.

"Scooter layin down restin'—and git rid o'dat cigarette would ya please? Da smell makes me sick at the stomach," Marjean said with uncharacteristic sharpness.

A sickness at the stomach? Did the tears mean Marjean was expecting again? Mason wondered. One night recently, when Mason had reached for his wife after she had bathed with her one bar of fine lemon soap and let down her corn silk hair, Jane had raised her foot and caught him squarely in the stomach with such force that he had nearly puked and came close to being kicked out of bed.

"My capacity for pumping out babies is not limitless, you know!" his wife had seethed. "You want to be like the po' white trash from the hills trailing fifteen chilluns' into town behind you?" she had asked, her voice ugly and sharp.

"Is Scooter sick?" Mason asked of Marjean.

"No."

"Well, kin I see 'em?"

"I reckon," his wife said sullenly, going back to a tiny garment she was repairing. Mason saw tears fall on the little shirt.

Scooter was lying in the sparsely furnished unheated room covered by a heavy quilt. He seemed to be fully dressed even to his shoes. He was lying quietly staring at the ceiling.

"You a rich man? You got time for layin' around in broad daylight?" Mason asked, attempting humor when he saw how beaten down his friend appeared.

"You know I ain't got no work no mo'," Scooter responded without moving or inquiring about Mason's presence. "But I wuz jus' thinkin' 'bout you. I wuz gonna git up and come down dere."

"Anythin' wrong?" Mason asked edgedly.

"Gawd damn right. Somebody done been in heah and stole every damn dime of ourva money! Every penny I done scraped and saved for years!"

"Naw!" Mason burst out, more surprised than not. "You say stole? Well, where was it? When did it happen? How much was it? Who do you think did it? Why?"

Jane was right. Again. Mason felt disaster drop over him like a storm cloud. He felt hot and sick and about to throw up. Mason looked for the slop jar out of the corner of his eye, just in case.

Scooter kicked the quilt from around his feet and sat up on the side of the bed in the small room. It was clear he had been crying too.

"Man, oh man!" he howled, putting his face in his hands. Mason moved over to his friend, sat on the side of the bed and patted Scooter's shoulders. He knew nothing else to do. He felt waves of nausea pass through him, and he kept swallowing in an effort to keep from throwing up.

When Scooter finally got a little control of himself he told Mason the following story: In the fifteen years that he had been married, he and Marjean had managed to save four hundred dollars. Not so bad if you still had a job. Last year they had given serious thought to buying a house, something of their own with half the money, but then the Panic hit and everybody with any sense was scared to death to spend a dime. Their money had always been hidden in their house, but now they found a better place than they had before—a little black potbellied stove that Scooter said he had planned to get a length of tin chimney for and vent it to the outside of the bedroom they were in, but decided it would be a smart place to hide their money. They would leave the tin chimney lying by the stove as if they were going to vent it outside any day. Well, that unhooked up stove musta been the first place they looked.

"Who?"

"Musta been one of dose mens dat is forever roaming through heah now looking for work, taking everythin' that ain't nailed down. Who else?"

"How you find out that money was gone? You check it every day?"

"Naw," Scooter said, not minding telling his friend everything. Mason could help you. Mason had graduated from high school and he, Scooter, had only finished the sixth grade, so Scooter had always had great respect for Mason's better schooling.

As for Mason, who did not get respect and admiration from many, it was good to have Scooter to talk to after your own wife had denounced you as the biggest fool in Arkansas.

"Naw, fact is we hate to look at hit at all, 'cause when you look, that means you 'bout to take. Wit' no jobs no wha, hi long dat money gone last? You ax hi we found out hit was gone? Well, we went a tad over at Christmas—cakes, pies, few little toys, candy, fruit, and all. So we low on flour, sugar, salt, pepper, lak dat. And I hate to admit it, but we had to replace near all the regular provisions too. Rice, and lard, beans, Irish potatoes, onions, jus' about everything we don't put up in jars. So Marjean went to git three dollars to go ta town wit'. Dats when we knowed da money was gone."

"You talk to the children?"

"They don't know nothin' from nothin'. Dey never knowed wha da money was hid. And on top o'dat," Scooter said, eyeing Mason pitifully.

"Marjean expectin' again," Mason said, finishing his friend's sentence.

Scooter looked at Mason as if he were the smartest man in the world. "Hi you know dat? She ain't that far yet."

Scooter finally thought to ask Mason if he had heard of anyone else "gittin' dey money stole?"

"Just me, Scooter," Mason said in a voice nearly too mournful and low to be heard, but glad to share this pain, to rub it around, thus spreading it and making it less intense like one did with a bumped knee.

Richard "Scooter" Fend shot up from his bed.

"What did you say?! Dey done got you too? You joneing, shoally!"

"Naw sir, I wish I wuz."

Scooter hollered for his wife, he was eager for her to hear of this double misfortune that was a crying shame!

The three of them crowded into the bedroom.

"We double sorry, Mason—and terribly surprised!" Marjean said.

"Triple sorry," said Scooter with a smile so anxious and bitter that it was merely an upward flicker of his lips. " 'Cause to tell you da honest ta Gawd truf, Mason, me and Marjean was kinda lookin' to you and Jane to kinda help us over the hump until we got back on ourva feets. So, hi much dey git you fer, if you don't mind mah axing, old buddy?" Scooter said.

"Close to six thousand dollars," Mason lied. He was not afraid of contradiction by Jane later. The woman, he knew, was secrecy itself.

"Six thou...?" Both of the Fends let out yelps of surprise and admiration.

"Boy! I didn't know you peckerwoods wuz dat rich!" Scooter said, his voice filled with awe.

" 'Was' is right, Scooter. I'm sitting here trying to be cool, but I feel like I'm 'bout to bust wide open!" Mason said, again feeling the surge of fear he first felt when he saw the cut paper.

The pale and wan Marjean sat on the side of the bed and whispered tearfully, "What is happening Mason, what is happening?"

Mason Biltree told the couple Jane's idea about the Negroes striking back.

"Can't be!" Scooter burst out when Mason had finished. "Niggers sho' ain't dumb enough to go up against the Klu Klux Klan!"

"I think y'all should git on over to Mistah Stassen's house fast as y'all kin." Marjean said. "He in charge. He'll know what to do. Y'all think dey done took any money from him?"

"Hell no!" the friends answered in unison.

"And mark my word, Marjean. Nothin' in this world is gonna convince me niggers is behind this! They wouldn't even dare!"

Louis D. Stassen was over in Lee County. His wife, Theodora Stassen, said he would be back tomorrow. So Mason and Scooter got back in Mason's truck which Jane Biltree finally decided to let her husband drive, and headed for Mason's five acres.

On the way, Scooter squirmed in his seat, hardly ever confident enough to advance an idea, thus the nickname Scooter—his squirming and scooting around was his way of letting you know something was on his mind and he hoped you had the good sense to notice his scooting and ask what it was.

"Quit polishing dat truck seat wit' yo' ass, and tell me what's on yo' mind," Mason said around the cigarette clenched between his teeth.

"Well, I was jus' thinkin'."

"Really?" Mason said sarcastically, not in the mood for hemming and hawing.

"Well, hit's jus' dat..."

"Come on, Scooter. Come on, Scooter!" Mason encouraged.

"Wouldn't it be a good idea, maybe, I mean, since we have to wait until tomorrow any hi?"

Mason stopped the truck, pulled over and sat looking expectantly at Scooter, his cigarette hanging from his lips. Waiting.

"Wouldn't hit be an iddy, maybe, to talk to mo' den jus' you and me about dis money lost thang? Not dat I agrees wit' what Jane be sayin' atall, though she pret smart fer a woman, see what I mean?" Scooter said finally.

"You mean Woody and Pongee and Sneel?"

"And mebbe Otha and Vernon and Claymont thrown in fer good measure, huh?"

"Seems like a pretty good idea to me!" Mason said, causing Scooter to smile as he always did when one of his ideas was found acceptable to his good friend Mason, who was, after all, a high school graduate.

Mason and Scooter visited them all, and with very little prompting the story of a mysterious thief who had visited six of the eight men came to light. The six men were pitiful to see, to talk to, for they were shattered and ruined men, dead broke in these disastrous times, with not the slightest hope of employment. They did not have to search long for a common thread: All of the six men who had now gathered themselves with the others in the bosom of Vernon Kenzie's large shed and repair shop had Klan ties. All six of the men who now found themselves "cleaned-out" had been present at most of the lynchings that had occurred in the twin towns. Five had been present in the Colored Woods that night when Tom Leak's high spirits were silenced forever.

Each man inflated what he had lost to the others—as if it mattered now. Each man lied his loss double. And Scooter, with his admission of his real loss, had always been the poorest among them—now he turned out to also be the most truthful.

The men in the repair shop cried to each other that they had lost a total of thirty thousand dollars. Actually, their loss was less than a quarter of that much, but who was to know?

FORTY-NINE

Power often followed money out of the window, and these men were not anxious to admit the loss of either—especially to those outside of their circle of friends. Louie D would be back tomorrow and they would wait for him to make the decision about whether the sheriff should be called in.

No one had ever waited for dawn as eagerly as these men waited for their leader, Louie D, to come home from Lee County.

Louis D Stassen was not happy to be confronted with a new set of problems, especially of this magnitude, for over in Lee County he had been severely reprimanded by a representative of the Grand Dragon. They had heard how "sassy and out of hand" niggers were getting in Phillips County—the murders, the jail breaks, the poisoning of livestock, and the tree incident. There was just no end to it and "by Gawd, niggers just could not be allowed to run over white folks" the way they were doing and he, Louis D. Stassen, had better get a hand on matters or else!

Louie D's new determination was met with a new crisis that was, in many ways, worse than all of the other incidents put together. The group of men in Vernon Kenzie's repair shop had collected others, and when the Klan leader walked into his yard on the day of his return, he found twenty-four panic-stricken men looking to be soothed, pacified, and re-directed. When Louie D heard their tale, saw the teeth-chattering fear in their faces, he experienced such fury and frustration that he was hardly able to contain himself, to be the good level-headed leader that the situation called for.

Someone had attacked the Grand Knights of the Ku Klux Klan?

"Pre-pos-toe-rus!" Louie D thundered and sputtered as convincingly as he could, but even though he was the Exalted Cyclops, he felt nearly as hopeless and powerless as the men in his living room felt—although he was not about to show it to men so angry and scared and restless that they seemed more a mob than a group of friends.

The Cyclops knew the question the gathered men dared not voice, the answer they wanted to know, but were afraid the knowledge would destroy them all completely. Had Louis D. Stassen, Exalted Cyclops of South East Arkansas, been robbed too? No one dared put forth such a question, and Louie D, having just returned from Lee County, had not had time to check his hiding place yet.

The panicked men sighed and shuffled, and stayed longer than they needed to in Louie D's "meeting room," wearing welcome as thin as a pie crust, Louie D thought. Truth was, Louie D was tired and anxious for these men to leave. Thoughts about the safety of his own money were uppermost in his mind, especially since the men had ferreted out a possible relationship between loss and Klan connection. It all made sense, but they wouldn't dare! Would they? Not to an Exalted Cyclops. *No Lawd!*

But Louie D was uneasy, agitated and woefully weary.

"Y'all jus' git along home nah, boys," the leader urged. "Everythin' gone be took care to yo' satisfaction. I kin guarantee dat."

The men had been waiting to hear these exact words, though they did not know it, waiting like children, like sheep, to be led to the green pastures of assurance, safety, and security.

Louie D was back! Why, he might even be able to recover their money, some of the sheep hoped. Louie D would make it right for white people in this town again. The sheriff had failed. The mayor had failed. Now only Louis D. Stassen held the keys to the Golden Gates of reinstatement and power. The men put all of their trust in him and moved slowly out of his front door.

Louie D listened until he was sure the last truck, car, and wagon had left his place along with their mouthfuls of lies about forty-five thousand dollar losses. He would wait another few minutes to make sure somebody had not forgotten something and doubled back—maybe to see if they could find Louie D scurrying around, perhaps looking for his money.

Theodora Stassen had heard everything from the next room, and when the men left she came in "tremblin' like a sheet on a clothes line," Louie D thought, and colorless as a haunt. He told her to sit by the stove with him and they would wait "ten minutes or so" together, warming up and simmering down.

The twin towns, sitting auspiciously as they were, Old Steward being on the very banks of the Mississippi River, had been in better times plagued, the residents laughed, with the money-making noise and dust of sawmills twenty-four hours a day, stifled with the golden sweet and acrid scent of Muellers soap factory, and prevented from naps during the day by the clunkety-clunk of Walter T. Reeves' chicken processing machinery, the largest in Arkansas. Now the twin towns were nearly silent day and night. It was a scary kind of quiet that meant heartache, hard times and, in many cases, near starvation.

Louis D. Stassen and his loyal wife now sat motionless, waiting in wrenching silence. It was the worst ten minutes of their lives.

When it was time to move, to check their hiding place, both Louie D and his wife found themselves moving slowly—not jumping up and around as one might expect.

"Nah, sugar, don't worry yourself none. Dat money right wha we put it. Right exactly wha we left it. Of dat I am certain," the husband said, looking into his wife's eyes, beaming all the courage and confidence he could to her with soft looks and hard squeezes of hand. His efforts were almost a prayer.

Louie D and his wife walked into the bedroom and approached the badly painted picture of lillies that hung on the bedroom wall that was papered with large orange and yellow flowers with dark brown leaves on a cream background. Behind the painting of lilies was the plastered wall holding a flat metal box. In this box was the wealth of the entire Stassen family.

Louie D's two daughters and their husbands had nothing to speak of but children and debts. When money was needed, which was often, the girls always made their way to daddy's house. So all that the Stassen family owned was now in this little box. Theodora had wisely suggested that some of their money should stay at home—this was the amount, thirty-six hundred dollars, that had escaped the Panic. The only other money the Stassens had was the one hundred dollars Louie D always carried as "flash" and the five dollars in Theodora's pocketbook.

"You ready, honey bunch?" Louie D asked his wife, as they started to very carefully peel the loose paper back from the wall. Both noticed immediately that the paper seemed slightly moist.

"Gimme the hammer, sweetie," Louie D said, sweating as they finished their careful removal of a single wide strip of wallpaper.

When Louie D plastered the wall, he always used circular motions, not very tidy, amateurish. *What did it matter?* he thought. The wall was made to be busted down, after all. As his wife shined the flashlight on a much neater-looking job, Louie felt his neck and shoulder tighten but he did not lose courage.

"Stand back a little bit, honey bee," Louie D advised as he, with shaking hands, swung hard enough to break the thin plaster, sending the little piece of holding chicken wire to the floor along with small chunks of plaster, revealing a smallish opening. Theodora aimed the flashlight into the dark hole and together they peered into the relatively shallow space before reaching in. They looked back at each other with wide and frightened eyes, for the flashlight fell on empty space.

Like a man falling from a cliff and reaching for a small tree branch, a leaf, anything, Louie D, the Exalted Cyclops of Southeast Arkansas, plunged his hand into the space that held his life. His wife held the flashlight up very close so there could be no mistake. Louie D ran his hand once more around in a circle, then he flattened his palm and felt every corner. With perspiration dripping from his chin, the man once again flashed his light in every recess of the small space, begging it to produce what he knew to be there no longer.

Louis D. Stassen looked at his wife, his face an awful thing to see, and she quickly burst into sobs.

"They done got us, too, ain't they? Oh, my Lawd! Oh, my Lawd!" she wailed, and feeling her ankles weaken, she sat on the side of the bed and fanned herself with an old fan from Petrie Funeral Home, with lettering that read, "Serving West Steward/Old Steward Since 1904."

Suddenly Louis D. Stassen sunk to his knees in front of what had been the hidden safe, and Theodora rushed to his side. Louie D felt odd, the right side of his body felt very weak, then numb. He tried to speak.

He thought he said, "Sugar cakes! Help me up. I can't seem to get up!"

But all his wife heard were garbled sounds from his lips, and all he heard from his faithful wife of thirty-seven years was her loud and terrified hollering.

"Louie D done had a stroke!" Aggie Pratt came flying in to tell Lela Bailey a few hours later. "When he fount out dat money was gone he fell out! Nah he up at da hospital!"

"Well," Lela said quietly. "Well, well Jesus," was all she said.

Now all of the Klansmen and everyone else knew. The mysterious robbers had got Louie D too! And without Louie D's direction, his men's rage and frustration knew no one direction, but flew around on a current of rashly conceived notions.

"Let's burn nigger town down!" Parker Wilson shouted. His cousin Willie "Red" Oakes, still deeply mourning the lost dog for which the sheriff had not come up with even one suspect, seconded the suggestion. A number of harsh ideas were advanced, but some of the more sensible older men prevailed—up to a point. It was suggested that strong efforts be made to try and find out who was responsible for the lost money in the next few days. No one had any concrete ideas about how to go about this, since dogs had been tried and, in each case, when sniffing the houses, yards and the emptied hiding places, the dogs had rared up and become hysterical with coughing and sputtering and barking, alerting the men that a powerful anti-tracking potion had been used, and forcing them to admit, however grudgingly, that they were up against forces to be reckoned with.

There were shouts of Northern niggers—outsiders. There was talk among the more informed of Communists, but all anybody knew for sure was that they had been hit, and hit hard, and now most had been brought to complete ruin.

And there was something else in the air that they had never thought they would live to experience: Fear of the Negro.

FIFTY

I mpoverished, angry and often hungry for the first time in their lives, a number of the men who had been robbed, or were afraid of being robbed no matter where they hid what they had left, decided to make an appointment with the mayor.

The mayor, Robert McShane, with his formal manner, was still more a part of them than this new sheriff, Ansell Morrisey, who was for giving the Colored a fair shake, they heard.

It was Tuesday. Their appointment with the mayor was for Friday at two o'clock at his office in Old Steward. It could not be soon enough, because the slick disappearance of the Klansmen's money was getting wide play, not only in the twin towns but all over Phillips County and beyond.

"I betcha niggers is a-laughing at us all the way up in Chicago, Detroit and New Yawk!" some of the Klansmen lamented. "Laughing at the Klu Klux Klan! Kin ya beat dat?"

One of the consequences of the cash losses was that money belts of all types sold out all over the county, and the consensus seemed to be what one old man was heard to remark: "If a nigger, or anyone else gets mah money, he gone have to take it off mah ass—and I keeps my pistol close to wha I keeps mah ass!"

In the meantime, a number of white men—not all of them Klan—found that they just could not stand idly by after the latest incident. Many were nearly dead broke due to unemployment or theft of funds or both, and they were so completely miserable, they were open to any plan that would show the black people that they still controlled these towns and would not be messed with!

Things had actually gotten so bad that some of the white men were ashamed to show their faces in White Town, where a few white women had been openly heard to voice the opinion that "if perhaps y'all would leave 'Them' alone 'They' would leave us alone, and we could go back to having some sleep in this town." But that line of conversation was always quickly followed by "Can you believe niggers is actin this a-way. Well, who else? I never thought I'd live to see the day!"

On Wednesday morning, a number of Louis D. Stassen's friends went to visit him. His doctor had explained that Louie D could hear but could not speak. Not knowing what else to say, they told the old man, who looked pitifully frail and gray in his hospital bed, that they were praying for him and that they hoped he would soon be better and home soon.

But whether or not their voices and promises of prayers offered him comfort, Louie D remained little changed within the busted shell of himself. With his good hand he squeezed each visitor's hand hard when they were ready to leave, and most of the men departed with tears in their eyes. Tears for an old and fallen warrior, and perhaps a tear or two for their own reduced circumstances as well.

The Circle was having one of its many small meetings in Lela Bailey's kitchen, and just she and twelve others were present in this special planning session.

"Well, I know some of you are not much on prayer," said Rev. Clayton, rising from his chair to open the meeting, and directing eye contact to two of the known hotheads in the group, Will Henry and Silas.

"I sho' ain't!" Will Henry said boldly.

"OK," the pastor said, laughing and endearing himself to everyone. "Those of you who are against prayer keep your seats. I'm asking the rest of you to stand for a few minutes and hold hands while we ask the Lord for staying strength and for guidance."

"Oh, shit!" Will Henry exclaimed loudly.

The minister pretended not to hear him and everyone stood, even Silas Benson and Will Henry.

When a rough circle was formed and heads were bowed, Rev. Clayton began to offer a prayer.

"Please make hit a short one," Will Henry begged.

"Excuse me," Rev. Clayton said, making his way over towards Will Henry, as Lela and some of the other women stared at the big red headed man and sucked in their collective breaths in disbelief for Will's lack of respect for this man of God.

Rev. Clayton moved around the circle and, to everyone's surprise, grasped Will Henry's large light reddish hand in his small jet black one.

"You know, Will, I don't believe you are as big a devil as you like to make out," Rev. Clayton said looking playfully up at the big man. "Now, I'm a small man, but I have a mighty strong grip. Interrupt this circle once again and I'm going to squeeze this hand of yours so hard you gonna holler for Sunday! Do I make myself clear?"

"Well, go 'head on, Reverend!" Aggie giggled, and even Lela, who had nearly given up on Will Henry's ability to behave "nicely," smiled at Will Henry's face, which had colored even redder than his natural ruddy coloring.

Still holding Will Henry's hand, Rev. Clayton said, "Shall we focus ourselves for prayer?" his voice becoming serious, his manner dignified.

Before prayer, Rev. Clayton always called for a moment of silence and focus, and the room was silent now and not so much warm as cozy. Cozy with the shared feeling of friends, safe inside of their black skins, each person present extending personal safety—both real and imagined—to the other. For the first time in their black lives they were not alone in their predicament of color. They had each other inside of a loving circle. They had a ring of planning, prayer, and of real power.

All of the women—and many of the men—shed tears as they held hands, and if someone had asked, "why the tears?" They would not have been able to answer. Perhaps their souls, more than their minds, knew the need for the tears, and maybe both past and present joy and sorrow had melted somewhere in the common air and was now spilling over into the consciousness of them all, causing tears to moisten cheeks both smooth and grizzled.

The sobbing was sketchy but had become audible, and knowing the healing, relieving, and cleansing power of tears, the reverend let the group weep themselves dry.

After a few minutes, Rev. Clayton found that Will Henry's hand had completely relaxed inside of his own, and the pastor begin his prayer. He asked for strength and wisdom, for courage and safety, for guidance and direction, "and most of all, sweet Jesus, for freedom from the bonds of hatred."

"Amen!" the room intoned.

After the very short prayer, everyone in the room seemed totally calm and ready to begin their meeting on a positive note as the pastor had suggested.

"We getting' mighty big, ain't we?" said Dave's mother. "Since two months ago, seventy mo' folks done put in tah join up," Lela mused, passing around the slices of cake, pie, and tea she had prepared.

It was true. The little group of eight original members had grown at first to forty and then to a hundred. Now even more wanted to join. Each victory brought in more membership requests. The disappearance of the Klan money alone brought in scores of smiling, back-slapping members who wanted to be a part of a group of Colored folks that were "at last actually doin' somethin', instead of sittin' around moanin', groanin', complainin' and getting' dey ass whipped!" But Dave thought it wise to keep their numbers relatively low in order to better control and inform the whole group.

Dave explained to his worried mother that the membership was again closed and this time it would stay closed at one hundred, and that the organization was still tightly controlled with ten good captains, each with only ten or so men and women each, so that every member was very well known to each captain.

Dave smiled benevolently at the group. "We are nearly completely independent of the white stores," he said proudly.

At each Circle meeting, members brought their captains something that could be used in the community, even if it was only one egg, a pocket handkerchief, a penny, an old clean blanket-just something. The captains delivered everything to Lela Bailey and her staff to be given out as needed to those in the community with emergency needs. In this way, no one in real need had to go begging the white man for charity. This system had vastly reduced the Colored community's need for store credit.

"Dat's right!" Aggie shouted out. "Honey, ain't hit beautiful? Da store owners is about to die trying to figure out hi come we ain't up in dey face every minute beggin' fer credit! Hi we still so fat and fine down heah in Colored Town when dey pullin in dey belts in White Town! Lawd ain't hit pretty!"

"OK Aggie, nah don't go crazy on us!" Will Henry said, laughing at Aggie's excitement.

Aggie had long since been moved from the relative isolation of her hill house and now lived in town, close to Helena's place, and they were great company for each other and had surprised everyone with the closeness of their friendship. Helena and Aggie and their four children left Lela's first with their two volunteer guards. The children, especially Merry, loved the guards. She said they made her feel like a royal princess in a story book.

Living mostly independent of the white merchants had been one of the Circle's proudest moments, bringing tears even to Rev. Clayton's eyes.

White store owners in both West Steward and Old Steward were feeling the pinch—badly—as more and more blacks, who were the majority population in both towns, took their business for the things they could not grow to the Jones Brothers, the only large black grocery store in the twin towns, and Jones bought and stored all of the dry food products, coffee, sugar, flour, beans, rice, in their large warehouse for the Circle. The Jones Brothers got, if not rich, more comfortable; and even the little black mom and pop stores had never done so well. Everybody was pleased except, of course, the white shopkeepers.

The Jones Brothers did not have everything, but they came so near to it that nobody minded if a Colored person spent a penny or nickel with a white merchant once in a while. In fact, it was all but encouraged, because while it denied the shopkeepers any real money, it had the advantage of keeping them confused. At first they thought they were being boycotted—now, with a Colored customer drifting in once in a while, they were not so sure.

"But still," Nadine Canton began in her comical and frank manner that caused heads to turn her way expecting a laugh, "a Colored person kin go into all but the Jew sto's and ax to have fifty dollars worth o' stuff put up on the counter, and dat person will have to wait and wait and wait until all de white folks is served first, bad as dat white main might need dat money. Chile, some time dey want yo' money so bad dey come justa slobbering—but naw mam, naw suh, you Colored, you got to step back and wait while Miz Ann gits herself a nickel wortha gum drops.

"Well," Nadine continued, her mouth set for the telling of a story, her audience for the hearing of one, for she was rather famous for rough and plain speaking to Colored or white. "Well, I waited nigh on to sebny years to git to tell the white folks to kiss my old ashy black ass—and Lawd knows I sho' is enjoyin' mahsef nah! Excuse me, Reverend, Miz Lela, and da rest o' y'all fer mah bad talk," said the totally unrepentant Nadine, as most of the room laughed out loud.

Seeing the barest flicker of a smile that the Rev. Clayton could not hide, Nadine was greatly inspired to continue.

"Sometimes I gits me five dollars, and I put hit in singles, den I put cut paper in between, so it look like a nice pile. Nah y'all know five dollars is a good piece o' change dese days, and plumped up dat way hit's a-nough to drive any sto' main crazy! Well, anyways, I puts dat money in mah hain up near mah face, and I say 'oh me, oh mah! I sho' would lak to buy me somethin' 'nother wit' dis heah cash money, but ahm sixty-nine years old and my legs ain't no mo' good for standin' and waitin', so if I got to wait in dis line and keep getting' pushed back even 'til all dese nice white folks is served—'specially seein' as hi I was heah furst, and specially seein' as hi mah money green lak every one else's.

" 'Well den...' " Nadine continued, nearly choking on her wheezy old laugh. " 'Well den, maybe ahm jus' gone have ta take dis heah twenty dollars and go wha dey serve you furst come, furst serve, Colored or white. Yes suh! I know me a coupla sto's lak dat'—which o'cose I doesn't." The old women wheezed out a laugh and the room laughed with her.

"By nah old Mistah Travis 'bout to pee on hissef lookin' at me and mah money. He says, 'Nadine, pleeeese! Jus' wait a minute! You know hi hit is. I'm gone git over dere to you fast lak a rabbit, and I thank ya! Jus' don't go no wha!' "

By now the room was rolling with laughter, imagining Mr. Travis' predicament, knowing how badly he wanted and needed what he thought was twenty dollars in his cash register.

Knowing she now had the Circle in the middle of her palm, old Nadine moved in for the kill: "Well nah, Mistah Travis done come jus' a-sweating tryin' to satisfy dese two old white folks—one want a nickle can o' snuff, da other a large ten cent can o' sweet peas—and old black me standing dere waitin' to spend twenty dollars—or so Travis thinks. Nah, jus' when old Travis fittin' to git 'round ta me, in walk Miz Gantry, and anybody what know Miz Gantry know she hinkty. She ain't 'bout to let no nigger woman git in head o' her! And Miz Gantry take da longest time to git her choice of a dime's wortha cookies! 'Da goils is comin' over fer a little tea, Mistah Travis, so gimme two sugar wafers and two lemon creams, and three butterscotch—no, make dat two strawberry creams, and one lemon cream'—and on she went. By nah Mistah Travis 'bout ta fall out fer dead, and heah I stand, da soul of patience, singin' a lil' song to mahsef, flapping dat money back and forth in mah hains once in a while talkin' out loud 'bout what I wanna git. 'Need me three pounds o' sugar, I does, and least five pound o' meal, den I sho' needs a sack o' navy beans. Some coffee fer sho', and oh Lawd, a sack o' rice and... I reckon one o' Mistah Travis' helper boys gone have to pull a wagon to take me home what wit' all I needs!' "

The entire room was now tittering, even Lela and the reverend could not hold back and their shoulders shook with mirth, because knowing Nadine Canton, and how she liked to "git on white folks' nerves," they felt they knew how this story must end. So the whole room, needing hilarity after days and weeks of tension, waited patiently for her sharp as a knife punch line.

"Well, jus' 'bout den, I believe Mistah Travis coulda *kilt* Miz Gantry wit' her dime fer cookies. He say, 'Nah hold on Nadine! Hold on Nadine! Lawd knows I'm a-trying ta git ta ya!' I wait 'zactly one more second, den I say real loud, ' Mistah Travis! Da Colored is a patient race, but I can't wait all day long wit' mah bad legs. Thank ya kindly, but ahm takin mah twenty dollars cross town!' And wit' dat I turned on my heels and flew out dat sto'. And chile, I wuz never gone buy a *thang* no how!"

The room exploded in loud and sustained laughter that provided as much relief as the group's earlier tears.

"We is a Circle of stone, ain't we?" Aggie enthused. "A sho'nuff Circle of stone which nobody can break!"

There were two short reports: Reza Mae Long stated that when the rumor got around that money was missing, the graveyard money was immediately discovered to be missing also, and no one knew who to suspect, certainly not her.

Omar Williams reported that of course they all knew that the clean-outs had not been one hundred percent effective, but that everything had turned out very "satisfactorily," which was the word Dave had used. Omar did not mention how surprised and pleased he was to hear that Louis D. Stassen had suffered a stroke. He knew such revengeful gloating would not have sat well with either the Rev. Matthew Moses Clayton or Lela Bailey. After all, Louis D. Stassen was a human being—"one o'Gawd's chirrens," Lela was likely to say—"although a real bad one."

PART FIVE

We smile, but, O great Christ, our cries
To thee from tortured souls arise.

FIFTY-ONE

The man was excessively raw boned, very tall, and his lack of flesh made him seem even taller than his six feet three inches. In his youth he had been a handsome man, if your taste ran to yellow Negroes tinged with red and covered with freckles. Truly a strong wind would have blown him and his large grip across a street, and he knew it, so he clutched it tightly with hands as bony as claws, as if it held treasure—which it did.

His clothes were clean, pressed, his shoes well shined. He was definitely not one of the "hard luck boys" now roaming America's towns searching, waiting, hoping.

He wore a long heavy coat of good brown wool that covered his thin frame loosely like death cloth. The coat was too heavy, but he was so often chilled now, even in fair weather, that he dared not be without it. A light woolen scarf, gloves of fine leather, and a woolen cap pulled low and covering his ears completed his "git up," he called it.

The man had taken some care with his dress. He wanted to look nice, for he was coming home.

No longer young, his skin was dry and dull, his checks hollow, and his eyes, though still alert, were sunken and rimmed in darkness against the paleness of his skin. But in all fairness, none of this loss of good looks could be blamed on the natural passage of time that comes to all.

The slightest exertion made him cough—a loose effusive cough that he tried to keep short and unoffensive, and which he took care of with one of his pounds of clean white handkerchiefs.

The man wanted to see Old Steward again, thinking it might be the last time he would see this town. It was Thursday and past noon. The shops that had not gone out of business had no customers to show for their anticipation. As he made his way slowly down the blocks, he noticed that the stores were much shabbier than he remembered. Some merchants stood in their store windows looking hopefully for the stray customer that did not come.

There was the five and dime, with its big glass windows, full of peanuts freshly roasted. There were also socks, thread, candy, combs...a little further down was Neiman's Dry Goods and Ed Hanly's pharmacy.

The grip was like a vessel filled with rocks and his legs had begun to feel like lead, but he was determined to see a few things in Old Steward before catching the bus home, determined not to give in after walking only two blocks. A hot cup of coffee would be good, but he didn't feel like sitting in the back—the "crow's corner"—of Chester Hunter's café no matter how badly he needed coffee.

The man had always disliked Chester and noted with guilty satisfaction that the café held only one diner, a seemingly poor white one hunched over the last sliver of pie, draining the last drops of coffee from his cup. The man looked through the window and smiled at the busted red leatherette counter seats repaired with black tape. It tickled him that hard times—really hard times—were now pinching some of the fattest butts in White Town, just as they had always pinched the majority of those in Colored Town, from birth to death. But here he had not seen the dreaded soup lines, the pitiful apple and pencil sellers he had seen up north—not yet.

He was tired now, too tired to continue sight seeing. His days of hopping freights was over for good—gone like good whiskey—but what a ride it was while it lasted! But, yes, the days on the road were over and done.

He walked towards the bus line to board a bus that would take him to West Steward. He figured he had dallied as long as his strength would allow.

Lela was cooking regularly now for the guards who had huge appetites, and this suited her fine. One of the men had just left her back door smiling and inquiring about dinner which Lela liked to serve around two o'clock in the afternoon.

Beef steak with candied sweets. "Lotsa gravy on da steak so you can spoon it over da sweets," Lela had said. Turnip greens. Biscuits. Fried pork chops. A corn pie. Beets and onions, sliced fresh tomatoes with black pepper and salt, and a big peach cobbler for dessert.

The guard sped off to tell the others, his face covered with lustful anticipation. Lela threw her head back and laughed at his enthusiasm, thinking what a pleasure it was to cook for people who really enjoyed "dey somethin' ta et."

There would be plenty left over for Helena and Aggie and their children and for Dave—and for Rev. Clayton and his family, for Lela had hammered four large steaks, blessing the Lord as she pounded the tough beef. The reverend was right—thank you, Jesus! The Panic had not—through God's grace—caused the Bailey family to miss one meal!

What a nice little wife the reverend had, Lela mused. And many were surprised at how readily Lela had accepted Quella Clayton, plus the fact that the reverend had a seven-year-old child, but had "neglected" to marry until a few months ago. Lela squashed pious criticism by saying, "Well, nah dats betwixt da reverend and da Lawd, don't you think? 'Member when da Lawd said he who is wit' out no sin throw da furst rock? Da reverend is a good main. A good Christian, I believes. Much mo' so den many what done been married up proper fer years!" And that ended that.

At first he thought he had arrived at the wrong house, yet how could that be? He knew every plank and nail of his home, even though he had not seen it in years. He was home alright, but who were all of these young Colored boys who had surrounded him and insisted on searching him, patting him up and down? What on earth was going on here? He didn't know any of the young men—or had they grown so much since he left?

Suddenly the litany went out: "Dave's father!" Dave's father, man! "And the scrawls and suspicion turned to smiles, to awe, to welcome. The powerfully built, angry looking young man, who had been the wiry, gentle little Silas Benson when Rex had left West Steward, stepped forward wide-eyed and apologetic.

"Oh, me! Ahm sorry, Mistah Bailey, we got orders ta—"

He was cut short by an older man.

"Rex? Rex, is dat you?" Roger Mulright, the furniture maker, who was now captain of the guards, asked.

Roger Mulright's face was a mirror and Rex Bailey now saw himself in it, and was gripped by a shivery fear as old Mulright tried to smile, to appear unshocked by his thinness, his dry, drawn appearance.

"Well! Go on in, boy!" Roger said with strained and false gaiety. "Lela gonna be mighty proud to see ya; I'll 'splain 'bout dis security stuff later."

But Roger and the guards could not peel their eyes off Rex, and he knew that as soon as he left the yard, their voices would start to buzz with talk, with inquiry. Where he come from? Where he been? Why he so po'?

Lawd, Lawd! He had delayed as long as he could, even months, trying to gain weight. He had done everything he had heard of: drank oceans of thick yellow cream, ate tins of sardines and piles of nuts with their rich oils, slept often and late in well ventilated rooms in good Colored rooming houses, took cod liver oil and herbs of all kinds, shapes and forms, ate beef steaks until he could stand no more, but he had continued to lose weight—and to lose ground. Finally, he had to come home before even that was lost to him.

Rex moved reluctantly towards the last few feet of his journey; he moved toward Lela Bailey's kitchen, he moved towards Lela's all seeing eyes. It had been years since he had been home and it seemed like forty or fifty.

"Ahm always bringing relatives!" Roger tried to joke. "First Helena, nah you."

Oh, mercy! Helena was home too! Rex thought with a jolt of surprise.

Roger went in with Rex. Since Dave was up on the car line or over in Epps, Roger wanted to be there to catch Lela if she fainted or fell or hollered out in pain when she saw the skeletal remains of her husband.

Lela was facing her husband when he walked into her kitchen, but she did not immediately look up from her slicing of sweet potatoes, for she had become accustomed to extra noise in her backyard, people coming in and out.

Roger spoke first.

"Miz Lela, hi 'bout a hot cup o' coffee fer a gent whats been on da road?" the furniture maker said making every effort to joke and to smile for Lela's sake.

"Hi, sugar bee!" Rex called out hoarsely, trying to sound casual and cheery as if lost years and lost pounds were of little consequence in this relationship.

Lela looked up, dropped her potatoes, her knife, dashed around the table and grabbed Rex and held on to him for dear life, her face buried in his bony chest so that he could not see his death that she had noted, in the flicker of an eye, on her face.

LawdhavemercyJesus! He got da consumption!

Over his protests, Lela put Rex to bed immediately using the excuse of his long and tiring journey. Rex was extremely grateful for Lela's good sense, and much to his shame he fell asleep in the warm, soft bed almost as soon as he stretched out his long legs.

Two guards were sent for Dave and Helena.

"Go git me mah chirrens," Lela said, trying to remain unruffled, but the tears gushed with a mind of their own. "Tell dem dey daddy home. And bring me Aggie Pratt if you kin find her. I wants to send her somewha."

When Dave was located, he told the sentries he would pick up his sister, and when they arrived they fairly ran into the house.

They found their father in a deep sleep. Lela quickly and quietly explained the situation to them, and when she did, Helena went to her mother and just held her.

"The best doctors money can buy!" Dave exclaimed, his voice unsteady.

"Hit's too late. Too late, son."

"No! I'll go get Dr. Echardt right now! I'll get John Candle!" Dave said, his voice filled with emotion.

Lela finally agreed, knowing they had to try, knowing Dave needed to feel that he was doing all he could.

By late Thursday afternoon Henri Echardt had made his examination of Rex Bailey and got his suptum cup, although he knew he didn't need to make a smear and stain it and look under the microscope for the deadly Tuberculosis bacilli. The good doctor also knew he didn't need an x-ray to tell him that Lela's husband had a hole in his left lung big enough to walk through.

He would take care of Rex Bailey as well as he could, but he could guarantee nothing, because regrettably, there was no medicine, no treatment for his condition. No. Sometimes in the young and in less advanced cases—but then Rex was not young, his condition was not new. The doctor's voice was quiet, full of despair and regret.

"Madame Bailey, you and Dave and me can sit down and talk about vhat ve are going to do next for your husband, yes?"

The doctor then got up and washed his hands very thoroughly at the kitchen sink, and dried them on the soft towel that Lela offered.

"Now put that towel avay for vashing, Lela. You vill need a special bag for the things your husband vill be using, yes?" the doctor said in the German accent that thirty years in the American South had not completely faded.

"Yas, o'cose."

The three of them, wife, son, doctor, continued to talk quietly while Rex slept.

The doctor laid down the rules: The grandchildren could not visit with Rex at all. Masks had to be worn by everyone when inside of his room. Gloves, gloves, stacks of gloves had to be bought for handling his food trays, bed pans, anything he used. Large bottles of disinfectant must be bought to scrub down the walls, the floors, once a week. Disinfectant should be added when washing the one set of dishes he was to use, and all of his bed linens must be boiled and air dried in the sun when possible. The middle room was fine, but Rex must always sleep alone.

His room must be thoroughly aired out for thirty minutes each day, if possible, in all weather except rain or snow. Fresh fruit, juice and fresh vegetables, lots of fish, meat in moderation, and yes, heavy cream, sardines, cod liver oil, if one believed in that popular regimen now going around—it couldn't hurt if it didn't help.

And piles and piles of handkerchiefs. Once used they were to be burned. Always. The father would have days of feeling better than others, but he would grow progressively weaker.

Yes, of course. Especially in Rex's case—the case of being Colored—home was better, more comfortable than any sanitorium if one had the means of the prescribed care that was ordered, and the Baileys obviously did. But they must keep very quiet about his condition. In fact, Dr. Echardt was running a grave risk in not reporting Rex to the health authorities, he explained. In White Town, some neighbors panicked and demanded that a similar case be hauled off to the T.B. Sanitorium all the way in Little Rock.

Both Lela and Dave assured Dr. Echardt that such a thing would not happen in this neighborhood.

Dr. Echardt left. He would take no fee from Lela as usual. He would look in on his patient each day as usual. Lela blessed his name. As usual.

Twenty-five minutes after the white doctor had left, John Candle, the old herbalist who had spent many years "back home in Africa," walked in Lela's door. Aggie Pratt had been sent to fetch him, and she had carefully outlined the situation as it had been told to her so that he could come prepared with his potions.

Everyone knew the old man was not fond of leaving his house, but would come up the hill in a car for Lela's sake to visit her dying husband.

John Candle unwrapped himself from the blanket he was wearing, and asked to be shown into the "sick room."

"Nah, lessee heah, boy!" he called out almost cheerily. "You sho' done went and got po'. What you do dat fer? Ain't you been eatin'?" the herbalist joked as he opened his crocker sack and began to set out his jars, bottles, tins, his cigar boxes tied with string. "Well, I got somethin' dats gone put some meat back on dem long bones o' yourn!"

John Candle's very manner—brusque and playful in this instance, and very confident—inspired trust. Dave looked at his little mother and smiled, and Aggie smiled and squeezed Helena's shoulders to give her courage, for she had been in constant tears.

"He a powerful lil' ol' main, honey! Ifn anybody kin help Mistah Rex other den Dr. Echardt, hit's John Candle!" Aggie promised Helena.

The herbalist continued to fish around in his sack. He set a deep yellow salve among the other potions that he had already lined up on the edge of the dresser. He opened the jar, and beckoning Lela to come closer, he explained how it was to be used in his absence, although this evening he would apply it himself.

When the jar of yellow salve was opened it smelled strongly of mint and lemons, and was, he said to be rubbed on the chest and back "nice and slow" for at least fifteen minutes every evening, then wide pieces of red flannel must be placed on the chest and back and tied with cotton strips. The salve was to be wiped off every morning, not washed off—for Rex was never to put water on his body again, but was to be wiped down daily, with another solution, this time a brownish one, which John Candle provided in a quart jar. He said he would send more later, as soon as he made it up.

There was green tea, boiled and drunk, four cups a day before meals and at bedtime. This tea kept the bowels open and removed "poisons" from the blood stream. Also, there were little bricks of bee pollen held together with a secret "glue" that had great power to knit up holes and cavities, such as the one the herbalist knew Rex had in his lung. He was to mash a brick in honey and eat it every morning.

"He gone be alright. Don't y'all worry y'all's self," the herbalist said to the little family. He had stayed with the stricken man for more than an hour, talking and explaining his medications, and although he washed his hands when he left Rex's room, he had not worn a mask or gloves as he applied the salve to the sick man's chest and back.

When the herbalist was finished, Dave put his hands in his pocket as if to offer the odd little man money before he sent him back home with sentries in one of the trucks.

The man stared up at Dave angrily.

"I know you ain't puttin yo' hains in yo' pockets fer me!" he said haughtily. "Nah git on outta mah way fore I bust yo' brains out!"

The women laughed as David pretended to retreat in fear and alarm.

"Lela, gimme some tea cakes ta take home—you got some? I be back Sattiday."

Lela gratefully gave the herbalist the entire glass jar that was half full of cakes, and John Candle motioned for Dave to take the jar to a guard. Then the ancient man pulled his blanket closely around himself and was gone.

FIFTY-TWO

Lela had polished the chimneys of three large coal oil lamps, trimmed the wicks and sat them in the middle room she had prepared for her husband. Even after all his "world travels" as Lela called them, Rex still preferred the homespun reassurance of the warm and kindly lamp lights to a stark electric bulb that dangled in the middle of the ceiling revealing more than you wanted to see.

Everything had been purchased and made ready. The piles of rubber gloves, a whole cardboard box of very soft white cloths to be used for handkerchiefs, then discarded in brown sacks and burned. Stacks of washable face masks to be used and then boiled with soft lye soap and disinfectant. Another table in the room contained Rex's special dishes and napkins.

The sick man's bed was thick with plump goose down pillows, fresh white sheets, blankets, and beautifully sewn quilts. In the middle of the bed set Rex, like a king in hand-stitched silk pajamas, laughing and joking with all who came to visit as if he had nothing more than a hang nail.

All of Rex's many friends wanted to visit, and they sat around the bed in chairs, draped in sheets, wearing masks, and listening to their old buddy's adventures of the road. They were allowed to stay only one hour, but the company was so good and the stories of Rex's travels so fine, that they bagged their sheets and masks with reluctance when it was time to go.

"Boy, y'all sho' look jus' lak da Klu Klux Klan coming in heah in all dat white!" Rex laughed. When laughing brought on a fit of productive coughing, he used his handkerchief discretely, discarded it just as discretely, and continued on with his jokes and tales as if it was the most natural thing in the world to know you were very near the end of your spool of thread.

Lela had spoken to him gently about his illness, and he had said without skipping a beat, "I know I got da T.B.'s, Lela, dats why I came on home. Sugar, I'm sorry to come dis-a-way, but I wanted to come *home*."

After resting a few days, Rex announced that he felt much better and would like to get up and walk around a bit. Both Dr. Echardt and the herbalist had recommended a little bit of exercise to keep the muscles toned and strong. So Rex, wrapped in wool blankets and dressed in long drawers, went for a ten minute walk around the backyard. The guards, having heard of his condition, gave him plenty of room.

When he returned to the kitchen he pronounced himself "feelin fit 'nough to fight," but Lela and Dave noticed that he seemed quite out of breath.

Sitting in his soft chair, draped with blankets and wearing his mask, Rex asked to be brought up to date on what had been happening while he was away.

"It's a long, long story, Daddy," Dave said.

"Well start on hit, son," Rex said, affectionately placing his hand on his son's knee and biffing him gently on the cheek.

Before he returned, Rex had decided that he would not live the rest of his life apologizing for having left, or regretting not having stayed and lived out his life in West Steward like a good family man. He had heard that the good Baptist vengeful were already pronouncing his illness punishment for leaving a po' lil' wife to make it the best way she could. Death for lack of responsibility. Death and suffering for the sin of seeing the United States. *Lawd have mercy! What did niggers know anyhow?*

The father and husband's strong comfort was that he had not come back empty handed. *No Lawd! Dear Father Gawd!* He had been spared that. He had certain things in his grip, things that he would take out real soon—tonight maybe, if his strength held. Yes, it was all about strength now. But first he wanted to know, had to know what had happened here in West Steward while he was gone.

Dave and Lela took turns telling him everything. Why Dave had left the mill and started his own business, but not how successful it was, for even now the son and the mother did not wish to overshadow Rex's part—the money he never failed to send home, which had been adequate and then some.

They told Rex about the murders in White Town that were still big news, the Duster family and how they were spirited out of town, about Aristotle Gillis, the jail break and the burning of the Old Storage House, the burning of the Lawrence family, the lynching of Billy Binder and Tom Leak, all people he knew, and about various other beatings and intimidations and how they had retaliated. Dave told his father about the Circle with great pride and his father listened with great dismay.

When Lela and Dave were finished, Rex shook his head several times in utter disbelief.

"You mean Colored peepers is fightin' back?"

"Yes, sir!" Dave said, smiling. Then thinking more closely about it, he added, "Now, Daddy, don't let this frighten you. I'm safer than I've ever been before."

But Rex looked at Lela. "Is dat right, Mama?" he asked with hoarse hope, his voice lined with fearful concern.

"I believe hit is, Rex. Hit took me a long time to come to dat iddy. I was just scared, scared, scared! All da time. Every time Dave went out after dem last murders, I just start to prayin' for him, for all our boys. 'Cause you know white folks is slick. Dey don't intend to let you git da best o'dem fer long."

"Well...dats just what I means," Rex said, his voice tailing off.

"Stand up, Dave! Damn! You done got to be a big nigger, boy!" Rex exclaimed, injecting humor into the conversation to dispel his qualms and uncertainties. He was glad Dave could not see his heart and the nervousness that it held. He had never heard of the Colored man winning this kind of battle anywhere and he had been all over the United States. Could this Circle, as they called it, do here what had not been done anywhere else in all of the forty-eight? Protect black people from white folks? Rex had his doubts, and as deep as they were, he decided to keep them to himself.

For now he would return to his comfortable bed and sleep. He had sat up too long and coughed too many times. Although he felt an urgency now to open the grip, he was afraid the old suitcase would have to wait for now.

Although Sallie Poindexter was quite stout, she had never learned to make a really good cake, so she was more than grateful when Aggie Pratt started to give her slices, then whole cakes from Lela Bailey's kitchen. Aggie told Lela that she thought the occasional gift cakes were a good idea since Sallie was the mayor's housekeeper, and that one day those cakes would yield valuable information. Aggie was right.

Seeing Aggie in White Town on Saturday, Sallie said, "Hey, girl! Come over mah house Sunday eveing and bring me some o' Miz Lela's tea cakes. I got somethin' ta tell ya."

Aggie pretended to pout because Sallie requested Mother Bailey's cakes and not hers, but she promised to be at Sallie's at six o'clock on Sunday evening.

Lela made the tea cakes especially sweet with a ginger glaze as Sallie liked them, and Aggie took a quart of buttermilk along also.

When Sallie had left her three children in another room to listen to the radio with their father, she took several of her three dozen tea cakes, placed them on a plate between her and Aggie and poured two glasses of buttermilk. The rest of the cakes she hid on top of her kitchen cabinet.

When Aggie was settled comfortably in Sallie's middle room, at her dining table with a bright lamp between them in the "unelectrified" house, Sallie said in a low voice, "For quite a spell I been believin' da mayor got him a snitch. He know too many lil' small thangs 'bout Colored Town, ya know? So, I say one day ahm gone find out jus' who dat is. What I knowed hit weren't no Marko Horton no mo', but hit was somebody—and Lawd, hi I hates a snitch! Dey cause mo' mess! Or worser! Well, you always been nice to me, and you got nice frens, in all, so I say if I finds out, ahm sho' gone tell Aggie Pratt. Hit may do some good."

"Did you find out, girl?" Aggie asked, feeling that she must have. Why else would she be sitting at Sallie's dining room table right now?

"Sho' did!" Sallie exclaimed. "Dis snitch come secret lak and I never see 'em. He come after ahm gone on home. I say dats alright. One day deres gone be a slip up."

"Yeah?"

"Last Thursday night I be called on to stay over a little to serve up dinner to da mayor's big men—important folks. Dey got business to be talkin'. Dey eat somethin', dey move to da parlor and start to drinkin'. I hang around mo' den I has to, 'cause I know pret soon tongues gone git loose, speakin' gone git loud. I thought dat snitch name might come up and hit sho' did—Benjamin Carter, da black dog!" Sallie spit out. "Kin you 'magine old nigger lak dat? Somebody outta whip his ass!"

"Well!" Aggie exhaled. This was indeed news she could use, and her feet moved involuntarily under the table, as she was anxious to go and let Dave know.

Aggie started to work on a polite leave—taking speech, for she did not wish to spend the rest of the eveing gossiping with Sallie, she had the information she needed and she wanted to go and do her work of informing on the hill.

Sallie noticed her anxiety between bites of tea cake and gulps of milk.

"Dats not all I wanted to tell ya, Aggie," Sallie said quietly.

"Naw? Honey, what you done told me is a belly buster!"

"Uh huh," Sallie said, taking her time. "Well, see what you think 'bout *dis!* Dat meetin' was all 'bout da disturbances whats been happenin' in dis town of late. Ahm standing outside da doe where I can hear but nobody can see me, see. Da mayor say he gone have Sheriff Morrissey pick up Dave Bailey on Monday moaning—tomorry. Say he da leader or somethin'. I thought you'd want a know. Dave is nice. He once lont my husmon five dollars fer rent and food."

"What!?" Aggie exclaimed. "Da sheriff gone pick up Dave Bailey?"

"Yas, dats right. Dats what I heered. Say Benjamin Carter say he da one dey all follows—he da one what tell everyone what ta do. Da mayor was very strong on dat. He say Benjamin Carter tell him lots o' stuff. 'Cose he didn't know mah ear wuz at da doe."

"They gone pick Dave up fer what?" Aggie asked, trying to maintain her self control and not show how chilled and hot and dizzy she had just become.

"Gone ax him some questions, he says."

"Listen, Sallie," Aggie said, regaining a little of her composure. "Please, please don't say nothin' to nobody 'bout dis heah, OK? Hit might mean somebody's life. Not even to Mistah Poindexter, OK?"

"OK. Fine. I understands."

"And thanks a lots, girl. I owe you two cakes!"

"Well, dats alright wit' me! Jus' don't forget about 'em—and Aggie?"

"Yas?" Aggie was sweating, now raring to go up the hill, to warn Dave, to tell them all.

"I hope y'all can git somebody to kick Benjamin Carter's old gray ass!"

Aggie ran all the way to Lela's and burst in the door.

"Sorry. Sorry, 'scuse me!"

"Aggie, whats goin' on? Sit down here, girl," Lela said, her heart beginning to race.

"Wha Dave?" Aggie asked, trying not to shake. Dave was out somewhere, but could be found.

Aggie told Lela what Sallie had said. There was a knock on the door. It was one of the guards.

"I saw you runnin', Miz Aggie. Is everything all right?"

"No! Go find Dave fast as you kin!"

Dave was brought back within twenty minutes. When he heard what Aggie had to say, he sent for Peter, Omar, Will Henry, Rev. Clayton, and LaSalle Peabody. This was the emergency team, the Inner Circle.

When the men were at Lela's table, Aggie told her story again.

"Gawd damn it, dat's tomorrow, excuse me, Reverend, ladies," Will Henry burst out.

Dave knitted his hands thoughtfully.

"If the mayor just wants to talk," he said finally, "then that's no problem. May be interesting. We'll see what's on his mind."

Omar took out his super sharp razor and opened it.

"Maybe he'd like to talk to dis," he said menacingly.

"Put that thing away, Omar," Rev. Clayton said quietly. "Perhaps Dave is right. Let's not get unduly excited without cause," he said to Will Henry, who looked confused at the use of the word "unduly."

"When white folks call black folks in to 'chat' it's hard not to get excited," Peter Frauzinou said with disgust in his voice.

"If dat mayor knows anything, he know not to start no s-h and there won't be no i-t," Aggie said, without apologizing.

"Listen," Dave said, "I'll put on my good suit, sleep with my stocking cap on so my hair won't be too nappy, wear a tie, shine my shoes and go see the mayor. OK? No problem."

In a corner with a cup of tea Helena looked worried, and Lela had been praying silently ever since she had heard the news. She also had one of her very rare headaches.

"No cause to worry that I can see," Rev. Clayton agreed. "Not now. Not yet. Let's not cross bridges before we come to them, my dear friends."

FIFTY-THREE

Arriving at seven-thirty in the morning as he did, Sheriff Ansell Morrissey thought to catch Dave Bailey off guard, possibly still sleeping. He knew that he did not sell his tamales on Mondays, so he probably had a lot of time for leisure, for sleeping.

But Sallie and Aggie had done their work, and at seven-thirty in the morning it was the sheriff who was surprised when he and his deputy, Ferral Banks, drove up the slight incline to the Bailey house. Dave Bailey was standing outside casually dressed in a suit, his hands in his pockets, waiting. If the sight of Dave surprised the sheriff, the numbers of men with him on the porch stunned both the lawmen. There were at least twenty "rough looking men on the porch with Bailey," Ferral Banks would later tell interested parties up in White Town.

So. They had flushed out a big hound, maybe the big hound, Sheriff Morrissey thought, trying to smile a little—but the number and looks of the Negroes on the porch ruffled the sheriff's feathers a bit. He was not used to a show of unity amongst Negroes—at least he guessed this was what the presence of the other men meant.

The smile left the sheriff's face more quickly than it had appeared, and pretending he did not know who Dave Bailey was, the sheriff walked up near the porch followed by a sweating deputy.

"Dave Bailey? Which one of you boys is Dave Bailey?"

No one answered. Dave cocked his head to the side, amused.

Lela pushed forward in her old heavy green sweater.

"Did you say *boys*, Sheriff? Well, as you kin see, dere ain't no boys out chere on dis porch. Mebbe you better start over," Lela said with a raise of her chin, her eyes defiant.

The twenty men with Dave sat in the swings, on the porch railings, leaned against the walls. They were all wearing jackets or coats except Dave Bailey. They stared at the sheriff and deputy, silent and waiting, their faces blank.

422

The sheriff scowled. Deputy Banks looked as if he didn't know whether to stay or run. He stayed a few paces behind the sheriff and continued to shed water from every pore in the coolness of the morning.

"Dave Bailey! Step out—please," Sheriff Morrissey called loudly, wondering what action he should take if nobody moved.

Dave stepped slowly down the three porch steps.

"Yes, Sheriff? What can I do for you?" he asked so suavely, so quietly that all the men on the porch howled with laughter. The men were already playing this scene to their sons, grandsons: "Den he, all six foot fo' o'him, dressed lak a rich white main, he say, real quiet lak, he say, 'Yes, Sheriff. What you want?' Not no 'yes suh, boss main, suh, please, suh,' Naw! None o' dat! Not Dave Bailey!"

"You are to come with me! The mayor wants to see you!" Sheriff Morrissey said more forcefully and harshly than necessary.

Damn! The sheriff reprimanded himself, for he thought he heard his voice almost echoing and felt that he sounded like a whining fool. He braced himself for the laughter of this porch full of Negroes. There was none.

Dave smiled down at the sheriff, who was four inches shorter than himself, and cast a look of amused disdain at Ferral Banks, a head shorter than the sheriff and "wide as a bail of cotton," the joke went.

"The mayor, you say? Must be powerful important!" Dave said, still smiling, and showing no sense of fear that such a summons would have caused even a year ago.

"You got dat right!" the deputy exclaimed loudly, putting in his coin's worth.

Dave squatted down and took his time wiping his already polished shoes with a little rag. At this stooping motion, the sheriff had jumped back, his hand coming near his gun. The men on the porch tittered at this show of uneasiness by the Law.

Damn niggers! Acting like a buncha monkeys, the sheriff thought.

"Shall we put the cuffs on 'em?" the deputy asked hopefully.

Before the sheriff could answer, Will Henry burst out, "Ain't nobody puttin no cuffs on nobody 'round heah!" Then he stood glowering at the fat deputy.

"Now, now," the sheriff said trying to ignore the angry outburst. "That ain't gonna be in no ways necessary. Now, come on 'round and get in back wit' my deputy, please. And we'll be on our way," the sheriff said, not liking the near begging tone of his voice.

"Why sure, Sheriff," Dave said amicably, and began walking down the path to get into the police car.

Lela cast Peter Frauzinou a pleading look, and he pulled her over and kissed her cheek.

"Mother Bailey, you don't have a thing in this world to worry about."

Lela straightened her small shoulders and smiled up at Peter. "I know I can depend on dat, so I ain't gone even think about hit no mo'," Lela said, trying to believe her own words.

The sheriff's car moved away with Dave in its back seat. At the same moment all of the men who had been on the porch ran for cars and trucks. They were going to follow Dave. They were going to see the mayor, too.

Omar, Peter, LaSalle, and Will Henry were in the head truck. The other men divided themselves up between waiting trucks and cars. All were heavily armed, their faces lit with determination, and even smiles.

As the entourage proceeded down the car line about two blocks, people began to notice and call out, "Well, I'll be! Will y'all look at dis! Hey! Where all y'all goin'?"

"We all goin' to see da mayor!" Omar sang out.

Ansell Morrissey suddenly realized that he was being trailed by a procession and he abruptly stopped his car, got out, and walked back to the first truck, which had also stopped.

Sheriff Morrissey addressed himself to the white looking Colored boy while thinking, *Could a boy with eyes this pale, hair this straight, skin this colorless really have nigger in him?*

"Now what y'all think you doin'?" the sheriff asked tensely.

"I beg your pardon?" Peter asked blandly. "What do you mean, Sheriff?"

The sheriff's jaws tightened as he looked into the cold grey eyes of the truck driver.

"You know what I mean! Why y'all following my car? The mayor wanna see Dave Bailey by hisself. Not all of Colored Town!" the sheriff said angrily, feeling that he'd better get a hold of this situation right now or he'd find himself answering to the mayor. This trail of trucks and cars was outrageous. Another slap in the white man's face. He wished for the second time this morning that he had had the presence of mind to bring more men with him.

"I really don't know what the problem is, Sheriff," Peter said, unruffled. "Me and the men you see behind me—and you—are simply going over to Old Steward to pick up some provisions. Is there now a law against shopping in Old Steward, Sheriff?" Peter asked, casually taking out a stick of gum and chewing it slowly as if he had not a care in the world.

The lying sonafabitch! If he had his way! But he did not. The mayor had been very clear: No trouble. Avoid a ruckus at all cost until we can talk to the leader.

So he, Ansell Morrissey, the high sheriff of both Old Steward and West Steward had to put up with stares and snickers all the way across town and into Old Steward as he was trailed by a pack of coons—and only God knew what they were up to!

The sheriff and his deputy entered the Court House and Business Building at 8:10 a.m. with Dave Bailey, looking serene, in the middle of them. The three of them proceeded to the second floor and the sheriff went into the mayor's office while Dave sat outside on a hard cold marble bench with a nervous Deputy Banks. Dave whistled. The deputy scowled; the whistling seemed disrespectful to him, and he cast Dave several disapproving looks in the few minutes they were seated. Dave ignored the deputy and continued to whistle and tap his feet, the picture of cool casualness, happy to be annoying Ferral Banks.

The sheriff spent several minutes with the mayor, no doubt informing him that Dave had not come alone.

After a few minutes the sheriff came out looking surly.

"Gwon in," he said impatiently.

Dave stood up, pulled down his jacket, straightened his tie, and walked into the mayor's office.

It was the thing that Robert McShane noticed first—appearance. This one looked carved in dark wood. He would bet Colored women found him good looking. The height, and the carriage. Erect, graceful. And surprise—this Dave Bailey was extremely well dressed. A good dark wool suit, nicely matched tie, highly polished shoes. This Bailey fellow made a very good impression.

The mayor was shorter in height and thinner than Dave had imagined he would be, having glimpsed him only once quickly, in person. But he had presence. In some ways this mayor reminded him of his old boss Dayton Holyoke. He had the same gentile air about him, the same spirit of command. This was no "po' white trash" in front of him, as he knew Ferral Banks and Ansell Morrissey to be. The man in front of him knew the rules of a gentleman—but whether they extended to a black man remained to be seen. Dave thought the office was a bit overdone, especially the blue silk drapery, but overall it was tasteful, masculine, low key, and elegant—like the mayor.

Mayor McShane came around the desk and extended a well-manicured hand. Dave grasped it and thought, *Round one.*

"Please have a seat," the mayor offered, pointing to one directly in front of his desk.

It was not the one Sheriff Birkens had been so uncomfortable in, but a large soft leather chair tufted and nail beaded.

Dave sat, looking at the mayor quietly with a questioning expression, and the mayor looked into the eyes nobody failed to notice, everybody commented on. Big, pretty eyes, said the ladies. His few enemies thought differently: *That nigger looks right through yo' ass! Don't miss a damn trick with them big eyes!*

"You wanted to see me, Mr. Mayor?" Dave asked politely.

The mayor noticed immediately that Dave was as about as relaxed as he had ever seen a man. There was not a shred of fear or anxiety about this meeting with the mayor. No quick and unnecessary movements of the body, and the mayor bet that his speech would remain quiet, smooth—not full of rushed air, hurried and stammered, showing nervousness to the world. And he was right. Dave looked sincerely interested. That was all.

His calmness caused the mayor to feel ill at ease; it made him feel in some ways that he would not even recognize himself, that he was meeting not just an equal, but a person possibly *superior* to himself. It was an experience he had not had in decades and he did not like it.

"Yes. Yes, indeed," Mayor McShane said, coming around the desk and sitting on the corner of it, which put him above Dave.

The mayor had thought over his approach. He would be low key, dignified, open. And yes, even friendly—for now.

"As you know, Dave, we have experienced a lot of problems of one kind or another in the last few months, serious problems. I need not go into them. You are aware?" the mayor said, looking around the room, at the floor, anywhere but in the face that held those eyes.

"Yes."

"Well, what I wondered is this: do you know anything about any of the things that have happened? Who's behind it, why things are happening—like that?" the mayor said slowly, thinking how badly he had phrased the question.

"Me?" Dave asked incredulously. "Me?" Dave asked again. "Well, I wonder if you care to be more specific, Mr. Mayor."

"You're right, Dave. I should be more specific. Much more specific. First, let me start with the fact that I keep hearing your name around town."

Dave gave the mayor an empty look.

"I mean, you and your mother are very well respected people, obviously. So, what it gets down to: when I've asked people if they were in trouble who they would go to in Colored Town for help, most of them said Lela Bailey or Dave Bailey without hesitation. Why is that?" the mayor asked, sitting on the edge of his desk, shaking his foot a little, thinking that maybe he had asked a good question.

"Easy question," Dave said, smiling and crossing his long legs, still the picture of complete relaxation. "My mother used to be a practical nurse, a helper to Dr. Henri Echardt, in Colored Town for years, so she was in and out of everybody's house and they got to trust her and call on her for free medical advice when the doctor wasn't around. Finally people started to ask for all kinds of advice. Mama helped when she could, which was most of the time. She's pretty level-headed.

"Now, as for me, I'm a small businessman. Very small businessman!" Dave laughed, mocking himself. "I sell hot tamales up on the car line. People know me. They also borrow money from me—small amounts. Folks like a place they can get a little piece of emergency change. I try to be generous. But," Dave said, laughing again, "I *loan* money. I don't give it away. They have to pay it back—eventually."

"I see," the mayor said, feeling that he was coming up dry. "And what is your rate of interest?"

"Interest? Oh, I don't charge any interest."

"None?" The mayor asked, allowing the pale blue eyes to light fleetingly on the coffee face.

"No. Never did. These are just small loans—a dollar, maybe up to ten dollars—among friends, Mr. Mayor."

"I see."

Dave waited.

The mayor's left foot continued its delicate dance.

"The murders. The jail break. The burning down of the Old Storage House. The poisoning of livestock, the killing of the dog," the mayor shotgunned, taking a chance, bunching the questions together. "You know nothing about any of those happenings?" He turned slightly and matched Dave's stare with his own mirror blue one. At that moment the sun came around the curtains and illuminated Dave's face, turning it golden. The room was very still, and the faint smile that the young man's face had held since he entered the mayor's office faded from his face.

Dave looked at the mayor for a long moment, as if weighing what had been asked. Finally he said utterly without concern, "Of course I know about all of those 'happenings,' as you call them. Every last one of them. I live here in West Steward," Dave said.

This was a clear rebuke, as if to say, *What do you take me for? Of course I know. I was here when it all happened.*

The mayor's foot stopped its dance, and he looked sharply at Dave and looked away, not seeming to take offense.

"But I have absolutely no idea who did those things or why. None whatsoever. Why are you asking me?" Dave asked.

"I thought perhaps you could help me get some of this mess, some of the problems we have been having in the last months straightened out."

"Oh, and how is that?" Dave asked, truly interested.

"Well," the mayor began, "since you and your family are so highly respected in Colored Town..." McShane trailed off, not quite knowing where to go from there.

The mayor had painted himself into a corner and he knew it, and he was sure Dave knew it too. There were many 'well respected' Colored people in Colored Town. Mrs. Keller, the principal of the grade school and high school for one, and the minister of the largest black church in the twin towns, Rev. F.W.T. Edison, and Pate Aclavin, the contractor, to mention a few. There was only one reason Dave Bailey sat before him this morning—Benjamin Carter. He led the jail break. He burned down the Old Storage House. He got the Dusters out of town because their son Ralph was a suspect in those murders. Everything that went on against the white men in the town, Dave Bailey was the guiding hand, Carter told the mayor. He had figured it all out.

This well dressed, mannerly man? Could it be? Yet he was imposing. He surely could lead something if he had a mind to. The mayor was sure of that. And he was proving quiet and smooth, to the mayor's dismay.

Robert McShane knew that Benjamin Carter had been passed over at the mill in favor of young Dave some years ago. Carter was a grizzled middle aged man who did not even know enough to wear a deodorant, and was never going to have all of his own teeth again. Was his story about Dave just a case of simple jealousy that had escalated into revenge? Did he hate the man sitting before him enough to try to get him killed?

Sallie Poindexter burst into the mayor's office suddenly without knocking, as she had been paid to do. Dave turned around quickly, and she looked directly at him and he smiled and winked.

"Oh, 'scuse me, Mistah Mayor, suh! I beg yo' most humble partners! I just happen to notice dat Miz Evelyn Thesault—you know, yo' secretary?—ain't heah yet, so I thought you might be wantin' some coffee or somethin'? I got some nice pound cake I could slice up."

"Would you like something, Dave?" the mayor asked.

"No, thank you very much."

Sallie closed the door, smiling, her questions answered.

"Well," the mayor said, feeling the earth moving away from under his feet as surely as if a small earthquake had moved dirt.

"Perhaps you can tell me this," the mayor said, almost sighing. "Why have Colored people stopped shopping with merchants in the town? Surely you know that." There was a bit of ill concealed rancor in the mayor's voice now, acknowledging that so far he had been bested.

Each man, in this early match, was sparring, looking for an advantage, looking for something to take back to the troops, trying to get the upper hand in some way. The mayor felt that Dave Bailey knew a great deal more than he was ever going to tell him. It all came down to whether he believed Benjamin Carter or not. A moment ago the two men had been in silence, a moment between questions; the mayor doing his foot dance, Dave practicing his studied calm. Both had been looking down.

By chance both men had looked up at the same time and in that fleeting second each had looked directly into the other's eyes and saw the truth. In that fleeting prism of time, Mayor McShane knew that Benjamin Carter had told him the truth: that the man before him was highly intelligent—even brilliant. No slacker himself, McShane realized that such men were to be negotiated with. It could be lethal to try to outwit them.

In *his* transient moment, Dave saw that the mayor was penned securely to the wall, and he also felt a wavering in the mayor, a lack of desire for blood sport. He also thought that things were possible now that in the past would have been unthinkable. Seeing this truth, Dave decided to push to the limit.

Dave sat up and forward in his chair, and the mayor, sensing a change in mood, moved around and sat in his seat behind the polished desk, in front of the silk drapery, and waited.

Dave pressed his palms together and placed them under his chin in a thoughtful manner. He began by telling the mayor a brief story: "There is a woman in Colored Town by the name of ...well, her name doesn't matter. Three months ago, her very elderly mother died down in Alabama. She left three insurance policies to this woman. When this woman, who is well known and very well liked in our community, had taken care of all of her mother's business, she had some money left. This woman was poor and had been doing without for years. We were happy to see her go to town to stock her larder with food, to buy new clothes and shoes that were badly needed. To make a long story short, this poor woman never got anything— not in town, Mr. Mayor."

The mayor sat forward with interest, frowning. "No? Why not?"

"Because she is proud," Dave said quietly, then he let his words soak in.

"Proud? What do you mean?" The mayor's eyebrows shot up quizzically.

"Proud," Dave repeated. "The woman had money to spend and she wanted to spend. She said she wanted something she could never afford to buy before: toilet water, good chocolates, a gold ring, a fur piece for her suit, things like that. Her ship had truly come in." Dave smiled. "But everywhere this poor woman went, she had to wait and wait and wait until others were served. The lady is seventy-one years old and her back is no longer strong, not to mention her legs. I mentioned that this lady is very proud. She said, 'My money is as good as anybody's. If they don't want it, I will not beg them to take it.' "

"I see," said the mayor, beginning to understand.

"There are three good store owners in and around these towns," Dave continued. "All Jewish. This woman went to the one that has his shop up in White Town. She asked him if he could get her a store bought dress, shoes, and a hat or two. There was one catch: She wanted to try things on for fit first, just as...some other customers are allowed to do."

The mayor lit a cigar. Almost automatically he offered one to Dave, who politely declined. The use of the word "others," meaning whites was not lost on the mayor. He sat back, listening.

"Well, Meyer is nobody's fool. I guess he reasoned that since over eighty percent of his customers were Colored anyway, he had more to gain than lose. It was a business decision Meyer made, not a moral one. Meyer had everything the lady wanted. He didn't even try to charge her extra, as she figured he would."

The mayor gave a tight little smile and lifted an eyebrow to show that he understood the reputation of the Jews as thieves, warranted or not.

"I like Old Meyer," Dave said, careful not to buy into any hint of anti-semitism that the mayor's little smile reflected. "He was fair, and he was smart. His business expanded beyond anything he had hoped for even in these times."

"Did his...other customers stay with him?" the mayor asked as diplomatically as he could.

Dave laughed and looked directly at the mayor to show that he understood the use of the word "other" that they both now found so convenient to use.

"No. Of course not. But Moishe Meyer is a happy man. He has lost some customers, but no money. Quite the opposite. Colored people are coming from miles around just to shop at his store, to be served on an equal basis, to try before they buy, to be treated fairly, politely," Dave said. Again, the smile was gone from his face. "When people are proud, Mr. Mayor, and are consistently treated with disrespect as if one is doing them a favor to take their money, well..."

The mayor waited for more speaking. There was none. Dave was finished.

"Oh, come on, Dave! You surely cannot ask me or the merchants to advocate equal treatment in these stores! The customers wouldn't stand for it. That's revolutionary. That's just not the way things are! Surely you don't think that as mayor I can change things like that? This is *the South*, fellow!" The mayor was clearly angry now, clearly frustrated.

The smile returned to Dave's face. It was a smile akin to the smile he had once given to Grant Fromm back at Detroit Mill. It was a smile of victory a-coming—of winning without a fight, of meeting The Man on the dance floor and out-stepping him.

"Oh, no, Mr. Mayor!" Dave said evenly. "I'm not asking you to do anything, nothing at all. I'm simply answering what you asked me. I'm telling you why people stopped shopping up in White Town and in Old Steward. The woman's pride spread, that's all. And most people have decided that until they are treated with respect as others are, they'd rather shop where they are treated fairly. It's as simple as that. Of course you still have some Negroes shopping in the twin towns—a few."

"Like who?"

"Oh, like Benjamin Carter and friends of his, people like that, I expect," Dave said, looking directly at the mayor.

"I see," said the mayor. "I see." He was thinking that of course this man would find out that Benjamin Carter was the reason he was sitting here now. Poor stupid Carter. The mayor actually felt a bit of pity for him, because he knew his ass was grass now.

"Now, how store owners and other merchants feel about how they are going to deal with the situation as I have explained it to you is up to them. People have a right to spend or not spend their money wherever they please. I'm sure we can agree on that, Mr. Mayor," Dave said smoothly.

The men stared at each other, neither smiling.

Clever. Very clever, the mayor was thinking. *A boycott. Somebody started a boycott. And it's working. Boy, how it's working! These so-called dumb niggers are putting solid businessmen out of business!*

Dave gave signs of getting restless, his body language asking, *Is that all Mr. Mayor?* But he sat politely in his chair, trying not to fidget or cross and uncross his legs too often.

Suddenly the mayor said, "That is all. You may go. Thank you for coming in."

Dave stood, turned and opened the door quickly. He knew the mayor would not want to shake his hand as he departed.

And now the mayor was certain. This man taking his leave now in his elegant attire, his black good looks, was everything Benjamin Carter had said he was and more. He was The Leader, and there wasn't a damn thing he could do about it— unless he wanted these two towns to explode, perhaps into something the South had never experienced since Nat Turner.

The very next thing the mayor did was get Benjamin Carter in his office and grill the living shit out of him. He gave him certain imperatives, and a large sum of money—twenty-five dollars—some of which he was to quietly spread around in Colored Town until he came up with some answers that led somewhere, the mayor told him, or he was going to have to find himself a better boy.

Benjamin liked money more than he feared Dave and the Circle, and he was also foolish enough to believe that no one knew of his "work" for the mayor.

Back at home, Dave shared everything with the Inner Circle.

"Ladies and gentlemen, I think we may have won something," he told the assembled group. "Give it another few weeks, let them get really desperate, then we'll send a few test cases out with money in their pockets and see if they can get served on a first come, first served basis everywhere or if these crackers want to starve to death!"

A great cheer went up in Lela's kitchen, and Dave received hugs, claps on back, smiles.

Over the noise Dave said, "You have your boycott, Reverend. Are you satisfied with it?"

"Very much so, Dave. Especially since no lives have been lost—I mean in boycotting. It's not the kind of boycott I imagined, but it is effective. That's what counts. Yes, we seem to be makin' a little progress. Praise the Lord!"

FIFTY-FOUR

I t was easy, Aggie told Lela and Helena, because Sadie Carter, old Benjamin's wife, had "da three L's so bad she didn't know what ta do!"

"The three L's? What on earth is that?" Helena asked, and Lela sat forward to hear too.

Aggie laughed, enjoying being somewhat mysterious, having knowledge that others did not as usual, even if she had to invent it.

"Why dats da long, loud, and loose lips!" Aggie giggled. "She were easy to git all da lowdown I needed, cause she talk forever! You ax her one thing she tell you answer ta ten!"

From Sadie Carter, Aggie learned in short order that Benjamin Carter had a sister in Alabama, a brother in Mississippi; she had even learned their addresses, which she carefully wrote down. Aggie also learned that Benjamin was a big believer in voodoo, often thinking he had been "fixed" when his luck turned bad, often seeking to put a "fix" on others. Benjamin believed in good luck oils, charms and the like, and carried a "sack" for good luck, Sadie said, that he thought protected him from evil spirits and haunts.

"Chile, I jus' 'bout passed out, I wanted to laugh so bad, but 'cose I had to keep a straight face," Aggie said.

Two days after Dave's meeting with the mayor, Benjamin Carter went to the car line to Jones' Market to buy a pound of spicy pork sausage, which the Jones brothers ground themselves. He was never seen again in West Steward.

A very dark-skinned man, heavily muscled, stopped Benjamin as he walked along and forced him into the back seat of a car that held two other men, whom Benjamin did not know.

"Did you check to see whether he had a gun or knife?" the driver asked Omar Williams.

"If he do, he better eat it!" the man who had pressed the gun to his temple, that Benjamin now recognized, said.

"Y'all gone kill me?" Benjamin was finally able to ask through dry lips. They had been driving for perhaps fifteen minutes, going, he thought, further and faster into darkness.

No answer.

Benjamin was burning up. Sweat had plastered his shirt to his back and ran between his thighs. He wished they would let him out to pee. He had never known such urgency in his life.

One of the men in the front seemed to be reading his mind.

"Don't you piss in dis car, nigger, or we'll shoot yo' ass heah and nah!"

The car crackled with laughter as they continued to push further into the night. Carter was sure they were out of West Steward now.

Once more he tried his dry tongue.

"Why y'all doin' dis?" he began.

"Shut up!" Omar yelled.

Finally, the driver approached a thickly wooded area and stopped. Benjamin Carter was ordered out of the car. It was pitch dark. He had no idea where he was.

"Uh, man! You sho' funked up dat automobile! Don't you put nothin' under yo' arms? Shit! You smell worser den a skunk!" the man who had been sitting next to the driver said.

Benjamin, now suddenly as cold as he had been hot, found himself in the middle of a three man circle. The men were slowly becoming visible even in this dark. He only knew Omar, but they seemed to know him.

No one spoke, and the wind whistling through the trees seemed to take on a whining tone, extremely high pitched and fretful.

"Well, Carter, what shall we do with the mayor's snitch, huh? A Negro so rotten that he goes to da mayor and says dey got a leader down dere, mah good Mistah White Mayor, dats so bad dat he should be lynched! Nah, Benjamin, I ax you, what kind of Negro main is dat?" the man who had finally spoken asked, almost pleasantly.

Benjamin Carter was nearly struck speechless.

Lawd in heaben! What was goin' on?

Nobody, nobody but the mayor knew he had made dat statement!

"I don't snitch fer nobody!" he retorted hotly.

"Oh, quit lying, nigger!" Omar said, moving closer to Benjamin, causing him to move backward so quickly that he stumbled and fell, got up quickly and continued to alternate between hot sweats and chills.

"You got twenty dollars snitch money laying in yo' pocket rat nah. It were twenty-five, but you done tried to spread some of that snitch fee around to catch a fish, didn't ya?" Omar said ominously. He had put the gun away, and now had in his hand his preferred weapon, a straight razor that glinted a bit, even in the dark.

"You have a sister by the name of Edwina Carols living in Grover, Alabama at 1315 Faulkner Avenue, Route 6, Box 12; you have an older brother over in Highland, Mississippi, on Gates Road, Route 2, Box 6. Both o'dem has six chirrens. You know, Carter, when you a snitch you kin end up hurting yo' entire fambly. Even yo' old mammy. You know what I mean?" asked the man who had been sitting next to the driver.

Lawd have mercy! Dey knowed everything! Benjamin thought, his knees sagging, his teeth beginning to chatter with cold fear.

"We gone stay here in da South. Dis our home, even though every day peepers is leaving in droves. No, suh. We ain't gone be runt off ourva land where so many of our kin have done died—ome due to niggers jus' lak you, Mistah Snitch," the driver said again. "Dis Southland belongs ta us as well as white folks—maybe even mo' so, since we da ones done worked da dirt, built da biggest portion of da houses. No, suh! We ain't gone be drove off."

"Dats right," said the other man. "And hi many killin's, poisonin's, or anythin' else been solved lately, Mistah Benjamin Carter? None! Dats hi many. So you see, things can be done nice and easy wit' doubt da White Man ever findin' out shit!" the man explained, taking credit for both deeds done and not done.

"What we means is, Mistah Snitch, when dat sun come up, you better be short coupled and long gone, heah? Take yo' twenty dollars and git yo' black ass on some way outta heah!" Omar said. "I mahself doesn't lak dis plan to let you loose at all, but boss say we got to spare yo' worthless behind."

Benjamin Carter, who considered himself the most fortunate man in the world, was left standing in the middle of "no wha in the middle of da nite." He was told to go as far North as he could get and never return, not even to visit his relatives in other southern states. "If you do, we'll know it," he was told, "den all hell gone break loose on yo' soul as well as yo' body!"

Benjamin did not know what the men meant exactly, but he believed them.

After walking for miles in the dark, the snitch reached in his pocket for a handkerchief to wipe sweat from his face and neck. His fingers felt something he had not put there. He lifted the thing out. It was a small red flannel sock, pulled together at the top with string. When he moved it in his hand, it made a slight clicking sound.

Bones.

Benjamin recognized what the sack was instantly and he began to sweat even more. With trembling hands, and went through all the pockets of his jacket. Another one! This time a black sack of rough material sewn top and bottom. Benjamin knew what was probably in it: black cat hairs, bones from a poisonous snake's tail, hair from the private parts of a whore, red pepper, perhaps a toe nail from a dead man's foot.

"Oh, Lawd! Oh, Lawd!" Benjamin hollered. "I done been fixed! Dem mens done fixed me! Hep me somebody! I done been fixed!"

Benjamin Carter ran through the woods until he couldn't run anymore. Leaving his jacket somewhere in the woods he dashed through the dark stumbling and panting.

Out of breath, his clothes torn by his mindless run through the trees, Benjamin came upon a Negro man on the road in a truck.

"Please!" he hollered. "I'll gie you five dollars to get me on away from heah!"

FIFTY-FIVE

✻

When Robert McShane heard that Benjamin Carter had disappeared, he was "perturbed but not surprised," Sallie Poindexter had heard him remark to an aide.

"'Cose nah, I believes dat ol' Carter bein' done left 'bout knocked Mac Mac's drawers down about round his ankles—he jus' won't admit hit. Chile, he aint looking none too happy dese days!" Sally remarked to Aggie.

"Preposterous, scandalous, unbelievable!" Mayor McShane had told his wife, Violet. "We are practically being held hostage by these damn Negroes!"

In the middle of the month, the mayor had gone to a large grocery store to see for himself if what they told him was true—that business was bad and getting worse.

"Our Negroes just don't shop with us no more," the storekeeper complained, his shirt hanging noticably slack on his back even as his cans—peaches, peas, tomatoes—sat folornly on their shelves gathering dust, like wall flowers waiting to be asked for a dance.

McShane watched the grocery line for a while. There were four whites in the line, and two Colored women trying to buy a nickle's worth of coffee and a nickle's worth of dried beans. The two Colored women kept getting shoved to the back of the line. After the four whites were served, the storekeeper waited on the Colored women in a friendly manner, inquiring about their health and their families. The mayor thought the women were sullen.

McShane put a pound of coffee, a pound of sugar in his basket, talked with the storekeeper a moment who professed to be real proud to see him, and left. As the mayor walked outside he saw Dave Bailey. He seemed to be just standing and he was alone. He seemed taller in the street than he had in his office. And blacker.

Dave was dressed casually this time, in khaki pants, a wool jacket and a cream-colored rough shirt opened at the collar. He was hatless, his hands in his pockets.

"Well! Dave Bailey. We meet again," the mayor said as his aide eyed them from the official car. He was getting out to take the mayor's package.

"Yes. How are you, Mr. Mayor?" the young man said, smiling broadly. "How is everything?"

"Fine. Fine. Doing some shopping. And you?" the mayor asked, his eyes narrowing.

"Oh, just passing the time," Dave said, still smiling. "Just passing the time."

I'll bet! the mayor thought. What was he doing up here in White Town just standing and looking? Then it occurred to the mayor in a flash: *Why he was doing the same thing I was doing! Watching the grocery line. Watching the effectiveness of the boycott!*

"Well, have a big day," the mayor said rather tartly to Dave as he took his leave.

"Same to you, Mr. Mayor!" Dave called with the same smile, as the mayor and his aide moved back towards the official car.

The mayor hesitated in his car, telling his driver and aide to wait. He wanted to see if the two Colored women who had been in the store addressed Dave when they came out, if they gave him any kind of report.

But Dave was watching the mayor's car out of the corner of his eye, and noting that his car did not move immediately, he quickly walked to his truck and drove off, before the two women he had planted had a chance to talk to him and thus alert the mayor.

Smart, Dave thought. The mayor figured out that those women had been sent to shop in that store as a test. That's why he sat watching. Dave was still smiling as he turned down Hickory Street to visit with Peter Frauzinou.

Smart, the mayor thought. Driving off like that before the women had a chance to come out and talk to him. Seeing Dave reminded the mayor of an unpleasant task he had not completed and must do immediately. McShane had not broached to the businessmen the reason the majority of Negroes were no longer shopping in their stores. He thought his reasoning was sound. He would let things cool down a bit, then he would tell the businessmen himself. He was trying to find a way to break it to them without seeming to take the Negroes' side—which of course he did not. But now two weeks had passed and he still had not talked to the Businessmen's Board.

He had decided that when he met with the board, he would tell them the unvarnished truth and let the chips fall. Then it would be out of his hands. It would be their decision. Then they must shit or get off the pot. That was for damn sure.

McShane knew that to be a successful mayor, to advance from a hick town to something larger, like governor—yes, like governor. There, the dream he had dared to name finally had surfaced. To be successful one had to keep the peace—be progressive, innovative. In short, McShane knew he had to cut a better hand than he had now, because these towns were just sinking into cesspool of problems.

What would you do, Mr. Mayor, if you were in our shoes? That's what the businessmen would ask. He would throw the question right back at them. Maybe he would say, "Gentlemen, do you want to make money, or starve, and be white? It's really *your* decision." The mayor decided he had to keep the ball in their laps at all times. And he would not let them blame the "cousins," the Jews, as they were prone to do—for he knew these men. If they took their frustrations out on the Jews, that would present another problem.

The Jews have taken our customers! they would holler. No, he would have to explain as quietly as he could that they made a decision that was right for them based on profit. "And gentlemen," he would say, "who wouldn't take drastic steps in times such as these? Why don't y'all go on home and think all this over? Y'all don't have to make a snap decision. Just think on it, and let me know what you come up with, say in a week? OK."

The men would leave angry, blaming the sun, moon and every black man that ever farted, but they would leave, and make decisions they could live with. And whatever decision the men made, the women would live with also.

Maxey Joe Blue was the first storekeeper in West Steward to cave in. For years he had run a very successful store similar to Dave's on the outskirts: candy, pickles, pickled pig feet, oil sausage and crackers, cookies, salted peanuts. The pregnant women, Colored or white, could not resist his stock, and since the Depression, there were more women expecting than ever, as their husbands were home both day and night.

Dave watched each day as the heavy-bellied women, three quarters of them black, waddled into the store and left with what they had to have: the salt, the grease, the sugar in little brown bags. So Dave decided this would be a good store to target directly.

Aggie's women had approached the expectant black mothers house by house. Would they consider buying from the little Colored stores instead of Maxey Joe Blue's?

"Just for a little while? You try to help us and we'll try to protect you if you ever need protection, OK?" Aggie promised, revealing more than she thought smart.

The women knew that somebody was at work for Colored in these twin towns now. They had all heard the stories. Yes, they would go where they could be served with respect, as long as it wasn't forever, 'cause Maxey Joe Blue did have the best of everything—the biggest stage planks, the best chocolate drops, more peanuts for a nickel.

The word boycott was never mentioned. Soon after the Colored mothers had been diverted to the little Negro mom and pop stores, Maxey Joe closed his store one evening and came home in a panic and told his wife, "I done lost all my Colored customers overnight! I dunno why. I can't sell no sour pickles wit' peppermint sticks jugged down in 'em fer da woil! No big moon cookies, no stage planks, no pickled pig foots, no oil sausages, no cherry chews, nothin'!"

When Maxey Joe Blue asked one of his former best customers, Iozta Reeves, why she now seemed to prefer old Clarence Baker's store to his, Iozta, pregnant mother of nine, who had been coached, told Maxey that she was big as a bull and "mah ankles is swole up, and I caint stand round all day waitin' behind white ladies while dey make up dey minds. Clarence don't have much stuff as you, Mistah Blue, and hit ain't put out near as pretty as yourn, but you don't have to stand around waitin' all day lak a dog."

So that was it.

"Lawd Gawd Almighty!" Maxey told his wife, "Deres two expectant white wimmens in particular look lak dey wuz tryin to put me clean outta business! Dey hem and dey haw. Nah dis, nah dat. Wait! I done changed mah mind! All dis goin' on while I'm standin dere watchin' Colored women wit' money justa burnin dey fingers git tired a waitin' after while. Nah, Iozta tell me dey all takin' dey business to da little Colored sto's! Lawdy!" At this point in the telling Maxey Joe Blue was so consumed with frustration and rage that his handkerchief was soaked from mopping his face and neck.

Truth be told, it was that anger and frustration—and *need*—that twisted decades of rules out of their proper shape, not any moral sense of right and wrong.

Maxey Joe simply could not stand seeing black women walking out of his store with money in their hands-not when he had five children and a wife to feed. So, one day he said—and not too pleasantly, either—"'Cuse me, Miz Bassy, I hope you don't mind if I just wait on Fannie Delores heah since she ready wit' her order and you not? Thank you, mam! You so kind," Maxey had snorted.

For the white women that complained that Colored were being served before them, Maxey Joe whined that he had to, that he had children and a wife to feed and these were hard times, real hard times, therefore he couldn't let one penny—not one red cent, he emphasized, slapping his hands together and rubbing the sweat from his brow—walk outta his store. Besides, he thought, Colored made up a good percent of his customers anyhow.

"First come, first served! Nah, dats hit! I done made up mah mind. Shit! Da Klu Klux Klan don't pay none o'mah bills!" Maxey reasoned. "Peckerwoods wanna jack me up 'bout dis, wanna mess wit' me 'bout dis, dey gone have to do so in front o'mah shotgun!"

And that was that. The mighty walls of segregation crumbled first at Maxey Joe Blue's candy store. The Circle knew it was a victory that would have wider implications—for no sooner did Maxey Joe start to use "need" as a reason for serving blacks on an equal basis than the other shopkeepers start giving Maxey Joe himself as an excuse: "Well nah, what kin we do? Maxey Joe using da first come first serve thing, and look at da money he making, even ifn hit is walking in penny by penny. Shoot! Peepers comin' from miles around to be served fo' white folks."

And they were. Negroes from Epps, Ketta, LaBima, Tricktoo, all around West Steward, wanted to see this equal service thing for themselves—and they brought at least a nickle to spend with Maxey Joe Blue.

So Maxey Joe became a reluctant hero in the eyes of the out-of-town Colored who did not know how this equal treatment business came about, and the Circle chalked up more victories as several smaller stores followed rapid suit. Of course the larger, more expensive stores did not change their policy, because having very few Negro customers in the first place, they had little to gain or lose.

FIFTY-SIX

Rex Bailey had gained weight in the few weeks that he had been home. His appetite was good, his coughing less frequent and racking, and on two occassions he felt well enough to stay out of bed almost the entire day.

When John Candle paid his third visit, it was clear that Rex was his favorite "patient."

"Well, hi is Mistah Long Bones tahday?" he asked jovially. "You sleeping good? You eatin' good? Yas, yas, I kin see dat you is, you filling out right nicely in da face."

After his examination, Rex told him, "I got somethin' fer ya in dis bag," and held up a small cloth tobacco sack with pull strings at the top. "If you don't want hit, don't come to dis house no mo'. I mean hit!" he said with faux irritation and anger.

The herbalist took the bag and shook it, and listened to the delicate clanking it made.

"What's in heah, Rex?"

"Ain't you got da sense to open hit up? Hit's a snake."

"Oh, good. Dats alright den. I do love snakes," the little man said dumping out five gold coins in his hand.

"Dis fer me? My lands!" the herbalist asked, stretching his small eyes.

"Naw. Hit's fer da devil," Rex snorted.

"Aw, Rex I can't take dis. You know dere ain't any charges fer what I does fer you."

At once the gentle, soft core of the herbalist, hardly ever glimpsed by anyone except those closest and dearest to him, revealed itself to the sick man, and the sweetness of it was so unexpected, so cloyingly intense that it left both men silent.

Rex spoke first. "You can't take dem coins? Den git on outta mah house you lil'old rascal! I ain't playin'."

John Candle's shoulders started to shake with mirth, then out of control, he rocked back and forth in a chair that he had fallen into, tears rolling down his face.

"Awright, awright den! I guess I got to keep dese old coins or git put out. Is dey gold?!"

"Naw. Where would a po' nigger git any gold at? They only five quarters covered over wit' paint."

The herbalist looked crestfallen for all of the second it took him to reexamine the coins and assure himself once again that they were indeed gold. He began to laugh again, a high hoop filled with the pleasure of an unexpected and valuable gift—for he did love gold.

Late on a Sunday evening after Rex had eaten a very small amount of one of his favorite meals, baked chicken with giblet dressing, he asked Dave to go fetch Helena and the children. "I'm 'bout ready to put on mah show," he stated happily.

Rex wore a mask because of the children, and Basil loved it. It made his grandfather, whom he had not met before now, appear even more mysterious. With his wife and children and grandchildren around the kitchen table, Rex had Dave lift his large grip up on the table, and with a playful muffled drum roll, Rex opened the grip with a flourish from his seat at the table.

With ceremony he removed a lovely large silk scarf with red peonies on a light green background. He had "come by hit" he said in Chinatown in San Francisco, California. He handed the scarf to his wife, his eyes crinkling in a smile behind the mask.

Lela took the beautiful scarf from her husband's hands. It was quite heavy, probably filled with bars of sweet soap, she figured.

"What's in heah Rex?" she asked seriously.

"Open it, Grandma!" Meredith said with breathless exasperation.

Everyone smiled and leaned forward in anticipation, as Lela nervously fumbled with the slippery knots in the scarf. Finally she undid the knots and mouths flew open.

"Aha!" Rex exclaimed merrily, kicking up his heels from his chair. "Thought hit was some old candies, didn't ya?"

Lela spread the contents of the silk scarf on her kitchen table. After counting, Lela found she had five packs of single dollar bills, each pack containing one hundred dollars, held together with golden cording.

"Lawdinheaben!" Lela exclaimed. "Where did you git all dis money, Rex? Is dis all fer me?"

Rex reached over and circled his wife's waist with a bony arm. He rubbed his mask against her arm very quickly and moved back in his chair again, already a little tired from his efforts.

Seeing that Lela was about to burst into tears, Rex said, "Oh, my Gawd! Don't let 'er turn on da hydrant!"

Lela laughed at her husband and checked her tears. "I think you musta robbed a bank!" she exclaimed.

"Please don't say that in front of these rascals, Mama!" Helena said. "They'll have it all over town!"

While Dave had gazed at his father's suitcase with casual interest, Helena's eyes had hardly left it. She eyed it, smiling as if it held great and mysterious riches.

"Dave, reach in dere and git dat white handkerchief. Hit's just plain white, not pretty lak yo' mama's scarf, 'cause you's a main. You was da only main dis house knew whiles I was away, so I brought you a little somethin' to show you hi much I appreciated you looking after yo' mama all dose years." Rex was getting a little emotional himself, so he reached out and patted Dave's head playfully to hide his feelings, and then sharply drew back his hand.

"Boy, you sho' got you some nappy hair!" his father laughed. "And you didn't get hit from me!"

"Well, don't look at me!" Lela tossed back.

This comment caused the family to laugh loudly.

Dave opened his white handkerchief and let out the excited, surprised whoop his father expected. His handkerchief had bills in more serious denominations: five packs, each containing ten dollar bills, five hundred dollars tied loosely with brown string.

They saw Rex's cheeks move up, smiling, broad and pleased behind his mask.

"Daddy, where did you get?—" Dave began, real surprise filling his voice.

"None of yo' business, nappy head!" Rex teased. "Ahm the daddy in dis fambly. *I* ax da questions."

Lela gawked at her husband, a look of profound amazement and love on her face.

"Nah, don't go looking at me lak dat, Lela. I ain't robbed no bank, I tole ya!" Rex said, giggling and coughing.

"Dave, deres another sack in dere fer you. In dat corner."

Dave could not immediately locate it under his father's clothes, so Rex struggled up from his chair and pretending to be annoyed, he thrust his hand into the grip and pulled out a bulging white cloth tobbaco sack pulled tightly at the top with red string.

"Here, boy," he said as if the contents of the sack were of little consequence.

Dave opened the heavy little sack and dumped the contents in his left hand.

"Daddy! Is this—"

"Gold." Rex said, giggling like a school boy.

Dave turned and looked at his father's masked face in awe now.

"Some from California. Some from Alaska. Some Colorado," Rex said simply. He lifted the mask momentarily, had a few sips of hot tea, and then pulled the mask down again.

"Getting' hot under dis thing," he complained.

"Well, I never!" Lela exclaimed looking at the sandy looking lumps of gold.

"Give my mother somethin'!" Basil demanded peevishly.

Rex threw back his head and laughed at his grandson.

"Lawd! Ain't he a little bugger!"

"How much gold is this, Daddy?" Dave asked, now staring at the magical suitcase as it revealed its treasure.

"Don't know!" Rex shouted out. "Never had it weighed up. Figured you'd do that—or jus' save it as a souvenir from yo' pappy."

The gifts continued to pour forth from the old grip. A heavy 22-carat bracelet and matching ring for Helena, from an East Indian shop "in one o'dose lil' neighborhoods in New Yawk City," Rex told his daughter. A package of money, ten twenty dollar bills, were lined up neatly in a red enamel jewelry box. Helena was stunned.

Her father started to laugh and cough and complain, "Lawd at da looks on y'alls faces! Y'all gone send me off to bed wit' a fever from laughing 'foe I finish puttin' out what I done brought!" With this he reached into the grip and brought out a fine black lace mantilla from New Mexico and gave it to Helena.

"Dem Catholic wimmens wears dese on dey heads to church. I guess you could too, if you wanted to."

There was a huge blue wool shawl with silken balls for fringes, which Rex handed to his wife. He also reached in and placed a lovely box with inlaid mother of pearl from

New Orleans in Lela's hands. There also was a delicate looking turquoise and silver necklace Rex said he had bought off a "red Indian" over in Wyoming.

By now, Rex's wife was past being astounded. She took her presents and stared at each one of them as if they were from the moon. Her looks of consternation were hardly less than those of Helena and Merry. Even Dave had become quiet with wonder and amazement.

The disgouging continued for others. A silk and lace waist, pure silver earrings, and fancy silk pajamas made by a Chinese woman in San Francisco, who could not believe the length the pajamas had to be to fit because of Dave's height.

Finally, Rex said, "I got somethin' fer grandchillen, too."

"Hooray!" Basil shouted, but Meredith St. Quatran remained quiet, watchful, eyeing the grip greedily, expectantly, and viewing her grandfather with renewed respect, even if his English was no better than her grandmother's.

Rex pointed to an item wrapped in rough cloth and Dave lifted it out of the grip for his father. Rex took it and unwrapped it himself and presented it to Basil.

It was a novelty mechanical bank, a black, clownish fat man with a little red hat on the side of his head. The man had a palm out. When you placed a coin in his palm, he put the coin in his pocket.

Basil went wild with joy.

"Alright, since you likes dat so well, heah you somethin' else," his grandfather said. "Look in dat corner."

Basil dived into the grip and found the small brown sealed envelope his grandfather said was his, and promptly ripped it open and dumped three twenty dollar gold coins in his hand.

"Thank you, Father Rexy!" Basil screamed, running around the table to hug his grandfather's neck before he could be stopped. Then looking up innocently at his mother he asked, "Am I a rich boy now, Mother?"

"Lawd, Lawd! Ain't dis boy a pistol!" Rex laughed, his whole body shaking.

Meredith eyed her brother's shiny coins and waited.

"And nah, little Miss Merry—what you want out dis grip?"

"Oh, just anything, Grandfather," Meredith said modestly.

A knowing look and wry smile passed between the adults in the kitchen who knew better. They knew Meredith wanted the most, would be the hardest to please or impress, even at her young age.

Her grandfather handed her a large fold of fine white cotton eyelet fabric, hand finished and exquisite, very suitable for a lovely summer party frock.

"Thank you. Very nice," the girl said, barely able to conceal her dissapointment. Where on earth would she wear such pretty material down here, she wondered. Merry's displeasure did not matter, for both Lela and Helena had already laid a pattern and stitched a garment in their heads with Merry's fine fabric.

A promising looking black enamel box revealed things Merry did like: a necklace of gold hearts and a gold bracelet with seven small gold hearts attached to it.

"Oooooh!" Merry purred, her eyes widening with pleasure. "I like this!" She exclaimed.

"You gone lak dis, too," Rex teased, reaching for a small soft pouch of red leather. The pouch contained five twenty dollar gold coins. Meredith was struck dumb.

"I never seed no gold coins befoe," Lela said. "Dey beautiful!"

"Well, goodness, gracious, Grandfather! You must be a very rich man!" she gushed, little beads of sweat breaking on her nose. She wondered if there was anything more for her in this magical grip.

"Yes, I is. Ahm rich in what counts da most in dis life: love and fambly. An nah dat y'all got somethin' to remember old Rex by, I'd better git me a short lil' nap. I'm gittin' plumb wore out. But wait! I almost done forgot deres one more somethin' fer fambly." Rex reached over from his chair and pulled out a dark blue velvet pouch with initials woven on its front in heavy golden thread.

Meredith's eyes sparkled and she reached out her hands to receive this beautiful bag that she knew must be hers.

Rex fell back in his chair laughing again as he handed the bag to Helena.

"Fer yo' husmon, fer Norman," Rex said, trying not to scowl, for Helena had told him a little about why she was home. Lela had told him more.

It was a solid gold pocket watch, heavy and ornately carved.

"Oh, Papa! That was so thoughtful!" Helena cried. She came over and rubbed her father's hand and arm in a soothing manner.

"Norman will love the watch. It is just beautiful!"

"I ain't no educated main," Rex said almost apologetically, "but I try not to be the biggest fool in the world. I tried to pick nice things."

Lela was near tears again.

"What you gone cry fer, old gal?" Rex teased. "You don't lak yo' presents?" he joked and was immediately seized with a fit of coughing. "Ahm getting' cold—and tired. I think I should go to bed nah."

When Rex was comfortably put to bed under his beautiful quilts and blankets, he asked everyone to gather around. Then he spoke to them quietly and with great dignity as he lay propped on his pillows.

"After being away for a while, I didn't wanna come back empty handed and sick. I struck gold three times, in three different places; not no million dollars, but enough to 'low me to come home da way I wanted to—proud and wit' a lil' somethin in my grip. Not raggedy and po' and begging."

Lela reached out and lovingly adjusted the quilts and pillows that needed no adjusting, but she was wise enough to keep quiet and let her husband finish what he had to say.

"Dat suitcase have a false bottom. I has some mo' money in dere, some gold coins, and five insurance policies for ten thousand dollars altogether. Nah y'all know you can bury somebody nice—real nice—for two, three hundred dollars. The rest o'dat money made out dis-a-way: half to my wife, half to be split between mah two chirrens."

There was no end to the secrets of the suitcase, it seemed. The family gazed at each other, dumbfounded and not at all happy that Rex had mentioned himself and funeral in the same sentence.

"Nah all y'all git on outta mah room!" Rex said, taking off his mask. "Dis mask could steam somebody ta death!" he laughed.

The morning sun crept over the yellow faces of the dandelions, lighting them like puffs of pure gold. But this morning, John Candle was not looking for these little flowers, but the small white flowers that grew close beside them in late May and early June. He knew it was too early—it was only the last week in April, but he could not be blamed for looking and hoping because Rex Bailey was not getting better; in fact, he had begun slipping away. And only the white flowers, dried, crushed and steeped into a tea, would give him any chance at all.

The nine pounds Lela had so praised Rex for having gained were not healthy pounds. When John Candle had pressed Rex Bailey's ankle with his thumb yesterday, the pressure had made a deep dent, which remained in the flesh for a long while. Excess water. Edema, John Candle knew. Rex was also struggling to breathe, and trying to hide that fact by talking less.

And there were other signs: a mealy texture to the skin, sunken eyes with black circles under them. Rex's face had always been a smooth, light reddish brown. Now it was mottled and spotted like a peach bruised and going bad.

Now the herbalist searched in vain for the small pale, blossoms that might save Rex, "daughters" of the seeds he had brought back from Africa and planted long ago among the dandelions in the yard in the back of his house. But his search was in vain. The daughter flowers from the mother country were nowhere to be found.

Finally, early in May, Lela admitted to herself what she had been hiding for more than two weeks. In spite of wonderful food and the best of care, Rex was getting worse. Tomorrow she would call in Dr. Echardt, the real doctor. John Candle was good, but Rex deserved all the help he could get now. He was swelling up, restless and sweating. He could no longer sit up and hold a conversation, nor was he eating.

There was something more wrong with him than just tuberculosis, for Lela had never known consumption to "act this-a-way," she told her son and daughter.

John Candle had said, "Go head on an' git Dr. Echardt, Lela. I done done the very best I know hi."

"I knows you has," Lela said kindly.

"And wit'out all my herbs—you know dem white ones I'm waiting fer-never did come up yet."

"I knows."

"Well den," the herbalist said, his voice subdued and resigned. Rex was too restless now. John Candle knew his heart was giving out. "I'll come on back by tomorry."

Every morning when Lela awoke, she said a brief prayer before rising, thanked Jesus for her blessings, then lay in bed a few minutes listening to God's world, she called it: the songs of the birds, if it was summer, perhaps a dog barking in the distance, a train's mournful whistle from as far away as Old Steward, the wind in the trees, a cow mooing. It was amazing and beautiful Lela thought, how sounds carried out here, especially when your house was on a slight hill.

But this morning, after hearing Dave leave, she heard nothing. Not a sound of any kind. The house was not just silent, but still. Then, suddenly she knew. What she was hearing was the stillness of death. Lela rose stiffly, her eyes beginning to blur with tears. She sat on the side of her bed for a few moments, then she stood up, put on her robe and slipped her feet in the blue satin slippers Helena had brought from Chicago. Still she had heard no sounds whatsoever. How strange, she thought. Not even a dog's bark!

Lela made her way toward her husband's room, which was only a few steps from her own, but today it was the longest walk of her life. Rex was laying on his side facing the door. His eyes were closed. He could have been sleeping, but Lela knew that he was dead. Lela got down on her stiff knees with difficulty and thanked God that Rex had made it home, had not died on the road "amongst strangers," she said. "For dat I thanks you, Almighty Father!" Lela held Rex's hand and rubbed it gently.

Although Lela's face was wet with tears, she felt at peace as she released her husband's hand—and his soul—to the "Good Master."

Suddenly, there was a small twittering in the trees, and Lela heard Witlow's bull let out a strong bellow. The morning sounds, the welcome, comforting sounds of the day had returned.

Lela struggled up from her knees. When Dave came back, they must go and fetch Helena and Rex's grandchildren, then they would go to Craig's Funeral Home and make the arrangements.

FIFTY-SEVEN

✸

Helena had remained distracted for several days because her attempts to call her husband found the phone disconnected. Her few letters to Norman in the last months had been returned—addressee unknown. Helena had no idea how to contact her children's father anymore. He did not know her father was dead. Helena was beginning to wonder if Norman himself was still alive. She knew she would have to go to Chicago to find out as soon as a decent period of grieving for her father had passed.

Three weeks after Rex Bailey's death, the goodwill gifts and solicitous visits slowed to a trickle, and things seemed to be getting back to normal for the Bailey family, so after a brief discussion with her mother and brother, Helena decided that it would be a good time to finally go back to Chicago to search for her husband. The children, Meredith and Basil, would stay with their grandmother for the few days of her absence.

Arriving by cab, Helena found the Chicago house at 4812 Grand Boulevard so improved it was difficult to recognize. Helena got out in the warm May air and stood and stared. The window sills had been freshly painted, the narrow front lawn manicured, the whole front of the brownstone had been tuck pointed, and the most amazing thing of all was the fence, new, tall, proprietary and imposing, guarding the beautiful building in stately dignity.

What had happened here? Surely old Miss Silverstein, the owner, was not putting out this kind of money during a Depression! This thought was pushed out by another. Had Norman gambled, won money, and bought this place? And was he hiding from her, marking letters address unknown? Was having a different phone number a part of the ruse?

Anger replaced admiration and wonder. Helena, well dressed in a rose-colored outfit with matching hat, strode up the steps to the front door and rung the bell. When there was no immediate answer, she pushed the door gently, found it open, and walked in. After all, this was her husband's flat.

Helena's mouth literally dropped open when she beheld the beauty of the room. There was the ebony piano Norman had paid too much for, draped in a lovely multi-colored silk fringed scarf. The parlor floor was so highly polished that it resembling liquid caramel. But the furniture had all been changed. Now it was all rich dark green, overstuffed and expensive. Colorful oriental rugs were scattered about the wooden floors. The curtains were a billowy satiny white. Elegant prints and bright paintings lined the walls.

What was going on? Norman must have really hit it big this time! And he hadn't sent a penny, Helena fumed, even though it turned out she hadn't needed anything from him.

"Hallo! Can I help you miss?" Helena spun around, picking up her grip which she had set on the floor. She faced a good looking man in early middle age, medium brown with a shaggy mustache. He was slightly stout and dressed in paint splattered work clothes. Perhaps he was doing some work for her husband.

"I'm sorry. I didn't hear the bell," he said graciously, assuming that she had rung it.

Helena smiled uneasily, though not out of fear of the painter, who seemed a nice man. But something was not quite right here.

"I'm looking for my husband, Norman St. Quatran. I'm Helena St. Quatran, I'm a day early. My husband is expecting me tomorrow," she lied.

The man looked puzzled for a moment. "St. Quatran?" he repeated. "Now, where have I heard that name before?" he asked Helena, studying the ceiling.

"Oh, yes! Yes," the man said, remembering. "Why, I bought this piano from a gentleman named St. Quatran. I remember now because St. Quatran is not a common name."

"You bought this piano?" Helena said in a small voice.

"Five months ago. It was a pretty good deal, too, but I imagine you know that. Or should I just shut my mouth?" the man said, laughing. "Name's Kedvale Lamps," he said, extending a large gritty paw. "Sorry, my hands are a little bit dirty. I'm still painting this place."

Helena had gone pale, and Kedvale Lamps noticed it and the slight unsteadiness of her legs.

"You're looking for your husband? Here? How long has it been since you've talked to him, Mrs. St. Quatran?" Kedvale Lamps, asked frowning.

The question sounded like a reprimand and Helena's ears stung and reddened with embarrassment.

"Would you care to sit down, Mrs. St. Quatran?" the man offered with concern. "Coffee?"

"No. No coffee. Just a seat please. Thank you."

Helena knew she was going to have to reveal something to this man in order to perhaps find out where her husband was. She had seldom felt so humiliated in her life.

"I used to live here, you see," she began. "My husband and I have been separated since last December."

"I see," Kedvale said sympathetically.

Kedvale Lamps told Helena that he had bought this house from Ronda Silverstein, the old white woman who owned it. He owned a funeral parlor, Lamps and Miles. Perhaps she had heard of it?

Helena confessed that she had no idea where her husband was, and was in fact searching for him. The man gave Helena Norman's last known address. Kedvale explained that Norman had given him the address "just in case." He had not said in case of what, and it was just luck that he had kept it in his billfold.

The East Forty-third Street neighborhood the undertaker had directed Helena to was showing signs of wear. The still sturdy greystones and brownstones had kitchenettes for rent signs in every window, and dirty, often torn curtains flapped out of the many screenless windows.

Helena shook her head. She knew what these Chicago kitchenette buildings held—twelve or more families where only three should live, over burdening the plumbing and filling the pockets of white landlords who lived in Hyde Park, Kenwood, South Shore, or further away. These new-to-the-city Colored families, seeking freedom, found only another kind of lynching—not of the body, but of the spirit.

Three young men set on the porch in the May sunshine eating greasy sandwiches; one sat in front of a plate of greens. Having already lost the gentility of the South, they made lightly lewd comments to Helena's inquiries.

"Mistah St. Quatran? Sho' wish a fine lil' mama lak you wuz looking for me, baby! Whoo whoo!"

"Mistah St. Quatran live way back in Number Eight wit' Danny," They informed Helena in their thick as sorghum molasses accents, and stopped to watch her as she climbed the stairs.

"Jus' look at dat booty move up dem steps! Lordy have mercy!" the boys wailed.

Helena felt perspiration gather on the forehead. She was assailed with thoughts of turning back.

With Danny? Who was Danny? she wondered as she walked down the hall as if in a dimly lit nightmare. The stench of cabbage, urine and poverty assaulted her nostrils, even as shouted curses, the sound of heavy falling objects, and the sure sharp tinkling of breaking glass battered her ears.

Good Lawd! What kind of place is this? Helena wondered as she dabbed at her forehead with her scented handkerchief. Finally, she stood shaking before Number Eight. Helena knocked quickly and too softly.

"Is dat somebody at da doe?" a young female voice asked.

"Well move your lardy ass and go see!" The male voice was strident and demanding, drunken perhaps, but even so the enunciation was perfect. It was Norman—her husband!

The door swung open and an empty-eyed young woman wearing the cheap wraparound dress that hiked up in the front stood before Helena. She was largely pregnant.

"Hey! Is you looking fer somebody? My name is Danny but I ain't no boy as you can see," she laughed.

The girl was chubby, dark, barely out of her teens and not at all pretty, but with a wide trusting smile. Helena saw her husband lying on a cot in a corner of the small room. He had one arm flung over his eyes and had not moved. He seemed drunk or sick.

The room was one of the infamous kitchenettes, so cramped that the entire space could be taken in at a glance. The communal bathroom was far down the hall.

The place was filthy, and a pot of something was boiling over on the tiny two burner range. A scent rose up from the place that was a mixture of things dirty, rotting and unbearably sad.

Helena stepped into the kitchenette onto a linoleum floor. The pattern had long since worn away, revealing the shiny black underbelly.

"Hello, Norman," Helena said loudly to her husband. The girl, Danny, turned from the little pot on the stove, confused.

"Y'all knows each n'nother, miss?" she asked with wide eyes.

"Oh, yes indeed."

At the sound of his wife's voice, which could be surprisingly loud and firm, Norman Newbridge St. Quatran had sat up and looked around, finally focusing his bleary eyes on Helena.

"Helena? Is that you, sugar? Well, I be damn!" Norman tried to struggle to his feet, failed in the attempt and remained sitting on the cot, a smile appearing, fading, then reappearing on his lips like some crazy flicking picture. Finally he asked, "Well, hi you been, sugar?"

"I was about to ask you the same thing, Norman," Helena said tersely.

Heavens, he looked awful! Helena thought. Norman was thirty-nine and looked sixty. Sobering up moment by moment, his face was losing a few of its flabby creases, but Helena still could not believe how terrible her husband appeared. And he was so thin!

Now Helena knew there was no need for the long talk she had envisioned on her way here, the talk that would clear up and straighten out their separate lives. It was all here before her. Norman's final slide all the way to the bottom of the heap. Perhaps it was a journey Norman had been on all his life, but she had simply refused to see it, Helena thought.

Helena felt genuinely sorry for the girl. Her future would be as empty as her wide and vacant smile.

"Norman was my husband," Helena said softly to the girl.

"He wuz?" The girl exclaimed. "Well kin you beat dat!? Hi he git a pretty lady lak you to marry him? He look lak an old dog ta me, but I laks 'em!" the girl said, smiling.

"Shut your Gawd damn mouth, Danny!" Norman bellowed sullenly.

Helena pulled up a soiled chair. Danny did not seem offended when Helena wiped its seat before she sat down. She was busy slapping mustard on bread and fitting sausages between the slices.

"Nah, I'm gonna run git me a orange pop from da sto'. Norman, you wants a grape, right? Will you excuse me Miss? Ahm gone be right back. You got a dime, Norman?" Norman did not seem to have a dime, or even a nickle.

Helena opened her purse and gave the girl a dollar. "Thank you, mam! The delighted girl exclaimed. You want a nice cold pop too? Hi 'bout a Coca Cola?"

"No, no, and please keep the change."

Thanking Helena again, the grateful girl lumbered out of the door.

Helena turned to her husband, who had not moved from the cot with its dirty blanket and unbelievably greasy pillowcases. "I'm here for a divorce, Norman," she said quietly. "I have been living with my family in Arkansas since before Christmas."

"Awright," her husband said as if he was not surprised and did not care.

"Is that all you have to say, Norman?" It surprised Helena that after nearly fourteen years of marriage, she felt nothing for this unkempt man except the sort of distant and wavering pity one might feel for a stranger one read about, in trouble in another city.

"Well, what else is there to say, Helena? You see the shape I'm in," Norman said defiantly, lifting his unshaven chin briefly, then hanging his head again. He did not ask about the children.

"Is this your permanent mailing address, Norman?" Helena asked, gently.

Catching the hint of pity in her voice, a single tear slid down her husband's face. "Yes," he said, hanging his head even lower, "I guess it is."

Helena looked away, caught up in a confusion of feelings that she had denied just moments ago. She had to get out of here—quickly. She stood, and fumbling in her purse she separated three hundred dollars from the four she had.

"Here," she said walking over and placing the money in his hand. "Good luck," Helena said, and turning quickly before Norman could speak, Helena grabbed her grip from the grimey floor and practically ran out of the door, down the hall and out the front door.

The three young men still on the porch were a blur as Helena hurried down the steps to the sidewalk, desperate for breath, gasping for fresh air.

It was only much later, after she had returned to Arkansas, that Helena realized that she had forgotten to give Norman the watch her father had brought him.

PART SIX

We sing, but oh the clay is vile
Beneath our feet, and long the mile;
But let the world dream otherwise,
We wear the mask!

FIFTY-EIGHT

✦

May broke into the warmer month of June 1931. Too quiet in these towns, the anxious at heart thought.

Things had changed some for the better, Negroes thought, but the cousins Willie "Red" Oakes and Parker Wilson still swore to "git even wit' da slick niggers," who they still thought had "taken over." The cousins were not alone in thinking that niggers had gotten "the best of us this go round."

But as slick as niggers had turned out to be, there were other considerations to take up a body's time, that caused even thoughts of burning down coon town to take a back seat. That other thing was the economy.

In the first quarter of 1931, things had never looked bleaker for most people. If it were not for the work of the Circle, a great number of Negroes, especially those on the outskirts, out in the New Addition, in Epps, Kitta, Tricktoo, places around West Steward, would have quietly starved to death—eating pride and drinking courage.

But Lela and her band of caring friends, always careful to "cry po'" for the benefit of white folks, fed scores, then hundreds of hungry Colored people several times a week now—thick rich soups, boiled eggs, bread, milk, delicious bread pudding rich with what was still plentiful—eggs, milk and butter.

Occasionally, poor white men wandered into the church line, stripped naked of prejudice or shame by slack bellies. No one was turned away because of color.

"Lela's ladies," they were called, also repaired the sparse number of clothes they now received and passed them out to the most needy. When F.W.T. Edison began to show an amazing lack of compassion by complaining that "trifling niggers and po' white trash" was dirtying up his church, Lela told Dave about it, and she and Dave had very quietly moved the soup kitchen to a large empty building down the street. This building, a large old Victorian house, was purchased by Dave Bailey, and much to Rev. Matthew Moses Clayton's delight, it became his temporary church. To F.W.T. Edison's dismay, one third of his parishioners followed Rev. Clayton to his new church, christened New Spirit Baptist Church.

One rainy day in the third week of June, when it was so warm that Lela and Helena found themselves sitting in the swings on the front porch watching the warm sprinkling rain, Aggie Pratt appeared looking glum. It was a false glum that Lela knew well—the proper face for a sad story that Aggie was bursting to tell. But Aggie liked to play coy, because Lela prided herself on knowing almost everything that went on in Colored Town.

Aggie liked to tease Lela by starting out saying "O'cose you know," which meant she was hoping that Lela did not know. This tack both annoyed and aroused Lela's curiosity as both she and Aggie knew it would. So it had become a game between them.

"Go 'head on and tell yo' story, girl, afore you bust!" Lela said to Aggie as the young woman took a seat across from Lela and her daughter in the other swing, the only porch in West Steward with two.

"O'cose you know," Aggie began, shaking her parasol down, so that it could drain on the porch, "Ray Jean done up and left Omar high and dry!" Aggie confided, properly lowering her voice, although there were none to hear for miles around except the guards, who already knew.

"Naw!" Lela said stopping the serene rhythm of her swinging, coming to the edge of her seat.

"Yas mam! Sho' did. Ray Jean done put dem chirrens wit' her mammy and she herself went off to Georgia to stay wit' her oldest sister awhile 'til she cool off—yassah!"

"Well do, Jesus!" Lela exclaimed. "When all dis happen?"

"Why Mother B! Dis all done happen up last week," Aggie exclaimed, letting a certain amount of outrage for Lela's ignorance of the matter seep into her voice, nearly pushing out the respectful tone she normally used when talking to Lela.

"Mother B, you shoally ain't gone tell me you don't know why Ray Jean done left Omar? Nah you know Omar done left and went to Chicago don't you?"

Dere! She had stung Mother Bailey twice. Aggie could not remember being so pleased. Did Helena see the way her mother's mouth just dropped open? A story like this and Mother B didn't know anything about it! But, it was not a pleasant story, and since Lela knew and loved both Omar and his wife, folks had tried to keep the nasty details from her ears—and they had succeeded.

With Omar working for Dave, and his wife Ray Jean selling her pies and working in Dave's store, the Williams were doing extremely well during this Depression. Omar was very responsible, but he was young and wanted to spend a little having a good time on weekends. So ironically, Omar and Ray Jean had begun to quarrel over money. It all came to a head one evening when they went to a picture show and Omar discovered that his wife had not only popped a big bag of corn to save money, but she had made some molasses candy and brought a quart jar of lemonade. She had it all in a sack along with some fried chicken.

No picture show popcorn, no cold peach soda water, no Power House candy bar, no chili after the show? It was too much!

"Awww, Ray Jean!" Omar complained.

"You ain't spendin' ourva money on no junk!" his wife hissed in the small lobby of Wellsir Barr's Theater, over in Old Steward. "Spending on junk when folks, black and white, is starving!"

Omar exploded. "Gawd damn it! I works too, ya know! You done got so you don't care nothing 'bout nothing but some money!" He stormed out of the picture show and into the street. The sight of his wife with her crocker sack of food burned him up, he said later.

"I don't know if he push Ray Jean or she stumble and fall, but the quart jar of lemonade fell on the cement and broke and the popcorn spilled all over creation," Aggie said. "And Ray Jean hit the ground so hot she wuz smokin'! She told her mammy he hit her. Maybe he did. Anyway, he left her right dere layin' in da street dirt. Peckerwoods was looking! Niggers was looking!

"Well, after dat, things wuz bumpy betwixt husband and wife but not total ruint—not 'til he took off after Mae Bell Lewis, dat is," Aggie said, looking innocently at Lela, knowing what a "startalation" that bit of information would cause.

When Lela was too stunned for a response, Aggie puffed up like a pigeon and continued her gossip. "Well, any hi, back 'round 'bout da time Mae Bell had 'bout fell out wit' Sheriff Birkens, she was out in da Colored Woods jus' a singing and singing loud as she could. Some of da Circle mens was out dere long wit' Omar and dey heard her. Omar made hit his business to talk to her, and..." Aggie trailed off, overacting a bit with the flourish of a natural teller of tales, "one thing led to another—if y'all knows what I means!"

"You mean," Helena began with wide eyes, interested even though she didn't know the principles well.

"Perzactly!"Aggie said triumphantly. "Chile, dey started slipping 'round together a little bit. I ain't never took wit' da iddy o' no woman taking somebody else's main, but then she run off and wuz gone, so I didn't think no mo' 'bout it. But nah he in Chicago looking fer 'er. See hi dat turned out!"

Lela was trying to keep up with this doozy of a story but now found herself lost. "Uh-uh! Dave sent Omar to Chicago to look for Ralph Duster. Da Dusters say Ralph went to Chicago, not Detroit, and dat he don't write dem hardly at all. Dave told Omar to go look up Ralph and let us know hi he doin'. Hi he really doin'. Den maybe we kin write a good letter to his mama. She must be worried to death over dat ramblin boy. He aint run off after no Mae Bell Lewis, chile! You telling tales!"

"Nah, when you knowed me to tell tales?" Aggie asked indignantly.

FIFTY-NINE

Omar Williams got off the Illinois Central train at LaSalle Street in Chicago, sauntered over and took a cab "lak a rich nigger," and headed straight for the California Club—the only address he had for Mae Bell in the only letter she had wrote him since she had left.

"Know wha the California Club is?" he asked impatiently.

"Sho'! Everybody know where that is, boss man. It's jumping!"

"Mebbe you heered of Miz Mae Bell Lewis? She sings at the California Club."

"You mean Mae Bell? Miz Bell? Oh, yeah! If that's who you mean. Yeah. I heard her once. She sings real nice—she have 'em jumpin'! You know her?" the driver asked, thinking he might get a tip after all because this man might not be the country fool he looked like.

"Yah, sure I know her," Omar said, leaning back and smiling, pleased that Mae Bell was good enough to still be at the club, and pleased at the new way the driver looked up in his mirror at him now.

Omar turned his attention to the people on the street. Man, this town was jumping! Everyone looked so clean and fine—much better than he expected from what he had heard about how bad things were, especially in the big cities. Everybody looked fine to him. Suits, hats at a confident angle. High heeled shoes with nice dresses. Shit, these people were beating the hell outta the Depression!

But as the cab neared his destination, where the buildings were not so amazingly tall, the neon signs so large, as he approached the South Side of Chicago, the scene changed. The Colored people were not dressed as well as the sprinkling of Negroes he had seen downtown. They were clean, but their clothes did not ring with success, their hats were not tilted so confidently on their heads; however they still had a certain upbeat spirit, Omar noticed, that he did not see in the twin towns, had not noticed in Memphis.

"Well. Here she are," joked the young driver when he pulled up in front of the California Club after twenty minutes.

In daylight, the club was not impressive. It resembled a large storefront—which was what it had been—with wide panes of glass on two sides, a door in the middle. The windows were festooned with gaudy, even tacky displays of somebody's idea of a California street scene. There were six or seven cardboard palm trees behind the windows, their bark painted dark brown, with leaves that resembled green spinach. From these "leaves" hung bunches of garish fruits, some improbable—grapes, plums, apples, lemons, coconuts, bananas and oranges.

Seeing Omar's disappointment, the friendly cab driver said, "Wait 'til you see her at night! All them fruits is all lit up and there's lights in that tree bark too!"

The driver recommended a boarding house operated by one Miss Bette that he said was clean and cheap.

"You'll like it, although you looks like you could afford better."

Omar found Miss Bette's to his liking, rented a room and took a hot bath. Later, he ate the three disappointing mealy tamales he had bought on the street in his room, slept and waited for the California Club to open.

That evening, just after dark, Omar dressed carefully and walked the six blocks from the boarding house to Thirty-Fifth and State. As he walked, he enjoyed the good music wafting from almost every open club, and marveled at the vibrant life of Chicago's Colored community, that knew how to enjoy itself even during hard times. He marveled proudly at the small shops and little restaurants, all owned by Colored.

Hungry again, Omar bought a pig ear sandwich from a street vendor, sprinkled it with vinegar and ate it walking. It left his fingers sticky. He went into a barbershop, asked to wash his hands, and reluctantly left a nickel in the plate above the sink.

When he finally arrived at the California Club, he saw that the taxi driver had been correct. The windows of the club were much prettier at night. Omar pushed the doors open and stepped into the dark, nearly empty room. He quickly staked out a seat at one of the tables up against the wall facing the door and sat down. The tables were small, jammed close together and covered with bright green cloths. Each table held a round glass flower pot with a lighted candle in it. The palm tree theme had been carried out inside the club as well, and trees were painted on all of the walls, even on the ceiling. The club was medium sized. Crowded, Omar felt it would hold one hundred and fifty people at best.

The stage was shallow but ran the entire length of the room and was draped in gleaming golden fabric. The whole effect was "stylish and classy," Omar thought.

The pianist and drummer took their places and began to play softly as the place started to fill up rapidly.

Omar studied the menu by the dim light, although he was not hungry now. The cab driver had told him the food was real good here, but Omar found himself shocked at the prices. Even coffee was a quarter a cup, and there had been a fifty cent cover charge! But then Omar supposed that the people who came here were "sporting people," entertainers, fancy women, people the Depression had not burned so badly yet.

When the waitress came by Omar ordered coffee. When she returned with it, Omar asked her if she knew Mae Bell Lewis.

"Mae Bell? Sure. You a friend?"

"Yes! Yeah!" Omar felt his heart pounding.

"She back there getting' ready. You want me to give her your card?"

"Card?" Omar asked stupidly.

The waitress smiled. She handed Omar a piece of paper.

"Write down your name and I'll give it to her. My name is Holly. I'll be your waitress tonight. OK?"

Holly disappeared for a moment and when she returned she seemed to be pointing some woman his way.

She was very thin and dark. From across the dim room he could not see if she was pretty or not. Although she was a little too thin for his liking, she had a shape that wouldn't wait! A regular Coca-Cola bottle. Her long blue dress seemed made of fish fins that glistened and glinted in this candle-lit room. As she moved closer, Omar could see that her hair was fashionably curled and her face heavily made up. But it wasn't until she stood above him that he actually recognized her.

"Mae Bell! Girl, what have you done to yo'self?" Omar exclaimed, not meaning the question as a compliment.

"Omar! Boy, what are you doing here?" Mae Bell cried. Nearly all of her Southern accent was gone. "Come on, stand up! Let me hug your neck! Did you come to see me? I must say you are looking well—very well!"

The woman spoke rapidly in a sort of breathy, hoarse manner that was as new to Omar as the twenty or so pounds Mae Bell had dropped, along with the heavily painted face and the husky voice she now affected.

Mae Bell took his open mouthed scrutiny as flattery. He was too shocked by her new good looks to speak, no doubt.

"Come on! Gimme a hug!" Mae Bell insisted.

Omar stood up and allowed himself to be enveloped in a mist of floral scent so strong that it almost made him sneeze.

"Well!" Mae Bell demanded. "Ain't you gonna say anything?" she teased.

"You look so—so different," Omar exclaimed, meaning it.

"I know!" Mae Bell cooed. "So, what brings you to Chicago? How long you been here? How long you gonna stay? Where you staying at?"

Mae Bell took a seat and crossed her "big fine legs," Omar used to call them and waited.

He had lusted after her all the way to Chicago—Mae Bell, Mae Bell his heart had beat. He could see that wild hair that was only half straightened. He could feel his face in it like before. Several times before. He remembered the slightly musty smell of her armpits. Her ample hips. Her almost mannish swaggering walk. The oily coffee-colored skin that had probably never known the powder puff. The rough, often chapped lips that she greased with vaseline in the winter to keep them from cracking, lips that rarely held lipstick.

But now, who was this woman sitting before him, who walked with careful floaty steps, and had given up loud and boisterous for quiet and hoarse? *My Lawd, she looks awful! She ain't Mae Bell no more,* the man thought. He would not, could not dream of getting in bed with all of that powder and paint, with those gallons of perfume. His desire had become water poured out of a cup into the dirt. The Mae Bell Lewis he had known was gone. *My, Gawd! Where wuz her hips?* he wondered.

But Mae Bell looked at Omar's still stunned face and saw what she wanted to see: the old desire so heavy that it had driven him all the way to Chicago to see her!

Before the band started playing too loudly for them to hear each other, Omar told Mae Bell that he was actually in Chicago looking for Ralph Duster. His mother was worried to death about him because he didn't write. Dave had sort of sent him, but naturally he came to look her up while he was here.

"Re-a-a-a-ly," Mae Bell said knowingly, not believing a word of Omar's story.

"Have you seen Ralph Duster?"

"Sure, he come in heah a lots. Use ta always be wit' a different woman, nah dere seems to be jus' da one."

Omar asked Mae Bell to tell him something about the young man, something to tell Miss Lela back home.

"Alright, but I don't think Lela wants to tell his mama dis! He don't work, dey say. Say he lives offa wimmens. He has changed. He calls himself Lee now. Please don't call him Ralph! He looks—different. You'll see. He dresses fine. He flashes a roll. Now hi you gonna flash a roll in dese times unless you outside da law?"

"He in da games?"

"Dats what dey say. All night long he gambles, plays, drinks, big times. He's living a fast life. The city has near ruint dat boy!"

"I hear the fast life can be dangerous," Omar said, mimicking a line from some picture show he had seen. It was after ten now and the club was nearly full.

"You better believe hit! I seen'm wit' lotsa wimmens," Mae Bell said, now back into the "flat," speech of rural Arkansas. "But deres one little bitty yellow one dat gives me the shits, honey! She dangerous. She cut him once for messing around. I hope he knows how to keep his wimmen straight now."

Mae Bell told Omar she was so glad to see him, but she had to leave and get dressed for her eleven o'clock show after the comedy act.

Standing up and rubbing the back of Omar's neck affectionately, Mae Bell glided towards the back of the stage, promising to meet him after the show. As soon as she left, Omar beckoned to Holly, who was more than anxious to have this well-dressed, hopefully good tipping man in her section.

Omar laid a king's ransom for a waitress on the table—one dollar, Holly's salary for the evening.

"I know you can't sit down wit' customers," Omar began, "but I kinna lak Miz Mae Bell. What kin you tell me 'bout her. Is she got someone special now? Ahm tryin' to see what mah chances might be, know what ah means?" Omar pushed the dollar at Holly and saw the mixture of desire and caution on her face. She wanted that dollar, sure, but she didn't want to get Mae Bell in no trouble.

"Aw, come on, sugar drops," Omar pleaded in his good natured way. "I laks da lady. I certainly ain't gone do her no harm. Ahm tellin' you the honest ta Gawd truf, honey plum."

The flat country accent that would not be denied, and the honest dark sincerity of Omar's face, gave Holly the little push towards the cash that she needed. Holly took the money, folded it carefully and slipped it in her brassiere.

"What you wanna know?" she asked in her high little voice, stooping over so Omar could hear her over the music and background club talk. "I don't want to hurt your feelings, mister, but Mae Bell got a regular man—over there." The waitress pointed. "He just came in. Name of Bass Stuyvesant. What I don't want to hurt your feelings about is that she likes hi yeller mens—only. Because of her son. She says his daddy was a very light-skinned Colored man and she looking for a proper looking daddy for her son, Birkey. Mister Bass comes every night Mae Bell is here."

"He pay her rent?" Omar asked.

"Yes, I think so."

"She living wit' him?"

"She *leaving* with him every night."

Omar peered at Bass Stuyvesant's wolf-like features through the candlelight.

"Just a whole lotta yellow gone to waste if you ax me!" Holly volunteered.

"You a rascal, Holly!" Omar said, laughing.

"Well, he sho' ain't good lookin'," Holly said.

Omar ordered another coffee. The show began, and still no Ralph Duster, but Omar waited because he wanted to tell the folks back in Arkansas he had seen a Chicago night club act and had seen Mae Bell Lewis perform.

The comedian was extremely funny. The band was smooth as cream, Omar thought, although he much preferred blues to jazz, which was all this high classed band had played so far.

Finally, at a little after eleven an announcer said, "Ladies and gentlemen! Miss Mae Bell!"

Mae Bell Lewis walked on the stage to a loud round of applause in a cherry red gown that sparkled as if it would flame up under the stage lights. She began a low crooning song that Omar had not heard before. Her voice was still wonderful but it was not the wild, free, boisterous style Omar had enjoyed in the woods. Still the crowd seemed to love her, because after Mae Bell had finished more songs in basically the same style, the audience had applauded loudly and long. Omar applauded too, but to tell the truth, he wished he was back up the hill at Princess Thelma's where they had *real* entertainment.

Mae Bell was coming to the end of her numbers.

"Finally," she said, "I would like to dedicate a special number to an old friend from back home who came all the way from West Steward, Arkansas to hear me perform tonight. Mr. Omar Williams, please stand up and take a bow! This one is for you!"

Omar was pleased and delighted, but Mae Bell's yellow man cast him a look of surprise and displeasure. It was that look that suddenly made Omar realize that he was being used to make someone jealous.

"Alright! Get ready everybody, 'cause this is one of those old down home tunes," Mae Bell yelled.

As soon as the band began the raunchy beat Omar recognized the song. It was a sort of made up audience participation song named "Shout and Call," and the way it worked was that the singer would call out something about someone's man or woman and then point to a person in the audience at random to finish her thought in a rhyming, comical, or dirty way. "Shout and Call" always brought down the house back in Arkansas. Omar was curious to see what it would do here. Evidently, Mae Bell had done this song before because when she shouted out, "I got a main who's black and greasy!" a pretty brown-skinned woman hopped up and yelled back, "But when he gets to lovin' me he drives me crazy!"

The band yelled the rollicking response, "Oh yeah!"

"I know a gal—she big and fat!"

A little black man hollered out, "But I want y'all to know I lak hit lak dat!"

"Oh yeah!"

Mae Bell threw out about twenty "Shouts and Calls," and everyone was laughing so hard at the responses and the band was playing so loud and merrily, the audience was clapping and singing so wildly, that Omar began to have a good time in spite of his earlier disappointments.

Two good male singers followed Mae Bell, and by twenty minutes to one Ralph Duster had not shown up. Mae Bell had reappeared—at Bass Stuyvesant's table. She cast Omar a nervous look, and Omar was beginning to feel funny sitting alone all night. He signaled Holly again and told her that when Mae Bell was alone to tell her that he would be back tomorrow, Saturday night. He also asked her not to say anything to anyone about "their little talk." He pressed another fifty cents in Holly's hand. The waitress looked dizzy with gratitude.

"When you come back tomorrow, please sit in my section again!" begged Holly.

The next night, at exactly nine-thirty, Omar walked into the California Club again. The club was very nearly full but the table he had sat at before was empty.

When he got closer to the little table, he saw a large reserved sign on it.

"Reserved for you!" Holly said, coming up behind him. "I was hoping you'd hurry up and come on," the waitress said as if talking to an old friend. "I wasn't gonna be able to hold this table much longer!"

Omar smiled, thanked Holly, sat down and ordered a catfish dinner and a quart of strawberry soda. He had not eaten since breakfast.

"You know that young man you told me to look out for? Lee? I remembered who he was. He hasn't come in yet, though. I'll let you know when he does," the waitress said pleasantly.

At about a quarter past ten, Holly came by Omar's table. "He's here," she said, pointing discretely to a tall, thin young man that had just entered the room.

"Want me to bring him to your table?"

"Naw. Let's wait awhile," Omar said, looking around to find Mae Bell's yellow man staring at him in a tight-lipped manner, as if he didn't know what to make of seeing him back again.

Ralph Duster, now called Lee Monroe, had taken a seat just two tables away from Omar. With Ralph was a very short, bright-skinned woman, older than he and far from pretty. Her eyes were large, protruding and black as two hard coals. Her lips were so full that they seemed to take up the entire bottom half of her face, and her nose spread out under her eyes like a v-shaped fan. Upon first seeing her, one was either so struck by her ugliness that they stared in disbelief or averted their eyes and did not look at Vishy Hoffman again.

After about fifteen minutes of watching the odd couple through the haze of smoke, Omar squeezed between the tables to where Ralph Duster and his lady sat. Now he could see that the little woman was much older than Ralph, perhaps by more than ten years. A woman so ugly and old with an attractive young man must be supporting him, Omar thought.

"Hey, Ralph," Omar said in his most jovial manner. "Don't know me no mo', huh?" He smiled broadly. "I'm just an old homeboy from West Steward—Omar. Omar Williams," he said standing at the table and extending his large hand.

Ralph Duster had actually jumped when Omar called his name, and the little woman's head had spun around and regarded Omar with narrowed, shiny black eyes. She neither smiled or offered a greeting.

Omar's smile remained fastened on his face as he noticed the quick and dangerous movements of the two: Ralph Duster had slid his hand inside of his jacket pocket where he kept his razor with lightning like movements—and kept it there. The little woman's hand went inside of her pocketbook—and stayed.

Damn! Omar thought. *What's going on heah?*

"Dave Bailey and Lela. Aggie Pratt and Peter!" Omar said hurriedly. "Don't you remember them from home, Ralph?"

"Ohhhhh," Ralph said, recognition finally seeping into his skull.

"Yeah. Well. Siddown, man. Yeah, I know you," the young man said, removing his hand slowly from his jacket. The little woman, taking note, also closed her purse, not removing her eyes from Omar's face, not smiling or making room. "The light ain't so good in here, ya know?" Ralph said with a thimble full of apology.

"And I'm real dark! So we got a problem," Omar laughed, taking a seat.

As an afterthought, Ralph reached over and shook Omar's hand.

"What ya doin' up heah?" he asked, his eyes narrowing suspiciously. "You know I'm using the name of Lee Monroe up here."

"Visiting," Omar answered. "Just visiting, Lee."

"Oh," Lee said, uninterested in pursuing reasons.

"Well, everybody back home is fine!" Omar said, comically emphasizing the fact that the young man had not asked—come to think of it neither, had Mae Bell Lewis. She hadn't asked about a soul back in West Steward, not even her friend Aggie Pratt.

"So they all fine? Well, that's good," Lee Monroe said absently. He didn't seem to give a second thought to the men who had taken no small risk to save his life and get him and his family out of town.

Omar could not believe Ralph's appearance. His hair was so slick to his head, it was obvious that he was hot combing it and wearing a stocking cap at night. He was also thin as one of Mr. Green's peppermint sticks, and his watchful eyes were sunken back in his head. Omar could see his shoulder bones poking through his good suit. His snow white shirt was too big around the collar, his face and the skin on his hands seemed thin and dry as an old man's. The young man seemed agitated and sat facing the door, watching everyone who came in.

When a male singer sang a jazzy song that Omar did not care for, Ralph smiled, and smoked, and applauded in a dreamy manner that made Omar wonder if there was some hidden meaning in the song or if there was something in his cigarette.

Omar wanted to escape the table and the rat-like eyes of the silent, little ugly woman, but he also had certain questions. Where did he live? What kind of work did he do, Was he married?

But when he did broach these questions, "Lee" gave no evidence of hearing him, and the ugly woman finally snapped, "Leave him 'lone! Can't you see he listnin' to his music!"

"Well, excuse mah black ass!" Omar said heatedly, as he stood and made his way back to his table, where he sat glaring at the two, who seemed to have already forgotten him.

Presently an extremely well dressed, thick-shouldered, narrow-hipped, thuggish looking young man approached the table of Mae Bell's man, bent down, cupped his hand and whispered something in the yellow man's ear. The news was met with a scowl and Bass Stuyvesant snapped his fingers for his waitress as if he were the King of Egypt, gave her a whispered message, made a show of handing her a bill, and hurried out of the restaurant with the muscular young man right behind him.

Mae Bell must have been watching behind the curtains, because the minute her man set foot outside of the door, she ran to Omar's side.

"Hey!" she said in a friendly but hurried manner, never taking her eyes off of the club entrance. She was all dressed in tight green satin and wearing more make up than ever.

"Sorry about the other night. Me and Stuy had a run to make!"

"Slow down, girl," Omar said. "And sit down. What you 'fraid of?"

"Nothing! Nothing," Mae Bell said as if totally surprised that Omar had picked up on her emotions.

"You sho' you kin talk to me, Mae?" Omar said with deliberate slowness in contrast to the woman's fast rattle. "'Cause I don't want no Chicago shit."

"Oh, Omar!" Mae Bell exclaimed, easing into the chair, trying to appear calm, but still watching the door. "Everything is fine. Sure I can talk. So. Hi is everybody back home? How is you? What is Henry Birkens up to nah?"

"Everyone fine. Everybody send dey love, but you know the sheriff got fired. He went back to North Texas where he got another sheriffing job in a little town what ain't got but a few hundred peepers in hit."

474

"No!" Mae Bell exclaimed. "Dat little? You joneing! How about that? Well den what about Aggie? Aggie? Lela? Dave? Dey ain't done forgot about me?" Mae Bell asked, slipping easily back into "flat" Southern speech, seeming to forget about the old sheriff altogether.

"Oh, no! Fact is dey ax me to look you up special."

"Dey did?"

"Sho'. I'll tell 'em you doin' good. Real good."

Mae Bell smiled a broad happy smile that could light up the darkest corner.

"Well give dem all a hug from Mae Bell."

"I will," Omar promised, amused and pleased by the fact that when the young woman was talking about "down home," her face took on some semblance of the old Mae Bell he knew.

He wanted to ask her about Bass Stuyvesant, but thought he'd better keep questions short about that one. "So, you gonna marry dis Bass Stuyvesant? What he do for a living, Mae?"

"I guess so," Mae Bell sighed without looking at Omar. "He rich. He what dey call well-connected. He knows everybody who anybody. He can give Birkey all the things I want Birkey to have. So yes, I guess I'm gonna marry 'em. I don't know what he do for a living, and to tell you the Gawd's truth, I don't care. I may not never make hit big—real big—as a singer so I gotta look out."

A hard bitter expression had come over Mae Bell's face that made her look tired, older, suddenly enveloped by the reality of her situation.

"Mae, what 'bout love?" Omar said softly.

"Bass could have near anybody he wants. Hi yeller to teasing tan, on down—but he chose me. He calls me his chocolate doll. Dats me." Mae Bell gave a humorless small laugh. "Listen, I'm on in a few minutes. I gotta git back. Can we have breakfast tomorrow morning? We ain't talked about back home."

Mae Bell reached inside of her bosom and took out a warm white card. "Dats mah number. Can you call by eight o'clock?"

"Listen, what about Ralph Duster? He looks—well, used up!" Omar persisted, holding on to Mae Bell's tense arm.

"He is. I tole you he living a fast life, honey. And been living a fast life since he stepped off the train. Don't hit a lick at a snake. Women take care his little ass. I'll tell you all about hit tomorrow."

Once more Mae Bell looked anxiously toward the door as Omar took the card with her personal number.

"I know a nice place. Hit's jus' lak eating in yo' own kitchen. The food is good and plenty. And yo' money won't spend. And Omar—don't worry 'bout me. Bass is real good to me, money wise. I can take care of myself. Until tomorrow den?"

In a puff of green satin and wild honey suckle Mae Bell was gone, at almost the exact moment that her yellow man re-entered the club—alone—and took his seat.

But Mae Bell didn't start her act for another forty minutes.

SIXTY

O mar never kept his date with Mae Bell. By eight the next morning he was on the bus for the long ride back to West Steward, Arkansas, back to Ray Jean Williams, even if he had to beg to get in the front door.

Much later that same day, Omar told the Circle his impressions of Chicago, although he admitted he had not seen a great deal of the city. Everybody was fascinated by what he had to relate about Ralph Duster.

Lela clucked her tongue.

"Dat boy 'bound to come to no good end," she said sadly. "Why? His mama and daddy think the world o' dat boy and dey do dey level best to bring 'em up right, but jus' seem lak he been wrong from da beginnin' for some reason or another."

"You gone write and tell his mama, Mother B?" Aggie asked.

"Naw, Aggie, I ain't. Gone say Omar saw 'em and he 'pear to be jus' fine. Ahm gonna say don't worry, 'cause sometimes chirrens don't see fit to write." Saying this, Lela looked straight at her daughter Helena, who flushed a pretty beige rose.

Finally Omar got the town report, even though he had been absent only a few days. The town was relatively prosperous for the times, thanks to Negroes coming from "everywhere" to test the new equal service they found in West Steward and Old Steward stores, and the store owners would be the last to admit it, but they were delighted to still be in business—niggers or no, Dave laughed.

The talk turned to other things.

With Dave's help, Rev. Clayton had founded his own church which was "doing great!" Peter said, smiling broadly. "And guess what?" Peter's smile was held so long and was so intense that Omar knew it held some type of secret. "His wife is expecting."

"She showin' some nah," Aggie piped up, unable to hold the news a minute longer.

"Naw!"

"Yeah!"

"Well, I'll be dog!" Omar said. "That's real good news, real good."

"Dey'll be heah in a few minutes. I done baked his favorite, a jelly cake." Lela told the Inner Circle.

"Every cake is his favorite!" Dave said, and everyone laughingly agreed.

Presently, Matthew and his pretty little wife, Quella, arrived. He looked better than anyone could remember. He looked rested and peaceful. Matthew Moses Clayton looked almost happy.

"Well!" he boomed expansively as he entered the door. "I see the gang's all here—or most of the gang."

This was new too. No one could remember Matthew ever being so light in spirit, so loud in voice.

Lela enlightened them as to the reason for this new Matthew: "I guess having a man's family wit' 'em—and another one on da way—and having yo' own church and hit growin' real nice and not having so mucha worry 'bout everybody getting' kilt no mo' jus' naturally lightens you up, don't hit, Reverend?" Lela asked, smiling.

The security guards were not so tense these days, so they took turns in Lela's kitchen enjoying the good cakes, coffee, and tea with the Circle, relating and listening to the stories that were told: Louis D. Stassen, former head of the Ku Klux Klan, was losing ground. He had had another stroke, and was now completely paralyzed on his right side and still unable to speak. One of the cousins, Willie "Red" Oakes, had left West Steward. Since his wife had re-married and taken his son back to Oklahoma with her, Willie had taken to the bottle daily.

"Got po' as a snake. Look lak a walkin' dead main. Next year, he woulda been gone as a goose, dey say, if his sister hadn't come and took him back wit' her to North Carolina. Nobody had heered from him since."

The sentries were called off by the Circle on August 1, 1931, but caution was still exercised and guns were still pushed down in belts, carried everywhere in jacket pockets, and in the small of backs, and the great cache of weapons were still available if needed.

The double murders were still unsolved, and that fact continued to cause a certain prickliness and suspicion between the races, although the Law had informally announced in diverse places that the crime was much too clever to have been committed by a member of the Negro race.

On September 15, 1931, Jessie Inez Clayton was born to the Rev. Matthew Moses Clayton and his wife, Quella. The healthy little girl was delivered by Dr. Henri Echardt, who charged no fee, but promptly demanded two sweet potato pies from Lela as payment.

"Why I got to do da bakin'? I ain't had no baby!" Lela teased, as she made the pies, throwing in a rich lemon walnut pound cake for good measure for Dr. Echardt to share with his patients.

Inquiries about the future were now frequently being made by the larger Circle.

"Sit tight," Dave had said. "I'm going to call a meeting soon. We'll deal with the future then."

The Circle had met so often at Lela's that it was strange to transact business elsewhere, but the Circle agreed that since all the wives would be invited as well as Lela and Helena it was best to meet in the Boise Café's empty dining room.

Dave was presiding and the meeting was called to order at seven one evening in the cozy, colorful dining room that was always crowded with a mostly white clientele right up until closing time at six o'clock.

When everyone was comfortably seated, all faces turned expectantly to Dave. The Inner Circle members were very curious as to what Dave would say. Even Lela professed that Dave had not discussed the contents of this meeting with her.

Dave surprised Matthew by asking him to give a short prayer, and Rev. Clayton made everyone laugh by saying, "Short? I'll pray as long as I want too!"

"Amen!" exclaimed Lela.

However, Matthew did keep his prayer brief and then Dave stood to address the group: Peter and Rachel Dora, Will Henry Mead and Emmie Lorraine, Omar Williams and his wife Ray Jean, Lela, Helena, Aggie, LaSalle Peabody and his wife Cutha.

"We've been through a good deal together, haven't we, friends?" Dave began.

There was a chorus heartfelt agreements.

"And we've had some decent victories, some solid victories, I'd say."

More applause.

Dave then went into the story of how ironic and humorous it was to see white shopkeepers now watching trains, buses, ferries, and the few cars and trucks that people owned looking for Negroes. Because Negroes coming in from small surrounding towns to test for themselves the first come, first served practice in both Old Steward and West Steward brought unexpected prosperity to these towns when other little towns were barely surviving, and many were near starvation.

"Boy," Dave said, mimicking an old black man. "I ax dat storekeeper could I try on a suit. O'cose! Sho'! Why not? Shucks, he woulda let me try on some long drawers so long as I had me some money!"

What the old black gentlemen did not know was that the white storekeeper would then set the suit the Negro had tried on aside so that only Negroes were trying on certain suits, and whites had another whole set of suits that they tried on. Never were whites and blacks trying on exactly the same clothes at any time.

Most Negroes knew this after a while, but they didn't care, since the objective was to be able to buy something that actually fitted you.

"I asked you here today to tell you how grateful I am that more of us did not get hurt or killed in these last few months during our period of trouble," Dave said to a chorus of "Amen!"

"But there is still work to be done and I'm not going to talk all night about it. I'll just say this: the men and women who joined us are still with us, as you know. The important thing to remember is that we are still together, functioning, feeding, clothing, and looking out for each other as necessary. And we are not asking the white man for *nothing!*"

A loud and sustained round of applause went up from the group of friends.

"We are continuing to look after each other's security, and we still have it in our minds that we will defend ourselves if necessary."

"Dats right!" Will Henry shouted. "We will always try to talk, or whatever, before fightin'. But if we have to fight we'll fight!" Will Henry shouted again. Aggie turned and looked at Will Henry curiously.

"Will, is you been in dat homemade blackberry wine again?"

"None yo' business, Miz Aggie Pratt!" Will said, snickering.

"Will, behave now," Rev. Clayton said kindly to the large redheaded man.

"Yassah, boss main." Will answered with comic respect.

Dave cast Will Henry a look, as if to say, *Are you finished?*

"Next Tuesday, I plan to meet with the larger group. Naturally, I want all of you to be present when we meet with the full group in Matthew's church, as we begin to make the basic plans for the future of our organization. We intend to stay together. And we intend to stay strong. Oh, yeah!" Dave said, bobbing his handsome black head up and down for emphasis.

Another sustained round of applause. "Well, that's it. The rest of the stuff is personal. Very. Nothing I say can be discussed outside of this room, OK?"

Dave, who had been standing in front of the group, now asked everyone to gather around the tables that had been pulled together. He took a seat at the head of the tables, which held glasses filled with chipped ice and bottles of soda water. Nobody touched the drinks; even the always hungry Omar waited anxiously and quietly to hear what Dave would say.

Pretty green curtains flicked at an open window, as the overhead fan helped push the still warm air around the room with a gentle whirling. It was the only sound in the room.

Dave took a long sip of his root beer, looking over the top of the glass at the people he loved like family, and at Peter and Omar, the birth brothers he never had. The serious and thoughtful LaSalle, good decent Rev. Clayton, and even the wild, hot headed Will Henry Mead, who was thoroughly loyal and lovable. Then there was Aggie Pratt, perhaps the female counterpart of Will Henry—sweet as the flesh of a hickory nut on the inside and as hard as its exterior shell if you didn't know her.

"This Depression won't last forever," Dave continued. "I've been doing a good deal of reading. Depressions or Panics are cyclical. They come and go," he said making a circular motion with his arms. "After this one is over, I plan to go into some kind of business, the house building business or something. We don't have a Colored hotel within a hundred miles of here in any direction.

"We have very few decent sized businesses of any kind. That's going to change. As you know my father had some luck out West. He struck gold—more than once— and he left insurance policies. Without stretching out the story of the plan, here it is: There is now enough money for the Circle, I'm talking about the original Circle, to go into business as soon as this Depression is over. I have in mind a Colored picture show on the outskirts, a nice inexpensive café, and why not a bank where Colored can borrow to start a business?"

The Circle sat in stunned silence as Dave continued. "Everyone will continue to get paid—in fact, I'm going to raise the salaries by five dollars a week, even though we will still sell the tamales on the weekend as usual as a cover for a while. The rest of the week will be given over to making plans for the future—our future.

"I see Omar and Ray Jean opening a nice hotel in Old Steward where most of the businesses are located. LaSalle and Cutha—how about you opening a picture show? Will Henry and Emmie might open a café. And Aggie will get the store over in Epps and a stationery specialty laundry if she wants it."

In truth, there was the money stolen from the Klan members, which was a drop in the bucket compared to the stash that had come from Mr. Dubbins' forty-two years of squirreling away cash in scores of places, and Rex's gold and insurance policies. But Dave claimed that nearly all of the money came from his tamale business and his father's good fortune, and those who knew better—or not—kept silent and accepted this as the truth.

"I will furnish *all* of the start-up money as open loans," Dave continued. "When all of our little businesses are very successful, then you can begin—then and only then—to start paying back your loans, which will be put in a common pot to loan to other entrepreneurs in Colored Town outside of this group. Is that agreeable to y'all?"

Suddenly the room burst into loud standing applause. All of the women were in some state of tears—even his mother and Aggie.

"Man, oh man, oh man!" yelled Will Henry. "Emmie, we gone have our own business, you heah? And ain't no white folks gone be able to tell us no *nothin'*!"

Will continued to stand and applaud as Rev. Clayton smiled his approval of Dave's plans, his eyes moist.

Lela glowed at her son's generosity, so filled with gladness she could shout.

Later, Dave was to ask his mother if he had done the right thing. "Seems I'm always trying to solve problems with money, Mama."

"Did you do the right thing? You axin' me dat when you seed the faces o'those friends o' yourn tonight? I don't think I'll ever *live* to see that much happiness ever again! Lawdhavemercy, Dave! We do what we kin do with what Gawd gies us—and he done gie you plenty! I jus' praise his name you dat much of a main to wanta share what you got. 'Cose you done right!"

SIXTY-ONE

❋

Theo Farriday decided to go fishing on Sunday instead of going to church. He liked to think that God enjoyed quiet too. Sometimes the hooping and hollering and shouting that went on at his church gave Theo "the headache." Nope, missing one day of church never killed nobody, Theo thought, as he ducked his line in the water, zipping up his jacket at the same time.

It was a warmish October day and Theo planned to have a good time all by himself. He had lied to his wife, telling her he had some work to do for his new boss, Omar Williams, who was working on opening a nice hotel over in Old Steward for when the Depression was over. Then, slipping his pole and his fishing bucket from the shed he headed for his favorite creek. His wife did not like his working on Sunday and missing church. Theo told her the work paid six bits. His wife shut up, but told him she wanted to see the six bits when he returned home.

At first Theo thought the glint he saw as he sat quietly with his line in the water was a bow dollar. Wouldn't that make Fannie Mae happy! Theo rested his pole on the wood prop he had made, his eyes following the sun on the glint he saw in the water. Now it seemed bigger than a dollar—maybe a tin can, he thought.

Theo took off his shoes, rolled his trousers up, and placing his feet carefully on the slippery stones, waded out into the water towards the shining object. The thing was wider and longer than it had appeared from his perch on the bank, and Theo stooped and dug around it with his fingers. Luckily he came upon the handle end of the object because, when he dusted back the dirt and silt, he saw a large hatchet and found that the blade was still sharp enough to cut the paper that his ten cents worth of lunch was wrapped in.

Theo sat on the bank on his jacket and examined the hatchet, pleased with his find—a sturdy, well made hatchet with a long, balanced handle. The wood was still tight and unswollen from its stay in the water, the blade was unrusted—it was in altogether fine condition.

Now who would toss such a good old hatchet in the creek? Theo wondered. Well, it was hisn nah. And what a find it was! Theo rinsed it carefully, although it was already clean, wrapped it in some of the newspaper he had brought along, then placed the hatchet in his cloth sack. He would show Mr. Williams his great find later today when he took him some of his catch. Now he was sure to catch a bucket full of fish, for suddenly Theo Farriday felt lucky.

Theo caught five fish. He wrapped up two for Omar, then he took the fish and the hatchet to Omar over in Old Steward, a fifteen minute bus ride away.

After Omar had thanked Theo for the fish, he examined the hatchet that the young man had found.

"Whew! Sharp bastard," Omar whistled. "Look, hit still cuts paper," he said, running a sheet across the blade, "and hit's been under water."

Omar turned it over carefully and examined the handle—and the hairs stood up on his arms and his neck. For at the base of the handle were three small initials: R. A. D. And that wasn't all. On top of the handle there was another mark: a line with one dot at the top of the line, one at the bottom.

Omar remembered that Dave and Peter Frauzinou had mentioned that Ralph Duster said he marked each one of his tools against theft with three small, but deeply carved letters—R. A. D. for Ralph A. Duster, plus the line and two dot "code" on the handle. "Jus' to make sho' "—and there, on this hatchet, Omar found the initials and the markings.

"Theo, I'd lak to buy dis hatchet," Omar said quietly, trying not to arouse the man's suspicion.

"Oh, naw suh!" Theo laughed. "Hit ain't for sale. Dat bugger is sharp! I fount hit, Mistah Williams. Fer dat reason I'd kinda lak ta keep hit."

"I know what you means," said Omar pleasantly. "Nah, hi much you think such a nice hatchet lak dis cost?"

"Oh, I reckon on about a dollar and a quarter. Mebbe even down a dollar and a half. Hit's made real fine."

"I'll gie you seven dollars for hit," Omar said calmly.

"Seven dollars?! In cash money?" Theo asked in disbelief. Already his hand involuntarily pushed the hatchet towards Omar, already the seven dollars was being spent up in White Town in Theo's head. A pair of red knob toed shoes, some BVD's...

Lela Bailey picked up a letter from her post office box on her way back from White Town to buy tea. Always one to "feel" things before they happened, Lela felt the heavy weight of sadness in it.

When she got home she placed the letter on the kitchen table and prepared to get comfortable before she opened it. The woman took her favorite old cracked cup from the shelf, poured a steaming cup of tea, which was nearly always on the back of the stove, sat down and opened the envelope, which she had already noted was from Nebraska. She opened it slowly, wondering about its contents since it was so thick—far more than the one or two pages she usually received. In the left hand corner was the name Lurlean Kane, who used to be Eunice Duster when she lived in West Steward, Arkansas.

Lela unfolded the six sheets and read the letter slowly. Then she read it again to make sure she had read it correctly. After the second reading, Lela did a rare thing—falling back in her chair she burst into heart-breaking sobs. Hearing his mother's sharp outcry, Dave rushed from the middle room where he had been working on his plans, shock and dismay on his face, for Dave had never heard his mother so upset, not even at the death of her husband. Something terrible had certainly happened, he thought, his heart tight with concern.

"Mother?" Dave said, coming into the kitchen. Lela stopped Dave by handing him the letter.

"Read hit," she said hoarsely, her face covered with tears.

Dave took the small pages in unsteady hands and read:

October 27, 1931

Dear Missus Bailey,

How is you? Fine I hope. Well things is not so fine wit us. We got another letter worse than the one what tole us my son Ralph had been kilt. Miss Lela we always try to live right. I don't no why we has so much trouble from our boy Ralph. He gone now but the trouble is still coming from him. I had my oldest girl copy the letter we got from a woman in Chicago. When you read it please please burn it up. I ain't got the heart to burn mines yet. Lela pray for us. My husmon and chirrens just feel so terrible bad but my new pastor say trouble don't last always and after while sorry will be wiped from our brow. Thank you. We love and care for you all very much.

Sincerely,

Lurlean Kane. Husmon and chirrens

P.S. One good thing. Things is gittin worser here wit work but Smitty still able to hole on to his job. We was gonna tell you about Ralph's death way before now, Miss Lela, but I just didn't have the heart, you understand?

Having read the cover letter from Lurlean, Dave laid it on the table and faced the carefully copied pages that accompanied it. They began:

October 8, 1931

Dear Mrs. Kane,

My name is Vishy Hoffman. Your son Lee Monroe and I were friends-really more than that. I wrote to you before. I am the one that buried Lee after he was found dead in an alley near where we lived. I was a friend to Lee a lot longer than most of Lee's lady friends, perhaps that was because I was a little bit older than the girls Lee used to run with and he seemed to look up to me. Me and Lee use to enjoy the picture show and listening to music together. I have a job. I work downtown in Chicago in a hotel kitchen. I help make all the salads and desserts. I used to bring a lot of good food home, so we always ate real good. We even sold some of the stuff I brought to our neighbors. I use to bring home leftover meat and rolls, and big trays of those little cartons of cream and butter that served only one, and packets of sugar, and tea. Stuff like that.

Lee told me lots of private things like his name was really Ralph Adam Duster not Lee Monroe. Lee worked off and on, but he mostly seemed to get in fights with the bosses a lot and quit. When he worked he gave me money, so I don't regret nothing I did for him. Lee always told me that if anything happened to me there is something I want you to tell my mama. That's why I am writing to you now. But I had to think about it. That's why I didn't write it in my first letter where I told you Lee was dead.

What I have to say is real bad, but Lee made me promise to tell you. Over and over

486

he kept making me promise. I don't know why. Sometimes he was strange but we got along fine most of the time. Lee told me to tell you that he killed them two white folks up in White Town in West Steward. He told me—he wrote it down—they names was Leon Baycott and Luxury Tweedle. He said to tell you he knew what he was doing all the time and that he wasn't having no fit or nothing, and that he wasn't sorry one bit. He said he took all of his bloody clothes, rinsed them in a nearby creek and took them back to Colored Town. The blood was still wet so it came out pretty good he said then he balled the overalls and shirt and socks up in a cloth sack he had with him and put them all in the hot soapy water of some washer woman's soaking pot in the backyard of somebody's house. He laughed when he said that. He said some white man is probably still wearing those overalls to this day. He said it was real early in the morning and nobody saw him. He said he bathed real good in the creek, then put on the change of clothes he had in another crocker sack and as I said, took the bloody clothes back to Colored Town. He said he throwed the hatchet way out in the creek. He says he throwed a knife in the creek too. He said it was pretty chilly that night, but he never felt cold-and he never caught a cold.

Lee said he remembers everything real clear. He wore rubber gloves. He said he knew he left some foot prints but that couldn't be helped. He said he just felt they never would catch him and I guess he was right. He said he knew what he was doing but he couldn't stop himself. He told me all about his problems with Leon Baycott. When he went up to the house he said he knew Leon Baycott would be with the woman because her husband was out of town, it didn't bother him none to kill her too. He said you his mother—and his daddy too—did not notice that he had changed clothes because his clothes was all the same—overalls and a shirt.

Well, I have told you like he wanted me to. But I still don't know why he made me promise. I sure wouldn't want my mother to know nothing like that about me. It would come near to killing her. They certainly can't catch him now because he's already gone.

Mrs. Kane, people are saying things but I didn't have nothing to do with Lee's death. I loved him too much to ever hurt him. I hope you believe me because it is the truth. There was no insurance policy. Lee had let it lapse. I told you I buried him myself out of what I make, as best that I could.

Yours very truly,
Vishy Della Hoffman
436 E. 39th Apt. 3C
Chicago, Illinois

"Mama, I'm so sorry," Dave exhaled after he had finished the letter. "That was the worst thing I ever read in my life."

"Ain't hit doe?" Lela said, her voice grief stricken. "Dat po', po' fambly. Dey sho' been hit hard."

It was not Lela's nature to either blame or question God when misfortunes struck, so she just stated her oft repeated phrase for such occasions: "Da Devil is sho' a busy main ain't he, Dave?"

"He sure is, Mama. You gonna burn this letter?"

"Gawd yes! Take dat poker and lift one o'dem eyes on da stove and stick dat thang in dere right nah!" Lela exclaimed.

Dave did as he was told, but he regretted not being able to show the letter to Peter and Omar.

"That boy was as crazy as I thought he was," Dave mumbled.

"Yes, crazy. LawdhavemercyJesus!"

Dave would tell Omar and Peter that the unbelievable letter he had to burn definitely solved the murders—and in a way no one had ever anticipated.

SIXTY-TWO

G enerally, Dave was optimistic, but reading the paper this morning, December 12, 1931, had taken a little of the wind out of his sails. He had read that the German banking system had collapsed and three thousand German banks had closed. Dave knew that the Depression was world wide, but that Germany, having relied heavily on the United States, was hit especially hard and now more than five and a half million Germans were unemployed. *My God!* Dave mused. *When will it end, and what is next?*

The fire had gone out in his fireplace, leaving the young man chilly and ill at ease. Reading the newspapers and listening to the radio almost made him feel that maybe he had no right to dream when so many were suffering. He sometimes felt as if his family were at sail in a luxury ship, while the wide sea foamed with misery around them. Even the generous plans for his friends did little to erase Dave's needling feeling of having too much, being too comfortable.

Yesterday, Helena had dropped by and asked, "Since you are a man of leisure now, I mean complete leisure, why can't we go digging again?" Helena's cheeks were rosy with excitement. Digging was the greatest adventure to her.

So they had waited until it was beginning to get dark, and Helena had donned her head-rag, overalls, and slipped her cotton gloves in her pockets, and they had headed for the Dubbins Place, which Dave now owned and kept loosely guarded against prowlers—if security was too tight, Dave figured, people would begin to wonder why.

In less than an hour Dave and Helena had come upon a large heavy five gallon glass pickle jar. Inside the jar was a well preserved thick leather pouch that held nine hundred dollars in one dollar bills.

"This place is a treasure trove!" Helena cried, but Dave felt an increasing sense of uneasiness as he looked in the hole where the jar had been buried, at the foot of a rotting tree. Dave felt almost as if he had uncovered a grave and lifted out the bones just to satisfy his curiosity. Seeing the frozen and unhappy look on her brother's face, Helena asked him what was wrong.

"I don't know," Dave said truthfully. "Hard to explain."

"Try," said Helena. "I'm listening."

"Not now," Dave said, more sharply than he had meant to.

"OK," Helena said, glancing at her brother. Dave tenderly reburied the old jar as if it was indeed a coffin, and they walked back to the truck with the pouch in a sturdy cotton sack they had brought.

"How much do you think is still left around here somewhere, Dave?"

"Hundreds, maybe thousands of dollars, Helena. We'll probably never find it all."

"Are you going to try? I mean to find all of it?"

"Probably, yes, maybe. From time to time," Dave answered uncertainly.

On the bumpy road back to Dave's house, Helena guessed at some of what was bothering her brother. "Dave, does having so much money bother you?"

Dave drew in his breath sharply at this accurate perception, thought that now his sister was gaining some "mother wit" like Lela, like all mothers were entitled to inherit at a certain age.

"Sometimes, yes," Dave answered frankly, looking straight ahead.

"Dave, do you have any idea how many people you can help with money, and how badly jobs are needed? You told us about your plans. Do you have any idea what a hotel, a bank, a large café, anything where we could hire a sizeable number of Negroes like you've planned would mean to this community? And the pride, Dave! Think of the pride Colored people would feel seeing we had something decent of our *own* built by a *Colored* man."

"Well, I must say I never thought of it that way."

"Why, Dave Bailey, you could be a role model for a whole passel of little nappy headed boys—and girls."

"Are you talking about my hair again on the sly?" Dave smiled, feeling a little lighter, thinking that maybe the fabled "mother wit" had more value than he thought.

"Good grief! What do you have to be blue about? You're the most generous man I ever saw! It's your money. You're supposed to enjoy some of it—and Lawd knows it's going to take a heap of money to do what you're thinking about. More than even you have now, I expect. We'll probably have to come and dig every day once you get started in," Helena laughed.

Dave was quiet for several minutes as he drove along the unlit road. Finally he said, "You have given me an entirely different view of things. You've got a good little head on you. Thanks. I mean it," Dave said warmly.

When Dave called on his new girlfriend later that evening, he thought she looked beautiful, and wondered how he could have ever thought her barely pretty after Adrianna James. Women could transform themselves with "powder and paint," Lela called it, and Dave had seen even his mother do it.

Looking at Lorine, Dave knew his mother was right when she had noted that Lorine Zena's face had character—"and when yo' face got character and nice high cheek bones, you become a real beauty when you gits old. Nah Adrianna, she got one o'dem faces dat fades early. She pretty nah, but at sixty her face gone start to look lak an empty sausit casing!"

"Mama!" Dave had laughed. His mother rarely spoke ill of anyone, but her dislike of Adrianna ran deep. He sighed with deep pleasure. His mama had said the Lord worked in mysterious ways, and his mama was right—again. With Lorine there would be fulfillment and joy, he thought and he sent up one of his rare and brief prayers: "Thank you Lord," he said.

And Lela was also thoroughly pleased with Lorine Zena, the contractor's daughter and a college graduate, who not having found a husband at school, had recently returned home to her family.

"I tole you, Dave, da Lawd gone send you a nice somebody!" Lela had exclaimed, her eyes bright with joy. "Nah look who he done sent! A nice and pretty girl you done met up wit' in Rev. Clayton's church of all places! Ain't dat a hallelujah!"

"Two thangs I bet ya don't know!" Aggie Pratt announced as she sat with Helena drinking hot tea onw Sunday afternoon after church.

"I'm sure there's more than two!" Helena answered good naturedly. She had long since learned to let Aggie have her way with her stories.

"You don't even know yo own mother is courting?" Aggie said slyly, grinning from cheek to cheek.

"Courting? Courting who?" Helena asked, truly amazed. How could Aggie know something that personal about her mother that she did not know? "Who is it, Aggie?"

"Why, Mistah Railing!" Aggie exclaimed as if that fact should be self explanatory.

"Who is he? I don't believe I know a Mr. Railing," Helena asked, as Aggie enjoyed her her sincere surprise.

"You don't know Mistah Arnell Railing?" Aggie asked, scandalized by such ignorance.

"Aggie will you quit playing and tell me!"

"OK, OK! Well see, Mistah Railing done all ways likeded Miz Lela. Dat's da second thang. His wife died four years ago, so he a widow. Real nice Christian gentleman. Since he know Mother Bailey's husband gone but she still got one, he can't say nothin' see, but nah..."

"What does he do?"

"Why he da watermelon main!" Aggie said, as if this statement made everything perfectly clear. "'Course he got lots other thangs too. Butter beans, sweet peas, pecks o'sweet taters, all dat stuff. He come by three times a week. He buy from farms. Sell in town."

Mr. Railing had been giving Lela free watermelons, his choicest—those that were sticky at the stem, dripping honey, he said—melons that were white on one side where they had lay on the ground away from the sun, losing their color and getting sweeter by the day. Arnell Railing was an expert on watermelons.

"You think Mama's interested in this Mister Railing?" Helena asked, a little taken aback by Aggie's full knowledge of the goings on.

"Enough to let him pick her up fer church, sit wit' her, den escort her back home—and try to stay fer some tea," Aggie said. "She 'cept all his gifts, so I think she laks him too. At least a little."

"So this is what you call courting, Aggie?" Helena asked, noting that there was room for misunderstanding here.

"Don't you? You ain't noticed cause you don't go to church—and yo' mama ain't said nothin' ta you and Dave cause she ain't made up her mind 'bout Mister Railing yet I suspicions. Hit's too early after losing Mister Rex, you see."

"But he's nice?" Helena asked with a shadow of concern.

"Sho'. Nice old feller. 'Round 'bout sixty-five. Got a little money. I ain't never heered nothin' bad bout 'em."

"Does Dave know?" Helena asked.

"Mens never knows nothin' 'bout love befoe wimmens. Dave will be surprised as shit to know Miz Lela still got some feelin' for mens."

Helena could only laugh and shake her head.

Robert McShane sat in his spacious office with Sheriff Ansell Morrissey for their weekly meeting.

"So. Still no good news on the Baycott-Tweedle thing? It's been more than a year, can you believe it?"

"I'm 'fraid not, Mr. Mayor. And the trail is about as cold as milk in a mouse's tits in the dead of winter," the sheriff said.

The mayor smiled across his desk at the sheriff's colorful answer. McShane got up and went around to the left of his desk, and taking out a small key ring he opened the handsome rubbed mahogany cabinet and took out two short, heavy crystal glasses and a quart bottle. Prohibition. So what the hell? The staff was gone home and everybody who was anybody had a stash of the good stuff somewhere, or knew someone white or Colored who could get something worth drinking.

Morrissey squinted at the bottle the mayor had set on the desk.

"Strained peach brandy?" he asked hopefully. Some of that homemade stuff could untie your shoelaces if it had been handled right, the sheriff knew.

"Home peach my ass!" The mayor exclaimed. "This is Kentucky sipping whiskey, peckerwood!"

Both men laughed. They liked each other. The mayor saw before him a competent man, sensible, the total opposite of Henry Birkens. Generally, the mayor liked the way Morrissey kept things quiet—at least White Town thought the sheriff was the one responsible for keeping the lid on things. Of course, the mayor was smart enough to know it was the Negroes themselves, especially that tall black one, that Bailey boy, that kept order in Colored Town. The thing that mattered was that order was being kept and he and Sheriff Ansell Morrissey were receiving the credit. Perfect. Robert McShane prayed to a God that he did not really believe in that things stayed the way they were. In time even those killings, as grisly as they were, could be put in the category of a good tale to be told around the potbellied stove at the general store. In time.

Peckerwoods loved horrible tales. Negroes too—all the Colored maids he and his wife had hired in their time loved to tell stories of haunts, of headless riders in the dark clanking chains. The more awful the story the better. In time, if this thing was not solved, it would become a part of healthy, scary myth, growing wilder in falsehood and embellishment with each passing year.

The two white men sat quietly for a while, enjoying the end of a work week, the good liquor and the good company.

Finally Ansell Morrissey said, "You know, Mr. Mayor, the only consolation I have about those killings is this: Colored didn't do it. Couldn't have. It's just too smart a crime. Why, to this day we haven't come upon a thing but a set of footprints, those long narrow ones you know—and even that disqualifies nigras. You know why? Because all the nigras I know got these big old wide foots. They may be long but they're most generally real wide, probably from walking barefoot over in Africa," the sheriff laughed. "Nope," he repeated, shaking his head, feeling the warm pleasantness of the whiskey spread from his chest to his toes. "Not a nigger-type killin'," he allowed with certainty, just as Henry Birkens, the sheriff before him had been convinced.

"Much, much, too smart a crime. But don't worry, Mr. Mayor. One day that killer is gonna slip up. Then we gonna lay hands on him, sure as you born to die," Sheriff Morrissey said without conviction.

"And the Klan? What are *they* planning now, I wonder," asked Robert McShane, surprised that they had been so quiet lately.

"Nothing, I expect. Not a thing no more. Since Louie D's failing health, the Klan has settled right on down. I think dey what I would call very *dis-spirited* nah. Whatever dey wuz planning is done gone out the window. Dey got no real leadership no mo'."

Warmed by the liquor, the sheriff left the mayor and drove down the car line toward Colored Town in the soft evening breeze. The scent of good coffee from somewhere wafted on the wind. Peaceful. Real peaceful.

Sheriff Ansell Morrissey was pleased with the peace and harmony now being experienced in the towns. The majority of the merchants had decided it was in their best interest to serve the Colored on an equal basis which started white folks to eating regularly again, and trouble began to die down in the twin towns. For this quiet and peace, Ansell Morrissey gave himself full credit.

The sheriff felt his Negroes were an orderly lot. Now of course, there were a few jickey heads, a few petty thieves, and wife beaters amongst them, but overall things had simmered right down.

The two unsolved murders could almost be forgotten. Almost. Had it been more than a year since it happened? God Almighty what a hornet's nest that thing had stirred up! And after all this time there were fewer clues than ever.

SIXTY-THREE

The last day of 1931 dawned colder than usual, and Lela Bailey donned her heaviest coat as she made ready for the Watch Night services which began promptly at ten that evening. This time Rev. Clayton's new church was ready, and he proudly opened it for his first large gathering since he had started renovating with the money Dave had given him. This church building had new dark pews and a fine wine-colored rug ran down the center aisle, all the way down in front of the altar rail. There was a nice sturdy pulpit, even a good used piano that some members thought a real church should do without, because a piano made some church music sound like blues, and folks were shouting for the wrong reasons when it was played.

New Spirit Baptist Church, which had been a large home in the past, had been converted and could seat up to three hundred, and had a nice sized social room and kitchen in back of the sanctuary. On the side of the church, in the west wing it was called, was the pastor's office, and a small library. Matthew was comically delighted with it all.

At nine-thirty most of the members were in their seats. Arnell Railing, the Watermelon Man, had been glad to take Lela in his truck, but none of the "younger people," not even Aggie, could be persuaded to come out to the services. Will Henry said flat out that Watch Meeting was a service for old folks.

At ten o'clock, the serious business of "praying in the New Year" began. There were testimonies, and spirituals, confessions, and resolutions, right up until eleven-fifteen. Then the Great Dirge began from New Spirit Baptist Church, and indeed from a great number of black Protestant churches across the nation. The Dirge that had its rhythmic birth in Africa. Slow and mournful it began: *Before this time another year, I-oh-I may be dead and gone... If you get there before I do just tell my Jesus I'm coming too!*

A singer might suggest another mournful line and the sorrowful lament would trail it like black crepe. The wailing and moaning, which served to cleanse the debris from the soul, continued until shortly after midnight, after which there were hugs and kisses and wishes for a happy prosperous New Year all around. The less spiritual all over the towns shot off their pistols and yelled and drank the strongest drinks they had to welcome in the New Year.

At New Spirit Baptist, hot drinks and light snacks were served and after the shooting stopped, everyone went home feeling refreshed and ready to face another year with Jesus.

January 1, 1932, a brisk, cold day. *A new year!* thought Lela. *Lawd!* So many things had happened, so many totally unexpected things had come about in just the space of little more than a year! Lela mused. Lela Bailey sat at her large table in the spacious kitchen, a hot cup of her ever-present red sassafras tea in front of her, wondering what another year might bring.

Lela often enjoyed the quietness of her big house. The quietness was good for sorting things out, and perhaps piecing them together again. But too much quietness had a way of spilling over into loneliness if you were not careful, Lela mused—because in the quiet, you had nobody to face but yourself. The silence caused Lela to float a question she had pushed to the back of her mind forward. That was the question of Arnell Railing and his recent proposal of marriage.

Too soon. Too soon after the burial of her beloved Rex whom no one could replace—even though he had spent almost as much time on the road as at home over the years.

Arnell. He was a good man, a clean man. Kind he was, and a hard worker. And not bad looking, if looks were a consideration—which they were not.

Love did not enter Lela's mind either. Hopefully it would—in time.

A nice old fellow. A good Christian. At nearly sixty, Lela wondered if she had a right to expect more.

The Lord had been good. Lela knew she certainly didn't need taking care of money-wise. Arnell didn't know this—not yet.

Lela smiled as she looked at herself in the mirror and viewed what she had not paid much attention to in years—her appearance. A medium brown-skinned woman with a decent length of "good" hair, all of her teeth, and a smooth, barely wrinkled face watched her as she turned her face from side to side, looking for sags and blemishes. Pleased, Lela noted there were none.

Her oldest friend, Mother Clarence, had told her a few days ago, "Girl, you take 'em! He a *nice* old somebody. You know what he said 'bout you da other day? He say, 'I loves dat woman's cooking. And she don't look lak no booger-bear either!' "

So, not a booger-bear, a truly ugly person. That statement pleased Lela more than she cared to admit. Yes, she had made up her mind. She would marry Arnell Railing in a year or so, if he would wait that long. And she would do her very best to be a good wife. She expected she and Arnell would get along just fine.

Up at the stove to pour another cup of tea, Lela noticed out of the back window the air was swirling a little of the rare snow West Steward, Arkansas could expect each year. If it got heavy enough, Lela decided that she would go find her grandson Basil and introduce him to the delights of gathering clean snow from the low sloped shed in the backyard to make fluffy snow ice cream.

What unexpecteds would come with this new year? Who knew? Right now, Lela thought it was enough to enjoy the soundless, peaceful whirl of the snow.

ABOUT THE AUTHOR

Verne Jackson has worked as a social worker in various agencies, as a Medical Lab Supervisor, and as a substitute teacher. She has a masters degree in Public Administration. Jackson currently lives in the South Shore area of Chicago.